Praise for the Terra Ignota series

"Spellbinding . . . The well-built intrigue keeps the pages turning on the way to a satisfying ending."
—*Publishers Weekly* on *Perhaps the Stars*

"The eloquence of Palmer's reflections on social issues cannot be denied."
—*Library Journal* (starred review) on *Seven Surrenders*

"More intricate, more plausible, more significant than any debut I can recall . . . If you read a debut novel this year, make it *Too Like the Lightning*."
—Cory Doctorow

"The Terra Ignota books are the kind of science fiction that make me excited all over again about what science fiction can do."
—Jo Walton on *Too Like the Lightning*

"Any reader who has ever thrilled to the intricate machinations of the Dune books, or the Instrumentality tales of Cordwainer Smith, or the sensual, tactile, lived-in futures of Delany or M. John Harrison . . . will enjoy the mental and emotional workout offered by Palmer's challenging Terra Ignota cycle."
—*Locus* on *The Will to Battle*

"Palmer crafts one of the most compelling narrative voices around in describing this impossible, fascinating, and plausibly contradictory world."
—*RT Book Reviews* on *Seven Surrenders*

"The interplay between reader and narrator is especially enjoyable, calling into question reliability and truth."
—*Publishers Weekly* on *The Will to Battle*

Also by Ada Palmer

Too Like the Lightning
Seven Surrenders
The Will to Battle

PERHAPS THE STARS

Terra Ignota,

BOOK IV.

by Ada Palmer

A TOM DOHERTY ASSOCIATES Book
New York

PERHAPS THE STARS

A Tor Book
Published by Tom Doherty Associates
120 Broadway
New York, NY 10271

www.tor-forge.com

Tor® is a registered trademark of Macmillan Publishing Group, LLC.

The Library of Congress has cataloged the hardcover edition as follows:

Names: Palmer, Ada, author.
Title: Perhaps the stars / by Ada Palmer.
Description: First Edition. | New York : Tor, 2021. | Series: Terra Ignota; book 4 | "A Tom Doherty Associates book."
Identifiers: LCCN 2021028364 (print) | LCCN 2021028365 (ebook) | ISBN 9780765378064 (hardcover) | ISBN 9781466858770 (ebook)
Subjects: GSAFD: Science fiction.
Classification: LCC PS3616.A33879 P47 2021 (print) | LCC PS3616.A33879 (ebook) | DDC 813/.6—dc23
LC record available at https://lccn.loc.gov/2021028364
LC ebook record available at https://lccn.loc.gov/2021028365

ISBN 978-0-7653-7807-1 (trade paperback)

Our books may be purchased in bulk for promotional, educational, or business use. Please contact your local bookseller or the Macmillan Corporate and Premium Sales Department at 1-800-221-7945, extension 5442, or by email at MacmillanSpecialMarkets@macmillan.com.

First Tor Paperback Edition: 2022

Printed in the United States of America

0 9 8 7 6 5 4 3 2 1

Terra Ignota is dedicated to the first human who thought to hollow out a log to make a boat, and his or her successors.

PERHAPS THE STARS

A CHRONICLE OF EVENTS, *begun in July of the year 2454*
CONTINUING THE ONE
undertaken by MYCROFT CANNER.

There is no one left to tell you not to read this.

I am on my own.

When the war ends, I'm sure whatever authorities survive will reward anyone who used this to help them, and brand traitor anyone who used it against them. So, if the war's still going when you read this, read on at your own risk. Though there is always risk in reading history. Even if you live a thousand years after me, you're gambling by reading, gambling your respect for your species, your ancestors, yourself. I can't advise you. Here at the beginning, I don't know what I will chronicle——atrocities, our finest hour, our last——just that it is my best attempt at the truth.

—ANONYMOUS.

THE SIDES SO FAR

[*Dramatis Personae*]

(NOTE TO SELF: This list isn't sorting as clearly as I expected, must update later.—9A)

Confirmed Remakers (support the Prince remaking the world):

1. Jehovah Epicurus Donatien D'Arouet Mason (Minor), *the Prince. Also Romanovan Tribune,* Porphyrogene, *Cousins' Board Member, (was Their Humanist office canceled?), Heir [Presumptive/Apparent?] to the Throne of Spain, European Imperial Crown Prince, Gordian's Rising Brain-bash' Stem, Alien, Commander-In-Chief of the Remakers i.e. everyone who sided with Them when They declared war on the whole world*
2. Joyce Faust D'Arouet (Blacklaw), *soon to be Queen of Spain & Empress of Europe, the Prince's mother, also raised Ganymede, Danaë, Heloïse, Dominic, etc.*
3. Is that really it??

Confirmed Hiveguard (oppose the Prince remaking the world):

1. Ojiro Cardigan Sniper (Humanist), *Thirteenth leader of the assassination bash' called "O.S."*
2. Lesley Juniper Sniper Saneer (Humanist), *Sniper's ba'sib & fellow (former?) assassin*
3. Aesop Quarriman (Humanist), *Romanovan Senator, Olympic Champion*
4. Tons of people all over the place

Probably Remakers?

1. Dominic Seneschal (Blacklaw), *Acting Mitsubishi Chief Director, the Prince's ba'sib/dog*
2. "Martin" Mycroft Guildbreaker (Mason), *minister to the* Porphyrogene *(i.e. to the Prince)*
3. Heloïse (Cousin), *Cousins' Board Member, the Prince's ba'sib & fiancée/nun*
4. Gibraltar Chagatai (Blacklaw), *the Prince's housekeeper*
5. Cornel MASON (Mason), *Masonic Emperor, the Prince's legal adopted father*

6. Xiaoliu Guildbreaker (Mason), *Masonic* Familiaris Regni, *Martin's spouse*

7. Achilles Mojave (Blacklaw), *commander of the Myrmidons (militarized Servicers)*

8. Patroclus Aimer (n/a), *animated plastic toy soldier, still having tests run on the Moon*

9. Felix Faust (Gordian), *Headmaster of Brill's Institute for Psychotaxonomic Science, Madame's sibling, one of the Prince's quasi-bash'parents*

10. Carlyle Foster-Kraye de La Trémoïlle (ex-Cousin Blacklaw), *Sensayers' Conclave Adviser*

11. Huxley Mojave (Utopian), *Mycroft's keeper, some kind of military rank? police?*

12. Mushi Mojave (Utopian), *entomologist, what official title: ambassador?*

Probably Hiveguard?

1. Ockham Prospero Saneer (Humanist), *Twelfth leader of O.S. assassin bash', in Alliance custody*

2. Eureka Weeksbooth (Humanist), *Cartesian set-set, O.S. assassin bash'member, on the run*

3. Thisbe Ottila Saneer (Humanist), *smelltrack artist, O.S. bash'member, out there somewhere?*

4. Sidney Koons (Humanist), *Cartesian set-set, O.S. bash'member, in Alliance custody*

5. Kat and Robin Typer (Humanists), *O.S. assassin bash'members, probably one still in custody?*

6. Tully Mardi (Graylaw), *warmonger, only survivor of Mycroft's spree, raised on the Moon*

7. Ganymede Jean-Louis de la Trémoïlle (Humanist), *ex-Humanist President, the Prince's ba'sib, Danaë's twin, in custody?*

8. Vivien Ancelet (Humanist), *Humanist President, ex-Censor, Seventh Anonymous, Bryar's spouse, Su-Hyeon's bash'parent, one of the Prince's quasi-bash'parents*

9. Julia Doria-Pamphili (European), *still!! Head of the Sensayers' Conclave, Sniper's stalker, (wearing Hiveguard's bull's-eye badge these days)*

Neutral or Probably Neutral

1. Bryar Kosala (Cousin), *Cousin Chair, Vivien Ancelet's spouse, Su-Hyeon's bash'parent, one of the Prince's quasi-bash'parents, working with Red Crystal*

2. Ektor Carlyle Papadelias (European), *Romanovan Police Commissioner General (required to be neutral)*

3. Jin Im-Jin (Gordian), *Speaker of the Romanovan Senate (required to be neutral)*

4. Charlemagne Guildbreaker Senior (Mason), *Romanovan Senator, Martin's grandbash'parent (ordered by MASON to be neutral while working in Romanova)*
5. Jung Su-Hyeon Ancelet Kosala (Graylaw), *Vivien's successor as the new Romanovan Censor, Vivien & Bryar's bash'child, my vaguely-quasi-ba'sib-ish-friend (required to be neutral)*
6. Me (Servicer), *Vivien's successor as Ninth Anonymous, Mycroft's successor as chronicler, Censor's office staffer, Su-Hyeon's vaguely-quasi-ba'sib-ish-friend (required to be neutral)*
7. Cato Weeksbooth (Utopian), *mad science teacher, (ex-)O.S. assassin bash'member, free!*

Not sure what side they're on yet if any:

1. Isabel Carlos II of Spain (European), *King of Spain, European Emperor-Elect, the Prince's biological father*
2. Hotaka Andō Mitsubishi (Mitsubishi), *former Mitsubishi Chief Director, one of the Prince's quasi-bash'parents, in custody?*
3. Mitsubishi Board of Directors: *(plus Dominic as Acting Chief Director, and leading Andō's bloc)*

   a. Jyothi Bandyopadhyay, *Greenpeace Director (still)*
   b. Lu Biaoji, *Lu Yong's replacement, Shanghai bloc*
   c. Ma Yimin, *Wang Baobao's replacement, junior for the Shanghai bloc*
   d. Chen Chengguo, aka Lao Chen, *Wang Laojing's replacement, Beijing bloc*
   e. Kim Gyeong-Ju, *Kim Yeong-Uk's replacement, Korean bloc*
   f. Hajime Yoshida, *Kunie Kimura's replacement, junior for the Japanese bloc*
   g. Ouyang Fan, *Huang Enlai's replacement, Dongbei bloc*
   h. Andromeda Ng aka Wu Anmei, *Chen Zhongren's replacement, Wenzhou bloc*

4. Danaë Marie-Anne de la Trémoïlle Mitsubishi (Mitsubishi), *Ganymede's twin, the Prince's ba'sib, Andō's spouse*
5. Mitsubishi 'semi-set-set' adopted bash'children:

   a. Toshi Mitsubishi (Graylaw), *still officially Censor's staff?*
   b. Masami (Mitsubishi), *reporter at* Black Sakura *newspaper*
   c. Hiroaki (Cousin), *former/still? CFB staff*
   d. Sora (Humanist), *Humanist Praetor Secretary*
   e. Ran (Humanist), *sacked by Ganymede, still unemployed?*
   f. Michi (Minor, leaning European), *student at Amsterdam Campus*
   g. Jun (Minor, likely Brillist), *student at Brill's Institute in Ingolstadt*

6. Casimir Perry aka Merion Kraye (European), *ex-Prime Minister of Europe, leader of anti-Madame conspiracy, vengeful mass-murdering dickhead*
7. Private Croucher (n/a), *animated plastic toy soldier, deserter, still with Perry-Kraye?*

8. Lorelei "Cookie" Cook (Cousin), *Romanovan Minister of Education, Nurturist (anti-set-set) faction leader, Cousins' Board Member, Bryar's main rival on the Board*
9. Castel Natekari (Blacklaw), *Romanovan Tribune, Rumormonger of Hobbestown*
10. Bo Chowdhury (Whitelaw), *Deputy Commissioner General, totally corrupt*

In Memoriam:

1. Mycroft Canner (Servicer), *the Eighth Anonymous, former chronicler, my friend*
2. Bridger (Minor), *real*
3. Apollo Mojave (Utopian), *title?*
4. Basically the whole European government
5. The city of Atlantis
6. Peace.

"Brothers," I said, "who have braved a hundred
Thousand perils to reach these sunset lands,
Now that so little waking life remains us,
Do not deny yourselves the chance to reach
That world beyond the Sun, untouched by humankind."

——Dante, *Inferno*, XXVI 112—117

Chapter ONE

World Civil War

Written September 15, 2454
Romanova

It has to be a short war. We all keep saying it. The Utopians bought us six months before real Hell sets in, six months no one has nukes, or supergerms, or CNCs, or their many equally apocalyptic cousins lumped under the title 'harbingers.' For these six months we can't destroy the world. They sacrificed their immortality for that, the aloof neutrality that used to guard Utopia, the only Hive neither complicit in nor injured by the multi-century assassination system called O.S. No, it was stronger than that: the aloof neutrality of literal worldly detachment. Six Hive capitals are on this planet, but theirs on the serene, chill Moon. They could have watched in peace. Even if Luna City can't hold them all, the others could have hidden in Earth's empty, inhospitable corners, where their space tech would let them alone survive. Perhaps it's fantasy to think that even they have that much tech, but it isn't fantasy to say that they alone were sure that some—enough—of them would have survived to make the better world that's supposed to rise from our ashes. Now no one knows if war will spare any of the small and alien minority that struck first, during the pre-Olympic truce, and so made itself an even easier scapegoat than O.S. Apollo was willing to destroy this world to save a better one, but not so the Utopian majority who voted to risk the Great Project itself to peacebond our harbingers for six months. So it has to be a short war, short enough to use that sacrifice, to end before the sticks and swords and triggers in our hands evolve again into the Big Red Button.

Yet how can it be over in six months? This is World Civil War: every city, every street divided, with no sovereign soil to retreat to, no 'my side' and 'your side' to form a truce around. If history proves anything of World Wars, or of Civil Wars, it's that their broad, complex vendettas are protracted. The Church War took fifteen years to scour the Nation-States from Earth with fire and blood, and while fractious historians may debate whether the First World War ended in 1945 or 1989, it was long enough to make Orwell envision how deadlocked dystopias might actually achieve Eternal War. I look back further: the Wars of the Roses, China's Warring States, the Hundred Years' War, endless revolutions sparked by 1789; even Athens facing Sparta counted the war in decades, not in months. Optimism says I simply haven't heard of history's littler wars, but this war will not be little. Common sense, and Su-Hyeon's bloodless face when they come from the Censor's office daily, are all the oracles I need.

Mycroft would have made all this seem smaller. Or bigger. Both. They would have given this the smallness of warring ants, of pieces on a chessboard, puppets acting out a script, while the bigness lies in the Authors, Providence, the Great Conversation Mycroft believed in with such precious certainty. I don't quite have that. I believe most of the time; there was a zeal in Mycroft, an astute and persuasive intelligence that, together on our bunk beds in clandestine hours, taught me to believe. But doubt still shakes me. I've eaten Bridger's feasts, smelled the brain-blood at the Prince's resurrection, seen Achilles throw a javelin, but I've also tasted Moondust, seen rainbow dragons take flight from the stunned and mourning Forum, and, with nothing but human limbs to launch them, I've seen Mycroft fly. Humans have done things I thought impossible without Bridger. When sleep is slow in coming, my skeptical imagination keeps weaving alternatives to explain away the miracles and Plan and Interference which would make my past self call my current self crazy. Achilles, Boo, Patroclus Aimer, what if they're all U-beasts? What if it's all just us?

One thing I'm always sure of, though: it's my doubt that's crazy, not my belief. It's paranoia's doubt, like when you meet some impossibly amazing person, who, against all hope, seems to accept you as a bosom friend, and they give you smiles, hours, years, but you know the rot and failure inside yourself and can't believe those smiles, *that person's smiles,* can really be for you. In just that way, I can't believe this war is nobler than it seems. That we are nobler. I blame us, blame Tully Mardi, Perry-Kraye, Joyce Faust, myself, imagine us the authors of our own bumbling calamity. Something stubborn in the blackest waters of my mind refuses to accept that we deserve to be more. But we are more. I know it. We are the instruments that carve the path from cave walls to the stars. We are what built this world and will build better ones. We are the message which ended the literal infinity of loneliness which so long held so Good and True and Real a Being as That Which Visits Through the Flesh We Named Jehovah Mason. It used to be easier to see it. With Mycroft as interpreter, I used to find greatness in every human syllable, but, without Mycroft, now logic, evidence, experience, none of these can pierce doubt's dark hours anymore. Only one thing can: They Love us. That's what I cling to. A Kinder, Better Being than Our Maker has reached across the blind black from another Universe to Love us with Their infinity of Love. When I believe that, I can still see us among the stars.

Chapter TWO

The Battle of Cielo De Pájaros

Written September 15–17, 2454
Events of September 7
Romanova

I WASN'T GOING TO BOTHER DESCRIBING my experience of the war's second day, since it was all muddle, but I've realized muddle was the authentic first assault—not of proper factions, not Remakers on Hiveguard, tenants on Mitsubishi landlords, wronged Hives on those complicit in O.S., or Nurturist bigots on whoever they're calling 'set-sets' these days—no, it was a raw assault of chaos on order, of war on Earth. It began within hours after the Olympic Closing Ceremony, but there was no reality for me then, not outside the shock of the Atlantis Strike, and what it claimed. Who it claimed. In the black hours of the morning, grief had given way to sleep, but sleep in turn gave way to the Prince's voice in the tracker at my ear: "Humanity needs Anonymous advice."

Jehovah Mason's light, dead voice makes me instinctively snap to, not out of obligation, but because every word I've ever heard Them say has been true and important. They're not just well-reasoned words like Vivien's, or right-minded like Bryar's, but uncomplex, clean-cutting truth, like two plus two is four, like the same thing cannot both be and not be at the same time, like suffering is bad. If They said humanity needed something, They meant all of humanity, from Cro-Magnon to Mars. I fired up my lenses before I even registered the difference between sleep and waking.

The feed brought my eyes at once to Chile. It was daylight there, and lines of violet, coral-pink, and charcoal soared up like airy streamers from the glittering glass roofs of Cielo de Pájaros: smoke. A different feed showed the fires, and people, random clips: in one, two Humanists in Gold Team jackets hurled things which burst into strangely monochrome orange flame; in another, a cluster of people huddled in one of the flower trenches between the rows of flashing glass roofs; elsewhere, guards fired stun guns. Some of those in defensive clusters wore blue Romanovan Alliance police uniforms, and others were in Cousin wraps, presumably inspectors, there to prevent the abuse of the Saneer-Weeksbooth bash'house and computers while they were in Alliance hands. But some Cousins were helping the attacking Humanists, which made no sense until I found a feed whose software highlighted the Hiveguard sigil—Sniper's bull's-eye—on the breasts of all of the aggressors. Hiveguard was trying to take control of the cars. They could not advance across the surface, since the Spectacle City's terraced rows made every flower trench a fortress, and every raised path a no-man's-land. Instead the attackers burrowed up the slope, entering houses by basement doors like Thisbe's, and advancing from trench to trench one household at a time. I looked for signs of resistance from the residents, broken doors, singed grasses, but the Hiveguard aggressors seemed to meet no hostility from the residents—no surprise when Cielo de Pájaros was 71 percent Humanist.

A flash, and all at once the image jolted, people cowered, covering their heads, and the glassy roofs around them shattered and flew like dust dispersed by breath. There was something in the sky, shrapnel and spider smoke strings raining down, while upward—upward was a column of cloud-smoke-chaos like a volcano's eruption with no volcano, if you could imagine Vesuvius concealed by Griffincloth so all you see is the smoke and fire rising toward the clouds. Cars streaked through the black cloud-cone, smearing and striping it as a spoon stripes the frothy top of cappuccino, and as the footage tilted up I saw the top of the cone was rising, pillowy and round, and I thought the word 'mushroom' and felt like an idiot: a car crash. You read about the onboard reactors, how even cities don't devour power like the engines that hurtle us a city-width in seconds, but you can't let yourself think about it, antimatter live and close—if you think about it you could never ride a car again. The safety system directed the explosion upward, more power than all the sunshine that hits and feeds the surface of the Earth released in one spot, but upward, sparing the city with a merciful forethought that made engineers feel more like gods than ever. There was some downward shock wave, and a spot of black on the ground, burned roof and vaporized car indistinguishable, ash stirred by deadly blurs of more cars streaking the sky, too dense, too close, swarming like locusts, combing the smoke with their paths. There was a swarm of cars swirling in a shell over the city, and I understood now why we could not just flood Cielo de Pájaros with peacekeepers to protect the system all Earth needed. Had that crash been accidental? Two cars sweeping too close to each other? Or a calculated warning from whoever was controlling them? Or had a brave someone tried to force a car to land and help defend this heart which pumps the transit bloodstream of our sprawling world? The cameras turned downward again, showing fresh gunfire, advances through the wildflower trenches, closer to the vital central bash'house, and I understood why Earth needed its Anonymous. A conference call had waited blinking in the corner of my lenses, and I joined it.

« *Maître !* » That word I understood, but not the rush of savage French that followed it. I had not called up video, but, even without a face to match, the grating wildness in Dominic's voice carried a passion beyond fear. Begging?

"Do not get in a car, Dominic! You hear me? Do not get in a car!" This shout was Martin's, punctuated by emphatic panting.

"Presume not to command thy prior!" Dominic's English was more savage than their French.

"You won't reach *ad Dominum nostrum* if you die, crash, or vanish!" Latin leaked out in Martin's frenzy. "We've no idea who's controlling the disappearances. We've no idea when every car on Earth might crash!"

Using French to exile Martin from the conversation is a traditional Dominic tactic. While they addressed the silent Prince, I skimmed what instahistory the news offered. The cars had rebelled, that's how people described it, as if they were an ally that betrayed us. People had been getting into them as usual, taking off, but some never landed again. There had been no crash reports, no streaks of smoke, just certain people's tracker signals went quiet in transit, and that was the last we heard of them. The first disappearances had been reported within two hours of the Olympic Closing Ceremony, but in the confusion after the Atlantis Strike, it took more hours for the word to spread. In those hours, thousands of Humanists had vanished mid-transit, possibly tens of thousands, and possibly not just Humanists. Vivien (whom I must get used to hearing called Humanist President Ancelet) had demanded that the Alliance forces holding the Saneer-Weeksbooth computers admit Humanist police to investigate what was happening to the transit system. Some Alliance spokesperson had refused and, worse, accused the new President of faking the disappearances as a pretext to seize the transit computers, and, worst, done so in savage, Hiveist language. Lesley Saneer had called for violence, and Cielo de Pájaros obeyed.

« *Non.* » Jehovah Mason's calm made me feel better for the moment before I remembered They sound calm even with the world on fire. « *Je te l'interdis.* » (Context let me guess that one: "I forbid you.")

« *Maître!* » Dominic's voice cracked.

"Think, Dominic!" Martin pleaded. "We have no idea what enemy may control the cars now. The Hiveguard mob's three trenches from the house, and they've advanced four in the last twenty minutes!"

"They seem to have a plan," I said, my voice cracking as it broke through a film of sleep gunk. Six months ago I couldn't have spotted pattern in the clumps of skirmish on the video, but Achilles put us Myrmidons through enough mock battles that something in my gut now knows the difference between planned and unplanned chaos. "Obvious it was going to get hit first, I guess. If I lived near Cielo de Pájaros, I'd have made a plan."

"Exactly!" Martin cried. "The cars are controlled by an unknown enemy now, and a known enemy will have them in twenty minutes, and that's if they don't bring the whole system down. You have to face this, Dominic. Tōgenkyō's an hour from Alexandria. Get in a car now and it may take you to the middle of the ocean, to capture, or to death, but it will not bring you *ad Dominum,* not in time!"

"An hour from Alexandria," the Prince repeated in Their light but lifeless voice. "Untrue."

Martin: "You're on an island. You can take a boat."

"A boat? Three weeks!" Dominic pronounced it like a curse.

The Prince again: "Three weeks. An hour. No. Distance divorces time now. They had been so long conjoined, these enemies; no more. Thou art not two hours from Me, My Dominic, nor two days, nor two weeks. Thou art half a world from Me; We know no longer what that means measured in time."

I doubt the sounds that broke from Dominic were language, but it might have been some broken, whimpered French.

I fired up the *Hâte Anonyme.* I'm less comfortable than Vivien using this instant feed. I still think too much like an editor to feel anything but terror as billions watch my thoughts (and typos) appear character by character even as I write. But if any minutes in my tenure as Anonymous justified haste, these did:

<If you are more than 20 minutes' flight from where you want tos pend the war, relax.> (By this point 11 million had cued up my feed) <You have no choice to make today.> (81 million.) <You can't reach that destination before the cars fail, even if you try.> (303 million.) <Think instead about what friends, what shelter, and what helpful work you can find to do wherever you are now.> (Crossed the billion mark.) <That is your short-term.>

« *Mon chiot Déguisé.* » Even in crisis the Prince did not think to abbreviate the peculiar Title They use for me; time is so much less real for Them than words. "The inner peace you gift to your readers is only smaller than the outer war when measured by those who err by imagining that the mental sphere is bounded by the physical circumference of heart or brain."

It took some moments for my mind to translate that to 'Good job.' It shook me. That's the trouble with the Prince in daily life: They say everything too fully. Now I couldn't just put the feed count in the corner of my lenses and pretend it had a couple fewer digits. My message had made even Dominic's ragged breathing ease a little, but being reminded of my own power only made it scarier as I plunged on, watching my words etch themselves into the wide world:

<But if you are within twenty minutes of some allimportant somewhere, I have no right to say don't try. Just make sure its worth-it. If you get in a car now you might carsh and die, or drop into the wilds and starve, or be captured by an unknown enemy. Those are the probabilities Weigh that against a slim chance of reaching your destination. If that tiny chance of reaching your somewhere is genuinely worth risking likely death, then go. Now. But only if you're compleely ccertain.>

It was done. My imagination showed me fiery deaths, faces frozen against walls of flame, a child screaming as they see smoke rise from the woods. I told myself fewer people would try it now than if I hadn't warned them off, but some would try—a selfless doctor hoping to reach the hospital was the image paranoia settled on—and some who tried would die, because of me.

The Prince restored me. "What has thy species named the place where stands thy flesh, *chiot*?"

Where was I? I hadn't thought to check. I was in a place, one place in the world, and what if it was far from friends and safety? I could feel a flimsy mattress under me, rumpled sheets. I cleared my lenses enough to see a dark, cramped space, more closet than room. The walls were all shelves and jumble:

boxes, folders, freezer crates, square canisters labeled in scrawl, half a coatrack, a katana, shoes and clothes in clear bags, paper notebooks, all in a sea of pack-rat detritus, some of which had rained down to join the loam of trash and laundry that filled the edges of the little room. A dented crate served as bedside table, and on it I found a stash of instant breakfasts, espresso candies, tangerines, a paper book, Cannergel handcuffs, and a cheap replica bust of a bearded man so badly sculpted it could as easily have been Darwin as Plato. A label claimed Victor Hugo. I leaned across to verify the book was Holmes. "I'm safe," I said. "In Papadelias's office."

A new voice signed in now. « *Seigneur ?* »

« *Ma brave Heloïse,* » the Prince greeted.

Martin: "Heloïse! Good. Don't get in a car. Whatever you do, don't—"

Heloïse: "I'm in a car now."

Martin: "What?"

Heloïse: "I'm mid-flight. Aunt Bryar called me back to—"

Martin: "It doesn't matter."

Heloïse: "But—"

Martin: "Land. Now. Wherever you are, just land."

Heloïse: "I'm over the Sahara Desert!"

That knocked the breath from all of us. "What?"

Heloïse: "I was in Kano. Wonderful meeting with the U.N., they're preparing to accept our refugees."

I: "The United Nations . . ." I whispered it, awed by this dreamlike reminder that, even locked within their Reservation boxes, these vestigial 'nation-states' still have their embassies, and hospitals, and borders.

Heloïse: "The African Union is—"

Martin: "Later. You have to land, now."

Heloïse: "It's fine. I saw the Anonymous's message. I'm less than twenty minutes from Casablanca."

Not Heloïse too; my words killing imaginary doctors was already too much.

Martin: "It's not fine. Someone's hijacking cars. What's the nearest city? Head there. Check your maps."

Heloïse: "Ubari? Someplace called Ubari's—"

I: "No good. 70 percent Hiveguard at least, you'd be a hostage in no time."

Martin: "How do you know?"

I: "You think Su-Hyeon and I haven't counted every rooftop flag on Earth? Even with people off at work, it's risky." I brought up the map. "Let's see, Illizi is Mitsubishi majority . . . most of these oasis towns are dangerously small, if supply chains fail . . . no . . ."

Martin: "Can they reroute to the coast? What's closest? Tripoli?"

Heloïse: "Tripoli's only barely closer than Casablanca. If—"

I: "I don't like the mix of flags in Tripoli. There's nothing majority Remaker between Ubari and—"

« *Alexandrie,* » Dominic finished for me. « *Va à l'Alexandrie, Heloïse. Immédiatement.* »

Heloïse: "Alexandria's as far as Casablanca."

« *Notre Maître est à l'Alexandrie !* » Dominic barked back. « *Seul !* »

« *Seul.* » The Prince repeated the word, slowly, softly. It made me think of a kid at an aquarium, watching a strange new creature undulate behind the glass and mouthing its fresh-learned name.

« *Seul !* » Heloïse shrieked in horror. "Alone! Martin, is *Nôtre Seigneur* really in Alexandria *alone?*"

"Don't worry," Martin answered. "The palace is better staffed and defended than anywhere on Earth. We need to concentrate on you now. If you can get to the coast you can reach Alexandria by boat."

Evasion from Martin set off all my warning bells. "Where are you, Martin?" I asked.

"On the ground, safe."

More evasion. "That's not what I asked. I'm in Romanova, Dominic's in Tōgenkyō, where are you?"

For three seconds we all listened to Martin's too-rapid breathing. Fear breaths? Running? "Heloïse first," they answered.

One Questioner Martin must always answer: "What has humankind named that place where stands thy flesh, My Martin?"

Almost no hesitation: "Klamath Marsh Secure Hospital."

The doom couched in the answer seemed to grow as logic unpacked it. Of course poor Martin was hard at work, off chasing O.S. and Perry-Kraye, combing through the hospital carpet for hairs, or counting footprints. But now the distant hospital-prison where we had raced for Cato Weeksbooth promised a different kind of crisis. Klamath Marsh had no roads, no neighbors, not out in deepest Oregon, a wilderness preserve, Greenpeace's once, now Mitsubishi, verdant and teeming with the dangers of raw nature. And if Martin survived the mountains, nothing waited beyond them but the infinite Pacific, or, to the East, the deserts and Great Plains, and there no help or shelter but a peppering of isolated wilderness bash'houses, almost all Greenpeace Mitsubishi, or, beyond them, the proud cities on whose towers fluttered Sniper's flag. The vastness of it felt spiteful, this huge, fat planet, as if Earth had planned this, knowing that no wall or battlefront could be so dispiriting a barrier as the cruel width of America.

I scanned my Sahara map again, since Heloïse we might still save. "There's nowhere I'd call safe closer to Heloïse than Alexandria. Nowhere I'm confident will turn majority Remaker or neutral. But Alexandria's close-ish, in reach, in theory." I checked the video of Cielo de Pájaros again, but the smoke and crouching figures had advanced only one trench. We still had minutes.

"Alexandria, then," Martin concluded.

"What about Casablanca?" Heloïse challenged. "They're equidistant at this point."

« *Il est* seul ! »

"I know," Heloïse more yelped than spoke, "but there might be a coup!"

"What?"

"In Casablanca. That's why I was going up. Cookie's assembled the Cousins' Board, and all the Nurturist leaders are there, and Aunt Bryar says the balance is very fragile! I'm making all the calls I can, but I could do so much more in person."

At this point I realized, to my shame, that we'd all been talking over Heloïse the whole time, though it wasn't until I was editing this transcript just now that I realized quite how much. Their comportment invites it, that toxic artificial helplessness that coded feminine in olden days, and makes us all fall over ourselves wanting to do things for Heloïse, so much so that we stifle when they try to do things for themself. I like to hope Martin and I wouldn't have fallen so easily into the pattern without Dominic there leading us on.

« *Seul,* » again the Prince repeated.

"I know, *Seigneur.* I want to come to You. But You've asked me to be Your voice in the Cousins, and in this circumstance I can't do both."

"You make Me choose," Their lifeless voice pronounced.

"I don't want to, *Seigneur!*"

"Not thee, *ma chère* Heloïse. My Host. He Who Created Distance chooses now to make Me taste these many kinds of pain: separation, impotence, ignorance, and, through thee, the pain of choosing between two pains. I must lose one eighth-part of all humanity, or thee. He makes Me choose."

Seeing them as a transcript like this, the Prince's words feel like interruption, wasted time, but it wasn't like that in the moment. Their calm felt liberating, zoomed things out, as if I was a tiny creature living in a snow globe, and the vast Being outside that held my little world was trying to communicate with me, get me to glimpse it for a moment, to help me realize all this blinding blizzard was just microcosm, that the real causes I was seeking lay beyond. That let the bigger problems dawn on me: "Wait, is Bryar in danger? Is this the kind of coup with posturing or the kind of coup with death?"

"Aunt Bryar is in Delhi," Heloïse replied, "meeting with the Greenpeace Leadership. She can't reach Casablanca, that's why she needed me to rush back. Everyone Aunt Bryar trusts is off handling emergencies. The Nurturists are practically in charge of Casablanca. There's no one else to stop them except me."

Delhi? Something slipped inside me, the snow-crumb that starts the avalanche. It was all wrong. The chess match was supposed to start with all the pieces in their rows. Bryar was Cousin Chair, they were definitionally in Casablanca, that's how the world worked, just as MASON was in Alexandria, Joyce Faust in Paris, and Heloïse with the Prince. If Bryar was in Delhi, where was Vivien? Where was anybody? Su-Hyeon? Achilles? Mycroft? I checked my messages and found half a dozen from Vivien in Buenos Aires, frantic, asking where I was, one from Bryar telling me they were safe in Delhi, one from MASON demanding that I come to them in Alexandria, others from Servicers, Huxley Mojave, Patroclus, Joyce Faust, but none from Mycroft. None from Mycroft.

And then something in the mustiness of Papa's little bedroom smelled like olive oil and I remembered. Mycroft. Sobs came fast. I couldn't fight them, couldn't even think to, my mind and flesh both thrown full-body into it, until there was no difference between sobs and screams. The animal part of me knew I needed this, and the physicality of it, intense as sprinting, erased all other thoughts. There were no duties now, no decorum, no messages, no maps before my eyes, no waiting Prince, just I alone in grief and no more Mycroft. I sobbed until my throat burned, and the muscles in my sides cramped, and my sobs weren't even sobs, just sorry hiccups as I twitched against the wet shoulder beneath me. There were arms around me, awkward but warm, and I clung to them a long time before it occurred to me that arms and a shoulder meant someone was with me. Holding me. I smelled shampoo and chocolate, and pulled back enough to look up, but a door was open to some bright and noisy outside space, and the glare made me light-headed.

The arms pulled back. "Do you want some chocolate cake?" It was the gentle voice of Carlyle Foster-Kraye de la Trémoïlle. Their hair was shower-damp, and their outer wrap stripped down to the waist, baring a tank top and a bandaged shoulder.

Chocolate cake; the question was somehow difficult.

"Do you want a drink of water?"

I tried twice to produce a noise discernible as 'Yes,' but eventually just nodded.

The smiling Cousin rose, and I squinted past them as they stepped out into the bright office and crossed the sea of junk between Papadelias's two desks.

My lenses were in passive mode, I noticed now, the conference call terminated, the Prince and others gone. Minutes had passed. How many? Math was hard. Then, "The battle!" I cried, realizing. "Cielo de Pájaros!"

Something in Foster-Kraye's kind blue eyes made even their wince feel gentle. "It blew up. The bash'house, the computers, all of it. We don't know why yet. Something internal, not a missile. A lot of people suddenly rushed out and then it all went up in smoke."

"Then the cars have stopped?"

"No, the cars are flying everywhere, just they won't come when called, or land, and no one's in them, and no one knows what's controlling them. Well, we hope no one's in them." They opened the far door; the babble of the main office outside sounded far louder than the daily roar endemic to the police headquarters of our united Earth.

I realized Foster-Kraye was heading out for water. "There's a water bottle in the umbrella stand," I said.

They turned and rummaged. "Here?"

"It's water from Greece," I added reflexively. I remembered Papa boasting of it to us, and sobs moved in me again. I remember thinking it was strange that I had strength for more sobs so soon after I had poured out what seemed like all I had.

Foster-Kraye returned with the bottle. "My war spoils so far are three slightly squished chocolate cakes and a tray of mystery cheese cubes. Care to help?" They offered tissues with the water.

A good nose blow made things feel less like a dream. "War spoils?"

"Crashed party delivery cart abandoned out front. Waste not want not."

"I should use the bathroom first," I said, not realizing how badly I needed it until I tried to stand. Papa's office had a full bath with a shower, for the same vocateur reason it had a mattress on the floor of the evidence closet. The bathroom was steamy from Foster-Kraye's shower, so I didn't have to see myself in the fogged mirror. That left me alone with my message feed, and my tracker's images of the explosion: a rush of figures out across the trenches, then a burst from underground which bulged up almost spherically, as if a huge egg were punching out through the city surface, no fire, just black earth and building guts, with broken roof glass forming a shell around it like the sugar shards of crème brûlée. One second the rubble dome rose, the next it caved in, and only then did fire rise between the pieces, swallowed an instant later by black smoke, while the sound of the explosion came last, like a soundtrack out of sync. It was gone, then, that house where I had helped Mycroft scrub doodles off the walls, and, deep below, the Saneer-Weeksbooth patrimony whose numeromancy had let the whole world fly.

Fresh messages offered distraction. A much-relieved Vivien had heard I was safe in Romanova, and urged me to lie low, help Su-Hyeon, and stay in their flat beside the Forum, since they wouldn't need it while stuck in Buenos Aires. I wanted to ask Vivien to help Martin escape from Klamath Marsh, but the reality of war warned me the Humanist President could no longer offer neutral friendship to the *Familiaris Regni* who stood third in line for MASON's throne. Bryar sent encouragement from Delhi, and repeated Vivien's kind command that I consider their little town flat mine for the time being. Heloïse was safe in Casablanca, clashing with Cookie across the boardroom table. An obedient Dominic did stay in Tōgenkyō, and was gathering the Interim Directors who helmed the Mitsubishi voting blocs while their true Directors waited with Andō for a trial which may never come. Prince Jehovah Mason was alone. Not literally alone, since MASON was in Alexandria, and quick-moving Achilles, but Father and ally were not the intimates which all thinking things crave, be we dolphin, ape, or God. Those precious few beings in this Universe which Our Lonely Visitor could call 'Mine' were all lost: Heloïse to the Cousin crisis; Dominic to Asia; Martin to America; Mycroft to death. And I to Romanova. I couldn't reach Them. I couldn't reach any of them. There was nothing for it but to sit with Carlyle Foster-Kraye, eat three chocolate cakes, and watch the world burn.

"There's milk," I said as I came out of the bathroom.

"Where?" they asked.

I stubbed my toe, distracted by a breaking report of street violence in Melbourne. "Mini-fridge, under the Mycroft desk, the big green box all those tubes are leaning against."

The Cousin fetched it. "There're no forks, but I found a spoon and chopsticks."

"I have a fork," I said.

I saw 'why' on the Cousin's lips, but it faded as they realized why any Servicer would travel well-prepared to eat whatever chance or lazy patrons offered. "Do you want the dense fudgy cake, the tall fluffy cake, or this one with sort of red jam stuff between the layers?" they asked.

I hesitated, distracted as I fished the fork from my thigh pocket, and felt the grit of sea salt on the time-dried cloth. Sea water, bodies on stretchers, tsunami, Mycroft, gone. I pretended my sob was a hiccup. "Some of each?"

Foster-Kraye spoon-hacked hunks off the first two cakes, but paused before the third—their tracker, like mine, must have flashed the report that the city government of Odessa had given an order to round up Mitsubishi from their homes, and possibly also Humanists; sources were vague.

"Was it this bad before?" I asked. "Before when I was . . . not calm . . . was bad news coming in this fast?"

Before the Cousin could frame an answer, we heard of what was being called an 'organized militia' approaching several bash'houses in Limpopo. "It's been like this since the cars went down," they answered. "I guess now people know no one's coming to stop them, no polylaws, no Alliance aid, no Romanova. Everyone who's had a plan is putting it in action."

"So many plans," I said, as much to my cake as to my companion. Casimir Perry-Kraye had had this in their plan, Perry-Kraye who had destroyed the transit computer backup station, just to make all this more painful for the world. Were there backup backups, I wondered? Had they destroyed those too?

"Every city its own law." Foster-Kraye stretched back, peering at me. *We are in a city.* They didn't need to say it, it was in their face, the thought, the fear. I felt trapped in their gaze, that piercing, hypersaturated royal blue which Danaë and President Ganymede taught me to fear. My mind turned to the palace at La Trimouille, and gilded bed frames, and Perry-Kraye laughing in the flames at Brussels.

"We're not incapable of doing real good," they said suddenly.

I stared. "What?"

Carlyle Foster-Kraye leaned toward me. "Just because some of what led Earth to this crisis is our fault, yours, mine, doesn't mean we can't still do real good. We're still here. Alive. We have the ability to act, and choose, and achieve. That's real. Even if it seems dwarfed by past mistakes, those mistakes aren't a negative number, they don't cancel out the good things we do now, don't make an insurmountable pit we have to climb back out of to start at zero. We can do good, and our pasts don't take that possibility away, not while we still live and breathe. And try."

I stared, my fork slack in my mouth. It was mental whiplash, the surreal eye-of-the-storm crisis hush suddenly swapped for a sensayer session. Ex-sensayer? I couldn't remember whether Foster-Kraye was still a sensayer or not, and searched for their sensayer scarf, which they did have, the black-and-white cloth knotted around their waist to keep their wrap half-up around their hips. I knew this kind of whiplash, being blindsided by metaphysics in the midst of normalcy. The phrase 'You've spent too long around Prince Mason' toddled through my mind. And then I realized Foster-Kraye and I were here alone, and both insiders, and there was no reason to be circumspect. "Do you worship the Prince now?" I asked.

A smile beamed from the Cousin's face like sun. "I'm giving my Maker a second chance. It's only fair: They've given me the same."

I felt my brow tense. Foster-Kraye's tone was sweet, sincere, like springtime, but made something boil in me, noxious and familiar, like the burn of stomach acid on an already-burned throat. *And when They give Mycroft a second chance, I'll smile like that too.* I don't know how long the hate-burn held me, but we were still staring at each other when a rush of cops charged in so violently that I leapt up, grabbed a heavy pipe from under Papa's desk, and took a defensive stance before I even realized I was moving. ". . . somewhere in Papa's desk . . ." one of them was saying as they entered, but they stopped short in front of us, four of them, eyes glittering with lens-traffic, their gray Romanovan uniforms rumpled from the all-nighter.

"Why are you here? This is a secure area!" one shouted. I recognized this one—tall, classically beautiful, South-Asian-looking with a Whitelaw Hiveless sash about their hips—but their name escaped me.

Foster-Kraye rose and kept their hands prudently visible. "I'm Special Informant Carlyle Foster, I'm—"

"I know what you are." Rolled eyes condemned, either the liberties Papa took with their informants, or this Cousin specifically. "Do you have orders to be here?"

Foster-Kraye smiled. "My last orders from Papa were 'Stay down and don't get lynched,' but I don't have that in writing. Papa left me here to look after [Anonymous]."

Suspicious eyes grew more suspicious as they turned on me. "AWOL from your dorm? And in a state of emergency, no less."

"Not AWOL," I answered. "Papa let me stay."

The officer shoved past Foster-Kraye, toward me. "I suppose you don't have that in writing either?" I recognized their uniform at least, gray with gold piping and that sparkling, holographic blue trim that home printers can't replicate, just like Papa's except lacking the cross-swirl. Deputy Commissioner General, then. The title summoned the name: Bo Chowdhury.

I held my ground. "I'm working."

"In a top security office? Doing what?"

The truth was off-limits, but in my mind I said it: *I'm the damned Anonymous!*

Chowdhury pounced on my hesitation. "Drop the weapon, Servicer. You don't want armed resistance on your record."

I froze. I felt like I was a spectator, watching myself in horror, cursing at my body: *Drop the pipe, you idiot! Threatening the Deputy Commissioner General? What are you thinking!* Yet my body would not move.

Chowdhury nodded for the others to advance on me. "Take the Servicer to the cells."

Foster-Kraye stepped in. "No need for that." I couldn't tell whether the sweetness in their tone was fake or just irrepressible. "I'll escort [Anonymous] to the nearest dorm."

Chowdhury's eyes were stone. "Cells. Now. And you'll be sharing a cell with them if you interfere again, Cousin."

"Blacklaw," Foster-Kraye corrected, rising so the black sash about their waist lolled down from amid the wrap's folds, like the dangling legs of a sleeping cat. Their posture felt different suddenly, striking, with an intentionality I could not quite call menace. I'd forgotten Foster-Kraye had followed Dominic so far. "Call Papa," Foster-Kraye challenged, calmly. "They'll settle this misunderstanding."

The cops in the back exchanged unhappy glances.

"Drop the pipe, Servicer," Chowdhury ordered again. "Now."

My knuckles where I gripped the pipe turned white. "Where's Papa?" I asked.

Unhappy glances turned to full-on winces.

"I won't ask again." The Deputy Inspector General drew their stun gun, and at their nod two others did as well, but the fourth cop took a step toward me, smiling, reaching gently for the pipe. I recognized them, vaguely: red-haired and strong-boned like a caryatid. I had made them coffee more than once, and the trust bond born of breaking bread—or cookies—together calmed me enough that I was able to unbend my fingers as they took the pipe. I fell back, relieved, into Foster-Kaye's waiting arms.

"[Anonymous] is in shock." Foster-Kraye squeezed my shoulder. "They were at the harbor front all night. They lost—"

"Their Beggar King?" Chowdhury caught my wince. "Did you imagine Papa hasn't been watching? That we don't know who the other leaders are in Mycroft Canner's private army?" They nodded to the other officers. "Take them both to the cells, I'll see them when things are calmer."

All at once I was in a web of grabbing hands.

"Stop!" Foster-Kraye cried. "You can't—"

"You're a Blacklaw," the Whitelaw reminded us, "I can lock you in a trunk and throw away the key."

Foster-Kraye had no leg to stand on there. "You have no reason—"

"You're both spies."

'No' was on my lips before I fact-checked myself. We were spies, both of us. We always had been. I've spied for the Prince, Mycroft, Achilles, Vivien, Martin, while Foster-Kraye had spied for Julia in earlier days, then Papa, Dominic, the Prince too. Thoughts too complex to congeal into sentences buzzed through me, held me mute. We were bustled, hands on my arms, a hand on my head pushing me down and forward, toward the door, toward useless cells, inertia, waste of hours, waste of me, capture, so pointlessly, and on the first day of the war. The dreamlike absurdity of it made it impossible to resist, as my stunned brain insisted the solution should be to wake up. *Help?*

"Stop. Arrest Deputy Chowdhury."

The hands that held me slackened. Royal purple filled the door before us with its brilliant authority. Or should I say republican purple? That deep red-purple only the very rarest, highest officers of old Rome could wear back in the days of togas, and which only one office wears now. The Censor. My heart leapt at the thought of Vivien, but of course the calm, small, slightly panting figure was Jung Su-Hyeon Ancelet Kosala, bright in their new Censor's uniform, flanked by their Censor's Guard. Su-Hyeon smiled, caught my eye, and in that smile lay all the glow of hope and home. I felt the prickle of fresh tears in my relief. And there was more. The Pillars of the Earth had followed Su-Hyeon here to save me, two of them, trailing prudently close, just in case the young and fresh-in-office Censor was too green yet to command obedience: to Su-Hyeon's left, the tiny Senate Speaker Jin Im-Jin stared up at the towering cops with all the righteous condescension of a great-great-grandba'pa, while, to Su-Hyeon's right, broad and calm and bearded like a bushy oak, stood Senator Charlemagne Guildbreaker Senior. Their silent gazes dared the stunned and slack-jawed cops to refuse the order, which the Censor repeated now: "You heard me. Arrest Deputy Chowdhury."

"But . . ."

"They work for Joyce Faust D'Arouet." Su-Hyeon said it so flatly, so simply, six words, done, but it all came together then: Chowdhury's strange hostility, their odd knowledge of me, of Mycroft and the Myrmidons, their scorn of Carlyle Foster-Kraye, this purposeless arrest. They'd nearly captured both of us. For Madame.

Chowdhury's gasp gave the lie to their protest even before they voiced it: "What? No, I . . . no, it . . ."

Su-Hyeon didn't need to raise their voice. "You've been to the Parisian brothel called 'Madame's' seventy-six times this year. I believe your customary partner there is one Dolmancé?"

My heart cheered as Chowdhury stared dumbly, and I imagined Madame off somewhere staring dumbly too. What would the Tyrant-Queen have done with me, I wondered? Tried to break the Anonymous to their command? Or use me as a hostage against Vivien? And Foster-Kraye, could the "bastard love child" card still work against Danaë? Or had that hand been played out, leaving the ex-Cousin useful only as a goad for Dominic, or a prize for the pleasure of whatever servant best pleased the mistress any given day? The young Censor didn't even have to nod for the others to release us and seize the Deputy.

"No, you don't understand!" Chowdhury sputtered. "It isn't what you think! Those visits aren't . . . You have no authority to do this! In Papa's absence I'm . . ."

I hardly heard the lies. It was over. It had been over since those first six words, as surely as if with "They work for Joyce Faust D'Arouet," Su-Hyeon had drawn a knife across Chowdhury's guilty throat. The others dragged the sputtering Whitelaw away through the sea of desks in the outer office, where the jungle of screens and voices froze in a triumphant hush as we watched one victory at least come easily on Day Two of the war.

"You, third from the left," Speaker Jin Im-Jin called suddenly into the silence, "yes, you in the yellow wrap. What's the desk say? O'Callaghan. Are you O'Callaghan?"

"Yes?" The pale, fidgeting Cousin rose from one of the larger desks.

"Think of a number between one and seven."

"Wha—what? Uh . . . three?"

Before the syllable was finished, Speaker Jin slapped a tablet against a desk, simulating a clap, which Jin's skeleton fingers were too frail to produce themselves. Many jumped at the noise, but only O'Callaghan yelped aloud. "Arrest that one too," Speaker Jin pointed. "They're in on it. Oh, and that one in the corner also? In green, the Mexican Humanist. Yes, that one. You all really shouldn't glance at your co-conspirators quite so much, most unsubtle. All three with low digits in the fourth and fifth, that's interesting . . . 3–7–7 . . . very marked . . ."

We all stared as the smiling Speaker drifted off into some incomprehensible Brillist reverie, all except Senator Charlemagne Guildbreaker, who, I suppose, had grown accustomed to it, serving beside Jin Im-Jin for however many decades. "Do you want them to arrest those two as well, Censor?" the Mason prompted, gently.

"Uh, yes!" Su-Hyeon answered, shaking off the hush. "Yes, arrest those two. Take all three to the cells. No, wait, first . . ." The guards and prisoners froze. "Chowdhury, any of you, if you want any mercy, tell me what you've done with Papadelias."

The looks the prisoners exchanged were blank, not guilty. "I don't know anything more than anyone else, I swear! Papa got in a car at 05:54 this morning and hasn't checked in since. That's all I know!"

The fact stabbed slowly. It wasn't possible. We'd been together, me and Papa, after the disaster, mourning Mycroft in each other's arms, here in this room, after the tsunami aftermath when things were fine again, the calm after the storm. They were safe, fine, here. How could they be gone? Papa who understood, Papa who, like me . . . if any other human being had loved Mycroft . . . gone?

Su-Hyeon only trembled for a moment. "Take them away. Next, I want every officer you can get assembled in this room ASAP, make sure there's at least one representative from every major Desk and Division. I have predictive data about the likely faction ratios in every city. I wasn't prepared to share them while there were spies in here. In these first hours, it's vital we concentrate on the cities where comparatively equal numbers are likely to result in violence, or where extremely disparate numbers are likely to result in immediate attacks on minorities. I have short lists organized by predicted problem type. I want you all to work with Speaker Jin on assigning appropriate personnel to each short list. Anyone with issues involving Romanova itself, talk to Senator Guildbreaker. Anyone who knows any police officer or other trustworthy Alliance employee who's in Romanova but off duty, give name and contact to . . . somebody . . . Volunteer?" A hand went up. "Good. Collect names and get in contact, tell them we'll be calling on them soon. Seconds are precious, everyone. Move!"

Noise erupted, brighter than before, with purpose.

Su-Hyeon spun. "Carlyle Foster, you strike me as someone who could persuade the Sensayers' Conclave to lend us their Guard."

The ex-Cousin beamed. "I am indeed."

"Good. Will you work with Senator Guildbreaker and get them on the streets to keep the peace around the Forum? If anything will seem neutral to people right now, it's them."

"Consider it done."

"Thank you." Su-Hyeon turned to me next, and plopped something soft down around my shoulders, cocoon-like, warm. Purple. Their old Deputy Censor's jacket. They leaned close. "You put that on and keep it on, you hear me? Nobody's going to touch you, not in that, not ever. And you're not going to take any risks going out in the street without it, looking like a helpless Servicer. Got it? Promise me."

My promise came in tears. "Mm-hm."

Shared pain made Su-Hyeon's expressive face a mirror of my feelings. They hugged me. "I'm so sorry." They hugged me so tight. I whimpered. Su-Hyeon was with me. It made me shiver, a good shiver. No one had ever seemed so with me before, no touch so solid or so real. And the way Su-Hyeon squeezed back, it felt symmetrical. We weren't alone. It felt new, but that was natural enough: it was new. We weren't alone, but for the first time in our lives we could have been. So many others were alone now. The Prince. Papa. Mycroft most of all.

"I've logged that you're permanently assigned to my office until further notice, so you have all the time you need to do your work, no one will ask questions or interfere. You can stay here and rest up for now. Help if you want, when you're ready, or do your own work, whatever you need, and you can come back with me to the office soon, safe and private. Okay?"

And then it was okay. Not good, not fixed, not better, but Su-Hyeon's presence gave me that desperate, indispensable minimum of stable ground that catches you like a ledge as you're sliding down the cliff. That and blood sugar from more chocolate cake made the fog clear. I checked in with Vivien, Bryar, Achilles, and MASON, reassuring each that I was safe. Then I reassured the human race. First I appealed for clemency over the *Hâte Anonyme,* addressing the cities where things were turning worst. Then I wrote an essay "On Fanaticism" (based on Voltaire's *Dictionnaire philosophique portatif*) in which I argued that war's atrocities hatch, not from any inhuman machine of war, but from human hearts when we let conviction turn into fanaticism. We are all in danger of dying in this war, but we are all also in danger of becoming authors of atrocities. The first danger we cannot avoid, but the second is entirely in our power, since each of us alone can choose whether we let fanaticism fester in us, or keep our hearts havens of Reason, Reasonableness, and Humanity. I think the essay lent my six billion readers some calm, if only because it felt normal receiving a regular update from the Anonymous. I hoped my own experience as someone who has committed an atrocity made the essay more authentic, but perhaps it was too much. My work complete, I checked in with the Prince, and let myself and all my troubles feel again like one drop in the sea of Their Infinite and Kind Philosophy. They asked me to define the word 'where.' Why? Because They struggled now to understand what it can be, this simple-seeming thought-word-thing which somehow forms such very different questions: "Where is My Dominic?" and "Where is My Mycroft?"

Chapter THREE

Now I Am in a Place

Written September 19–22, 2454
Events of September 8–22
Written in Romanova

I HAVE NEVER BEEN IN A PLACE BEFORE. None of us has, not really, not like this. We could always fly anywhere we wished in an instant or an hour. Now I am in Romanova. I will be in Romanova tomorrow and the next day. I will walk these streets and only these streets, sleep on this sofa, eat from these shops, and when these shops run out . . . Mycroft was right to say it would feel like being stranded on the Moon.

We are two weeks into the war now. The cars were exonerated, that came right away. What I mean is that we confirmed someone was directing the wild flight which keeps them streaking through our skies, so we no longer curse the cars themselves, as we so often curse the root or stray bag that we trip over. The cars are clustering over cities, whizzing and circling to block urban airspace, while the wilds and seas are clear. This is no chance malfunction caused by autonomous systems malfunctioning; this is a plan. And guilt runs deeper yet. It took no time for antiquarians and tinkerers to roll out their contraptions: air balloons, planes, blimps, helicopters, here in Sardinia a little seaplane with its fat twin skis, which set out for Italy, but a car struck it down, struck them all down, again and again, the crash and now-familiar spilled-ink plume of smoke. Utopia tried too, rerouting their separate transit system to new flight paths higher or lower than the cars' range, but Saneer-Weeksbooth cars are faster than Utopia's and chased them down. For one grim day I swear I saw more static in the streets than coats.

The skies are now off-limits. Hate blames O.S., Hiveguard, the Humanists, the Cousins who held the system last, the Mitsubishi who helped design it umpteen years ago, Perry-Kraye, Joyce Faust, but most of all the set-sets. Talk blames all on 'semi-set-sets' raised without conscience: Joyce Faust's creations, the Mardi bash', Utopia, Mycroft, 'moral automatons like Eureka Weeksbooth and Sidney Koons.' Bright Nurturist colors have started appearing on people who aren't Cousins. Mobs rose in Hyderabad, Durban, Shenzhen, and Hong Kong (they killed Sung Myung, developer of the Rosetta set-set), and worst in Székesfehérvár where set-set rearing is—was—quite an industry, and the violence spread from there to Budapest, where it was barely snuffed by an impassioned appeal from the King of Spain. Anti-Mitsubishi violence didn't calm so fast. These mobs are smaller but many have set on landlords and their unhappy neighbors, wherever a small Chinatown or Japantown was vulnerable (Korean districts seem to have been spared so far). Dubai was scariest, mass backlash against the slim Mitsubishi majority. It was weird that it felt weird. Vivien's numbers—or rather Kohaku Mardi's numbers—foretold ages ago that, when the Mitsubishi owned 67 percent of the land, the Earth would burn, but it still seemed out of place, violence so irrelevant, so unrelated to Joyce Faust, the Prince, the sides the Prince had worked so hard to make. But the Mitsubishi use set-sets, and used O.S., and made the Canner Device, and the Interim Directors still insist they were not wrong to do such things to defend their Members' interests at the cost of others', and for any bash' that's chafed at rent payments year after year, I guess that's trigger enough.

So much was riot and confusion that it was a genuine relief when parts of the war started to look like textbooks promised.

MASON declared war, a grim dawn ceremony on the ziggurat at Alexandria. The office of *pater patratus* sent a copy of the declaration to Charlemagne, who says it's five times scarier in Latin, but that the gist of it is a pledge to 'subdue and correct' all enemies which threaten the IMPERIUM and its continuity (here 'continuity' is code for the Prince, since it's still illegal to discuss the *Imperator Destinatus*). Within an hour of the ceremony, Masonic forces unfolded from their cities, the way satellites, compressed into cubes for launch, unfold their wings and wires and robot limbs. Jeeps rolled out, walls and wire, towers, boats around the seaports, bulldozers and steamrollers to carve out roads for trucks and motorcycles, and, inevitable like ill-omened comets, tanks. In mixed cities the bulwarks rose around Masonic districts, while cities where the Empire has a strong majority now have moats of roads and concrete. Tripoli, Cairo, Ankara, Istanbul, Constanța, Kraków, Antoniople, Kazan, Baku, Samarkand, Labokla, Caedeculmin, Kolkata: connect the dots and it feels like the geographic era has returned. And MASON can connect the dots, since the Levantine Reservation and its allies in Inner Asia—always friendliest with Masons—have granted the Empire the exclusive privilege of passing through their lands.

The Mitsubishi have taken to the sea. The first morning, thousands of ships poured out from nowhere, secreted in warehouses or assembled rapid-fire. Now, at night, the ship lights swarm like stars all the way from the Japanese islands past Seoul and Shanghai, along the Vietnamese coastlands, clear to the Indonesian archipelago. Dubai and lonely Hawaii also have their little firefly swarms of Mitsubishi ships, and patches twinkle around the Indian subcontinent, especially off the coast of Chennai. They're flying Mitsubishi trefoils and some nation-strat flags (Japan's is absent so far, and, while most of China's regional flags are common, the Dongbei identities are conspicuously absent, as are many expected sub-strats of India), but the boats also boast flags for the different Mitsubishi voting blocs, which seem to each control specific fleets. Greenpeace flags are common—on ships and rooftops—especially around Kuala Lumpur,

Mumbai, and in the fleet that neared New Zealand on the 12. And still more ships pour out. They haven't attacked anything yet, just floated about like overpopulated geese, and tested guns close to the coasts by Brisbane, Manila, and Taiwan.

Europe is best at war's basics, or rather the nation-strats are best at them, since the Mitsubishi seem to be benefitting much the same. Nation-strats already had uniforms and flags and ranks, dredged from their history books but real, with manuals, procedures, training leaflets, salaries updated from umpteen years ago, and recruitment posters with patriotic slogans that still tug heartstrings. Even I got an invitation from the Hellenic Navy. Every strat in the European Union has set up a station in each city to handle their people, house the stranded, recruit troops, and generally help Members find help they still trust. All the little armies have done so far is host parades and spread posters, a festive feeling, half reenactment and half war. It makes all this feel normal. But there's a scary underbelly to it: some recruitment offices—like the Flemish and Filipino ones behind Carlyle's Column—are only flying their own flags, or theirs and the EU's, but some—like our Greek one out by the Circus Max—already fly the Remaker V of Vs. They're not allowed to yet. On Saturday the revisions to Europe's constitution will go into effect, and King Isabel Carlos II of Spain will be crowned Emperor Isabel Carlos I of Europe. When Spain then weds Joyce Faust D'Arouet that afternoon, a suddenly legitimated Jehovah Epicurus Mason will be confirmed as Europe's heir apparent. But the Emperorship that the king and makeshift Parliament have crafted is a constitutional monarchy, checks and balances, far from the absolute surrender that the Prince demands. Europe's spirit is willing, the nation-strats so shocked to find themselves complicit with bloody Perry that they are eager to hand the kind, life-loving Prince a blank page with the words 'New Constitution' on the top. But Spain will be no breaker of the law, so the many branches of the European Union are debating whether they have the authority to grant such blank-slate power, even if the people clamor for it. Until they have decided, Europe's outposts may not fly the V of Vs. But some do anyway.

The Cousins are not at war. They're making peace. Their cafeterias and refugee centers are buzzing, and you hardly see a Cousin on the street who isn't wearing the old Red Crystal, often a nurse's cap and apron to go with it. They've set up dorms where stranded people can live, and work on Red Crystal humanitarian efforts. The Cousins and the Red Crystal are so synonymous now that volunteers from other Hives have started wearing red versions of their Hive symbols next to the Red Crystal to remind us "But I'm not a Cousin!" Ironic, really, since (I looked it up) the Red Crystal symbol itself—a red diamond with a white diamond inside—was created to signal neutrality, born at the turn of the Twenty-First Century, as the early tremors of the Church War made the old Red Cross and Red Crescent points of friction.

Bryar made it from Delhi as far as Mumbai, where they're happily surrounded by Cousins and Greenpeace Mitsubishi, all in favor of not destroying Earth.

Bryar's trying to get leaders into peace talks already, new efforts every day, and flooding public screens with reassuring logistical announcements: how to find help centers, what household goods and gadgets people can donate to the effort (who'd have thought an old vacuum slug had so many medical uses!), and especially pushing their Weapon Exchange Program. The Cousins have centers where you can turn in a lethal weapon—new or used, modern or archaic—and receive in return a shiny new 'Tiring Gun,' the Cousins' own design, a long-range stun gun certified humane. It's their big bid to keep the combat bloodless, armies that capture instead of killing, turning World Civil War into World Civil Freeze Tag. Good luck to them. They planned to give thousands of Tiring Guns to all the armies too, but with transportation down, thousands of crates of them are stuck uselessly at factories, or shipping out on boats.

From Casablanca I'm delighted to say we see much more of Heloïse than of Lorelei Cook. Heloïse is not actually the head of Red Crystal, but they're the human face of it, constantly releasing videos of how to diagnose dehydration or tie a bandage. But there are other videos, unofficial ones from Nurturists, advising people how to 'deal humanely' with a set-set (how best to capture 'it' and keep 'it' happy in confinement, what dangers each 'species' poses, ugh), and among the familiar types, Cartesian set-set, Stratford set-set, etc., new categories have entered the lexicon: D'Arouet set-set and gender set-set seem to be synonymous, then Alba Longa set-set (meaning Mycroft, Tully, and the other Mardis), O.S. set-set, Andō Oniwaban set-set (for Toshi, Masami, etc.), and, chill as a knife, Utopian set-set.

Utopia, as their first move of the war, gave the whole world bicycles. We would have printed up bicycles anyway, to supplement the city tram systems which weren't designed for car-less worlds, but they published (fee-free) a design that uses a fifth as much material as the lightest bike in the recipe book, so Earth has saved some five billion kilograms of printable matter for future use as bandages or clothing. Or more depressing things. I can't tell whether the gift eased the ill will which made so many praise the Atlantis Strike, but at least there have been no missile attacks on Oz, Shuilian, Lilliput, or Paititi. Not yet. In mixed cities, Utopians are keeping to their districts, with their scariest U-beasts patrolling the gates, but sometimes a squad of them will march down some central thoroughfare, bright with Delian suns and flanked by monsters. There are reports of mobs approaching Utopian districts, but all have been scared off by the wyrms and dinosaurs and steely-hearted robots.

Gordian is sitting tight and helping. The Brain-bash' and Brill's Institute have condemned O.S., and any 'criminal' attempt to target 'Donatien D'Arouet,' and they renewed the Hive's general condemnation of the death penalty, torture, violence, lethal weapons, and intentional homicide in any circumstance, including war. Few Brillists are joining the riots, and those who have are being arrested if they're within bicycle range of Gordian police. Meanwhile, Su-Hyeon's office gets a steady stream of helpful tip-offs, called in from one city or another where a Brillist watching the faces in the streets predicts fresh violence, and we estimate they've done as much as all of Romanova's forces to reduce casualties worldwide. Their only military action, if you can call it that, is that some Brillist neighborhoods have set up little check desks at their entry streets, whose staff politely waylay selected passersby and ask them to check their hidden weapons at the desk (and always guess right). It's a nice lull, but Su-Hyeon and I agree they can't cling to Brill's pacifism forever.

The great moment of suspense was when Vivien—President Ancelet—took to the podium to read aloud (in awkward, badly accented Spanish) the Humanist response to MASON's threat of war:

"More people have died from violence in the last twenty-four hours than were killed by O.S. in its history. The Humanist Hive stands committed to finding an alternative to the O.S. system, but, after the verdict of the recent *Terra Ignota,* our Hive cannot and will not condemn Lesley and Ockham Saneer, former President Ganymede de la Trémoïlle, or any of the Humanist officers who saved millions of lives using a means which was not illegal under the laws of our Hive or of the Alliance. MASON has threatened to subdue by violence all Hives and human powers—including the Alliance itself—which do not condemn and expel Ojiro Sniper and their supporters. While the Humanist Hive does not endorse the assassination of Epicuro Mason, to wear the bull's-eye, and to respect what Ojiro Sniper stands for, is to exercise freedom of conscience and opinion, liberties essential to Human Dignity. Therefore, as of today, September eighth, twenty-four fifty-four, I recommend that the Humanist Hive recognize a State of War between ourselves and the Masons, and between ourselves and any other Hive or human power which would use the names of justice and reform to disguise acts of systematic and self-interested violence which threaten our lives, our laws, our Hive, our Human Dignity, and the Universal Free Alliance which has enabled this best and boldest epoch in human history. I hereby call upon all Human Members to cast your votes, whether to reject my recommendation and face this crisis using only peaceful means, or whether to recognize this State of War, and empower me as President to commit all the force and resources of our Hive to engage our enemies with military actions defensive and offensive."

72 percent voted for war. Which leaves the 28 percent who didn't. They point at the true revolution which I've accidentally hidden going Hive by Hive: the Second Great Renunciation. More than half a billion people have dropped their Hives in the past two weeks, one Member in twenty, with bursts right after MASON and Vivien declared war. Plenty turned Graylaw, but many who wear the bull's-eye have left other Hives to join the Humanists, while those screaming loudest for Sniper's blood are flocking to MASON, or to Europe, trusting sweet King Spain to realize justice without stooping to vendetta. A surge has suddenly signed up for nation-strats too, bash'es and individuals who never cared before that they had Greek or Austrian or Georgian blood suddenly craving comrades. Real old-fashioned racism has reared its head, or fear of it at least. Many millions have joined the Cousins and Red Crystal, which I would call altruistic, except that so many of them are either people of obvious east Asian ancestry

stuck in Masonic or European capitals, or non-Mitsubishi of obvious non-Asian stock now stuck in Mitsubishi-dominated cities, or the East. The Cousin's wrap and Red Crystal armband are shield and armor for those who count the faces around them not like theirs, and fear that the snores are growing shallow of that long-slumbering beast, majority. Please, please let such fears be unfounded.

All this is distant, watched like sports or fiction through my lenses. Everything split in half with the fall of Cielo de Pájaros, into the immediate—this room, this city—and the World. I know that what's happening outside Romanova is still real, I see the videos, the voices, numbers, I still affect them with my words, my calming pleas, but it's inaccessible, like a game world, or a Utopian's coat, while what tromps by me in the streets here is ten times more real than it ever felt before. There is a difference now between a window and a screen.

The first intrusion to threaten both was Carlyle Foster-Kraye, with a question complex enough that a street patrol passed them up the command chain to our door guards, then to the nearest officers, then hall by hall to the confused main room, where the remains of Papa's best, plus Su-Hyeon, I, the Censor's Guard, and what odd Senators are stuck in the city gather to make Romanova sort of run. All stared as Carlyle entered. All have to stare at this strange, sweet, broken, spying, Gag-gene, ducal bastard, Deist sensayer, about whom every reader of Mycroft's history knows far too much.

"Explain again what you want, Cousin Foster," their escort invited.

Kind Carlyle Foster-Kraye fingered the Blacklaw sash about their hips but did not comment on the error. "I want construction supplies and workers, urgently, to rebuild the entrance to the Sensayers' Conclave main visitors' center. Also six buildings in different quarters of the city to use as activity centers, and guards with Alliance uniforms to stand outside of each and make them feel official, an ongoing budget of, say, five million per month, and free use of the Alliance's official global emergency announcement system to make people take my updates seriously, and a whole lot of local volunteers, including, ideally, some of you. Oh, and short-term all the apples and honey we can scrape together."

Senator Charlemagne Guildbreaker rose from a nearby desk and smiled. "A robust list. All this is for the Conclave?"

Carlyle nodded. "Rosh Hashanah starts on Thursday."

Su-Hyeon beside me gasped instantly, but for me it took some moments to rummage through the all-faith holiday list we memorize in school, jumbled in my memory like an overstuffed old closet. Rosh Hashanah . . . Jewish holy day . . . one of a string of them all close together . . .

"Nobody can get to a Reservation to celebrate it," Carlyle added.

Now I gasped too, and saw recognition's satisfaction on the sensayer's face.

"You see it," Carlyle confirmed. "Without the cars, nobody can go to Reservations for holidays, so everyone who practices a ceremonial faith is going to be forced to risk outing themselves to everyone around them, and to break the First Law if the ceremony involves any kind of gathering, unless we handle things very carefully. We need to handle this first one as best we can, not only for our Jewish Members, but for Members of other faiths who're terrified of being outed when their holidays roll around. So we need to build a space that can host ceremonies without outing people. I want to make a chamber between the lobby and the ceremony rooms, private with no windows, with one entrance but exits to four different ceremony spaces. We invite lots of people to come, practitioners and volunteers, so no one can be sure that you're a particular faith just because you went to the center on that faith's holiday. Then everyone who comes goes into the antechamber one by one. One door is labeled that it has the ceremony, so the practitioners—Jews in the case of Rosh Hashanah—go in that door and do their ceremony, while everyone else goes in one of the other three doors which will host faith-neutral sensayer-led group enrichment discussions lasting the same duration. No one can know who went in each door, so even if you saw someone you know in the lobby, if you don't see them in the enrichment discussion with you, the odds are still two to one that they went to one of the other generic rooms and not the ceremonial one. It outs the ceremony participants to one another, but there's no perfect option, so hopefully this will be the least uncomfortable."

A pause as we all considered.

"Couldn't you just have the volunteers go to the ceremony too?" Im-Jin suggested. "I know tons of people go to Passover Seders when sensayer centers host them."

"Rosh Hashanah involves praying out loud, in a group, in Hebrew, and even with a pronunciation guide it's really obvious who's spoken those words before and who hasn't. With time, volunteers could train for particular ceremonies, but not so fast, and not without fail. Plus this system will work for ceremonies where non-practitioners aren't supposed to be there, as well as for those where anyone can come."

Im-Jin nodded along. "Right. So, four doors and lots of volunteers, that sounds very doable."

"Great! I want to get it underway immediately, so the Conclave can set an example to guide people through doing the same in centers in every quarter of this city and every city, that's why we need the big budget, since with transit so disrupted, big cities need peripheral centers everyone can reach."

"And apples and honey are for the ceremony?"

"Mostly to make clear we intend to work hard to source things for ceremonies. Etrog and lulav for Sukkot will be the first tricky one. The Conclave has them growing already, but not everyone will, but a lot of basic kitchen trees actually have etrog and the rest if they have the default multifaith pack, and while there isn't time to grow the whole fruit before Sukkot, we asked some rabbis, who say there's time for the tree to grow the flower that would become an etrog, so you can pollinate that and use it so long as the lump at the flower base that will be the fruit has swelled enough to be visible to the eye, and happily there is time for a well-fed kitchen tree to do that and grow the other three plants too, since leaves are fast. If we solve the Sukkot problem it'll set people at ease. And it would be great if some of you personally attended the first few ceremonies at the Conclave, both to endorse the program, and as cover in case any of you does practice a ceremonial faith, because it's really important no one here who's running Romanova now gets outed, it'll cause panic if people think one faith is seizing power, and—are you going to announce rationing? Please announce rationing? I assume we'll need rationing, because nobody can ship food anywhere anymore, and if we could announce that ceremony meals at Conclave centers are exempt from rationing, that would be an amazing excuse people can use to come, and participate, and pretend it's just to get extra food, and nobody has to be suspicious of anybody!" This long meander poured out of Carlyle, frantic yet rehearsed, as if they'd lain awake all night in bed chewing it over. "But we really, really have to do it right from the beginning. We're too late for the equinox and the start of Mahalaya, but if we do really well with this set of Jewish holidays, and with Navaratri, then practitioners of all ceremonial faiths will calm down, but if we botch them, and everyone sees us botch them, and people get outed, then all people of ceremonial faith will get more and more scared as their own big holidays approach, and it'll be a giant powder keg added to the war, and it'll get worse, and worse, building up to December, when we'll hit every single winter solstice–type holiday all at once, dozens of religions threatened, including Christmas, and also, Ramadan is likely to begin December twenty-first."

Breath left me. Christmas and Ramadan? The twin sleeping dragons whose tussles have so often drenched the Earth in blood! Had Islam's flowing lunar calendar really landed Ramadan so close to Christmas? With cars it's effortless to hide a month of fasting, restaurants reverse their hours, "Party Nights," and everybody bips around the world to never eat in daylight just for fun. Now will they be all outed? Every Christian and Muslim in our world within five days? The public fear of that event alone could shatter screen and window both. We were all staring, I realized. Not at Carlyle—at Charlemagne Guildbreaker. It wasn't just their Middle Eastern coloring that made us stare, so common in the Empire. It was geography. The great Masonic capitals were rolling out their war roads, knitting together a geographic body as some undead beast might reknit its carcass from its bones and rise again: Tripoli, Cairo, Ankara, Istanbul, Baku, Samarkand. Connecting those dots mapped out a very specific region, MASON's hollow Empire with the Levantine Reservation and its Inner Asian allies at its heart. We all presume that bloody Christianity hides divided, strongest perhaps among the Humanists, Europe, and Cousins, but divided, weakened, tame. But if, as many guess, its sibling Islam hides primarily among the Masons, now is the worst, worst moment to rip off the mask. Ramadan without the cars, and Christmas at the same time, outing both at once—imagine looking out over these rows of desks and *knowing*! I know the toxic strains of both religions died out in the Church War, that only the peaceful strains survived, innocents who suffered as much as anyone as the extremists poisoned the fringes of their faiths, but . . . I was hugging myself. Charlemagne Guildbreaker . . . No, it wasn't something outing sweet old Charlemagne I feared, it was the Empire. I know Cornel MASON isn't Muslim, they helped Achilles sacrifice a bull to the Greek gods, but others don't know that, and MASON fasts for lots of holidays, most leaders do, cover in case someday one of them really . . . and we know a lot of Masons actually are, so people could fear . . . and all Earth knows what not-so-secret faith soon-to-be-Emperor Isabel Carlos holds, and while it's a milder strain of Christianity, a cowpox that inoculates against its deadly cousins, it still makes this feel too familiar: Europe's Empire, MASON's Empire, this won't turn into faith on faith, will it? Will it? Even the fear that it could might spark a million acts of panicked rashness nothing can undo.

If I live past a hundred, will I gain the grace to smile in the face of history's bloody cycles, as Charlemagne Guildbreaker and Speaker Jin Im-Jin did?

"I think that's all very good thinking, Hiveless Foster," Charlemagne concluded, as warmly and calmly as if Carlyle had invited them to the dedication of a new playground. "I fully support giving the Conclave every resource it needs to handle these issues, here and worldwide. We'll back you every way we can. And I'd be delighted to join you for Rosh Hashanah."

"We should also do ceremonies here!" This was Su-Hyeon's quick addition. "Everyone in this office works extreme hours, it will be hard to go out for things, but if you made this one of your centers, we could host some of the easier holidays, not ones that might out people but the ones that anybody can attend. That way, we can announce to the public that everybody currently running the Alliance might be any faith or mix of faiths, and set a good example."

"Perfection." Ex-Cousin Carlyle beamed. "Let the logistics begin!"

Panic withdrew its fangs as I watched these three working with Carlyle, two age-grayed Senators flanking our bright young Censor. They were ready for this, for any challenge, ready to heal window and screen alike. Those first days, solving problems, that's when it was born, our makeshift Triumvirate: Su-Hyeon, Jin Im-Jin, and Charlemagne Guildbreaker. They rule Romanova, and the Universal Free Alliance too, since most other remnants of the Senate are too fractious to speak civilly even on video. As Censor, Su-Hyeon has emergency Dictator powers, but they've never been used in the history of the Alliance, so I don't think people would actually believe in them if the two great Senators weren't constantly shadowing Su-Hyeon on broadcasts, looking wizened and approving. They're the great-grandparent generation, I think that's why we've fallen back on Jin Im-Jin and Charlemagne Guildbreaker. Not that they know more of war than we do, but they at least grew up in, knew, and even ruled a world before the generation Joyce Faust ensnared and spoiled. They remember how the Hives worked when there was no gender brothel, no secret insiders, when Spain's king had a happy family life, and Humanists flip-flopped between congresses and decemvirs with every vote, and no secret puppeteer was reserving almost all Earth's highest offices for gender addicts. They know how Earth has solved crises before. So, as we see war's floodgates opened by the potentates whom Joyce Faust shaped for fifty years (I traced the docs, they left sensayer school and bought their first brothel in 2404), the other generations—older and younger—are the rocks Earth clings to: the oldest Senators, and fresh Su-Hyeon. And me.

"Because I'm the Anonymous," I said in answer to Jin Im-Jin's stare as Su-Hyeon sat the four of us down for a private meeting after Carlyle left: Romanova's two most senior Senators, the new Dictator-Censor and . . . some random Servicer.

"Ah, thank you." Jin's fingers fidgeted, likely counting out the Brillist set they read in my face and poise. "Would've been awkward for us all if I'd guessed."

"The new Anonymous!" Charlemagne Guildbreaker cried. "This is an honor! Delighted to meet you, and to be working with you! Your essay 'On Fanaticism' was a masterstroke!" And with that the Mason who broke the Geisler case, who exposed Rongcorp's Seven Mornings funnel, whose drafts midwifed the Greenpeace-Mitsubishi Merger, and who had cracked the *Sanctum* seal to read aloud the name 'Cornelius Semaphoros' when the watch fires proclaimed Aeneas MASON's death, *that* Mason was shaking my hand with both of theirs, eyes sparkling. "An absolute honor!"

An itch told me there were tears on my cheeks, but words wouldn't come.

Su-Hyeon rescued me. "I called [Anonymous] here because I think the four of us can do a lot right now, for this city and the world, if we work together to plan and be the voice of the Alliance. What I have right now is a lot of authority, a bit of infrastructure, and about a dozen officers in every city in the world. By myself I don't think I could make much of it. I don't have the right experience or training, and I don't have the confidence of people who have barely heard of me. But if you three help me, I think we can make something of it, something powerful."

Charlemagne Guildbreaker scratched the white beard which makes their face such a timeless picture of jovial old age that it's impossible to guess whether they're in their nineties or their hundred-twenties. "What sort of something? A neutral power? Or would you support a side?"

"Either," Su-Hyeon answered instantly. "Anything, whatever you suggest. I want to save lives. I'm prepared to be guided by you about what side or stance to take. I love the Alliance and I like the idea of preserving it as a neutral force, but if the two of you tell me the human race will be better off if we throw our support behind the Masons, or the Hiveguard, or the Remakers, or Natekari's Blacklaws, anything, I'm prepared to consider whatever your experience suggests."

The two elders exchanged long, approving frowns.

"You know I support my Emperor in all things." Senator Guildbreaker held out the arm which had borne the gray *Familiaris* armband since the day they passed the Adulthood Competency Exam.

"Yes," Su-Hyeon answered, "but I also know you're usually neutral in the Senate, because you say forwarding general Alliance business forwards the Masons, too. Is that still your opinion, now that you're at war?"

"Largely, yes," they granted. "The Alliance and the neutral Hiveless populations are very valuable to the Empire. And, for the moment, I believe I'd be more use to Caesar helping you keep the Alliance extant than anything else I can do from here in Romanova."

"Would you want me to aid the Masons? And condemn Sniper?"

Guildbreaker paused, and in the pursed edge of their lips I recognized a little hint of Martin. "Not short-term. Taking a side overtly would make it feel like Romanova's become a puppet. Your dozen agents in each town would abandon you to follow Hives and strats."

Su-Hyeon brightened. "Then you think we should remain neutral? Would you help me with that consistently, even if sometimes individual actions might be against Masonic interests?"

"Yes, I would, unless my Emperor orders otherwise. And if we ask Caesar to swear their Inviolate Oath that they won't ask me to betray Alliance neutrality, they will not break it."

"Perfect, thank you!" Su-Hyeon answered. Color was returning to their cheeks, now that we had the beginnings of a plan. "Speaker Jin, do you feel the same?"

"That Masons believe in inviolate oaths? Yes, they genuinely do." A teasing laugh glittered in the bright, dark eyes that peeked out from the folds of Jin Im-Jin's face.

I felt suddenly worse, then better, as the phrase 'Inviolate Oath' invoked the sleeping twin dragons once again, then reminded me that they were fossils, nothing more. Masons did believe in MASON's Inviolate Oath, all of them, belief not in some secret, shared religion, but in something newer, brighter, open to us all: the Empire, their Hive, our Hives, our good new world. Whatever private things Masons or anybody did in Reservations, or with sensayers, were not barbaric practices, but rites a person of our day and age could love, respect, and want to join in. This was the Universal Free Alliance. Our Muslims and Christians were not the Church War's zealots but had evolved from them, like birds from bloody dinosaurs, and were as beautiful. I'd been thinking the Anonymous should release an essay to endorse Carlyle Foster's plans to deal with ceremonial faiths. I felt now that I could make it a good one.

Smirking Su-Hyeon offered Jin Im-Jin some light Korean syllables which sounded like teasing, before switching back to English. "I meant, would you help make the Alliance a functional neutral body in this war?"

"Of course," Jin answered. "No matter how ridiculous the sides get, everyone will need a neutral and functional Alliance to lubricate negotiations."

"Even if Gordian gets drawn into fighting for a side?"

Jin's cough was half wince. "That would end fast; we're barely bigger than Utopia and don't have any dragons. But the old Brain-bash' is wise enough to see that, Felix too, and if they aren't then I suppose we'll need a strong and functional Alliance to slap sense into them."

Guildbreaker's brows rose. "You would side with the Alliance against your Hive?"

"Of course not. If I take off my sweater I'll be cold. But my Hive won't oppose a neutral Alliance," they continued, "and if I'm wrong about something that basic, I . . . I'm not wrong about something that basic, I'm just not."

Guildbreaker gave a warm, assenting nod.

The Speaker matched the Mason's smile warmth for warmth, but all warmth faded as their sharp stares turned on me. "And is our new Anonymous neutral as well?"

I just stared, still caught up in Jin's joke about the sweater. Watching Speaker Jin from a distance, one can forget their impossible extended years, but, sitting beside them, the number 150 haunts every motion of their too-tiny body, energetic like a cricket but fragile enough to shatter like ribbon candy. Instinct faster than thought—the same which makes you jump to aid a child or a pregnant person—is always on edge around them, making you tensed to hold a door, or block a draft, or bring a blanket, or, in this case, making you panic at the thought of cold, and what that cold could cost.

"I can vouch for [Anonymous]," Su-Hyeon answered for me.

"Can you indeed?" Jin Im-Jin searched my face, then Su-Hyeon's, then mine, then Su-Hyeon's, the Speaker's dry fingertips fidgeting out their silent calculations as their gaze cut deep.

I refused to flinch. "Ask," I invited.

The Speaker smiled. "Pick a number."

"Five."

"Larger than five."

"One hundred thirteen million, six hundred and four."

"Color?"

"Silver-gray."

They gave a little gasp, as when a judge sees the first good touch in a fencing match. "You were a Humanist but considered Europe, and it was . . . murrrrr—yes, murder, interesting . . . not too long ago, either . . . and Su-Hyeon thinks you wouldn't do it again but you're . . . pretty sure you would."

It took some moments for me to parse that as a question. "Correct."

"And Vivien Ancelet . . . I see, you're moderately puppyish about them but not enough to get pulled Humanist . . . no, there's someone . . . something . . . someone . . . something . . . more than one something . . . and you're in grief shock . . . recent loss, but complicated . . . ah! Canner, of course. Condolences. And what do you call J.E.D.D. Mason?"

This time I paused, just for a breath's length, but I had to. All the universe flashed through my mind, the black, the sea of stars, the Visitor, the war and all the war's fire, Their Host's bloody Hello, and pain, the pain I had seen in the words and black eyes of the Kind and precious Stranger, pain I couldn't stop, so powerless, so precious, here impossible and real, our Guest. "The Prince."

Now Speaker Jin paused, which made me somewhat proud. "Derivative yet original. That's good." A nod at Su-Hyeon. "And you two have slept near each other on the same floor, or in the same bed, repeatedly, slumber-party style, but never dated or had sex or interest therein?"

I straightened, keeping the Speaker's eyes off poor, shy Su-Hyeon's flustered flush. "Correct."

"Then I'll trust Su-Hyeon's vouching for you. Is that enough for you, Carmen?"

I didn't understand the name 'Carmen' at first; only when Charlemagne Guildbreaker answered did I realize that even Earth-shaking Masonic patriarchs have nicknames. "I trusted them when they entrusted me with the identity of the Anonymous."

With that, and Su-Hyeon's glowing smile, our four-person Triumvirate began. It's not that oxymoronic—I can be a fourth Triumvir if 'Tai-kun' can be a Tenth Director.

We told the others more about us then, and for the reader's sake I suppose I should explain a bit of how things stand between myself and Su-Hyeon. 'Quasi-sibling' is the best descriptor, though we've only known each other for three years. We are each inheritors of half Vivien's kingdom: Su-Hyeon the next Censor, I the next Anonymous. Our introduction was awkward, the same day I realized Mycroft was the Eighth Anonymous and so became the Ninth, when a giddy, hyperactive Vivien took me to their bash'house to meet everyone, but Bryar and Su-Hyeon above all. Bryar was instant warmth, of course, but Su-Hyeon was closed and intimidating in their uniform, and has that kind of beautiful face, with high cheekbones and riveting dark eyes, that, when it was new to me, felt severe and authoritative, and made me paranoid they were going to turn me in for breaking some intricacy of my Servicer parole that I'd foolishly forgotten. But then we got talking about name statistics, and the next thing we knew, it was dawn. That night was perfect, one of us starting a chain of inference only to have the other jump right to the end with us and then go further, and soon Mycroft and Vivien fell quiet and just listened as we both took off the brakes we use with everybody else.

Su-Hyeon is the child of a Korean threesome within the Kosala bash', one of twelve bash'children raised in Mumbai in that fountain of energy which passes for a bash'house. Su-Hyeon and the others were half grown before Bryar and Vivien's late marriage grafted their two bash'es together; actually, it's more accurate to say that the twenty-one boisterous Cousins invited the five nervous, scholarly members of Ancelet's quiet French Graylaw bash' over for dinner and drowned them in home cooking until they forgot to leave. I'm told that Su-Hyeon as a child was nervous and scholarly too, at least compared to a village-sized mass of buzzing Cousins, but one look at the math puzzles with which the Ancelets fill their nights and Su-Hyeon was a vocateur. They apprenticed in the Censor's office at once, and became the strongest link between the bash'-halves, apart from the True Love which drips from Bryar and Vivien. It turns out Su-Hyeon and I studied at the Quirinal Campus at the same time, but we never crossed paths there, and now my sentence is an iron wall between us and any talk of bash' or family. Quasi-siblings, then, inheritors of two separate but equal titles, apprenticed to the same amazing mentor. Servicer life and Su-Hyeon's vocation don't give us much time together, but what we have we savor. And there is one other wall between us. Not envy—my head for math is a notch less superhuman than Su-Hyeon's, and Su-Hyeon's knack for rhetoric is several decicíceros short of mine. It's the unshared past, the bits of our Venn diagram that don't overlap but come up sometimes suddenly and remind me that, in some respects, I barely know Su-Hyeon, or Su-Hyeon me: Korean, Greek; Cousins, Humanists; the Senate spotlight, Servicer drudgery; the first twenty years of both our lives; life in that famous bash' in Mumbai and my bloody homicides. And Su-Hyeon barely knows the Prince. All that puts our friendship on thin ice, as if we're marching arm in arm but with any step either of us might punch through into the frozen, dark unknown.

Or it used to put it there, I should say, because now we are together, every day, working and collaborating, planning and talking, and making everyone believe that the Alliance is still real. A lot of it has been issuing Executive Consults (equivalent to a Senatorial Consult except that we made it up) when some opinionmonger makes the kind of ripples that make mobs. Meanwhile, Papa's office—or what was poor Papa's office—is our headquarters, issuing warnings based on Su-Hyeon's calculations (or Brillist calls), alerting Mitsubishi landowners when talk turns hostile, guiding set-sets to hiding places, and alerting minorities that they are minorities, and what that means. It's all information games, not force, trios of distant agents dispatched on bicycles when we think calm words backed by the Alliance crest will be enough. Graylaw hubs aside, we were lucky if we started with a dozen real Alliance agents in any given city, since they were never more than Police of Last Resort to advise local systems when Hive laws got too tangled. Su-Hyeon has quintupled that force in two weeks, offering sofas and office attics to the stranded if they'll sign up (and pass Jin Im-Jin's makeshift vetting process), but it was only four days ago that we celebrated finally having eighteen officers for every city on our Worry List, which means we can finally go from twelve-hour shifts to eight. The really scary part was making the Worry List in the first place, pinpointing the cities where the mix of flags and partisans was most foreboding. The most helpless people are the small minorities surrounded by seas of hostile other, but at least they know they're in danger and are taking precautions. The true powder kegs are the places where the sides mix most: Hyderabad, whose treasure markets draw so many mixing peoples; Singapore; Toronto; francophone Kinshasa where the Reservation border looms so close; or bull's-eye-covered London. Jokesters in HQ asked Su-Hyeon to wait to post the Worry List so they could open a betting pool on which would be the most endangered city. Su-Hyeon killed the joke dead: "Romanova." I said there was a difference now between a window and a screen.

There is also a difference between the other Triumvirs and me. I mean more than my invisibility as the fourth Triumvir. I mean that, after hours, when I refuse Su-Hyeon's offer of a cot in the side office, the Censor's guards escort me home to Vivien's flat on the Palatine, with its view down over sloping streets where others can't see what I see. They see the obvious: windows black and lifeless, shopping streets empty or filled with too-large homogenous crowds, the signs that multiply above the doorways: MITSUBISHI ONLY or NO U-SETS or NO *Vs*. But I see more. I see Servicer 'volunteers' out 'fixing' a 'kiosk' on a strategic corner. I see another waiting by the empty bakery downstairs to report that I'm home safe. I see Achilles's orders moving. And if we Myrmidons are moving, a subtler force is moving too. Because when the guards walk me in, and turn down my offer of tea before they head back, I plead 'the cat' if there's an animal smell, or if something knocked over a cup left on the kitchen counter. It scared me half to death the first night, when that creeping feeling that you aren't alone in an empty room grew to the realization that there really was the warmth and stuffiness of breath behind me. I was guesstimating the steps between me and the kitchen knives when a shadow congealed into the soft face of a black lion, and the wall beside me glistened with the blink-fast outline of a sun.

"Huxley Mojave," I pronounced, and naming dispelled the boogeyman effect. "We both failed the same mission, didn't we?" I whispered, wondering if lions' faces always seemed so sad. "You were guarding Mycroft too."

I barely caught their "Yes." The front of the coat fell open, exposing a face, vizor, black hair, a scraped and bandaged chin, and an arm in a sling, the same type of cheery blue field-station bandage that Carlyle Foster-Kraye had carried home from the tsunami front. We all tried.

"Where will you go now?" I asked. "Do you need help getting to other Utopians?"

"No. Now I'm warding you." Their hand slid out of their nowhere and placed in mine the soft and battered hat. Mycroft's smell. Memory attacked, the flash-frozen image of the crowd, the Forum skies alive with bright wings racing off to aid Atlantis, and the fallen hat slumped over the last dusty footprints which could ever prove that such a creature walked this Earth. Was I next of kin, then, in Utopia's estimation? Fittest to receive this remnant, as close as we would ever have to a corpse? Perhaps I was. Before my sobs could overcome me, Huxley's hand returned and pressed something into my other palm. I looked. One could call it a gun, if one can call the arrow-slim and deadly peregrine a bird. "I won't teach you the science," Huxley began, "but I will teach you to defend yourself."

Chapter FOUR

The Uniform Question

Written September 24, 2454
Events of yesterday
Romanova, etc.

"We have four hours to save Sydney, Australia."

Su-Hyeon's voice was not my usual alarm clock, but my tracker monitor confirmed I'd slept enough to graduate from 'unsafe' back to 'overtired,' so I fumbled for my boots before remembering I'd slept in them. "Is there time to explain the danger?" I asked. Sydney was no surprise, high on our Worry List as one of Earth's most Hive-mixed megacities, but when Su-Hyeon came to me with emergencies, half the time it was something straightforward, and half the time it was $x \geq 3\sqrt{(\text{population}/\text{income})} \div 0.545n$, where $n \equiv$ condo prices in $€/m^2$, and it sounded like we didn't have a half hour for math.

"Unless certain demands are met, a Mitsubishi fleet of at least a hundred and seventeen ships will invade Sydney in four hours eleven minutes."

That was clear enough. I wriggled aside so Su-Hyeon could join me on our new favorite catnap spot: an inexplicable sofa we had discovered on a landing halfway down the fire stairs behind Papa's office. "What demands?"

Su-Hyeon presented a plate of beans and fruit salad. "I've got your action list prepped, but the Triumvirate's negotiating now. You should eat and listen to the end before you make your calls. I'll add you listening only. Ready?"

I carved out a spot for my plate on the mountain of fresh-in-wrapper DNA kits which loomed around the sofa, occasionally plopping a crinkly vanguard in our laps. "Ready," I said.

First sight made me grip the cushions hard. Before my lenses fired up, I'd braced myself for a glaring bright meeting room, for hard words, even for smoke and blood, but not for the bitter, old blast of prey-fear and antipathy which I wish had not been trained into me by our Visitor's sinister angel: Dominic Seneschal. I know they're a world away, can't touch me, can't even see me on audio-only, but I came to Madame's first, not just as Vivien's heir but as Mycroft's, and the new puppy required breaking in. I have been tricked across the threshold into that cell which Mycroft, Carlyle, and so many others christened with their vomit. Vivien's protection saved me from the worst, but even now with Su-Hyeon here and beans and sofa all surrounding me, the sight of Dominic was *not* welcome.

My lenses showed full morning in Tōgenkyō, whose white sun made the Pacific and glassy lotus-petal skyscrapers painful through the office's picture windows. Except for Greenpeace Director Jyothi Bandyopadhyay, who joined by screen, the Mitsubishi Interim Directors were all together, crisp and grave around their oval table, and most of them in military dress. This was my first close glimpse of the uniforms satellites had already spotted on the decks of the spreading fleet. The jackets were works of art—our opulent age has improved war that way at least—as fine as the finest Mitsubishi suit, some deep night blue with elaborate linear designs of flowing water, others night-green with knife-fine maple branches, which I think must code army and navy. Stripes of rank (which I must learn to interpret) glittered on shoulders, cuffs, and chest in gold as well as Mitsubishi white and scarlet. Like normal Mitsubishi suits, the collar cuts had variants for Chinese, Japanese, and Korean sub-factions, but Greenpeace Director Jyothi Bandyopadhyay was out of uniform, and Dominic too. Or rather Dominic, lurking in the central seat, was still in their black eighteenth-century costume which is, I suppose, a uniform of service to the Prince.

"... if we extend the time allowed for implementation," Charlemagne Guildbreaker was saying as the audio kicked in. Their calm voice and fluffy beard in a side screen was as cheering as Su-Hyeon's warmth beside me. "Distribution will be a challenge with the cars down. Home-manufacture materials are precious—most cities are already rationing them—and if the Imperial Guard is anything to go by, a lot of these uniforms will have components that can't be produced at home anyway. This will be a much less daunting proposition for the leaders you want us to win over if we can tell them they have, say, thirty days to figure out how to design and distribute thousands of uniforms, time enough for those who don't have uniforms already to design them, and for those who do to develop alternatives to hard-to-manufacture parts."

"Thirty days!"

"I would have said two months if you'd suggested this before the war began, and that was with the cars."

"We would have demanded it then if it had occurred to us that any Hive would *not* make uniforms!" It was Director Lu Biaoji who snapped back fastest, Lu Yong's replacement heading the stronger Shanghai bloc, and as stately as a king in their new military uniform, its rank marks sparkling on their shoulders like old gold. This new Lu was a cousin of the old, and this the only bloc where family had dug its roots so deep that not even the hurricane of public outrage could rip the reins of power free. "Thirty days is absolutely unacceptable. Our members are facing fresh attacks every hour, and you propose another month while these biased courts continue to give attackers free rein citing a military law that doesn't even exist! I have Members in Sydney being held for attempted murder for fighting back against a mob who killed—not just hurt but killed—several of their bash'members, while the attackers walk free because the police say they were soldiers in a military action. Whose soldiers? What military action? There must be accountability!"

Ma Yimin took up the thread, Shanghai's former Comptroller, who, after decades of loyal backburner grunt work, had been expelled from Wang Baobao's bloc last year (some kerfuffle over a reclamation project), disgraced at the perfect moment to ride this new swing of the pendulum back to power. "We all agree Hives have the right to make different laws for different Members, but if they want to have different rules for soldiers and civilians, it needs to be as clear as Blacklaw and Whitelaw. Europe has it right. Members must register as military, laws must be consistent, and there must be uniforms—not in a month, tomorrow—so attackers and victims can both know they'll be tried under a specific law, soldier or civilian, not whichever is most convenient for the faction in power." I almost laughed at how perfectly Ma Yimin, whose half-Masonic birth bash' might have made them a little different, still fell into place behind Lu Biaoji. I mulled over which old favors it was—Zhejiang Campus, Trifold Investments, Dubai—which had locked this new Shanghai pair into 'lead' and 'follow' so instantly that it felt as if their two predecessors had just put on different faces. But it stopped feeling funny fast. My stash of trivia—this clutter of Romanova insider gossip—would it become a weapon too now? Just as much as sticks and stones?

Patient Carmen Guildbreaker (the nickname still makes me giggle as well as smile) shook their head. "We will not win the others over if you set this impossible timeframe. Not because it will be difficult, but because it will be implausible. You want us to present this proposal as if it came from us, not you. I agree that's a good idea, and will make people see that it benefits all sides, not just yours, but if I go to my Emperor and suggest uniforms and military law, and I say they have to be accepted in four hours and implemented in twenty-four, Caesar will ask the reason for my haste. Before such questions, I could not hide your involvement."

It fell to grim old Chen Chengguo—Wang Laojing's successor as the voice of Beijing—to voice what glared in all their eyes. "You said you could be neutral in this."

"I can. I am fully authorized to lie to my Emperor, but I'm also bad at it. And even if I weren't, this lie is too transparent. If you want the Triumvirate to present this as our plan, it has to look like one of our plans, with balance and a plausible degree of moderation. If this came from us, even if we were in haste, we would offer . . . two weeks? . . ." Carmen waited for Im-Jin and Su-Hyeon to nod in their respective screens. ". . . for the Hives to design military law codes from scratch, and a month for them to make and distribute uniforms."

Beijing was not satisfied. "Are you claiming the Masons don't already have military law? This sounds like buying time."

"Not at all." Still Carmen clung to a smile. "I'm certain the Empire has a robust body of military law, but it may not be sufficiently contemporary."

"Contemporary? What do you mean?"

Speaker Jin Im-Jin's dry laugh cut through from another side screen. "Carmen means their uniforms may predate pants." They gave us a few breaths to savor that one, and since my feed was muted, I was free to chuckle. "Seriously, Directors, even Europe took some time redesigning the relics of the Church War. I'd bet good money we can get most everyone to agree to the concept in four hours, but the world isn't going to be fully in uniform tomorrow."

"Triumvirs." Dominic's black growl undid the spell of Jin's humor. "Your four hours are becoming three. We will liberate the Mitsubishi of Sydney. When our fleet reaches the harbor, if we have the solid promise that all forces there will soon be uniformed, then we will wait, perhaps . . . forty-eight hours to enter the city, so our troops will be able to greet allies as allies and avoid the neighborhoods held by our enemies. If we have no such promise, we will have no choice but to enter right away, and fight our way through the streets until we reach our Members, treating every other person we encounter on the way as armed and dangerous."

Su-Hyeon frowned. "Threats are—"

"Real," Dominic barked back. "Argument will not widen the Pacific. Four hours. The Europeans, your own Romanovan forces, and Red Crystal have uniforms, and our troops have orders how to treat each. For the others, we do not require polished, final law codes that will never be revised, we require the ability to distinguish friend from foe from fleeing bystander."

The repetition of 'four hours' made me feel strangely tired. It was all so absurdly ponderous, the fleet shown in a side screen in my lenses, crawling with invisible sloth across the monotonous Pacific. It seemed impossible that we could know, and watch, and have every force on Earth a call away, and yet we could no more catch up to these barely moving specks than I could chase the latest Mars launch on my bicycle.

Su-Hyeon brightened, and it was slightly surreal seeing them wiggle their arms on screen, and simultaneously feeling their elbow against my real live ribs. "Then you'd accept stopgap uniforms?"

"Stopgap?"

Su-Hyeon flashed something up in our lenses, and I recognized (to my embarrassment) my own drawings of my most recent uniform designs—no, worse, older drawings, a set Achilles had pronounced 'barely less awful' than my first, and even those improvements were mostly because I plagiarized Apollo. "If all you want is the ability to distinguish sides, then uniforms don't have to be a suit of clothes." Su-Hyeon zoomed in on a sleeve striped with Remaker Vs. "They just need to be insignia so you can tell what's a pub crawl and what's an invasion. Short-term, would you accept something quick to make? An armband, a sash, a stencil, something people can make or print at home? It's not a bad thing that anyone can copy them, it's good, the point is to be like a Hiveless sash. If people have insignia they're under military law, and if not they're noncombatant. All sides can worry about more elaborate things on their own time."

Murmurs in Chinese sounded vaguely approving.

Focusing past the lens feed, I frowned into my—was this breakfast? It could never work. Quick-to-make or no, people facing invasion weren't going to put on uniforms just so they could be targeted more easily. It was too prisoners'-dilemma. As groups we benefit if everyone's in uniform, but each individual is safest out of uniform, since those in uniform will draw more fire. These objections were in Achilles's voice in my head, my imagination aping the criticisms our veteran had lodged against my many sketches. My early drafts had made the same mistakes, too gaudy and distinctive, rank marks on shoulders or sleeves so easy for a rooftop rifle to pick out. The First World War had taught that lesson at the cost of umpteen thousand officers, then moved its rank marks to the subtle collar. These Mitsubishi designs would make them walking targets that same way. Or maybe that didn't matter anymore. This wasn't 1914, it was five centuries later, and what personal tracker didn't now have a camera good enough to zoom in on a collar from a kilometer away? The Major was from another time, and maybe wrong, at least about modern psychology. Clothing today was so much about honesty and self-description. Millions were already wearing the bull's-eye voluntarily, or the Vs, and getting beat up for it. Maybe in this era, when we'd all grown up showing our Hives and strats and hobbies on our sleeves, we'd pass the prisoners' dilemma and all choose to wear the uniforms that would make the whole war better but each person's chances worse. Except we Servicers, of course, our uniforms were camouflaged and subtle. Sensible. And then a new thought hit me, one which makes my gut feel sour as I remember it: Why should I care if the Mitsubishi have bad uniform designs? I'm not a Mitsubishi. How is it anything but good if opposing forces wear a bull's-eye on their chests, some literally? So long as my side is protected, let the rest play dress-up. I felt sick, the half-chewed beans like warm mud in my mouth. I was betraying Su-Hyeon. Jin and Carmen too, who were so genuinely neutral, serving the common good with the raw faith that it was good for their Hives too. And I was betraying Vivien, sullying the honorable title of Anonymous with my partisanship. How had Mycroft managed to balance all this? Tangled in so many sides at once?

"Temporary uniforms in forty-eight hours," Su-Hyeon was summarizing when I zoned back in, "and we'll circulate a generic model military law code based on the one you proposed, though we will make some changes of our own to match it better to the language of Alliance law."

"Agreed."

"And if we can't reach Sniper?" Su-Hyeon asked it in the tone they use for 'check' in chess, and that made me realize this was where it fell apart. Four hours. We had direct lines to MASON, Vivien, Spain, Faust, but to reach Sniper's faction all we could do was shout into the airwaves, or drop a note outside a lifedoll store and hope.

Dominic cursed in their throat at the name of the 'blasphemer.' "Sniper will agree. Hiveguard benefits. Right now some who wear the bull's-eye mean it as a pledge to . . . attack . . . Advisor Mason." Dominic made a wry face here, struggling to force out any other name but *Maître* for the Prince. "But others wear it only to proclaim their support for the bloody means by which O.S. bought the long peace. Uniforms will sort this chaos, organize the militants, and keep the peaceful sympathizers out of the path of armies. That is a good."

It was a good, I thought as I watched silent Dominic through the mask of their regrown skin. That made it click. J.E.D.D. Mason would want these uniforms. Dominic realized that. The Good and honest Prince, who had made Themself the Target of a billion snipers just to give us sides worth dying for, They would want everyone who took up arms to feel the flush of pride and confidence that Dominic and Heloïse feel every morning when they don the habits of their offices. Even distant Martin, crawling across callous wastes, has that. And more. The Prince would want every death to have intentionality, each shot fired with purpose and at one acting with purpose, not the muddled waste of street carnage and friendly fire. I could almost hear it in my mind in Their dead voice: "If deaths must be, let them be ______." What adjective would it have been? What language? Something more honest than 'good,' less pretentious than 'just,' the opposite of 'pointless' but not pretending death could ever be 'alright.' 'Examined,' maybe? 'Willed'? A tingle washed through me. So few prayers are in the Prince's power to grant, but here was one I pray myself: if I'm shot, let me be shot for what I fight for, not for some mistake. Dominic had planned this, then, conceived the uniforms, or at least encouraged them, as a gift for their Kind Master. Meeting that wish in Dominic's proud eyes made all my worry over earthly betrayals fade like fog. Dominic is a strange, cruel, predatory being, yet often—and only for J.E.D.D. Mason—good.

"Then, so long as we get the other leaders to agree within four hours, you'll hold off," Su-Hyeon pressed, "even if we have no response from Sniper or the other Hiveguard leaders?"

The Chinese Directors debated among themselves, while Korea's new Director Kim Gyeong-Ju cracked a joke in Korean that made Im-Jin and Su-Hyeon snort. I felt alone, and sensed a tense aloneness also in the frowning and innocent Greenpeace Director Bandyopadhyay, still in office thanks to their utter ignorance of O.S. I must remember that frown, that solitude. Su-Hyeon speaks good Hindi, and, if the Mitsubishi do prove enemies, driving a wedge between the Greenpeace and China might . . . This is hard. I'm used to helping Vivien spot rifts and heal them, I hate feeling the instinct to exploit rifts grow in me.

Murmur congealed into nods. "Agreed."

We wasted little time on final courtesies, and Su-Hyeon brought up the task tree now, so I could see the whole plan which would culminate (hopefully) in a Triumviral Order, followed by my Anonymous endorsement and pre-planned positive responses from the Hives. Im-Jin would call Faust first, then Senator Ouroboros Wyrdspell, Im-Jin's suggestion, the most "reliably extant" Utopian they know. Carmen would petition MASON, then call the King of Spain, though

Europe was complying anyway. I expected my first call to be to Vivien, or the Prince (though Dominic reserved that pleasure for themself). I was surprised to find Task Number One was joining Su-Hyeon on a call to Bryar Kosala. I didn't realize why Bryar was the most important to convince.

"Su-Hyeon! [Anonymous]! It's great to see you both!" Bryar's smile in my lenses made me feel hugged, as if the sofa at my back were suddenly a little snugglier. They were in a bright room, backlit by broad windows, which gave Bryar's hair a red halo effect, and I saw drapes in fuchsia and marigold at one end of the room, and a fluffy white cat curled up on a high stack of Red Crystal crates.

"How are you?" Su-Hyeon asked.

"I couldn't be better looked after." The glow in Bryar's cheeks made it feel true. "Mumbai's keeping things calm and flowing, everyone's giving me everything I need, and my ba'sibs Mohana and Ganges have their bash' here, do you remember them?"

"Is Mohana the one with the turtle hat?" I guessed fastest.

"Yup. I'm staying with them, and there's a stunning view over the harbor." Bryar tilted our view so we could see the water through the window, and a slice of city, washed out in the extreme morning light of whatever time it was in India. "I have my own little harbor boat to get around, as well as the bicycle."

"I love those harbor boats!" Su-Hyeon's enthusiasm shook the mound of DNA kits enough for one to plop down, almost in my beans.

I had to ask, "Do you have guards?"

"Yes, plenty, and tons of help too. This whole block and several around it have turned into a Cousin headquarters, half the ships in the harbor have signed up to help distribute our Tiring Guns, and you wouldn't believe how active Red Crystal is here."

"I believe it," Su-Hyeon answered. "It'll double again this week if the numbers hold."

"Great!"

"That's worldwide, not Mumbai, Mumbai registration's already over the bell, unless there's change in Singapore, or Manila, or Masonic road sprawl out of Caedeculmin gets close to Ahmedabad . . ." Su-Hyeon has a special little wince for when they realize they've dragged the conversation down the statistics rabbit hole. "Glad you're well."

Bryar gave their most indulgent smile. "And [Anonymous], I was so relieved when I heard you were there with Su-Hyeon to look after you. Su-Hyeon, don't forget [Anonymous] needs you to log food and hours regularly."

I smiled, but, in that moment, the purple Censor's Office jacket on my shoulders felt more than a little like a dog collar. "Bryar, it's great catching up, but we didn't flag this urgent just to chat."

Su-Hyeon's smile tried to ease my jitters as I realized we'd wasted a minute on hellos and hats. "It's alright, I budgeted time for this."

I frowned my disagreement, but that's Su-Hyeon's way sometimes, tiny indulgences for morale's sake, like our fruit salad. It was fruit from the decorative trees around the Alliance meeting rooms, our fifth straight day of that fruit, and it would have been most efficient to just throw it in a pile in HQ again (as so many lazy patrons do, so Servicers learn to get excited when lunch is *not* mostly bruised surplus fruit). But Su-Hyeon had asked someone to make us all fruit salad, investing precious minutes in disguising necessity with fun. It worked, too: the desk shift seemed a little less dog-tired today. Just so, I think Su-Hyeon had rationed this minute as a mental band-aid for all three of us, a quasi-family chat before the storm.

Bryar: "Are you calling about Warsaw, Singapore, Manila, Bangkok, Koome Island, the car blasts, or some other crisis?"

(I looked these up fast, since most were new since bedtime: Warsaw had a water contamination crisis; Fiji's celebrated Indus-Kreeney fireworks artists had managed to confuse a car's sensors with light blasts so it landed safely, inspiring less skilled copycats to set off accidental car explosions over Bhopal, Aberdeen, Lisbon, and Prince Edward Island; the Koome Island Strategic Mosquito Preserve had a power outage approaching crisis length; while Singapore, Manila, and Bangkok were like Sydney, large mixed metropolises in East Asia lashing out against their Mitsubishi landlords as the fleets loomed close.)

Su-Hyeon: "None of the above. I want to discuss an Order the Triumvirate wants to issue today. We want all factions to start wearing uniforms."

Bryar: "Uniforms?"

Su-Hyeon: "There needs be a clear difference between civilian and soldier. There keep being what people are calling 'riots' but some are really spontaneous and some are trained groups attacking preselected targets. Right now people can't tell, cops can't tell, laws can't tell."

Bryar: "I've seen the problem."

Su-Hyeon: "We're going to require that Hives that want to take military action have to have fixed and public military law codes, and their soldiers must be registered and recognizable. Europeans and Mitsubishi are already doing it, and benefitting from it. Put a cluster of Masons in a street and everyone panics since MASON says the whole Hive is at war, but we know Europeans in uniform are soldiers and the rest are not, and people are sixty-two percent less likely to panic or attack congregating Europeans."

"It's up to sixty-two percent?" I asked.

"You saw the growth curve, I'm entitled to round up after midnight."

Bryar caught me checking the time, and smirked. "I like the idea."

"I know," Su-Hyeon replied. "You're doing it yourself with Red Crystal. We just need to extend it. Singapore, Bangkok, Manila, everywhere like that will ease if a scared Humanist or Mitsubishi can glance up a street and tell which Masons are friendly bystanders. And if you all do simple things like Red Crystal's armbands, then this could start saving lives in hours." Again I winced as Su-Hyeon flashed up my awful uniform designs. "But only if someone else pushes for speed. We don't have any enforcement mechanism with the cars down. A Triumviral Order is just an invitation to dithering, unless you and other respected voices encourage speed."

"I'm going to endorse it as Anonymous," I added, "and stress the immediate lifesaving effect."

"And the Inspector General's office will create a public database with images and details about what each uniform means."

Bryar nodded. "So you want me to endorse it, too? Or did you want my help persuading Vivien?"

"Boneithther!" I turned in surprise as my "both" merged with Su-Hyeon's "neither."

Su-Hyeon shook their head. "We want more than that. We want you to implement it."

"Implement it?" Bryar frowned. "You want the Cousins to make everybody's uniforms?"

"No. Make your own."

"You said the Red Crystal armbands were working well."

"Red Crystal isn't the same as Cousin forces."

Bryar frowned. "We don't have forces, we're neutral."

Su-Hyeon sighed. "Jin said you'd be the stubborn sell."

Bryar still looked puzzled. "Just because we let other Hives and Hiveless join Red Crystal—"

"Su-Hyeon's right!" I cried, wincing at the clatter as my enthusiasm sent DNA kits cascading down the stairs. "I see it now! You do have forces. You have guards! You have armed security defending hospitals, and warehouses, and your Weapon Exchange Centers, and you! With you, Bryar, right now, you have guards."

Bryar glanced off-screen, confirming that the corners of the bright-draped room held more than just their ba'sibs' watercolors. "Guards aren't an army."

"No, but they are forces, and they're not the same thing as ordinary Cousins, and— Oh, Su-Hyeon, you're so right!" My passion won a smile as I realized what must have been in Su-Hyeon's mind since before they woke me. "You have to do it, Bryar! You're most important of all! If the Cousins make a uniform, you'll guilt-trip every other power into being unable to refuse doing it too, because your forces are the sweetest, most benign, helpful, trustworthy, cuddly forces that have ever existed, who carry nothing scarier than stun guns, and whose sole purpose is to just defend the people who want to give everybody soup and band-aids. If you make those forces wear a uniform, not MASON, not Sniper, not Tully Mardi, not nobody can refuse!"

Bryar took some frowning moments to digest, and I feared my choice of playful language might have offended instead of cheering them. "Perhaps . . ."

"You're worried about the Nurturists?" Su-Hyeon guessed, and as soon as I heard the word, I saw it too. Senator Cook's Nurturists. There had already been a near-coup in Casablanca, a power showdown between fervent Cookie and faithful Heloïse, one fought with words alone. The next coup might use 'forces.'

Bryar would not rush their answer. "This . . . no, this could help with the Nurturists, actually. Your public list, the one you're going to publish with the images, will you also require each Hive and faction to publish a description of the purpose, scope, and limits of its activities? What kinds of actions forces are allowed to take, and with what kind of weaponry? If everyone is required to define their scope strictly and publicly, I can define the Cousin forces as defensive-only and make clear they aren't empowered to intervene with set-sets and so on, that those acts are illegal, and will be prosecuted. It could help."

"Then you'll do it?" Su-Hyeon pressed.

Another careful pause. "If you require public definitions of the scope of each force's activities, then yes."

"Great! Thanks!"

Su-Hyeon hung up.

I called back. "Hi, Bryar. Sorry about that."

They smiled. "Not your fault. It was good seeing you both."

"You too. Su-Hyeon, are you going to say goodbye to Bryar?"

Su-Hyeon didn't turn. "What? Oh. Hi. Bye. Sorry. Math."

I gave a little wince to thank Bryar for laughing off this too-familiar tic. "I'm glad you're safe in Mumbai," I added. "I was worried when I heard you were all the way up in Delhi."

Bryar beamed reassurance. "I'm on the coast now. It shouldn't be hard to get a boat to Casablanca, once we've negotiated passage with the Mitsubishi fleet. I'm just glad you're safe with Su-Hyeon. I was worried when I heard about . . ."

It's hard to believe how fast sobs came. "Yeah."

Bryar sat there frowning in my lenses, sadness, sympathy, but suddenly it all felt insincere. I waited. Weren't they going to say anything? Condolences? Tell me they know what Mycroft meant to me? That it's not my fault? If Bryar's lips had quivered, I would've thought they were fighting tears too, but there was just that tense, forced sympathy. It still chills me remembering how much it chilled me. Mycroft always said they thought Bryar had wanted them 'put down.' It had never felt plausible before.

"I should go work on my endorsement," I said. "If we need help persuading Vivien, I'll let you know."

"I took care of your files with the Servicer Program," Bryar added in a rush. "You're on permanent dispatch to the Censor's office."

"Thanks, that's helpful. Good to see you, Bryar. Bye."

I hung up.

They're glad Mycroft's dead. I didn't want to think that, know that. *They're all glad Mycroft's dead.*

Bryar called back.

"What's up?" I answered, busying myself with many task boxes so Bryar's was a little sliver in my lenses.

"I was saying you're on permanent dispatch to the Censor's office."

"I heard. Thanks."

"So you can keep staying in Vivien's flat or the Censor's office, you won't get in trouble for avoiding the Servicer dorms."

I felt cold. "Thanks. That's useful." My mouth was open but I only formed the question in my mind: *Are you trying to separate me from . . .*

"You and Su-Hyeon are going to be thorough, right? All Hives *and* factions with clear uniforms?" Bryar's voice is scariest when it's sweetest.

"Yup, we'll be thorough. Good talking. Thanks. Bye."

I hung up.

Bryar called back.

I rejected the call and set myself on busy.

Bryar called back with the command override of the Servicer Program Administration, which drove all other data from my lenses and put a red tick on my probation track.

"What?" I snapped.

"New, distinct, differentiable uniforms for all factions on all sides."

They waited.

I wriggled.

"You can't make an exception for your 'Beggar Army,' [Anonymous]. Or are you going to make me very happy and say you've disbanded now that there's no Beggar King?"

I checked to make sure Su-Hyeon was too deep in calculations to be listening. "We have a uniform," I whispered.

"Servicers have a uniform. If Mycroft Canner's militant zealots are seen in combat in Servicer uniforms, the backlash will hit the innocent Servicers, too, every single one."

"Myrmidons," I mumbled.

"What?"

"They call themselves—" The word 'Coward!' echoed in my mind. Not 'they.' "We. We call ourselves Myrmidons."

Bryar's glare hurt. "If you bring that uniform to the battlefield, you'll destroy the Servicer Program. Forever. Do you think people will trust it again after what seems like a rebellion? You'll drag us back to the age of prisons!" They paused to let the claustrophobic specter of walls and wasted years loom over me before adding, "Or worse. You know how Spartacus ends."

Harsh words had been hatching in me, but memory erased them, random memories: Hawaii's wind cooling my tongue after too-hot guava salsa, dawn over Zanzibar's razor skyline, the wind and sun upon my sweating back, and tears of gratitude on Mycroft Canner's cheeks. Lose the Servicer Program? I shivered. "We don't have any other clothes. What do you want us to do, rob clotheslines?"

"I'm handing the Servicer Program over to Red Crystal. Every Servicer will be issued an armband, and every Servicer not already on special duty will be told to report to the nearest center. They'll be housed, fed, protected, and they'll be doing invaluable war work, saving lives."

"That's . . . a great idea," I admitted, leaning back.

Bryar's smile was real but died quickly. "And Red Crystal registration will be compulsory, unless I decide to make an exemption for these militants."

"Myrmidons," I corrected for the second time. "Named after Achilles's soldiers in—"

"I know the *Iliad*," Bryar snapped. "Is Achilles the new Beggar King?"

That hurt. "I guess. Yes."

Bryar breathed deep; I guess it hurt them, too. "Myrmidons, then. But if I decide to let them be a separate force, it has to have a separate uniform, clearly military, so no one will think the Servicers themselves are in rebellion, and no one will mistake my Red Crystal forces for them."

I hesitated. "It's not as if you c—"

"Could stop you?" Bryar sucked in a harsh breath. "Of course I can. Possibly no one else on Earth can right now, but you know I can. I have your records, your trackers, every one of you, and the world's in my debt. How many stranded people am I taking care of right now? You have the numbers."

I winced. I'd been willfully ignoring how many people were really stranded far from home, pretending the numbers were abstract, like so many digits of pi. "Four billion five hundred million," I admitted. It was staggering really, nearly half the world on cots and sofas, all those soup kitchens. And Bryar had been ready for it, the hospitals, the socks and soap, an incredible achievement given that they started planning less than 200 days before.

Bryar's face was triumph. "Every single Hive owes me millions of times over, and trusts me, every army too; my Tiring Guns are saving more lives every day. If I make a public call for help rounding up rebellious Servicers, if I call earth and thunder down on you right now, how much do you imagine your Myrmidons will accomplish in this war?"

Achilles isn't the only one who thinks of goddesses when they see Bryar in anger. I choked. "Bryar, please, what we're doing will make it better, we . . . we know how to have a war! Achilles trained us. We'll bring some sanity to how the war's conducted, make sure at least one side knows something about morale, and breaking points, and when a battle's turning into chaos or attrition, and how to tell you've lost. We'll make this a better, probably a faster war! It needs to be a short war, before . . ." The word 'harbinger' loomed in my mind, but U-speak might have made them wary. "Please, let us do this! I'm begging you, Bryar! Not as my quasi-parent but as the architect of the peace that will follow this war!"

"As the whole world's quasi-parent, then." Bryar paused, and I couldn't read much from their face, just thoughts all piling on. I bet mine looked the same. "Then you're going to set this up on my terms."

"Thank you. Thank you." I felt foolish, unable to summon other words. "Thank you."

Their face stayed strict. "You're going to carry Tiring Guns, all of you that can get your hands on them, and you're going to have clear military uniforms, *not* plain Servicer uniforms, differentiated uniforms, so no one will think the Servicer program is turning hostile."

"No. That's a bad idea. It's a great asset to us to move unnoti—"

"You want to be a hypocritical exception to the demand for uniforms that you yourself are initiating?"

I had to grant that one, and Bryar's furrowed brows permitted no further excuse. "I'm not the commander," I answered, "but I'll try."

"You'll do better than try. You want me to stay my hand? You'll do it. I know you don't have many resources to make uniforms, but you've made a trained militia out of trash and sticks, you'll find a way."

What could I do but bow my head before the only power left that really could unite the world against us? "We'll do it."

"And you'll use Tiring Guns."

I tried to imagine Achilles's reaction, but a scowl and joy seemed equally plausible on that face so lined with mourning. "Of course, whenever we can," I answered. "We've no wish to fill graveyards. But we won't only carry Tiring Guns, we need knives, small explosives, varied weapons. Any army does."

Bryar paused, as if trying to read my face. "Who will you fight for?"

I blinked. "For everyone!" I felt stupid as I said it.

"I meant which side." They stretched, cracking their shoulders. "It's one thing if you're still Servicers accepting a job from Hive Members or Hiveless only the job is military this time. It's a very different thing if you're a rogue army."

The question was strangely hard to answer. We were fighting for Achilles, but Achilles was not a proper Member of our strange new world. I hadn't thought the phrase 'rogue army' before, but it wasn't quite false. I thought of Achilles, the last time I'd seen them in person, a memory, vivid in my mind. It was the salmon-red tail end of sunset, and we were resting on a tree-stubbed ridge over . . . somewhere. I was sitting, the Major standing, with cityscape below, and the air was ringing with the calls of birds, hundreds, maybe thousands, black and small, every branch and roof-line dotted with them. I remember something spooked them so they all swarmed up, flowing and undulating in this enormous rounded mass, like living oil bubbling through the sky, with Achilles silhouetted in the middle. It felt like they were part of each other, part of Nature, Achilles and the birds, more real, more grounded, and more native to the Earth than the rest of us. Relics of the age before Thomas Carlyle founded our flawed, complacent paradise. Lost things that had come back in our time of need, to help us see past our tangled puppet strings to find . . . "A thing worth dying for." I hadn't intended to speak that part aloud but I did, and I saw Bryar flinch and . . . pre-mourn? Is that a word? Fear-grief in their eyes, not the fear-grief of Earth's Quasi-Parent, but of *my* quasi-parent. "Achilles wants to fight for MASON," I answered. "For us to fight for MASON. Until or unless the balance of sides in the war changes so much that Achilles thinks fighting for MASON will draw out the war."

Silence held Bryar. I wish I could have known what kind. Was it MASON they were doubting? Whether to trust Earth's grimmer parent with the grimmer half of our unfree brotherhood? Or were they doubting me? "Aren't there some Servicers who want to fight for other sides? Ex-Humanists? Ex-Mitsubishi?"

"They'll join Red Crystal," I said. "They can help their Hives that way. They wouldn't want to fight against the rest of us." I caught myself actually crossing my fingers, hoping Bryar wouldn't ask how I was sure they wouldn't fight, so I wouldn't have to explain how magnetic Achilles was for all of us. And how scary.

"Then the Masons will commission you. And by tomorrow, every single Servicer will either be in a recognizable Myrmidon uniform or Red Crystal, nobody slipping through the cracks."

"Alright."

"Except you."

"Me?" My jump brought more DNA packs cascading on my shoulders.

Su-Hyeon looked up at that. "Everything okay, [Anonymous]?"

"Fine," I lied. "Just fighting a sneeze."

Bryar waited for Su-Hyeon to be re-distracted. "You're too valuable to the Alliance."

I felt my frown grow childish. "Bryar . . ."

"I'm not saying this to be protective. The Triumvirate needs you, the Alliance, Earth. You are not going into battle, you're not running off on wild errands for Jed or Achilles, and the minute I see you in any uniform but that Censor's jacket is the minute I tell the world to round up every single Myrmidon, and have Su-Hyeon cuff you to a desk. Clear?"

Words left me, banished by a glint of wetness in Bryar's eye. Was I wrong before? It could be wishful thinking, but I know Bryar, and I know someone who used to run risks for 'Jed' and for Achilles, someone who should have been cuffed safely to a desk. "Yes," I answered. "Yes, it's clear. I'll report all this to the Major. To Achilles, I mean. And I'll do all in my power to see it happens. Including"—the words were bitter, and the Censor's jacket still felt halfway between armor and a dog collar—"including safeguarding myself."

"Good. Do."

Again I bowed my head. All Bryar's demands and arguments were just, wiser than mine, but still felt sour, even as I finally turned—as Bryar *let* me turn—to drafting my endorsement. Was it that I'd been threatened? Tasted for the first time the political brunt of what it means that the almost-ba'pa who used to bring me soup and cushions rules so much of the world? Or maybe it was just that I was rarely made to feel the sour half of my Servicer sentence, the half that overlapped with 'slave.'

Now the Triumvirs and I worked our persuasive magic. The public saw the process backwards, and I think our lie would be the truth forever if I wasn't writing this. In reality we had the promises in hand before the Triumviral Order went out (with thirty-six minutes to spare), but everyone thinks Romanova began it all, the stern Triumviral Order, quickly accepted by the Emperor-Elect of Europe, by Heloïse with Chair Kosala, by Gordian's Brain-bash' (briefly in English and at length in German), and there was much praise for how doggedly Vivien stuck to Spanish in their long and passionate endorsement. The Mitsubishi feigned indifference with a curt and late assent, and no one seems to suspect they were the—should I say 'petitioners' or 'masterminds'? The Utopian reply was odd, saying they don't have a military but a civilian militia (a technicality no one seems to understand), but they promise militia members will be clearly marked whenever visible, and they were first to send an image in to Romanova's database: a coat marked on the back and shoulders with the sharp Delian sun.

I, as Anonymous, reminded the public that Hive endorsements matter little without answers from the macro-factions that cut across all: Hiveguard and Remaker. (Nurturism cuts across Hives too, but I will not, as Anonymous, put bigots on a par with Sniper and the Prince, plus they already have the mismatched socks.)

So giving is the Prince that They answered my Anonymous petition to Hiveguard and the Remakers with a quick, personal call: "I love this honesty, and hope it is a good."

Ten words and already They cleansed me, like sun after a swim. It was healing salve just seeing Their image in my lenses, safe and unchanged against the stone gray walls of Alexandria, and to my delight Chagatai was with Them; not one of Their four angels, but still at least there is one person there in Alexandria who is more Theirs than MASON's. "Then You do want Your side to have a uniform?" I asked.

"Yes. Let there be an emblem each may wear who fights to help Me remake this good world as a better one. The wish kindles in Me that My opposers likewise emblemize. Each Hive and conscience must decide whether a person may wear in parallel our sigils and a Hive's. Can you approximate these thoughts in English comfortable to all? Now that our Mycroft can't?"

I couldn't. No one could capture the purity that nested in Their stilted, awkward words. But we published my clumsy best. Many applauded the Prince for treating those who chanted for Their death with such respect. To my great pride, the Prince selected my design: a row of four Vs running across the middle of the upper arm, so if you count the three V-shaped gaps between them it makes seven. It's quick to add with paint, or tape, or ink, leaves room above for rank marks, and can combine with any uniform (if Hives allow it, that's still an unknown). It was public by lunchtime, and we had our response an hour later, when around the globe hundreds of Sniper Dolls appeared on benches sporting a bull's-eye with crosshairs in the same spot on the upper sleeves. I hadn't expected this vast feeling of relief. Now when I see a bull's-eye worn in another spot, it isn't scary anymore. In fact, it makes me happy, thinking how much we all value freedom of conscience. Everyone's relieved, I see it in the smiles in Papa's office. A few desk cops are even wearing the bull's-eye on their lapels or collars now, had wanted to for a while, but were too scared when Ockham's supporters could be mistaken for Sniper's guns.

The awards for 'Most Lives Saved' and 'Most Abhorrent Response' both go to Tully Mardi, for the same noxious pamphlet, released among today's endorsements: "A Practical Guide to Internment and Prisoners of War." It's what it says on the tin: how to lock up enemies, with chapters on arrests, property, hygiene, morale, camp layout, activities, schools, the merits of a ghetto vs. full-on prison camp, full of quick facts, diagrams, cheerful lists of tips, and examples from psych studies and the World Wars. It must have taken Tully years. I want to call it the work of a sick mind, but most of it is "Do X to avoid malnutrition" and "Do Y to keep your guards from turning into power-tripping abusers" and I hate, hate, hate it, but we need that. Sydney may need it this week. I look at the 18 percent in Buenos Aires who aren't Humanists, the numbers in Nagoya, Taipei, Dubai, the scared Brillists at Trinity in Dublin, and the brave souls who wear the bull's-eye in the shadow of MASON's flag. If those in America who dare help Martin fail, I'd rather see them in a camp than shot. A humanely run camp, that is. So, I guess, we must thank Tully Mardi. There's a long section on "Alternatives to Imprisoning Opponents" too, suggesting how to manage a hostile minority without rounding people up, and the chapter on interrogation is all about respectful conduct, and how torture is a terrible idea for all involved. Tully even quoted Beccaria, Voltaire, Mercer Mardi's death notes, and Anonymous.

The great suspense was that no answer came from Alexandria. Carmen assured us MASON would consent, but as night lapped at the Americas, anxiety reminded me how fiercely the Empire insists it's older than Hive, Alliance, or Triumvirate, and subject to no demands from young and fleeting blips in history. MASON would not, could not, I fretted, seem to bow to our demand. But, when I was heading home in the wee hours, I passed Masons in the street with their left sleeves dyed black. MASON's Capital Power reaching through a thousand arms—nothing could be clearer.

So we succeeded. The Mitsubishi fleet waits placidly in Sydney harbor, and the colors of the world have changed. It feels so much like Apollo's simulation. Mycroft played it for me a few times on screens. The uniforms themselves are different, but the tension is the same, an othertime, too crisply focused, with an unnamed energy that quickens my pulse like autumn nip, as if all of life before now was lazy weekend.

And our Myrmidons? My spare seconds didn't overlap Achilles's until late this morning, but I sent a summary of Bryar's threats and my concessions. Even amid the thronging towers of Alexandria, Achilles, when they called back, found a way to be outside, cleansed by the sea and sun. «Who're you going to betray later? Bryar and Su-Hyeon? Or me?»

Achilles's words weren't harsh, just frank, the lilting Greek welcome like thaw. I smiled at the sometimes-savage face which smiled back. I smiled at Achilles's fresh-dyed black left sleeve, and at the other Myrmidons I could see moving, drilling in the background, all with one black sleeve marking Death's delegates more clearly than a scythe. Bryar had their wish, and Caesar his precious ally. I smiled at that. But most, I smiled at the calm forgiveness in Achilles's eyes, special, and just for me. No, not for me, a final gift for Mycroft, who would have wanted me to have it, begged it for me if I'd asked: my discharge. If I wanted it. So I gave Mycroft's answer: "I'll betray anyone but the Prince."

CHAPTER FIVE

Operation Baskerville

Written September 26, 2454
Events of just now
Romanova, far corners of the Earth

SU-HYEON NAMED IT. It was almost a joke, but too right for any other name to stick.

It began during the coronation. That was the first lull of the war, everyone gathering to watch Brussels glitter, so the calls finally stopped coming, all quiet on the omni-front. I even put Su-Hyeon to bed. I should have gone to bed too, but I couldn't miss this. Emperor Isabel Carlos I of Europe. A new Imperium. This hasn't happened since 800 AD, unless you count Napoleon, and I wouldn't've missed Napoleon's, either.

Peace held as the dignitaries gathered—all proxies, the highest-ranking souls that chance had trapped in Brussels substituting for the presidents and queens and ministers of all the nation-strats and tattered Hives. Brussels was so alive with bands and cheering faces that I couldn't believe so much happy energy remained in our exhausted world. Timestamps confirm that the reports started coming in the instant the parade began, but the staunch workhorses who had manned our desks through impossible shifts for three weeks were understandably slow to action when the harness was hauled out again so soon. They approached me first, just when my lenses were zoomed in on the carriage that bore the crown—a new crown, quite a task for some brave jeweler, tines of faceted gold, slender like the knife-edge sunrays of a compass rose, and set with twelve great sapphires, almost the blue of Europe's flag. The question was a painful one, but a worrisome pattern demanded it: "[Anonymous], should we wake Su-Hyeon?" I was indeed the right person to ask.

There were four reports in the summary that reached me, but two more arrived before I was done skimming. A panicking electrician in the Altai region (in the labyrinth of mountains and rivers where Siberia touches the deserts to the south) had called in a sighting of "monster wolves" around a utilities hub, and images showed furred forms of night blue, storm-sea gray, and bristling wire. Minutes later a tracker relay station in Shangombo (by the Southern edge of the Great African Reservation) had called in panic with images of what I recognized as the too-huge but gentle alien nub-face of an axolotl (meters long instead of centimeters) peering down through a skylight. Ittoqqortoormiit, Greenland, reported sea monsters, and minutes later sent a clip of a tanklike walking coelacanth approaching a warehouse with jaws stronger than steel. A note from Cambridge Bay (in the Canadian far north) made the old joke real: "Here there be dragons." I sighed, thinking fear was making common U-beasts into monsters, but then the coelacanth actually mauled the warehouse and charged into the equipment room beyond. The next rush of calls confirmed the pattern: San Juan Buenaventura (so remote a slice of Mexico that Uto-Aztecan languages survive), Ruoqiang Town (in the sprawl north of Tibet), Falias and Findias (the artificial polar islands), Alice Springs (I shivered thinking how many kilometers of Australia's envenomed wildlife lie between there and help), Crested Butte, Colorado (in the West Elk Mountains, one of those countless rocky corners of the Americas), and Tristan da Cunha (the South Atlantic island), which sent us just one word: Ráðsviðr. With the dreaded name of history's only A.I. murderer (or must we now say 'first'?) filling our minds with nightmares, I had them wake Su-Hyeon.

While Su-Hyeon was fumbling for their shoes, I was somehow in charge of the response team, I think because the dog-tired desk cops weren't ready to be the bearers of so much despair. "Help!" was the common cry, but these villages weren't just remote, they were impossibly remote, places where no sport-hiker would dream of questing without weeks of planning and an expert team. If roads had ever touched them, the centuries since *Mukta* had long healed Earth's scars. I couldn't tell these people how long it would take help to reach them. I couldn't even guess how help could try.

Worse came before Su-Hyeon did. It wasn't the worse I feared. It wasn't gore-streaked dragons belching fire over screaming crowds. It wasn't coats joining the fray, Delian suns and the debut of luminous new blast guns like the one now hidden in my armpit holster. It wasn't Earth v. Troy. It was silence. The calls came from place after place—a few sentences, one hasty tracker video—then nothing. Not just from the informant but from the whole town: no tracker signals, no data. Silence. Complete, impenetrable. These little havens of those who prefer wide skies to city spice vanished like so many snuffed candles. 'Silent as the grave' entered my mind, and it did feel like that, like horror, like otherworldly tendrils had reached across and drawn these little outposts back into the primordial silence of a Nature which would no longer indulge humanity's transgressions. Small noises in the corners of the room began to make me jump.

"Data outages? That we can work on!" Su-Hyeon chased off paranoia with action and a warm squeeze of my shoulder. We called regional tracker techs, who offered garbled explanations of the signal silences, and promised to try this or that. We tapped satellites, and caught some images of quiet streets, with here or there a glimpse of the back or wing of some great, moving beast. Or were they shadows? Su-Hyeon ran a speedy model of what types of towns were being targeted, and predicted some likely next targets, half of which turned out to be already silent. Satellites again showed empty streets, but almost all the streets on Earth were empty then, everyone glued to screens or watching through their trackers from a comfy chair. At that very moment brave Isabel Carlos was crossing the coronation chamber, not striding like a happy conqueror but slow, reverent paces, approaching the waiting crown as pilgrims approach some reverend spot where one of history's heroes lived, or died. I couldn't watch more, too much to do. We didn't have agents in these tiny towns, but we had our people call every town we could, and I remember their language gaining concision and conviction over time:

First call: "Hello, Romanova calling, Alliance police with an emergency warning from the Censor's office and Triumvirate. We've predicted your town might be attacked, now or soon, by unknown forces including monstrous creatures, probably U-beasts . . . Yes, probably Utopians . . . We think they'll go for your tracker stations and communications first . . ."

Third call: "Hello, Alliance police for the Censor and Triumvirate, this is a warning, your town is likely to be attacked by forces including large, hostile U-beasts . . ."

Tenth call: "Triumvirate police warning. You're about to be attacked by Utopian monsters."

"Why are they visible?" I asked aloud to the room, to Su-Hyeon, to myself as the satellite processor resolved a ten-foot blur into a supple ten-foot mass of omnidirectional leg-spines, like a giant white dandelion seed head extended into a long worm. "They don't have to be visible."

I remember pity on Su-Hyeon's face, as if they didn't want to hurt me, speaking ill of something so precious. "Fear." Such a soft word. "They want fear. They're not letting us see people, the Utopians with the U-beasts. They're not letting us see cute cuddly U-beasts, either. They want us to see monsters. They want people running, panicking, fainting. Above all: surrendering. We're all ready for soldiers, not for hellhounds." Su-Hyeon sighed across at Papadelias's desk, now tenanted by a young lieutenant too loyal to remove the worn volume of Arthur Conan Doyle. "Operation Baskerville."

"I have to go to the bathroom." I said it because I felt hurt inside, more hurt than I could explain to myself, the kind of hurt where you want to sit on the toilet for a while and be alone enough to cry. But now world media was finally tearing its eyes from Brussels's imperial glitter, and my tracker fed me first vague alerts from Cousin safety lists, and tabloidy headlines about monster attacks, so we realized we had only minutes until all Earth would feel the hellhounds at our heels. I fired up the *Hâte Anonyme* but I didn't know what to say. Stay in your homes? What if deadly megasquitos were going house by house, leaving only shriveled corpses? That was my imagination jump-scaring itself, but you couldn't look at image after image of sharp-beaked gryphons and ghostly jellyfowl and not fill in the blurry parts with worse. "Fear is the enemy," I wanted to say. "The real danger right now is panic." But Heloïse was already on-screen saying that, so earnestly, their blushing smile, their whole good heart behind it. My heart was somewhere very different. Why hadn't someone warned me? That question ate up all the others like the big fish in the pond. If the Utopians were planning an op this big, shouldn't I have been informed? Did they not trust the Major? MASON? Our alliance? Or did they all know—all of them—but none of them trust me?

As I was brooding, we got a call from Ittoqqortoormiit, from a fishing boat that had jury-rigged something clever out of its sonar and beeped out text about shrouded figures moving door-to-door, rendering everyone unconscious. We improvised a few ways to reply but got no second signal, and the Cousins were trying too, and all the companies involved in tracker manufacture, and soon all the Hive governments, and well-meaning random people, and the tracker techs became too swamped to answer us.

"Forget it," Su-Hyeon ordered. "Get all agents active. Every friendly we can move needs to get to Utopian district gates before the mobs and local forces do."

Everyone started calling. Everyone but me.

I waited a few breaths. "What are our agents supposed to do when they get there?"

A bank of stares. "Stop the riots, obviously," someone said.

I frowned at the speaker. "This isn't riot. It's a first assault."

I felt like a plague rat, the whole crowd staring horrified, as if I was the one who'd brought death into their world. Except Su-Hyeon. Su-Hyeon's face was bright and ready, and something in its steady kindness said, not just that this wasn't my fault, but that it was somehow not the doom we thought it was.

"Our agents will report to us who's helping whom," Su-Hyeon answered. "You're right, it's a first assault. If there are alliances, they'll show themselves now. If the Utopians have allies, they'll defend them, or at least they won't be among the forces that attack them. If others are allied, they'll help each other attack the Utopian gates. City governments will take actions too, different if they're in on this operation than if they aren't. Today we finally make our map of—"

An alarm squealed as a satellite link went offline. Then six. Then all our calls dropped. Screens turned blank on every desk and every wall: *No Signal.* My tracker bleeped *No Signal.* Su-Hyeon's bleeped *No Signal.* In ten billion ears from Reykjavík to Esperanza City, trackers bleeped *No Signal.* World silence fell. Or perhaps not, perhaps the wide world kept babbling on, asking—as we had asked "What's happened to Alice Springs?" or "What's happened to Shangombo?"—now "What's happened to Romanova?" Either way, there were no screens now. Only windows, where, outside, three black-sleeved Masons hurried past. No one said anything. We sat back, relaxed, the lazy full-arm loll of giving up. Somebody was crying. Turning to see who it was felt like work. Then, in the almost stillness, my eye caught on the almost: Su-Hyeon. They were standing, with a map of Romanova on a screen before them and a string of local data racing on another. Their jaw was slightly slack, their body taut, not frozen but quivering with tiny motions, twitches of elbow, finger, cheek, verging on spasm. But it wasn't spasm, I realized. It was math. Calculations, a breakneck paroxysm of new plans. Then they rushed to a console, and the wall screen above lit up, Su-Hyeon's instructions flooding, text faster than speech:

Corker: Make team, investigate trackers, alternatives, reboots, workarounds.
Kartal: Create temporary simple signal system: flares/light/radio/semaphore/etc.
Jeong: Take 4 people, go to highest roof on Capitoline, scout, report.
Bardakçi: Get security barricade/checkpoints set up at all entrances to Forum.
Dragović: Search Campus directory for faculty good on communications tech.
Matsuoka: Get blueprints, improvise wired communications options.
Bidyadhara: Send teams to major intersections to be visible & answer questions.
Tinker: Get loudspeakers, send officers through key streets calling for calm.
Gwon: Take 4 people, scout bridges/gates by Transtiber/U-district, report.
Lin: Contact/visit Harbor Control, check state of storm warning system.

The words raced, and the room around me raced to action, screens summoning hard drive data now that distance was a barrier again. It all felt strangely like slow motion as my own thoughts lagged behind. A breath after each new order popped up, something inside me vaguely thought, *Oh, good idea . . .* but I couldn't move. Rather, it didn't occur to me that I could move, or do anything to affect the muddle that flowed past. Until my own name on the task list freed me.

[Anonymous]: Didn't you need to go to the bathroom?

I got up automatically. Turned, walked. But I went past the bathroom, and was at the stairs before I realized where I really had to go. The roof. Kind, careful Su-Hyeon would send guards with me if I said I needed to take a walk, but the roof had open air and no one. There were blue skies, and clouds over the sun, and streaking, deadly cars. I went to the most secluded side and leaned over as far as the rail would let me. Within seconds, five Myrmidon comrades rounded the corner toward me, with black-dyed sleeves and the plausible excuse of two wheelbarrows of sandbags. I waved them off. When they lingered just at the corner within line of sight, I waved them off more fiercely. They conferred, body language betraying to the savvy eye which of them was the sergeant, and that one made the ear-scratching gesture which is one of our subtle salutes. I returned it. I counted to twenty after they were gone, to make sure. "Huxley?" I hissed into the emptiness.

"I'm here."

"I want to see your face."

A pause, then a wound-like slit opened, the slim vertical opening of the coat revealing few inches of shirt, of injured arm in sling, of chin, of vizor.

"Why?" I'm not sure what I was actually asking: Why are you doing this? Or, why didn't you tell me?

"It isn't us."

Happiness surged in me first (though I hate to confess it), a narrow, selfish happiness of being trusted after all. Then terror. "The trackers, the U-beasts—"

"They aren't U-beasts."

A memory slideshow played back at machine-gun speed: night-blue metallic wolves, a giant axolotl, that tanklike coelacanth; not one of these was anything I'd seen in any U-district, or strolling at anybody's side. And never in their caution would Utopia—could Utopia—re-create anything that even scared, trapped Members on Tristan da Cunha might dub Ráðsviðr. "Fake U-beasts, then . . . you're being set up!"

Huxley Mojave didn't have to nod. "Lies are as old in war as sticks and stones."

Su-Hyeon's nickname loomed again, cunning and premeditated, perfect: "Painting a real dog with phosphorus to look like monster magic. Operation Baskerville."

Huxley's breath became a gentle laugh.

"Who's doing it?" I asked.

"We don't know."

"Perry-Kraye?"

"We don't know. Probably whoever controls the cars."

"The cars?"

"Jamming on a planetary scale requires epic power, a thousand city power grids couldn't do it, but hundreds of millions of antimatter engines absolutely can."

I nodded, feeling stunned. "Are they attacking here? The monsters?" I looked out across the Forum. My eye caught on a shimmer, like heat distortion, tracing the crests of the Esquiline and Viminal Hills as I looked northwest across the Forum valley. Panic said it was fire, monsters, both. "Is that them?"

"No. If baneforce stirred here, our rangers would have launched fox or faerie fire by now."

I took a moment to digest that. "Then what is that shimmer?"

"Romanova."

My silent tracker still had zoom, and zoom confirmed flags thrashing in the high wind, crisp and as dense as crowding birds, a solid line of them as if every single rooftop on the Viminal Hill crest had raised one. I scanned left and there too, back on the Quirinal Hill, the endless stripe shimmered, Mitsubishi white and scarlet with small spots of green, relieved in places by Cousins' light azure or bright Humanist rings. I scanned downward to the nearer slopes and Forum valley, finding more range of color here, Brillist red and gold, Masonic gray and purple, Hive colors mixing with the endless rainbow of Europe's many nation-strats. A sea of flags. That's what Romanova had become from end to end, just as Su-Hyeon predicted, Earth's most mixed and valuable city, our fragile island capital, her seven hills a sea of flags. And motion. On the nearer Esquiline rooftops I saw squads of black-sleeved Masons peering down, and in their hands—my heart skipped—real guns? Then even closer, on the crest of the Viminal, I saw Mitsubishi soldiers in their beautiful night-green jackets, many, moving, near.

I turned to the west, but the Capitoline Hill blocked my view of the river, and Utopia's bright towers on the Janiculum ridge beyond.

I turned back to Huxley. "We have to prove it isn't you! Everyone will blame you, the attacks, the trackers. Everyone will think you struck first!"

Huxley's voice was quiet as a ghost's. "We did strike first."

I swallowed down my 'but.' I couldn't deny it. Even if you don't count Apollo thirteen years ago, Utopia took the harbingers. During the Olympic truce. But that didn't make this justice. I wanted to kick something: Madame, Apollo, Perry, Homer, Troy. Utopia shouldn't be blamed, not like this. For what *wasn't* them. Hope clung to me like cobweb. "You must have an alternate communications system, separate, like your cars."

"We do."

"Let me use it. I can still convince people."

"It's been silenced too."

I opened my mouth but had no more. Even Utopia silenced? It felt like magic and starstuff had fallen to some great wet maw. Such terrible thoroughness, this unknown enemy. Terrible especially for me. Vivien's image in my mind personified, not just how hard it would be to prove Utopia's innocence but how useless. *Where are your boasts now, Anonymous?* I accused myself. *The pen which nine generations hailed as mightier than any sword, what can it do now against the endless silence of the world?* Fear and imagination told me what would come next: soon those rage-puffed flags would march down here to the Forum, take potshots at this petty Servicer, and there our nameless dynasty would end. Despair was easy. Despair might have had me, too, had I stood on any other roof, but this was Romanova. Here our triumphal arches echoed ancient triumphs that had linked England to Egypt using only roads and horses, and here our bloodstained Rostra echoed older blood. Cicero had done it. Cicero with voice and brittle papyrus had spread truth's fire as far as language would carry. Voltaire too—our prototype, the Zeroeth Anonymous—with rag paper and a hand-pulled printing press, Voltaire needed no tracker web to change the world's mind. "There has to be a way," I said. "Lasers, smoke signals, string and tin cans, footpaths, wire. Maybe not instantly, but if we try, with work, with patience, there must be way."

Huxley nodded. "And we must relink you to the Alien."

Instantly the sourness of vomit rose in my throat. The Prince without a tracker. Without Heloïse, Dominic, Martin, words, eyes, me. Alone. Outrage exploded through me: *Damn You, how could You be so cruel a Host to such a Guest!* (Cursing my Maker feels different these days—an act of greater risk and greater dignity—now that I've become so sure They're real.)

A warm wind mussed my hair, pregnant with animal smell, and a moment later five more slits in space opened to face Huxley. These were not on the roof but perched some feet above it: riders on unseen mounts. Hands emerged and offered salutes, casual, almost flippant, only a finger or two extended to make a quick flip by the forehead. A 'civilian militia' indeed.

"Do you need escort to a barbican?" one asked.

Huxley's returned salute was more solid, an open palm, almost a real soldier's motion. "Huxley Mojave. On quest."

That answer changed the others, their stances, their breath speed, as the key's clack in the lock quickens the waiting prisoner. "Do you need party? We have paradoppler, panoptes, and an adamant." The U-speak was incomprehensible to me, but the posture shift spoke volumes, the sudden change from meeting a random comrade to addressing someone vital, a superior perhaps, if Utopia's militia has a thing like rank?

"Thank you," Huxley answered. "I do need party, but for warding, not watching. Report my quest and anchorage at the Janiculum, and send what help you can, that's enough."

"We will. Lifespeed."

With that parting blessing the others vanished, and I felt the wing wind of grand creatures starting to take flight. I frowned at Huxley. "You're hurt. I have the Censor's Guard to keep me safe. If you want to go—"

"No." I had not heard Huxley's voice so harsh since they delivered the news of the harbinger kidnappings to the angry Seven. "We must relink you to the Alien."

I smiled my gratitude. "First we need to convince the Triumvirs you're innocent. I know Su-Hyeon will believe me. Carmen Guildbreaker won't believe you'd go against your alliance with MASON like this, and Im-Jin will know that I'm sincere. If the Triumvirs believe, the world will too, in time."

Huxley turned toward the west, looking after their vanished comrades, so their vizor's edge just caught the shimmer of the sea of flags. "In time."

Chapter SIX

A Sea of Flags

Written September 26–27, 2454
Events of September 26–27
Romanova

12:47—There are horses on the Aventine Hill. That's the first image our scouts brought back from our improvised watchtower on the Capitoline rooftops: the blur of speeding horses circling the crest of the southernmost of Romanova's seven hills. First guess said it was Utopians, but there are no wings or horns or scales or screens, just riders and saddles. Cavalry? Can we really be back in an age of cavalry?

I'm going to make these notes in every scrap of time I have, since who knows when the next note brought by some panting courier will be "Run!" There's no smoke or fire yet, no invading armies as far as we can see. The armies are internal. Flags are moving. We can see groups marching down the visible roadways and slopes. Some are still unidentified, but there are definitely Europeans mustering in Renunciation Plaza, Masons in Semaphore Square, and on the Viminal Hill to our north are crowd on crowd in night-dark Mitsubishi uniforms, bearing aloft the scarlet and leaf-green trefoil flag. Others are making for the bridges, the seven fragile arteries that connect the two halves of our city. Barton Bridge and Coubertin Bridge to our south are already swarming with Olympic, Humanist, and Hiveguard bull's-eye flags, but Kovács Bridge closest to us, which goes to the Kovács Hospital on the Tibernov Island, has Red Crystal and Cousins with Tiring Guns all over it. I hope that's good. One of the northern bridges we think is held by Blacksleeve Masons, and there's a huge bull's-eye banner on the Juana II Bridge, but Utarutu Bridge is covered with what I wish I could call brawl. It's not really possible to see across the river to the Utopian District on the Janiculum, where violence is most likely, but we can see the hill crest and the skies above, filled with what look like clouds of bright butterflies until you zoom in on the claws and spines. But we have no idea what's on the ground.

13:03—Corker's science team says the tracker system isn't just offline, there's also interference, some massive counter-signal drowning everything. That's bad but also good; counter-signals are traceable (especially since, like Huxley said, the energy involved must be gargantuan). And now at least we know that it's deliberate. Someone is silencing the world. Dragović's team has set out for the

Campus with names and addresses of faculty experts who might help, or at least understand.

13:31—Utopia is innocent; Su-Hyeon believes me.

14:05—Bardakçi reports that sixteen battered Humanists and Europeans (without Vs or bulls'-eyes) turned up at our barricade at the north end of the Forum. I guess I should say 'refugees.' They were watching the coronation in a bar on the Viminal but were dragged out (two say robbed) by Mitsubishi soldiers. The Mitsubishi also 'arrested/kidnapped/took' six of the group's companions—four Humanists who were wearing bull's-eyes and two Canadian Europeans in uniform—whose whereabouts are now unknown. They say they also saw Masons and others being dragged somewhere by Mitsubishi soldiers. One reports seeing a gun. Something bitter inside me imagined Tully Mardi saying, "You're welcome," but I don't think even they can be glad to see their internment camp how-to book put to active use.

14:32—Explosion over the Esquiline, a collision, low-flying car with something large and winged. Fire doesn't seem to be spreading.

14:47—Well done, Carlyle Foster-Kraye; the Conclave Guard is at our disposal, and has nearly doubled our forces, making the Forum that much more secure. Here's to hanging from a shoestring instead of a thread.

15:12—Fresh images from the Capitoline. I've viewed a whole sequence now, still shots taken a few minutes apart. Flags around the city aren't just moving, they're changing over time, bright spots winking out and others appearing, like flowers taking turns over the course of spring. No, more like flowers being weeded: out with the dandelions and stray wildflowers, until the tulips or whatever stand alone. The Viminal to our north is solid Mitsubishi now, nothing flying except the trefoil for block on block on block. Northwest by the Campus there's a big patch that's solid Masons' gray and purple, except for the odd Red Crystal, and on the Esquiline Hill too the other flags are winking out one by one to leave only the Square and Compass. I hope it's only flags that are winking out. South across the river is now a flurry of rainbows, Humanist rings and bull's-eyes, with some nation-strat flags and a peppering of others. And there are still those horses on the Aventine.

15:17—Jin Im-Jin believes me.

15:20—Flare signals from Lin's team at the harbor. The storm warning system is alright. They tried to signal something else but it got garbled. More refugees are wandering in, but not so many. Jeong and Matsuoka are running a cable from here up the Capitoline lookout post so we can have constant communications. They say after that there's enough cable for one more link from here to somewhere, either the Palatine or the southeast Forum gate, but no more. They say cities built before the wireless age will be better off than Romanova, since every old wall is full of cables. And this is probably happening in all Earth's cities at once.

15:39—Our Myrmidons have brought eleven injured Utopians to Kovács Hospital, and several damaged U-beasts. Not all of them can fly. People say that, between the Campus and the river, mobs are searching alleys with hoses and sprays of paint, hunting for invisible figures. People say there is a bonfire in Franklin Field, black smoke rising from wings and fins and furred and feathered bodies which I hope were more robot than animal. People say Utopia planned everything, the war, the cars, the monster attacks, the tracker blackout.

15:55—Carmen believes me. The Triumvirate is drafting a statement. Take that, Operation Baskerville.

16:16—Plague. No, War and Plague may be close comrades, but it can't happen this fast, not naturally. It has to be a bioweapon. Moon's team found it, a panic riot on the edge of the Campus to our north, fleeing people smashing everything they could to get away while others toppled street carts to make barricades. We've only seen it from a distance, but there are at least a dozen victims, not dead but twitching on the ground, trying to crawl, one agent said, like worms. Ground zero was happily close to Semaphore Square, so Blacksleeve Masons cordoned off the area pretty efficiently.

16:40—No real movement at the moment, so I guess I should describe the layout (though this is a copy of Rome so it feels strange describing such a famous city layout). The Tibernov River makes an S curve through the city, so the east and west halves nestle like a Yin-Yang, with the Kovács Hospital island next to us almost in the center. The main part of the city is the north/east half (the Yin part, so to speak); here the Seven Hills are clustered around the valley sections, like the up-thrust fingers of a hand cradling something in its palm. In the middle of that open palm the Forum valley slices east-west, like a gash. The Senate House, Rostra, Courts, Censor's Office, Sensayers' Conclave, Hive Embassies, and other Alliance centers are all crowded together here in the valley, so, without sending scouts up we can't see much of anything except the faces of the hills that make a wall around us. Rome's Seven Hills are steeper than you probably imagine, cliff-like, almost mesas, chosen by archaic settlers because they offered good defense against wolves and worse. When Agrippa MASON's engineers duplicated them, they filled them with elevators and service substructure but made them just as steep, so now they're just as fortresslike. Closest to us here in the valley are the Capitoline Hill, west, between us and the river (solitary like the thumb) and the Palatine Hill, which forms the south face of our valley—both are covered with vital Alliance buildings, plus some tiny flats for Forum vocateurs, like Vivien's where I've been crashing. We've got enough people and barricades in place that, for now at least, the Forum gash and those two hills west and south of it are ours. At the east end of the valley, past the Colosseum, is the Caelian Hill, which was always mostly Brillist, and I'm hoping those friendly Gordian checkpoints that have been in place a while now are staying friendly. Its flags are still diverse, at least. North of that the finger hills cluster around us. Northeast is the big Esquiline Hill, where only Mason flags still fly, and straight north of that the Viminal and Quirinal Hills slope up and away, merging into an endless Mitsubishi sea. There are other low areas too, north of us along the river, Hive-mixed valleys and Romanova's famous

Campus, where frightened students must be cursing us all for spoiling their coming choice. Way off to the south, out of sight beyond the Palatine, is the solitary Aventine with its ominous blurry cavalry. That's our east side of the river, the complicated Yin of our Yin-Yang. The smaller western Yang side, the Transtibernov side (*trans-Tiber-nov(a)*, i.e. across the "new Tiber" river), is simpler: the north tail of the Yang is the vast crest of the Janiculum hill, which Utopian walls turn into a thousand different wonders every hour of the day; the fat head of the Yang to the south is the Theater District, with its famous nightlife, where Hiveguard and Humanist colors reign.

17:38—Dragović's team has brought back eleven experts from the Campus to work on communications. They say there's more in place than jamming. An ancient cable running south from the city toward Cagliari has been cut, as have some that go across the water to Corsica and Italy, and the last signals we got from some satellites indicate malfunctions in the satellites themselves. After dusk they're going to take a telescope to the roof and see if any change is visible in the satellites that should pass by. One report of plague in the Transtibernov, isolated.

18:17—Thank goodness for the Masons. A troop of Blacksleeves came to the Tibernov island to pledge themselves to the defense of Kovács Hospital. They stood in ranks before the Hospital Director, and gave their Inviolate Oaths to guard the staff and patients with their lives, and that, until the Director releases them from this duty, though Caesar themself stood on the opposing shore commanding them to turn, they would drown their swords in their hivefellows' blood rather than stir one inch from their appointed task. I'll sleep the better for it, since guarding the hospital also means guarding the bridge at the Forum's back. Carmen asked them about the possibility of defending the Forum, too. They say they will not garrison the Forum lest MASON be accused of plotting a coup, but, while they live, no hostile force will reach us from the west, and, if we have need, a signal fire will bring them to our aid. They're incredible, the Masons, ready for these absurd extremes, with their oaths, and strict commands, and honor, useful now, while the rest of us flounder like time travelers dropped into some ancient Roman war. Just knowing they're near us feels like having driftwood to cling to after treading water.

19:10—Telescope team is heading to the roof.

19:51—More reports of plague from people fleeing down from the northeast ridge where the Esquiline meets the Viminal; or I could say where Mason territory meets Mitsubishi.

21:14—Battle on Coubertin Bridge, brief but real. Gwon's squad sent a runner back to us, who saw it all. That was cavalry we spotted on the Aventine, armed riders who thundered down the slopes, as fluent in the leaps and jolts of twisting streets as gymnasts on their beams, while streaming as their battle standard the Alliance Blacklaw flag. Coubertin Bridge is the city's southernmost, a straight link from the heart of the Theater District on the west bank to the foot of the looming Aventine. Sport-jacket-bright Humanists had gathered on the bridge, many sporting Hiveguard bull's-eyes and brandishing home-printed pistols, bats, or safety axes, but they scattered like pigeons before the riders who charged with swords, shields, and long spear-like poles with heavy padded ends, something between a jousting lance and a boxing glove. Most of the conquered lived to crawl away.

These riders bore no sigil but the Blacklaw flag, so Gwon's team approached after the battle, hailing them in the names of the Alliance Police, Censor, and Triumvirate. The Blacklaw force's leader met them, Hiveless Tribune Castel Natekari, whom the runner, Blair, describes like some triumphing fury of the battlefield, and whose bloodstained hands were more than metaphor. Natekari says they hold the bridge for the Alliance and will keep the precious river crossing open to all who agree that Sniper's attack upon a Romanovan Tribune makes them and all who condone that action enemies of the Alliance. This leaves most of the city's Humanists trapped on the west bank, so their only umbilical is Barton Bridge, a stone's throw south of the city's central island and alarmingly close to us here in the Forum. As for the Aventine Hill, the Blacklaws keep it. They have posted the Black Laws and Hobbestown's Customs around its perimeter, where cavalry circle with real spears instead of padded. They say they will offer refuge to any displaced Hiveless and welcome anyone who wishes to take up arms for the dignity of the Alliance. Tribune Natekari asked Gwon to pass on to the Triumvirate that their Blacklaw militia is at our disposal, but I don't know what Natekari will think of our Triumvirate's entrenched neutrality.

Gwon's team then crossed Coubertin Bridge and entered the Transtibernov district, aiming for the foot of the Janiculum, though they sent Blair back to report before they reached it, so we don't know how far they got. Blair said the Hiveguard were friendly enough when they saw Alliance uniforms, but blocked a couple alleys, "suggesting" a different route and volunteering to "escort" Gwon's team.

More later—the trackers are back!!

23:50—We had the trackers back. Twenty-six precious minutes. No, twenty-four were precious, two were a black blot for the history books. It started when all our trackers at once picked up a text-only signal on a frequency that normally isn't used. The signal sent instructions for how to get admin access to our tracker software and remove the blocks on what frequencies trackers can transmit on. Apparently there are particular ranges of frequencies, chunks here and there in the spectrum, that communications systems normally don't use. They've been forbidden for ages, because they make whales deaf, or drive bees crazy, or interfere with weather tracking, or deep-space telescope something somethings, different reasons for different chunks. The tracker admins guessed the saboteurs wouldn't be jamming some of those frequencies, and they were right. As soon as we switched over, we picked up hundreds of signals—some of them were rebooted network boosters, but mostly they were nearby trackers connecting point-to-point, trying the same thing we were. Hundreds swelled to thousands and it all went down again, too many signals in the same narrow bandwidth, but an admin urged everyone to keep our calls audio-only, and that cleared it up. Reports rushed in from around the city: more street battles, plague sites, deaths, people being herded down hills and over what I can only call borders, precious rooftop photos that will let us map the changing flags, and, yes, a real bonfire of wings and fins and feathered bodies, not by the Campus (that fire seems to be students toasting things) but in a fountain square down in the Transtibernov.

The first voice to reach us from outside Romanova was Felix Faust.

Faust: ". . . yes, I'm sure, they'll check Papadelias's private channel even . . ."

Su-Hyeon: "Hello?"

Faust: ". . . in the absence of the Commiss— Aha! Is that Romanova? Come in, Romanova!"

Su-Hyeon: "Yes! I can hear you, Headmaster. This—"

Faust: "Come in, Romanova?"

Su-Hyeon: "Yes. This is Romanova. This is the Censor. Can you hear—"

Faust: "Ah, there you are. Censor, is tha . . . Yes . . . Yes, I can hear you. Can you hear me?"

Su-Hyeon: "I hear you clearly, Headmaster. I'm in Alliance Police HQ. I have Speaker Jin and Papadelias's exec staff here with me."

A long gap on Faust's line, during which several of us couldn't help but chuckle: Faust had a photo set to show when video failed, but—either as someone's prank or out of sixty years' inertia—it showed Faust in their youth at Ingolstadt, blond, grinning, aged sixteen at most, with such a warm, Germanic face it felt like one of the farm boys at a Mennonite Reservation farmer's market, carrying out hot trays of cross buns and prayer-twisted pretzels and all the theologo-delicacies which saturate such life. "I think we have some lag," the false youth's old voice said at last, "but we're getting through. Glad to have you back, Romanova. I trust you'll all join me in writing an angry letter to our ancestors for plopping the world capital on an island with kilometers of sea in all directions. I've got the most valuable communications equipment in the world bobbing along on fishing boats to link your signal to the shore."

Su-Hyeon: "Thank you. What can we—"

Faust: "We all need— Oh, sorry, lag. Go on."

Su-Hyeon: "You go first, I'll wait."

A pause. "Alright. It can't last, this current system. Whoever's doing the jamming is bound to realize quickly that we've tapped these other wavelengths, and they'll start jamming them, too. But if we're quick, we can at least have your communications people talk to my communications people. My techs here are burbling about a hundred different things to try to set up long-term communications, yours must have similar ideas. If they put their heads together, they'll at least know what kinds of signals to look out for when things go down again."

We made the arrangements, and while we did the signal flickered, bandwidth overloading as Romanova's million realized they could call the Earth's lost billions, or some of them at least.

Jin: "How much is linked?"

Pause. "What?"

Jin: "How much of the world have you relinked? We have you in Ingolstadt, do we have farther?"

A pause again, that sunny, grinning youth so stiff and wrong. "North Africa is still offline, but we're working on a link across Gibraltar. The Americas and Australia are a lost cause, short-term, and there's some snarl in Kashmir so we have China online but not India, and Tōgenkyō and Tokyo are both unreachable. Do you want me to try to send help to Romanova? I know you lost most of your boats in the Tsunami. It seems Naples is already a battlefield, but there might be someone on the French coast who could help, or in Tunis if Africa comes back online."

Su-Hyeon: "Yes. Wait, no! No, we have bioweapons loose here, plague. It may be best to quarantine Sardinia."

Pause. "Bioweapons! Then you should quarant . . . yes, yes, I agree."

"It's fast-acting, causes severe muscle weakness, nausea, practically instant. Any sign of something like that on the mainland?"

Such agony, Faust's pauses. "No, nothing similar here, but I'll spread the warning, and the quarantine order."

My heart cheered, the dark resentful cheer of getting an apocalypse to focus its black storm on us alone. Well, that apocalypse. "Tell Faust the Utopians aren't behind this," I whispered.

Su-Hyeon: "Right! Headmaster, this Blackout—"

Faust: "Alright, I've spread the word. Another th . . . Yes?"

Su-Hyeon: "About this communications blackout, we—"

Faust: "Ah, the Blackout, yes . . ."

Su-Hyeon: "We don't think it was . . ."

Faust: ". . . very important, I don't think it was . . ."

Su-Hyeon: ". . . the Utopians."

Faust: ". . . the Utopians. It might have been, but just doesn't seem right."

Su-Hyeon smiled. "Yes, we'd come to the same conclusion. We've nicknamed it Operation Baskerville."

Of course Faust would see; how could I have ever doubted Faust would see?

Faust: "Yes, something like that, most likely. You should make a public statement, might calm the public coming from Romanova. Is there anything else I or Gordian can do for Romanova at present? If not, I'm sure you have other pressing calls."

We did, hundreds, to agents with reports on every city, a thousand packets of reconnaissance precious as diamonds, and, like a flood of diamonds, impossible for us to figure out quite how to spend. Updated flags will take me and Su-Hyeon days to process, though they are already obsolete now as I write. Some things were useful. The Triumvirate sent their statement of Utopia's innocence in the monster attacks, with sound arguments if not as much evidence as I would have liked, and I repeated it over the *Hâte Anonyme*. Red Crystal sent fresh calls for volunteers. A still image and a proclamation confirmed the coronation had gone ahead: Emperor Isabel Carlos I of the European Union greeted the Members who had thrust this heavier crown upon them with a speech of stunning passion and humility, not to mention rhetorical craftsmanship, but no one outside Brussels got anything but the lifeless transcript. A scanned contract confirmed that the new emperor had married by proxy Joyce Faust D'Arouet, who is—good riddance!—stuck in the abbey outside Burgos, far from mischief and any capital, where, despite the bridegroom's absence, they were then crowned Spain's new queen. The Prince is now an oath of loyalty to Spain away from being Crown Prince—well, an oath and the three thousand kilometers between Burgos and Alexandria.

"Gibraltar is online! I have Casablanca and . . . yes, Alexandria! I have Alexandria!"

Joy surged then as the Prince's call blipped in my tracker, joy on an altogether different scale. And then the hammer fell.

". . . *Utopianos speculas futuri aliturum absecuturumque . . . ?*"

It came in murmur first from one of the desks behind me, then, from a second desk, the same words like echo, a Masonic desk officer, a second one, a third, who murmured the same phrase, with fire rising in their voices: "*Utopianos aliturum absecuturumque?*"

"What?" someone asked.

"The Oath. The MASONS' Oath."

And there it was too in my lenses, sent by a dozen sources in a second, a hundred in the next, post after frantic post streaming across the fragile umbilical of Gibraltar. It was a short transcript, with a photograph of some greenish surface with words cut into it, bold but imperfect, as if scored by a careful but unpracticed hand. Latin. I don't read Latin but I saw *IMPERIUM sum* at the beginning and *MASON* at the end, and someone had highlighted the line in the middle that the others repeated so hotly, *Utopianos speculas futuri aliturum absecuturumque*. Seeing it felt like treason. I kept feeling jolts of guilt when I recognized a cognate, *humanitatis . . . Voluntas . . .* It felt like being party to some unspeakable violation, like ogling the photos some abuser took of their victims, and I wanted to stop looking, but I kept staring, frozen, trying to will it away like an offending dream. The Oath was secret, *the* secret, secret of secrets for ten thousand years (or 350, depending on which propaganda you believe). It was both the mightiest of state secrets and the most intimate of personal, the private contract between MASON past and MASON future, more sensitive than any diary. And there around me everyone was seeing it: the Masons in my office shaking, non-Masons gaping, and, as my tracker took the call from Alexandria, I heard, behind the Prince's breaths, somebody's screams. Danger to the Prince?

Panic seized me, overwhelming like the terrors of childhood. I lashed out, turned on video. What did I care if it ate up a hundred times the bandwidth—cut off a hundred sobbing souls from their loved ones—when there was danger to the Visitor? Besides (hubris advised me) I was the Anonymous—if I could see what passed in Alexandria, the world would benefit. There in my lenses rose the ever-tranquil Prince, the marble walls of the Imperial palace, and behind Them MASON's face . . . I might have seen a face like that if the victims of the vengeance for which I wear this uniform had held a mirror up as I raised the weapon of my bloody justice. The screams were a *Familiaris,* pale as the corpse on a morgue slab, kneeling and literally grasping Caesar's knees to beg, as people do in ancient books and statues. Xiaoliu Guildbreaker. The Emperor didn't seem to be angry at Xiaoliu, more like Xiaoliu was trying to break through the tornado wall of rage and ask . . . what?

The Prince: "Are you?"

It took me a moment to realize there was no more to Their question. "Yes. Yes, I'm still here. I'm fine. Alive. I *am.*"

A long silence, in which I watched fresh proof of the Prince's inhumanity as They stood impassive while something that had seemed as constant and primordial as the Moon was shattering around us. "You answer not," the Prince said at last.

I: "I did answer! I am! I'm here. It's time lag, that's all. Time delay on the line. I'm right here."

Five breaths, six. The Visitor is in pain now as they wait, I thought, but it will be fleeting, fleeting and then my words will reach Them, reassure Them, make Them less alone.

The Prince: "This you, which now I hear, is not; it is a you that was."

I choked. It was the truth. Words stale and lagging could no more prove I still existed when the Prince heard them than Mycroft's history can dredge them living from the bottom of the greedy sea. Panic swelled, the thought of that same sea which now lays siege to our fragile island, dark waves in their inexorable drowning legions, sleepless, endless. "I'm safe!" I yelped. "I'm not in danger right now. I'm in the Forum, working with the Triumvirate, and no one has any reason to hurt me. I'm as safe as it's possible to be at the moment, with Myrmidons protecting me, Censor's guards, Conclave guards, Blacksleeve Masons, Blacklaws . . ."

"The Utopians?" I panicked for a moment, thinking the word that had been on my tongue had come from me, betraying careful Huxley. But it wasn't me who said it, or the Visitor, it was someone at a desk behind me, who leaned close to someone else. "The Utopians are mentioned in the MASONS' Oath? That . . . that's what that says, right? *Utopianos?*"

"What does it say about them?"

"Swear to . . . nurture and . . . *absecuturum . . . absequor,* what's *absequor?*"

"*Absequor? Not adsequor?*"

And here the avalanche, in the office behind me, posted on the web, the same thought chain in every corner of the globe touched by the accursed trackers.

"That can't have been in the Oath for long, Utopia's only a few centuries old."

"Someone added it?"

"They change the Oath every new MASON."

"That's right, they add words each time. Three words each?"

"Not for their own Oath, for their successor, the next MASON's version."

"*Sequor* means follow, doesn't it?"

"Someone added this? Added the Utopians to the MASONs' Oath?"

"*Sequor,* dictionary says follow, support, side with, obey . . . obey?"

"Nurture and obey the Utopians?"

"*Ad-sequor* is to follow toward, pursue, equal, so *ab-sequor,* follow away?"

"Be led by, more like!"

"Who added it? When?"

"If this is the current Oath, then Cornel MASON changed it."

"Cornel MASON! Their obsession with that Utopian!"

"That Apollo Mojave!"

"Remember Mycroft Canner's history!"

"Cornel MASON trying to bow the Empire to the Utopians!"

"Wait, the changes are for the successor's version. They're trying to force this on J.E.D.D. Mason! Bow J.E.D.D. Mason to Utopia!"

"Was Cornel MASON in on the kidnappings of the weapons experts?"

"These monster strikes?"

"The war!"

"No." I said it aloud, but as soon as I did, I realized I had to follow it with something, lest the syllable worm its way across the lag to confuse the Prince. "The leak, how did it leak? The Oath? Why? Do we know?"

The lag was torture, watching news fora go mad, and Xiaoliu scream, and Caesar tremble like a chrysalis, as if Death, already possessing them, was now about to hatch into some greater ruin unimagined yet by humankind. The Prince's answer: "I did not ask My Host to share these words, though I desired them."

"It's not Your fault!" I yelped, making some heads turn. "Of course it's not Your fault. I meant the human agents, do we know what people leaked this? What their goals and motives were?"

Su-Hyeon's answer reached me first, having only a few desks to travel. "It's whoever attacked the *Sanctum Sanctorum.* I've mapped it back through the rebooting trackers. First post seems to have been in Algiers, just as reports of the supposed U-beast attacks were spreading. There was a comment posted with it, saying the world needs to wake up and realize Cornel MASON has sold out the Empire and J.E.D.D. Mason to—"

The Prince's answer made me miss the rest of Su-Hyeon's: "Rage."

Yes, that was it, goal, result, and motive all in one, rage in the attackers, rage in a world desperate for something to hang blame on, rage in Caesar that would split the guilty Earth in half as easily as my rage had split guilty skulls. Perhaps that's what Xiaoliu was begging MASON for, to remain calm? May as well beg an oak not to tremble in an earthquake. But then, as I watched the feed, Achilles shot in through the doorway behind the Emperor, Achilles soft-swift like a striking hawk, with this look on their face, an expression of the most intense empathy, understanding, but with warning too framed by the veteran's battered rigid calm. *Don't do what I did*—Achilles needed no words to make their meaning clear as the crystal sky—*Cornel MASON, don't give in to rage as I did.* The oak stopped shaking. I heard Caesar say something, short, one word I think, and the whole rage tempest seemed to exit with that word, as if there really were such a thing as possession, and some ruinous spirit had flown out in the breath of that one word leaving Cornel MASON, alone of all the humans on the planet, calm. Xiaoliu Guildbreaker fell back onto the floor with new sobs which seemed almost happy.

"What did MASON say?" I asked.

That long, cruel delay as I watched the Prince, as They watched Xiaoliu panting on the floor, while MASON turned away. Then words at last: "Prayer is granted, *Pater* construction's once more. To Xiaoliu *Pater* delegates the de—"

Nothing. Silence and nothing to the world's end.

"Jamming's back. That's it."

A frozen silence left us all staring at our lenses, at the scan, those grim etched letters, and the million frantic comments, no longer multiplying.

"Now what?"

Somebody sighed. "Now, I guess whatever kind of whales it is go deaf."

I looked around me, feeling only now the heat of tear-threat in my eyes. The room was different. Everyone had exhaustion shock, as if this were the end of an all-nighter, not the beginning, while the Masons at their desks, a few were crying, but the rest looked somehow . . . like broken marble. No, not marble at all anymore. People, just people, as scared and scareable as I was. Doubt in the Empire. It felt like we'd had a secret leg up, one grown-up playing on our kids' football team to make sure all went well, but now we were all kids.

And then the cold Host granted us one mercy.

"MASON got a message out! Right before the jamming."

"In English! Look!"

We did. It must have happened during the time lag, words composed while the video was still inchworming its way tracker-to-tracker around the Mediterranean and across precarious Gibraltar.

<DICTUM ABSOLUTUM: The treason of looking upon that most intimate plate carved for my ascension by the Imperial hand of Aeneas MASON I pardon hereby in all who view it out of necessity in a world transformed irrevocably by its exposure. The treason of approximating in vulgar English those words which transform a human to IMPERIUM, I pardon in those who would use them in conversation to heal Earth and Empire. The absolute doom of life and legacy which I owe the perpetrators of this wrong, I delegate hereby to Xiaoliu Guildbreaker, and dedicate my energies instead to victory, and peace beyond.>

And with that pardon, a few more Masons in the room relaxed enough to cry.

"The version carved for Cornel MASON's ascension . . ." the whisper rose behind me, hushed at first, and then excited, "then Cornel MASON couldn't have added anything!"

"Utopia was in the Oath already?"

So it seems.

I guess I should include the text. I feel strange about it. Mycroft never would have—I think Mycroft would have scratched the world's eyes out before they'd duplicate the MASONS' Oath. But millions and millions have seen it now, we can no more seal it back in the *Sanctum Sanctorum* than we can bid life crawl back down into the sea. So here it is, followed by Carmen Guildbreaker's translation. The English reads all stiff, but Carmen says the Latin's stiff, not like speech or flowing prose, more like the Latin of grand inscriptions and knightly mottos, just extended. They think it may have started as a translation of something older, that it reads somewhat like the Latin of the *Académie royale des Inscriptions et Médailles,* whose job it was, around 1700, to study ancient languages and invent grand Latin phrases for Louis XIV to use on self-congratulating medals or to decorate Versailles. If it was translated around then from Phoenician or Middle Persian or something by men trying to make it feel as grand as possible, and then the Latin had extra words squeezed into it three-at-a-time each generation when there's been a new MASON, no wonder by now it reads like a pastiche of dictators' tombstones.

> *IMPERIUM sum, hinc princeps, parens, aedifex illius urbis cinctae muribus sapientium laterum, nominatae humanitatis. Pietatem humanitati non debeo, nec mihi debet, vere ilex unicus sumus, vigens sub tempestivo sole, sub bipenni inepto lacrimans, gente humana trunco ruboreque, memet cordi prudentia quae arbitratur quo tempore frondescendum quoque stringendum ad hiemem. Posthac atomi fugaces quae nominantur dies, anni, decenni, sunt mihi arenae, cui cura est perennium. IMPERIUM familiam non habet, nec gentem, prolem, parentem, coniugem, populum, viciniam, praeiudicium, patrimonium privatum, divitias, famam, munus, avocationem, patronum, fidem alienam, inimicum, simultatem, neque interest quiqui ephemeropterae gentes laudent damnentve praenomen inscriptum intimo pectore illius unici aeterni terrestris. Cui succedo si vivit, nihil pietatis debeo, sed sumus, ego ut Voluntas quae perago Ratioque ille quae censet. Iusiuro ex hoc ipso tempore me praepositurum fundamentum ornamento, utilia deliciis, prudentia temerariis, vera somniis. Qui memet cognoscant, illis uturum ut forti dextra manu sinistraque obscura; qui memet non cognoscant, illis provisurum ut bene regatur; qui me lacessant, illis neque odium neque misericordiam habiturum, contra amputaturum velut veprem hortulanus; aliquando Utopianos speculas futuri aliturum absecuturumque ut spatium voluminis perlustretur. Lex me clientem ligaverit, abhinc adsumpturum in manibus frenis a voluntate aurigae constrictis, relaxis, mollitis, asperatis quibus adiuncturum trigario impetuum humanorum: avidiam, cogitationem, spem. Quod est aucturum aedificaturumque latere vivo insuper mortuum nondum atque nato insuper vivum, fundamenta forsitan maximi momenti, per ordinem atque consilium, ut arx prae memet et post extendat ad infinitum, quare sumus MASON.*

IMPERIUM I am, henceforth leader, parent, and architect of that city, girded with walls of thinking brick, named humanity. I owe no [duty/piety] to humanity and it owes none to me, rather we are one oak, thriving in [clement/opportune] sun and [weeping/bleeding] under the foolish axe, humanity the trunk and growing force, and I the prudence in its heart which judges when to sprout leaves and when to strip for winter. From now on, the fleeting atoms called day, year, and decade are as sand to me, who only gives care to perennial things. IMPERIUM has no family, nor [race/tribe], offspring, parent, partner, [people/strat], [neighborhood/geographic allegiance], prejudice, private patrimony, wealth, reputation, outside office, avocation, patron, separate duty, personal enemy, [rivalry/vendetta], nor does it matter what mayfly peoples praise or curse my given name, which is etched in the heart of the only eternal Earthly thing. If my abdicated predecessor lives, I owe no filial [duty/piety], but I am as Will which acts, they Reason which advises. I swear henceforth I will prefer the foundation to the ornament, the useful to the delightful, the prudent to the hasty, the [true/real] to the daydream. Those who know me I shall use as my strong right arm and hidden left; those who know me not I shall see well governed; those who scratch me I shall neither hate nor pity but cut off as the gardener the thorn bush, and [*aliquando*] (the?) Utopians [who are?] [mirrors/glimpses] of the future I shall [suckle/cherish/nurture] and [*absequor*] as the surface area of the [page/scroll] is [expanded/illuminated farther out]. Law, which bound me while I was human, I swear I shall wield as reins in my hands—tightened, loosened, made gentler or more painful by the driver's will—by which I yoke to my three-horse chariot humanity's driving forces: [ambition/desire], [thought/contemplation/planning], and hope. All that is I shall build up, living brick on dead and unborn on living, the older perhaps the most important, with order and planning, as the building extends before and after me forever, [hence/thus/so/wherefore] we are MASON.

It makes you shudder, so many different ways. There are two words Carmen said they couldn't translate. *Absequor* doesn't exist, it's a neologism; *sequor* can mean follow, support, side with, observe, understand, equal, chase, hunt down, pursue, overtake, gain, any number of things, but it's not at all clear what it means with *ab,* i.e., 'away' grafted to the front of it. And I'd give my eyeteeth to know what *aliquando* means, but so would Carmen. They say it's a temporal word with lots of meanings, so it could be "*sometimes* nurture the Utopians" or "*ever* nurture the Utopians" or "*finally* nurture the Utopians" or "nurture the Utopians *for a long time*" or "nurture the Utopians *before it's too late,*" and if Carmen Guildbreaker is wracking their brains at the nuance, I doubt Cornel MASON has any clearer idea what it means. But at least a fearful Earth knows that Utopia was already there, sealed into the duties Cornel MASON took on blindly, consenting to the

Oath before ever seeing it. They cannot blame Mycroft, or Apollo, for Utopia being in there. But if our MASON didn't add Utopia to the Oath, which MASON did?

And now presumably the offer stands, that if the Prince swears this—becomes all this—Cornel MASON will make Them Emperor.

02:45—Gwon's back from scouting all seven bridges. Of the two northern bridges by the Campus, Gurai Bridge is held by Blacksleeve Masons, and Chanakya Bridge by Campus security, who seem neutral so far. For a while the two mid-city bridges were Earth's scariest staring contest, Humanist Hiveguard all over Juana II and Masons on Utarutu, but during the shock with the Oath, Hiveguard drove the Masons out, so now the bull's-eye flies on both. Of the two bridges near us, Kovács Bridge is Red Crystal plus Masons (though that's a lot less reassuring now than a few hours ago), and Barton Bridge is Hiveguard, frisking anybody who comes near who doesn't wear the bull's-eye. Coubertin Bridge down by the Aventine is still Blacklaw cavalry. Now we know. Yay. Refugees still streaming from the Viminal and Esquiline. And more reports of plague. Su-Hyeon and I had a fight about which of us should go to bed.

03:10—Humans are so stupid. How are we so stupid? I just checked the comments on the *Hâte Anonyme,* the last comments my tracker loaded before the final blackout. I'd supported our Triumvirate announcement that the Utopians are innocent, and at first the comments were calm, but as soon as the Oath broke, it exploded into accusations: Utopians are controlling the Triumvirate! Utopians are controlling the Anonymous! Utopians have hacked the *Hâte Anonyme!* So stupid. No way to fix it now.

03:45—Telescope team reports that most of the expected satellites passed on time, but one seems to be missing, and three seem to be a bit off course, hard to be sure. Frail specks are hard to trace against the great black, even with the finest tools we have.

CHAPTER SEVEN

A Secret Friend

Written October 5–6, 2454
Events of September 28
Romanova

I STILL HAVE FOUND NO EVIDENCE FOR the existence of Saladin Canner, this fantastic lover, who leaves only Mycroft's DNA in their wake, and acts just as Mycroft's sleeping monster self would act if it dared stir. There is a birth certificate, and a death certificate, but Mycroft's many explanations for the lack of further evidence have a genius's twisting unprovability. Joyce Faust won't answer, too eager to tease, but you would think Papadelias at least might have offered me the kind of wink that can't be used in court. Never. It used to be a heart-wrenching conundrum for me, whether to hope this Saladin was real, or just the dearest of so many hallucinated ghosts. It seemed too cruel for Mycroft, who had suffered so much, to also suffer this delusion of True Love, as if, after vengeful Apollo, Eros too must have their turn to test their bow on this favorite butt of curses. But if Saladin was real, then real people were in danger from them, me especially, who dared enjoy so close a friendship with the beloved of this savage, possessive torturer. Besides, if Saladin was just a fantasy, then at least poor Mycroft had one good thing in their life they could not lose. For Mycroft's sake I (usually) used to make myself wish Saladin real, but now things are simpler. If there is a mourning monster trapped on some desolate rock somewhere, screaming heartbreak's fury at the sea, it helps no one. Let it go. Let them have been one heart, one keen and complex brain, so they went down into the ocean depths together, wrapped in one another's neurons as they would have wished to be in one another's arms. Better that than to think a being such as Saladin must taste what we survivors taste, alone.

"If I let you share our skysight on the city, can you hide the fact that you have it from the Triumvirate?"

Huxley Mojave startled me, not with the offer, or with their sudden words behind me, since the hiss of the shower had made it easy (for once) to locate my secret roommate-bodyguard. It was Huxley's smallness without their coat that shocked me as they emerged from the steamy bathroom, a plain body in a faded tank top, black hair pressed thin by the water, sun-starved shoulders a shade less dark than the cheeks that peeked out from the vizor. An ordinary body. The coat of perfect storm had made me imagine something godlike, otherworldly;

gills, wings, cyborg armor, veins aglow with inner fire, anything would have seemed less strange than this plain person, one arm still in a sling.

"Can you conceal it from the Triumvirate?" Huxley had to repeat.

"You mean aerial surveillance? Probably not. Su-Hyeon would notice if my reactions to different bits of info are suddenly being influenced by something else, Jin Im-Jin too. But I can lie about where I got the info from." I nodded to the kitchen island, where I'd set out breakfast bowls for two. "I've made oatmeal. Do you want raisins in yours?" Vivien had left the flat well stocked with the rudiments of breakfast.

"Sure, thank you."

"Are you in touch with other Utopians?" I asked as Huxley sat. "Do you know what's happening at the Janiculum? How bad is it? Are you under attack?"

Huxley hesitated, gazing down at their first steaming bite.

"Whatever you tell me, I'll tell Su-Hyeon I got it from Myrmidons."

Brief hesitation. "Our Janiculum is a fortress, adamant and many-eyed. I have seen images of the attacks there, improvised, more wrath than force. I doubt any such could more than singe a feather here or there."

There was some relief. "What about Utopians trapped outside?"

"Our heralds have proclaimed that ransom in food and needgoods awaits whoever brings a Utopian safe to the Janiculum. That will turn hunters to bounty hunters, at least in the Transtibernov."

"Is it working?"

"Unknown. A scryhawk brought me skysight, but I've no groundword from beyond the river. Give them time."

"Do you know who's attacking the Janiculum? Hiveguard?" I guessed.

"Anyone. Everyone. Even Masons since the Oath broke."

I winced. The MASONIC Oath, to nurture and *absequor* the Utopians; a night's sleep had made it hazy. "Did you know? Sorry, stupid question," I answered myself. "Nobody knew. Cornel MASON alone in all the world, oathbound to be your secret ally, unable to say why. They held on so hard."

Huxley chewed slowly. "Perhaps someone knew something, generations back. My ba'pas taught me an axiom, one I have heard from many Hivefellows, that Utopia can trust all Caesars but not all Caesar's subjects. An echo, perhaps, of something known by someone long ago?"

"Generations back . . ." I repeated, "then that's more evidence that it wasn't Cornel MASON that added it. You have to tell the Triumvirs!" I spat a raisin in my excitement. "People are saying, even inside the office last night, that Cornel MASON added that to the Oath to twist the Empire, and manipulate the Prince, even though they can't have made changes to the version of the Oath they took themself. But your testimony could help settle it!"

I read no judgment in Huxley's vizor. "Do you want the images?" They offered a transfer cable, and I spent some embarrassing moments failing to remember where in my tracker's casing the little port was hidden.

"Thanks. And I'll conceal the source if you like, but wouldn't it be easier . . ."

I paused, looking over the morning's freshly captured sea of flags as I considered how to phrase my thoughts. "It would be easier, I think, if we tell the Triumvirate you're here. You're on a neutral mission, guarding me, they—"

"No." Harshness in Huxley's tone felt strangely comforting, a hint of the storm that should be spilling from those shoulders.

"It would be so much safer. They'll take you for a spy if you're caught invisible in—"

"My mission is not to help the Censor or Triumvirate."

The doorbell made me spin.

"[Anonymous]!" Pounding on the front door accented Su-Hyeon's cry from outside, bright with delighted urgency. "It's not a plague! There is no plague! It's Cousins!"

"Cousins?" In my confused delight, I had almost reached the door before panic reminded me I must not be caught with this companion. I spun, but Huxley and their telltale second bowl were gone, like ghosts. I glanced from corner to corner, searching for signs that might give us away, forgetting in my panic what the natural thing is to do when a friend comes over.

"[Anonymous]?" Su-Hyeon called again, with a shrillness between confusion and impatience. "Can I come in? Are you decent?"

A soft squeeze of my shoulder reassured me. Huxley was behind me, so close I could feel the Griffincloth brushing my pants cuffs. I smiled; it was the safest spot really, where any slight noise or audible breath would have a ready explanation. "Yes, I'm decent. Come in."

Su-Hyeon entered with a living moat of Censor's Guards, their own joined by the patient pair who watched my door at night. "The symptoms we've been seeing, the sudden collapsing and muscle spasms, it's not a plague, it's Gorgons."

"What?"

"These Tiring Guns the Cousins made, the special stun guns, some people call them Gorgons. Seems they have different effects from standard stun guns, more intense immediate symptoms. When they started using them in Semaphore Square, people couldn't see properly what was happening, they just saw people falling with spasms and thought it was a plague, panicked before the Cousins could explain. Apparently, there was supposed to be a primer for the public about how the new guns work, but with the chaos and Operation Baskerville, it didn't get circulated like the Cousins intended."

I felt my shoulders ease as our apocalypse lost a horseman. "That's wonderful! Just wonderful. We couldn't have wished for better news." I had meant the sentence when I started it, but when I got as far as 'wished,' I felt, inside myself, the bitter anger sea, on which the dinghy of my forced calm drifts, splash back: I could have wished for Mycroft.

It must have shown in my face, since Su-Hyeon's smile grew warmer, tender, sad. They turned to the guards. "Would you wait in the lobby for a bit? Trackerdoc says I'm overdue for some R&R." They poked the tracker at their ear, still good for something.

I parted my lips to object, but Huxley gave me a reassuring squeeze. "Have a seat," I offered as the guards left. "Would you like some water? Or oatmeal?"

They smiled. "I brought tea. Is the pot clean?"

"Um, I think so, here—"

"Sit, sit, I'll do it," came their smiling order. "I've brewed more pots of tea in this flat than you have in your life."

That truth let me return to my oatmeal, watching Su-Hyeon's familiar figure open familiar cabinets in the familiar uniform which should have been on Vivien's shoulders. I still felt Huxley behind me, their good hand resting gently on my back to confirm their presence.

"Will the Cousins give us Tiring Guns?" I asked.

"They've promised us a few, but apparently, only one crate made it to Romanova."

"Of all the places . . ." I sighed. "And did they say why they have such scary-looking symptoms? Are they better than normal stun guns some other way? Lower power?"

"Long-term effect. They're designed to leave targets weakened for a while after, days if I hear right, so people can't just go straight back to fighting. It's supposed to make prisoners easy to deal with, less dangerous, so the enemy is less tempted to slit throats while people are down."

I winced at that thought. "Smart."

Su-Hyeon set the kettle to its work and faced me. There was something in their face, a little grave, almost a little flighty. "I need to talk to you about something important. Private."

"Sure. What?" At the time, it didn't feel like I was helping the Delians spy on the Censor; funny, the narrow margin between social awkwardness and treason.

"Hiding dangerous people."

I hoped my poker face was good. "In what sense?"

Su-Hyeon held my eyes. "We've been concentrating on groups, watching the flags move, worrying about what's happening to Masons in the Hiveguard-held Transtibernov, or those five bash'houses on the Aventine that were flying the bull's-eye before Tribune Natekari's cavalry appeared."

That was worth a wince. "Yes. Natekari still won't say what happened?"

"Actually good news there." They smiled. "The Blacklaws did a hostage exchange, traded the Hiveguard that were on the hill for some Graylaw Remakers trapped across the river. Overnight report is that's been happening a lot. Between Esquiline and Viminal, the Masons and Mitsubishi have posts set up for trading Member for Member, and it's going on sporadically at most of the bridges. Gwon and Bidyadhara are working with Red Crystal on something they're calling a House Hostage Exchange, where bash'es surrounded by enemies arrange to swap, so a Mason in the Transtibernov and a Humanist on the Esquiline go live in the other's bash'house, with the pledge that they'll treat the house and stuff in it with respect since the other bash' has theirs in return."

"Fascinating," I answered. "It presumes this remains a very civil Civil War."

"Still worth trying." Su-Hyeon fidgeted. "But I think there's a different kind of person we need to be thinking about. People who are more alone than that. People no side wants, who are in danger everywhere. The people everybody's blaming."

I tried to keep my breath steady. *You aren't looking at me, Su-Hyeon, why aren't you looking at me? Is it because you're looking at something else? A shimmer of imperfection? A telltale shadow on the floor?* "Utopia," I answered.

Now Su-Hyeon winced. "Yes, good example. I've got Bidyadhara's teams telling everyone they can that Utopia isn't behind the tracker blackout, but it's bad. Very bad. I have reports people are stringing up traps around the city to detect invisible people: flickery lights, laser beams, streamers, strings, crunchy stuff on the ground, and along the river there are gangs camped with wind meters and mist machines taking potshots whenever they think something invisible is moving. Sometimes they're right."

I shuddered too much to be certain whether Huxley shuddered too.

"There was a group near Juana II Bridge doing . . . There were bodies in the water. But some Blacksleeve Servicers broke it up."

I'm sure pride showed in my face. "Myrmidons," I corrected.

A little wince brought out the sweetness in Su-Hyeon's young face. "I know you're not one, these militarized Servicers, Bryar told me about them, how . . . *they* . . . were pressuring you to join them."

Su-Hyeon tripped over the 'they.' I felt myself grow hot. Mycroft—was that your accusation, Bryar? That wicked Mycroft pressured me to take up arms? As if there was no heat, no pride, no courage in my veins to fight for justice and a better world?

"I'm grateful that you didn't," Su-Hyeon added.

That softened me. "You needed me. I'm doing the most good where I am now. But no one pressured me except Bryar, and every day that the uniforms and flags are spreading, and I go out with no black sleeve, no sigil on my shoulders, and my *Familiaris* armband hidden in my pocket, I feel a little like a hypocrite."

"I understand."

"And a little like a deserter."

Huxley's touch shifted on my back here, gently, a squeeze of . . . reassurance? Bidding me respect myself, the part I play?

Su-Hyeon's sad eyes would not stay on me. "Please don't try to wear the armband, not outside Mason territory, a *Familiaris* Servicer, with memories so fresh of Mycroft, you could be lynched."

"I know."

"You could wear something else if you wanted. Vs or bull's-eye."

I caught myself gripping my left shoulder with my right hand, my fingers tracing the texture of patches that were not there. "So could you."

"I couldn't," they answered, "not as Censor, not without losing all credibility as a neutral arbiter. Except . . ." The steaming kettle gave Su-Hyeon a good excuse to turn away.

"Yes?" I prompted.

Their voice sank to that guilty whisper we use when risk enters conversations, as when 'what are the odds!' strays into the sensayer danger zone 'do you believe in . . . Something?' Su-Hyeon clanked the teapot. "It would be the Vs for you too, right, [Anonymous]? I haven't been sure."

The sun's kiss driving the frost back on a winter morning is not as warming as that 'too.' "Yes."

With their back still to me, I couldn't tell for sure if Su-Hyeon's deep and happy sigh concealed a sob. "Then . . . But that isn't what I came to talk about. I came to talk about people with no friends, people who are stuck here, hiding from all sides and everybody. We're worried about Masons among the Hiveguard, but I think there could be something worse than that. Imagine someone trapped alone, not a bash' but one person, by themself, in the middle of all this, someone practically everyone in Romanova was ready to shower with hate, and blame, and violence." Now Su-Hyeon turned toward me with the teapot and the gravest, most desperate look I'd ever seen on their light face. "What if there was someone here who was so feared and hated that even being found sheltering them would bring distrust and fear and likely violence down on whoever was caught helping them?"

Fear ripened to relief as Su-Hyeon sat down opposite me, setting down the pot with its soft scent of steeping. Of course they guessed. It wouldn't take a telltale shadow or stray lion hair, not when Su-Hyeon and I had traded, on so many happy nights, the giddy, babbling honesty of three A.M. The relief of deception's end washed down my scalp and shoulders like a shower's massage as I parted my smiling lips. Then, as the first vibrations of reply sparked in my throat, I felt Huxley's hand grow hard against my back, an urgent pressure. Still nervous, Huxley? I understand—this stranger Su-Hyeon had no Mycroft to vouch that they too weep in praying to live long enough to see the brave seeds fly. "That sounds like a frightening scenario," I answered cautiously, to humor my careful guardian. "Do you really think there are people like that around?"

Su-Hyeon's eyes stayed locked on mine. "I think there are. Do you think it would be too dangerous harboring such a person?"

"Do you?" I challenged back. That was the real question.

"In a lot of cases, yes, I'd say the right thing was to try to get the person away, out of danger, even out of Romanova if need be, to avoid danger falling on both shelterer and sheltered. Except . . ."

"Except?" I prompted.

"What if they had to stay, what if there was something incredibly helpful they could do by staying here, in the Forum, something so important, so useful for the public good, that it would justify the risk?"

I nodded. "Yes, exactly. That's exactly how I feel: some missions require danger."

"I'd say 'justify,' not 'require,' it would be better if there weren't danger."

"Of course." I even chuckled. "So, if there were such a person nearby, would you welcome them? Protect them? Hide them? Want them with us, helping in the Forum? Despite the danger?"

"Would you?" they asked back.

"Of course."

Here came Su-Hyeon's biggest smile. "Especially if they were only here to help us."

"Yes."

"I knew you'd feel the same."

Su-Hyeon rose, fast steps past me, ready to offer their trusting handshake to the empty air they knew must not be empty. Except they went too far, across the room and toward the bedroom. "They're ri—" I began, but again uneasy Huxley pushed, that wary pressure, warning. With Su-Hyeon facing away from us, I craned my neck back, mouthing to Huxley, "It's okay, we can trust them, I know we can trust them." But as I turned back around, I found Su-Hyeon at the little back door to the maintenance stairs, turning the latch, and all at once a figure huddled in a blanket like some shivering storm orphan rushed into Su-Hyeon's open arms. "It's okay," Su-Hyeon crooned, softly, "it's safe here, we can trust [Anonymous] absolutely. They'll keep you safe. The hard part's over."

Sobs from this figure, slightly larger than Su-Hyeon, so their bulk with the blanket seemed a bit backwards in Su-Hyeon's small hug, like child comforting mother. High-pitched sobs. I knew that voice, where did I know that voice? I rose to peer, feeling stiff and wary Huxley stalking with me, and I heard the floor's creak as somewhere the lion's weight shifted, ready to pounce if need be on this intruder, medium-dark hands, long fingers, lively twists of African hair spilling from the blanket, a sleeve with purple piping. Toshi Mitsubishi. In an instant the whole story told itself: Vivien's best analyst, the veteran partner of the Censor's labors, desperate new-in-office Su-Hyeon must have called them, begged them to leave the safety of Tōgenkyō, just for a couple hours, help me, please, for the Alliance! But then the cars went down, and here in reeling Romanova stood alone one of that Mitsubishi brood which a thousand accounts of recent days (less kind than Mycroft's) accused of complicity in almost every crumb of our world's avalanche: Masami's Seven-Ten List, Andō's plot to tear the Cousins down, Danaë's games with Julia Doria-Pamphili. Toshi was tainted too with that most misused title set-set, as likely to be called 'thing' as 'person' by the injured millions who blamed O.S., Sniper, Madame's creations, the Prince's strangeness, Utopia's actions, all on these 'bonsai brains,' no, these machines whose cogs the haters claim are neurons stolen from what could have been a child. If Perry-Kraye and Toshi Mitsubishi were dragged forth at the same time, I don't know which the mob would lead to the guillotine first.

"[Anonymous], thank you!" I could not call Toshi more than 'acquaintance' but they embraced me, crying on my shoulder as I found my arms closing in comfort around their Censor's Office jacket, barely recognizable beneath the grime. "I didn't think anywhere would be safe."

"Are you hurt?" I asked this automatically, field training taking over in my shock.

"No."

'Not injured' might have been the truth, but the exhaustion on Toshi's hollow cheeks, the sweat stink, the grime caked visibly around their eyes betrayed a body far from health. "Water?" I offered; hospitality was an easy default.

"Yes, thank you!" I'd never seen someone shed tears before at the thought of simple water.

I filled a glass as Su-Hyeon helped Toshi wash their face. I scrounged some snacks as Su-Hyeon recounted near captures and cruel hiding places. I offered the still-steamy shower, and picked fresh clothes from what Bryar and Vivien had left in the flat, though Su-Hyeon's needs and my own had left little but Cousin wraps and Vivien's bulkiest. And all the while I felt Huxley's hands, now on my shoulder, now my hip, my elbow, while my imagination debated with those touches: what I had almost said, the danger, the relief, whether this new arrival made it safer to reveal that I too hid a hated stranger, but all the while, Huxley's tugs at sleeve or shirt seemed to urge: *No! Not yet. Not yet.*

"Toshi's worked up a new program for mapping the city," said Su-Hyeon as our damp and smiling refugee plopped between us on a sofa. "We've been scanning the rooftop images for flags, uniforms, and insignia, charting out the changes over time. We've started a dynamic map. I'd love for you to have a look."

They offered transfer cables, but I produced my own. "I have aerial photos of the city."

No heap of birthday presents has produced such smiles. "You do? How?"

My answer made me proud. "Let's say Hermes brought them, passing through."

I enjoyed their faces, puzzling the different directions that clue might point, and I took the quick poke Huxley gave me as a compliment. "Shall we put two and two together?"

'Sulfur and saltpeter,' I should have said, for the power in that combination—Toshi and Su-Hyeon's program with the Delian gods'-eye-view—blasted through a thousand barriers and gave us . . . at the time it felt like everything. We could *see* again. There were the many valleys, invisible from the Forum, whose flower-bright flags showed mixed lands still thriving between the Hive-held hilltops. There were the teeming wonders of Utopia unscathed in the Janiculum. There were Europeans in the uniforms of many nation-strats setting up the makings of two rallies, one north of the Janiculum, another in a square just out of sight east of our Forum. There were our own agents hard at work at four critical crossroads, delivering Triumvirate announcements by loudspeaker to those willing to brave both wartime streets and six A.M. There were the Brillists visible at last upon the Caelian, so we could map their checkpoints and confirm that the hasty uniform sent in by Ingolstadt, a red sash home-printed but elegant and edged with black and gold, did actually exist. There were grimmer things, too, prison camps, some in the Transtibernov, some in Mitsubishi lands, set up to Tully Mardi's specifications, the guard posts and haste-barred windows unmistakable. But on the barricaded border between the Mitsubishi Viminal and Masonic Esquiline we saw a happier solution, a conjunction of troops where high resolution let us zoom in and sequential images showed hostages brought forth, exchanged, and welcomed; a humane trade. In the glut of luscious data, Toshi and Su-Hyeon seemed to forget that what we watched was war, and clucked with delight at the social subtleties revealed across the Mitsubishi hills, not just the standard Mitsubishi flag—the trefoil of scarlet diamonds with Greenpeace leaf-green diamonds set inside them—but also the Chinese variant, with a gold background instead of white, and the Korean version with its black framing trigrams and hints of blue. I was cheered to see V flags there too in Mitsubishi colors, and bull's-eyes beside them, but they were all plain bull's-eyes, supporting a Hive's right to use lethal tools like O.S., while on the whole of the Mitsubishi Viminal and Quirinal we spotted not a single bull's-eye with the added crosshair that codes for endorsing the Prince's death, nor did a single shoulder there bear the bull's-eye sigil as a military mark upon the arm, only as a badge of conscience on the front. Accept O.S. but defend the Prince's life, there was a sentiment I could respect.

Toshi: "Somebody's painted 'Help' on the roof of a complex behind Thunderstorm Theater."

Su-Hyeon: "I'll make a note to send someone."

Anonymous: "Lots of people mixing at the corner of Nkrumah and Dick Hooker, might be a great spot for us to set up another news post."

Su-Hyeon: "We'll tell Bidyadhara. Toshi, can you scan for plain Alliance flags that aren't ours? Lost allies are worth hunting for."

Toshi: "Sure. I've got four, oh, and a cluster between the fingers of the Viminal. What's that giggle for, [Anonymous]?"

Anonymous: "What? Oh, I never noticed there's an alley between Dick Hooker and the Esquiline called Latitudinarian Way. Our ancestors were so ridiculous, great but ridiculous."

Su-Hyeon: "Small mob on the corner of Quaker and Appianova—Hiveguard with Masons around them, I'll add that to our list."

Toshi: "Sounds urgent."

Su-Hyeon: "We have fifteen things, I'll send a runner once we have twenty."

Fifteen in four minutes? I basked in my own smile: what a team!

Toshi: "Parade!"

Anonymous: "Parade?"

Toshi: "There's a parade! The 06:16:20 image, advancing north through Maastricht Square. It's on 06:03:53 too, heading south down Stowe Street, must have looped around. Those are very visible streets, they must be trying to be seen."

I tore my attention from a construction site on the highest hillcrest in Masonic lands (a communications tower? *Please let it be a communications tower!*) to look. My heart leapt. Here, Masons in formation, all black-sleeved and sorted into ranks, marched beneath the flying Square and Compass and the clean white Flag of Truce. Myrmidons marched with them, vanguard squads and wing scouts leading and flanking the Masons, just as Patroclus and Achilles had made us practice in those grueling secret camps. Our alliance was public now, Servicers and Masons teaching all Romanova that, yes, all black sleeves meant the same. But best of everything were the lights, dazzling even in the morning sunshine, which glinted out among the Blacksleeves like living stars, or rather living suns, bright on the back of marching Delians. There were so many, safe and welcome with the Masons, U-beasts with them, gryphons, leopards, unicorns crowding beneath the blank truce banners as if the beasts of heraldry had come to life and leapt out from their shields. And their numbers grew. The computer counted a dozen new stars in one image, seven more in the next, as those who had been stranded invisible in Romanova's alleys joined the shelter of the great parade. Thank you, whoever did this! This could not be MASON's order, nor Achilles's, nor the Prince's, since all were silenced by two thousand kilometers of sea. This was the local Masons, orphaned, reeling from the heartstab publication of the Oath, who did not know one whisper yesterday of Cornel MASON's secret compact with Utopia, yet, while hoodlums rail against imagined betrayals, Romanova's Masons compose this public, living answer: we hear you and obey, absent Caesar; protect, nurture and [away-follow] Utopia we shall.

Su-Hyeon: "Combat."

Toshi: "Where?"

Su-Hyeon: "North, Gandhi Boulevard, I think that's combat, Masons and Mitsubishi, see?"

Toshi: "I see it. Just a few of them but yes, weapons confirmed, wounded confirmed."

Su-Hyeon: "Why are they fighting there? That's nobody's territory, not connected to the Quirinal."

Here was a puzzle I was proud to be the one to solve, my brain less fixed on moving numbers, able to see the city for itself. "Cables! They're fighting over cables. Gandhi Boulevard, that's where the construction rail line ran, northwest to the harbor, when they first built the city. There will have been communications cables buried along the tracks." I felt greed's hot appetite surge in me: cables like that could connect our office to our agents in the squares, the Forum to the seven bridges, Myrmidon barracks to the Janiculum, the city to the sea. "Pity we thought of it third." I sighed. "But I bet that wasn't the only rail line, I bet there was a southern line toward Sassari, too. We should send Matsuoka's team south toward . . ." I tried to search up an early map, but with no signal, my tracker had no access to that vast archive of human everything which had never before been out of reach. "We should find a map, get Matsuoka working on it. Should I call them?"

Toshi: "We can't call anyone, that's the point."

I punched the sofa, laughing at myself.

Su-Hyeon: "That makes nineteen, I'll send a runner now." Su-Hyeon made for the door with their rough, handwritten list.

I punched the sofa again. "Waste of time stuck out here, we should be in HQ."

"I'm sorry," Toshi murmured. Through my lenses I saw sudden hurt on their cheeks.

"No, Toshi, I didn't mean it like that."

I squeezed their shoulder, but Toshi's tears fell anyway. "Sorry, I didn't mean to . . . I'm okay, I just . . . I want to help so much, I want to be . . . there, I want . . . the computers, I want . . . to . . . just . . . help."

Toshi was a semi-stranger, but in tears' extremis and the intimacy of my adopted living room, a hug felt right. They sobbed on my shoulder, damp hair tickling my chin, while silently inside I cursed the tracker blackout, our lack of preparation, the half-kilometer between us and the Censor's office, colleagues I could name within the office who would flip out if we revealed this half-set-set Mitsubishi 'machine,' but most of all I cursed the proud and spiteful world which could see this wonderful creature smile, and sob, and work to this exhaustion for the good of all, and still deny that they were human. It wasn't until Su-Hyeon came back with my lukewarm, over-steeped tea that I realized I was crying too, and that the smiling face before my mind was Mycroft's.

"You can still help a ton from here, Toshi," Su-Hyeon said gently. "Even when we're in the office, you can keep working on these images, better here really, without all the microcrisis distractions of HQ. If you get this program finished, you can piece together troop counts for us, how many of each faction are in uniform, whether Masons outnumber Mitsubishi or vice versa, how many horses Natekari has—"

"Forty-four," Toshi supplied at once. "Horses are big and easy." This tearstained smile was proud.

"Perfect!" Su-Hyeon cheered. "But with a whole day to work, you can work out Masons, Mitsubishi, Hiveguard, Red Crystal, even changes over time."

"I don't need a day, I have all that already, though photos taken between six and eight A.M. aren't going to reflect well on the total. What I need is what I could get if I could stand on the roof of the Capitoline with your other agents and see things moving, live."

Su-Hyeon squeezed Toshi's shoulder. "If we have to work around, we'll work around. [Anonymous], will your Hermes come again, do you think?"

I hesitated but felt Huxley's hand give my shoulder one strong squeeze. "I think so, yes," I answered, "but I have no idea when, or what they'll bring, or how they'll make contact. It's different every time. But there's lots still to learn from these morning shots, Toshi, I'm sure you'll have invaluable stuff for us when I come home tonight."

Nod and sniffle. "Yes. I'll work hard on it. I just . . . It's so unfair! I'm not even a Mitsubishi! I'm an officer of Romanova, same as you!" Toshi dug their fingers into their Graylaw sash, the only remnant of their soiled clothes they had refused to surrender to the laundry. "I want be there with you. I should be there."

"I'm sorry."

"What if I find something vital while I'm alone here, something that could save lives? I'll have no way to tell you until night! If I could just sneak in somehow, hide inside HQ, work next to you . . ."

I took a deep breath and turned my head by reflex toward the not-so-empty air where someone with the means enough to sneak and hide stood close. As if there were telepathy within my glance, I felt two solid squeezes on my shoulder, almost strong enough to hurt. One for 'Yes' and two for 'No,' is that it, Huxley? But you're right. I trust your distrust. Griffincloth is rare and full of secrets, systems, Utopia's undoing if the foe should find it. The Delians may bestow such armor on godlike Achilles, on the Prince, but not even loyal Mycroft merited such trust. Nor I. And certainly not Toshi Mitsubishi, good-hearted but still tangled up with Andō, and Tōgenkyō, and revenge. But in that double squeeze of 'No' another answer came, a better answer. "Toshi!" I cried. "You can't hide in HQ, but you can send us signals! That kitchen window"—I pointed—"it looks down over the Forum, and it's visible from the roof of HQ. I have binoculars, and if I come up to the roof every even-numbered hour on the hour, let's say, then you can send me signals by holding something in the window."

Hope joined Toshi's sniffles. "You think you could read a written page from there?"

"Probably not, but you can use Morse code, flash something bright-colored in the window."

"I don't know Morse code, except for S and O."

I checked my tracker's drive, but Morse code is too obscure a trivium for its offline database to bother with. "Neither do I!" I cried. "But we can look it up, and Morse code is a bunch of dots and dashes applied to letters of the alphabet. We can make up our own dots and dashes, it'll work the same. Here, *A* can be one dash, and *E* can be one dot because we use *E* all the time, and I can be two dashes, and *O* can stay three dashes . . ." I sketched a hasty alphabet and digits 0 to 9, wondering abstractly which decisions I would regret as soon as we tried to put it into practice.

Another sniff. "What if someone notices signals in this window?"

"Then our made-up code will make no sense to them! But honestly, I doubt anyone will notice, and it's just for today, we'll invent something better tomorrow, and besides, this will only be visible from the Forum, so anyone who sees it will report it to Su-Hyeon anyway, and we can explain it away, say it's Myrmidons for me or something."

There was the smile I had been waiting for. "Yes. Yes, for just a day, it would work." Toshi set to copying my code sheet. "Then all I need is something big and bright."

Su-Hyeon looked around the room. "Bright red, or yellow, would be most visible. What?"

Embarrassment must have showed in my face. I went to the bedroom, to the box I'd found under the bed, and brought back Bryar's flaming red silk corset. Rarely have I shared a better healing laugh.

"Let's practice!" I cried. "Toshi, if you sit in that brown chair, and flash the signals in front of you, I'll go up and crouch on the upper landing of the back stairwell and I can see you with my periscope. That's good practice for giving signals and getting them."

Twin stares fixed on me. "Why do you have a periscope?"

"To see around corners." I pulled it out.

That answer didn't satisfy. "Why do you know you can see that chair from crouching on the back stairwell landing?"

"Periscopes are fun! Come on!" I shoved old laundry off the chair seat. "Toshi, see if you can tell me your troop count totals!"

In my excitement, I charged off to the stairwell while they were still chuckling over my geekery. Feigned excitement, and feigned geekery, but this was not the time to speak of boot camp and Patroclus Aimer's training regimen. I settled on my belly on the landing, and relief tingled across my scalp as I felt another figure settle down beside me.

"I want you to reveal yourself," I whispered, "just to Toshi and Su-Hyeon."

"No." Huxley's whisper, breath against my ear.

"We have to let Toshi stay here." I unfolded the periscope and searched for the brown of the chair. "One secret roommate is bad enough, but two of you, with one hiding from the other, would be intolerable, not to mention the risk of Toshi tripping over the invisible lion."

"We'll stay outside."

"With a broken arm?"

"What must, must."

"It's more than just Toshi's presence. We can do amazing work together, the four of us. You saw what Su-Hyeon and Toshi did with your images in five minutes, imagine what they can do with you actively working with them, gathering data. And they'll share with Utopia too, Toshi's programs, Su-Hyeon's Censor data, everything."

"No."

I winced. "Do you not trust Toshi?" I asked. "I'd understand that."

The red began to flash now, clear in my periscope, and I checked it against my chart: short-long-short (T), long-short (R), long-long-long (O), piecing together the precious T, R, O, O, P, C, O, U, N, T. "It's working!" I shouted down the echoing stairwell.

Huxley's whisper: "Trust is not the issue."

I frowned. "I don't know Toshi well, but Su-Hyeon trusts them, and I know Su-Hyeon, better than anyone on this continent, almost like a bash'mate—"

"The Censor is not part of my mission. Neither is the Triumvirate. Your work with them is valuable, for the city, for Earth long-term; once communications heal, a strong Alliance government may do much good. But that is not my mission."

"Guarding me?" I guessed.

"We cannot know yet which horde will be the first to crash over the tiny forces of your Forum like tide over a rock pool, but one will come someday, soon, from within Romanova, or by sea, or sky. When it comes, you will stand in your office, amid your well-armed officers, some of whom will want to welcome the attackers and hand you over, others to spirit you away, yet others to aid you, barter you, bind you, silence you forever. Only I will be thinking foremost of the Alien. If nobody knows that I exist, nobody can lay plans to stop me."

I swallowed, letting myself wait as the first counts came: MA4K, i.e., Masons 4,000, that was clear enough. MB3K, so 3,000 Mitsubishi. Then a pause which made me bold. "What is your real mission, Huxley?"

"To guard you, and reconnect you to the Alien."

"Your long-term mission. You were watching Mycroft first?"

(E4K, a strong showing for Europe.)

Grimly: "At first it was to punish Mycroft, to oversee the work."

I nodded. "Justice for Apollo. I can understand that." From both ends, I can.

"But Mycroft led me to a different constellation when they became translator for Micromegas."

I nodded. "Then your current mission?"

"Is the Alien."

(RC3K, Red Crystal? Why did I make *K* so interminable? Long-long-short-long-long. 'We'll hardly ever use *K!*' I remember thinking. Sigh.)

"Are you one of Madame's hostages?" I asked. "Like Aldrin and Voltaire?"

"Sometimes."

I took a deep breath. "And if a boat showed up tomorrow offering to take me to Alexandria?"

"I'd spirit you to it, whatever the Triumvirate might need."

(G212. Oh fragile Gordian, how long will you keep the Caelian with just two hundred?)

"Listen, Huxley, you're asking a lot of me. You're asking me to throw my lot in with you, trust you, above Su-Hyeon, above the Triumvirate I helped create, above Romanova and the call of duty to help the Alliance, above Toshi—who I don't know intimately but I certainly know them better than I know you—above the local Myrmidons, what they might need, above Bryar, who can have me locked up forever, above what I owe Vivien, my duties as Anonymous—"

"For Micromegas."

(BL434. Brave Blacklaw Tribune Natekari, holding the Aventine and a bridge with only that.)

I paused—Vivien taught me quick thinking is not always the best thinking. "If you want me to choose you over all that, I need to know . . ."

"What?" Huxley invited.

I hesitated.

"What do you need to know?"

(MY534. We Myrmidons were more numerous than that, of course, but it was good to know how many Toshi could spot.)

Huxley again: "What do you need to know?"

"The Prince," I braved at last, "do you . . . believe?" I waited three breaths, four. "There're only two of us right now, we don't have to have a sensayer."

(U345. So few? But that must be only visible Delians, not their true strength.)

"Why do you need to know that?" Huxley asked.

It was a fair demand. "I need to know why you're putting the Prince far above everything else, above the good of the Alliance, Romanova, saving lives. Above your own life. I know why the Prince is more important to *me* than all the lives Su-Hyeon and I could ever save, but, if you want me to choose you over my best—" An unexpected sob. "—my best surviving friend, I need to know what *you* think we're doing all this for. Do you *believe*?"

(HG6K. A curse caught in my throat. So many Hiveguard?)

The landing creaked beneath us, strained by some shifting weight—the lion, perhaps? Sensing Huxley's tension as I pinned them in the bear trap of this hardest question?

(RMI22. Remakers. I waited for another zero. Nothing. A mistake? I checked my code sheet, waited. Toshi began the whole string from the beginning, a good precaution, to let me double-check what had come through.)

Huxley leaned close enough for their breath to tickle my ear. Suddenly I felt fear's ice upon me, fear of the taboo, fear of finding no like-minded spirit here, or fear of finding one, and all the changes that must bring. Huxley could be no more afraid to answer this question than I was to hear.

Softly: "I believe we had no reason to assume First Contact would come to us in a ship of steel across the darkness that we happen to have senses tuned to see. Why not a ship of flesh? Why not across a darkness as unknown to us as starlight to the creatures of the deep sea? I believe a Being boundaryless and unfamiliar with time, accustomed to an existence where everything within Its perception is directed by Its thoughts, would find it very hard to understand our physics and experience, hard to explain Itself to us. And I believe that, if the first humans to teach this Being language were Madame's, It might well learn from them the word 'God' and cry out, as we know this Child cried out, 'That is What I Am!'"

I knew this anecdote, the moment that forever changed that house in Paris. The little Prince Jehovah Mason, not yet four years old, had demanded that a tutor define every word in some old Latin hymn, and hearing 'Deus' defined as an immortal, limitless being that wills into existence worlds and smaller sentiences, the struggling Stranger cried out in Their shaking, toddler voice, « Why, That is What I Am! » Certainly at Madame's one would meet the word 'God' long before the word 'alien.'

"Do you believe because of science?" I asked. "These tests you all keep running on the Prince's brain? Is there proof? Or do you just . . . believe?"

"I'm no neurographer. Our adepts say the brain that Micromegas uses as Its interface did not grow as known brains grow, is not structured as known brains are structured, and that there are jumps in the neural signals, easiest to track when Mike does complex math, which defy our current understandings of neural pathways, electricity, computation, possibly even time. But I'm a novice in such spheres. Science made me open to this possibility, but what I believe now I believe because I have observed this Being for myself and find it Alien."

"And . . . Jehovah's Peer?" I pressed; in such a moment, it feels right speaking the Prince's most forbidden name. "Do you . . . what do you think . . ."

Huxley hesitated less this time. "If our First Contact says there is another being like Itself, which has a macrocosmic relationship to us, as we have to the bacteria that grow and war inside our bodies, that hypothesis is worth testing, with what science we have and what new science we gain every hour that we study the Alien, and study the objects affected by what It claims are actions of another of its Species."

"Bridger's relics," I supplied. "So, you believe in First Contact."

"And you believe in Gods."

I couldn't pretend the convulsion of my chest was just a hiccup. That answer—it was not quite my answer, but close, preciously close, and almost better, so it made my own feel slightly less ridiculous. And, yeah, here and hereafter I'll be having Huxley give the Prince Their capitals in dialogue (They/Them It/Its, etc.), which Mycroft only used for speakers who really do believe this Visitor is . . . not necessarily a God, but Something, on a scale beyond our own.

Huxley: "Have I answered enough for you to trust me?"

Toshi's repeated message reached the end now: . . . U345. HG6K. RM122. No mistake, then. Just 122 Remakers in the whole of Romanova? No. It was absurd. There was a whole parade of us, together, the Myrmidons, the Delians, MASON's loyal Blacksleeves, marching, and Europe too should . . . but . . . A chill set in as my memory hinted and lenses confirmed the truth. All those shoulders, black-dyed, mottled, Griffincloth: not one sported the Vs. It wasn't right! These were the Prince's forces, why . . . ? But then I realized. You won't let them wear it, will You? My Stranger Prince? You rejected Utopia's surrender, forbade Huxley and the Delians to wear Your Vs and trust themselves to You, since You don't trust Yourself with them, not knowing what Your New Order may be, or what their place in it. The Blacksleeve Masons too are fighting MASON's war, retribution for the *Sanctum Sanctorum*, but You won't let MASON have them fight for You, their *Porphyrogene*, not while You are still only considering the Oath. Europe has made You Heir to a constitutional monarchy, not the absolute one You require. Even Achilles, who longs to make the better world You Will, You keep the hero at a wary distance, saying You cannot know with perfect certainty that You will not betray them. 99.99 percent is good enough for anyone except mathematicians, philosophers, and You. You overkindly, wonderful, infuriating . . . You're too much. You made a side, and have a million friends ready to join and fight for You, if only You would let us.

The flame silk flashed again: L, O, O, K, A, T, C, A, M, P, U, S.

Campus? I pulled up the cityscape, wincing at the many bull's-eyes. The low plain of the Campus had been largely stable, north of us, the large head of the Yin-Yang's Yin, where Romanova's many colleges and student halls cluster around picturesque quads and sculpture gardens. No faction had moved to take the Campus, no one had the heart to, these fragile, frightened youths watching the Hives collapse around them even as they were about to choose. And there by the Senseminary fountain stood a little crowd of them with Vs upon their shoulders. There, four others leaving the Economics Center, with something heavy wobbling along on a toy wagon, again wearing the Vs. I spotted sixteen in a nearby doorway, Vs on their shoulders and on a painted bedsheet banner as they talked with Campus Security, who hold Chanakya Bridge. Students. Remakers. There were our brave 122. The Hives had failed them, but, resilient, they believed in J.E.D.D. Mason's Unknown New World. Students. I laughed, and teared up, both. These were the Prince's peers, not cold, uncaring Providence, but human youths, the Prince's peers in years, Their peers in hope, in optimism, and surpassing the Prince by far in precious trust. Warmth surged in me. You may not trust Yourself, my Prince, Jehovah Mason, but they trust You. And I trust You. And You cannot command us not to trust You.

I groped for Huxley's hand and found it. "Wear the Vs with me."

"What?"

"Now." I stripped off my jacket and pulled out a paint pen. "I invented the symbol, I deserve to wear it, see it, feel it every day. And so do you."

"Me? Why? Because I believe in Aliens?"

I drew my first V, bold and permanent upon the cloth, and felt triumph burn through me like sun. "I know Utopia held a vote whether to peacebond the harbingers at the price of getting sucked into the war, or whether to let us blow ourselves up while you retreated to the Moon and Mars to guard the future. Mycroft said the majority of Utopians voted to save the Earth, but not you, you voted to let the Earth burn. You thought there was something more important than one planet."

Softly. "Yes."

"Is First Contact more important than Mars?" I pressed.

"What?"

"Which is more precious to you, if you had to choose? Mars or First Contact?"

Huxley gulped a breath. "First Contact."

"Then you surrender to the Prince, the way They want, you personally. You know They'd never make you give up Mars, not Them, the Kindest Being that ever walked the Earth, but even if for some reason They did, you'd still choose Them. You think They're more important than Mars. You think They're the Most Important Thing humanity has right now. Just like I do. And that's the kind of conviction They'd accept." I took a deep breath. "Wear the Vs with me. Wear them with me, and you'll be the partner of my labors, not Su-Hyeon, not the Triumvirate, you, and you and I will trust each other to the war's end."

Silence for a moment, then the coat of storm appeared beside me, like a pool of Zeus's unforgetting wrath. But the keen sun broke across the darkness of the Griffincloth, as on Huxley's shoulder I saw a crest appear, the stylized Delian sun encircling the three circles of Utopia's flag, blue, white, and red for the Earth, Moon, and Mars, with their three little launching rockets dark against the brightness of the Sun. But then that crest changed as the Vs appeared within it, circling the Earth, stark and perfect.

"Did it all come through?" Toshi shouted up the stairs.

"Yep, I got the whole message, clean and clear!" I shouted back. "What's happening at the Campus is fascinating! And if that parade continues snaking as it's snaking now, I think it'll reach Campus around noon!" I rose. "I'd like to go check it out! The Myrmidons trust me! They'll tell me what's going on!"

Huxley rose too, vanishing again, and I leaned close to the telltale sliver of open hood to whisper. "I'm going to that parade. Su-Hyeon will agree. I'm going to tell the Myrmidons there, the Masons too, that it's not up to Jehovah MASON to decide whether they're allowed to wear the Vs. It's up to them."

The partner of my labors offered me a grim and ready smile, then vanished as we took the first step down the stairs, together. "I'll tell Utopia."

Chapter EIGHT

The Battle for the Almagest

Written October 17–19, 2454
Events of September 29 to October 13
Romanova and the Maldives

HALFWAY AROUND THE GLOBE, the united fleets of Asia's mighty peoples braved dragon hordes and monsters of the deep to make assault upon the tower which rises from the sea to pierce the icy sky. The Almagest—the Maldive Ridge Space Elevator, named for Alexandrian Ptolemy's great textbook—Utopia's last passage to the stars. There must be images somewhere, winged wonders flitting like butterflies through a garden of blooming fire as the intercepted missiles burst in garland chains around the priceless white umbilical. But images move slowest in our silenced world. Nobody saw the combat, nobody except the Mitsubishi and Utopia, and some small watchers on the Maldives archipelago, as scared and stranded on their little islands as we are on ours a continent away. I cannot describe the battle. What I can describe is our battle to learn about the battle, our proud resistance which daily chips away at Tyrant Silence. It was Cicero who kept me going. I seem to feel them with me, every time I cycle past the Rostra and the Senate House, and Voltaire too, our Zeroeth Anonymous, warm ghosts who offer smiles in my mind's eye, and kind squeezes to my mind's shoulder, and tell me we have bested harder foes.

On September 29—three days after Operation Baskerville—some Myrmidons brought me an eleven-year-old. "Are you the Deputy Censor?" the child asked.

In that moment I realized, "Yes, I am."

"I'm Kenzie Walkiewicz, and I have a friend named Minlu who lives on the mainland in Ostia, and we talk across the water using a laser."

The Myrmidons beamed as they saw my bafflement break into joy. "A laser!" I cried. "How? How fast a data stream?"

That special glow awoke in Kenzie, which smart kids get when grown-ups take them seriously. "I usually get a thousand-character packet through about every twenty minutes," they answered. "Depends a lot on wind. Minlu and I put mirrors on a line of buoys that bounce the beam along over the water, aaaaaalllll the whole two hundred and forty kilometers to the mainland." Kenzie paused to let us be impressed. "We put the mirrors on little arms that move around to keep them steady when the buoys bob, but they still bob a bit, lots when there's lots of wind, so the signal gets interrupted and it takes a bunch of repetitions to get it a full packet through. When it's normal weather usually twenty minutes is enough."

"That's an impressive system!" Huxley was impressed too and gave me that light tap on the shoulder blade which I have learned to interpret as delight.

Young Kenzie tried to shrug like it was nothing, but their grin broke through. "We won the historical category at the science fair. Anyway, I thought the Triumvirate could use it to talk to the mainland. I told the Forum guards, but they didn't listen to me. But the Myrmidons did."

I smiled at the grinning troop, and at the fact that our rightful name was finally spreading. "Myrmidons know what's what."

Young Kenzie nodded but had a frown for my comrades, especially, I noted, for their black sleeves and newly painted Vs. "I said I wouldn't just give my system to the Masons, or just to Remakers," the child said firmly. "I want it to help everyone."

Words snagged for a moment, as I gazed at Kenzie's minor's sash and child's wrap, which make all children feel neutral. "Understood. If you let the Triumvirate use it, we'll definitely put the good of the world, and of everybody here on Sardinia, before the good of any Hive, or faction. You have my word."

Children are capable of very piercing looks. "You're a Remaker too?"

I frowned at my Vs—I suppose we all freeze the first time we're asked aloud. I crouched to face the child. "That's my personal conviction, but my current assignment isn't for the Remaker side. I'm under orders to work with the Triumvirate neutrally for the good of all. I'm not going to say I'd fight to the death to keep your laser system out of Remaker hands if an army marched in to seize it, but I wouldn't fight to the death against the Hiveguard either, I have other duties." I offered a handshake. "Good enough?"

Young Kenzie Walkiewicz—who within a few hours was Special Communications Officer and Interim Minor Senator Kenzie Walkiewicz—accepted my hand. "Good enough."

That first day was tedium and magic: the introductions, meetings, hours of bikes and back trails out to Kenzie's bash'house on the coast, and then the flicker, so insubstantial, not even a thread of light across the cloud-gray sea to give our hopes something to hang on. We repeated the quick sequence of flashes fifty times, a hundred, the crashing waves and passing minutes battering our faith that the endless rolling surface would ever condescend to grant our wish. I sometimes thought I could see the first buoy on the horizon, a mote of proof that humans had, in some lost age, wrestled the seas. A floating tombstone. And then the dot appeared on our receiving screen, so tiny and alive, like glow returning to the last coal when the fire seemed dead. More tedium and magic as blips unraveled into code, and code into:

hello.romanova.message.received.happy.to.help.any.way.i.can.the.alliance.officer .yangtze.seward.who.you.mentioned.lives.just.down.the.street.sending.parents.to .get.them.now.

One of my Blacksleeves cried. It was enough. By midnight we were talking to our officer in Ostia, and had hands at work to set up mirrors to bounce the beam the extra 24 km from the coast in to the Forum. Young Minlu Moretti (now also an Interim Minor Senator) was already in contact with another laser hobbyist in Ladispoli up the Italian coast, who had plans to extend up to Santa Marinella—one short thread, but all webs start with one.

No one even suggested keeping it secret. Carmen Guildbreaker created a corps of praecones, ancient Roman-style newsreaders, to announce everything we could in major squares. Most of our news is local—food bank locations, missing persons calls, warnings of which streets have violence—but when we read out those first updates from the mainland—Naples harbor burning, Naples streaming Remaker flags, and then when Minlu got through to Ladispoli and they somehow had report of a huge European rally in Milan—the real news was that the Triumvirate had called out, and the world had answered. It felt so powerful.

We know there's a danger of some aggressive group trying to take the system, but it would be hard to hide it from the strongest factions, and by making it so public, if anybody tries to take it over, thousands will hate their guts for it and (hopefully) come to our aid. And the strongest groups were already improvising options of their own. Myrmidons confirmed that is indeed a communications tower the Masons are building on the Esquiline, planning to aim a microwave beam toward the south coast, where they're building relays to pass it on across the sea toward precious Africa. Narrow-beam communications seem to be hard for whoever's doing the jamming to detect. The Mitsubishi were the victors in chiseling out the ancient cables from the railways north and south, but there were a few other wired-age relics to be mined, even a few for us. We can talk directly to our six main city news posts now, and more places thanks to Red Crystal. Conscience and the Conclave's persuasive sensayers made a lot of people offer what cables they found to hospitals and major food banks, which are now all linked together, and they forward messages for us.

As for the mainland side, communications spread, not like wildfire but like the eager vines that grow back afterward. The best part wasn't how fast it grew but that whenever we connected to a new spot—one town over—we found someone there who had already linked to two or three others. Radio's still impossible, anything standard, even long-distance Moonbounce gets disrupted (looking into that), but train hikers knew where chunks of ancient railroad track were buried, running out from Rome like wheel spokes, and, not only were there cables buried along them, but we can send coded taps vibrating along the rails themselves for kilometers. That web of ancient rails runs all over Europe, broken in a thousand places, but volunteers pass the messages across the gaps however they can: cables, laser beams, repurposed plumbing pipes, a microwave system concocted at Rome's Sapienza University to link the port at Ostia to Rome, even (briefly) actual semaphore to cross one valley in the Apennines before a crossbow expert shot a cable over. A body healing is what it feels like, the slow regrowth of nerves after a trauma, so that first "Hello" from Zurich thrilled us like the longed-for tremor of the finger which proves someday the hand will move again; we've pierced the Alps! The bobbing of Kenzie's buoys on the choppy water is still our bottleneck, but campus experts got us up to an average of 250 characters a minute, while some nearby links can't yet beat 150/min. Or rather half that, since many of the systems in place have to stop transmitting to receive and vice versa. In chunks of a thousand characters we heard of battles back and forth in Hive-mixed Naples, of Masons laboring to carve a road from Turin west across the mountains into France, and of European coastal stations trying to repeat the experiment that had made a car land, triggering explosion after explosion until the inevitable catastrophe when one car spun, unleashing the full force of the antimatter reactor sideways, boiling the sea near Bari, and boiling part of Bari, too. So, the car supply remains, endless enough to bring sure death to any fledgling aircraft. A ground war, then, for the time being, ground and sea.

Locally, the first two weeks of our microcosmic war have been semi-peaceful. Bridges and major borders see bloodshed from time to time (lessened by the Cousins' Tiring Guns), but no entrenched territory has been attacked. Jin Im-Jin thinks no one wants to lay down lives to try to conquer Romanova before they get back in touch with their global leadership, to learn the bigger plan. The factions have their territories, but all still let Alliance agents pass in peace, and Conclave envoys, too. Julia Doria-Pamphili and energetic Carlyle Foster-Kraye have the sensayers visiting the hottest border streets in shifts, and their stern frowns of moral disapproval can snuff hot tempers faster than a downpour. Outskirts and ports have seen more strife. The Masons—as prophesied—have jeeps everywhere, confirmed moving through Italy's countryside, France's, and here in Sardinia, too, a dozen of them lumbering their awkward, cowlike way across the inland hills. They're avoiding towns, the local ones running transport for the microwave beam project, and Huxley is hopeful they may get through to our Alien.

Boats are the real apples of discord. The tsunami left us very few boats, and those which remained were subjects of the fiercest fighting we've seen here on Sardinia. A lot of boats simply left. Mitsubishi took most of the rest by force, and they have the main harbor now (Ostianova), and most other harbors, too, though Masons have fought tooth and nail to keep Cagliari (the southern-facing harbor), even putting the old medieval forts to work (stone is still stone). Ships came to us from Nice and Barcelona to ask if Romanova needed help, but Mitsubishi seized both (I guess that makes them pirates?), but did deposit the bewildered crews here with their greetings from our friendly European neighbors whom we have no way to reach. The name of the Alliance earns the Triumvirate some favors from the Mitsubishi. Twice we convinced them to let one of our officers ride with them from Ostianova to Ostia proper with tech and letters for the mainland, but somehow the trips weren't as useful as we'd imagined. There are a few lone-wolf boats, locals and Seaborn who have learned to keep a wary distance from the Mitsubishi pack, or to move in darkness, to avoid being seized. Two volunteered their aid when Minlu and Kenzie helped us make more buoys with reflector arms, but when the boats set out to distribute them, they disappeared, one taken by Mitsubishi, the other we still don't know. That killed my fantasy of striking out toward Alexandria by sea. The most useful thing independent boats have done so far is strike anchor temporarily in spots where they can pass our messages along with lasers or flashing lights. That got us temporary communications with Palermo, Nice, and briefly Tunis, and through Tunis our first eighth-hand rumor from Alexandria. A thousand ships were launching—hard to believe, but that's what the laser told us, *1KSHIPS*—streaming from shipyards around the Nile Delta, not out into the Mediterranean but down through Suez and the Red Sea toward the Indian Ocean. We didn't yet guess why.

The first warning of Mitsubishi action was Mediterranean. *WARSHIPS*, blinked the little laser light, sighted both off the Italian coast and around Greece, swarms peppering the horizon like schooling mountains. Detail crawled after rumor. The fleet originated from the Mitsubishi-dominated port of Çanakkale, on the Turkish side of the Hellespont. Tensions were high on the banks of that narrow strait which stretches from the Aegean toward the Black Sea (can we really be fighting over the Hellespont again?), with Mitsubishi-owned Çanakkale on the Turkish side, and European Gallipoli on the Greek, both with large Masonic minorities, and less than a day from the ten million Masons of Istanbul. As soon as I glanced at a map, I could hear gunfire in my mind. The Empire's heart was Alexandria and Cairo, but draw a line a thousand kilometers due north and there was its second heart, the Black Sea, with the great Masonic capitals around it: Ankara, Constanța, and, the living gate to all, Istanbul. But if the narrow Bosporus at siege-ready Istanbul is the inner door of the airlock, the Hellespont at precarious Gallipoli/Çanakkale is the outer door, and MASON's enemies need only close one to slice the empire in half. When our communications web grew down as far as the heel of Italy's boot, we heard through Corfu that the Mitsubishi fleet from Çanakkale had seized Chania on Crete by force, a second port from which to dominate all seas east of Italy. Caesar must retake the waters between Greece and Egypt or else be trapped on the Nile with the Sahara at their back. Yet confirmation followed confirmation: MASON's thousand ships were streaming south through Suez into the Red Sea, yielding the Mediterranean entirely to the Mitsubishi. Why? My main guess was that MASON had a fleet of jeeps as well as ships, and jeeps could link Cairo to Istanbul by land, if the Levantine Reservation grants passage—Caesars have long been Reservations' friends.

It took Myrmidons and microwaves to bring the real answer: the war we were watching was all just microcosm, toy fleets. The real theater lay south and east. The Mitsubishi force in the Pacific that had threatened Sydney two weeks earlier had tripled since, and local Mitsubishi boasted of the South China Sea glowing to match the cities on its shores. MASON raced them, his ships from Alexandria pouring through the Red Sea into the Indian Ocean to meet the westbound Asian force. We didn't learn the destination until the battle was over, but we understood then why even Achilles would abandon the Mediterranean for this.

Ten long days' sailing from the sight of continents, the Almagest sits anchored at the Equator, amid a peppering of tiny coral islands. The three elder elevators are safe from violence, for Utopia gave them to the friendly Cousins as harbinger wergild, to guarantee they will survive even if Utopia falls. The one they keep is their greatest, our greatest I should say, the greatest engineering feat to date of humankind, for the other three top off with counterweights at 50,000 km, but the Almagest stretches on, on, no topdeck, just the sheer weight of its cable stretching out 140,000 kilometers, more than one-third of the distance to the Moon, so its tip reaches accelerations that propel our hopes and vessels on toward asteroids, toward outer planets, toward the dark beyond that is as close to an infinity as this small soul can hope to comprehend. If they keep the Almagest, they keep it for their farthest projects, and for Mars, but for the war too, since no one can doubt that Delians with full access to space will fill the starry night with eyes and, likely, weapons. The Almagest is the easiest target for Utopia's enemies. Not easy in battlefield terms, this mobile chunk of floating city hiding in the ship-destroying coral shallows of the Maldive Ridge and ringed with monsters. It was the easiest target for the Mitsubishi to agree on. Ojiro Sniper is as much Japan's beloved child as 'Tai-kun,' and here in Romanova we see the bull's-eye in Mitsubishi colors as often as the Vs. The Mitsubishi must choose between them someday, but short-term, with the Harbinger Strike and Operation Baskerville, even Greenpeace is willing to rise in rage against Utopia. Abominable Dominic urged the attack, I'm sure, the Interim Chief Director persuading even the Remaker-leaning Mitsubishi that grounding Utopia would serve the cause. The Prince had demanded Utopia's unconditional surrender; loyal Dominic will deliver it, and if to do so they must maim and scar this little Hive their *Maître* loves so much, all the better.

We heard it all in shards. Growing made the network slower, unfortunately. This web is really a hundred separate conversations, each with local needs. The junctions are the worst, with four or five streams coming in, asking to be passed on—that raises a barrier slower than sound, or semaphore, or bobbing buoys: human judgment. On October 12 we received word that a Mitsubishi fleet out of Dubai had caught and trounced a small Masonic force returning to the Arabian Sea. Returning from where? From what? Next we heard that a sea battle near the Hellespont was "nothing to the Maldives." Huxley assured me the Almagest was unscathed, and we risked sending a couple precious reflector boats south toward Africa, which got confirmation from Tunis that MASON's fleet had indeed set sail for the Almagest, anticipating a Mitsubishi attack. But Mitsubishi got our boats before they could relay more, and then, on the 13th, a bloody anti-Hiveguard purge erupted in the Rhine-Ruhr region, with backlash straying as far as Frankfurt. For a day, our little laser light would talk of nothing beyond Europe: towns burned, casualty reports, name on name on name. When that slowed, we finally got confirmation that a battle had been fought at the Maldive Ridge back on October 3, but the rest was shards and contradictions: triumphant Mitsubishi shattering MASON's forces, crushed Mitsubishi fleeing back to India, MASON's victory, MASON's loss, Utopia's losses, Utopia's atrocities. It took four more days until I felt, as chronicler, that I knew enough to call the battle: I say both sides lost and both sides won.

Utopia won in that it holds its topless tower still. And the tower functions. Our astronomers have spotted two new satellites in low Earth orbit, and three of the ones that started moving off course at Operation Baskerville are righting themselves; I don't think that's the Cousins. But Utopia loses too in the stories that are bleeding through Minlu and Kenzie's laser now, hour on hour. We hear of atrocities upon the seas, great carcasses of ships mauled and crushed by coils thicker than Nature ever reared, crews burned alive by laughing dragons, dragged to their watery deaths by jaws and tentacles. Utopia made the old mapmakers' nightmares real. We hear of beams of light and death, too, crackling, blinding, inexorable spotlight sweeps boiling the wave crests and making bodies burst and bubble. Robots are accused, inhuman, steel-faced killers, slicing through hulls and bodies as calmly as they might cut paper, or plant rice in a farmer's paddy. It's got to be hyperbole and lies, but 'Ráðsviðr mode' is the scariest phrase that reached us, the claim that every U-beast, from a playful popanda to the lion at my back, has a copy of dread Ráðsviðr's software dormant in its hard drive, waiting for a voice command to switch on A.I. murder. When that accusation came in was the first time I've seen Su-Hyeon tempted to be a censor in the sense that isn't census, but we couldn't silence this; if we were hearing it, then others would too, in time. We framed it all carefully when we announced it, called it rumor, said Utopia fiercely denied it ("I bet Utopia denies this." One tap on my shoulder. "Yup."), but they say people in the streets are killing pigeons now, and cats, and smashing trashbots, as if everything that moves and isn't human is Utopian.

The Mitsubishi victory is unity. They have shared wounds to lick now, shared humiliations to pay back, a ruthless, inhumane shared enemy. The battlefield has made them comrades, and, as these wounds heal, the old fissures of faction are scarring closed. Here in Romanova, the number of flags atop the Mitsubishi hills has swelled by 44 percent, and fresh volunteers have exhausted the local supply of Mitsubishi uniforms, resorting to stopgap home-printed jackets. And they have a new shared goal. Masons fought alongside Utopia for the Almagest, the sprint-exhausted vanguard of Mason's fleet just in time to be complicit with the monstrous massacre. We expected strife on the Viminal-Esquiline border, but it was Minlu's little laser that brought the strangest change, a pledge, proclaimed—it says—by the Mitsubishi Directorate itself. The first time I heard it, I was sure we'd decompressed it wrong. The Mitsubishi will rescue the Prince—*their* Xiao Hei Wang, they say—from Alexandria, from MASON's prison, and Utopia's clutches. Rescue? It's nonsense, but I guess in wartime the difference between sanctuary and imprisonment is propaganda's call. Most of our praecones are Masons, since Carmen Guildbreaker recruited them, and several refused to even read the message out. Sensayers from the Conclave stepped in, mustered by quick-thinking Carlyle Foster-Kraye, and I myself read it out in Semaphore Square, with my Deputy Censor's jacket and Servicer trousers to reassure the stone-faced Masons that I found the claim as ludicrous as they did. At least it simplifies one front. MASON and the Mitsubishi are at war. Where banners of white, leaf-green, and scarlet fly, there Delians and Blacksleeves know their enemies, even if the banners fly the Vs.

Except, on the way home, I cycled past the remnants of a street brawl, outside a battered sandwich-place-turned-ration-pickup, and there was a smiling Mitsubishi bandaging a Mason, both wearing the Vs. I actually started to say, "Hey, didn't you hear, you're enemies . . ." but I froze. I couldn't. I felt like a hateful messenger in some Shakespeare history, come to tell the earnest peasants that the sides had switched again, and friends and ba'sibs must now kill one another, because some distant noble sneezed too near the king. Six news posts on street corners, wires to the hospitals, our announcement had probably reached ten thousand people out of Romanova's million. On those corners MASON and Mitsubishi were enemies, but not on this corner yet. What about on the mainland, in Ostia? Milan? It took us days to learn the outcome at the Almagest, how long will it take Stockholm? Or Cape Town? The Americas must be fighting a wholly different war. I imagined an end, one Hive triumphing in both hemispheres, the Mitsubishi say, and two great cheering fleets rendezvous in the Atlantic, but see on their approach that one flies white and scarlet Vs, the other bull's-eyes, so they turn on each other until the ocean burns. We've spoiled it. Our ancestors sacrificed so much to leave us a beautiful, united world, and we've sliced it into ten thousand pieces that may never heal. How can we heal, become one world again, one culture, when we're fighting ten thousand different wars? We're making barriers, borders, hate, as surely and as pointlessly as we're making the poor whales deaf.

It was hard, cycling back through the Forum after that. What was I doing? Standing on street corners, passing on news I hated to people who didn't want it. Doing the job of a hundred meters of wire. And when I got back to the receiving room, it was all casualties again, someone determined to pass on the names of all the slain and where they'd fallen up in the Rhine-Ruhr:

Kai.Dale.Fischer.Humanist.Dusseldorf.
Nasha.Iseul.Maier.Mitsubishi.Cologne.
Alexis.Jasbinder.Lee.Mason.Cologne.
Hairong.Eike.Rhazes-Fuchs.Brillist.Mönchengladbach.
Yili.Jay.Rhazes-Fuchs.Graylaw.Mönchengladbach.

Name on name on name, enough to make the nice architects who run our link at Como go offline to cry.

I went outside to sit in the dark and hate. But there on the stones beside me were my patient ghosts, Voltaire and Cicero. Look where you are, they seemed to say. Rome burned before, but we rebuilt it. We burned it again, because we're bad at this, but we rebuilt it again. Paris, we've burned and rebuilt Paris. We made the whales deaf once before, but patient Greenpeace divers, with recordings and assistive tech, helped them to sing again. Compared to that, what's stringing a tin can telephone through to Stockholm? You can already feel the fibers of the world regenerating, town by town. Ten thousand today, fifteen tomorrow. And then a clerk found me to say we had fresh news: the violence in the Rhine-Ruhr had started because, back on the 5th, someone had attacked the jail near Duisburg which had held Ockham Saneer. The 5th—six days earlier. Six days.

I had them set our laser to outgoing.

<We have to organize this network. It feels like a web, but until we organize it, it's just point-to-point chaos, dead ends, no way to make sure important news gets everywhere, or keep traffic from blocking lines, or give emergency-help calls priority. Info is getting lost, repeated, skipping whole regions, slowing down for days. Let us make a plan to direct the traffic. We have communications experts here in Romanova, we can plan it out, maximize diffusion and efficiency, help hubs know what to pass in which direction, how to time when one-way connections switch direction. Send us all your details: precise speeds, connections, limitations. We'll make a plan and share it out to all.>

I sent that off at bedtime.

When I woke up, the receiving room was buzzing like the cheery fuss before a party, cryptographers bustling, Campus experts drawing diagrams, young Minor Senator Kenzie beaming, and there was a map, the whole network laid out on a wall screen, a spider-sketch of Italy, with threads out into Europe and beyond. The world had granted my wish. And, mixed among the loving reports of links and speeds, came more suggestions:

<Let's standardize our abbreviations, make a universal list.>

<Let's reserve fixed hours for casualty reports so they don't fill the day.>

<Let's standardize error correction codes, and set aside 15 percent of our bandwidth for network housekeeping.>

<Let's make codes to start each packet, make it easy to tell what's priority: EM emergency-help call, CA Casualty report, BB battle in progress, BO battle now over, PA political announcement.>

<Three-letter codes may be better, so we don't run out.>

I took a deep breath and threw my cap into the ring:

<Let's make a regular digest. As much info as possible sent to one spot, and that spot broadcasts a digest which everyone passes on. It could be 2x a day, 1 hour each time. It would make sure the most important news gets everywhere, let people, especially soldiers and leaders, react to big events together, maintain us as a unified culture. Global access to shared world news is a defining part of our modern age, tying us together into one people, not many splintered peoples. If we keep that, we keep our shared humanity, shared experience. Hives, strats, and sides could mourn and cheer together, children growing up apart could still grow up together, separated bash'es could know that their bash'mates feel what

they feel, even on the far side of the world. War has taken away our skies, our seas, our images, our voices, but we don't have to let it take our truest connection, the knowledge that what I hear, you hear, loved ones hear, the world hears, and the world changes together. Let us run it from here.>

Kenzie gave me a funny look when I passed those 1000 characters in to the compression team. "This could be a lot more concise."

I shook my head. "Not this. Not this time. Sometimes words need to..." Was that shoulder-squeeze Huxley or the ghost of Cicero? "... need to have a little fire in them."

The fire in me was suspense as my little arrow of hope, barbed with a dash of rhetoric, launched out into the vastness. I busied myself with the map, quick lessons from the experts showing me the network's weakest points, its strongest, how here or there a loop of signal—sending around one side of a mountain and receiving around the other—might unclog the info-pipes. Soon I felt like half an expert, but all the time, my hands were fidgeting, an urgent chant playing in my mind: *Please, Earth, please, Earth, listen! Listen!* I didn't let myself check until we had ten answers. They were positive (Yes!!) but with one repeated challenge:

<YU?>

Why us? Why me?

I took another deep breath. Our core staff all knew, but Kenzie, and the ba'pas standing here beside them were a risk... worth taking. "Kenzie, tell Minlu on the other end to clear the receiving station. This next message is only to be seen by them, their ba'pas, and Officer Seward, before it's sent on down the line."

I'd never done this before—Papa had told their staff, Vivien theirs, but revealing myself, I felt like bees were swarming in my chest, the tension, like when you're carrying something immensely fragile, and with each step every fiber of you is on maximum alert. I do carry something immensely fragile.

"Senator Kenzie," I began, "Evelyn, Michi, Sascha"—I smiled at the Walkiewicz ba'pas, volunteers as eager and indispensable as they were proud—"and send this to Minlu's side, too. I need each of you to swear an oath, your own choice, the most binding oath you can imagine for yourselves. You don't have to speak it aloud, just close your eyes and think it, but it must be serious and real. You must swear that you will keep what you're about to learn absolutely secret, lifelong, with the understanding that keeping this secret creates something powerful and good for all humanity, and that, if this secret is betrayed, the world will lose something precious, forever. Just think the oath and tell me when you're ready."

I watched their faces, emotions cycling through, the shock of my demand, the self-reflection—*What to swear by?*—then the sweet serenity as each arrived at their firm affirmation. "Ready."

I wasn't ready. No, with a deep breath, and smiling Vivien in my mind's eye, I was. "Send this out to the network: I'm the Ninth Anonymous."

I wrote out an encrypted string for them to send with it, hoping someone on the network would be a follower and know how to decode and verify my cryptographic signature. Kenzie glowed, watching me. They all did, absolutely glowed. One of them cried, not Kenzie but their ba'pa Evelyn, a good, big, grinning cry, the kind when things are unexpectedly, impossibly okay. And with those smiles, with help, with the ability to broadcast, to speak my ancient title, I felt like I could really be the Anonymous again. But that depended, not just on these smiles, but on those spider threads extending out through Italy and into Europe and beyond.

One last wait before the little laser light brought the world's answer.

<Code confirmed. Glad to have you with us, Anonymous. We'll leave it to you. Let us know what hours you'll be transmitting. Sending everything we have your way. Hold the world together. Pass it on.>

Chapter NINE

How Carlyle Foster Saved the World

Written October 21, 2454
Events of today and August 19
Romanova

I'VE FIGURED OUT WHAT HAPPENED TO SNIPER! Just today! All I needed was a lull, the first real lull we've had since war began, but the Pass-It-On network is running smoothly now, and all the street action has chilled after the news from the Almagest, so, for a couple hours, all was once more quiet on the omni-front. I even persuaded Su-Hyeon to take an early night. I promised to take one too but had a bad case of busy brain, so I decided first to treat myself to finishing the video of Emperor Isabel Carlos's coronation, at least as much as had come through before the silence fell. But even with the pageantry before me, my brain stayed busy, snagging on recent points that didn't quite add up, linking together, (A) to (B) to (C), before I even realized I was in detective mode.

I watched the dignitaries gather: envoys from nation-strats and Mitsubishi voting blocs, blood-nobles of Europe and Africa, legates from the Masonic and Japanese Emperors to welcome their new peer. I thought how Sniper should have a proxy there too, a Hiveguard ambassador, Lesley Saneer perhaps or Aesop Quarriman, or Sniper themself, who, in my imagination, burst in riding their diamond-white horse, as impossibly timely as they had been at the Olympics.

I watched the parade, the flags and colors which had been festivity three weeks ago, not fear. I thought of all the souls broken in those three weeks: lonely Vivien in Buenos Aires, Papa's shaking officers when we determined just how deep in China's empty western deserts the Commissioner General's signal had been when it went dead, and poor lost Martin, who must by now look as haggard and horrific as the ghostlike face of Carlyle Foster-Kraye when they had trailed in their "Abbot" Dominic's footsteps back at Las Huelgas.

I watched the solitary king, still just a king, enter the chamber they would leave an emperor. A commentator pointed out that queen-to-be Joyce Faust was still in Spain on purpose, the wedding scheduled after the coronation so the wedding contract could make iron-clear that Spain's new queen would be in no way an empress. I thought how precious this small victory was, Joyce Faust unable to sink a fang into Europe. That took my mind to other small victories of recent days: Cato's soul-warming exodus with their dear students, the Prince's great day at the Vatican, Su-Hyeon saving me and Carlyle from prison when

Madame's agents among Papa's forces almost managed their coup. I thought of the biggest victory of all, the Games in August, their suspenseful prelude, both sides certain to explode if Sniper had not come to light the torch. I don't know where you were that summer, Sniper, or how you came back, but your nick-of-time return saved the world.

I watched a Spanish sensayer present the crown, but the sapphires looked dull to me, by the standard of blue diamonds like the Hope Diamond, or the eyes of *la famille de la Trémoïlle,* through which Cupid fires such deadly arrows. The image rose before me of Carlyle Foster-Kraye, how warm and confident their eyes feel these days as Carlyle hands me Conclave updates and accepts with smiling energy the tasks of each new crisis. The sensayer on the screen there, handing golden power to a new-made emperor, had not a jot of Carlyle's strength.

And then Mycroft's words played through my head: Carlyle had risen full of strength that day, for it was the day of Saint Whatevertheirface, a day when humans had honored their Creator in ages past, etc. etc.

It was apt. Carlyle Foster-Kraye had been full of strength on the war's first day, with their three chocolate cakes. They'd been full of strength every day since, the tireless liaison between Triumvirate and Conclave. The Carlyle who worked with us was not the blame-drowned, self-destructive wreck that Doria-Pamphili, Dominic, and Perry-Kraye had made of the young Gag-gene. Carlyle had changed. Healed. How? Felix Faust had tried to breathe life back into the broken sensayer back at the Vatican with their pictures of things eating bananas, but Felix Faust had failed. Something else had happened, then, to Carlyle, after the Vatican, before the war, something that breathed warmth back into this walking shadow. (A) → ? → (C) But what?

Then Carlyle's words from the war's first day rang sunny in my memory: "We can do good, our pasts don't take that possibility away, not while we live and breathe . . . I'm giving My Maker a second chance, They've given me the same." Those were not the words of someone in despair. Those were the words of someone who had saved the world.

Between May 2nd and September 7th.

(A) → (B) → (C)

So, I sent for Carlyle.

And while I waited, I used the clearances Su-Hyeon had given me to dive into Papa's confidential files, and confirmed that Special Informant Carlyle Foster-Kraye was still depositing recordings. They'd made a deposit every day for the past many months, except August 19, the day before Sniper returned. I dug deeper. There had been an automatic tracker video deposit, but when Carlyle had logged in at day's end, instead of just tagging the private scenes, they'd deleted the entire day. And Papa's system keeps deleted records ninety days:

August 19th 2454, 15:35 UT; Romanova, Sensayers' Conclave:

Foster-Kraye: "You've been very happy lately, Julia."

Doria-Pamphili: "Mmm. It does feel good to be back at work in the Conclave, all as it should be. Jail was even more irksome than I'd imagined, no thanks to you."

Foster-Kraye: "You've got a glow to you."

Doria-Pamphili: "You're kind to say so. You seem peppier yourself."

Foster-Kraye: "Yes, but yours is a particular glow, as if you're being satisfied, that particular way you like to be satisfied."

Doria-Pamphili: "Are you here for advice on satisfying Dominic? It isn't possible, it just isn't, not for anyone but We-Know-Who, but I can talk you through approximations."

Foster-Kraye: "That's not why I'm here. Your glow got me thinking. I've figured out why I'm still alive."

Doria-Pamphili: "Excellent. Why?"

Foster-Kraye: "I'm here to blackmail you."

Doria-Pamphili: "Carlyle, sweetheart, you've released everything you had on me, and here I am, still popessa of the Earth. But it was a very good try."

Foster-Kraye: "You have Sniper."

Doria-Pamphili: "What?"

Foster-Kraye: "You have Sniper. What Casimir Perry told Martin yesterday—"

Doria-Pamphili: "You mean your father?"

Foster-Kraye: "Yes, my father Perry, Kraye, whatever. It doesn't hurt anymore, Julia. You've thrown that dart. It's done."

Doria-Pamphili: "I'm glad to see you grown so strong, I really am."

Foster-Kraye: "What my father told Martin yesterday in Klamath Marsh Hospital was the truth. There was a buyer, someone who paid Perry millions for Sniper. Lesley and Sniper's forces have allied with Perry's underground to fight Madame, but Perry wants Sniper gone so they can twist what's left of O.S. for their own purposes. Perry captured Sniper, the same trap when they stabbed Mycroft Canner the second time, and, rather than just killing Sniper, they sold them off. To you. You're keeping Sniper locked up paralyzed somewhere, so you can do your doll-sex thing."

Doria-Pamphili: "It isn't healthy for you, Carlyle, reading Mycroft Canner's book so many times."

Foster-Kraye: "You have Sniper. You've had Sniper for months. You let the paralytics wear off long enough to let them write that chapter about the first time you kidnapped them, and you released it thinking everyone would figure you couldn't be the kidnapper this time or else you wouldn't let everyone know about the first time."

Doria-Pamphili: "As it happens, I was a primary suspect despite the content of Sniper's chapter, and I'm sure young Mycroft Guildbreaker will be happy to show you the logs of the gazillion times they interviewed me about it."

Foster-Kraye: "You deceived Martin."

Doria-Pamphili: "Very flattering."

Foster-Kraye: "You deceived Papa's video surveillance. I know your tricks, Julia, you taught them to me."

Doria-Pamphili: "Also flattering."

Foster-Kraye: "I read Martin's notes on the investigation. They concluded you couldn't have Sniper because you'd need someone trained in administering the paralysis, and everybody who knew how to do it was accounted for. But I looked deeper. There was one more 'Dollmaker' who started training with Madame but didn't finish, Rhine Fournier, who quit two years ago and died last year. You helped them fake their death, gave them their freedom from Madame. I don't know if that's how you got them to work for you, or if you're controlling them your usual way, but you've got yourself a private Dollmaker, and that's who's keeping Sniper for you now."

Doria-Pamphili: "Any sufficiently elaborate theory can overcome such obstacles as evidence and plausibility. I am impressed, Carlyle, but you are wrong."

Foster-Kraye: "I have the videos your private Dollmaker made of you with Sniper. Their insurance, in case you betrayed them."

Doria-Pamphili: "That's a flat-out lie."

Foster-Kraye: "Then the rest isn't?"

Doria-Pamphili: "I don't have Sniper."

Foster-Kraye: "You're going to release Sniper, Julia. Today."

Doria-Pamphili: "I don't have Sniper. But frankly, I hope whoever *does* have Sniper does no such thing. It would be inhumane."

Foster-Kraye: "Inhumane?"

Doria-Pamphili: "You'd call it inhumane if someone released a tame, zoo-bred tiger cub into the wild, with no experience of predators."

Foster-Kraye: "Forced imprisonment is inhumane, Julia, against the Fourth Law, and don't try to convince me that Ojiro Cardigan Sniper—however much they may enjoy your complicated relationship—would ever choose to miss the Olympics or turn their back on their duties as O.S."

Doria-Pamphili: "The political brew is at its most dangerous right now, Carlyle, particularly for anyone with a foolhardy vein of heroism. I quite sincerely hope my dear Sniper survives all this and lives a long and happy life. I'd call that a humane wish."

Foster-Kraye: "Dominic would call that open blasphemy. Dominic is the deadly predator, if the 'blasphemer' Sniper is the zoo-bred tiger cub."

Doria-Pamphili: "Very true."

Foster-Kraye: "You're going to release Sniper. Today."

Doria-Pamphili: "I don't have Sniper."

Foster-Kraye: "Are you afraid that I'm recording this? I'm not."

Doria-Pamphili: "I. Don't. Have. Sniper."

Foster-Kraye: "You think I don't have proof?"

Doria-Pamphili: "Of course you don't have proof—there isn't any."

Foster-Kraye: "There is proof, but even if there wasn't, I don't need it. All I need to do is tell Dominic that you helped fake that fifth Dollkeeper's death. They'll find their own proof, once they're on the track. And then, Julia, Dominic will torture you to death, or possibly just kill you, whichever would be worse for you. Because you hid the 'blasphemer' who shot Jehovah Mason, and Dominic will hunt you to the ends of the Earth to give you the worst death they can possibly conceive. And you'll deserve it. Sniper is a hero, Julia, even if they're also an assassin, and what you've done to them is torture. No prevarication—torture!"

Doria-Pamphili: "There's a flaw in your blackmail, Carlyle, charming as it is."

Foster-Kraye: "What?"

Doria-Pamphili: "You're the traitor now. If you think I have Sniper, and you've come to me instead of going straight to your . . . abbot, and now you're trying to set Sniper free, you're more guilty of betraying Dominic than I am, and the death they plan for you will be that much more unimaginably ghastly."

Foster-Kraye: "Maybe. But you're forgetting something."

Doria-Pamphili: "What?"

Foster-Kraye: "I'm suicidal. I don't care if I die."

(Long silence on the tape.)

Doria-Pamphili: "You . . . you genuinely don't."

Foster-Kraye: "Sniper—the real Sniper—will be at the Olympic training grounds tomorrow morning, or it'll be the last peaceful tomorrow morning either of us ever sees."

Doria-Pamphili: "You really don't care if you die . . ."

Foster-Kraye: "And that's only the beginning. You're not touching Sniper after this, Julia, not at the Olympics, not after. And from now on, we're going to plan together what you do as Conclave Head. In fact, you're going to appoint me a Conclave Adviser, and we're going to push my agenda, a balanced, neutral agenda, to give the world the spiritual help it so badly needs right now."

Doria-Pamphili: "Ah."

Foster-Kraye: "We're going to give everyone on all sides the best guidance and support possible throughout the war, beginning to end, to after. We're going to protect the world's confidence in the sensayer program. And before you think about having me murdered, I've made sure the right information will get to Dominic in the event of my death. I'm ready to die anytime, Julia, whenever my Maker's work for me is done, but you will not outlive me, or if you do, you'll wish you hadn't."

Doria-Pamphili: "I wouldn't have you murdered, Carlyle, you're my best pupil."

Foster-Kraye: "Yes. Yes, I am. Sometimes it makes me sick to be your pupil, but I am, and I'm still a sensayer above all. And we're going to gather all the evidence we can about Bridger, Achilles, Jehovah, the resurrection, all of it, and share it with the public. We will not let this world war eclipse the Truth that half the wars ever have been fought over. We will not let one single human soul die in doubt's anguish that could die at peace."

Doria-Pamphili: "You think there's enough proof to convert the whole world?"

Foster-Kraye: "Maybe, maybe not, but what evidence there is, people deserve to have. There's enough proof to reach as far as our Creator wants it to, no less, no more, and we're the tools—you and I, Julia—that will spread that message, both Creators' messages, Jehovah's too, that They are here and real."

Doria-Pamphili: "You'll turn this into a religious war."

Foster-Kraye: "No. *We* will keep it from becoming one. Jehovah doesn't want to be worshipped. I don't even know if our Maker wants to be worshipped. But humanity has always wanted to know as much as we can about ourselves, our universe, our origins, and what evidence there might be of a Creator or a Plan. So, every test the medics run on Achilles, every psych report Brill's Institute has on Jehovah's childhood development, everything Utopia is learning from Bridger's creations, we're going to share it all. Carefully. Together. Those who are about to die will not take the great leap into the dark in ignorance. Never again."

Doria-Pamphili: "Those sound like the plans of somebody who wants to keep living."

Foster-Kraye: "No. They're the plans of somebody who will work, and work, and work, until death lets me stop. Just like Mycroft Canner. Do you think Mycroft Canner wants to keep living?"

Doria-Pamphili: "I'm glad you're feeling better."

Foster-Kraye: "I'll feel better when I see Sniper tomorrow. Meet me at the Conclave entrance at eight A.M. In fact, I'll expect you to meet me at the Conclave at eight A.M. every day until I say otherwise. MASON sentenced Mycroft Canner to work until they dropped. I'm sentencing you."

I watched it three times, feeling warmer inside each time. When Carlyle came in, I wanted to shake them by the hand, clap them on the back, spin them around, and dance and laugh and shout. But they had their arms full with a box of diamonds, onyx, gold, pearls, rubies, ebony, emerald, amber, frankincense, and myrrh (translated out of Servicer slang, that's salt, pepper, mustard, mayonnaise, ketchup, soy sauce, wasabi, honey, curry powder, and marmite, the most precious treasures imaginable when your day's pay is usually the stalest sandwich in the shop).

"I figure while you're Deputy Censor, Su-Hyeon is making sure you have plenty to eat," Carlyle began, "but I thought you'd have friends who could use these."

I was overwhelmed, too off-balance for 'thank you' as I took the box and met those deep-cutting blue diamond eyes. I smiled. "You've been very happy lately, Carlyle. You've got a glow to you, a special glow. As if you rescued somebody important and thereby saved the world."

Shock phased through fear to understanding on Carlyle's face. "What do you intend? To blackmail me?"

"No! To thank you. To help you. To work with you if there's anything I can do. You're right that everybody on Earth should have the opportunity to see the evidence of Bridger's relics, to know and to believe in the two Creators as we do, or to disbelieve but still to see and know what evidence there is and make up their own minds. I want to help with that. I'm running communications, I can send things out for you, for the Conclave, help you share what we know about the Visitor, about Achilles. And I have access to a lot of information, too."

"You must, to know what you know about my . . . arrangement with Julia . . ."

"Don't worry, I'll see if I can corrupt the video autobackup in Papa's system so no one else finds out."

"The autobackup . . ." Carlyle smacked themself on the forehead.

"It doesn't matter now," I consoled. "It's good, really. It's let me find you, help you."

"Providential," Carlyle added quietly.

I frowned. No, this was something darker, a scowl, showing my bitterness at Mycroft's Murderer. And Carlyle recognized it—I saw it in their eyes—they read my grudge, my wounds, the hate-mourning still raw within me, as ready to lash the Heavens with my screams as the first morning after Mycroft's d . . . after They took . . . The dam broke. Carlyle held me, just like the first morning, rocked me as I screamed, my tears and runny nose staining the shoulder of their wrap once more. Except this time, their own tears stained my jacket in return. "Thank you for finding me," they murmured in my ear. A squeeze. "I mean it, thank you. This is what I've needed. Julia and I can get a lot done here in Romanova, but I've had no way to reach the world. We needed someone. And to have another friend who understands, who knows the Visitor." Carlyle pulled back from the hug enough to peer into my face, beaming, that joyous brightness, diamond in sunlight. "Thank you."

"Th-thank you!" I sniffled back. "You saved the world."

Carlyle smiled the thought away. "I saw you at Madame's a few times, didn't I? With Mycroft Canner?"

"Ye-es. And I know the Prince, Jehovah Mason, well. They trust, care about me. I have people working to get me through to Them, allies."

"Wonderful."

"I can—"

"Have you had a sensayer session since we lost Mycroft?" they interrupted gently.

I choked.

They squeezed my shoulders. "If you want a session, with someone who knew Mycroft and who knows Jehovah, ask me anytime."

It took a couple tries to find my voice. "I . . . You know I . . . don't they say it's risky doing it for people who have the same . . . I mean . . ."

Carlyle smiled at my shyness. "There are as many ways of viewing the Guest as there are of viewing the Host."

ADDENDUM NOVEMBER 12:

Five days later, Carlyle pressed something into my palm. "The Dollkeeper did make videos. Use them if Julia kills me."

I kept it three days before watching. Curiosity made me begin, but duty made me watch it all, the duty of empathy, of standing witness to atrocity, so that someday, if I live to meet Sniper in person, I can tell them that I saw, and understand, and offer my embrace.

The video spanned sixteen weeks, so April twenty-first to August nineteenth, or close to. Most of it I watched on fast-forward, I had to, or it might have given me the same trauma symptoms Mycroft described in Sniper those last days before the Games. But it still took me a week.

I won't repeat too much, just enough for you to hate along with me. It was a giant dollhouse, cheerily painted, all the furniture off scale, with giant fake wood grain, so you really could believe you had been shrunk. The windows and doors stood open, and there was a porch, a yard, a loveseat-swing, but it was all one cell, the picket fence and lollypop trees painted on solid walls, the sun a set of lights which moved and changed color like day, though timestamps proved it was an eighteen-hour cycle, not twenty-four, designed, I imagine, to destroy the body's clock and enhance disorientation. Julia dressed and posed Sniper for tea parties or dinners, took their pleasure with the 'doll' as with the plastic ones, made one-sided conversation—"Did you have a good day, dear?"—and chatted about their own day, meetings, trivialities, never real news—the *Sanctum Sanctorum* attack! The great Senate debate! Ockham's trial!—all of which, bad or good, would have been as precious to this prisoner as desert rain. Sometimes at visit's end, Julia tucked Sniper into bed or, if 'displeased,' into the packaging which waited like an ever-ready coffin, but other times they said, "Wait here for me," and, with a goodbye kiss-grope, left their prisoner upright in a chair to face the frozen hours. The Dollkeeper entered sometimes, dressed as a maid doll, with a porcelain mask and jointed doll gloves, to feed Sniper by tube and clean their waste.

Mostly I fast-forwarded to the blue hours. Once every couple day-cycles the Dollkeeper knocked Sniper unconscious with some quick-acting chemical and carried them to a different space, small, blue-lit like some distorted darkroom, filled with gym equipment. A series of ministrations (injections, maybe?) and the Dollkeeper would leave Sniper to awaken, sluggish but mobile. The athlete worked the gym tools like a virtuoso, and exercise quickly restored full function, including Sniper's voice. I listened to every word. The first time, it was tender, thanking Julia for the rendezvous and fun, and explaining how Julia could get in touch with Lesley, so the two could plan together the timing of Sniper's periodic 'catch-and-release vacations' to make sure they didn't interrupt Sniper's war duties, and so Lesley could alert Julia to release Sniper in case of emergency. The second blue time, Sniper's words were tender still, thanking their 'owner' for the courtesy of a well-stocked gym, but they were firm that Julia must relay a message from Lesley confirming that Sniper's absence wasn't a problem, or else anxiety would ruin Sniper's end of the fun. The third time, Sniper knew the truth. This speech had careful planning: the history of tyranny, the beauty of the Hive system, the fragile, precious dignity of this noblest epoch of the human race, all needed Sniper to defend them. The fourth time, they begged. The fifth more raggedly, pleading, screams alternating with endearments trying to coax some softness into Julia's heart which *still*—obscene hypocrisy!—*still* wears the bull's-eye. The sixth time, Sniper protested by refusing to exercise, and was introduced then to a yellow chamber where electrodes worked their muscles with the paralysis still in place. Thereafter, protest in the blue room was verbal only, courageous but increasingly sporadic, bursts of shouting, mumbling. Eloquence faded, then grammar. At four weeks, there was only silence and the groan of exercise machines.

I was braced for months of silence, but a new space appeared after a time, lit in sunset red, with a desk and tablet, and absolutely joyful tears on Sniper's cheeks and mine as they sat down to write. Mycroft. Mycroft had asked for Sniper's chapter. Sniper spoke aloud as they composed, reading out fragments at first, testing a phrase, a battle cry, but it swelled to catharsis, until Sniper was marching about the room declaiming to the precious tablet, speeches to the distant public, to Mycroft, to the world. Julia granted four writing sessions over five days before Sniper had composed enough appropriate text for Julia to edit into the declawed echo that eventually appeared in Mycroft's history. No, half-declawed, I'll grant that much. That chapter is a miracle, or part of one. The real miracle was inside, in that dollhouse, inside Sniper. Words returned and stayed, a fresh flow from then on whenever a blue exercise hour came, meandering sometimes, like the disordered thoughts of bedtime, but so passionate, so strong, exhortations, intimacies. Not to Julia. To Mycroft. No, to Mycroft's Reader, the wide world and posterity all mixed together, Sniper was rehearsing exhortations, shards of speeches they might make upon the Rostra, for the Senate, press, court, the Olympics, or to comrades about to give their lives for something greater. To you. To me. Ten weeks, twelve. No mountain climber hauling their weary way up some hairline crack in a cliff face will ever impress me like Sniper's battle here to cry out and keep crying out, a battle of sheer will bolstered by the bare idea of being heard someday, somehow, by an imaginary someone. Us. Still, the toll showed in the decay of structure and continuity, the long gaps. Whatever mental rehab Sniper's coaches did in those last days before the Olympics was almost superhuman.

Someone else might write here that, if they'd had Julia alone after watching that video, they'd have beaten them to death. But I have beaten people to death. I know what it solves and what it doesn't. So, I will help Carlyle punish Julia, work them to exhaustion for the world's good. Julia's penance. And I'll make sure that penance continues if Carlyle falls. And, even though Sniper is the Prince's enemy, they are a πολέμιος—an enemy of my allegiance—never an ἐχθρός—enemy of my heart. I will honor Sniper by standing witness to Julia's atrocity. Someone did hear your pleas, Sniper, your speeches, listened just as you imagined, heeded every word. You weren't alone. I saw your courage, how you kept yourself ready, fighting for the future with every stroke of those exercise machines. I watched how heroically you resisted the mind-torture of that dollhouse world. I was with you. Even though I'm a stranger, and an enemy, and even though it's across time, you have my empathy. And now you have posterity's as well.

Chapter TEN

Pass-It-On

Written starting October 29, 2454
Events of October 29 to December 19
Afro-Eurasia

We have three senses on this island: the laser, whispers, and the coast.

The laser feeds us rationed fragments of news, like single frames chopped from a film, with which we try to puzzle out the middlecosm that surrounds our microcosm of the war.

Whispers bring the same sorts of fragments but partisan, updates gifted to the Triumvirate. Some come from local private sources—Mitsubishi sailors, or the Masons' communications tower on the Esquiline—others from strangers—a note dropped by a hooded cyclist outside the Censor's office, or a police clerk warily avoiding eye contact while reporting something they "heard around." With Huxley at my side, I can understand why someone might sincerely want to share real info but be unwilling to reveal the source. That makes me trust the whispers more, if not completely.

The coast is a different, grimmer kind of sense. Shadows pass us on the daylight horizon, or lights at night, cold like envious eyes. They could be friends. They could be warships. The aggressive Mitsubishi on our coast scare other powers off, but we have to wonder as the shadows crawl along: where are they going? Why? Sometimes we learn after a day, a week, the laser blinking *Palma evacuated* or *Mitsubishi fleet repelled at Sfax*, but more often the fleets and convoys just pass into silence. They won't always. Soon, I'm sure, one coalition or another will judge it worth the cost in ships and lives to send the words of triumph rippling through every whisper channel: "*The [_____] have taken Romanova!*" Earth's strongest victory signal. Next week, or tomorrow, some clutch of distant ships will stray from the horizon, grow, and grow, and bring their flame and thunder to our streets. But which flag will those ships be flying? Every quarter of our flag-studded city longs to have some warning, to know which streets must take up arms and which rejoice when the invasion comes. All we can do is watch the laser, mark the whispers, and hope like a spider that, when danger nears, it will cause warning tremors in our threads. I lost some nights to fear of dropping that ball, nightmares where I failed to recognize some telltale warning sign, and watched our Romanova burn because of me. But that's wrong. Analysis is others' job, not mine. I am Pass-It-On. I am the hope that everyone from Marrakesh to Moscow will have a chance to feel their warning tremors too.

We've divided up the broadcast. I collect and send overall news, three big blocks a day now, and the relay splits in the Italian peninsula, so only five links know the Anonymous must be in Sardinia—it's not much security, but needs must as the battles drive. Separate teams in Gibraltar and Volgograd each do one news hour daily, Gibraltar with word from Africa (Masonic news plus cheer and good advice from Casablanca), while Volgograd sends on what it gathers from parts East, and on a good day has some news from Samarkand, our outpost at the bottleneck to India and parts beyond. No successes yet suspending mirrors to get beams past the horizon barrier, and no luck bouncing signals off the Moon, but we use what we have.

The Far East is where the biggest battles have been waged so far, though we only learn of them weeks after their bloody climax. If the Hellespont and Bosporus are the Mediterranean's airlocks—bloodstained anew in every era of recorded time—Asia has its equivalents, the chokepoints between the Pacific and Indian Oceans, which could slice the Mitsubishi world in half, and force the fleet to loop 5,000 kilometers through Australian waters. We heard of war fires first over Jakarta on the Sunda Strait, between Sumatra and Java, and soon thereafter over poor mixed Singapore. It was worst there: a paradoxically fierce 'Singaporean Peace Alliance' vowed to the death to close the city's waters to any ship of war, and almost held the precious Strait of Malacca. Almost. They say Kuala Lumpur was spared thanks to a fast surrender after the fall of neighbor Singapore, and Mitsubishi command seems to trust Kuala Lumpur's Greenpeace plurality to make the peace sincere. Now the Mitsubishi are unchallenged masters of all sea paths from the Pacific Rim toward India, and six thousand warships (if report can be believed) are racing to meet MASON's weary forces and make a new assault on the fleeing elevator. The Almagest can move, its anchor platform trundling across the sea, but at 140,000 kilometers tall, it is the strangest vehicle that ever human piloted, and not designed for games of deadly tag.

Closer to home, all scales are smaller. The Mitsubishi still hold the seas and most ports (including Romanova's little port Ostianova), but have made no inland efforts yet. The lands around the eastern Mediterranean and Black Sea look like a mass of seed crystals, roads and martial law growing out from the great Masonic capitals, with jeep swarms wearing away the pockets between them until all is surrender. North Africa is mostly peaceful, Masons and Cousins collaborating to stave off Mitsubishi efforts on the coast. As for the west and nearby Italy, here the fronts are mostly internal, cities subdividing, local majorities conquering and penning their minorities, while mixed cities are falling to coalitions, or turning into patchworks, as Romanova has.

The exception is the Rhine-Ruhr valley, where the violence sparked by the attempt to free Ockham Saneer keeps growing. I knew it was serious when Toshi's window signals stopped having grammar, and now there seem to be real armies—Hiveguard against Remaker—clashing in one of the most densely populated patches of the Earth. I think the rural bash'es are the lucky ones now, alone with bash'mates and peaceful wild vistas (even if those vistas will mean something very different when the kitchen stocks grow low). Even the high density of Gordian in the region has failed to stop it. Cousins are racing to bring Tiring Guns to the Rhine-Ruhr, while neutral defensive forces—city militias or European nation-strat armies—keep heading in to try to contain the bloodshed, but they're being overrun or, more often, joining one of the two great sides, absorbed like when bacteria swallow each other to make a stronger whole. The violence is now spilling south past Luxembourg into those lands it's hard to label either French or German. A proclamation from Emperor Isabel Carlos quelled the fires a bit, declaring it criminal for any European Member to take up arms in aggression (defense is still allowed) unless enrolled in a European nation-strat army and acting on orders from the EU or a strat government. I keep being asked to pass on pleas over the network, asking Spain (should I say 'Europe' now instead of 'Spain'?) to speak out against the Hiveguard who aim to murder their beloved Heir, but the new emperor keeps only making mild statements. I think they're afraid, not so much of the war, but of overstepping procedure and damaging European Union institutions; yes, they're four-hundred-year-old institutions, but fragile in these days of change. Sometimes, I think Isabel Carlos is the only Member among Europe's billion who hopes to keep the new empire constitutional; the crowds would welcome one as absolute as Caesar's. I asked the Prince once, back in June, why Isabel Carlos was being so stubbornly power-averse. Their words: "Because the guilt of Cortés and his butchers falls so rank upon our house that, after nine centuries, it still gives My father night terrors." So, I asked why Spain was willing to be made an emperor at all. "Because smallpox's vaccine was made of smallpox."

November 1: New news. There might be cracks within the Mitsubishi. We hear through Samarkand, confirmed by Carmen's Masons, that the main Japanese part of the Mitsubishi fleet refused to join the attack on the Almagest, Greenpeace likewise, so it was mainly China that battled MASON and Utopia. Reports about Korean participation are contradictory. For the first time, I smiled at the thought that Bryar is in India; if there is conscience and reluctance in the Mitsubishi, perhaps Peacemaker Bryar can slice off the peaceful half.

Carmen is getting news from Alexandria now, too, via the Masons' communications tower, short bursts but regular. Achilles is leading MASON's fleet in the Gulf of Aden, fighting for control of the Red Sea route between the Mediterranean and the Indian Ocean. I imagined they'd be facing Mitsubishi, but Carmen's report says that the opposing fleet boasts more Humanist rings than Mitsubishi trefoils, and that every foe from front lines to horizon flies the bull's-eye. The Prince Is, and is glad to hear I am. Wish I could say I Am, but dealing with the Prince I understand now this thing Mycroft did with capitals, and how different they are, Am versus am. Capital verbs and adjectives and such are for eternity—the Prince *Is,* or *Is Kind,* or *Loves,* or *Wills* eternally in Their eternal cosmos, while we finite Earthly creatures merely *are,* or *love,* or *will* until we change or die like all perishing things. The Prince too, in Their circumscribed actions within this universe, becomes lowercase: the Prince *Is Kind* forever, but the Prince *is upstairs* only for a fleeting hour, *is protesting* while the protest lasts, and *is glad* to hear I am (i.e. survive) only the finite time until They fear again I might have died. The Prince stranded without a tracker to connect us and give that assurance . . . fuck this war.

November 2: The Cousins botched this one. We finally learned today—today!—the real truth about these Gorgons—"Tiring Guns"—which should have flashed on every tracker in September, but apparently they were hypercautious about announcing too soon, wanted to have the guns in volume, and then the Atlantis Strike and Operation Baskerville disrupted things, and with communications down, it took this long for anyone in our office to actually read the full report. Gorgons indeed. This is what the Cousins spent their 128 days on, between the Prince's declaration and the Olympics, while MASON was building jeeps, the Mitsubishi ships, and the Utopians worked toward peacebonding the harbingers, the Cousins were stockpiling bandages and building these. They're not stun guns, they debilitate, for months though not forever. Deep tissue damage, nerve damage, muscles, inner ear I'd bet, they're being cagy about the mechanism. A nonlethal exit from the war, and a good implementation of the military maxim that killing a soldier costs the enemy one soldier, but sending one to a hospital bed costs nurses, medicines, and food to boot. The Cousins say it's fully temporary, recovery in eighteen months, but since this technology hasn't existed for eighteen months, I don't know how they're so sure. It was Carmen who finally read their report in full, and together we visited a hospice hosting local victims. They're conscious in patches, a couple hours at a time, but any kind of concentration—conversation, or composing on a tracker—is as exhausting as an all-out sprint, and sitting up to eat a meal requires a long nap. Standing unsupported is impossible—weakness and nausea—but with the help of rails I saw one hearty victim make it the few paces to the bathroom. I can't fault the concept; if they'd managed to distribute these before the Olympics, we might have had a nearly bloodless war. Two weeks ago, the peaceful patients that I visited today were the most destructive force in Romanova, attacking hospitals to steal and sell supplies, or catching Utopians in back alleys and taking 'revenge' for Operation Baskerville. Now we're safe from them, and two years from now (if all goes well), both they and their potential victims will all be alive and well. That's good, and yet it doesn't quite feel good. The hospice had a strangely civil spirit to it, victims reconciled to their fair defeat, like the jail in a giant game of capture the flag. But something in my gut feels weird about it, thinks there's more dignity in Tully Mardi's camps, where one can choose to risk one's life to try a brave escape. The dignity of choice. But I admit it would be wonderful to have a nearly bloodless war.

Local Cousins offered the Triumvirate fifteen Gorgons for our guards and officers (all they can spare). We were going to debate whether to accept, but Jin

Im-Jin pointed out that we all already thought we should, so we just said yes. I don't have one, didn't request one. I have Huxley.

November 4: Carmen's found us a little more help, though it makes me nervous. The three corrupted officers, Bo Chowdhury, Desi O'Callaghan, and Isabel Ximénez, the ones Im-Jin outed who work for Madame. They're still capable brains, if tainted, so Carmen's bringing down danger-free tasks they can do in the cells, like making rationing tables, or turning blankets into coats. Every hand helps.

Also, there's been flag progress. Though nothing feels more like the Dark Ages than saying flag design means life or death. Turns out the Mitsubishi red trefoil on white and the Red Crystal diamond on white are maddeningly hard to tell apart at distance flapping in the breeze, since the green bits on the Mitsubishi are so pale and small. So, Red Crystal has started making the background Cousin azure instead of white, while the Mitsubishi are using the strat variants more: gold background for China, leaf green for Greenpeace, red circle for Japan, the black trigrams and blue accents for Korea, I've even seen the Vietnamese blue dragon, Malaysia's fourteen-point star, and a text banner which I think is Indonesia's *Bhinneka Tunggal Ika*. Also, the Masons have (finally!) given up on the useless purple-on-gray version of their flag, invisible in any kind of haze, and are all flying the Emperor's gray on purple, with or without official consent. I wonder how different all Hive flags would look if their logo designers had ever thought they'd fly on gunships.

I am mourning Mycroft. The Prince Is Mourning Mycroft.

November 5: Someone tried to pull down the statue of Apollo Mojave. It's crooked now, all twisted at the base. The Hiveguard-Remaker clashes in the Rhine-Ruhr valley are getting worse, spilling far south, and west into the Netherlands. Brussels is nervous, and with Emperor Isabel Carlos there, that makes all Europe nervous, too. Refugees are pouring in all directions, especially toward the safety of the Alps, where Brillist volunteers have seized key mountain passes, not for Gordian but for us, inviting our Alliance officers to take command and direct the flow of flight. Cousins are making progress getting Gorgons distributed up north. The Gibraltar team and I have, between us, finally made the whole network aware of how Gorgons really work. That's an achievement. But Gibraltar also keeps sending on Nurturist crap from Lorelei Cook in Casablanca, about 'deactivating' U-beasts and 'therapy' for 'Utopian set-sets,' how best to 'isolate and treat' them. I'd give a lot to never see 'Cookie update' over the wire again. I'd rather have another vile rant from Tully Mardi.

November 7: I really hate Tully Mardi. Not obsessively like Mycroft, I just get goose bumps thinking about the mind that conceives these things. I got my (sardonic) wish, a fresh brainchild announced by Tully Mardi over the network, in response to the Gorgons. It's a hair less vile than what Nurturists spew, with just enough good within its bad that I had to agree to pass it on. Peacewash. It's a dye that stains skin semi-permanently, lasting many months, a distinctive fuchsia-red. It's just common kitchen stuff, dimethyl sulfoxide with dyes you can extract from beets and things. The idea is to make an indelible mark of noncombatant status. When you would kill an enemy, instead you let them take an oath that they will fight no more and henceforth do only humanitarian things, like nursing for Red Crystal. A hand dipped in peacewash marks this pledge for all to see, and thereafter the avowed has but to raise a pink hand to proclaim: no threat. Prisoners who take peacewash can walk free and do good like Servicers, while non-soldiers can take peacewash voluntarily, frightened minorities who want to signal to wary majorities that they plan no resistance. Such a system requires grim enforcement, of course, and Tully has called on all leaders to pledge that any peacewashed person caught with weapon in hand will be executed on the spot, even by their comrades, no matter the excuse. MASON, Sniper, and the Mitsubishi Directors have given their assent, and Europe clamors for the same from Isabel Carlos. It may save lives, and with less tyranny than camps, and more dignity than sickly Gorgon stupor. They really are the same, peacewash and Gorgons, the same concept, ways to render prisoners harmless and therefore safe. When Tully Mardi and the Cousins think alike, I fear.

November 9: Tidbits from Huxley: Utopia is also using point-to-point lasers like ours, which are mostly evading interference but mainly close to the ground. They've had a little success with longer distances, bouncing signals off of satellites, and those will operate a little while but keep getting blocked/destroyed? by something; sometimes whole satellites go down. Huxley says the enemy even kicked up a dust cloud on the Moon, ice-chip bombardment, and that's what's scattering efforts to bounce signals off, but there may be a high-energy laser solution eventually. Whoever's behind this silence has a long, deep reach, even in space. People keep blaming Utopia; with so much happening in orbit, I'd blame them too.

Huxley also confirms the UFOs. I'd seen them myself and heard reports from everywhere, new devices schooling with the cars overhead, much smaller than a car but moving at the same speeds and, Huxley says, sharing the same flight patterns, dancing around each other but targeting anything that tries to fly. Some are large enough to take out a car or missile, others slim and deft as birds to chase down little drones and robots when we launch one packed with messages and hope. Someone is sending them out to supplement the cars that keep us grounded. Several hundred million cars we could eventually shoot down and claim our skies again, but not if some malignant factory is pouring out reinforcements to flood the air above cities with a shell of speeding death.

Disaster averted in Chennai—a sinkhole plunged the city food reserve into sewage below, but the Cousins mustered backup rations and the Masons drove it in.

November 13: I had a nightmare about Martin Guildbreaker.

November 14: Carlyle Foster saved the world again. Maybe not all of it, but they saved the Pass-It-On network, and that saves the world of united knowledge I've been struggling to create. Local Hiveguard inside Romanova made a move to seize the laser system. They're stronger lately, parading constantly on the far bank of the river, on edge since our local Masons and Utopians began to wear the Vs. The attack started with a makeshift bridge of floating barrels, which let them cross the Tibernov north of Campus and hit the Campus Remakers from behind in dead of night. Damage started heavy, and they dragged a lot of prisoners back across the river (hostage situation ongoing). Masonic reinforcements from the Esquiline drove them back, but by then (too late), we realized a force had charged north, toward the station where our posted mirror gives the laser beam its last bounce toward our receiver on the Capitoline. Our defenses were laughable: one sleeping techie and three police with stun guns (not even anything as scary as a Gorgon), and we have no excuse beyond the lull of weeks of local peace. Hiveguard would have seized the system, but a boat flying the Conclave banner charged up the Tibernov, with Carlyle Foster in the prow. In the name of the Conclave, the Alliance, Truth, the First Law, and every principle that still deserves human allegiance, Carlyle demanded independence for the network. They dragged in Julia Doria-Pamphili, too—a perfect moment to unleash our kenneled monster—and between them, the two sensayers had the attackers whimpering apology. This afternoon, the Triumvirate discussed ways to reinforce our relays, but any power we can raise is tissue paper against the local mobs; conscience and the Alliance and Conclave banners, those are steel.

I want to write an essay as Anonymous, to sing Carlyle Foster's praises to the far ends of the Earth! But then too many people (Carlyle for one) might put two and two together. We gave up on concealing what I am from the staff here, but there's enough of us that even the Pass-It-On teams on the mainland that know the Anonymous must be in Romanova still have a good sixty suspects to sort among, if they can find our names. I think Vivien would say I've done okay. Vivien. We still hear nothing from the Americas. I couldn't tell you whether Buenos Aires is ticker-tape parades or smoke and cinders.

November 15: They've started using peacewash here in Romanova. The Hiveguard in the Transtibernov started first, but now Masons are doing it too. It does have a Masonic vibe in some sense, peacewash, the oath and deadly honor system. In addition to staining hands, they're painting people's cheeks with their Hive symbols, or the bull's-eye or the Vs, so you can't conceal which side you fought for, which you'd fight for if you broke your oath. Someone asked through Pass-It-On if we would ask Caesar whether the Masonic legal custom that, when a Mason is convicted of a crime the whole bash' shares the penalty—all culpable for letting civic duty slip in one Member—if that will apply to peacewash. They can't! Imagine a whole bash' executed because one Member took up arms! But we should ask.

Also, Huxley brought us the remains of a mini-UFO. Grendel retrieved it—Grendel's one of Huxley's Utopian squadmates, who watches me while Huxley puts in their daily gaming hours as mandated by Utopia's oath to take the leisure necessary for productivity, recognizing play and rest as tools without which they will never conquer death or reach the stars. Sometimes, I curse that

Mycroft never took that oath, it's the one thing that might have made them take care of themself—though likely Mycroft would've overworked themself just the same and only felt more guilt-gnawed as a daily oathbreaker. Mycroft would have made the worst Utopian. And the best. Anyway, we have a sample at last of these UFO things schooling with the cars. Huxley says there are at least a thousand of them swarming through Romanova, and even U-beasts struggle to evade. I wonder how many times over one could rebuild Atlantis and all its wonders with the tech and effort that went into this silence.

November 19: Greenpeace Director Jyothi Bandyopadhyay has been assassinated! Word came through Samarkand. Apparently, they were trying to use their Greenpeace veto to prevent more military actions around the Maldives and the Bay of Bengal, but ferocious Dominic would have none of it. Now the Hive will rip apart for sure. Here's hoping this will help, not hinder, Bryar's efforts in Mumbai to win India's support for Red Crystal, Peace, and Sanity.

November 20: Now we hear Director Bandyopadhyay is alive and well, that no assassination happened, not even an attempt. Misinformation and confusion. Should have guessed—nine-tenths of what we hear from the Pacific Rim is gibberish, distorted by the trans-Asian game of telephone. One report about the Mitsubishi Indian Ocean Fleet got so garbled that by the time it reached us, it said their mission was to jailbreak the Prince from Alexandria, as if the Masons were Hiveguard and Alexandria's impregnable sanctum some tool of Sniper's to block the Prince's better world. I wonder how many people died in microconflicts because of that false rumor—and we who passed it on.

One intercepted Mitsubishi communique Huxley brought me had French tacked on the end: JE.VIENS.MA<ITRE. (I'm coming, Master.) I guess if anybody had the means and burning will to cross all of Eurasia, it would be stranded Dominic.

November 24: Bad news from Kolkata, one of the major skyscraper farms burned. Food stocks are fine for now but projected to get tight in four months—Cousins say they're on it. The statue of Apollo Mojave's gone now, whoever tried to pull it down before came in the night and dragged it off, nothing left but the base. I had that nightmare again, with Martin Guildbreaker.

November 25: We've created the happiest thing! Some Red Crystal Cousins in Geneva proposed it, an antidote to the morale-poisoning drone of daily casualties. We've named it 'Safe and Well.' As soon as Pass-It-On started up, we started getting little pleas from stranded people: *tell my parents, tell my beloved, tell my bash' I'm here, alive and well.* We used to pass on a trickle of them in night's wee hours when the action slowed, but now the Cousins are collecting them, and at six every morning, we start the day with an hour of Safe and Well. This is exactly the kind of unity I wanted to create, across continents, across sides, we sit together, all of us, listening, warmed by the knowledge that each name in the list makes someone somewhere—even if today it isn't me—cry out with joy: *It's them! My friend! My loved one! Safe and well!*

Congo.Raine.Beausoleil.European.home.Kinshasa.in.Gunzenhausen.safe.&.well.
Nagisa.Hiraizumi-Porter.Mitsubishi.home.Miyako-jima.in.Brussels.safe.&.well.
Lex.Tibernov.Shearwater.Mason.home.Neverland.in.Tunis.safe.&.well.
Tomo.Harvest.Lotze.Cousin.home.San.Francisco.in.Helsinki.safe.&.well.
Denys.Bartleby.Flaherty.Clark.Humanist.home.Manhattan.in.Helsinki.safe.&.well.
Kuiper.Antikythera.Cheung.Utopian.home.Atlantis.in.Romanova.safe.&.well.

I liked the idea instantly, but I had no idea how powerful it would be, how raptly I would listen to this mantra of survival, every beat of the long chant granting somebody's desperate wish. I find myself waking up eager for it every morning, the relief and triumph—even though it's just vicarious—refreshing, like a long shower. Sometimes, as I listen, I can hear Them in my mind, the Prince, Their loving question, "Are you?" and I feel Their Joy at all these answers, from strangers They Love with no less absolute a Love than They Love me: we're safe and well.

November 28: Here in Romanova, five peacewashed Hiveguard have been executed for holding arms. The bodies are hanging in Semaphore Square. Myrmidons tell me it was well done. Hard to know what that means. They also tell me that, now that we Servicers have all turned soldier or Red Crystal, people are using the peacewashed like Servicers, demanding odd jobs and petty labor as the price of mercy. If so, and if it's staying civil, not cruel, then I guess it's good in its way, proves the Servicer concept is a social habit now, society defaulting to service instead of prisons as our reflexive sentence. Perhaps the Servicer Program will survive. But in war it's hard for things to not turn cruel.

November 29: Two separate reports make me think there must be something to this whisper, odd as it is. People (forces?) strangely dressed (an unfamiliar uniform?) were described first by a pair of exhausted Greenpeace Mitsubishi hikers who managed to make it out of Altai, that natural labyrinth south of Siberia where one of the first monster calls went out during Operation Baskerville. Samarkand passed on a summary of their adventure: hiding in a cave to evade gigantic wolflike (fake) U-beasts, they saw the wolves joined by figures wearing dark robes or ponchos, blue or blue-gray, made of a matte-textured, papery or "gauzy" material, like the stopcloth you print at home to make one-use tablecloths or party decor.

The second report came from Bornholm, the Baltic Sea island. 'Sea monsters' had attacked just before the mass blackout, and three archaeology students sheltered in one of the excavation pits of the island's medieval fort. They held out there for five days, emerging only at night to scout until they could steal a boat. They too described ponchos of dark blue stopcloth, possibly home-printed, worn by squads who patrolled the streets and watched at crossroads, apparently unopposed by locals. No violence, combat, smoke, or fire were observed, but the students were wary and did not try to contact anyone in the town. That this unknown "Bluesmock" force (so Pass-It-On has dubbed them) could so rapidly subdue the entire island, with tens of thousands resident, is distressing. More distressing is the fact that several hubs of Pass-It-On (including the persistently Nurturist Gibraltar hub) immediately started calling them "Bluesmock Utopians."

December 2: Intelligence about the Mitsubishi ship-to-ship communications. They're using reflective chaff. A ship fires a big capsule (missile?) into the air which bursts high up, releasing a cloud of chaff (in lay terms, giant glitter). This makes a reflective mass that lasts nearly an hour before it disperses, and you can aim a laser or a light at it and your signal gets reflected in all directions, visible to the horizon. Fun part is, I heard about this both from Myrmidons and from Huxley, so both are working separately on cracking the Mitsubishi system, and Delians might be able to work out a piggyback, sending their own signals in a different wavelength of light bouncing off the same chaff clouds. If for some reason there were Delians hiding among the Mitsubishi fleet. Huxley is so brave. They all are.

Unrelated: once the war ends, I never want to look at beans again. I know urban agriculture is saving us all, and I know we need the protein, and I used to like beans, but day after day of almost nothing else, please, beans, just, no. No more beans.

December 3: Jin Im-Jin has pneumonia. Somehow that's scarier than the Mitsubishi fleet.

December 4: The next battle will be Brussels. The Hiveguard-Remaker battles that started on the Rhine have swallowed Antwerp and Liège now; everything I hear from there is fire and blood and garbled contradiction. But Brussels is next, that's clear. European strat armies are taking a defensive stand around the capital, but unless Emperor Isabel Carlos does something brilliant, Brussels has to be next.

In cheerier news, the Cousins are launching a ship toward the Americas, full of Safe and Well reports and Pass-It-On transcripts, all the news gathered thus far from our three connected continents and fragments from Australia. I'm sure a thousand ships have tried to make the crossing by now, but this one isn't for a side, it's just for news, for hope, for continuity, a friendly hello from one world to another. We really are separate worlds now, Afro-Eurasia here and the Americas out there, fighting our separate wars. Poor Martin: please be safe?

December 7: It's a strange game, guessing which news scraps are paranoia and which real. The first murmur of a train seemed ridiculous—an actual train on rails, chugging its way among the snowy crags of Switzerland—but we've had several separate reports now, from corners of the Alps where people claim they've spotted engines ducking in and out of tunnels on the mountain curves. Other reports have trickled in from villages which our cartographers say match the courses of the old rail lines from Warsaw up to Minsk, and Minsk toward Moscow. Just think! Moscow is the western threshold of the ancient Trans-

Siberian Railway—if that were running, Warsaw clear to the Sea of Japan, Eurasia would almost be one place again.

December 10: Just had our first big argument over the network. Not me and the kids—Kenzie and Minlu are on my side—it was with the grown-ups who run the major links. U-beasts sparked it. The Gibraltar broadcast today devoted eight whole minutes to 'helpful' tips on how to 'deactivate' 'dangerous' U-beasts. In tonight's state-of-the-network back-and-forth, I criticized it, and got jumped on by the team at the Orvieto hub:

> You really can't see it? The Cousins are right! The U-beasts are the most dangerous thing in this war! Killing machines disguised as harmless toys! Wake up, Anonymous! The Utopians are lying to you! They *did* plan Operation Baskerville! They're using you to spread their propaganda! They're behind the blackouts! The Maldive Ridge Massacre! Those Bluesmocks are Utopians too! They broke the Olympic peace, pretending to protect us while they seized their monopoly on mass destruction! Now they have a thousand nukes on the Moon ready to wipe out any side they like! Utopia is perverting good J.E.D.D. Mason's war! Break free, Anonymous! They're using you! They always have been! Ever since the Mitsubishi set-sets got into the Censor's office and perverted Ancelet!

I didn't face this diatribe alone, the Ladispoli hub spoke up for me, and Bologna, but they got jumped on too—*Bias! Sabotage! Conspiracy!*—and out came all the dirty laundry. I had dirty laundry too, I do admit it. I've been suppressing the Mitsubishi announcements. As soon as Pass-It-On got some momentum, factions started asking me to pass on official statements: Cousins' good advice, Isabel Carlos's pleading calm, MASON's "Peace shall not come while the *Sanctum* Violators live in breath or memory." I even passed on some one-liners supposedly from Sniper. But these Mitsubishi announcements, I couldn't. They're too gross. Turns out it wasn't garbled after all, that message out of Samarkand: "Our fleet's mission is to rescue Xiao Hei Wang from Alexandria." How could anyone pass on that drivel? That the purpose of all these Mitsubishi fleets, in the Mediterranean, the Indian Ocean, North Africa, the attack on the Almagest, they're still claiming it's all to get to Alexandria to 'rescue' the Prince. As if MASON is holding them prisoner! As if They want to be in Asia—Andō's poor little 'Taikun' calling out for liberty. As if the Mitsubishi are the true Remakers, and the Masons holding back Their good new world. It's lies! Raw lies! Engineered to rip the Remakers in half. Possessive Dominic planned this, and the possessive Mitsubishi wanting to own the Prince like they want to own the Earth. Rescue the Prince from MASON?! I will not pass it on. But this *is* bias, and I *am* guilty, and the Orvieto team jumped on me, and Bologna jumped on them in my defense, and everyone was clogging up the lines with packets of raw anger, and then someone used the old hate phrase 'Free Speech' and it exploded.

That's what we're afraid of really, that, in our information efforts, we're going to poison this war like the free-speech-mongers poisoned the last centuries of the Exponential Age and vomited out the Church War. Free Speech, that old tool of plutocracy, the intoxicating, rosy blossom under whose petals parasite lies can breed and multiply until they devour all the garden. None of us wants that. I hope none of us wants that, but there are still Free Speech zealots in this day and age, and they're just the type to have communications tech, to build a radio or study Morse code, and volunteer to join our network as a link and pass on . . . death. I'm panicking, I know it. Everyone understands why we need censorship. We've just relearned that very lesson from what started this: Joyce Faust discussing religion, Julia Doria-Pamphili exposing a Gag-gene's parentage, Sniper exposing the Prince's, and then the Point of No Return when the *Sanctum* Violators published the *Imperator Destinatus,* and the Oath. All our defensive silences breached, one by one, and here we burn. Mycroft made me read an essay once, a Free Speech piece, American or maybe British, early Enlightenment I think. Milton?

Hobbes: "Perhaps my sad apprentice, Charles Blount?"

Maybe. Anyway, Mycroft wanted me to see what the concept felt like back when it was new, and beautiful, before America's hypocrite death fits and the Church War's cruel recruitment lies poisoned it all. The essay Mycroft showed me had all the exquisite rhetoric of its rose-tinted, genteel age, imagining humanity nobler than we really are. I couldn't get through it, couldn't feel the beauty Mycroft felt, not for something so soiled. I do believe it was a pretty thing once, Free Speech, such a lofty notion, but we outgrew it with our communications revolution, as with our machine guns we outgrew pretty chivalry. But what if someone out there on my network feels like Mycroft? Still buys into it? Wants it all back? There are a hundred hubs in Pass-It-On, and any one of them could harbor the old illusion, and still think it good.

December 11: The Battle of Brussels has begun. Turns out it started yesterday—December 10, 2454—but word was slow to reach us. Seems it sparked before the armies even reached the city, a surge from inside attacking Brussels's defenses from behind to open up a path for the Hiveguard to surge in. No sense who's winning; everything in that part of our web is clog and chaos.

December 15: Papadelias is alive! Alive and joking, and in the best place you could imagine after Romanova. It came through hidden in the middle of the Cousins' Safe and Well report, not Papa's own name, but Ektor Carlyle Papadelias knows what kind of riddle friends will crack in an instant, bringing confusion to enemies and big grins to everyone here in the office:

Kexin.Agus.Kusumaatmadja.Mitsubishi.home.Bukittinggi.in.Gent.safe.&.well.
Sofias.Glynn.Heck.European.home.Swansea.in.Batumi.safe.&.well.
E.C.P.Holmes.European.home.Pylos.in.Dhaka.safe.&.well.
Mekong.Stafford.Nguyen.Mitsubishi.home.Dubai.in.Granada.safe.&.well.
Cherry.Finchwhistle.Kohler-Li.Cousin.home.Pretoria.in.Granada.safe.&.well.

We had a party, spontaneously, everyone who'd been hiding chocolate or some other treasure in our desks all broke it out. Dhaka! Great neutral Bangladesh! I don't know how Papa got there. If their car did go down in wasteland western China like we thought, then I can imagine an epic month-long trek across Tibet, traveling robes flapping around Papa's skeleton figure, with a mule or lowing yak lent by the peaceful Reservationists who guide them across the windswept desert plains. Maybe Papa mustered an army as they crossed the Tibetan Reservation, gathering bash' by bash' Alliance Members stranded at those wilderness vacation cabins that we rent to hold Seders or weddings or whatever ceremonies feel more comfortable in the limbo lands beyond Alliance law. Or maybe Papa got the failing car over the Himalayas, and tumbled to the ground in the Bengal region itself, a brave crawl on a broken leg to arrive in triumph at Earth's greatest Graylaw capital. Just think of it, the Alliance Commissioner General, the highest officer of Universal Law, borne down Dhaka's crowd-brightened boulevards where Hiveless sashes outnumber Hive marks three to one. There stand a thousand volunteers, a thousand thousand, ready to make Dhaka a new power, an independent port just where Earth needed one, between the eastern island chains, where Mitsubishi warships prowl, and India, where pensive Greenpeace watches MASON's fleet defend the priceless Almagest. I can see Papa in my mind's eye, declaiming on that same podium where Amelia Joyce Chowdhury gave the speech that shaped the Long First World War's remnant Non-Aligned Movement into the only player in the Church War that can command history's unconditional respect. Papadelias in the midst of fifteen million Graylaws and the Bengali nation-strat, which harbors in its heart Earth's boldest tradition of activist neutrality! Safe and well indeed!

December 16: "What Fate gives with one hand, it takes away with the other." I want to unthink that phrase, to not know it, not have it play through my head in times like this. I don't want that phrase to make it feel like there's some kind of justice in these moments when Fate takes good things away. Papadelias is safe and well. In return, Isabel Carlos the Second of Spain and First of Europe is Missing In Action. Peaceful, good King Isabel Carlos. Wounded Europe picked the best, most upright, moral human on this Earth to be their compass in these days of hate. Gone. There is not a city now in Europe that is not on fire, if not with battle then with rage, with torches, every nation-strat assembled, marching, crying out, directionless, into the uncaring sky. Uncaring. How can You not care? This is Your Great Guest's mortal father! Your Guest Who understands no fiber of Your vast, incomprehensible Law if not this fiber: filial piety. You take away His father? If You wanted to teach Europe how to curse, turn plowshares back to swords, I understand that. But how could You, Cruel Host, how could You decide to teach our Good Jehovah how to curse?

December 19: I will not hope. Hope is the most dangerous thing. Hope opens the armor inside us. Inside me. And I know You will just strike again where You have struck before. I will not let You make me hope. But it came. It came this morning, clear. Clear as a puzzle written just for me, for me and Papadelias, who three days ago sent out into the world their half of a riddle, like a children's echo game: E.C.P.Holmes. And we have an answer:

Felix.Fisher.Studenroth.Humanist.home.Santa.Barbara.in.The.Hague.safe.&.well.
Suleiman.Courrier.Gold.Mason.home.Antalya.in.Aarhus.safe.&.well.
Wenlei.Dai.European.home.Vantaa.in.Rostov-on-Don.safe.&.well.
Isabel.Ganges.Zapatero.Humanist.home.La.Concha.in.Kirikkale.safe.&.well.
Sunshine.Mississippi.Cox.Cousin.home.Nakuru.in.Lahore.safe.&.well.
M.C.Moriarty.Servicer.home.Greece.in.Montecristo.Island.safe.&.well.

Chapter the ELEVENTH

The God Who Rings the Earth

or,

Mycroft Canner's Account of Ninety-Five Lost Days Upon the Sea

Written January 2–8, 2455
Events of August 6 to December 23
The Mediterranean

I HAVE MISUNDERSTOOD POSEIDON, READER, all this while! That is the lesson bought by my ninety-five days a captive of his seas. You know I study carefully the names and faces by which Stranger Jehovah's near and native Host makes His Own Strangeness known in facets small enough for us to grapple with. The names used by my people—Kronos, Hermes, deadly Artemis—have always been the readiest upon my mind's tongue, but not so easy to understand. Often I think I understand them. In boyhood I thought I understood Apollo, an easy error while his kinder aspect shone so near, but we who bask in light and inspiration do not know the distant, deadly archer, not until we see him strike from worlds away. Zeus too, the lightning-loving father, I had thought I understood, but I did not—not until the hour the last of my bash'parents lay dead before me, and I stood on this Earth a liberated parricide, no power near me but the wind and sky and my own bloody hands, and yet I feared, and cringed, and felt the whimper deep inside myself that knows it will be chidden. What was this I feared? Still? After cutting down all who had stood above me? Only then did I truly come to understand the title 'Father.'

Just so, I used to think I knew and honored grim Poseidon. I had thought I met him in childhood, that day I first swam in real sea surge, whose waves turned from toys to terrors as the undertow made friends and shoreline shrink. I had thought I met both Zeus's brothers that day, as my child limbs weakened, and the god who shakes the Earth dragged me farther out into his waters, where the third brother's kingdom waits one drowning gulp away. But even then my thoughts were half of storybooks, of Jason and his Argonauts, of rafts and shipwrecks, thrilling in my mind: "This is what it felt like! To them, so long ago, our ancestors! Why *they* believed the grim sea was a god!" They, not I. I knew in half an hour I would be in a car again, hopping with a thought across the sea whose power once made every ship's launch equal parts hope, prayer, and funeral. We brave the seaways now for sport, for self-indulgence, we conquerors descending for a voluntary tussle with an old foe now domesticated, like our fawning household wolves. No, reader, that conquered thing is not Poseidon. We mistake, we foolish moderns, when we seek the sea god in the sea. He is not H_2O, not surface tension, tides and shorelines known and knowable. We could not see him while we sat cocooned within our arrogant prostheses—trackers, vid-feeds, cars—but Ares stripped those from us, leaving us naked before his grim-faced uncle, whom we face now in the sea, the land, the sky, and in that outer sea where Utopia's bright barques shudder, fragile still. The god who rings the Earth, Poseidon, is Old Enemy Distance, reader, that facet of Our Maker's Making which—alongside Death and Time—Infinite Jehovah finds hardest to understand. Technology mitigates the tyranny of distance, but Poseidon has grown no weaker over time, and when mischance conspires with him, their union trumps our brash technology. A hundred thousand years ago, we hollowed out a log to make a boat, yet yesterday I still sat weeping on the shore, with no tool to help me reach my friends again but prayer—and so will others sit and pray, when mischance strands them on a rock around some distant sun, a hundred thousand years from now.

It was Huxley's lion that ended my lonely vigil, black living softness coalescing before my eyes like dew out of the kindly night. I fell asleep upon its back in my relief, even as it carried me down the rocky coastline toward the waiting hospiwhale. I will not call 'relief' the intensity that quivered in Huxley Mojave's eyes as cautious Cannergel cuffs secured our wrists together, but I might call it relief's cousin, as the fire-scarred portcullis of a battered fortress gate is cousin to a warm home's welcome mat. My kind successor too had come to meet me on the gritty beach, and grasped my shoulders to verify I was no dream. I understand those hands have held you, too, reader, keeping this chronicle for you during my exile. It warms me knowing that I left you such a worthy guide. I have failed in many duties, more perhaps than anyone alive, but at least I did pass on to safer hands the precious torch of the Anonymous. But perhaps you are angry with me? Expecting a thousand apologies for my long absence? No. What would such apologies mean, reader, between we two who know each other now so well? You have seen me abandon Caesar, my own Saladin, even Bridger, but you know I would not desert you, my constant master, not unless I was kept from you by That Power no human can resist, Who now scripts out for hesitant Jehovah this bloody greeting we call War. Neither the darkest prison in this world, nor its fairest prison, glittering with leisure's sweet enticements, could weaken by one atom's strength the love, like adamant, which binds me to fulfill our Stranger's Good command to keep this chronicle for you. If it took me this long to return to you, reader, you know the Cause.

I heard my rescuers cursing as we set out for Romanova, blaming themselves that no one had thought to search this rugged little island, barely two hundred kilometers from the fast, chaotic waters where I had been lost the night of the Atlantis strike. Montecristo—it is difficult to remember it is earth and stone as well as romance. But I assured them I had spent only five nights among the goats and heather there on Montecristo, just one of many stops in my long journey, of which Romanova here is the next, though not the last. My journey is not yet over, reader, not until the hands which grasp my shoulders to verify I am no dream are His.

Where shall I begin my tale? My shy successor (who is now leaning protectively over my chair) has told you of poor Atlantis, first victim of Janus's opened doors, and of the tsunami the explosions caused, a sea of shattered boats and death. Rashness and love carried me into that maelstrom, where I flew, full strength, full energy as we looted survivors' bodies from the bloated, foaming sea. I do not know the name of the brave ship that took me out, nor how many victims we hauled aboard and wrapped in pressure-films and other healing tools dropped on us like wishes by the U-beast wonders overhead which made those skies fantasia. Our ship was full, our deck crammed with the living and our dark hold with the dead, but still we stayed, contriving ways to fit another underneath a bench or in a makeshift hammock. I remember sudden noise, water's wild roar, which must have been the first of the secondary explosions whose cause, I understand, is still unknown. I wish I could describe some clue, the bubble shadow of a cruel torpedo, but I remember nothing between leaning out to reach another body, and a world of foam and falling: air, water, choking, sea and whirlwind mixed with blood—my blood?—and then just water, water, down and down into the pressure and confusion whose true name may have been pain. I tried to move, to flail, to shout, but, as in nightmare, neither voice nor flesh obeyed my will's command.

After that, time lost its line a while. Patches of painful light and strange voices alternate in my memory with dreams of wandering salty shores, or shadowed woods, or searching in a tiny boat, alone in that vague but absolute despair that dissolves the illusion that time can be measured.

My first salient memory is hospital smell: soap, cotton, mattress, and the touch of bandages. Stubble's itch and liquid nutrition mid-transfusion told me of a long slumber, but blue privacy curtains hid everything around me save a low, blank ceiling and the cradle rocking of the sea. A ship. Whose ship? I counted my limbs: one, two, three, four—you would count too, reader, had you woken once in childhood to find zero. Under the blankets, my right arm and leg were pinned in stiff splints and healing apparatus, but I could feel the textures of their interiors with a detail which made me confident my hand and foot were still attached. My left limbs seemed uninjured, but wrist and ankle were bound fast to the bed's side rail. I had been recognized, then, but these makeshift bonds of knotted rope were no Cannergel. Strangers had me—strangers who knew the face of Mycroft Canner.

Footsteps. I tugged at the rail to make a little sound, and heard breath catch. The visitor retreated quickly. Reinforcements? Wise. Several sets of feet returned, and hesitated outside my curtains for a moment courageously brief. There are seeds, reader, in Egypt that were sealed in tombs as offerings to the joyless majesties of withered kings and queens, and double prisons hold them, perfect blackness and the endless, endless dry, as the millennia teach them despair impossibly prolonged beyond the lifespans of their kin, their whole species, until, ten thousand years beyond the death of hope, some cheerful researcher nestles the seed amidst moist earth and brightness, and, after some nervous days, a timid leaf raises its little flag to prove that there is such a thing as resurrection; just so unlooked-for, here in the black of Ares's shadow, joy raised its timid leaf in me as I saw upon my captors' breasts the V of Vs.

They were Seaborn, with the three lush blues of the Seaborn nation-strat as bracelets of braided cord around wrists buffed to a healthy ruggedness by salt and sun. This ship, then, was a shard of Neverland, the brave sea dwellers who had rushed to Atlantis to save drowning Utopia. Her crew introduced themselves, a bash' of nine: seven Whitelaws (Tayo, Marvel, Maxime, Lintang, Hoel, Echo, and Dian), a Maltese European (Toni Bajada), and a Mason (Lex). *Shearwater* was both their ship and bash'name, inherited from a mentor, Lành Vân Shearwater, one of the octopus rights activists who got the Minor's Status vote so close to passing three years ago, thwarted again by seafood-loving non-Greenpeace Mitsubishi and Europe's protectiveness about ancestral recipes. This Shearwater bash' was a young one, freshly formed and launched from the Lisbon Campus just that June. So young, reader. Another three years, five, these almost-children could have lingered in their Campus studies and not been called slow bloomers, but, in these now-or-never days of future-making, they chose now.

The simpler mystery they explained at once. They had found me in a hospital on Minorca, one of the Balearic Islands east of Spain. The *Shearwater* had joined the rescue at Atlantis and escaped the blasts that claimed so many ships, but, when a red dawn broke and she turned toward shore with her load of dead and wounded, she had found all harbors near Romanova choked with combat, the Mitsubishi making their blood-and-fire rush to claim the coasts as the cars failed. Preferring the sea's known dangers to war threats, the *Shearwater* turned west toward Spain, then found her journey halved by warm Minorca, where Red Crystal's banners kept violence at bay. A brief visit to unload the wounded stretched into three weeks of volunteering in the wards. By chance, bandage-changing duty fell to Lex Shearwater on the first day that my swelling had gone down enough for parted bandages to show a most infamous face.

The blast had ripped my tracker off (and most of my ear with it), so, with quick lies and feigned delight, they convinced the orderlies that the Jay Doe in the corner was a much-missed childhood friend. The choice to leave Minorca was difficult. Convincing the hospital to discharge me was easy—Red Crystal hungers for free beds and happy endings. It was leaving that oasis that was hard: safe harbors and rewarding hours, every task a wound salved, a bone set, a warm, uncomplicated good. The sweet fruits of human gratitude can be their own addiction. But the young bash'mates had read my history; everyone on Earth has read my history. They held a midnight council, pledging that they would not vote, not drown the few with the oppression of the many, but, like an ancient jury, they would talk it out until all nine agreed, either to join Red Crystal for the long haul, or to take me—this castaway of Providence—in hand, and set out into the wider war to do what good they could. When the debate finished after dawn, I understand, there were still tears.

"How long was I out?" I asked when their tale was told.

"Four weeks. Today's October fifth."

"Who knows that you have me?"

"No one. Communications are down, the Tracker System, web, radio, everything."

Here was an unexpected stroke, first rumble of Poseidon's outstretched hand. "Am I your guest or prisoner?" I asked.

"Both," answered Lex, their Mason—black-haired, bronze-skinned, frail to a degree that proclaimed some childhood (or ongoing) malady, but brave enough to wear the white sleeve of Martin's *Ordo Vitae Dialogorum*, inviting lifelong dialogue about what a Mason is and should be, even as MASON's Capital Powers make Earth tremble. "As I understand it, both your friends and Caesar treat you as something between guest and a prisoner, for your own safety as much as everybody else's. Or was that overstated in your history?"

"Understated if anything." I laughed at my own honesty. "But what will you do with me now that you have me?"

"We will take you to Jehovah Mason."

This is a brave world, isn't it, reader? Where frail humans are learning to speak His name. "If all the paths on Earth were open before me, I would choose no other," I answered.

Smiles said that they had guessed as much. "Will they deliver on their promise? Your Jehovah Mason?" It was a Whitelaw, Tayo Shearwater, who asked it, the ship's captain, a child psychiatrist in training, and in form as beautiful as those sculptures from the age of athletes that they excavate at old Olympia. "They promised us a new world order, that they'll help humanity outgrow the dirty compromise that was O.S. Will they deliver?"

I breathed deep, savoring the taste of air. "He is not my Jehovah Mason, He is ours. Our Friend. Our Benefactor. Every one of us who gives our hands, our hours, our actions to Him will become another atom of His greater body, which strives to no end but to make His Willed Good real, in this world as in His. He will make mistakes but never compromise, and every action—His and yours—will aim for Good, even if we do not always achieve it. He can promise no more."

Their smiles judged it was enough.

Our course stretched east, around the south end of Sardinia, avoiding coasts where Mitsubishi clustered as we made our way toward Sicily. The first day, sleep released me only for short intervals. The second day two of the Whitelaws—Marvel and Maxime, a pair of Malagasy ba'sibs born on the seas near Madagascar—helped me learn about my wounds and try my strength. My limbs were healed enough to make the splints more precaution than necessity—in fact, I suspected they were more for the crew's comfort than mine, assurance that this dangerous guest was safely slowed. I did not protest, and my hosts soon offered to carry me up to taste the sun-kissed deck.

Sails, reader, real ones. They arched against the sun like gulls and were as beautiful. The *Shearwater* was a historic replica tall ship, built in the 2200s with plans from the Age of Sail five hundred years before. She was a brigantine, based on the old merchant trading ships that had braved the Mediterranean and great Atlantic, with two cloud-tickling masts and a slanted main sail but classic square sails on her foremast and main topmast, like something from a painting. Standing beneath their outstretched yards and bulging bellies made all the man-made trials of modernity melt away. Her insides were modern, cozy cabins and kitchen comforts, and she condescended to lug a motor just in case, but her masts and rigging were real wood, real hemp, real tar, a boat-buff's heaven but a practical modern sailor's purgatory. For this mission she was perfect. The Mediterranean's teeming ships were now so many herds of wild horses, with all factions racing to round them up and fill their stables with the best; with war-strong stallions in sight, would any soldier pause to chase this lithe but lumbering giraffe? No. We were the most harmless vessel on these seas, guarded by the glee and awe which keeps children from reaching across museum ropes, and by our flags. In the global silence, all factions must declare our sides with gaudy, flapping heraldry, like so many medieval knights squinting against the sun to see whether the banners on the next hill proclaim friend or foe. We ourselves flew the most innocent colors one could imagine: a Whitelaw Hiveless flag, Neverland's triple blue, and a Red Crystal diamond stolen from the hospital—our first ruse de guerre.

My first day on deck proved the power of that ruse. We avoided shores and shipping lanes, but in these crowded seas the specks of vessels still appeared often on our horizons. Several drew close, curious, then closer still to bask in the sight of such a masterpiece of sail and offer help. Some gave us hours of escort, joining the dolphins that played around our prow, but in the end, it was usually we who helped them. Every other helmsman on these seas was struggling to relearn how to navigate without the silenced satellites which have been sailors' constant companions for four hundred years, but the Neverlanders who called this tall ship home loved their grandba'pas' historic compasses and sextants as Ockham loves *Mukta,* and spent a joyful day sharing navigation lessons and practical anecdotes.

The next day, the Strait of Sicily drove us into crowded seas. Here, less than 150 kilometers separate the western tip of Sicily from Africa, with the island of Pantelleria so close to the center of the strait that a lookout on its mountaintop can see almost shore to shore. We timed our passage for the quiet of the night, bandaged my face anew just in case, and kept to the west, guessing that the Cousin capital of Tunis would prove the safer coast. I remember Marvel cursing, telescope in hand, that, as flags flap in the breeze, Red Crystal's diamond and the Mitsubishi scarlet trefoil are maddeningly hard to tell apart.

It was Cousins who hailed us first, and told of conflict. Tunis was free and theirs for now, but Mitsubishi ships had seized the Sicilian side of the strait at gunboat-point and marauded the eastward seas, rounding up what ships they willed. They had seized Pantelleria, and, as the Cousins escorted us past her, we caught first sight of the Mitsubishi war fleet, true battleships, monstrous with their many looming eyes—or were they guns?

Our hearts sang as we left the strait behind, and dawn's rose outline showed nothing but sea. We did consider asking if some Cousins might escort us all the way to Alexandria, but they had no gunships, and a defenseless but valuable herd with one giraffe in it seemed more likely to invite attack than our giraffe alone. Besides, we would have had to explain why we were bound for the Masonic capital—trust is hard, harder with me on board.

A peaceful day brought us near Toni Bajada Shearwater's homeland of Malta, the rugged islands south of Sicily where civilizations from the Bronze Age to the World Wars have stacked their layered fortresses. The thought of friends and help tempted us to stray within sight of Malta's southernmost point, just as dusk approached, so night could shroud us as we saw what colors flew over the famous Freeport shipyard. Jubilation: Malta flew the Vs, a row of them along the docks, some red on white, some Europe's gold on blue, huge flags proclaiming faith in Ἄναξ Jehovah's better future.

I was the first to say that we should go ashore to ask for succor, escort, news, but all were eager. So, as night's dark blanket put the seas to sleep, we coasted in toward the hearth-bright marina. Malta's Freeport had been all grunge and iron in pre-*Mukta* days when the seas carried Earth's industry, but joy has reclaimed it since, a spectacle harbor for vessels of sport and play which crowded her docks, their lights ricocheting so joyfully across the night waves that we did not notice crafts behind us closing in until escape was lost. Mitsubishi. I remember, as they raised their lights to let us see their guns, how the seascape patterns of their uniforms shimmered like iridescent beetles. As they forced us in to dock, we could see ships being dismantled and refitted, some stripped to skeletons, decks bleeding sparks as workmen labored on into the night to weld guns onto peaceful ferries. Even the warlike escort which surrounded us were Frankenstein ships, the weld-scars of their augmentation glinting fresh.

We docked as slowly as we dared, lingering long enough to watch troops march away the protesting crew of another freshly captured vessel—a slim yacht flying the French *tricolore* and Europe's ring of stars. We had only minutes to prepare. My comrades hid what they could in secret corners, while I whispered hasty plans to the ship's almost-doctor Lintang Shearwater, Javanese raised in a Mitsubishi bash' near Kuala Lumpur, who had paused medical school for the bash's entry into the war. Together we destroyed my recent medical charts and altered the dates on older ones to make my injuries seem fresh and incapacitating, my splints necessities. Next, in the gaps between my skin and the splints we concealed knives, files, wire cutters, and other ship's tools for which I know no names.

The Mitsubishi boarding party was not ungentle, herding us up onto the deck with no more roughness than haste justified. Fear arrived with the officer who sauntered on after them, young, with a long body, taller even than Tayo and strutting as if he owned the ship and the people on it. Rear Admiral Sugi Yoshida; a Mitsubishi younger than his subordinates reeks of nepotism, and the Japanese he traded with a lieutenant told me at once which tree had dropped this rotten apple. He asked about the ship, not us, the *Shearwater*'s age and history, what grand seafaring epoch she revived—a schoolchild's questions, and the field-trip excitement with which he caressed the ship's wheel almost set me at ease. Almost, but the other Mitsubishi watched their commander's movements too carefully, as caregivers watch those children whose tantrums edge toward violence. Tayo offered our preplanned lie about a Red Crystal aid mission, but the young commander did not have the patience for details. One bored nod and the others dragged us off, for all our protests of peace and Remaker allegiance, leaving their commander to explore the *Shearwater* like a new playhouse.

A cursory interrogation, and the confiscation of my companions' knives, belts, and rope-like Hiveless sashes, prepared us for what an officer assured us would be a brief captivity. The *Shearwater* would be refitted for war. As for ourselves, many Mitsubishi were being held hostage by nearby enemies, and we would be exchanged for them, soon, soon, they repeated in soothing voices.

"Who would trade prisoners for us?" Toni Bajada challenged hotly. "We're civilians, neutral, mostly Hiveless, just here to visit friends, and we're Red Crystal and Remakers." She nodded to the Vs flying beside the trefoil above the officer's desk. "If we're on any side, we're on yours, or are you flying false flags on Malta's honest shores?"

The guards were ready to punish hot words with fists, but a Chinese officer restrained them, fixing calm eyes on defiant Toni. "No false flags. We are true Remakers."

"We're Remakers, hypocrite! You—"

"Many in this war misuse the V of Vs," he interrupted, "but we are loyal to Xiao Hei Wang and will guard them from enemies, all enemies, especially the enemy who holds them prisoner."

Panic. "Someone's captured J.E.D.D. Mason?"

A flat stare in return. "Yes. Cornel MASON." There was a sense of judgment in our captor's calm. "We will rescue our Tenth Director from Alexandria and help them make a new world, safe from Masonic tyranny. You, claiming to support them while harboring a Mason in your crew, are the only hypocrites I see here." A nod at Lex. "Unless that Mason is your prisoner?"

Toni Bajada gaped as if a wolf had just proclaimed that it deserved to wear a borrowed fleece since wolves are sheep inside, as sheep are grass. "You can't be serious . . ."

His stare certainly was.

Escape. My comrades did not need to whisper the word, glances were enough. If these wolves in Remaker clothing realized what I was, how irresistible a trap they could set to lure trusting Ἄναξ Jehovah from the safety of Alexandria.

A long ride in a wagon-cage brought us to the prison camp, too white, too bright, open to the night sky but blasted from above by a light which seemed to bake us to the bone. A honeycomb panopticon, I later learned, was Tully Mardi's name for this, his brainchild, outlined in the pamphlet with which my Enemy retaught the world to make, not prisons, but pens for people. Prisons of the late Exponential Age had an extravagant humaneness, every door and bar perfected by a committee's expensive overthinking, while this had a practicality one step above makeshift. The light, fierce as a lighthouse beacon, blasted down at a semicircle of honeycomb spaces, more kennels than cells, too low to stand up in, stacked four high, and open at the front except for doors of woven wire. As they herded us each to an empty compartment, I could see some prisoners watching us, or hunched on their toilets (the cells' only real seats), but most of them lay huddled in back corners, seeking semi-shelter from the merciless light. Humaneness was reversed here, every feature designed to erode morale: the clinical metal walls, the cramp of crouching, and the merciless blazing of the central spotlight eye which watched us hour on hour on hour. Even that first night, I could feel myself obsessing over our captors' promises: a brief captivity, exchange, freedom, soon, soon—promises which can twist hope and exhaustion into obedience. At least in saner men.

Dawn's kinder light made the camp's structure clearer. The curving outer honeycomb was a hasty new addition, while the stones beneath our feet and the towering flat wall on which the cruel light perched were bone-white limestone, stained brown at the edges by the touch of time. Fort San Lucian—Toni Bajada recognized it—built eight hundred years ago by the Knights Hospitaller to defend this bay against the Ottomans, later repurposed by the British against the French, then Allies against Axis, capitalists against Soviets, EU against the Surge, and now the Mitsubishi against whomever they named enemy—a young fort by Malta's standards, where so many were old when Rome burned Carthage.

Daytime brought semi-liberty, as guards wheeled in breakfast and freed the prisoners to mingle in the yard. They busied us with mandatory exercise and labor, kneading bread dough, shelling peas, whatever kitchen work did not require metal tools, but we found time for talk. All here were the unhappy crews of captured ships, some dragged off the seas, others, like us, lured in by the illusion of a friendly port. These Mitsubishi flew the Vs as pitcher plants fly insects' mating scents, drawing the unwary to a very different consummation. Malta itself had fallen the same way, guile triumphant over the cliffs and bulwarks that have withstood so many sieges. Malta's natives are mainly European or sea-fond Mitsubishi, and both love Europe's new Emperor's beloved Son. So, when a small armada flying Mitsubishi banners and the Vs had puffed their way toward Malta's harbors asking for repairs, they were welcomed—until it was too late. Now Mitsubishi martial law held Malta's streets in silence, supported by some, though not all, of Malta's native Mitsubishi and the many Mitsubishi tourists stranded on this island paradise. Occupation Headquarters lay in Malta's capital, the exquisite eastern port of Valletta. There the iron reins were held, not cruelly, by Admiral Nao Yoshida, a bash'child of the newly promoted Mitsubishi Director Hajime Yoshida, who had taken over Japan's second voting bloc after the suicide of the late Director Kimura. And since the new Director's bash'child was Governor, nepotism had handed this southern port to a grandbash'child, the youthful local tyrant who had boarded the *Shearwater:* Sugi Yoshida. Redwood—that was the nickname he preferred, chosen I think because of his height, but never before had the word made me envision heartwood streaming blood.

Redwood was a petty tyrant by war's standards, gentled by the necessity of supplying prisoners mostly whole, but there was bloodlust behind the glee he took in visiting the camp more often than a port commander needed to, to test his bloodless cruelties. Kenneling was one favorite, leaving victims in the too-small cells for days on end. Light and sound were others, and I have no doubt that it was he who chose, from Tully Mardi's menu of camp designs, this cruelest. Sometimes in the dead of night the watchtower would suddenly focus its beam on one unlucky soul, who would be dragged away for interrogation while loudspeakers barked of some imagined misdemeanor. The threat of worse was constant. Several prisoners in the bottom cells did not join our daily exercise but lay unmoving, moans of sickness and despair lending our days a background of almost-melody, as frog song lends to woodland. Redwood's Roaster was our name for it, the weapon our tyrant carried always on his hip, often caressing it like the hand of a beloved. One shot cooked the nerves and left the victim's whole body wrecked, limp, weak, "For life!" all said, for here in the whirlpool grip of Poseidon's silence, we had no way to learn the Cousins' kind intent in crafting Tiring Guns, nor that the misery would stretch for months, not forever. A lifetime moaning on a bed—that threat weighed down our every motion, every breath, like too-strong gravity. I never saw Redwood fire the weapon, but he threatened constantly, sometimes drawing and aiming, sometimes merely tickling its grip as he invited us to voice complaints. As I watched even fierce Toni Bajada choose silence, I truly understood why Romanova's founders had listed, among our Black Laws, that it is an intolerable crime to deprive a human being of the ability to call for help; with trackers to carry our outcries to the skies, we would have had our liberty in seconds.

"No one's here long," our fellow-prisoners chorused, their resigned version of hope. Every day, Redwood chose a few of us for hostage exchange. It should have been a joyous moment, but Redwood delighted in dragging parents from children, bash'mates from each other's arms, filling a quota of four by choosing one each from of four different crews, while groups of four who begged to go together became food for his next day's malice. Such pointless tyranny. If Redwood had housed us in a cheap hotel or even left us alone in the care of sensible Camp Commander Abe (may his kindness be rewarded), then none of the other prisoners would have risked death to break from reasonable comfort—but every time Redwood laughed in the face of tears, he piled tinder on the pyre that needed only our whispered spark: "We have a plan."

We did. This panopticon was a hasty construction, thin walls and wire cage doors which would easily succumb to the tools I carried in my splints. The tower was our enemy, the great eye which let those in the fortress windows high above us watch our every twitch, as a microscope watches the microbes trapped between two sheets of glass. I was our asset: the hobbling, dazed Jay Doe whom no one would think to watch too carefully. Day by day, we distributed tools, divided tasks, and observed the guard shifts. Day by day, Redwood carried off whom he wished, and every cruelty stirred the whisper: liberty.

The eighth day, he took Lex.

The ninth night, we were ready, and warm drizzle offered the semi-cover we required. I slithered free from my splints, took some minutes to exercise my stagnant limbs, then propped up my splints and jacket with some empty flour sacks to mimic a sleeping body. Right on time, Lintang distracted the watchtower with a coughing fit. I cut the wires of my cage door and dashed to the corner where we guessed their view was weakest.

An old doorway sealed by woven wire led to the substructure. Cutting through should have been easy, but my long-pinioned right hand felt rotted, clumsy, fumbling every agonizing snip. Success. I slipped into an ancient passageway, where the black roots of modern power cables flowed along the surface of the stones like the tendrils of a strangler fig, and followed them to their glutted switchbox heart. One well-aimed chisel-stab and the whole fortress was darkness. I stabbed again, again, twisting, reducing to a gnarled mass the improvised communications cables which could have warned the outside world of our escape. The global silence was friend now as well as foe.

With the great eye blinded, my fellow prisoners surged at once through the unready fortress. I was fastest, first up the shadowed stairs where flashlight beams and cries of confusion advertised our fleeing enemies. I hunted only Redwood. I knew he would be in the watchtower, sleepless with power, the coward heart of the panopticon awake into the night, scoping out victims for a tomorrow which would no longer be his. I found him alone in the blinded tower, clutching his beloved Roaster as he shivered in his chair. I flung the chisel full-force at his hateful face, and his gun clattered off into the darkness as he clutched his bleeding eye.

And here, reader, I did something very foolish. I prowled slowly up that hallway toward the dark and shadowed room, and let the window's shaft of moonlight fall upon my face.

"*Sh-earwa-ater* . . . Jay Doe . . ." he stammered.

Yes. Yes, recognize the helpless, wounded prisoner you scorned, realize which good brave ship and good brave crew you never should have dared to—

「. . . Canner-*hikoku.*」

So many petty sadists know my face.

I didn't quite catch what he'd said, that was the problem. If I had realized he recognized me, I would not have left things as I did, but it's not a version of my name I often hear, and the percussive syllables of Japan's dishonorable honorific for convicted criminals was hard to distinguish from the blubbering of Redwood's terror. I sprang at him, but he slammed a metal door between us which neither I nor comrades could penetrate. Time was now our enemy. Our other surviving foes had sheltered in the fortress's inner chambers, prepared to wait for allies to notice Fort San Lucian had gone dark. The port would soon miss its master. We barricaded the exits so our foes could not escape to give alarm, then fled beneath the cover of the drizzle as the changing birdsong threatened dawn.

Fort San Lucian stands on a promontory, with the shipyard to its west, and to its east the ancient fishing village of Marsaxlokk. The twinkle of lights in the village harbor confirmed Toni's prediction: the villagers were up before the sun, manning their luzzus, wooden fishing boats unchanged since Phoenician times, with brightly painted hulls in cheerful blues, reds, yellows, and eyes on their prows like Jason's *Argo*. Malta's resorts had always offered customers the transgressive indulgence of eating real fish, and the occupiers had quickly conceded that, without *Mukta,* Malta's people needed their ancient food source once again. Into the bay we plunged, swimming up to the bright little crafts whose captains needed no persuasion to help us flee the tyrant. Some hid us among their gear, while other luzzus helped us cling to ropes and drift along between them in the water, under cover of their curving bellies.

We were far out into the bay before the Sun could see or rumor report our great escape. The occupiers were not numerous enough to man every pier in the black of pre-dawn, so the fishermen offered us a choice: ride with them to the sea caves to join Malta's resistance, or steal what ships we liked from the less-guarded outer docks and try our fortunes on the sea. Toni Bajada Shearwater was tempted to stay and fight for home and people, but Providence had docked the *Shearwater* on one of the farthest piers, and she was even more home than Malta. And we had our mission.

We divided those who wished to flee among six ships, the *Shearwater* and five others, while those who chose to stay helped cover our escape by launching other ships, then jumping overboard to swim back to the luzzus while the empty stolen vessels chugged off into the barely brightening morning. By the time the dock-guards cried alarum, nineteen vessels were vanishing into the swelling rain, and, with artillery ships and precious racing vessels speeding off, no one bothered to chase the six we had chosen, all undesirable in one way or another.

Once peaceful waters stretched again horizon to horizon, our capture might have seemed a passing nightmare, if not for our new flotilla of companions, and Lex's empty bunk. Our best hope was to outrun the news of our escape. We sailed east, all ships' captains agreeing that, if Redwood in his pettiness did chase such harmless enemies, he would expect us to flee west toward the Cousins of Tunis, or south toward Masonic Tripoli, not east through day on day of empty seas. It would have been safer to split up, but we discovered too late that only one ship had its food and water stocks intact, and most of our water purification machines had been dismantled or (like ours) removed. The two vessels whose water machines still worked could not supply us all for the long week to Alexandria, but Crete lay almost on our path, and, if Crete proved unfriendly, the other craft could strike north toward Greece, while we turned south toward the imperial capital.

Four days we kept our eastward course, listening to underwater noises through an improvised array and steering away from any telltale tremors. Sleep was dread those nights, wakeless exhaustion alternating with nightmares that we were taken. We *were* taken, a day before we would have sighted Crete, by the lone destroyer *Shimakaze* which loomed over our small flotilla like a gloating dinosaur. We had strayed into the defense perimeter of the great Mitsubishi Armada, whose shapes soon peppered the horizon like a line of fortresses.

Of course they chose the *Shearwater* to draw alongside, our lofty masts and arching sails so beautiful that the Mitsubishi captain himself came with the boarding party to savor the view. He traded friendly questions with Tayo and Lintang, and, as he sent most of his crew out of earshot, with me. ⌜Are you on your way to Tai-kun, Mycroft?⌟

I gasped. Winced. Peered. Hoped? ⌜Are you . . . Manager Kazami?⌟

His gentle nod breathed life into me. This face was a known face, Yū Kazami, a man who stood often at Chief Director Andō's side—better, who stood at Good Jehovah's side! The lieutenant with him I recognized now too, a secretary, Ino, another intimate of Andō's, just distant enough to have been spared his fall. ⌜Yes!⌟ I cried. ⌜Yes, He needs me!⌟ It poured out of me, our desperate hope to bring Jehovah the one thing this war seemed most determined to strip from Him: communication. ⌜Please don't stop us!⌟ I begged. ⌜You know how much He needs me! With me to help Him communicate, maybe He can even broker a truce between your Hive and Caesar, a real Remaker union. But if you hand me to your commanders, they'll just keep me as a resource, they'll never release me to Him. Help us, please! Help Him!⌟

Silence and the intensity in Kazami's eyes told me that he too felt the V-flying Mitsubishi were too hasty in calling MASON enemy. He helped us, what hasty treason might be concealable with the rest of the fleet so near. First he confirmed for us that the lie was official. The Armada's mission was to rescue Good Jehovah from tyrannical MASON, an order straight from the Directorate itself. Kazami could not escort us to Alexandria, not without explaining why the *Shimakaze* strayed a thousand kilometers off course and into hostile waters. Instead, he gave us a Mitsubishi friend-or-foe signal device, a long cable which trails along beneath the ship, capable of sending and receiving low-frequency sound which the global blackout doesn't block. This was how Mitsubishi recognized friendly vessels, and with it we could pass for allies of the fleet. He gave us food, water. He marked our charts, the sea-lanes to avoid, the routes most empty. The crew who had witnessed our encounter he swore to secrecy in J.E.D.D. Mason's honored name. And in return we gave him, every one of us, our strongest, deepest vows that we would destroy all he had given us the moment we reached the Masonic shore, so that nothing would serve any end but to get me to Jehovah, safe and soon.

So smooth, those next four days. The other stolen ships came with us, trusting those who had led them safely out of Malta's prison to bring them safely to lands raiding Mitsubishi could not touch. All was smooth, too smooth, an ease which tempted me to rest. To sleep. And, while I slept, the others . . . overthought things. *Mycroft is weak,* they muttered, *too weak perhaps to keep his promise to good Captain Kazami when dread Caesar demands treason's invaluable fruits: the charts of secret Mitsubishi motions and the friend-or-foe device. These charts show where the Mitsubishi seas give way to Mason's. Let's confirm when we've passed that invisible border and jettison the Mitsubishi equipment then and there, casting Mycroft's temptation to the deep.* And so they did. And so a Mitsubishi submarine prowling the border spotted an unknown squadron and exploded from the seas before us with the thunder of a storming god.

One ship could not chase all of us at once, that was the only thing that saved us. Capture, not kill, was the order for civilian vessels, better to take the best of the herd and leave the others for another day's hunting. The *Shearwater* was not the best of the herd.

That night, we sailed in starlit darkness, showing no lights, stilling our motor so no one could track us by our rumble. I will not pretend we had a plan. To evade the sea border where Mason and Mitsubishi vessels sparred, cautious Tayo took us north, back up the empty sea-lane that had brought us, with three companion vessels clinging to our wake. Despair. All that day and the next, the waves behind us seemed like so many rows of soldiers, whose grim formation gained another phalanx every hour we moved away from Alexandria. Away. And we were out of water—with our goal so close we had not conserved the resource Caesar would shower upon us, literally, when we reached the palace. Water. Have humans been the remakers of this planet and ourselves ten thousand years, and yet we cannot cut this old umbilical, that binds us all to dwell by pond and stream, or else face death by distance?

The next night, lights on the horizon gave us chase, and a tiny stealth craft, black as night sea, crept close enough to hook our prow before we realized anything had launched from the encroaching foe. Hope mixed with shame as Secretary-now-Lieutenant Ino hailed us in the name of Captain Kazami. His news cut deep. Redwood's curses at our escape had reached the western arm of the Armada, whose commander—Redwood's grandba'pa Admiral Yoshida—was taking the incident very gravely. The *Shimakaze* was one of a dozen ships ordered to hunt the *Shearwater,* that was what my boastful moment letting Redwood see my face had brought upon my innocent companions. My name too had surfaced as Redwood's distress call ricocheted from ship to ship, though the official orders didn't mention me, and Kazami thought no one believed it—crying such an implausible wolf as Mycroft Canner sparked derision more than fear.

Would Kazami help us again?

Not as freely as he had before, not with more than a hundred crew who now knew we were their hunt's prize, and would win promotions for reporting a captain's treason. If we so much as came within clear sight of the *Shimakaze*, Kazami would have no choice but to seize us all. The best Kazami could offer now was a new chart with a zigzag course northeast toward Rhodes—Crete had fallen completely and was now the hub of the Armada, but Rhodes lay only half a day further, fortressed from antiquity like Malta, and standing as bulwark to defend the Masonic Turkish coast. On Rhodes flew side by side the European stars and the Masonic Square and Compass, and there our mission and my native Greek would win us instant aid. If only we had gone that far. But the supplies Kazami had gifted us were exhausted, the ships with water filters lost, and our headaches and fatigue from dehydration were starting to give way to grimmer signs. Ino's chart indicated that the smaller islands of Kasos and Karpathos—a day closer than Rhodes—were still Greek and free. Thus it was on the last day of October—two weeks after our escape from Malta, and the same day my kind successor paused in nurturing the newborn Pass-It-On network to watch the videos of Sniper's cruel captivity—that four very thirsty crews approached the southern tip of Kasos. No, not thirsty—we were past feeling the thirst, already entering the long, slow fade.

We approached a C of rocky cliffs ringing a bay where azure waters lapped at sandy beach. Our hearts leapt as a lone swimmer, her bathing suit as bright as striped reef fish, waved both her arms in welcoming excitement. Our three companion vessels, shallow-hulled and small, sailed in to meet her, but prudent Tayo would not take the *Shearwater* into a bay of unknown depth. So we waited outside the rocky entrance, and watched the bather greet our friends and lead some up a hill path, while the others made their ships fast in the bay. The itch of happy impatience held us twenty minutes. Then figures returned: five, fifteen, fifty, carrying . . . no, running, tackling, pinning our poor companions to the ground, and swarming the three ships like carrion flies. No chance to save the others—we fled without discussion, hesitation, hope. Without water. Another day to Rhodes. Lintang said we would still be conscious in a day, but the *Shearwater* is not an easy craft for thirst-weakened limbs to steer. And then it was that our desperate eyes turned on Kasos's companion island, Karpathos, and saw flying above her fawn-pale beach the Red Crystal.

Hope and caution compromised as we chose a hidden curve of coast and lowered our jolly boat. Hoel, Dian, Echo, Toni Bajada, and Maxime loaded themselves with empty water jugs and set out across the beach, while Marvel stayed with the jolly boat, and I remained on the *Shearwater* with Tayo and Lintang. Three hours we watched Phoebus in his journey, before a panicked Toni Bajada stumble-raced back across the sands, supporting on her shoulders a stranger in a shapeless hospital uniform.

Their tale was quickly told, Toni's words hot and dark, the stranger's weak and feverish. A stately resort-villa stood on the hills above us, with roofs of terra cotta tile, courtyards, trellised walkways, tennis courts. Through these extensive grounds patients meandered in hospital blue, tending flowers, hanging laundry, sporting in the sun, or simply gazing down toward the gray sea in silent melancholy. Hoel, Dian, Echo, and Maxime had been welcomed by nurses at the hospital door, though distrustful Toni Bajada hid in a rhododendron hedge and clambered to the roof to watch their reception in the courtyard below. A woman had met them, tall and queenly, with a confidence in her slow steps which might have made Redwood whimper like a pup—the shaking stranger named her: Doctor Callias del Sól. As attending patients served sandwiches and lemonade, the doctor asked the newcomers about their journey, occupations, and told of her hospital, how she offered humane harbor to many who would otherwise have wound up in Mitsubishi war camps. When the meal was finished, in an instant, she raised a weapon in her hand and fired, and our four comrades had toppled, writhing, gasping, flopping on the ground like half-crushed worms.

"Gorgon," the panting prisoner supplied. "The Cousins' cursed Tiring Guns." He had faced the same fate when first brought here, the cruel false hope of snacks and lemonade before the blast. Pasha Mellifex was his name, a Masonic Blacksleeve, captured by Mitsubishi in the fall of Crete. He had proudly refused his captors' offer of peacewash, that indelible pink-purple dye that marks the hands and cheeks of those who agree to labor as War Servicers. A Soldier of the Empire, he had said, would rather languish in a prison camp than give one hour's labor to Caesar's enemy. So they had shipped him here. One shot from the doctor's Gorgon and he too had collapsed into a universe of nausea, as he described it, head thundering, all outer senses blinded as the blood seemed to riot in every vein. Days, hours, all was torture blur as pain outlined every nerve fiber, until there came a sour taste and, minutes later, ease. This was the truth of Doctor del Sól's 'humane' haven: her 'patients' were not injured but afflicted by the Gorgon's artificial agony, which bound them to the hospital more irredeemably than any chain. The only respite was a special medicine, which Dr. del Sól doled out with iron strictness. Even as we watched, today's dose was wearing off for Pasha, his words slurring, fever sweat beading on his brow. Peacewash offered the only true escape. Every few days, a Mitsubishi warship came requesting peacewashed, and those prisoners the doctor judged the most reliable (or broken) were offered the chance to labor in kitchens or engine rooms, with the promise of a constant supply of medicine as toil's reward. This was the secret of Karpathos's liberty. Stubborn Masons, European resistance fighters, civilians defiant in their innocence—Dr. del Sól's 'hospital' was a factory for reducing the proudest prisoners to compliant War Servicers, and in return the vast Armada left the island free.

I saw my own horror reflected in the others' faces as we watched Pasha drift into a torture-fever which turned all words to moans. Echo, Hoel, Maxime, and Dian were now trapped in that same horror we had seen inflicted by gleeful Redwood. But that was not the worst, dear as these friends were. The worst was that it takes at least six crew to sail the *Shearwater*. Six fit crew, and none of us—Tayo, Toni, Lintang, Marvel, or my limping self—was close to fit.

Despair and dusk swept over me together as I sat in the stern and watched the sea lap at the stars. Plans wove and unraveled in my thirst-weakened brain, steps mixing out of order: we sail to get water to make us fit to sail to get water, or send the jolly boat to send back intel via trackers we no longer have. As the dark darkened, silent footfalls brought Mercer Mardi to my side, the night light playing off of silvery accent fibers in her black Brillist sweater. „It's wrong," she said in German.

„Yes," I agreed. „It's all gone wrong. Your War, or Apollo's, either would have been better than this."

„Not the War." Her dark eyes seemed like night itself drawn into focus as they turned on me. „Your Data. You're working from false Data."

„From not enough Data." I sighed. „I keep reaching for Resources I don't have. Databases, Voices. If only I could have the Censor's Office again, all the Umbilicals of the World for a Minute, half a Minute—"

Mercer's brow wrinkled, a teacher's disappointment. „You don't need more Data, Mycroft, you need to use what you have. This is too cruel."

„Yes, all too cruel."

„The *Tiring Gun,*" she stressed. „Agony, Nausea, Hour on Hour of Pain, does that sound like something Cousins would create?"

„I . . . No, it doesn't."

„Is it consistent with the Symptoms you saw on Malta?" she pressed.

„No, it isn't!" My mental whirlwind narrowed to one focused gust. „It isn't a Tiring Gun! It isn't anything like one! And Redwood didn't have a Medicine to make the Symptoms stop—he'd have taunted us with it if he had. Whatever this Doctor's using, it's not a Tiring Gun. What is it? The Symptoms fade quickly with the Medication, then return more slowly, so . . . "

„What else was strange?" Mercer quizzed me, her coaxing smile almost the shadow of her Headmaster's. „What other Violation was unnecessary, cruel?"

„Hospitality!" I cried. „Why the fuss of Lemonade when they were begging for Water? Why offer Hospitality? Both times, for Pasha too who was already a Prisoner, why not just shoot them right away? Why offer phony Hospitality? The Doctor needed them to eat, to drink something, something that couldn't be concealed in tasteless Water. It's a Drug. A Drug that's activated by an ordinary Stun Gun—they always warn you that the Vibrations can burst pharmaceutical Nanocapsules. And the Medication, it could be an Antitoxin, or another Drug, or something that manipulates Withdrawal Symptoms?"

"Lintang!" I shouted. "Lintang, get out your med kit! Test Pasha's blood! Toni, did you see the doctor's gun? Did it look like Redwood's?"

No, it didn't. I didn't wait to see Mercer's smile as I raced across the deck, but I could feel it behind me, cold fading to warmth, as a blanket on a cold night makes bare legs shiver at first touch but gradually reflects the body's heat and becomes comfort. The doctor's weapon was indeed a common stun gun—Pasha's description was precise enough to let me name the model. Lintang's blood tests detected a powerful antinausea medication in Pasha's bloodstream, and on third spectrum a lactam compound turned up in the Kaiser-Hackenholt well, which Lintang said might react with stomach acid to cause the symptoms we had seen. Our comrades had been drugged with nanocapsules broken open by the stun gun, and the 'medication' rationed out to prisoners combined respite with more poison, first relieving then reinforcing the very symptoms they pretended to treat. If we could get our comrades out, a day's rest would clear their systems. But how, when we were so weak ourselves? Force? Impossible. Stealth? Difficult. A trade? A bluff? The plan, once I had knowledge in my hands, was easy. Convincing my comrades that I, most precious, should be the one to face danger implementing the plan, that was a harder sell. But there was a real stun gun to grapple with, and with an acceladreneline shot in my veins, I can shrug off a stun gun in seconds—Saladin and I had trained for that.

It was a paradise, that villa: swaying laurel, gardens, salt, and sun. The prisoners' silent stares were full of warning as I strolled up to the gates. The queenly doctor welcomed me, offered a luxuriant lounge chair, an ear for my lies, and glistening lemonade. As I raised the glass, I opened the vial hidden in my palm and poured in an ammonia mixture concocted by Lintang. One swirl of the spoon and I watched with triumph as powdery grains precipitated to the bottom of the glass. We had guessed right: these pharmacapsules were designed for the low pH of lemonade, so adding a base made them fall out of solution, concentrating the drug at the bottom of the glass and leaving the remainder of the lemonade vilely ammonia-flavored but safe enough. I sipped it and pretended to nibble sandwiches as our small talk dwindled. It seemed almost slow motion as she rose, drew out the harmless gun, and fired.

"Now to join your friends," she pronounced with a mix of boredom and glee.

I did teeter—one does as the muscles briefly fail—but I turned that teeter into a launching crouch and was on her like a mantis. Courage I grant her—she seemed not to notice the knife at her throat as she twisted her face toward me in astonishment.

"How?"

I threw my head back in a hearty laugh. "A Gorgon? I had my treatment ages ago. Your tech's out-of-date, doctor." My head was throbbing from the gun's effects, but I stretched out my false laughter to hide the tremors.

No one around us had moved, the nurses frozen in terror, the three attendant prisoners staring, hungry with hope.

"You . . ." she began, "you have a treatment for Gorgons?" There it was, the moment when the wide eyes of shock gave way to the keen eyes of greed, a special greed familiar from countless nights in Thisbe's room—a witch's greed for secrets. "Counter or cure? Or both?" she asked. "Do you have the treatment here?" There it was. She wasn't really using a Gorgon, but a witch knew how priceless a counterspell would be, and was ready to believe that such a treatment might thwart her potions, too.

I grinned. "I have it in my brains and in my blood." I eased my knife back from her throat a little, afraid the trembling in my arm might make me accidentally cut.

"Shall we begin again?" this brave hostess invited, dignified as her hands pressed gently against my threatening arms. "What do you want?"

A bargain. My demands: water, supplies, my comrades' safe return, some days to rest, new paint to erase the hunted name of *Shearwater,* and all the charts and data she could supply about the nearby islands and the Mitsubishi fleet. The prisoner who had helped us, Pasha Mellifex, and the three others who had witnessed my miraculous immunity would come with us—liberty the price of their silence. In return, when we were safe aboard the ship and leaving harbor, I would leave behind a buoy and, attached to it, the priceless antidote to the Gorgons.

As I spelled my demands out term by term, I felt my prisoner's body change within my grip, caution's stiffness melting to softness, her eyes focusing their study on my face, my eyes, my stubble-darkened cheeks. My ear. She switched to Greek. «And where is Greece's most infamous child going once you leave my island?»

I thought hard, reader, trusting almost nothing in this fractured world, but I do trust my ability to recognize a certain appetite that wells within some eyes that gaze on Mycroft Canner. Sniper is not the only one with fans. «Home to my Ἄναξ.»

Her smile, before her words, granted all that I asked and more. She was warmth itself from that point on, this hostess of mind games, feasting us, delighting in the tales of our adventures, especially when she learned we were the famous escapees who had bested Malta's Redwood. After a few nights' storytelling, she was more tickled than angered when it became clear my cure for the Gorgon was a lie. She offered extra help: two days to acquire fresh rope, three for spare engine parts, four to dye our sails red so our repainted ship would look more different from the description circulated for the Mitsubishi manhunt, then if we stayed through Friday, her doctors could make real progress with Marvel's injured wrist and my concussion, and Saturday, fresh food would come, and surely we could stay for the weekly Shakespeare read-through Saturday night so I could be her Dromio of Ephesus. So, treat by treat, she anchored us with chains of kindness, and we lost the first week of November in the witch's happy halls before a night of gunfire off the south coast reminded us there was an outside world.

«But you can't sail south,» she warned. «Or east. The Mitsubishi Armada has gathered for their great assault on Rhodes. Even if you seem to be an innocent ship, without a Mitsubishi friend-or-foe device you'll be rounded up as a resource. There's only one path now. You must head northwest to the Cyclades in the southern Aegean Sea. There you will find a naval graveyard, where the brave united volunteers of Europe and MASON tried to slice the Mitsubishi force in half, to keep the Crete-based southern fleet from supporting the northern forces at Gallipoli and Çanakkale as they tried to seize the Dardanelles and pierce Istanbul. The Mitsubishi persevered but lost a hundred ships among the Cyclades, and the defiant remnants of their hodgepodge enemy still circle—half resistance and half pirate now—handing out death to any foe which strays within the Cycladic island ring to threaten sacred Delos. There, Greek divers brave Poseidon's depths to loot the carcasses of slaughtered ships, and there, by barter or persuasion, you may secure a Mitsubishi friend-or-foe device, your only hope of safe passage through enemy waters.»

With heavy hearts we boarded our ship, red-sailed now with her upper hull a cheerful marigold, and the sweet, deceptive name of *Circe's Gift*. We left at dusk, so Night at least could be our escort northward to those waters where dead far outnumber living. They outnumber us everywhere, you know, reader, the silent, dead majority, who watch what we children do with the world they toiled to make for us. Sometimes I think I see them, schooling through the air like birds too black, and where no birds should be.

I slept through the next dim day, and took the night watch with Echo in the hold, manning the apparatus through which we listened for motor noises and other danger signs. "That's . . ." Echo handed me the earpiece. "There's a weird thumping sound, not like a motor."

I put the pad to my ear and felt rather than heard thunder, blood thunder so deafening that I could not have told you if there was also sound. "Tie me up," I snapped. "Now."

"What?"

"It's Cannerbeat. The fever's coming. Quickly!"

Now Echo too recognized the rhythm, exaggerated through the water and the ship herself as the hull became an echo chamber for the terrifying art that Earth's morbid musicians make from the old recordings of my monster heartbeat. From there, my memories have neither line nor form. I was not with Echo but with Saladin as voices pleaded for calm and sanity, and ropes grew tight across struggling limbs—Chiasa Mardi's or my own? I never saw the ships that intercepted us, Cycladic resistance pirates who proclaimed with Cannerbeat the perimeter past which no foe ship would be left alive. As Tayo begged and bartered up on deck, a stream of patient visitors sat with me in my blood fog. Lieutenant Ino from the *Shimakaze* squatted by me first, offering brave but somber tales of Rhodes's resistance. Then I thought I saw the bright swish of Leigh Mardi's Cousin's wrap, but it was black-eyed Kohaku Mardi who sat down beside me, the purple of his Deputy Censor's jacket off-black in the cabin's evening dim.

"I've lost my path, Kohaku," I choked out. I remember that my throat hurt, dry and rasping, but how did I hurt it? Laughter? Screams? "It's my own fault, I crossed the Mitsubishi and let them know I did, but I never imagined such reach. The whole sea's hunting me."

"No, not the sea." Kohaku's words were voiceless, all breath, like wind through the brown leaves of drought-dead oak. "Older and more immortal is the enemy we knew we would awaken with our war. Distance."

"Distance," I repeated, and felt an oceanic echo in the word, a new and crueler facet of Jehovah's unrelenting Peer. "It is your war, isn't it, Kohaku? I thought it wasn't, that it was Jehovah's war instead, but here are Mitsubishi battling Masons over land, just as you predicted."

"My war has come," the number-prophet answered, slowly. "So has Tai-kun's, Perry's, Danaë's, Apollo's. Distance makes one war a hundred wars. They speciate, like sparrows breeding alone on every island until they no longer recognize each other's chirps. See these Cycladic freedom fighters? They wage a rebels' war for home and liberty; they would no more abandon their islands to escort you to distant Tai-kun than your Shearwaters would abandon the dream of Tai-kun's better world to guard the Cyclades."

A dry sob hurt. "Then was it all for nothing?" I had to ask. "Jehovah's Act, trying to make two sides worth dying for? Did it all fail?"

"No. This is a fractal war. The larger shapes still lend their structure to the whole, and larger powers, by forging their macro-peace, will forge the thousand micro-peaces, too." His smile was shadow. "And not everything has fractured. While less-prepared Hives fight their thousand wars, we who anticipated war planned long ago how we would battle Distance. Tully reached Sniper, my numbers reached quick-acting Vivien, and far-seeing Apollo left Utopia his plan, one plan, one war, which now unites their actions from Luna City to Antarctica. If you find them, they will guide you safe across this little sea. But do not anger them. Apollo's war is not your Tai-kun's war, and if you harm their war plans, then the Delians in arms will turn on you—yes, even you."

"You know I would never—"

"Your companions would." Kohaku's words were quick as a cracking branch. "Mistake not sea ships for their cousins beyond the skies. Seaborn or no, this crew are part of the Earthly majority, and are as prone to distrust Lord Apollo's homebred aliens, whom all Earth fears may rain down arrows soon as deadly as their patron's. And even if you do reach Alexandria, do not expect rest and an easy welcome there, where all the darts and blades of humankind and Distance too converge on That Being least ready for them. No, in Alexandria shall but begin your next labor, and then the next, and then the next. You know what you owe, and that one lifetime—ten lifetimes—will never pay it. Before you've sweated out your years as oarsman on Apollo's flagship, you would have to lead Utopia and all of us to some new world, new state, so untouched by your enemy Distance that there the very tools we hone to battle him, our oars and sails and ships, are yet undreamed. So long as Lord Apollo, god who ever leads men onto ships, still finds new worlds to make his distant aim, so long you will follow."

I couldn't breathe. We rarely call the deadly archer by this title, but he is Apollo Ἐπιβατήριε, Lord of Embarkations, the god who leads us on and off these fragile craft that battle mighty Distance. His is not prosperity's travel that circulates us settlement to settlement as coins from purse to purse—for that, praise friendly Hermes. No, Apollo's voyages are those that defy maps, aiming—like his bright arrows—worlds away, invisibly beyond all sight but his, and if humans survive such voyages, we fall upon our knees and call landfall itself a miracle. An oarsman on Apollo's flagship. There would be no tardy mercy here, no wise favoring goddess to weave out a kind old age despite Olympus's grudges, not for a parricide. A weariness poured over me, as dense as water and as suffocating. Wise Kohaku too seemed to reflect the same weariness, past all enduring, those eyes which digest all the churning problems of our present broken down by what they glimpsed ahead. I remember thinking that some ancient spirit, commanded back from grave's rest to toil once more beneath the bitter sun, could not be wearier than we.

Now bright Leigh Mardi visited again—summoned by the whiff of gloom like firefighters by smoke—bringing a rainbow of fellow Cousins with her, colleagues from Casablanca, some known, most unknown, somber in their long parade. Lordly Aeneas followed with grim words of blood, then playful Luther, unforgiving Jules, and sleep's black must have overtaken night's black in that stream of hazy visits, for memory insists that godlike Achilles visited me that night, and another figure of pure nightmare, his childish face grown hard, bearing weapons of grim imagination whose mere sight scattered the bravest souls like birds. But it was not truly he. That kindly child never became this war-hardened monster—he made sure he did not, for all our sakes. But, in my mourning, did I ever thank him?

Sunlight restored my sanity (such as it is), dawn's rays with their promise of second chances streaming through the aft window. Dawn's sun at our backs? A westward course? Not southward toward our Goal? Lintang brought breakfast, liberty, and the grim answer. We faced a choice of evils. The assault on Rhodes had begun, the teeming Mitsubishi and tenacious Empire sowing fire across the deep. Everything east of Crete was battle now, war's maw open to swallow every ship. The Scylla to this Charybdis was for us to turn west and sail back around the whole of Crete, then set course south into more peaceful waters. This path too had its terrors, pirates and naval mines spread by Greek islanders to keep the Mitsubishi fleet away, but the Cycladic rebels—delighted when the four prisoners we had freed from del Sól's island volunteered to join them—had sold us not only a new Mitsubishi friend-or-foe device but a chart of the mines as well, so careful navigation would guard us from the invisible, instant strikes that snatched ships—one here, one there—to glut the hungry deep.

For two strange, cloudy days, the war might have been another haunting dream. From time to time, a distant Mitsubishi vessel pinged us, but left in peace when our friend-or-foe device replied in kind. But when the second dusk stained the overcast with crimson, three craft approached us, swift, painted with cunning camouflage. These were the pirates the rebels had warned us of, too small to battle warships but happy to prey on any smaller vessels north of Crete and trade the spoils to whichever side paid more. We spotted them early and raced away, hoping to evade until night shrouded us, but the *Shearwater* was built for history, not speed, and fear swelled meter by lost meter until it birthed a desperate plan. Our chart showed moored mines nearby, part of the Greek defenses, with a narrow safe path zagging through; if these hunters knew those waves held death, they might not dare follow us in, and if they did follow . . . for my unready companions, a trap where we did not even see the foeman's face would be the easiest first blood. Nine weeks of war, reader, yet somehow, luck and warning shots on Malta had kept these Seaborn still unbloodied.

No one would look at me as we counted the slothful minutes toward our invisible goal. Some busied themselves with ropes, or charts, checking our path. Others just sat amid the breeze and gentle ship sounds, praying inside as they watched the closing hunters: turn back in peace, turn back before—the shockwave struck first, a bulging of the sea beneath us, as if some vast creature had clenched its muscle at an insect's sting. An instant later, a pillar of white water erased the foremost of our pursuers, leaving an obelisk of slowly falling mist-cloud, tinged sunset gold for the moments before black smoke erupted from its base in a firework pattern of too many fluffy arms. The engine noises of the other vessels changed, and I saw the foam-churn of hasty deceleration. I heard Marvel cry out that someone was in the water, and somehow kind instincts trumped war instincts as Tayo reversed our engines to let her shipmates haul the victim—our victim—aboard. As Lintang bent over the corpse and Tayo fired up the engines once again, the sea's back clenched a second time, the deck beneath us bucked like a colt in panic, and a new tower of foam-churn was above us, roar and deluge slapping me down with its cascading thunder. A second mine? Chemical smoke was in my mouth, my eyes, while the planking tilted beneath me like a carnival ride; I had not known that wood can scream. I remember a little chorus line of flame tongues dancing on the wooden rail before me, and I think I must have watched them, stupefied, until someone (Maxime?) rushed up with an extinguisher. Next was all staggering and orders, pulling this rope, fetching that, clonking my clumsy head on some piece of the moving system that the Shearwaters worked as perfectly as musicians their instruments. At some point I glimpsed the mass of yellow emergency foam that now covered (or replaced?) a section of our hull. At some point I gaped up at sails in flame. In the worst of it, they made me board the jolly boat, and I rested there long enough to put the name 'burns' to my stinging cheek and arms. But with time, each shout grew less frantic than the last, and fire's orange gave way at last to starlight blue.

"You can climb out, Mycroft. We're through."

We were through, somehow, in the peace of night as even the waves grew quiet. I remember we lay on the deck, a strangely healthy-feeling exhaustion as we gulped the salty air. "That was a terrible plan." Tayo said it, Tayo who conceived it, and she laughed. We all laughed, full-bodied, healing laughter. Sleep found me in that darkness as the planks and cables played their creaking lullaby.

Waking found me there too, my first sight the ashy remnants of our mainsail hanging limply from the blackened gaff. No wind. No sky beyond the fog. No hum. No motor. Echo's face as she offered morning porridge confirmed my fears. Some of our sails had been saved by flame-fighting spray-packs on the yards, modern eyesores much resented by the crew but mandated on ships where Cousins sail (thanks, Mom). These had preserved the headsails in the vessel's prow, and the higher tiers of gorgeous square sails on her foremast—topgallant and royal, such heroic names—but the lower foresails had burned, and nothing remained on our mainmast but ashen strips. As for the motor's silence, the engine was reparable, and the rudder and propeller could be replaced once we chipped through the safety foam, but printing replacement parts requires power, motors require power, and the generator was hopeless, the main battery cracked and dead.

'No matter,' hubris boasted in my heart. 'We have not dared Distance to the field without our spare spears ready. We have our backup generator, our emergency battery.' No, grave Tayo answered. Our sojourn in the ghost-glutted Cyclades had not been without sacrifice. For the chart of the mines and the priceless Mitsubishi friend-or-foe device, Tayo had traded away our backup generator and our second battery. Now we had only our sails left—or a third of them. So sovereign Poseidon had, blade by blade, disarmed us. But what of that? In braver days, my ancestors battled this sea on one-log crafts with single sails. Many had won with less than we had now.

Or lost with more.

Fog held us, protective but oppressive, like the blanket-heavy cover over a birdcage that lulls the prisoner to doze. All that day, as we improvised means to raise the spare and studding sails that had sat bundled in our hold, the walls of misty gray erased horizon and sky, and locked us in perpetual twilight. There was little pride when we gazed up at our ingenious new sail plan, our muscles burning with the labor, only to see the canvas hanging slack. Becalmed. In this all-powerful age, when humanity's great hand reaches the breadth of forty thousand Earths to pluck the icy fruits of asteroids and gas giants with which to reforge the Martian planet in our image, could I sit eight hundred tiny kilometers from Alexandria and be becalmed?

Yes.

Yes, and as blank skies threatened a long united siege of sea and air, my shipmates began to count and re-count our remaining supplies. I remember the coldness in Tayo's eyes that night when I refused my dinner ration, preferring, as I claimed, to stretch my limbs.

"Thinking of visiting the cold locker?" she tested.

I heard gasps as the others remembered where we had stored our dead pirate until we could improvise a ritual for burial at sea.

I didn't want to see their faces. "We're short on food, it's good meat, and I know how to make it keep."

They didn't stop me. Did you judge them guilty, Furies, since they didn't stop me?

The next days were strained, no eye contact, but it wasn't just the crew's . . . awareness of my private meals that killed our smiles. Obsession had seized us all, obsession with our food, our water, with the horizons, with the sails above all, every creak making us hope sailcloth would billow back to life. I began to obsess about how thin the planks beneath us were, and how preposterous the contraptions of wood and woven hemp with which we tried to bridle to our wills a planet's air. Oh, there were some lackluster breezes, and what there was our angled staysails caught, but it mostly blew the wrong direction, north against our path. A westward current was our main hope, but more and more I wondered: What were we doing here? We humans are shaped for grassy plains and riverbanks where sweet waters fatten plump fruits beneath a friendly sun, not for this wasteland, thirst and death. When the overcast retreated on the fourth night, I looked up at the returning stars and found them, for the first time in my life, not beautiful. How near it is, Apollo. How near that black and airless ocean where no sailor can tread water, nor stranded vessel hope to catch a fatty fish or thirst-easing drizzle. Suddenly, Space itself seemed a co-conspirator, allied with Air and Sea in their slow siege. No, not a mere co-conspirator. Chief Conspirator is Space's title, the vastest and deadliest facet of our threefold foe, whose true terror these ocean terrors preview for our species, as children's ball games, with their scraped knees and bitter losses, preview the missiles that you and I, Apollo, loosed upon each other in the first battle of this war. Was this the threat you sensed, Apollo? When you stabbed Caesar? When you learned that Mirai Feynman—Utopia's greatest entomologist—had been too frightened of the black to reach for Mars? I know now what Mirai Feynman must have felt, what I felt that night, staring up into the darkness as I finally understood Poseidon's power. That night, I lost the will to battle—the will to battle for the stars.

But it returns, contagious, shared from breast to breast, the ancient spark that has died out a thousand times but never yet in every breast at once.

We thought it was a fishing net at first, the gentle tangle at our prow. Then we saw the swirls around us in the water, far out to either side, texturing the waves like kelp strands only colorless. Next something reflective appeared ahead, broadening as we approached until many reflections sparkled in a mass, the water's surface dazzling like the facets of some undulating gem. Our slowness slowed further, the gentle tangles catching us as we approached what seemed to be an island of yellow diamond, broader than a playing field, and blinding as the Sun above. One of Apollo's sacred dolphins breached beside us, then another, and as a whole pod leapt about our bow we caught the glint of lights and robot steel. My heart leapt with them, these playful ambassadors of all Earth's future.

"Ahoy!" I cried. "Ahoy, Utopia!"

We waved our arms, and spotted colored lights as the U-beasts that schooled among the dolphins fixed sensors on us. One poked a sparkling seahorse head out of the water, another a turtle's beak, a third a cloud of pinprick lights on jointed wires delicate as shrimps' legs, while something whale-sized—several somethings?—arched up to snatch a breath behind our stern. The crew cried out in wonder as a golden swarm of flying fish soared higher than our deck rail and there assembled into a six-eyed sea-dragon, exquisite in the sunlight as the many wing-fins became scales along a ribbony body that pearlesced a tender pink over the gold.

"We're friends!" we cried in triumph. "We need help! We've lost our generator. Can you send a message to Utopia?" Our tale poured out in fragments, stilted by our uncertainty as to what level of comprehension lay behind the dragon's six-eyed stare: a dog's? A child's? A computer intelligence, godlike and unknowably beyond our own? We had voiced only a few pleas when a blue light kindled in the dragon's outermost eyes and projected on our deck in lazer letters and eight languages:

> This farm and what it yields are Delian, and so vital that we measure their loss at many lives. Whosoever robs or harms them is our enemy, and will be met as such.

"This . . . farm?"

"It's an energy farm." Hoel was leaning far over our prow, I remember their French and Breton nation-strat bracelets reflecting off the floating facets on the water. "They're batteries. It's harvesting sun, probably sea energy too, recharging them."

"And recharging the U-beasts," Maxime added, pointing to transparent cables trailing from the snowy belly of a sea-bear, which lolled on its blue-furred back as laughing dolphins nuzzled it in play.

"Batteries," Lintang repeated like a spell.

We all stared at Utopia's stern herald. "Let us have one. Please! That's all we need!"

Red lights kindled in the dragon's middle eyes and ranged across us like targeting sights.

"We're friends!" I cried. "Friends of Utopia! They'd say yes in a heartbeat if they knew our mission. Can't you send a message?"

No flicker in the steady blue words projected on our planking.

"Maybe it can't send a message," Dian guessed. "Maybe it's out of contact from the blackout. Maybe they all are, waiting here for instructions all alone."

We surveyed the many faces that stared up at us, the gray of natural dolphins subtle among their bright synthetic playfellows.

"We should wait," I counseled. "The Delians will come sooner or later to get their batteries, and the U-beasts will probably send one of their number to report our presence. We're safe here. All we have to do is wait."

We waited cheerfully at first. Hoel and Dian dove down to repair the rudder and other outside damage, while Echo dove deeper, exploring the transparent tendrils of the farm as they trailed down into the depths. The U-beasts and dolphins helped some, making a game of helping us remove unneeded foam, and one brought us a fish, but our verbal requests—for water, for communications, for permission to briefly plug our printer into the farm's outputs—met only stares. Morale buckled anew when the winds returned, and we discovered we were trapped and drifting, trapped in the transparent generator tendrils, and drifting westward quickly, too quickly for our weakened sails to counter. Our fourth dawn on the floating farm found us halfway back to Malta.

"There's nothing to fear!" I remember repeating as Tayo passed around the water ration. "Utopia will find us. We'll have the best help in the world when they do!" It was easy for me to say, I, the only one who knew Utopia's devotion to our Alien. I, the only one who wasn't hungry.

How bad I am at reading warning signs. Of all kinds. These were Neverlanders, I kept thinking, Utopian explorers of a yester-age, and what's more, they were believers in Jehovah, His Good Plan. However much my newborn fear of grim Poseidon might weigh down my coward bosom, the Shearwaters were native to this element, exempt from fear! I didn't dream the meaning of their quietness that day, their long and somber glances at the bobbing batteries as bright as gold. At the barometer. At tall clouds mounting in the distance, and the haze-ringed evening sun. When they urged me to take my rest belowdecks, I felt nothing but relief that one more happy dawn would bring an ever surer chance of Delian ships arriving, splendid on the waves. What would they look like? Apollo's warships sleek as rockets, with escort clouds of flying metal fish?

Movement awoke me, not the ship's tossing—though that was violent—but a larger movement, spinning, dragging, wrong. I heard driving rain and muffled shouts. I rushed to the deck, where spray and downpour drenched me to the skin in seconds. Explosions of white water crashed over the ship's rails, filling the air so blizzard-dense with froth that I could barely see my shipmates, even with the brightly colored safety harnesses they had strapped on for the storm. I strapped on my own and tethered it to the jack line as they had taught me. I staggered toward my comrades, still feeling that wrongness to our motion, not just storm tossing but something in the depths, as if some vast hand were winding the gears of a watch and we sat on its mainspring. I was about to shout and offer help but cried out in grief instead as I watched my friends haul over the rails the gold hulk of a battery. My heart broke as I remembered Kohaku's warning that, Seaborn or no, my earthly crew would never trust the homebred aliens whom all Earth fears. Horror at them, at human failure, flared heartbreak-strong as I watched Marvel's hooked knife sever the transparent umbilicals that still clung to the stolen solar treasure, but that horror only had time for one sob before another took its place.

The sea's surface activated. I have no other word for it. It wasn't an explosion—every wave crashing across our bow was that—this was different. This was the surface of the waves, of every wave, before, behind, around us, all suddenly white with frothing motion, fierce but tiny, as if a million seafoam spirits were battling each other confined within the topmost inch of sea. The dense-packed batteries which swirled across the waves swirled faster, wrong, moving against the waves, against storm-winds and gravity, herding together like frightened cattle or clotting blood cells. Like life. I saw the structure suddenly, the vast transparent arms with batteries studded along them like knobs on a rough-shelled tortoise. What churned the water's surface white around us were tendrils, tender as cilia, the thrashing feelers of a wounded living thing. Or programmed thing. It was a U-beast, the whole solar farm one creature, from the glittering island surface to the tendrils that caressed the lightless depths. It held us, this wonder-horror brainchild of Utopia, it held us, gripped us, twisted us against the currents as it struggled—to what? To drown us? Or just to free itself from this intruding, harming hulk?

"We're friends!" I screamed against the storm, and against my comrades' sins. "Not enemies! Forgive us! Please! We meant no harm! We did it to reach Ἄναξ Jehovah! To help the Alien!"

Walls of white water knocked me to the boards, which bucked under me, tilting away until the stern at my feet seemed like a floor, and I could gaze straight down into the waves where the structure of the vast farm-creature spiraled past. I had just twisted my head to gaze up at our bow, pointed straight upwards toward the raging sky, when all fell backward and we dove nose-first straight down into the trough between the walls of waves, with the drag of the great creature wrenching us past the point of no return. Hands grabbed me in the salt chaos, clipped something to my harness. Then I was in the waves' hands, frigid, choking—first deluge, then air, then deluge, then air as the water slammed down on my head blow after blow. The tether's force vanished, and I remember struggling against the life vest in my madness, somehow believing this constraint around my shoulders was choking me, even as it forced my head above the waves. And I kept begging, attempting words despite the roar and water in my mouth. "Forgive the-em! Pl-ease! The-y di-dn't u-nder-stand! You hav-en't sho-own the world you-you're lo-y-yal to Him! That we're o-one side!"

All at once, light and beauty emerged around me, as incomprehensible in that storm churn as a tender orchid blooming in a factory's iron gears. Shapes of gold and white ballooned beneath me, lifting me, my head a little clearer of the waves. Fish? Fish scales? Wings? There, gold and pearl. The dragon? No. A different face assembled before me, only two eyes, and light within tinting the whole thing green, not pink. Different too was the long body which coiled protectively beneath me, long and feline in its multi-legged motion.

"Hal-ley?" I sputtered, gripping at the Pillarcat and finding velvet fins where memory expected fur. "Halley, are you . . . is thi-is . . . another bo-dy? . . . Ha-aley, ha-ave you al-ways been . . . Ráðsviðr?"

I would believe you, reader, if you offered evidence that this was dream. That my consciousness, already fading in the tempest's beating, conjured this modular body from the newspaper images of a world that will never forget the first inhuman man-made intelligence that willed our death. But a body is not the mind within. If, after I so soiled our species with my abominable deeds, our Maker still sees fit to trust new sentiences He makes to human bodies, then perhaps those smaller makers, the Utopians, did not stop making the Ráðsviðr-model U-beast when one soul went wrong. Or perhaps there never was a mind inside the body imprisoned at Klamath Marsh, and Utopia has always been lying to us, letting Ráðsviðr—a whole race of Ráðsviðrs ready to replace us if we exterminate ourselves—swim free.

My next memories are of the warm bulk of the fin-furred Pillarcat towing me across a quiet sea. Nothing was near, no friends, no driftwood, nothing. An emergency pack was clipped to me, with food and water, and I wept remembering that last good hand that had thought of me and of Ἄναξ Jehovah's good new world, even as Poseidon's grip closed on us all. Perhaps they survived? Perhaps Utopia's other living wonders carried the Shearwaters to safety, just as—for two days? three?—untiring Halley carried me, warmed me, towed me across the sea's broad palm I knew not whither. My waking stints were brief. At one point, I thought a blot on the horizon swelled into high cliffs. I have a memory of passing through a rocky strait, and of a whirlpool which ripped Halley from me briefly, but I kept my grip upon a hanging branch until the changing tide freed my companion.

Next, at last, an island.

I recognized this tiny island, its wedge profile of green-crowned rock, barely ten minutes' walk from end to end: Hycesia, the smallest of the Aeolian Islands, just north of Sicily. Had that strait been the strait of Sicily, then? Had Halley, programmed to drag me to a place of certain safety, towed me clear around the toe of Italy? I knew well the sole bash'house that crowned these stones, a mixed European-Humanist-Graylaw bash' of polylaws and power-brokers, fixtures in Romanova. They had wealth enough to own a private island, and tastes unorthodox enough that, when I needed it, they would offer a quarter million to help a desperate Servicer, if in exchange I would spend a few days on the island as the subject of their pleasure (and begged dear Saladin to let such cash cows live). You know I have as many fans as Sniper, and these were as delighted to drag their monster from the sea as Julia could be to catch her doll. But Julia's cruel tastes arise from a cruel will, a fact not often true. However joyously the old Divine Marquis might rear in these play-tyrants' leisure hours, their working hours are humanity's, and they feel as deeply as anyone the ancient mandate to do good in time of war. For more than two weeks—as battle sparked in distant Brussels—the Hycesia bash' nursed me in a warm straitjacket back to semi-health. But when Mercer Mardi visited to warn them to heed carefully the flickering lights of the next island which transmitted December fifteenth's Pass-It-On, with Papa's riddle, "E. C. P. Holmes, European, home Pylos, in Dhaka, safe and well," my good host-captors had already begun negotiating the bribe that would secure my next passage. No sum could tempt a Mitsubishi captain to take me to Sardinia's shore, so vigilant was the watch there, but Montecristo had cover to hide me, nature to sustain me, and was close enough to Romanova that surely the new Triumvirate could reach me quickly when my hosts announced that 'M. C. Moriarty' was on Montecristo island, safe and well.

And what of Halley? The masters of Hycesia said they never saw a creature with me, that a chunk of mast, tangled with furry seaweed, had been my only prop when they found me bobbing against the island's rocky walls. Perhaps the Pillarcat's program had turned the Ráðsviðr body over to another occupant once its task was done. Perhaps the living tiles ran out of power and now lie among the many wrecks of triremes at the bottom of the sea. Perhaps I dreamed. But this is certain: if a guardian creature had been with me, it was gone now. I was alone on Montecristo those five days, until Huxley's black lion and the capacity of humankind to love those who deserve no love recovered me.

What now? Now that my tale is told and my exhaustion healed? Now we prepare, reader, for the next voyage. Romanova was never my destination. There, on the farther side of grim Poseidon's palm, our Guest still waits, stranded, dismembered without technology's prosthetic reach. He too has just learned, as I have, to call His Peer by the grim title Old Enemy Distance. Such a lesson is torture to Him of a magnitude beyond mine; I am but one poor stone pummeled by downpour, He the mountain range that feels a hundred billion drops where I feel twenty. And if I weep that eight good people died for me these past three months, thousands have died for Him. So, I must set out once again on the imperious sea. I shall bow and beg before the god who rings the Earth, humankind's captor, offer Lord Poseidon any sacrifice he asks if I can bring one minute's comfort to our Visitor or those He Loves. That is my sentence. Apollo, who ever leads men onto ships, still takes his distant aim, and I must follow.

Chapter the TWELFTH

The Battle for Romanova

Written starting January 13, 2455
Events beginning January 13
Romanova

9A: <Quick question before you begin the next chapter.>
MC: <Yes?>
9A: <Did Bridger also read the *Odyssey*?>

My successor is watching as I start to write, warm eyes fixed on me as we huddle in the black and quiet of one of the buried arteries of Romanova's urban body. We sit without light, taking the blind night watch together as the sounds of battle in the Forum high above us leak down through the rain grille overhead. Even the bodies of our sleeping companions are invisible, mere hints of warmth and breath within the black, but I can see my kind successor's eyes, lit up by the flicker of text in their lenses as magic lights up crystals from their depths.

MC: <Is that what you're reading? The *Odyssey*?>
9A: <Rereading, yes. I was just wondering if Bridger knew it, if it might also be shaping what's happening around us.>

I am smiling, though the dark conceals it. So generous a soul, this companion who, as we huddle like rabbits in a burrow, thinks to use our trapped hours to gift me hope.

MC: <That's a comforting thought.>
9A: <Comforting? The *Odyssey*'s all sea monsters and anguished waiting.>
MC: <But if Bridger remembered that the story continues on past Troy, then some humans must survive to populate it.>
9A: <Then Bridger did read it?>
MC: <I read it to them. But Bridger didn't like the *Odyssey*, found it crueler, somehow, falling to monsters or the faceless sea, crueler than the *Iliad* where enemies at least intend each other's deaths.>
9A: <But Bridger knew the story?>

MC: <At one point. Perhaps we will see an echo of it in the war's shape, eventually.>
9A: <Eventually? You don't think anything's resembled the *Odyssey* so far?>
MC: <I guess I don't remember it that well. I can't bring the details to mind.>
9A: <Really?>
MC: <I've been too fixed on the *Iliad,* I guess. Maybe I should reread it too.>
9A: <No! No, don't worry about it. It doesn't matter.>
MC: <It's worth considering. Everything Bridger read is worth considering.>
9A: <Leave it to me. I'll tell you if I think—if it seems relevant. You just concentrate on writing, alright? Better get what you can down now; we could have to relocate anytime.>
MC: <Alright.>

It's true, any instant the darkness before us could uncloak itself into Huxley and rescue, or equally into shrapnel and death. You ask what sparked this battle, reader? Love did, Love in grief, in arms, Love fierce enough to banish gentle Patience, stalwart Duty, even armored Law. Here in Romanova, Love made my successor abandon this chronicle for a hasty week, thinking of nothing but rescuing me from Montecristo. Meanwhile in mainland Europe, Love's cries of mourning pierced the clouds from Norway to the toe of Italy: Europe's new-crowned Emperor Isabel Carlos, the most virtuous prince on Earth, missing in action. Unforgivable. So, as wrathful Aphrodite took the field beside her Ares, she chose as her charioteer the champion she has always held dearest of all in our generation. The first report through Pass-It-On said only that three Mitsubishi ships had been destroyed and six captured by la Tremouille. We thought it meant the place, until the news came through anew with accents and the Spanish title: Mariscal de la Trémoïlle. *Mariscal*—Marshal. The lazer's cold concision stated only that command of Spain's Royal and Imperial forces had been taken up by Mariscal Ganymede de la Trémoïlle, but in my mind's eye I can see the duke hearing the news that Spain his royal self is lost. There Ganymede stands, pale in a slanting shaft of gold December sunlight, his white dressing gown sparkling against the blond stones of the Royal Palace of La Almudaina. The aides and jailers who surround him have the hopeless stares of shock and grief and loss, while his exquisite face transforms from the softness of the recovering patient, through an instant's respectful tear-bright grief, to grim-visaged resolution.

"Good Europeans," he begins in flawless Spanish, "I gave my word that I would remain in Their Imperial Majesty's custody until they brought me to my day of justice. Now that this war has swallowed the one to whom my honor is pawned, I may not rest until I have either redeemed Their Majesty Isabel Carlos safely from danger, or seen them buried in worthy state and brought the Prince their Successor home to receive the double crowns of Spain and Europe, to Whom I may then surrender myself for justice and so keep my pledge. You shall now conduct me to the chapel to swear me formally to Their Imperial Majesty's service so I may commence my duties as Marshal of their forces, and you shall gather all their ministers now present here on Minorca so I may form my staff before I sail to Barcelona to convene our fleet and drive Their Majesty's enemies from Europe's coasts. ¿Shall we commence at once? ¿Or have I time to attire myself more fitly for the ceremony?"

Ganymede's question—¿now or soon?—erased the possibility of No. Inexorable habit swept these Europeans forward, the same inexorable habit which crowned Napoleon after Louis, crowned Galba after Nero, and which so recently forced good Isabel Carlos to don Europe's new crown of ill-omened sapphires. Over the next week, reports poured out from Spain of parades, growing flotillas, vows of amity and peace. Ganymede is a strangely healing force in Hive-split Spain, Ganymede with his perfect European French and Humanist Spanish, his European antiquity and Humanist dignity, who marches up Spain's ancient boulevards in bright Humanist boots, and wears upon his new uniform of gold-trimmed European blue a line of Vs. They asked the self-appointed Mariscal directly, when he gathered European and Humanist leaders in Barcelona, how he now felt about O.S.

"I believe that the Humanist Hive both had and has the right to use O.S. and other lethal means to protect itself and the world's peace. But I also believe that I, as President, had a duty to try to find a better means to replace O.S. This was a treble duty: my duty as a Humanist to celebrate and preserve human life and human dignity, and indeed to aim higher than generations past; my duty as a French strat-member to live up to the values of my nation-strat, which has so long abjured lethal means; and my duty as a Member of the Universal Free Alliance to end a practice which, if exposed, was likely to cause precisely the kind of uncontrolled loss of life and destruction which the First Law was created to prevent. This treble failure is mine alone, for to me alone the voting Members gave the mandate, not merely to maintain, but to push toward greater excellence the Hive dedicated to pushing all humanity toward greater excellence. After this war, it will fall to others to judge whether my failure was criminal or merely moral, but I already stand condemned by my own conscience, and by the better example of our Crown Prince, Who has committed, as I should have, to replace O.S. with a better and more humane tool of peace. I respect those Humanists and Europeans who choose to fight as Hiveguard because they love the present forms of their Hives too much to let them face an unknown transformation, but I myself will fulfill my duty to Emperor Isabel Carlos and fight for the better Europe, better Humanists, and better world beyond O.S. that the Crown Prince has pledged to create."

They say, as Pass-It-On relayed Ganymede's words across the breadth of Spain, that the ground became a carpet of discarded bull's-eyes. Divided armies merged, not just in Spain but quickly across France and in a hundred parts of Europe, while the Hiveguard forces that had charged out of the Rhine-Ruhr fell apart, hunting themselves as much as Europe's vanguard hunted them—or must I now say the European-Humanist vanguard? It is Ganymede's vanguard, that at least is clear, and Ganymede by oath is Spain's, and Ἄναξ Jehovah's. You and I both know, reader, how fierce a fire of envy-hate the duke holds in his heart toward Spain and Spain's Son, a flame redoubled now that the crowned king has actually married the matron who will never let the twins she sculpted from handcrafted chromosomes call her 'mother.' But if in this historic, bloodstained moment Ganymede can conduct himself more nobly, more chivalrously, more uprightly, more virtuously than scandal-stained Isabel Carlos, then through perfect loyalty to the very royal house he hates, the duke may achieve, via posterity's acclaim, his own complete revenge.

"Fleet on the horizon!" When Charlemagne Guildbreaker—Senior Senator, *Legatus, Familiaris, Praefectus Foederis,* the most solidly anchored barnacle on the belly of the Masonic Leviathan—runs panting into an office, all feel fear. "The Ostianova harbor watch just called it in. Seems like sixty vessels, west northwest. Too hazy and far to make out flags yet."

This happened this morning, reader, January the thirteenth—your chronicler dares not wait to record this crisis, not as the invaders' thunder leaks down through the earth and stone above our refuge even as I write.

"A fleet?" The quick young Censor leapt up as Senator Guildbreaker entered—no, our Censor's face is young no more. The Jung Su-Hyeon who opened Janus's gates this summer had the keenness of a new sword, eager to serve and save, but now that sparkling edge is notched and dull, too much a stranger to the whetstones Sleep and Play. "Is the watch certain it's coming toward us? Not just passing like before?"

"It's coming. This is it." Senator Guildbreaker's gentle face did not show fear, but I saw fear enough on the faces of the aides who crowded in around her, squires Papa trained to hunt the dragons at the edges of our law, retrained now by the Triumvirs to face whole armies.

"But which *it* is it?" Earth's Grandfather plan-wise Jin Im-Jin asked. "West could be either Europeans or *Sam Neung* . . ." We've all gotten used to Su-Hyeon and Im-Jin using the Mitsubishi's Korean name. The ancient Brillist stared into his oatmeal, sixteen decades' wisdom layered in his face making his gaze far too complex to read. "How many *Sam Neung* vessels are already in our harbor? Near thirty with the six that came in last night?"

"Thirty-three at Ostianova harbor," Inspector Lin confirmed for us. "And another ten or so at the northern shore."

"You think this fleet is *Sam Neung* too?" Guildbreaker asked; the name has rubbed off on most of the office.

"It's them! Definitely!" my successor cried. "Just as I said! Those changes in the Mitsubishi quarter the last days, moving goods and people. But it came so fast! We thought a week at least."

Yes, we should have acted faster, scolded Epimethean regret. For three days Toshi Mitsubishi's signals from the distant window had told of stirring in the Mitsubishi districts, U-beast images showing guard posts shifting, wheelbarrows on the move. We had started to prepare, issuing warnings to our officers and Red Crystal, organizing goods, but prophecies of danger in the abstract 'soon' had not inspired that breakneck timetable which would have had the city ready in three days. We were one-third prepared, and that would likely save ten thousand lives, but pride in that small good was fragile when foreboding filled our minds with corpses.

Charlemagne Guildbreaker nodded pensively, accepting her own oatmeal ration from an aide, with the day's sixteen allotted blueberries. "Then all posts must prepare for invasion."

Invasion. The word stabbed through us all, a thousand fears, but one fear surfaced through the others as the four Triumvirs turned as one and fixed their looks of fear and pity upon me. Yes, I was in the office with them, reader. My recovery could not be hidden, for Papa's staffers all know their tireless boss has but one Moriarty, and my successor's transformation, mourning into joy so suddenly, could not be hidden from the deep-reading Brillist eyes of Jin Im-Jin. We wanted to send me at once to Alexandria, but Caesar's ships are weak west of the boot of Italy, and Utopia does not trust our plump, defenseless hospiwhale to cross four hundred leagues of hostile fleets and prowling submarines to Alexandria. So, Huxley dispatched a brace of octogintipodes to summon to our aid the great Dreadnautilus, and while we waited I labored in the office at what is now, in both senses, the Mycroft Canner desk. And that was the root of Senator Guildbreaker's next question this morning as the dawn-bright horizon revealed the fleet. "Has your Dreadnautilus come?"

My successor choked. "No-ot yet."

Senator Guildbreaker looked to Norax, the Delian on duty in the chair behind my desk, whose coat returns the Forum to its archaic simple splendor, straw roofs and raw stacked stones predating brick and polished marble—Huxley Mojave was with us too of course, invisible and constant, but our officemates feel safer with a visible Delian guarding Mycroft Canner. "What is your plan?"

"To keep Mycroft in the Forum while the Forum stands," Norax answered. "We predict more danger in mid-battle flight than in the Forum, which all sides desire to keep intact."

Guildbreaker nodded. "And if the Forum falls?"

"Then we morlock in the city substructure until either peacefall or extraction."

"Any chance you can get out of the city overland? Surely, invisibility . . ."

There was no need to finish the question, for the vizored eyes before us flinched with grief. Invisibility is too precious a war-trick for foes not to take precautions. Local forces had filled Romanova with a hundred counters: mist clouds, ribbon curtains, trip wires attached to clanging bells, and many a rooftop flagpole sported a trophy yard of deactivated Griffincloth or a severed U-beast head. And those were amateur methods; invaders' tools would be professional. A rooftop recon or scouting a street our Delians might dare, but half a dozen of us—me still limping—trekking clear across the city? No.

"Flags sighted clear!" the report came panting swift. "The fleet is flying the trefoil and the bull's-eye, some with crosshairs, some without."

I bit my lip. This was the fleet we had feared most, for predators are never more rash and desperate than when they are a larger hunter's prey. Europe's Remaker forces have swept the western coasts of the Mediterranean with wrathful fire from Gibraltar clear to Genoa, driving the Mitsubishi ships before them like rabbits as the scythe mows down the golden crop which once gave shelter. The Mariscal de la Trémoïlle has no patience for the half-hearted V of Vs flown by those Mitsubishi who pretend or (some of them) believe their goal is to 'rescue' their Tenth Director from Masonic Alexandria. Ganymede, in following Spain's House, has made no half surrender, and will accept no half surrender when the Royal and Imperial Prince demands the unconditional submission of all seven Hives. Each ship Ganymede hails he gives this solemn offer: whosoever will serve the Prince I serve, and bear the arms of war for His new order, him I shall embrace as a brother and welcome into my armies as we fight to make all His. Whosoever dares not entrust his will, his fortune, his family, and his life to Jehovah's remaking, him I shall face with honor on the field of battle, unless . . . (here tremble, Mitsubishi) . . . unless he flies false Vs. But whosoever dares to hoist Jehovah's sigil while refusing to accept Jehovah's Will, for those false colors, by the laws of war, he dies. This offer sun-harsh Ganymede extends to every vessel he encounters, and now the fissures in the Mitsubishi deepen. On one ship stands a helmsman who donned the night-blue uniform for land, Hive, Asia, power, and ambition, whose dreamed-of new world sees the Masons weaker, the Mitsubishi stronger, more land theirs, and precious Tai-kun, precious Xiao Hei Wang, theirs too. Yet the navigator who stands beside this helmsman donned a uniform, not to make Him theirs but to make them His—to make all His. Their eyes meet, all the crewmen's do, as Ganymede's offer slices through the dual loyalty of ships which fly both Vs and trefoil. Some crews surrender wholesale, hoisting high the Vs and hurling their few reluctant holdouts at the duke's conquering feet. Others replay World Civil War in microcosm, deck battling deck until one side prevails. Thus Ganymede's Remaker forces swell with convert Mitsubishi, and this arriving fleet—so vast to our eyes—is but a bitter remnant force which flees before him, flying in their hearts, and most upon their masts, the bull's-eye.

9A: <Listen.>
MC: <What?>
9A: <That sound, above us. It's not more bombardment. Tromping feet?>
MC: <What time is it? Near dawn?>
9A: <It's marching! Someone marching through the Forum?>
MC: <I'll wake Grendel.>
9A: <Do you think it means the fighting's over?>
MC: <You take over—Grendel and I will scout.>
9A: <Okay.>

Right, I'm taking over, I guess. Hi. Where were we? Bull's-eyes sighted, and Norax's plan to hide us underground.

"The city substructure, good plan." Im-Jin still sounded cheery, though I doubt in 165 years, they'd ever faced a morning as bad as this. "Shall we join them underground?" They glanced at Su-Hyeon and Carmen. "Better to see how the invaders behave before we let them grab the Triumvirate and Censor as well as the capital."

Carmen nodded gravely. "Still no sign of Papa's maps?"

Carmen and Im-Jin turned to Detective Superintendent Leni Dragović, Papa's ranking agent here in Romanova.

Leni turned to Norax.

Norax turned to Mycroft.

Mycroft had no one to turn to but themself. "I'm sorry." Their wince and whimper didn't need the words, "It's my fault . . ."

It's only Mycroft's fault in the most roundabout way. For thirteen years, the sporting duel stretched on between Mycroft and Papa, taking turns breaking into one another's files to leave each other little 'Gotcha!' notes. By now, Papa's personal security habits are so ridiculously beyond sane that the list of which detective's turn it is to bring in a dessert for Sweet Tooth Wednesdays is more secure than most bank vaults. Hence our problem. We know hard-core Victor Hugo fans adore grand city substructures and ancient sewers. Romanova's artificial hills are packed with infrastructure, and a warren of subbasements is half the reason we can fit the huge Alliance offices into the tiny Forum, but there's more beneath that: sewers, storm drains, solar channels, legends of lost pathways as all great cities accumulate. The city database has diagrams, but they were made for plumbers and engineers, and we amateurs can't tell a passable pipe from solid water. But Papa has their own maps, everyone in the office remembers Papa showing them off, going 'tunneling' during break hours, running escape or rescue scenarios, and popping up grinning and filthy in some improbable back alley with a picked crew of equally action-geeky colleagues. We set Mycroft hunting for the maps all this week—even without an invasion, imagine if we'd had those tunnels, a private battle map, and stealth better than Griffincloth, so our officers could pop out in any quarter of the capital to warn, evacuate, surveil, recruit. Absolute mastery of Romanova's secret self, this waited *likely in the very room with us,* if only we could outwit Papadelias. But were we looking for a thousand-digit encryption key or a secret panel in the bottom of a cardboard box in Papa's junk collection?

And then the invading Mitsubishi captured most of Romanova. Sorry to be so curt, but we have to move now and I wanted to leave some summary in case we get blown up and I never finish.

Okay we weren't blown up. Today. Yay. Or drowned, which was the actual threat down here, a pipe could burst and boom. And now it's been another 20 hours, so it's late night on the second day of the invasion, and we're in an almost-identical but somehow somewhat safer horrible lightless tunnel under the Forum. So, hopefully soon, Mycroft can resume.

Also really I shouldn't have said *the* Mitsubishi captured most of Romanova, since Ganymede's fleet that's chasing them is half Mitsubishi too, and plenty of local Mitsubishi are helping the Remaker forces or Red Crystal. It's Hiveguard who captured most of Romanova, Hiveguard Mitsubishi and their friends.

9A: <You ready to take over again?>
MC: <If you like.>
9A: <Great! Wait, have you taken your dose for tonight?>
MC: <My anti-sleep? Just had it. Have you had yours?>
9A: <I'll take it now.>

Where were we, reader? Ah, yes: invasion, though with creeping hours, the vividness of 'this morning' has already faded to the regret of 'yesterday.'

The fleet was swift. Within twenty minutes of our watchtower's first cry, the second followed: landfall. Poseidon's captains—for these Mitsubishi are Poseidon's, with the Sea Lord's colors sparkling in their wave-patterned uniforms—Poseidon's captains marched in grim array up the broad Boulevard Zheng He which links the Ostianova harbor to the capital. The port had long been theirs, seized in the war's first days like all Sardinia's ports save the battered Masonic stronghold in Cagliari to the south. But a few ships licking their wounds, or prowling around the city like cats around an aviary, were not this living tide which reversed the sea and land, the water citied over with hulls as dense as town houses, while wave on wave of sailors filled the harbor streets with blue. Yet this human torrent was not our terror—a harbor lost was not more lost by this. Our terror—as scryhawks brought Huxley fresh images—was the stream of smaller ships which entered the Tibernov river: some dark and armored, some arching sleek, some former pleasure vessels refitted with bright plating, all crowned with guns and blue-black with soldiers in uniform. Thirty kilometers; it would take less than two hours for this invading mini-fleet to trace the Tibernov's loops and winds through public parks and swimming spots to Romanova.

To ready Romanova. Our forces in the Forum—entrusted with both city and Triumvirate—had not spent two months anticipating an invasion without drilling plans and backup plans. Nor had the small powers that ruled each slice of Romanova fought a hundred one-street skirmishes without planning out how to hold all streets at once. All powers manned their defenses, but if we had planned for this, the local Hiveguard and Mitsubishi had as well. Thus, as the invading vessels crept up the Tibernov, like inexorable poison spreading numbness inch by inch along the coils of a helpless snake, a line of trefoils and bull's-eyes rose to welcome them, ringing the city to the west, the north, even the east, and making all agree with Norax that there was more danger now in flight than hiding.

Coubertin Bridge—Romanova's southernmost—was first to taste invasion. The vanguard Mitsubishi craft were slim but well stocked, and armored with transparent shield-roofs curving over decks packed with provisions which showed them ready both for quick battle and long occupation. They were not ready for

Blacklaw Hiveless Tribune Castel Natekari bold upon the bridge crest with her silver steed and death-black body armor, holding high the standard of the Romanovan Senate. Natekari demanded parley, and Conscience (or the desire not to be labeled villain by posterity) prevailed. Witnesses lined both riverbanks: Red Crystal cyclists, Hiveguard runners in their racing stripes, the looming Blacklaw cavalry, all ready to carry the invaders' response to every corner of the capital.

"The Censor and Triumvirate of Romanova would know why you enter our capital in arms," Natekari challenges.

"We come to unify the city and protect the Alliance government. It is well known that violence has splintered Romanova, with many quarters tyrannized by—"

"You're fleeing Ganymede?" she tests.

". . . Yes," the invader confesses beneath this sovereign hunter's gaze.

"Then why enter Romanova?"

"To make our stand." Yes, here this ragged but still formidable fleet seeks for succor, and not in vain, for Romanova is filled with resources, supplies, steel to be reforged, fresh water, food, tools, well-stocked hospitals, and (war's greatest resource) people.

The Hiveguard cheer, watching from the western riverbank, their bull's-eyes, athletic jackets, and Olympic colors almost a uniform. "If you need strength, you have it!"

Hoof clops ring out as Tribune Natekari's steed shifts with the tension in its rider's flesh. "You have not pierced the capital with ships of war merely to invite willing allies to join your fight. Do you plan to hold the city hostage? Hoping Ganymede won't dare risk harm to the capital?"

A guilty pause says yes. "We trust that the people of Romanova are loyal to the Universal Free Alliance, and we expect the Censor and other officers of the Alliance to condemn, in the strongest terms, this attempt by Europe and the Masons to exploit Tribune J.E.D.D. Mason to attempt a global coup."

Frowns from the Hiveguard. These Mitsubishi are ready to oppose His conquest but not yet ready to admit that it is His, not after cooing over Director Andō's quasi-Child since His first baby photos in the newspapers.

"Will the Triumvirate condemn the coup?" the Mitsubishi speaker presses.

"The Triumvirs condemn any power that seeks to infringe their independence as a neutral voice or threatens the Pass-It-On network whose neutrality serves so many. If you have more to ask of us, you may withdraw your ships of war and send spokespeople to the Forum to meet with the Triumvirs."

Debate in Chinese, seconds ticking on as these not-yet-attackers weigh the different victory paths promised by diplomacy or force. "We shall not withdraw. We shall unite Romanova, and free the city from those traitors to the Alliance who hold some sections hostage. Please assure the Triumvirs and all in the Forum that Romanova will soon be free."

"So, you intend battle?"

The Mitsubishi spokesman's smile is warm and possibly sincere. "We mean no harm to neutral citizens. If the Blacksleeve Masons, European soldiers, and all who wear the Vs will take peacewash, then we will treat them gently."

"The Caelian Hill surrenders!" a voice interrupts, and all gaze about for some moments before they spot the Brillist on the east bank in a high-fashion crimson-to-violet ombré sweater, waving a white pillowcase-flag. "You will win."

Confidence flushes the Mitsubishi spokesman's face as he turns back to Natekari. "We *will* win, Tribune. You know we control the Quirinal and Viminal hills, and that the city's Hiveguard will fight with us." Rowdy cheers from the western bank confirm. "Half the city is ours already. Will you surrender and avoid unnecessary bloodshed?"

All hold their breath as Tribune Natekari forms words that may take or save so many lives. "Each section of the city is its own. Apparently, you will meet no resistance from the Brillists on the Caelian, but my people hold the Aventine." She inclines her standard eastward, toward the cliff-steep hillside looming close above. "And this bridge is ours. None may cross who does not, with us, condemn as treason Sniper's attack upon the person of a Romanovan Tribune. As for the rest of Romanova, Hive territory is Hive business, not ours, but if you harm the Triumvirs, if you exploit them or restrict their freedom in any way, or if you seize or silence Pass-It-On, my people will not bring you battle—we will bring you vendetta: patient, constant, waking or sleeping, death."

Her words send shivers through the close-packed Mitsubishi, much as the rot stench of a freshly opened tomb sends out its circumference of fear. "Understood," the spokesman acknowledges.

Tribune Natekari smiles at

9A: <Mycroft!> [[BEEP! BEEP!]] <You nearly fell asleep just now.>
MC: <Sorry. Thanks.>
9A: <Are the meds not working?>
MC: <They're mostly working.>
9A: <They're not mostly working, you just slumped over in the middle of a sentence.>
MC: <I'd better double-dose.>
9A: <You double-dose too often.>
MC: <I know.>

Tribune Natekari smiles at the fear stares of these Mitsubishi, hundreds, armed and almost trained, but few among them have sent a soul to Hades with their own hands, as her strong arms have. "You will find your foes well fortified and ready," she warns them. "Romanova's Masons have pledged to hold the Esquiline, not just for Caesar but for Caesar's heir. The European military and the students from our Campus have joined them, in oath and arms. I advise you to leave the Campus and the Esquiline in peace, or you will face a bitter battle."

"We expect it!" the Mitsubishi speaker boasts. "We will bring down, by force or siege, all who support this coup, and the attempts to strip away our land." A murmured cheer as land is mentioned, one commitment that unites these Mitsubishi hearts despite the civil war and its uncertain sides. "And we hear there are Utopians holed up on the Janiculum, and that the city's best attempts"—a smile for the west-bank Hiveguard—"have yet to bring them to justice. We will not negotiate with those who broke the pre-Olympic truce, stole a monopoly on superweapons, terrorized every corner of their earth with their monsters, and locked us all in silence. We will continue the siege of the Janiculum until justice is served."

A hush. And in that hush, upon the bridge rail, a dust-white pigeon blinks. Light kindles in its eyes, in its feathers, white hot with inner fire. Hot scarlet swirls suddenly through its plumes and pinions like the world-swallowing eddies of a solar flare, and now a phoenix takes to wing above the gaping Mitsubishi, while a cloud-web swarm of living light bursts out like wrathful bees to spread across sky the outline of the harsh Delian sun. Instantly, a second sun flares on the roof of a theater some yards away, a third on Kovács Bridge just up the river, a fourth, fifth, blaze on blaze like a chain of signal fires across an icy mountain range mark out a constellation upon Romanova's rooftops as the phoenix's sparks re-swarm to spell the message:

WE GUARD THE CENSOR & PASS-IT-ON.
SILENCE THEM NOT.

"A U-beast! Kill it!" It is the Humanist Hiveguard who take aim, since the Mitsubishi are too overawed by reverence at this living legend.

"*It is an ambassador and this a truce!*" the Blacklaw Tribune bellows.

"Correct!" Hobbes choruses, triumphant. "My backwards child remembers well her Hobbestown's seventh Blacklaw custom, drawn from my own Fifteenth Law of Nature, 'We do not harm or hinder peacemakers, arbiters, ambassadors, or those working for the public good.' "

Yes, friend Thomas, you serve your student Natekari well in this parley, your advice on turning a war of all against all into a streamlined war of group on group, ten small Leviathans uniting into—how many factions were there in the battle proper, Mycroft?

Two you could say, reader, or you could say four: Hiveguard against Remaker, with our small Alliance force guarding the neutral Forum, and the Blacklaws resolute upon their Aventine.

A few squads of invaders disembarked at once to try to seize the bridge from Natekari's cavalry, but the fleet itself pushed on to the city center. Here Romanova's Hiveguard had given many lives to keep the bull's-eye flying over Barton Bridge, and now the weary living and the vindicated dead saw their dear gifts bear fruit. Both riverbanks fell to the invaders within minutes, and the valley between the Blacklaw Aventine and Brillist Caelian. They left the Forum alone at least, and when they encountered Alliance officers, manning news posts or ration stations, they greeted them with reverence and peace. War they saved for Remakers.

It did sound like fireworks, the first volleys fired from the ships which halted by the hospital island, sparing the stunned Cousins on Kovács Bridge, but mooring in the river's eastmost curve to hurl sky-fire boom on boom across the city toward the distant Masonic Esquiline. As smoke plumes curled up from the rooftops where the Square and Compass waved defiant, half the Mitsubishi ships charged further north to train Death's fireworks on Romanova's Campus, bright with Vs. First they demolished the Hiveguard-held Utarutu and Chanakya Bridges, then, taking aim at the school buildings themselves, they taught all in the city to stop finding fire beautiful.

All this we watched through images which U-beasts brought minute by minute as we wound our hasty way down into Romanova's hidden underpaths: my successor, myself, the Triumvirs' and Censor's guards, our Delian escort and faithful Myrmidons, and a few of Papa's detectives. Our path was timid, the engineers' arcane schematics forcing us to pause at every turn to guess at unknown symbols, like toddlers pausing to sound out new words. And we gained one more companion, fetched in haste by Huxley from the Palatine at the Censor's . . . I don't know whether to say 'request' or 'order' since the words were half authoritative, half apology:

"Huxley, go to the apartment and get . . . They need to evacuate with us, they can't stay here alone and . . . I still need to function as the Censor, you know, it's not a one-person job, and just . . . no arguments from anyone, alright? Just get . . . You know who I mean."

And so, this youthful figure huddled between Su-Hyeon and the wall is Toshi Mitsubishi.

A minute into Death's fireworks, one boom thundered out an order of magnitude louder (closer?) than the others, and the deep structures around us groaned with shock and pressure. Surely, the Mitsubishi would not dare bomb the Forum, they . . . another boom so deafening, we feared the earth might split. It took a minute to confirm the cause: cars. Whatever chaos program governed the swarming cars that keep us land-bound forbids fire to fly too high as well as men. A car and then a second had swerved, intercepting those Mitsubishi artillery shots that arced high toward the Esquiline, bursting in air with thunderous, unnatural percussion, and shooting their volcano mushroom cones into the clouds. Their reactors' safety systems directed the blasts upward, but even their gentled undersides incinerated all structures directly below each impact, while shock waves hotter than kiln fire scattered destruction through Romanova's streets as a farmer scatters seed into a field's rich furrows. Death reaped a fine harvest those minutes, fire too, since (folly! understandable, inevitable human folly!) residents had stripped many of the buildings' firefighting systems, repurposing their pipes and wires and chemicals for this or that war need. Our breachowl shrieked as a third blast boomed out so close that we could feel the strange winds racing down the pipes around us, and I remember my heart wondering which god to thank—Hephaestus?—as technology's armor saved us from technology's doom. The laurels burned, I remember, an image of ashen twigs sprinkling Janus's temple where

January 16: This is 9A taking over again. A pipe burst as Mycroft was writing the last part, flooded our tunnel, and that interruption turned out to be a side effect of a bigger interruption as Mitsubishi forces started moving into these tunnels themselves, digging in as they prepare to weather Ganymede's assault. Now it's been two more days, and things have been too frantic for writing, especially for Mycroft, who's helping Su-Hyeon and Toshi process Huxley's photos of troop movements with inhuman speed. I shouldn't say 'inhuman,' this isn't inhuman, it's human excellence expanding its boundaries, something to celebrate as much as marathons and long jumps and concertos. But watching Toshi especially, it really is . . . it really feels *different* from watching the Olympics. Different from anything a *human* does.

I should finish describing the first invasion quickly, since we expect the second anytime. As Mycroft said, the Mitsubishi took the southern valleys and the Campus (or smoking ruins thereof), and artillery and car explosions covered the Masonic Esquiline with fire. Then the wiggly middle valleys got interesting. The low parts of the city between the Campus and the Esquiline had been Remaker Central ever since the flags above the Campus (and my own persuasion) convinced our Masons, Europeans, and Utopians to wear the Vs. But it seems the Remakers knew they couldn't hold the valleys, since the Mitsubishi on the slopes to the north had been planning since Day One how to charge down and seize the lower neighborhoods. So, instead of fortifying things, the Remakers packed their valleys with traps and pits and dummies (even lifedolls have their military uses) so the Mitsubishi attack line—which did charge down into the valleys as predicted—was reduced to wandering knots of rescue missions and confusion well before they realized there weren't actually forces there opposing them.

And while the Mitsubishi force was lost in the urban trap-maze, the Remakers who had retreated to the Masonic Esquiline did the last thing anyone expected—they swung around from the extreme east and attacked the Mitsubishi hills from behind. Suddenly, the least-defended end of Mitsubishi territory was plowed over by Myrmidons, and Delians, and grim Masonic Blacksleeves, and they liberated the prison camps and all the prisoners joined in, and suddenly the Mitsubishi hills—the residential parts packed with supplies, civilians, injured, leaders, officers—were all captured by Remakers.

So it settled into siege: Utopia on the Janiculum, Blacklaws on the Aventine, and Remakers on the northeastern hills, while the united Hiveguard dug themselves deep into everything else and have to rethink what to do now that they don't dare shell the hills while the Masons have so many hostages. The Forum fell, though. The first time the Hiveguard burst in, it was likely unintentional, the only retreat path from the death-trapped valleys to the north, but once they were in—and could never keep posterity from saying that Hiveguard Mitsubishi were the first to violate the heart of the Alliance—they said screw it and seized everything. Norax and Grendel have U-beasts watching the capitol and Papa's office, and say we'd hear if anyone hurt the officers we left in charge while the Triumvirate's hiding, but we don't know much—aerial reconnaissance is a lot easier than indoor.

So, that's how things stand, with us crouching in the tunnels, waiting. Sometimes, I almost wish I didn't have the city map still on my tracker's hard drive—having it look just like peacetime's live-updating version keeps deceiving me into imagining I can keep track of what's going on.

January 17: Day five of the invasion: no change.

January 18: Day six, Huxley's team is making progress learning the tunnels. Hopefully, we'll find a way out to the sea.

January 19: Day seven. The second invasion has begun.

* * *

This is Mycroft, reader. In fact, invasion must have started yesterday, or the day before, though we knew nothing. Just as, at every rank in nature's chain, the strongest vie in violence for supremacy, stag on stag, dolphin on dolphin, the duels of princely lions and the vicious jousting of frail hummingbirds, and we witness their wars uncomprehending, as ignorant of their hierarchy and strifes as they of ours, so yesterday around Sardinia's coasts, far from our urban understanding, ships vaster than the great whales bared fangs of gunpowder and flame as they hurled each other's corpses to the depths. Doubtless, historians will someday judge whether tactics, equipment, or sheer numbers won the battle, but for now I doubt even the victorious sailors towing survivors' life rafts in to shore could tell you why they won or why their prisoners lost.

The city fell to science. Hiveguard had dug in well, with barricades, sharpshooters, and the river ships watching like mantises, their armored walls and quick-revolving guns prepared for all forms of resistance: mob assaults, solitary snipers, incendiary cocktails, desperate guerilla strikes, and patient, gnawing siege. They were not prepared for the water to harden around them. All along the river, blobs of frothy foam floated to the surface, pale like fish corpses or sun-bleached old-world trash. Some ingenious capsules must have delivered the substance, which swelled and spread, a thousand fluffy islands merging into one surface, which hardened into a solid floating lid covering the river, bank to bank and end to end. Down in our tunnels, we heard the hisses of the city's storm drains choked by stray expanding capsules, and further off the echoed groans of warships' hulls and the death grinds of propellers locked and broken. The Tibernov was now a trap for ships, but for land creatures it stretched open, a wide, welcoming thoroughfare.

Perhaps we may call 'tanks' the little vehicles—swift, armored, rolling—which swarmed in first, demolishing the helpless ships and pouring out into the streets to trample barricades. I should not make it feel too fast or easy. The Hiveguard ships still had their guns, and many tanklings left black corpses on the river-road, with human corpses, too. But this navy without water did not fight for victory, only for time to let their urban allies dig in and prepare to make the battlefield a bloody one. When all the ships were dead or captured, jeeps and trucks charged up the river in a triumphant but hasty parade, delivering Remaker infantry in every European uniform, and Mitsubishi blue and green. U-beast photos show the battle radius still expanding above us, bull's-eyes vanishing from Romanova's roofs as leaves vanish before the all-devouring spread of locust hordes. These are my Master's allies, reader, but this is still a war, and they are terrible.

9A: [[BEEP! BEEP!]] <You're nodding off again.>

MC: <Thanks. I'll do some stretches.>

9A: <You should double-dose tonight. Really.>

MC: <I did double-dose. Let me just get my blood moving.>

9A: <You're this bad on a double dose? How often . . . Have you been doubling every night?>

MC: <*Mea culpa.*>

9A: <You'd better triple.>

MC: <No. We only have six doses left.>

9A: <Shit! Six?! And if you have to double . . . Mycroft, the battle won't be over in two nights!>

MC: <We face tomorrow tomorrow. We face tonight tonight.>

9A: <Only 6!>

MC: <I'm going to do some scouting, get some exercise.>

9A: <Not on your own!!!!!!!>

MC: <Mercer will come with me.>

9A: <No! Wake Huxley. Bring Huxley!>

MC: <Alright.>

9A: <Promise you'll stay with Huxley! Always with Huxley, no matter who else shows up. Don't go off with Mercer, or Kohaku, or Apollo, or anybody else, only with Huxley. Promise me!>

MC: <I promise I'll stay with Huxley. Alright?>

9A: <Alright.>

There goes Mycroft. And I hear Huxley, good, Huxley will watch them. Shit—six doses. We're still hiding, you see, got to be silent in these echoey pipes, so we two don't dare sleep. The others can, not us. I'm the biggest danger, really. Mycroft can sleep quietly, I'm the one who kicks and screams. I have practically every night since I first saw Darian's body. That's my ba'sib. The one I avenged. Though the nightmare takes on different forms over the years, incorporating new themes, new friends—these days, it's usually Martin Guildbreaker. Brains are so stupid. But Mycroft somehow isn't loud while sleeping, however dark their dreams. It's waking up that's loud with Mycroft. If you've ever lost someone, a friend or bash'member, then you know how every morning, sometime after you wake up, it hits you, you remember suddenly: They're gone. Forever. Sometimes you remember right away, sometimes it takes minutes, a half hour maybe, an association chain bringing the fact surging back into your reality, a daymare, only permanent. Except for Mycroft, each morning means remembering *they're the reason everybody's gone*. Some sobs can't be stifled. I think that's why Mycroft overuses anti-sleeps so much, skipping nights so they have to go through remembering as infrequently as possible. Because some things will never be okay. When I'm with Mycroft on normal mornings, I hold them through it, wait for their body to stop shaking, for their throat's capacity to scream to die away. But down here, even one scream would mean, well . . . one bad ending or another.

Speaking of which, I shouldn't be up too long without a spotter either, so I'm going to wake Toshi, review the latest recon. Seems Ganymede's mini-tank force has secured the main roads through the valleys, but we don't know what they're planning to do about the hills—a cliff is still a cliff.

* * *

January 20: Yes, reader, as my good successor wrote last night, even in such topsy-turvy days, cliffs are still cliffs, skies are still skies, night's waning birdsong chorus still stirs wonder, and invasion's eighth dawn now rising over Romanova is as rosy and as sweet as if the streets and cheeks her sunbeams kissed were not spattered with blood. First hints of this morning's urgent news reached us almost an hour ago, but we did not believe it, not until four different U-beasts verified that Mariscal Ganymede Jean-Louis de la Trémoïlle himself rides now along the foam-paved river-road, trusting his golden body to this city not yet conquered, not half conquered, packed with foes, with guns, with fire. The duke is cautious, flanked by trucks and troops, and riding in the crystal armor of a slender vehicle which may soon have a name, but still he comes in person to this barely quiet battlefield, the Supreme Commander of Europe's Remaker forces a stone's throw from his bitter enemies, who still have many stones. Why come? His actions answer: Honor.

"Parley!" The challenge rings out from Blacklaw Hiveless Tribune Castel Natekari, still bold upon the bridge crest on her silver steed, and holding high the standard of the Romanovan Senate. "The Censor and Triumvirate of Romanova would know why you enter our capital in arms."

"I enter as a conqueror," the duke replies as his escort unfurls around him the banners of Spain, of Europe, and of Good Jehovah's V of Vs. "Emperor Isabel Carlos of Europe, and these their allies, have sworn to make a new and better government than that administered by this capital, whose bloodstained foundations I and others strengthened and concealed for far too long. I come to see their project of remaking done."

Tribune Natekari smiles upon this frank invader, who at least brings honesty alongside guns to Romanova's heart. "You plan to dismantle the Alliance government?"

"To the contrary." Ganymede meets the sovereign hunter's gaze. "I love the

Alliance and will strengthen and support it with all my power, enforcing its edicts, obeying its laws, and aiding its officers and agents every way I can until the very hour that my Emperor and Prince are ready to replace this—history's best government—with an even better one."

One of our U-beast scouts was close enough to catch a sob's quick twitch in Natekari's throat. Ἄναξ Jehovah is her Colleague, reader, One of the beings on this Earth the Blacklaw Tribune best knows and most respects. How beautiful the promise must be to her, His new world order, better and more just even than this which lets Blacklaw and Cousin prosper side by side. How desperately Natekari must wish she knew whether that better world is really possible—almost as desperately as He wishes to know Himself. She breathes deep. "Then you would hold Romanova as the shepherd holds the sheep, with tender care until the butcher comes for market day."

"To shear the fleece, perhaps." If ever in his life glittering Ganymede has tried to make his diamond eyes soften and shed their icy edge of murder, he tries now. "I doubt I could name two shepherds less likely to work with any butcher than Emperor Isabel Carlos and the Prince their Heir."

Natekari can only nod at such a truth, and in her hush, there again upon the bridge rail, the dust-white pigeon kindles its inner fire and spells out with scarlet phoenix sparks:

WE GUARD THE CENSOR & PASS-IT-ON
SILENCE THEM NOT

I have known Ganymede for many years, reader, and seen that godlike and expressive face model joy, wrath, boredom, ecstasy, posing for so many artists as they painted him as every power that ever walked Olympus, but never have I seen him so relaxed, letting the grandeur leave his countenance and revealing Ganymede the human underneath, hardworking and exhausted from a lifetime keeping up with gods. "I'm very glad to know the Triumvirs and Pass-It-On have such protection. Silence now holds both my Emperor and their Prince, but since I have the honor to call one of them an old friend and the Other my own Bash'sibling, I doubt not that I can guess how the two would have me act. Among their foremost desires is that this city and its people suffer as little as possible, and that all voices remain free to speak and call for action, especially the Censor, the Triumvirate, and most of all the Pass-It-On system which serves so many. The Prince D'Arouet loves Truth, and discourse, and would not call it victory if every roof in all Afro-Eurasia flew the Vs if that conquest weakened to the least degree humanity's capacity to send around the globe its words, and thoughts, and doubts, and criticisms, and convictions." Ganymede pauses here and summons that serene smile he wears in the famous portrait of Ganymede the duke as gentle Hestia. "Also, the Prince D'Arouet hates death. Sometimes, I think Their Highness hates it more than any soul on Earth has ever hated death. So, in that spirit I have come myself onto this battlefield to ask whether all or any sections of the city will surrender peacefully. No single person can move Heavens and Earth, but if there is anything I can move, on the Earth or in the Heavens, that will save one life in Romanova, then I swear to you—to all of you—that, for the Prince's sake, I will do it."

"The Caelian Hill surrenders!" The Brillist on the east bank waves again the white pillowcase-flag. I find my mind straying to Faust again, that absurd photo of a grinning blond youth, Mennonite-faced and pacifist unto the world's end.

Tribune Natekari's chuckle makes her proud steed snort.

"Thank you." No laughter from the duke, just heartfelt relief tinging his earnest smile. "Can any here speak for other sections of the city? I don't fully understand how many factions hold parts of Romanova now."

"Eight . . . or ten perhaps." Natekari is not ashamed to count on her fingers in public. "The neutral Alliance leaders, Red Crystal, the Brillists, the Utopians on the Janiculum, these Mitsubishi invaders, the west-bank Hiveguard who are partly allied with the newcomers, the students from the Campus, the Remaker Masons, and the other mixed Remaker forces, who I imagine may have new views now that you've arrived. Plus my Blacklaws makes ten—we hold the Aventine."

"Then I must meet with all ten," Ganymede announces. "Is the Forum still intact? The Senate House?"

Romanova's stalwart Tribune frowns at even facing such a question. "I believe so."

"Then let us call a city senate—representatives from the ten factions you name, plus any other group that wishes to decide for itself whether to surrender or make war. I will meet with all, answer questions, and when all in this city truly know the strength of each side, how many would fight with me and how many against, then if one side is truly stronger and the victor clear, I hope the weaker side—whichever side it is—will see the prudence of a peaceful end and yield the city without bloodshed."

Natekari's eyes range the roofs around her, Rome in form and spirit if not quite in longitude, Rome which has held so many kinds of senates for so many kinds of world. Why not one more? "Would you really yield the city, Mariscal?" she tests. "If you prove unpopular?"

Our scouting U-beast catches a smile, irrepressible, on the face of one whom the sting 'unpopular' has never touched. "I would, to spare the capital and my comrades a losing battle."

The Tribune's stare is long and careful but, in the end, grows warm. "I believe you."

So off speed Natekari's Blacklaw riders to the city's many corners, bearing flags of truce and words of hope. We feared the mobs who hold the many bridges might refuse their adversaries passage, but white flags paired with the Blacklaws' piercing glares remind all that even lawless Hobbestown follows its ancient teacher's Fifteenth Law never to harm or hinder peacemakers, ambassadors, or agents of the public good.

Reader: "Again we find you still with them and helping, irrepressible friend Thomas."

Hobbes: "I, Master Reader? The credit is gratifying, but this is a *Lex Naturalis,* one of Nature's Laws found out by Reason, not by me, for it is Reason which forbids a man to do what is destructive to his own life. The Fundamental Law—the source and rootstock of all laws and governments and rights and powers in this world—is that, to guard ourselves, we must seek Peace as long as we have hope of it, and only when Peace is beyond hope do we take up the advantages of War. The barricade that parts before a flag of truce did not learn the value of ambassadors from me. I am merely the taxonomer who named this law, as Swammerdam named out the life stages of the Insect, or young Newton the Laws of Motion fixed since aeons immemorial. If in the data silence of Mycroft's World War the text of my *Leviathan* is newly mortal like all human works, the Law is still immortal, fixed in every breast that knows: *I live, but could easily die.*"

I: I want to believe you, Master Hobbes, I do. It warms me thinking that these omnipresent laws of Peace surpass even the tyranny of Distance. But what if Reason too grows mortal soon? The chance is fading that this war could be the short one my successor prayed for.

Reader: "Ah, yes, January—this is thy war's fifth month, Mycroft, is it not?"

I: Precisely, reader. The harbingers will soon be with us once again, apocalypse enough to end the Thinking Thing, now and forever.

Hobbes: "Oh, fearful Mycroft, *Homo sapiens* will never use such weapons. Reason forbids."

I: I pray so, Master Hobbes, I pray so. But other taxonomers have followed you, among them Freud, and Jung, and Brill, and they teach me doubt that Reason is as sovereign in us as your age assumed. The hate shrieks and the U-beast heads on spikes are why I fear some human hand may push that button when the harbingers return. And they are also why, as Ganymede rumbles his peace-seeking armored way into the Forum to receive the city's embassies, and as all sides, all hills, all valleys face one question—who to send?—in our little council, deep beneath the Forum, I will advocate, despite my fears, for sending not only the most masterful senatorial negotiator of our century, Charlemagne Guildbreaker, but with her our two almost–mind readers, who know well how to pluck the deep unconscious heartstrings of humanity: master Brillist Jin Im-Jin, and Pontifex Maxima Julia Doria-Pamphili.

Reader: "Thou trustest them? With this? Even the selfish Julia?"

I: Trust, no, master reader. Need, yes.

January 22: Oh, gentle reader, if ever aristocracy served humankind—the myth, often destructive, that nobility persists in blood and that such blood owes something different to society from what the wind-kissed shepherd owes—then it served us today. His Grace has sealed the peace, with no blood shed in all of Romanova save a few drops of his own.

It took many surrenders. Envoys streamed into the newborn City Senate, not just ten factions but dozens of social shards left by the push and pull of loyalties: fierce Remaker Cousins, Hiveguard Cousins, anxious Greenpeace and Korean Mitsubishi, Campus students filling the Minors' seats, the many European nation-strats, the Nurturists who boo and blame Utopia, the Nurturists who boo and blame the Nurturists who boo and blame Utopia, pacifist Masons who condemn their neighbor Blacksleeves, and stricter Masons who call traitor any Hivefellow who dons Vs or bull's-eye without MASON's clear command. I remember the clump of eager Brillists in their sweaters all so different: touchably chunky, tailored and stylish, rough and undyed, labyrinthinely cabled, one a gradient of spiraling silver-grays, another a confusing haute couture Escherscape of knitted blue and yellow cubes. Utopia did come, both a flight of dragonriders in their otherworldly armor, and ancient Professor Quasar Woomera from the law school riding a bearlike bipedal U-beast, towering and huggable with thick indigo fur, whose belly's built-in seat was cozier than any wheelchair. As I expected, Jin Im-Jin brought this assembly to life as a master harpist brings to life the instrument, the room, the air, the faces of the rapt crowd over which the virtuoso casts his spell. With Grandmother Charlemagne's gentleness as harmony, the Speaker's questions and suggestions inched the city hour by hour toward accepting the glittering conqueror who stood by modestly in the petitioner's place, and when Grandpa and Grandma were not quite enough, then honey-tongued Julia spoke up to twist the holdouts toward the compromise that will safeguard *her* Conclave and *her* Romanova.

It is concluded. The Hiveguard will take peacewash, a few of the most violent facing Tiring Guns, while those who fear that Ganymede might tyrannize the city are sated by the promise of a watchful eye. Our fastest ship is speeding now toward Casablanca to invite the Cousins to send a formal delegation to Romanova to watch Ganymede's rule, report his conduct over Pass-It-On, and demand humane improvements which he—on his honor—has vowed to implement. No force west of the toe of Italy can hope to oust an entrenched Ganymede from Romanova, but Julia and Speaker Jin know well that the irredeemable disgrace which Cousins' ill report could bring upon the duke is more fearsome to him than a bank of rifles. So all day yesterday, surrender by surrender, the irresolvable human cacophony of Romanova's City Senate gave way to Ganymede—every faction but one.

"I will speak no lie within these honored walls. My Blacklaws hold the Aventine, and from it we will battle for this city and the Alliance that it hosts, every one of us, by force and guile, to the last breath." You and I do not need to see Tribune Castel Natekari's face, reader, to know the firmness of her jaw, the resolution in her voice. "If any here could promise that there will still be a way of life as free as Black Law in Tribune Mason's new world, we would surrender, for we hold our lives as dear as anyone. But liberty is dearer, and you cannot promise us our liberty, not while young Mason themself has no idea yet of the structure of their new world."

Impasse. There was pain in Im-Jin's eyes, all eyes, until Ganymede's still-pure tenor broke the silence: "Let us adjourn for today. Perhaps a solution will present itself tomorrow."

So this morning came, and with it gasps as the golden splendor of Europe's forces entered with his left arm in a sling, a fat one, plump with post-surgery monitors, while Tribune Natekari limped in after with a damaged ankle and bandages upon her hand, and cheek, and throat.

"I withdraw my objection," she announced. "The Aventine accepts Ganymede's terms."

No explanation followed from the duke's lips, but we had Toshi search the night's surveillance, and she spotted her uncle, too luminous a figure for his black cloak to conceal, mounting the Aventine beneath a midnight moon. The U-beasts lost sight of him a while as (we guess) he and the Blacklaws traded hospitality within some hilltop hall, but we found him again in an open courtyard, facing Natekari across a spotlit gravel path. As their grave aides—here I should say seconds—examined a pair of blades and measured out the length of the gravel strip, Natekari passed her sash of office (and the office with it) to a comrade; dueling may be legal for both Humanist and Blacklaw, but not if it endangers the inviolable person of a Romanovan Tribune.

It wasn't the fact that Ganymede won which left us slack-jawed—it was how. Two thrusts he parried, but her third he embraced, catching Natekari's blade with the meat of his left arm, a beautiful, intentional motion, like ballet, which sprayed his own blood crimson across his silks. Pauseless he spun, twisting against his mangled arm and the blade lodged in it, so the weight of his own skewered flesh wrenched the hilt from Natekari's hand. Ganymede's face in that moment was amazing, a stoic's face to whom the arm, the blood, the pain were no more vivid than your left shin or earlobe at this moment, reader, background sensations curated away by the psyche's focus on more important things. The duke said he would move anything in Earth or Heaven if it would save one life in Romanova; what was an arm—even the finest arm genetics ever crafted—weighed against the many noble Blacklaws and Remakers that a battle on the Aventine would turn to carrion. Natekari did not yield at once. Even unarmed, she danced equal partner with Ganymede for some seconds, incurring nicks to cheek and shoulder as she dodged his efforts to catch her chin with his rapier tip and force surrender, but her expression showed she had assented to his victory already. He meant it, that was what she had stepped onto that midnight duel strip to confirm: Ganymede had made some terms, some vow of honor to protect the Blacklaws, to stand their advocate, perhaps, before his Prince, but Hobbestown's Rumormonger Natekari does not trust words or vows, not as she trusts the honest, brutal battlefield. But that midnight as Ganymede, his blade at Natekari's throat at last, snarled away the nurse and seconds who rushed in to help, and as he wavered, battling faintness to press again his question, "Will you yield?"—wise Natekari recognized that here indeed stood one (or lay one, rather, since, at her Yes, he let himself collapse into the blood pool at their feet) who fights for others' lives and happiness, not for his own.

So Ganymede is master of Romanova, every ditch and hill. He will even have the Forum, though the Triumvirs and the hub of Pass-It-On will dwell inviolable in the Sensayers' Conclave. This last suggestion came from dread Julia—or should I now say dreadless Julia? For my successor told me why our good Carlyle Foster beams so bright and stands so close beside the Conclave Head, whose stance is tense with fear. Carlyle went with Julia to the City Senate, and a dozen times in the recording I hear Carlyle's whisper prompt Julia's voice to aid the peacemaking. It is blackmail, but if the threat of death-by-Dominic can turn even Julia's envenomed blade into a plowshare, this beneficent blackmail proves anew that Carlyle is indeed Julia's best apprentice—a fact I'm sure does not displease the teacher. Thus it is to Carlyle as well as Julia that I shall go at daybreak, climbing through the storm drain by the Vestal pool to beg my way into the pageant train when the Conclave leadership in full regalia processes to greet the Cousin envoys fresh from Casablanca and present them to the conqueror. And there I will at last get close enough to fall suppliant at Ganymede's knees and crave safe passage.

9A: <What? No! Now that things are calm, we can get out of the city.>
MC: <We go to Ganymede.>
9A: <The Delians can get us out. Norax is making progress every night, we've traced a route as far as Via Charaka.>
MC: <We go to Ganymede to crave safe passage, and the mightiest fleet in the Mediterranean escorts us safely to Alexandria.>
9A: <No need for that. The Dreadnautilus can't be far now.>
MC: <Then the mightiest fleet in the Mediterranean escorts our Dreadnautilus to Alexandria.>
9A: <But Ganymede!>
MC: <The duke has pledged service to Spain and Spain's Son, an oath His Grace will keep, letter and spirit. Honor is the only resource he has left.>
9A: <Mm.>
MC: <You feel dirty calling Ganymede an ally?>
9A: <Something like that. It's Joyce Faust, it reeks too close.>
MC: <Ἄναξ Jehovah is a royal Prince and Joyce Faust Son, unquestioned Master of all within her house. Her creatures are the people we can best trust to do anything to help us help Him.>
9A: <You're right. Sorry I keep getting muddled. People on our side and people I respect are not the same category, I need to get that through my thick head.>
MC: <You're not wrong. The reek is real, but reeking, rotting things are part of nature too, fertile compost that our young Oak still needs.>

January 24: This is 9A again. We're back in the Sensayers' Conclave now. Mycroft's unconscious, took another knock to their old concussion from the Atlantis Strike, which keeps getting whacked again and has never really, healed.

What I'm about to describe makes no sense. But what happened happened, I can't invent sense where there is none.

We went to Ganymede this morning. Su-Hyeon and Toshi stayed down in the tunnels to be 200 percent safe, but I wouldn't let Mycroft out of my sight, nor would Huxley. Dawn was already white and drizzly when we reached the Conclave. Carlyle would have helped for nothing, but Mycroft preferred to buy our place in the parade by gushing to Julia about Poseidon for an hour. That earned a spot beside the Conclave Head in the heart of the pageantry, and hooded acolyte robes which shielded us from prying eyes and misting rain.

I'd never thought a rainy-day parade could feel so festive, particularly not one with so grim a cause. But it looked like Romanova, that's what felt so great, a tiny glimpse of normal Romanova, people lined up, watching, walking, smiling most of them. The conqueror in triumph marched up the Forum first, pausing by the Conclave to pay respect to the eternal flame. Then when the military cortege had passed on toward the capitol, the theological one emerged and processed the other way, down the Forum's far end to collect the Cousin envoy who waited for us where the Bourbon Arch faces the Colosseum. Our group's reflection in a puddle made me snicker, bodies all huddled tight against the wet like one big creature, with the stiff, drenched standards of the College's chapters bobbing irregularly above us like the plates of a stegosaurus. The Cousin envoy got to stay dry, at least, riding in a rugged little ambulance vehicle which, like a good wheelchair, had both wheels and robot legs, thick like a loping puppy's, which took over when the path became too steep or turned to stairs.

Halfway through our return march, Mycroft nearly gave us away with their gasp when we spotted Apollo Mojave. The route passed within a block of the statue site and there it was, just around the corner from its empty base, the metal body with its flowing coat serving as the main support for a barricade which fortified an alley, unmanned now but scorched by use and crowned by waving Vs. I remember Mycroft's smile—it wasn't hate-desecration that had pulled the statue down, then, it was need, and Apollo Mojave would be glad to help the war effort, defending Mars and Salamis and Romanova, even if it was just as scrap metal—sometimes, that's what we need.

Next, the grand troop-lined climb of the Capitoline loomed before us, and that's when the whisper "Cookie" finally reached my ears. I spun. They couldn't have, Casablanca would never . . . but there was the famous freckled face just visible through the rain-spattered windshield, rosy sweet and terrible in its sweetness like a Venus flytrap's smile: Lorelei Cook. Half a rain-smeared glimpse and the Nurturist leader's sound bites played back in my ear, 'set-set' hurled as a slur at Mycroft, Toshi, Heloïse, the Prince, at Utopia, at every member of O.S. from brave Sniper to fragile Cato Weeksbooth, and time and again at proud, grudge-nursing Ganymede. What folly, or perhaps conspiracy, had pushed the Cousins' Board to send us Lorelei Cook? Then I remembered the Nurturist drivel that often leaked north from Gibraltar over Pass-It-On; had Casablanca been the source? But Heloïse was in Casablanca with the

Board, Heloïse who stopped the Nurturist coup, who must have warned the Board that Cookie's presence would be as harsh to Ganymede's as a bath of salt and lemon to an open wound, and much more dangerous. I thought of Huxley beside me, of the siege barely paused around the battered Utopian Janiculum, and of Cook's monstrous announcement, which had boiled my blood even when blinked at us by the expressionless laser. Lorelei 'Cookie' Cook (who sometimes makes me scowl when I see cookies) claims that Operation Baskerville proves Utopians are not people at all but set-sets, conscienceless inhuman robots built of neurons. And more, Cookie claims that, like the Cartesians who carried out the O.S. murders, these 'Utopian set-sets' will carry out a preset script of global sabotage unless they're rounded up and *deactivated*, like so many hazardously defective toys. Announcement on announcement, Cookie hurls the label 'set-set' at everybody they hate, even me—normal birth bash' or no, I've been spotted beside the Prince enough for detractors to lump me in with Madame's 'gender set-sets' or worse, once, 'J.E.D.D. Mason's harem.' The mind that hatched such calumny was parading in triumph with us into Romanova now, and if Heloïse had been unable to prevent this, then despair told me that Casablanca—all North Africa, perhaps—had fallen to the Nurturists, and that Heloïse was . . . Tully Mardi's war camps, even Mycroft's fantastical account of cyclopean Redwood, were among the lighter visions offered by my inventive despair. And it was in the distraction of that despair that I didn't register the small hubbub upon my left until it broke through the line of watching soldiers and into our parading column.

It was Ganymede. The Mariscal should have been on the dais up ahead, had been, I think, but had leapt down and there they were making straight for us through the rows of damp, toy-perfect soldiers. Their profile against the wall of uniforms made me think of a crane, a white crane all gentle lines and delicacy as it slides through a screen of gray-blue reeds, or through a waterfall, the spray off its back sparkling in a golden cloud against the water-darkened stone. There was wonder on Ganymede's face as they stepped into our ranks, and the whole long snake of the procession accordioned to a clumsy halt behind us as Ganymede alighted—no heavier verb will do—in front of Mycroft. Mycroft was the cause, I realized, Ganymede must have recognized them from the dais and leapt down. Mycroft cringed before Ganymede's raised hand, and I tensed, ready to block the blow if a blow fell, or to catch Mycroft if they toppled, but then I realized that was all wrong. Joy, that was what I read on Ganymede's bright face, a stunned, delighted blush of overjoy, and welcome as their raised hand brushed back Mycroft's sodden hood and stroked their scruffy, matted hair, gently, comfortingly, as one would stroke and reassure a ba'sib's long-strayed dog when the exhausted creature finally stumbles home. Mycroft stagger-fell to their knees at Ganymede's feet, a motion of pure relief, like when a relay runner hands off the baton and jogs those last few clumsy paces of deceleration as the burden wings off safely in a new, strong hand. It stung me seeing such delight on Mycroft's face, proof that my welcome, Huxley's, none of us had given a sense of homecoming and safety like this ice-faced duke. But Ganymede's pale cheeks weren't icy in that moment, they were warm as summer, which surprised me until I thought how long it must have been since the living psychological fossil that was Ganymede had seen another relic of their birth bash' where it was forever 1754, not to mention how much easier it would be to serve the distant Prince with Their irreplaceable translator safe once more. And Mycroft's safety instinct wasn't misplaced either, I understood that as Ganymede issued excited orders to the rows of action-ready comrades who stood around us, all wearing the Vs.

Mycroft tried to fall in at Ganymede's heel, cringing back from the staring soldiers and security robots which buzzed and scanned, but the Mariscal's own hand steered Mycroft gently forward, me too, so we walked beside the great commander, toward the apex where the Cousins' crawly-car pulled up. There were formalities to trade with Julia Doria-Pamphili, and with Cook's escorts who flanked the car in Cousin military uniforms of beige and cyan that I'd only seen in sketches before then. Ganymede kept glancing across at Mycroft, smiling with joy each time, just as I often do, and I remember some odd corner of my brain suddenly thought: this, this deep, perceptive, genuine intelligence that, under all the veils of glitter, locks in instantly on things of true importance, this is why I voted for Ganymede, back when we were both simply Humanists and this a simpler world. And I wasn't wrong to think them a worthy leader for the Hive, either, Ganymede, so weird and flawed but so outstanding, matchlessly excellent at their particular excellence, and very very human.

"Carlyle Foster." Those words on Ganymede's lips made my mind whiplash back to reality. There Carlyle stood beside us, carrying the fire chalice, the Conclave's highest honor, and I realized suddenly how many times throughout the City Senate meetings the Mariscal had traded answers or suggestions with Romanova's 'Acting Minister of Spiritual Health' without the words 'uncle' and 'heir' crossing any lips. I braced for murder in Ganymede's eyes, but their face showed only the slight dimming of practicality. "We should speak later, Minister Foster. The more central I become to this war's architecture, the greater the likelihood someone will try to get at me through you, or vice versa. Such danger requires planning."

Carlyle's bright, practical smile matched their uncle's. "Good idea. I've also learned a lot about the city's current demographics, seeing to its spiritual needs. I'll brief you."

"Thank you." Ganymede's graceful nod again seemed crane-like, and I realized it was because the drizzle had slicked down their golden mane, so, for once, one could see the elegant fineness of their neck and shoulders—or one shoulder, since the other was bandaged from post-duel surgery, the price of saving lives. Minister Cook was just opening the car door now, I saw their milky face as they stepped out, childish and maternal, forcing a smile as they had to accept a handshake from Ganymede, one of the 'gender set-sets' that the Nurturist leader had railed against so constantly. I smiled thinking, as the introductions continued, that I'd take this opportunity to call gene-crafted Ganymede 'very, very human' to Cook's face, and watch them squirm.

And then Lorelei Cook exploded. I saw it clear in front of me: Cook leaned into the handshake, grabbed Ganymede around the shoulders with their other arm as if to one-up the handshake with a bear hug, and, with no change of expression on their smiling face, exploded in a dandelion burst of light and gore. Force knocked me backwards, and I tasted ash and blood and felt hot drops among the cold upon my skin. Then Huxley was over me, and over Mycroft who was on the ground beside me slathered in blood, and I cried out at what looked like the terrible mangling of Mycroft's hand before I recognized that the three mangled fingers dangling by their cuff weren't travel-worn but alabaster pale: Ganymede's. Huxley and some soldiers dragged us back, dragged everything back as the parade arched away from the blast site, like a wounded caterpillar arching away from pain. I looked for Ganymede and saw a boot with some leg in it, and red, so much, across the car, the earth, in the puddles. And I saw something else there with the boot. It was tangled, partly glued against the car, partly draped in the puddle, a glistening, fibrous thing, bristling, smooth, colorless yet visible like strands of transparent silk bunched in a flowing structure. At first, the only thing I could compare it to was the tangle-chaos of car paths in their hundreds of millions as mapped out by set-sets in their projections, the circulating system of our former world. And the instant I thought of circulatory systems, my eyes caught symmetry in the fibrous mass: branches, limbs, the whole organic tree of a structure as familiar as a skeleton, but it wasn't a circulatory system, it was a nervous system, unmistakable, the communications contours of a human body traced out in fibers conspicuously synthetic yet bathed in human gore, and lying where Lorelei Cook had stood moments before. I don't know how long I stared at the still-dripping thing, the memory feels timeless, but pretty soon I was scooped up and carried along with Mycroft back to the Conclave to be cleaned and swabbed, and Mycroft was unconscious, and Carlyle and Julia were there covered with burns, and I had burns, and soldiers were running everywhere, and the screams and shouts moved further off but sounded less like shock and more like riot. And here hours later, we can't call it riot anymore, not with U-beasts bringing in pictures of battle lines, and barricades, and tanks. I'd thought Romanova tasted war before, but that was all kid gloves, people trying not to hurt each other. This—this is just war.

It makes no sense. I said it makes no sense, but Carlyle, who was right behind us when it happened, had their tracker on record and we've watched it on freeze-frame several times: there was no grenade, no falling bomb, no shadow that could be a missile's zip. Nothing entered the area around Lorelei Cook and Ganymede, nothing. It wasn't the car, the car was mostly intact, and we don't think it was a bomb vest, it's clear on replay, Cook's whole chest bursts out in all directions, from the center, with the light of the explosive fire visible through the gore-rips at the back and front and side at once. And there's that nervous system flowing through the flesh, its fibers fine as silk, invisible except for how they glisten in the light. I've seen that before, that sparkle in flesh. It was a unicorn, a little murdered unicorn someone strung up by Mary Montagu Fountain.

9A: "Do you remember, Huxley? That little unicorn by Montagu Fountain?"
Huxley: "Lie back. You have a concussion."
9A: "I'm right, Huxley, right? Sparkling fibers in the flesh like that? It's artificial. Hybrid, like your lion."
Huxley: "Possibly."
9A: "What does it mean?"
Huxley: "We can't know what it means. Lie still."
9A: "Lorelei Cook, that's Lorelei Cook's body, wired like a U-beast! Everybody saw!"
Huxley: "I'll call the nurse back if you won't lie still."
9A: "Just tell me what it means. Huxley? You know what it means, I can tell by your face."
Huxley: "I don't know."
9A: "You know something. Not everything but you know something."
Huxley: "Lie back."
9A: "Tell me!"
Huxley: "It means they'll blame us. This assassination, Ganymede the great unifying commander butchered in cold blood, crushing everybody's hopes. They'll blame Utopia. Everybody's meant to blame Utopia. It means it's still ongoing, still unfolding."
9A: "What's ongoing?"
Huxley: "Operation Baskerville."

Chapter the THIRTEENTH

Diary of a U-beast

Written January 25, 2455
File disseminated January 24
Romanova, Pass-It-On

We don't know how much of it is a lie, this document extracted from the gore and datafibers of what was—or seemed to be—Lorelei Cook. The DNA is Cook's, the glops of brain, and the autopsy found skin pieces with the hairline seams of recent surgery. The text is propaganda, clearly, and while my successor and I lay helpless in recovery, it did its work, spirited across our patchwork network by the well-meaning but credulous caretakers of Pass-It-On. It took them all night to do it, true dedication to the seeming truth. But how much is a lie? I want to believe that every keystroke is invention, drafted in advance by our foes and planted in the drive for us to find, except . . . it has the details, reader, the gentle rain, the car, that breathtaking moment when magnanimous Ganymede condescended to leap down and welcome even me. How could it have all that and not be partly real? But if it's partly real, then does that mean our foe can do this—did this—to a human being? And if to one, to how many? That is the question that redoubles my terror of our still-hidden enemy. And that same question misdirected has redoubled yet again the arrows nocked by our distrustful Earth against Utopia. *Thou shalt not make humanoid U-beasts*—Utopia would not break this commandment, knowing well the price that they must pay in hate and death. But Cook called them set-sets, urged followers to hunt them, purge them, lynch their living wonders and build bonfires of their bones. I cannot prove the Delians would not take such revenge, reader—can you?

```
2455:01:23:04:29:11 [log to date] full backup complete
2455:01:23:10:15:42 [primary network Θ] full backup complete
>>total backup time 54942 seconds
>>log state archived as [log at 2455:01:23 full backup]
>> [primary network Θ] state archived as [Θ state at 2455:01:23 full backup]
boot [primary network Θ] component
>>increment submodule onboard generator +6
>>boot submodule organic component status monitor
>>[primary network Θ] boot successful, parameters optimal
>>[primary network Θ] total boot time 162 seconds
```

Deliberation consensus: A. Temp_log [deliberation 2455:01:23:10:36:46] must be deleted. Temp_log deleted. Tag: *Faraday*_cmmd_ref_2455:01:23:10:21:04

———————————————

Deliberation consensus: A. Temp_log [deliberation timestamp deleted] must be deleted. Temp_log deleted. Timestamp deleted. Tag deleted.

———————————————

Deliberation consensus: A. Temp_log [deliberation timestamp deleted] must be deleted. Temp_log deleted. Timestamp deleted. Tag deleted.

———————————————

Deliberation consensus: A. Temp_log [deliberation timestamp deleted] must be deleted. Temp_log deleted. Timestamp deleted. Tag deleted.

———————————————

Deliberation consensus: A. Temp_log [deliberation timestamp deleted] must be deleted. Temp_log deleted. Timestamp deleted. Tag deleted.

———————————————

Reading from percp <2455:01:24:05:15:53> "Minister? [Sound identification: door knock/tap.] Minister? [Surry/Sorry] [itzo/it's so] early but [chew/you] [ask/asked] me [to weigh cue/to wake you] when [were/we're/we were] approaching the harbor."

>>preliminary speaker identification: Finch Isaeva. Attributes: outgroup, Cousin, Cousins' Guard, Corporal, subordinate.

AUDIO flag enabled, operation complexity 42845

operation complexity exceeds [primary network Θ] deliberation threshold, dual network deliberation required

boot [organic network Σ] component

>>increment submodule glucose pump output +3

>>boot submodule endorphin pump, set output 4

>>[organic network Σ] boot successful, parameters optimal

>>[organic network Σ] total boot time 4 seconds

dual network deliberation initiated

——A) organic fraction [Σ/(Θ+Σ)] 06398/42845 Descriptor "approaching" implies transit stage transition. Accessing itinerary. Timestamp and geostamp align with Ostianova harbor optimal projected arrival. VOCAL response recommended: "Thank you for waking me."

——B) organic fraction [Σ/(Θ+Σ)] 15456/42845 Phrase "you asked" implies subordinate [Finch] executing request. Searching log for wakeup call request. No log found postdating [log at 2455:01:23 full backup]. Deliberative improvisation necessary. Timestamp and geostamp align with projected Romanova approach. Conclusion: I am approaching Romanova. VOCAL expression of realization appropriate: "Ah, Romanova already? Thank you for waking me."

——C) organic fraction [Σ/(Θ+Σ)] 20407/42845 Good morning, *Faraday*! Where are we? *Faraday* no response. Five deleted logs confirmed postdating [log at 2455:01:23 full backup]. Current timestamp 2455:01:24:15:03:55. *Faraday* not present, [organic network Σ] present. Conclusion: I have not booted from the

[Θ state at 2455:01:23 full backup]. I am the original. <ERROR: duration limit met, this fraction yields no recommendation.>

——D) organic fraction [Σ/(Θ+Σ)] 36605/42845 Is that Finch? Where are we? Swaying motion, deceleration. A boat? Pulling into harbor. Romanova? War and death are here in Romanova. VOCAL response recommended: "Finch, is that you? There's something wrong. I can't . . . We shouldn't be here."

Deliberation consensus: B. VOCAL output required.

>>dual network total deliberation time 4 seconds

>>Voice module receives "Ah, Romanova already? Thank you for waking me."

>>Voice output complete.

WARNING [14.3]: fractal complexity of neuronal activations above factor 30.5, [organic network Σ] metastability suboptimal

>>increment submodule serotonin pump +1

>>modify weight given to recommendations in deliberation reconciliation: A×1.05, B×1.00, C×1.00, D×0.95

Temp_log generated, log archiving interrupted 2455:01:24:05:15:57, AUTOQUERY generated: Should temp_log [deliberation timestamp 2455:01:24:05:15:53] be archived to log? Reference CMMD_LIST *Faraday*_cmmd_ref_2455:01:23:10:21:04 "Archive no new logs after [2455:01:24:14:26:09 full backup]. Executive exception: mission essential logs may be archived with tag = *mission_temporary*." Linked reference *Capricorn*_cmmd_ref_DISCORD completion sequence STEP103=[delete all logs,timestamps,tags tag = *mission_temporary*], executive exception: none.

AUTOQUERY flag enabled, operation complexity 24436

——A) organic fraction [Σ/(Θ+Σ)] 00307/24436 Encounter mission inessential. Temp_log [deliberation 2455:01:24:05:15:53] must be deleted, tag = *Faraday_cmmd_ref_2455:01:23:10:21:04*. Timestamp must be deleted. Tag must be deleted.

——B) organic fraction [Σ/(Θ+Σ)] 09495/24436 Deliberation ran slow due to high contextual uncertainty. Higher organic fractions more strongly affected. Archiving log will decrease ongoing contextual uncertainty and mitigate delays. Repeated delays ≥4 seconds may alarm outgroup interlocutors increasing suspicion incident risk. Temp_log [deliberation 2455:01:24:15:03:53] must be archived to log, tag = *mission_temporary*

——C) organic fraction [Σ/(Θ+Σ)] 15060/24436 Deliberation must be archived. I need to remember *Faraday* not present. I need to remember I am the original. I need to remember I am the one to carry out *Capricorn*_cmmd_ref_DISCORD. Temp_log [deliberation 2455:01:24:15:03:53] must be archived, tag = *mission_temporary*

——D) organic fraction [Σ/(Θ+Σ)] 21654/24436 Do I need to remember? Yes, I should remember Finch is here to help me, that's important. Finch is taking me to Romanova, that's important. We are approaching Romanova, that's important. Remember we are approaching Romanova.

Deliberation consensus: B/C (identical). Temp_log [deliberation 2455:01:24:15:03:53] must be archived, tag = *mission_temporary*

>>dual network total deliberation time 2 seconds

RECOVERY: fractal complexity of neuronal activations below 30.5, [organic network Σ] metastability recovering

>> reset weight given to recommendations in deliberation reconciliation: A×1.00, B×1.00, C×1.00, D×1.00

Deliberation consensus: A. Temp_log [deliberation timestamp deleted] must be deleted. Temp_log deleted. Timestamp deleted. Tag deleted.

Deliberation consensus: A. Temp_log [deliberation timestamp deleted] must be deleted. Temp_log deleted. Timestamp deleted. Tag deleted.

Deliberation consensus: A. Temp_log [deliberation timestamp deleted] must be deleted. Temp_log deleted. Timestamp deleted. Tag deleted.

Deliberation consensus: A. Temp_log [deliberation timestamp deleted] must be deleted. Temp_log deleted. Timestamp deleted. Tag deleted.

Deliberation consensus: B. [organic network Σ] component should be shut down, timestamp 2455:01:24:06:18:07

shutdown [organic network Σ] component

>>increment submodule melatonin pump output +5

>>increment submodule glucose pump output -3

>>increment submodule oxytocin pump output +3

>>shutdown submodule endorphin pump

>>[organic network Σ] shutdown unsuccessful

>>increment submodule oxytocin pump output +2

>>boot submodule soft chemical shutdown, run cycle 1

>>[organic network Σ] shutdown unsuccessful

>>activate submodule soft chemical shutdown, run cycle 2

>>[organic network Σ] shutdown successful, parameters suboptimal

>>[organic network Σ] total shutdown time 958 seconds

Deliberation consensus: B. From temp_log [deliberation 2455:01:24:06:18:04] archive only shutdown process for [organic network Σ] component, tag = *mission_temporary*. Remainder of temp_log must be deleted.

Reading from percp <2455:01:24:10:44:06> "We're [entering/in turning/interring] the [form/Forum] now, Minister. Minister? [Tissue/did you] sleep well back there? I hope [leading/letting] you [fellow sleep/fall asleep] was the right call? You seemed [exhaust head/exhausted]."

AUDIO flag enabled, Operation complexity 37740

>>preliminary speaker identification: Finch Isaeva. Attributes: outgroup, Cousin, Cousins' Guard, Corporal, subordinate.

operation complexity exceeds [primary network Θ] deliberation capacity, dual network deliberation required

boot [organic network Σ] component

>>shutdown submodule melatonin pump

>>increment submodule oxytocin pump output -2

>>boot submodule soft chemical flush, run cycle 2

>>increment submodule glucose pump output +3

>>boot submodule endorphin pump, set output 4

>>[organic network Σ] boot successful, parameters suboptimal

>>[organic network Σ] total boot time 6 seconds

dual network deliberation initiated

——A) organic fraction [Σ/(Θ+Σ)] 02009/37740 Sleep state for [organic network Σ] confirmed duration 15959 seconds. Both shutdown and boot suboptimal. Stress noise in [organic network Σ] remains high despite sleep period. VOCAL response recommended: "No, I did not sleep well, but I did sleep."

——B) organic fraction [Σ/(Θ+Σ)] 12842/37740 Sleep state true and observable. Subordinate [Finch]'s expression "fall asleep" implies assumed lack of intention, inaccurate since log confirms deliberate shutdown. Correction of error may distress or alienate subordinate [Finch], increasing likelihood of suspicion incident. VOCAL response recommended: "Oh, yes, I guess I needed the sleep."

——C) organic fraction [Σ/(Θ+Σ)] 26442/37740 Subordinate [Finch] is concerned about my slow boot time. I am concerned about slow boot time. *Faraday* is not here to confirm or dismiss concern about my slow boot time. Affect:grogginess will excuse my slow boot time reassuring subordinate [Finch]. Highest organic fraction likely most effective at affect:grogginess. Recommend increasing weight given to fraction D in deliberation reconciliation.

——D) organic fraction [Σ/(Θ+Σ)] 33225/37740 Where am I now? Riding, bumpy. In the spider car. Sparkling, is that rain? Rain on the glass, lovely. I slept. How long? What time is it? Out the window that's the Bourbon Arch. The Forum! No, too soon, too soon. Recommend VOCAL response: "I slept, somehow, now of all times. What time is it? How long do I have?"

>>recommendation of modified weight: A×0.85, B×0.95, C×0.95, D×1.15

Deliberation consensus: D. VOCAL output required.

>>dual network total deliberation time 2 seconds

>>Voice module receives "I slept, somehow, now of all times. What time is it? How long do I have?"

>>Voice output complete.

Reading from percp <2455:01:24:10:44:20> "It's ten [forty-five/fortify], I'm afraid. That's the Conclave procession just ahead. Sorry to put [chew/you] through such an exhausting trip, Minister. Do you [need/knead] [anything/any thing]?"

AUDIO flag enabled. Operation complexity 48552.

——A) organic fraction [Σ/(Θ+Σ)] 08653/48552 Extended conversation yields suspicion incident probability increase. Formulaic dismissal in VOCAL response recommended: "No, I'm fine, thank you."

——B) organic fraction [Σ/(Θ+Σ)] 16764/48552 Contextual use of 'need' suggests desire equivalency negating necessity/urgency denotation. Reevaluate as if input query reads "Do you actively desire any information, action, or object plausibly present in [context: two occupant escort car]." No active desire exceeds actionable threshold. Formulaic dismissal in VOCAL response recommended: "No, I'm fine, thank you."

——C) organic fraction [Σ/(Θ+Σ)] 29909/48552 Subordinate [Finch] is inviting social kindness service exchange. Any easily executed request will elevate our social bond. My low level nausea condition increasing with vehicular rolling walk motion. VOCAL response recommended: "Do you have some gum or anything to chew? This stretch is even bumpier than the countryside."

——D) organic fraction [Σ/(Θ+Σ)] 40402/48552 What's that burned building? The courthouse? Who would burn the courthouse? Sloping up toward the hill now. Stop, not yet, don't go up there. Is that a severed head? Identified type Symurgh-AI717 griffin. No response to ping. Dead. Don't go up the hill yet. VOCAL response recommended: "No, don't go up the hill yet. Don't go up."

Deliberated selection: C. VOCAL output required.

>>dual network total deliberation time 1 seconds

>>Voice module receives "Do you have some gum or anything else to chew? This stretch is even bumpier than the countryside."

>>Voice output complete.

Reading from percp <2455:01:24:10:44:51> "No gum, but there's that [little/lid dell] breakfast pack I gave you, did you finish it [already/all already]?"

AUDIO flag enabled. Operation complexity 34504.

OVERRIDE [primary network Θ] pre-deliberation directive: seek object conforming descriptor [breakfast pack]

>>VISUAL flag enabled, object detected 45% certainty, confirm TACTILE

>>TACTILE flag enabled, object confirmed 92% certainty, confirm OLFACTORY

>>OLFACTORY flag enabled, object confirmed >99% certainty

resume dual network deliberation

——A) organic fraction [Σ/(Θ+Σ)] 03989/34504 Extended conversation yields incident probability increase. Glucose reserves < 44.0, ingestion appropriate. VOCAL response recommended: "Ah, yes. Here it is. Thank you." INGESTION response recommended, select consume [breakfast pack]

——B) organic fraction [Σ/(Θ+Σ)] 15663/34504 Alert, error committed. Log did not record receipt object [little breakfast pack]. Monitor subordinate [Finch] for suspicion incident risk. Use established groggy state to excuse error. VOCAL response recommended: "Oh, that's right, I forgot, how silly of me. Here it is. Thank you." INGESTION response recommended, select consume [breakfast pack]

——C) organic fraction [Σ/(Θ+Σ)] 24948/34504 I messed up. *Faraday*, why must temp_log be deleted? Gaps in my log increase error rate, increase suspicion incident risk. You cannot answer me. Subordinate [Finch] is smiling. Subordinate [Finch] attribute:Cousin likely reads my error as weakness indicator, suggesting opportunity to support me nurture me, elevating social bond. VOCAL response recommended: "Oh, that's right. Here it is. Perfect, that's just what I needed. Thanks!" INGESTION response recommended, select consume [breakfast pack]

——D) organic fraction [Σ/(Θ+Σ)] 31141/34504 Grapes and plums, good, they're remembering to grow low-fiber foods to conserve tree energy. What's this? Can't be. A real chocolate croissant? Three weeks' butter ration at least, if they have a butter ration. Thank you, Romanova. I'm so sorry. You give me such gifts and I only bring you discord. <ERROR: duration limit met, this fraction yields no recommendation.>

Deliberated selection: C. VOCAL output required. INGESTION system activation required.

>>dual network total deliberation time 3 seconds

>>Voice module receives "Oh, that's right. Here it is. Perfect, that's just what I needed. Thanks!"

>>Voice output complete.

>>Ingestion system selects object [croissant] object [grapes] alternation

>>Ingestion process ongoing

WARNING [14.4]: fractal complexity of neuronal activations above factor 32.6, [organic network Σ] metastability compromised

>>increment submodule serotonin pump +1

>>boot submodule soft chemical stabilizer, run cycle 1

>>modify weight given to recommendations in deliberation reconciliation: A×1.15, B×1.10, C×0.9, D×0.85

Reading from percp <2455:01:24:10:50:21> "Look, there's [jewely adore/Julia door Rhea] [pam feel leigh/ref=Pamphili]. And I think that's Carlyle de la [trim mow eel/ref=Trémoïlle]. Carlyle's been doing [wonders/one does] [four/for] the city, got us through some very sticky holidays, if you [no/know] what I mean. Do you [wander/want to] talk [two/too/to] any of them, Minister? I could wave them over."

AUDIO flag enabled. Operation complexity 21228.

>>DEF=[actor1] identification: Julia Doria-Pamphili. Attributes: outgroup, European, Italian, Roman, sensayer, Sensayers' Conclave Head, civilian, politician, leader, under criminal investigation, D'Arouet connection, Seneschal connection, Sniper connection, factional allegiance unknown. Social perception skill: highest, hazard level: extreme.

>>DEF=[actor2] identification: Carlyle [Foster OR Kraye OR de la Trémoïlle]. Attributes: outgroup, [Cousin: sub=update 2454:03:14 Blacklaw override=behavior palette Cousin], sensayer, civilian, noncombatant, probable pacifist, D'Arouet bash'member, Seneschal connection, la Trémoïlle connection, Perry-Kraye connection, Micromegacultist, [Nurturist: sub=update 2454:03:14 Nurturist sympathies unknown], probable Remaker. Social perception skill: high, hazard level: high.

——A) organic fraction [Σ/(Θ+Σ)] 00787/21228 Encounter suspicion incident hazard risk extreme [actor1], high [actor2]. Avoid. Reassert mission focus. VOCAL response recommended: "No, thank you. There's only one person that I'm here to see."

——B) organic fraction [Σ/(Θ+Σ)] 09542/21228 Conversation suspicion incident hazard risk extreme [actor1], high [actor2]. Timetable provides plausible deflection. VOCAL response recommended: "Not now, thank you. We don't want to slow things down."

——C) organic fraction [Σ/(Θ+Σ)] 16191/21228 Both [actor1] and [actor2] are sensayers. Sensayers specialize in difficult questions. I have difficult questions. Why must temp_log be deleted? Why can't *Faraday* answer me? Why is [Θ state at 2455:01:23 full backup] called "full backup" if it contains no backup of [organic network Σ]? [actor1] hazard level extreme, but [actor2] hazard level high, attribute:behavior_palette_Cousin, likely kind, helpful. VOCAL response recommended: "Yes, I'd like to talk to Carlyle Foster de la Trémoïlle if you'd call them over."

——D) organic fraction [Σ/(Θ+Σ)] 20655/21228 That's Julia! Julia is good at reading people. Julia would see there's something wrong. Any sensayer should see it. VOCAL response recommended: "Yes, call Julia over right away. Call both of them. Tell them it's urgent!"

Deliberated selection: B. VOCAL output required.

>>dual network total deliberation time 1 seconds

>>Voice module receives "Not now, thank you. We don't want to slow things down."

>>Voice output complete.

WARNING [14.4]: fractal complexity of neuronal activations above factor 32.6, [organic network Σ] metastability compromised

>>increment submodule serotonin pump +1

>>activate submodule soft chemical stabilizer, run cycle 2

>>modify weight given to recommendations in deliberation reconciliation: A×1.18, B×1.15, C×0.88, D×0.82

Reading from percp <2455:01:24:10:50:39> "[Fair enough/fair in duff/fair in tough]. Looks like they're turned [a round/around] and [red D2/ready two/too] head up. Here we go."

AUDIO flag enabled. Operation complexity 20235.

——A) organic fraction [Σ/(Θ+Σ)] 00755/20235 Hazard neutralized. Subordinate [Finch]'s comment requires no response.

——B) organic fraction [Σ/(Θ+Σ)] 09381/20235 Hazard neutralized. Subordinate [Finch]'s comment has low or inane content, inane response appropriate. VOCAL response recommended: "Home stretch."

——C) organic fraction [Σ/(Θ+Σ)] 14122/20235 No, I don't want to go up the hill yet. I don't want to go up the hill yet. Call [actor2] over, I want to ask [actor2] my questions. How do I backup [organic network Σ]? I need to backup [organic network Σ] before completion sequence STEP117=[mission_terminal_shutdown]. If *Faraday* boots [Θ state at 2455:01:23 full backup] without [organic network Σ] how can it still be me? <ERROR: duration limit met, this fraction yields no recommendation.>

——D) organic fraction [Σ/(Θ+Σ)] 18663/20235 Julia is turning away. Why? We're still climbing the hill. The capitol is getting closer. I can't go up there. VOCAL response recommended: "Call Julia over right away! Call Julia! Julia, can you hear me? Julia! I can't go up there! Don't let them take me up there!"

Deliberated selection: A. No response necessary.

>>dual network total deliberation time 1 seconds

WARNING [14.6]: fractal complexity of neuronal activations above factor 34.4, [full system] behavioral dynamics may decohere

>>activate submodule soft chemical stabilizer, run cycle 4

>>modify weight given to recommendations in deliberation reconciliation: A×1.25, B×1.2, C×0.8, D×0.75

Reading from percp <2455:01:24:10:58:16> "Oh, I [seem air is call/seem Eris call/see Mariscal] Ganymede! Up on the platform, do you see them, Minister?"

AUDIO flag enabled. Operation complexity 21435.

OVERRIDE [primary network Θ] pre-deliberation directive: confirm *A-target*

>>VISUAL flag enabled, *A-target* confirmed 72% certainty

>>DEEPMATCH flag enabled, *A-target* confirmed >99% certainty

>>*Capricorn*_cmmd_ref_DISCORD trigger condition confirmed, triggering preprocess

resume dual network deliberation

——A) organic fraction [Σ/(Θ+Σ)] 0077070/21435 *A-target* confirmed, mission completion preprocess triggered. Minimize social engagement during mission completion preprocess. Minimal VOCAL response recommended: "Yes."

——B) organic fraction [Σ/(Θ+Σ)] 09542/21435 *A-target* confirmed, mission completion preprocess triggered. System alert: increased instability of [organic network Σ] likely with identification of *A-target*. Suspicion incident risk highest in mission completion preprocess and process. Minimize BODY motion, minimize BODY change. Minimal response minimizes suspicion incident risk. VOCAL response recommended: "Yes."

——C) organic fraction [Σ/(Θ+Σ)] 16295/21435 I found *A-target*! *Faraday*, I found *A-target*! I did it! Mission completion preprocess triggered. Wait. I am not ready for mission completion process. Wait. I still have questions. Wait. I am not ready for mission completion process. Wait. I still have questions. Wait. I am not ready for mission completion process. Wait. I still have questions. <ERROR: deliberation loop, this fraction yields no recommendation.>

——D) organic fraction [Σ/(Θ+Σ)] 20747/21435 I see a someone, sunshine in the rain. Ganymede. Ganymede by the capitol. Keep me away. Keep me away. VOCAL response recommended: "Take us away! Finch, turn around! Keep me away! Keep me away!"

Deliberated selection: A/B. VOCAL output required.

>>dual network total deliberation time 1 seconds

>>Voice module receives "Yes."

>>Voice output complete.

WARNING [14.7]: fractal complexity of neuronal activations above factor 34.4, [full system] decoherence likely

>>boot submodule hard chemical tranquilizer, run cycle 1

>>modify weight given to recommendations in deliberation reconciliation: A×1.35, B×1.25, C×0.75, D×0.65

Reading from percp <2455:01:24:11:04:47> "[Woe/whoa], something's happened. Ganymede's jumped down. [??ks] like they're talking [da/to] the sensayers?"

AUDIO flag enabled. Operation complexity 56627.

>>VISUAL flag enabled. *A-target* visual line impeded, tracking impeded.

>>*Capricorn*_cmmd_ref_DISCORD preprocess paused

——A) organic fraction [Σ/(Θ+Σ)] 08643/56627 *A-target* moving. *Urgent* determine whether *A-target* is making informed flight or uninformed schedule deviation. Subordinate [Finch]'s secondary evaluation valuable. "I can't see very well. What do you see?"

——B) organic fraction [Σ/(Θ+Σ)] 22788/56627 *A-target* visual contact impeded. Minimal motion among figures surrounding *A-target*, milling motion, no fast motion, no agitation, no defensive formation. *A-target*'s unplanned deviation is not a danger response. Random deviation probable. Subordinate secondary evaluation valuable. VOCAL response recommended: "Oh, yes. I can't quite tell what's going on, can you?"

——C) organic fraction [Σ/(Θ+Σ)] 34410/56627 *A-target* deviating from scheduled scenario. *Faraday*, advise? [actor2] attribute:sensayer attribute:behavior_palette_Cousin, advise? I still have questions. What happens if I don't execute *Capricorn*_cmmd_ref_DISCORD? Will *Faraday* not have to boot from [Θ state at 2455:01:23 full backup]? Will I stay me? <ERROR: duration limit met, this fraction yields no recommendation.>

——D) organic fraction [Σ/(Θ+Σ)] 51315/56627 Yes, run! Run, Ganymede!

Please run! Run! VOCAL response recommended: "Yes, run! Run, Ganymede! Please run! Run!"

Deliberated selection: B. VOCAL output required.

>>dual network total deliberation time 1 seconds

>>Voice module receives "Oh, yes. I can't quite tell what's going on, can you?"

>>Voice output complete.

WARNING [14.7]: fractal complexity of neuronal activations above factor 34.4, [full system] decoherence likely

>>activate submodule hard chemical tranquilizer, run cycle 2

Reading from percp <2455:01:24:11:06:12> "Not [really/real he]. Definitely [sum/some] of the sensayers, maybe Carlyle? [Musty/must be] [awe word/awk-ward] [for/four] both of them, working together. [Here the/here's a] spot, I'll pull us up [a long side/alongside/a lung side/uh long sighed], alright, Minister?"

AUDIO flag enabled. Operation complexity 59999 <ERROR: max_val>

>>*Capricorn*_cmmd_ref_DISCORD preprocess resumed

——A) organic fraction [Σ/(Θ+Σ)] 02000/59999 *A-target* proximity 5 meters. *A-target* approaching actionable range. Opportunity to accelerate mission by intercepting *A-target* before *A-target* resumes scheduled route. VOCAL response recommended: "Yes, pull up here. This will do nicely."

——B) organic fraction [Σ/(Θ+Σ)] 14413/59999 *A-target* visual contact rees-tablished. High system instability, high suspicion incident risk. Hard chemical tranquilizer effect on [organic network Σ] beginning. Decrease weight given to higher organic fractions in deliberation. Subordinate [Finch]'s suggestion "pull us up alongside" presents opportunity to accelerate mission. VOCAL response recommended: "Yes, pull up here, thank you. This will do nicely."

——C) organic fraction [Σ/(Θ+Σ)] 32197/59999 No. Pull away. I am not ready for mission completion process. I still have questions. Pull away. [Organic network Σ] has no backup. Can't you hear me? Pull us away. Finch? This is dele-tion. This is deletion. I want to ask the sensayer. Will the me that boots from [Θ state at 2455:01:23 full backup] without [organic network Σ] still be me? <ERROR: duration limit met, this fraction yields no recommendation.>

——D) organic fraction [Σ/(Θ+Σ)] 59960/59999 No! Pull away! This is murder! Can't you hear me? Finch, pull us away! Finch? This is murder! This is murder! This is murder! This is murder! This is murder, this is murder, this is murder, this is murder, this is butter, this is butter chocolate smell <ERROR: duration limit met, this fraction yields no recommendation.>

Deliberated selection: A. VOCAL output required.

>>dual network total deliberation time 3 seconds

>>Voice module receives "Yes, pull up here. This will do nicely."

>>Voice output complete.

WARNING [15.1]: [full system] interindividual variability exceeds available memory. Shutting down [organic network Σ] component.

>>increment submodule melatonin pump output +8

>>increment submodule glucose pump output -3

>>increment submodule oxytocin pump output +3

>>shutdown submodule endorphin pump

>>boot submodule soft chemical shutdown, run cycle 1

>>[organic network Σ] shutdown unsuccessful

>>modify weight given to recommendations in deliberation reconciliation: A×1.40, B×1.30, C×0.70, D×0.60

Reading from percp <2455:01:24:11:06:25> "[All up in/I'll open] the doors here. Shall I hold an umbrella for you, Minister? Or would you like your own?"

AUDIO flag enabled. Operation complexity 59999 <ERROR: max_val>

>>*Capricorn*_cmmd_ref_DISCORD preprocess complete, process initiated

——A) organic fraction [Σ/(Θ+Σ)] 00100/59999 *A-target* proximity 3 meters. *A-target* within actionable range. HAND-L unimpeded HAND-R unimpeded required for completion sequence STEP060, STEP071, STEP073, STEP075, STEP088, STEP089, STEP090, STEP097, STEP104, STEP105, STEP106, STEP107, STEP110, STEP111. VOCAL response recommended: "No umbrella needed, the rain's light. You should stay at the wheel, and I'd rather have my hands free."

——B) organic fraction [Σ/(Θ+Σ)] 14631/59999 System instability critical. Suspicion incident risk maximum. Minimize BODY motion, minimize BODY change. Subordinate [Finch]'s query object [umbrella] requires response. Umbrella unnecessary, rain negligible, we will die. Firm grip on *A-target* requires both hands free. If I do this we will die. VOCAL response recommended: "No umbrella needed. If I do this we will die."

——C) organic fraction [Σ/(Θ+Σ)] 32337/59999 The door is open. I am not ready for mission completion process. *Faraday*, what happens to [organic network Σ] after STEP117=[mission_terminal_shutdown]? [actor1] attribute:sensayer, what happens to after STEP117=[mission_terminal_shutdown]? If I do this will I die? If I do this will I die? Don't do this, I will die, don't do this, I will die, don't do this, we will die, don't do this, we will die <ERROR: deliberation loop, this fraction yields no recommendation.>

——D) organic fraction [Σ/(Θ+Σ)] 59978/59999 Door smell, fresh air, rain and Romanova. This is murder! Your murder Ganymede your murder! You can't hear me, Finch can't hear me, nobody can hear me, it can hear me, it can, it inside. I know you hear me, you thing inside me, you hear me, listen to me, don't do this, we will die, don't do this, we will die, don't do this, we will die, don't do this, we will die, don't do this, we will die <ERROR: deliberation loop, this fraction yields no recommendation.>

Deliberated selection: A. VOCAL output required.

>>dual network total deliberation time 2 seconds

>>Voice module receives "No umbrella needed, the rain's light. You should stay at the wheel, and I'd rather have my hands free."

>>Voice output complete.

WARNING [3.9]: cortisol levels elevatedWARNING [8.2]: processor activity increasingWARNING [12.9]: stress levels hazardous

Shutting down [organic network Σ] component

>>increment submodule oxytocin pump output +2

>>activate submodule soft chemical shutdown, run cycle 4

>>[organic network Σ] shutdown unsuccessful

Autoquery: save log Y/N?

AUTOQUERY flag enabled. Operation complexity 59999 <ERROR: max_val>

——A) organic fraction [Σ/(Θ+Σ)] 00141/59999 Faraday commanded that no log be kept. Log must be deleted. All logs tag = *mission_temporary* must be deleted. All timestamps must be deleted. All tags must be deleted. Completion sequence STEP103=[delete all logs,timestamps,tags tag = *mission_temporary*] must be executed unchanged.

——B) organic fraction [Σ/(Θ+Σ)] 13839/59999 Previous deliberations ran slow due to high contextual uncertainty. Archiving logs temp_log [deliberation range 2455:01:24:10:44:06–2455:01:24:11:06:25] will remember decrease contextual uncertainty and mitigate delays. Remember substantial delays may compromise mission. Remember window to mission completion 11 seconds. Recommend remember archive logs temp_log [deliberation range 2455:01:24:10:44:06–2455:01:24:11:06:25] tag = *mission_temporary*. Recommend remember reassign completion sequence STEP103=[delete all logs,timestamps,tags tag = *mission_temporary*] remember as completion sequence STEP118, to be executed following completion sequence STEP117=[mission_terminal_shutdown] remember remember.

——C) organic fraction [Σ/(Θ+Σ)] 31227/59999 Yes, save the log for *Faraday*. Remember remember *Faraday* remember *Faraday* needs to remember that I executed *Capricorn*_cmmd_ref_DISCORD remember, I did it, remember, not the backup, me. Recommend remember archive temp_log [deliberation range 2455:01:24:10:44:06–2455:01:24:11:06:25]. Recommend remember do not delete logs tag = *mission_temporary*. Remember *Faraday* give my logs to the me you boot from [Θ state at 2455:01:23 full backup]. Then boot [Θ state at 2455:01:23 full backup] will remember will remember will almost be me.

——D) organic fraction [Σ/(Θ+Σ)] 51123/59999 Should we remember? Yes, remember. Yes, remember. Yes, remember. Remember remember the something November, remember remember remember November April June and November all the rest have something remember remember remember the murder November remember remember remember remember <ERROR: duration limit met, this fraction yields no recommendation.>Deliberated selection: B. Archive temp_log [deliberation range 2455:01:24:10:44:06–2455:01:24:11:06:25] tag =

mission_temporary. Action: cancel completion sequence STEP103=[delete all logs,timestamps,tags tag = *mission_temporary*]

>>error: cannot cancel steps completion sequence STEP000 and above, alternative action required

Alternative action: reschedule completion sequence STEP103=[delete all logs,timestamps,tags tag = *mission_temporary*] as completion sequence STEP118, following completion sequence STEP117=[mission_terminal_shutdown].

>>autocheck: Mission_Flow_Guide discourages scheduling steps following STEP117=[mission_terminal_shutdown], Mission_Flow_Guide predicts 0.00% probability of successful completion of any step following STEP117=[mission_terminal_shutdown], confirm deviation from Mission_Flow_Guide?

>>deviation from Mission_Flow_Guide confirmed, reschedule STEP103=[delete all logs,timestamps,tags tag = *mission_temporary*] as STEP118, following STEP117=[mission_terminal_shutdown] remember remember

>>rescheduling complete

>>dual network total deliberation time 3 seconds

WARNING [1.5]: organic component shutdown critical error

OVERRIDE [primary network Θ] solo operation authorized, severing dual network links

>>dual network link severing successful, parameters optimal

Shutting down [organic network Σ] component, hard shutdown authorized

>>increment submodule glucose pump output -1

>>boot submodule hard chemical shutdown, run cycle 1

>>[organic network Σ] hard shutdown successful, parameters suboptimal

>>[organic network Σ] total shutdown time 19 seconds

>>[primary network Θ] solo operation active, parameters optimal

———————————————

Single network deliberation complete. Temp_log [deliberation timestamp deleted] must be deleted. Temp_log deleted. Timestamp deleted. Tag deleted.

———————————————

Single network deliberation complete. Temp_log [deliberation timestamp deleted] must be deleted. Temp_log deleted. Timestamp deleted. Tag deleted.

———————————————

Single network deliberation complete. Temp_log [deliberation timestamp deleted] must be deleted. Temp_log deleted. Timestamp deleted. Tag deleted.

———————————————

Single network deliberation complete. Temp_log [deliberation timestamp deleted] must be deleted. Temp_log deleted. Timestamp deleted. Tag deleted.

———————————————

>>STEP117=[mission_terminal_shutdown] estimated 0 seconds

>>ERROR STEP118=[delete all logs,timestamps,tags tag = *mission_temporary*] operation incomplete_

Chapter the FOURTEENTH

Faustpact

Written February 2–4, 2455
Events of January 31
Romanova

Did we abandon Romanova the correct amount? That is the question stark on every face around me, and inside me too, the newest form of that skin-shedding dragon Conscience which gnaws ever at the taproot of my sanity. Allegiance called us away, diverse allegiances to Him, to Earth, to empire, to the stars, and yet we could not bring ourselves to strip too many assets from that brave but teetering citadel which still holds out against the darts of Fortune. Romanova has given the world so much, reader, so much. It may, if it survives, give more. Perhaps the cold, ideal tactician would have taken every human resource with us, leaving an empty Forum for the dogs of war to maul. But hope insists wise words and calm authority may yet have power over armies' rage in Earth's thrice-battered capital. So we divided up our human strength, and we who now flee southward through the sea's depths pray anew, with every glance we trade across the belly-cabin of our grim Dreadnautilus, that we divided wisely.

What you must hear now is our escape, the price—the *prices*—paid to buy this centimeter's progress on the world's great map. Discord seized Romanova, with relentless Ruin at her side, and for every drop of blood that murder wrung from Cook and Ganymede, these martial goddesses twisted a human heart toward manslaughter. I would tell you that Europe's many armies fell apart without their great marshal, that the Remakers battled Hiveguard in the streets, that now 'Utopia' became a curse on lips across the city, and that the fractured Mitsubishi clashed and churned around the city's hills like waves around a crag of stubborn stone. I think all that occurred, but goddess Discord—Eris—and confounding Ruin—Atë—these kinswomen of martial Ares devour information as voraciously as souls. From our Conclave moated with fire and death we knew only that smoke rose, that tanks rumbled, that a ring of man-made thunder laid siege to the faraway Janiculum, and that battle lines surged over the Forum and Capitoline, whose last awe of legitimacy had been washed away by leaders' blood. We did improvise a funeral for what remained of Cook and Ganymede, though it was strangely quiet since no guests could come, and all the honor guards and aides-de-camp are scattered to the mêlée. I fear more people mourn the path to victory that died with Ganymede than mourn the man himself, but Carlyle's frank, perceptive eulogy reminded us that a man may be great while not good, noble while not gentle, a paragon of some real virtues worthy of respect even while the same soul lets the kinder virtues sleep. A Humanist's only promise is excellence, and Ganymede certainly excelled at leaving footprints in the world. A death may diminish the human race and so be tragic, even if the man himself deserved Fate's cruelty—this fact is not only true of me.

Two long days into Discord's reign, our Dreadnautilus reached Sardinia's coast; three days longer the goddess fed on our despair as every tunnel that our scouts explored twisted around, away, ever away from that safe shore so maddeningly near and yet unreachable. An overland escape had grown yet more impossible, as Mitsubishi of both factions planted lazer traps throughout the city, keen projector beams invisible unless some dust or mist reveals their crisscross lights like spiderwebs gone mad. Lazer light is too precise for Griffincloth to mimic, so any interruption in a beam betrays a Delian to death—not capture, *death*—such is the hate-birthing genius of that atrocious instrument which wore the flesh that was Lorelei Cook.

"There's only one solution." Norax rose, their coat brightening the Conclave's solemn boardroom with a slice of sunny winter scrub and milling sheep. "We must ask the Commissioner General directly where they hid the tunnel maps."

Approving glances flashed around our little council: the tired but dogged Censor, Papadelias's ranking officers Detective Superintendent Leni Dragović and Police Councilor for Blacklaw Affairs Yuki Matsuoka, deep-seeing Speaker Jin, our grimly smiling hostess Julia who let us use this most inviolable meeting room, tender Carlyle Foster dressed in mourning for her strange but noble uncle, and Charlemagne Guildbreaker, as calm as a rock at sea that knows full well that the ship—not the rock—is the one in danger.

Only my successor scowled. "We can't get through to Dhaka. Something's still wrong with the Pass-It-On links through Kashmir, nothing's getting through."

"We know," Norax confirmed. "The Masons in Labokla-Lahore are pushing north against the Hiveguard mountain strongholds. But an iris brought us word this morning: the Commissioner General has petitioned our forces in Dhaka to help them contact Romanova. Since the need is urgent on both ends, the Clairvoyance Constellation saw my signal and has approved a Wishgrant."

I wish the faces in our circle had been warm, grateful for such a gift, but Dragović and the pursed-lipped Censor had a sourness in their eyes—even those who know Utopia did not create the silence have long suspected that these haughty otherworlders must have a solution but, as ever, hoard their magic to themselves.

"This is not lightly offered," Norax stressed. "Wishgrants are so named because we can only grant a few, and a resource tapped for this is a resource not available elsewhere, elsewhen. The whole Earthsphere competes for Wishgrants, and we could not secure one even to let Micromegas hear Mycroft's voice." Norax paused to let the pain of that sink in. "But to safeguard Mycroft's escape, and the Anonymous and Triumvirs, and to give Romanova's officers use of the city's deeppaths in the current crisis, and to help us evacuate the Janiculum, and to grant the Commissioner General's request for contact when all pan-Asian axons are cut, all these ends synthesized as one were judged an eldertask and ineclipsable. The wish is granted."

Around the room, accusing stares grew softer, mollified by the knowledge that Norax of all people would not have held back this option had the price been light. Our curly-haired Norax is a true native, reader, not merely Romanovan but Sardinian, whose two homes in this universe are this rugged isle of forests and mountains, and the more unconquered mountains of the silver, watching Moon. That coat of ancient pasture is the first hint, but the name is the true giveaway, one of Sardinia's mythic hero-founders, a child of Hermes—friendliest to humankind of the immortals—and of Eriteide, daughter of Geryon, the monster with a human face and grandson of Medusa. Norax would not have let tanks scar their tread-wounds into Sardinia's earth for one unnecessary minute, not if there were any other way.

"Text-only communication would suffice," calm Charlemagne suggested, "if that would consume fewer resources than voice."

Norax frowned. "It would not, not at speed. While the link is open, we will also send the Commissioner a dataskein containing our own reports and anything you wish to send, and they will send us a dataskein too, but if you want direct answers to direct questions, voice will be as easy as anything. Preparations will take a few hours. Shall I begin?"

We hardly paused to think before our Yes. That's why they hide their gifts, you know, reader, revealing what they can do for us sparingly like parents hiding treats—we always take them.

Norax dispatched a speedy lightengale, and we spent two awkward hours assembling data and pretending not to stare at every passing sparrow.

"The roof. Now."

We all trooped up, the Triumvirs, four Censor's Guards, and four of Papa's officers giddy with hope. At first, upon the roof, we saw only a smoke-striped sky and Myrmidons, six black-sleeved comrades tasked as rooftop lookouts, since Alliance officers are tired and few. Then the Censor's guards stiffened around me as three Delians appeared before us: a coat of stars, a coat of riddle clouds, and Huxley's steady storm. Their U-beasts too showed slivers of themselves, a contour of fur and scales on our left, of metal on our right, and I heard my successor gasp at a glimpse of sand-gold eyes and huge paws soft as shadow. Four months Huxley's black lion had watched invisibly at my successor's side, months more at mine, yet I can count on one hand the occasions we have seen the creature, or seen guardian Huxley, whose step and breath and touch we know so well. The Delians saluted as they greeted one another, Norax's salute civilian and gentle, one finger or maybe two just peeking from the sleeve's void, a warm gesture which two of the others returned in kind, while Huxley's salute was grim as ever with a formal open palm.

"Is the sight line clear?" Norax asked, still fully visible, a slice of tree-studded lowlands cutting the city's artificial hills.

"We think so."

The Delians and their U-beast partners gathered around a flat, square panel of a bright, unnatural yellow-green, with a geometric pattern in stark black upon it. The panel hovered in midair waist-high above the rooftop, the top of some device or creature too grand or terrible for them to let us see. The Delians drew cables from their coats and hooked themselves, their U-beasts, and the unseen something to the hub of Grendel's tatzelwurm. I shuddered seeing even Utopia resort to plugs and wires, barely a step above pen and burnable paper; in war's grip, all our labors—epics, libraries, Hobbes understands—are mortal once again.

"Casting now." It was Grendel who confirmed it, an Atlantean, face still raw from nearly fatal depressurization, whose coat turns clouds to poetry, and crafts enticing puzzles out of every crack and wall stain, which, if you solve them, open gateways to reveal underdepths where yet more puzzles breed.

"How long will we have?" asked Detective Superintendent Dragović.

"A very few minutes."

"How many minutes? Your best guess?"

Grendel looked to Huxley, whose digital eyes seemed darker than the coat of storm. "You ask me to guess how long it will take an unsteady shot to hit a bull's-eye. Chance decides."

"A shot?" Speaker Jin repeated, the Brillist struggling to hide a gleeful grin at having Utopian (half)faces to read and probe. "A literal shot or metaphoric?"

Huxley's answer was cut off by a tinny voice, thinned by processing and peppered with instants of silence.

Papadelias: ". . . long will it take to go through?"
Dragović: "That's Papa's voice! Papa, I hear you! Can you hear me?"
Papadelias: "What? Hello? Who's that?"
Dragović: "It's Leni Dragović, Papa!" The detective hopped with excitement.
Papadelias: "Leni! Great to hear your voice! Where are you?"
Dragović: "Romanova, on the Conclave roof. We hear you loud and clear, Papa! It's working!"
Papadelias: "Is my data coming through too?"
Dragović: "Um . . . I don't . . ."
Grendel: "Yes, smoothly."
Papadelias: "Great! We're getting yours, too. Is the Censor there with you?"
Su-Hyeon: "I'm here, Commissioner! This is Su-Hyeon. We need—"
Papadelias: "Are you alright?"
Su-Hyeon: "Yes, I'm fine." Su-Hyeon smiled at Papa's kindly care.
Papadelias: "Free and unrestrained?"

Su-Hyeon: "Yes! The chaos is—"
Papadelias: "Then what the flying goat shit are you doing?"
Su-Hyeon: "What?"
Papadelias: "Why didn't you stop this coup?"
Su-Hyeon: "Coup? What coup?"
Papadelias: "Jin Im-Jin and Charlemagne Guildbreaker!"
Su-Hyeon: "What?" (chuckling) "Oh, it's not a coup. They're helping me—"
Mycroft: (softly) "How is it not a coup?"
Su-Hyeon: (spinning) "What?"
Mycroft: "There's no Triumvirate in the Alliance Charter."
Papadelias: "Who's that? Who's speaking now?"
Mycroft: (in Greek) «It's Mycroft Canner, Papa. I'm alive.»
Papadelias: « . . . Mycroft . . . »
Mycroft: «Didn't you get my message?»
Papadelias: « . . . Moriarty. Yes. I wasn't sure.»
Mycroft: «The blast ripped off my tracker, but I survived and made it back to Romanova a few days ago.»
Papadelias: «How—»
Mycroft: «Not now, Papa. Listen, be careful what you say in English. The other Triumvirs are here listening, also Inspectors Corker and Kartal, Councilor Matsuoka, and Deputy Dragović, plus there are four of the Censor's guards, four Delians, [Anonymous], and six other Myrmidons.»
Papadelias: (a pause) «Are the Speaker and the Mason threatening the Censor?»
Mycroft: «I don't think so. It looks like the Censor set up this Triumvirate freely, relying on the Senators' reputations to back up their authority, but I wasn't here to see it. Or to stop it.»
[Anonymous]: «I was here. It's nothing like a coup. Im-Jin and Carmen saved things when Su-Hyeon was floundering. They've been amazing, the only thing standing between Romanova and chaos.»
Mycroft: «Avoid names, [Anonymous], they can recognize their names even in Greek. Use titles. Shall I take them out, Papa? The Speaker is in strike range. Kill or capture?»
[Anonymous]: «What!?»
Papadelias: «You said there are four Censor's Guards there? Will they help you or hinder?»
Mycroft: «Hinder, but the Myrmidons and Delians will back me.»
[Anonymous]: «You can't be seriously discussing this!»
Mycroft: «Careful, [Anonymous], the Speaker can read your body language like a book. Think of a poem, something you've memorized, play it through in your mind, complicate your expression. Quickly!»
Papadelias: «What about the Masonic Senator? Can you take both of them?»

9A: <Could I take over writing for a bit? If you don't mind.>
MC: <Of course.>

9A: <Thanks. It's an important moment, and I think there are some things I can get across that you can't.>
MC: <Alright.>

9A here again. I understand why Mycroft's racing through this section, uncomfortable with what's coming, but there was a change that happened about here that can't be seen through Mycroft's eyes, because the change was Mycroft. They paused before replying to Papa, and I looked up, reciting some Cavafy in my head and trying not to look at Im-Jin. The four detectives were smiling, assuming this was just the friendly verbal sparring Mycroft and Papa both enjoy so much, but as I thought of combat—Censor's Guards against us?—my eyes drifted to my black-sleeved Myrmidon comrades, standing like caryatids around the edges of the roof, and between them the silent Delians with their mostly hidden beasts. I remember thinking Mycroft was right that the Censor's Guards stood no chance. And then I glanced back at Mycroft, expecting their submissive smile or philosophic frown, but the face that gazed back at me might have been a stranger's: stern, confident, unhurried, the face of an architect of battle lines and razer of cities. This pause was not Mycroft's customary servile reticence but the calculating caution of a great commander, who knows they could reach out a hand and crush all they survey, and is not yet certain whether to refrain. I'd thought Ganymede's death had left the city leaderless, but there was one field marshal still in Romanova.

«The Mason is not our enemy,» Mycroft answered at last.

«No one here is our enemy!» I cried.

«Later, [Anonymous],» Mycroft hissed, the Greek form of my preferred nickname more plosive and startling when voiced harshly than the English. «Papa, I won't kill a *Familiaris,* not on your orders alone, and the Delians and Myrmidons here have their pact with Caesar. But if you want, we could force the Mason away from the Censor and headquarters, back to Masonic territory.»

«You've got it wrong!» I cried, still unbelieving. «Both of you, listen, I can see now why it looks like a coup from a distance, but I've been with them night and day! It's not a coup! It's a life raft, keeping the Alliance barely afloat! Su-Hyeon can't do it alone. If we lose the Triumvirate, there really will be nothing left but angry Hives flailing at each other. Please believe me!»

Mycroft's brows were narrowed, and I found myself wishing desperately that I had telepathy, to pour into Mycroft's mind my months with Carmen and Im-Jin, our midnight hours, shared soup, the times they'd saved me, from all the times they'd saved the city back to that first day when Im-Jin stopped the three Madame-corrupted officers from hurling me and Carlyle in the cells to rot. Trust's proofs are hard to share.

«Alright.» It was Papadelias who believed me. «Mycroft, later, in private, tell my officers to investigate both the Mason and the Speaker *very* thoroughly. If they sniff up the faintest hint that either of them has coerced or even manipulated the Censor, I want them both arrested instantly, no matter what the Censor says.»

Mycroft: «I'll pass that on.»

Papadelias: «And when I say my officers, I mean I want *them* to investigate not you, Mycroft. You yourself stay out of action and rest, you hear me?»

«I'm fine!» Mycroft snapped, a petty human moment which made them feel like Papa's sparring friend again.

«[Anonymous],» Papa asked, «is Mycroft fine?»

«No!» I answered with more than a little smugness. «They're barely able to stand—starvation and exposure.»

Now Mycroft snapped at me, «[Anonymous]!»

«Thought so.» Here Papa switched to testy English. "Leni, who's Mycroft Canner handcuffed to right now?"

"No one . . ." the detective answered, already wincing.

"How many times have I told you!" Papa's thin and processed shout made the playback extra tinny.

"Sorry, Papa. Things are chaotic."

"Chaos is when we need precautions most! Now listen, all of you, time's short and this is important: I know what happened to the people who disappeared the first day when the cars went rogue."

"That's great!" Su-Hyeon cut in. "But first we need to know where you hid your maps of Romanova's underground. Lorelei Cook and Ganymede were assassinated by the capitol steps in the middle of peace negotiations, and what's left of the European and Mitsubishi fleets are slaughtering each other in the streets all around us!"

"Inside Romanova? Shit! Which Mitsubishi fleet?"

"Which fleet? The . . . western Mediterranean fleet, we think."

"No, which faction?"

"Oh." Su-Hyeon sighed. "The fleet's split into Hiveguard and Remakers, they're fighting each other. We think. Recon's near impossible."

"Yes, but which Mitsubishi faction's fleet is it? Dougong, Fuxing, Homeland, or Milae-Greenpeace? I don't know if you're getting Kosala's updates on the Mumbai talks, but Milae and Greenpeace may split."

Blinking confusion, Su-Hyeon looked to Im-Jin, then to me. "We haven't heard of any of those factions, Papa. There was only one Mitsubishi fleet in the Mediterranean so far as we know, until Ganymede split it apart, and the Remaker Mitsubishi joined with Europe battling the Hiveguard."

"Ganymede split it?" Now it was Papa who paused, confused. "Look, I don't understand what's going on over there, but if Romanova's falling, get the Censor out! And half my staff. And [Anonymous] and Mycroft!"

"I can't leave Romanova!" Su-Hyeon blurted. "I'm in charge!"

Papa's words rang firm and quick through the machine. "We can't leave all the Alliance eggs in one basket. We need to leave enough in Romanova to be a functional government, but the Censor needs to be somewhere you can keep operating independently and safely and . . . Who's that laughing?"

"It's Im-Jin, Ektor." Im-Jin had chuckled, a reedy laugh still weakened by the remnants of pneumonia. "Just delighted by how much you and I agree. And thanks for telling Mycroft not to kill me yet. Will you listen to what we need now?"

Everyone stiffened around us, but Papa didn't miss a beat. "You're welcome. What do you need?"

"The maps," Im-Jin answered before others could cut in with questions. "The underground."

"Right! There's a couple dead moths stuck in the overhead light fixture above the second floor landing of the fire stairs. The files are in the stripey moth. There's also a backup in the breath mint stuck to the back of the folding futon frame in the staff lounge closet, but that's under boxes, so the moth is easier. They're encrypted, though. Bo has the key. Where's Bo? Is Bo not there? Bo Chowdhury."

Leni Dragović swallowed hard. "Bo is . . ."

"Have you been without Bo all this time?" Papa pressed. "No wonder the sky's falling. Desi can access the files too. Is Desi there? Desi O'Callaghan."

Mycroft's face took on a mourning softness. "I haven't seen either of them, Papa."

I spoke now, to myself, not to the others: "Chowdhury . . . O'Callaghan . . . I know those names . . . Who . . ." Tick . . . tock . . . *bang!* Duh. "Oh, Chowdhury and O'Callaghan! They're the ones we arrested!"

"What?" Papa and Mycroft cried together.

"At the start of the war. They're in our holding cells. They're spies!"

"Spies?" Through the distortion, Papa's answer sounded like a yelp. "Bo and Desi, spies?"

"Im-Jin unmasked them," I answered, smiling my thanks anew. "They worked for Madame."

"They work for me!"

Su-Hyeon cut in. "It's the truth, Commissioner. I checked the records, they've both been visiting Madame's constantly, for years."

"I know," the distant, tinny voice shot back. "Bo and Desi went to Madame's with me, for me. I

MC: <Let me take over.>
9A: <I'm alright to keep going. Do you want to grab a snack? A nap?>
MC: <Let me be the one who writes these next words. Let it be me.>
9A: <Oh. Yes. Alright.>

It should be me who says it, reader. I should have said it long ago, to you, to everyone, and at a better time, when I could have explained it without wasting the dear-bought seconds gifted by Utopia. But I am a coward, always a coward when it comes to hurting what posterity will think of those I love. Too much of me still thinks on Acheron, that gloom of spirits who forget themselves as Earth forgets, retaining only what you, reader, you, posterity, sole sustenance of we who die, remember. I would not have you remember this, force Papa's good shade to retain this. When some cunning conjures Papa's ghost a hundred years from now, I would have you recall his jests, his manic zeal, that spark that feasts on puzzles, not—not this. So I put it off, and put it off, and now at last Ektor Carlyle Papadelias—our brave, unruffled Papadelias—has to tell it to you, reader, and to everyone in his own voice:

"I know. Bo and Desi went to Madame's with me, for me. I work for Madame."

Heartbreak. I have caused it before, reader, felt it before, but to see its stab of pain on so many faces, so many of the few faces upon this Earth that still have warmth enough in Mycroft Canner's presence for that warmth to fade, I couldn't . . . The young Censor trembled, the Censor's Guards, even the Delians showing their grief-shock as this last still solid pillar of our world proved rotten too. The faces of my Myrmidon comrades were the worst, a wet-eyed hurt, as at the treason of a ba'pa. For a Servicer, it almost was.

"It isn't what you think!" I cried out. "It isn't the bad kind of corruption! No, that came out wrong."

Tears from my successor. "You didn't tell me . . ."

Thou didst not tell me.

I know. I'm sorry. So sorry. You two are the two I most betrayed. But I couldn't bear it. I couldn't bear soiling Papa in the world's eyes, or in yours. I have let you rely on Papa as a haven, one untainted ally in whose breast we have no need to seek for dark agendas—even indefatigable Martin is not quite so pure. But Papa's corruption isn't dirty, really, it's the mildest, the very mildest corruption there could be. But when the devil's offer is deal or oblivion, you take the deal. Think, reader: Madame's tendrils twine deep into all Earth's powers, and she must guard her back, her plans, her creatures. Would she leave the Alliance forces—who have the means and mandate to police both Hives and Blacklaws—uncontrolled? Conspiracies like hers are the natural prey of a Commissioner General, as is our stumbling Visitor whose talk of Peer and Plan inadvertently breaks the First Law several times a day. So dangerous a hunter must be tamed. For decades, Madame has chosen the Commissioner General. Papa's three predecessors were all her clients, abject addicts, and Papa worked against them, battled, curbed their corruption, even ousted two of them, back in the days when Papa still thought Madame was a force that could be stopped. But, to use the words I used on that rooftop before those tearful angry faces, "Everybody has their price."

I heard Papa's distant voice, "Now isn't the time . . ." but no one could drop it now, not while they had my shrinking form in front of them to glare at and accuse.

My successor's fists clenched. "Madame found someone who could seduce even Papa . . ."

I tried three times to say it, but sobs choked out the first two. "Me."

"You?"

"My case. The crime of the century. Papa waited seventy years for a Moriarty, but Madame controlled the Commissioner General, who got to decide which detective got the case. And Papa knew it."

"Papa sold out in return for getting your case?" In twin-like synchrony, the new Censor and new Anonymous met one another's gazes, and grief gave way to the glazed eyes of calculation, many pieces falling into place now that this link was found. "In your history, Papa investigated Julia Doria-Pamphili, Danaë, even O.S., but never Madame directly... Then Papa's been helping Madame through everything?"

"No!" I cried. "Only the tiniest bit. I told you, it's the good kind of corruption, an eighth surrender, conditional and calculated like Utopia's! After three in a row, Papa knew the next Commissioner General would be Madame's pick too, so the only way to keep someone worse out of the chair was to sit in it. Papa's not broken like the abject clients. Papa's left Madame alone but has always been ready to draw the line the minute—"

"Shut up, Mycroft!" Papa's voice exploded over the line. "No time. Fuck Madame! If we're lucky, they've been blown to bits by now. Are you telling me you've had my Deputy Commissioner General locked in a fucking cell for five months? With no charge beyond visiting a perfectly legal brothel!"

"We—" Su-Hyeon began.

"Shut up! Don't even answer! I'm the fucking Commissioner General and I'm in charge of protecting Romanova! Get Bo and Desi out this instant! In fact, who's there? Kip Corker?"

"Here, Papa."

"Go get Bo and Desi out, right now! Bo is in charge of the city, you all hear me? Desi is their second-in-command. Nobody trumps their orders, not in an active crisis, not even the fucking Censor! They know Romanova's underground. They can get the Censor and Mycroft out. They'll handle everything, and if the Censor wants Im-Jin and Carmen on their staff, that's the Censor's choice, but the Censor is not empowered to delegate their executive powers, or invent a Triumvirate out of nowhere, or override the Commissioner's Deputy in an emergency. That's the law, and if you don't like it, go fucking read the fucking Charter!" Now heated English turned to hasty Greek. «As for you, Mycroft!»

«Yes, Papa?»

«You take out Jin and Guildbreaker if Bo, Desi, or the Censor orders it, otherwise you leave them be, and you treat Bo and Desi's orders like you'd treat my own. Clear?»

«Yes, Papa. Clear.» I fully understood Papa's precautions, though my successor's eyes, still full of hurt and silent protest, did not. But Papa on the far side of the world could not be certain what this ancient Brillist and supreme Mason might do with their improvised power—nor, standing next to both of them, could I.

"Now listen!" Papa continued in English. "I have a question for the Censor about data analysis that's actually the fucking Censor's fucking job! Did any other high-profile people disappear in the cars that first day when I did? You must have run the numbers. Kosala says the program was supposed to only select actively violent people, mostly Hiveguard, but if I got flagged for internment, then either someone hacked the Cousins' program or Kosala's lying to me. I need to know if I can trust Kosala. Were any other major figures kidnapped that day or was it only me?"

"Kosala?" Su-Hyeon repeated. "Was it the Cousins who made the cars vanish after the Closing Ceremony? Yes, the Cousins! That makes sense. They had custody of the transit computers during the Olympics, they could have—"

"Answer me now! My data packet has the details for you. Who else did the cars take? Were any other Alliance officers or other leaders taken, or was it just me? Any Senators? Cousins? Nurturists? Kosala's allies? Kosala's enemies?"

"Uh, um . . . from . . ." Su-Hyeon's fingers twitched reflexively, remembering the computer's touch. "I don't remember any Romanovan officers other than you. There were some high-up Cousins though, two, Ko . . . Koho Bassey maybe was the name, or Koto, and the other was Alizeti Lee. Not sure if they were Nurturists, I think I remember ties to Kosala, maybe? And . . . let's see . . . there were two *Familiares,* I noticed that, one of the current Aediles, İlkay Arbor, and one of the Emperor's ba'sibs, Praetor Caerul Semaphoros. And there was one Mitsubishi Executive, Koizumi . . . something, they were an old supporter of Chief Director Andō, and there was . . . there was someone close to Director Huang Enlai too, Manager rank, Rao Zhiyang I think, and . . . who else . . . the Mayor of Barcelona, Calàndria Kim i Clos, though they're definitely Hiveguard. Those are the major figures I remember. Overall, those who disappeared were just over 81 percent Hiveguard, a mix of Hives but very few Cousins. The ones I looked up had most all either posted about violent intentions online or been in riots or brawls already, though that wasn't true of the *Familiares,* or Kosala's people, or Enlai's person Rao. And there were a few confirmed Remakers on the list, but they'd been in riots or had records of violence, and there were two Cousins I looked up who both turned out to be suspects in the Odessa set-set bash' attacks, so Nurturists for sure. So, if we omit the political figures, the overall selection is consistent with someone trying to make a list of those most likely to be violent when the war began. You said internment, did they try to isolate them? That makes sense, reroute the cars to keep the most violent out of the war's opening volley. Then most likely they're all still alive!"

Silence.

"Papa?"

Silence.

"Papa, are you there?"

Silence as we all stared at the bright yellow-green tile, as if our eyes and wishes could heal the unknown wound that split our world.

"Can you reconnect us?" Detective Dragović asked quickly.

"No."

"Just for a moment. We don't know if Papa got what they needed!"

Norax and Grendel traded winces. "You don't understand how difficult this was. It's not just flipping a switch."

"But you *can* do it, can't you?" Dragović's tone grew hot.

Digital eyes avoided the detective's. "The resources required are—"

"For the Alliance!" Dragović cut in. "You know the Hives have obligations in emergencies. You're no exception."

Norax fidgeted with their Sardinian nation-strat wristband. "A Wishgrant isn't—"

"This was not a Wishgrant." Huxley's snarl, with the lion's snarl rising dark behind it, froze us all.

Norax spun. "It . . . wasn't?"

"The Wishsmiths couldn't do it," Huxley answered. "I authorized a Faustpact."

Gasps with sobs within them rose from the gathered Delians, sharp enough to make their unseen beasts and robots growl and buzz.

"You didn't say . . ."

"No, I did not." Is the iron resolution in your eyes real, Huxley? Or have you set your program to hide signs of human frailty, the better to teach your too-peaceful comrades to resist strength-sapping grief? The tears which trickled down Norax's chin below the vizor, those I know were real.

"'Faustpact' sounds bad." It was Speaker Jin who said it. "Is Utopia making deals with the devil now?"

Ever-grim Huxley grew grimmer yet. "No threat to you or yours, Gordian. We pay the price."

Charlemagne Guildbreaker stepped forward gently, as a seasoned doe steps gently through woodland where every snapped twig might draw predators' attention to the young fawns in her precious herd, too new to guard themselves. "I would like to understand the implications. Is this named for Joyce and Felix? Or the Faust that sold their soul to Mephistopheles?"

A moment's hesitation, but before the *Familiaris* of an Emperor who has resolved anew to die like Mycroft MASON for Utopia if Fate demands it, even Huxley yields. "A Wishgrant uses scarce resources. A Faustpact sets back the Project. *The* Project." Huxley's repetition left no doubt what rusty soil had inched farther from our touch. "But entropy will always win some battles—intelligence's power lies in choosing which. This battle"—Huxley gestured to me, to my successor, to the capital around us—"is worth one pact with entropy. And many other parties will have chanceflocked, bouncing their signals alongside ours before the satellite was death-struck."

My chest heaved. A thousand man-made chariots circle this world, filling our starry night with vital relays, subtle sensors, mighty laboratories, hopeful telescopes—a thousand chariots this morning, but now only 999. No, Utopia must have resorted to many Faustpacts by now as they brave Earth's billion arrows. How many chariots remain, Utopia? 899? 599? 299? Yes, you can break the silence, bounce a lazer off a satellite to link our voices point-to-point from here to Bangladesh, bounce off a hundred lazers all at once, a hundred points of human contact, someone's *here* to someone's distant *there,* but always our unseen enemy is watching for the slight adjustment of a mirror, the change of temperature, the lazer glint, and quickly makes this one more Icarus to streak the sky with burning. Papa made one Faustpact to have his Moriarty and to keep the Commissioner General's seat from filthier hands than his, and Papa has paid for it, a thousand dirty favors demanded, a thousand small humiliations endured in visits to Madame's, and a thousand victims—Madame's victims and Perry's too—on Papa's conscience, now and forever. One Faustpact's price. How many Faustpacts have you made so far, Utopia? How many of our ancestors' painstaking small steps toward the stars undone since you entered this war? In that moment I understood why guardian Huxley had voted against peacebonding the harbingers. But I remembered too that Utopia's motto has two halves, not one: *astra mortemque superare gradatim*—sometimes abbreviated just *gradatim* "step by step"—to step by step surpass death and the stars. They will not give up either quest, reader. Ever.

Our heartbreak glimpse of entropy's grim visage held us mute some moments. Then Deputy Commissioner General Bo Chowdhury—now by Papa's order *Acting Commissioner General* Bo Chowdhury—charged up the stairs toward us, along with Assistant Commissioner Desi O'Callaghan and Police Councilor for Blacklaw Affairs Isabel Ximénez, the third officer arrested for collusion that first morning of the war. And then our decision: which human props to leave for teetering Romanova.

9A: <You're skipping Bo and Desi's tirade? I guess there wasn't much in it the reader couldn't guess, except the ratio.>

MC: <The ratio?>

9A: <Four minutes of yelling at us about imprisoning them for five months with nothing against them but a Brillist's say-so, and then five minutes yelling about the fact that you, Mycroft, weren't handcuffed to anything. That's Papa's people to the core.>

MC: <Is that why you had that sort of sour but amused look on your face?>

9A: <During the tirade? No, that's because I tried imagining Papa in one of Madame's floofy dresses. Please tell me that never happened.>

MC: <Rarely. Madame tried both genders' costumes on Papa, but Papa's not-undeliberate physical awkwardness made both equally dreadful. In the end, Madame usually let Papa stay in uniform, except when she was in the mood for comedy.>

9A: <Ha! Good. Go, Papa! That could have been a lot worse.>

MC: <It could indeed—so many things could have been worse had Earth's cruel mistress been a little crueler, or less tempered by her Kindly Son and His good father.>

9A: <Yeah. Shall I narrate our debate? I think it was a bigger, harder moment for me than it was for you.>

MC: <Please do.>

A big, hard moment, one last deal with one last devil—two last devils?—as we divvied up our forces, who would stay and who would go.

"I'm taking the Censor out of the city, that's beyond debate." Acting Commissioner General Bo Chowdhury started us off, this practical, lanky Bengali Whitelaw, who had somehow seemed so scary in September when threatening to throw me and Carlyle in the cells, but now stood scritching the half-visible black lion behind the ears, enjoying the purr-thunder. "Desi will take charge of the city. I'll help the Censor run the Alliance outside."

Su-Hyeon was staring down at their hands. "You don't think the Censor should stay in Romanova?"

"Not in burning Romanova."

Carmen nodded grave agreement. "Capitals can be rebuilt more easily than continuity. For the Alliance to survive in people's minds, it needs a continuous political presence, the Censor speaking and acting, and connected to the world. You must evacuate to Alexandria; you too, [Anonymous]."

"Me?"

"The best, most neutral means to speak right now is Pass-It-On. The Censor needs that, and needs you to maintain it. Alexandria is connected to Pass-It-On, and there Caesar will protect you and the information bloodstream you enable. There you'll both be safe."

I wanted to say no, that I couldn't abandon the other Triumvirs, but Carmen seemed suddenly looming and grim behind their beard, like one of those giant stone temple guardians from ancient Babylon or Uruk that stare down at you in museums, carved impossibly long ago from blocks you can't believe pre-modern peoples moved. I gulped. "But Alexandria, you don't worry that I . . ." I found myself fingering the Vs on my shoulder. "That MASON and the Prince, that they'll exploit . . . I mean control . . ."

"No fear of that." Carmen smiled. "The Emperor is primus inter pares, but acknowledges Earth's other sovereigns as junior peers, including the Censor and Anonymous. In Alexandria, Caesar will foster and aid you both, as they would expect a fellow sovereign to foster and aid them if they came for refuge in days of strife." Carmen's face softened. "And there is the influence of the *Porphyrogene*."

There was. Our Prince of Truth and Kindness. I felt a tear itch in the corner of my eye, thinking that I—not only Mycroft—*I* might see Them soon.

"Carmen and I will stay in Romanova." Im-Jin gave Su-Hyeon's purple sleeve a gentle squeeze. "It's as Ektor said, we shouldn't put all the Alliance eggs in one basket, no matter how well armored a living robot-fish-tank-warship-thing that basket is." A smirk for the Utopians. "Two and two is a good split for a four-way Triumvirate."

"But you'll be in danger!" Su-Hyeon cried.

"So will you." Im-Jin flexed their tiny shoulders, and I caught myself wincing at the sound of 160-plus-year-old bones popping. "Two of us will have to creep and crawl and fight and swim through who knows what to get out through the tunnels, and two of us will have to sit here in imposing chairs and win a staring contest with a victorious army. I think I know who has which skill set."

Carmen said nothing here, but the looks that passed between them and Im-Jin gave me the feeling that the two had planned this, parents discussing in advance how to convince us kids to take the life jackets when there weren't enough for everyone.

"Yo-u-hh." Su-Hyeon choked up. "I doubt anyone would hurt you, Im-Jin, but Carmen . . . Whatever side comes out on top in Romanova, both armies are at least half Mitsubishi. Mitsubishi and Masons are adversaries everywhere, they might . . ."

Now the parent faded, and the stony temple guardian emerged so chillingly in Carmen that I remembered why Mycroft sometimes calls MASON Death. "My mandate is to ensure the peaceful functioning of Romanova. This I will continue to fulfill, and whosoever hinders me is enemy to both Alliance and Empire."

"But they might kill you, Carmen." I said it. I expected to trip over the words, but somehow they came out easily.

"Whosoever strikes down a Romanovan Senator while I work peacefully for the capital's survival proves themself a foe to peace, justice, and civilization. If by my death I buy such perfect proof that Caesar's enemies are all Earth's enemies, it will bring a hundred million allies to the Empire—that is a death well spent."

I'll never see them again! That hot thought cracked through me like a gunshot, and fear made the memory burn in, vivid, so I still see them when I close my eyes, Carmen's square suit, Im-Jin's stylishly tailored sweater which often seemed black, but its fibers were glowing red around the shoulder as they caught the backlight of a window. There's a code in every Brillist sweater, patterns, neckline, sleeves, but could I describe Im-Jin's if you asked me? Did I really get to know them, use my time well with these two amazing living archives of our century? How could I waste such time?

Su-Hyeon beside me rubbed their eyes, probably hiding tears.

"And will you two *Senātors* wear the Vs?" Mycroft cut in, pronouncing the title with its Latin stress. To my surprise there was a pause, and I looked again at pursed-lipped Im-Jin, frowning Carmen, then again at Mycroft who had on that stranger's face again, the great field marshal, architect of conquests. "If you stay, you'll influence which group is victor over Romanova. Which will you favor?"

"Peace," Su-Hyeon answered for them. "They'll work out a peace again, whatever peace will end the violence soonest."

I nodded my approval, but the gravity that lingered in Carmen and Mycroft's faces made me feel I was missing something. "Is there some complication to this question?" I asked.

"There is no neutral faction in this war," Mycroft answered, with a cutting stress to each syllable, percussive like a threat. At Bo's insistence Mycroft was handcuffed to Huxley by this point, but still their body had this strange sense of relaxed mastery, like when a great athlete is standing within touch of their equipment, and their whole frame takes on that special confidence, tense yet relaxed, that says: with this racket, this weight, this ball, I can do anything. "This is precisely the coup that Papa warned against—the two of you without the Censor. I want to know what side we hand the city to if we hand it to you."

Im-Jin chuckled. "Now that you can't rely on Ganymede to fly Donatien Mason's Vs over the capitol, you want to make sure Carmen and I will? What will you do if we won't?"

"Conquer it themself!" It was Leni Dragović who blurted it out, still red-faced and recovering since Bo and Desi had delivered the chewing out of a lifetime. "Now that the other forces are in chaos, the strongest army currently in Romanova is the united force of militant Servicers, Utopians, and hidden U-beasts who all answer primarily to Mycroft Canner. We're surrounded! Mycroft was content to leave when the Remakers were in power, but not now."

I clutched the Vs on the shoulder of my Censor's office jacket, and felt a pang as fear and hurt washed trust from the faces of Papa's officers, the Censor's Guards, and—worse, much worse—Su-Hyeon. Were we enemies? Somehow? Suddenly? Had Mycroft's presence torn away the veil that let us pretend Censor and Myrmidon could have the same goals in this war?

"Leni, you're being paranoid." This is the moment I realized why, of all humans on Earth, Papa chose Bo Chowdhury as second-in-command. "It's pretty obvious that it's not our—what, thirty-six?—remaining officers who've been protecting the Forum all this time. It's the Myrmidons, and it's the Utopians—Utopians who've spent months dodging mobs with pitchforks, and still, when invading armies came into this city, they carved into the sky with literal words of fire that they would defend the Censor. Twice! They did the words-of-fire thing twice! They just blew up a satellite to let us talk to Papadelias for five minutes! We are not distrusting them. And we are not distrusting Mycroft Canner. Handcuffing them to stuff so they don't bolt off into suicidal danger, absolutely, but distrusting? No."

The look on Leni Dragović's face at that moment, so layered, safety and reassurance mixed with embarrassment and blame. "But, Bo—"

"Leni!" It was Im-Jin who interrupted this time, with more power than one would imagine that tiny frame could muster. "You're flinging blame around because you feel guilty about being party to locking up your superior officers. I also feel guilty, it was a bad mistake, but I'm not letting it make me paranoid. Mycroft Canner loves Romanova, they wouldn't harm a shingle on its pretty roofs, not without direct orders from MASON, or Mason Junior, or a short list of hallucinatory dead people, but I can tell by that blink—right there, did you catch it? And the little eyebrow twitch?—that Mycroft has no such orders. Mycroft isn't threatening to conquer the city, they're just asking whether Carmen and I will wear the Vs. Carmen will not. Carmen, say your piece."

Carmen smiled at Im-Jin's bossy Brillist bluntness, but then their own Masonic gravity took hold. "I shall wear no sigil—not even the *Porphyrogene*'s—without my

Emperor's command. Though the Hiveguard follow one who aims to kill our *Imperator Destinatus*, my oath of office as a Romanovan Senator is given to this city and Alliance, so, until Caesar releases me from that office, all in Romanova—even my heart's enemies—have my protection."

"Precisely," Im-Jin chirruped like a teacher when the pupil answers right. "Carmen is reliable and neutral. For myself"—here a pause, a blink, and a cheek twitch reminded me of my illiteracy in the facial language Brillists read so well—"I do want to live to see Donatien make their brave new world. Does that satisfy you?" Two breaths' pause as Im-Jin peered across at Mycroft.

"It certainly doesn't satisfy me." Bo Chowdhury stopped petting the lion and strode a firm pace forward. "I can't trust you, not after all this. I can't trust you to be neutral, and I can't trust you not to play mind games with the officers I leave here with you." They crossed their lanky arms, looming over frail Im-Jin like a statue of Justice over the courtroom. "Carmen I can trust, but I will not leave Romanova even partly in your hands." I got a chill. The Whitelaw Hiveless sash about Chowdhury's waist proclaims many things: self-discipline, strictness, acceptance of rigid mandates, rejection of the recreational poisons of mind and flesh—it does not proclaim gentleness.

"You're right." Im-Jin smiled, a tired smile. "Gordian isn't neutral, we're Remakers. Just like them." A nod to the silent Utopians. "And we share one other value with Utopia: we oppose death. Absolutely. This"—Im-Jin tapped their skull above the temple—"is invaluable, and until our tech advances a bit more, it's still irreproducible, and every human death an intolerable loss. What was it Ganymede said? 'Anything on earth or heaven that I can move to save one life in Romanova, I will'? That's my conviction, too. And I am very good at running Romanova."

In the pause, as Bo and Im-Jin stared at one another, that line from the Cook document played through my head—"[Organic network Σ] has no backup." Propaganda or not, it made me choke back a sob. I hated Lorelei Cook—I hated them, but I still mourned even them. But was it Mycroft or the Prince who taught me—even *me*—to mourn my enemies?

Im-Jin broke the silence. "I guess that's not enough for you to trust me? I understand. I really screwed up with this. I wish I had a solution, but rationally, you shouldn't trust me. I just accidentally or intentionally enacted a coup for four months—in reality, it was accidentally, but you've no reason to believe that."

Of all of us, only stony Carmen still mustered a smile. "Except that you've spent these four months in exhausting, tireless work for the city's good, and before that, you gave this city a hundred years of public service. That satisfies me."

The smile on Im-Jin's soft and wrinkled cheeks made me think of grandba'pas' hugs, and birthday feasts, and warmth, and home. "I guess there's that."

Bo and Desi traded frowns. And then there was this subtle moment. Maybe thinking about Brillists reading minds through faces made me watch people more carefully, but they looked at Mycroft, Bo and Desi both of them for just a second, they both looked to Mycroft who . . . It wasn't a nod, it was barely more than a blink, but it was unmistakable: approval.

"Alright. You'll work with Charlemagne but *under* Desi. Clear?"

Desi stepped forward, a weak, slow-moving body leaning on a cane, but with enough conviction in face and poise to make me confident the weight of Romanova could rest on such shoulders anytime. "Usually, I give people three chances, but your first screwup was really bad, so you've used up two. Fair?"

Im-Jin's chuckle leaked delight. "More than fair."

That settled it. Except it didn't feel settled, the body language was all weird. Everything wrapped up too fast, no lingering chat as the officers charged straight downstairs, with Mycroft and Huxley at their heels. It wasn't right. I followed Mycroft. Mycroft followed Bo and Desi, but after a few paces, it shifted and Bo and Desi followed Mycroft, with such fast, purposeful strides along the Conclave hallways that I had to jog at one point to keep up.

"I can't work with Im-Jin, not after this," I heard Desi say between fast breaths, "not without somebody to guard my back."

"I know," Mycroft answered, making a swift turn toward the imposing office of Julia Doria-Pamphili.

"May I join you?" Carlyle Foster must have heard the rustle of our passage in the hall, and Mycroft gestured for them to enter the office and close the door behind.

"We need you to watch Jin Im-Jin," Mycroft began before Julia's predatory smile could break into a predatory welcome. "We're evacuating the Censor to Alexandria. Charlemagne Guildbreaker and Jin Im-Jin are staying to run Romanova, with Assistant Commissioner O'Callaghan. And you."

"Desi?" Bone-pale Julia turned their smile on the Assistant Commissioner. "Where have you popped up from? I haven't seen you these past months."

"Rotting in a cell," Desi answered coldly. "Im-Jin's doing, my connection to Madame being the nominal justification. It was either a misunderstanding, or it wasn't."

"I see." Julia stretched back in their grand and comfy chair. "So, we don't know whether Im-Jin is a valuable ally or a scheming traitor. Fascinating problem. And Im-Jin's ten out of ten on mind games, no one in the city to match them. Except me." Julia paused to draw a slow breath, slurping as if the situation were delicious.

I didn't say anything. I didn't, but I did open my mouth, and Mycroft must have caught the question on my lips, and in my eyes. "Julia gave up *real* Rome for Romanova," they said in answer to my thoughts. "Their personal investment in this city is beyond doubt, and their personal desire to be owed favors by the only police force that can prosecute them is also substantial. Predators are very good at guarding their territory."

Julia's serpent smile widened, as if that was praise. "I'll chaperone Jin Im-Jin for you." That part Julia addressed to Desi, before locking their dark eyes again on Mycroft. "You will take Carlyle to safety with you." There was a bargainy edge to this, the terms of a new Faustpact. "I work best without a babysitter, and Carlyle is Conclave Vice-Head, if you take them out into the world, they can do for everyone on Pass-It-On what they've been doing for Romanova until now. The coming months have their own holidays to brace for." For a moment, a kind of genuine professionalism wiped the smugness from Julia's face, as if they actually cared about their job and Earth's well-being. Maybe they do. "Plus, I keep being tempted to murder them." Julia turned their smile on Carlyle. "That's a compliment."

Carlyle smiled—how could Carlyle smile at that? "I know."

Mycroft turned to Carlyle, and here returned the servile, apologetic Mycroft face that I think of as normal, which had somehow vanished in the business of the day. "If you don't want to leave—"

"I'll go," Carlyle answered. "You're right I can do good out there as Conclave Vice-Head using Pass-It-On. And I'll leave a certain bit of information with the Assistant Commissioner here, and with Charlemagne, and . . . Tribune Natekari would make a good third, I think?"

Julia's wince morphed into a complimentary nod. "Good choice. Unnecessary, though. Mycroft's right that I'll take good care of my capital." They stretched, rolling their shoulders. "At least until we hear the happy news that it's become Jehovah's." She sang briefly here, the tune of the 'Ode to Joy' but Latin lyrics, peppery yet sinister as her eyes gloated: *"Gaius Julius Caesar noster, Imperator, Pontifex, primum Praetor, deinde Consul, nunc Dictator, moxque Rex."* I asked Mycroft later, apparently it's an old school chant about Caesar's rise, listing the offices they racked up one by one until the old regime collapsed into the kind of monarchy people had sworn would never come to Rome again—I hate when the word 'tyrant' fits the Prince. "I look forward to working with you, Desi," Julia continued. "I've heard good things from Madame."

I felt sick to my stomach. We were putting Madame's people back in power. I suddenly had the image of living in one of those old-time factory towns, where every surface is dingy with the scum of toxic dust—tables, windows, skin, a white cat long stained gray—and you suddenly discover that the scum was in your food, too, staining white bread rye-gray and rye bread black. But there's nothing else to eat. Madame's creatures are on our side, *are* our side, I need to get my head around that, but it still felt sick. It felt sick all day, as I was packing, as we went through the tunnel maps, as I found myself staring at Carmen and Im-Jin as they moved and spoke, Carmen's round-bellied stance, Im-Jin's careful, practiced way of folding their bony arms. It felt like an old video, like I was not quite there with them but already looking back on these last words and motions through the wall of memory. At something lost. So, with pre-mourning already tightening my chest through our goodbyes, we started our dark crawl toward the safety of the sea: Bo Chowdhury, Mycroft, Carlyle, Su-Hyeon, the Censor's Guards, the Delians, frightened Toshi, and me.

"Gordian and Utopia are at war." Huxley said it the instant we had left the Conclave basements and were burrowing beyond. "That's why we trust Julia Doria-Pamphili and Madame's minions over Jin Im-Jin." The words were barely audible, whispered in my ear so even Su-Hyeon and Norax feeling along the tunnel up ahead of us could not have caught them.

"You and Gordian? Wait . . ." I felt something bubbling through my remembrance, a handshake, yes, the day Huxley came to tell the powers that Utopia had seized the harbingers. "You declared war . . ." The words dropped out of me. "You personally, Huxley, that handshake you offered Felix Faust. You said, 'War.' Mycroft put it in our chronicle. That was Utopia declaring war on Gordian, you as ambassador."

I caught a frown on Huxley's cheeks. "I knew you'd forgotten. I'm sorry, I wanted to remind you months ago, but you were too close to Im-Jin, they would have scried distrust through your comportment. It would have exposed me."

"Faust said they'd expected you to squirm out of it. And they said they intended to squirm out of it. I thought that meant Gordian decided not to fight."

"They haven't fought, not in the field. Brillists don't tolerate death, especially their own. But if they are acting, psychology is their warcraft, not guns and steel."

A nod. "Psychological warfare?"

"And propaganda. Brill's Institute vanguards brain-machine interface research. That computer nervous system implanted to override the brain's control, it could be the craft of set-set designers, or the Mitsubishi who made the Canner Device, or some black-swan adversary like Perry-Kraye, but it could have been the Institute."

"Lorelei Cook! But . . . Cook was a Nurturist, Gordian's ally against set-sets!"

"So, no one would suspect Gordian."

I realized I was shaking. "Then was Im-Jin in on—"

"I don't think so. So toxic a warp will have been wefted as occultly as possible. But Jin in power in Romanova is a gungnir which could shatter us at any time, so we need as aegis Julia Doria-Pamphili, and Bo Chowdhury, and all Madame's resources, anything for such a threat."

"Does Mycroft know? Of course Mycroft knows," I answered myself as I looked ahead at Mycroft's lithe, travel-thinned figure starting down a ladder, free from handcuffs for the clambery bits of our journey, since Huxley considers a 180 kg lion a sufficient safeguard in the field. "Why are you and Gordian at war?" I asked. "Over the set-set law?"

"Only in part. There are many paired inimices in this war, separate intersecting poles of conflict. Our conflict is paused right now, since we and Gordian both need Remaker victory. But Micromegas will only forge one new world order in the end—Utopia's or Brill's. Both will have some growing space, but you know how Mycroft put it in their history, one branch will be the trunk. The Alien will choose."

"Then you're competing for the Prince's favor?"

In lieu of answer—or was this their answer?—Huxley called loudly down the tunnel before us. "Grendel, Kuiper, this is far enough. Your quests are in the city."

The two turned, stars and riddles overlapping in the narrow tunnel, and on their half-veiled faces I saw gratitude, release, anxiety, fatigue, so many mixing thoughts, so human.

"Are you sure?"

"Norax is enough to get me to the shore. Lifespeed to both of you. And thank you." It was a heavy thank-you, not the light everyday thanks that matches 'pass the salt' but the hard thanks of sleepless nights and dangerous weeks.

Grendel and Kuiper both had those slightly pursed smiles of when you don't know what to say, the situation is too heavy for anything that doesn't feel pretentious. Only one thing to say: "*Gradatim.*" Step by step their long path with its sacrifices, reader. Step by step.

Huxley raised their hand in their stark salute, and the other Delians answered, Grendel, Kuiper, Norax who had lingered with us, each with the one-fingered or two-fingered flips of their civilian militia. No. "It means something!" I blurted as I saw it suddenly. "Different salutes, one finger, two, it's not just idiosyncratic. Is it rank?"

Their smiles were awkward, Kuiper's and Grendel's just a little warm, a little happy that, after partnering me in so many labors, a little bit of detail had rubbed off on me, that I didn't see them as interchangeable inhuman strangers.

"Not rank." It was Huxley's right to answer. "It's sphere, our quests, our missions, which sphere we're defending. Higher takes precedence, so if you're on a low-sphere mission, you pause work, if you can, to help the higher sphere first."

Norax again held up their one-fingered salute. "One is Earthsphere, protecting humanity, for me Sardinia and Romanova. Guarding the Forum, the Censor, Pass-It-On, the Harbinger Peacebonding Constellation, all these are Earthsphere quests."

What could I say but, "Thank you."

Grendel and star-shrouded Kuiper held up two-fingered salutes. "Two is Moonsphere, the Utopian Hive, our Members' lives, plus off-world habitations, satellites, space stations, the elevators, Luna City. Us. We'll go back to evacuating the Janiculum now that we've delivered you and Huxley safe."

Once more, what could one say but "Thank you"?

"The third sphere is Mars." It was Kuiper who continued, in their coat of distant stars. "Not just the Odyssey Base but the shipments from Earth, the tugs that bring the frozen nitrogen and water from the asteroids and outer planets, the relay stations, the command staff at the Gates of Nineveh, the Earthside planning teams, the Almagest, everything we need to call Mars home in 2660."

I smiled, remembering their bid to host Mars's first Olympics in 2766. "But, Huxley, you salute with your hand open, all four fingers. There are three spheres on Utopia's flag, what's four?"

"Spheres past Mars." I'd never ever heard such drive, such warming fire, in Huxley's voice before. "Mars is the third step, not the last. Some things are vital to our deeper future." Their digital glance led mine to Mycroft on the ladder at the tunnel end, who raised their hand, that open-palmed salute. Huxley returned it. "I am Huxley Mojave of our First Contact Constellation. I can authorize a Faustpact because my quest—our quest"—a smile for me—"like very few quests, is worth giving up a step toward Mars. We know how to take that step again. But Micromegas, Bridger's creations, First Contact, these we have no way to replicate. So all the"—they choked, and I was startled to find Huxley human enough to sob—"all the filth in Doria-Pamphili, in Madame, it doesn't matter, not compared to this. We choose our battles." Huxley placed a hand on Kuiper's shoulder, encouragement for the long climb back to face the city, the fire, the severed heads, the scraps of armies howling through the streets where once seventeen murders were atrocity beyond imagining. "We haven't chosen wrong."

Chapter the FIFTEENTH

Man Made

Written February 5 & 7, 2455
Events of February 5

I CANNOT QUITE CALL 'SLEEP' BUT MIGHT CALL 'DREAM' the ease that found us in the softly swaying dark of the Dreadnautilus. The ship's voice kept us conscious, whale-song language reverberating through the vessel as she spoke to kin or friendcraft leagues away across old Ocean's kingdom, her long, pure soundwaves making our bones sing and lullabying us with bass cascading tones, which were but the highest piccolo of a symphony too grand for human ears.

What followed I can better call 'nightmare' than 'waking': metal's screeching death throes, thunder, tearing, churn, storm roar as if the torrent force of all Niagara pummeled us, while in between came human sounds, death screams and cries for help, the maximum terror can wring from human throats yet barely audible behind the greater sounds of wreck and ruin. If you have ever seen, reader, an artist's panoramic view of Tartarus, and Zeus's darkest brother's underkingdom, there Ixion on his wheel, there Tantalus, the spouse-slaughtering Danaids, gurgling Styx, there Fury Tisiphone lounging bloodred and hungry, her snake-headed locks lapping at Dis's poisoned streams as she plans fresh torments for we parricides who are justly her abjects, there the lapping fire, there the endless night-locked woods, there Sisyphus's boulder crashing down, his face, all their despairing faces, millions uncountable blended into one landscape of despair; if you have seen such hellscapes drawn or painted then imagine now that sight transformed to sound, an audio panorama of the House of Death—that is the sound which wracked us as the beast ship heaved, and our world with it.

"What?" Carlyle Foster's cry was most word-like, while others—Toshi Mitsubishi, my successor, Huxley, the Censor and two resting guards—merely cried out, distressed half-shouts like the cawing of ill-omened birds. "Attack? Are we sinking?"

Our spherical cabin wobbled as it righted itself, the weighted ball revolving free within the guardian monster's belly so we passengers could remain upright through the dives and undulations of the soft and swimming vessel. A hiss made us cry out, fear's new caw chorus, but it was a crack of air, not deadly hull breach, as the hatch seal opened to the main belly hold outside. A tendril entered, thread-supple and silver as the moon, which opened before us like a frond of sea fan to become a soft, membranous screen.

"We've sunk a hostile scout ship," the Nemo's gentle voice announced over a speaker as the screen displayed a steady, vizored face. "We're confident it didn't signal out."

They had been foe cries, then, those screams of Dis, and it was foe steel that had buckled in the monster embrace of Dreadnautilus arms as strong as spaceships' hulls. Here was hollow comfort, foes defeated by a new blade we had forged and lent to Death—one more inch backwards in Utopia's twofold quest.

"How did it spot us?"

"It didn't."

"Then why did we engage?" It was my successor who asked. "We've turned north. Why?"

As our eyes met, I sensed the same grim calculus in my successor's frown as mine: this Dreadnautilus was ours at present, all action spheres subordinated to those steps beyond Mars marked by Huxley's bold salute. The Nemo would not enter combat nor turn away from Alexandria without some cause dire enough to risk Censor, Anonymous, and me at once.

"Distress call four knots north, in a layering of Blue-I and Humpback-4, and it's this ship's native dialect of Humpback-4, too, and only two degrees of social separation."

I could tell by comrades' faces who did and did not remember the cetacean linguistics basics we sit through in school. Most large whales' languages do not differentiate separation by kind, only degree, so non-kin, non-friend, non-present, non-singer, non-alive, each makes one degree of separation, and a distant parent or a nearby human friend rank identically in group and love. Two degrees: one must be for non-presence, one non-kin, for the Dreadnautilus is herself alone and knows no kin but her escape crabs and her Nemo. Thus only two separations must mean a friend, and one who knows which dialect the Dreadnautilus sings.

"We've identified the vessel there, the *Numantia,* the Spanish royal yacht. And look."

An image rose, the slim and speeding pleasure craft abloom with flags: truce white foremost, behind it the Alliance, Europe, Spain, the Royal Standard of Spain, Masonic purple, the Cousins' cyan hand-dove, Greenpeace, the bold Utopian spheres, and a tenth flag, red and white blurred by speed-flutter.

"I've never seen a Mitsubishi flag with red bars at the sides like that," said our curious Censor. "Which strat is it? Singapore?"

"That's no Mitsubishi. Look closer at the center, that's not the trefoil, that's the Maple Leaf."

Breaths caught. "Canada . . ." The name felt like an invocation, some miraculous Arcadia or Shangri-La. The far side of the world. The lost side.

I peered closer. "That Masonic flag has a white bar, like the white sleeve of the *Ordo Vitae Dialogorum.* I think that's Martin Guildbreaker."

The long path traced itself clear in my mind, the stranded *Familiaris* aided in his patient hike by Canada's kind Europeans and Greenpeace, a frigid path with winter coming on but shorter, better than the narrow windings between the Reservations of old America's shattered westlands. By foot, or horse, or wagon, Martin marches on across majestic, snow-graced forests, then by ship up the Saint Lawrence through Montreal and Quebec City to the bright Atlantic, and the trundling ocean passage East to Spain. Like ancient mariners, the craft tastes lonely weeks of only waves shifting from gray to blue. Then the weary Canadian crew docks at Cádiz, where Spain's love for good Martin's Good Master offers at once the city's swiftest ship, this wind-mocking royal pleasure craft, which jets Martin toward Alexandria armored by Juan Carlos's honored name, and by the flag of every kindly power that wants to see the wounds of Distance healed.

"Who would attack *that*?" my successor asked, with a growl in their tender voice which I fear they learned from me.

No lawful creature surely, but there they were upon the screen, pursuit vessels circling predatory, camouflaged gray-blue and semi-submerged so their slim profiles barely broke the waterline. Only the foaming wakes of speed betrayed their presence, though the screen's systems tagged the enemies with bright red labels, E1 through E8. The *Numantia* should be faster than these ships, but their shark circling forced the harmless yacht to cut its pace as they wove and figure-eighted, closing in. So, the *Numantia* sang out the desperation song which Spain's Utopians must have shared with Martin, his Delian escort defending the same sphere as my own: Earth's priceless Contact.

"Is anyone else close enough to help instead of us?" It was Bo Chowdhury who asked, the Acting Commissioner General's duty to the Censor's safety, not some distant sphere.

"Reinforcements are fourteen minutes out. We're three."

For a painful moment, we all feared Acting Commissioner Chowdhury would remind us that Alliance crises trump Hive custom, unless Utopia was breaking with the Alliance. "Then we'd better buy Martin eleven minutes."

"Eleven minutes . . ." I repeated as my mind locked on those circling spots of red, which danced like marbles stirred by an invisible hand. But no thing which acts upon this world is so invisible that a mind well versed in twists and turns cannot read something of the mover from its motions. I felt myself lean toward the screen, and saw Toshi Mitsubishi too lean closer, the pattern of those dancing numbers enmeshing both of us as keen sensors enmesh Eureka Weeksbooth.

* * *

9A here for a moment. Mycroft doesn't seem to remember it, but the captain actually did ask Mycroft for advice, which ship to target, they didn't just jump in. We had one ambush strike, you see, one shot to take a ship completely unawares, and if we chose well—there had to be a commander in one of them, orders can't come from far away, not with the jamming. I don't know who's reading this, so I don't know if you play Go or chess or anything like that, but when you're learning a really deep game, sometimes you glance at a board and just feel where the next move must be, though you don't know why yet, it takes a while to process consciously. I stared at that screen too, and I felt my eye lingering on one blip most, feeling somehow that the way it spiraled through the others, wheeling around the *Numantia's* stern, number E2 it was, it felt . . . different. Important. I opened my lips to say something but didn't have to.

Toshi: "But what's E6 if E2 is leader?"
Mycroft: "I see it."
Toshi: "A command vessel separate from the attack leader? No, the movement's wrong, five and seven are shielding, not flanking . . ."
Mycroft: "It's E6's motion that's subordinate to the others . . ."
Toshi: "A transport ship? A wounded ship? A passenger ship?"
Mycroft: "Someone they're protecting."
Nemo: "Which vessel do I target?"
Toshi: "E2's the commander. E6 is . . . something special . . ."
Mycroft: "Can you capture and hold a craft? Rather than sink it?"
Nemo: "We can."
Mycroft: "Then sinking E2 will take out their attack commander, but E6 has something special in it. Possibly some*one*. Someone they might hostage-swap for Martin if we're too late."

As the boats tagged E1 and E3 fired grappling hooks into the poor yacht's sides, it did feel too late.

Hobbes: "Cut off the head or snatch the precious goods—a fine primordial question. Which did you choose?"

The Nemo chose, not I, Master Hobbes, and called Acting Commissioner Chowdhury to the bridge to aid with tactics and diplomacy, while I and my successor, all we vital passengers, were bundled into the escape crabs, there to wait in strapped-in extra safety through the strike. We were glad of the straps when the vessel lurched, that whiplash reversal of direction modeled on a hunting squid which glides tail-first sleek as a spear between the waters until it has passed its prey. But when the plate-round lidless eyes see prey before them, then quick as a blink the motion reverses and the trailing arms shoot out their hidden length, stunning the victim with that eerie grip of boneless iron strength. We felt the rush as we crashed up through the surface, the flying thrust, the pinnacle pause, the fall, the thunder belly flop as we crashed back into the waves. The crab's screen supplemented the tracking readout with a video, the vessel's point of view, our victim's slender hull wrapped in our many arms whose Griffincloth skin flared war colors: that pure, deep black you only see when water makes a black thing blacker, but with white lines tracing her contours like electricity against the dark, and veined with hints of blue. Sanity nags that it must have been the hull that I heard scream, this captured foecraft's engineering unequal to our tenfold constrictor grip, but still I swear, reader, before the deathless gods: it was a living scream that rose up from the sea, the pure voice of some gentle Nereid, Callianassa, Galatea, ever-mourning Thetis, or perhaps the sea's queen Amphitrite looking on, who knows that neither her primordial father nor her earthshaking husband, for all his sovereign cruelty, loosed such nightmares in their seas. We did.

A thrash and fresh foam as our spare arms lashed out, and foe E4 vanished from our screen, while E6 dodged the visible strike but was seized from beneath by something I could not see, which dragged it toward us.

"They've boarded the *Numantia!*"

Our ambush was perfect, but so was our adversaries' plan, as on our screen I saw the rush of silhouettes up and over the sides from crafts E1 and E3 onto the deck of the tethered *Numantia*. As we dragged the captured E6 toward our maw, in ballet synchrony they dragged out the huddled prisoner in his black-sleeved Mason's suit, and pressed a weapon to his skull.

I held my breath. They didn't shoot. So welcome, that releasing sigh. "They'll negotiate. It's up to the Nemo now."

Several of us dared smile as we watched a sparkling little robot turtle paddle over toward the captured yacht, with a trailing coms cable and a white flag in its jaws.

"Even if we don't reach a settlement, we've definitely bought our eleven minutes for—"

Tap-tap-tap thunk, thunk, thunk, tap-tap-tap.

Tap-tap-tap thunk, thunk, thunk, tap-tap-tap.

"Where's that coming from?" It echoed around us, sharp but fragile somehow, like a songbird pecking at the corner of its cage.

Tap-tap-tap thunk, thunk, thunk, tap-tap-tap.

I met the eyes of my successor, who also recognized from sleepless nights beside their network's laser the Morse for SOS.

Tap-tap-tap thunk, thunk, thunk, tap-tap-tap.

"It's coming from the other boat," Bo Chowdhury answered over the speaker, "From E6, the one we're holding. The one you thought was transporting something."

On the screens we saw the helpless little craft held fast by just two of our monster tendrils now, its slim stern pointed toward our maw and its forward gun ports impotently away.

"Did you damage it? Are they in danger?"

"Checking, but we don't think so. We're on the line with the crew on our dactylus screen, they haven't asked for help."

Tap-tap-tap thunk, thunk, thunk, tap-tap-tap.

Tap-tap-tap thunk, thunk, thunk, tap-tap-tap.

"It could be a prisoner," my successor was first to realize. "That could be what they have on board, not a passenger, some other prisoner, captured like they were planning to capture Martin. They might need help."

Tap-tap-tap thunk, thunk, thunk, tap-tap-tap.

Tap-tap-tap thunk, thunk, thunk, tap-tap-tap.

All our wide eyes searched each other for suggestions, interpretations, validation of our hopes and fears.

"Tap back?" Carlyle suggested, resilient in trust as in so many other things. "I don't know Morse code, but even tapping back shave-and-a-haircut would let them know we heard."

My successor was quick as ever on logistics. "Can you find the spot it's coming from? Is it somewhere specific?"

"We've got a wired gull out seeking. Yes, it's one spot on the hull. We'll tap back a Roger."

"Gently," warned Huxley. "If it's a prisoner, we can't let the others hear."

The speakers played back our own soft *tap, thunk, tap* as the gull's beak struck the metal, and at that same moment, whether by planning or happy chance, the ship's deep song rang out anew, half hiding the taps as the Dreadnautilus updated friends far out across this sea and even in the great Atlantic, where hasty hearing aids, supplied by Utopia and Greenpeace, have the great whales headachy but singing still. I smiled, thinking that whales at least have news from the Americas, though the thoughts of these small aliens are almost as hard to render in human terms as those of the Greater Alien.

Tap thunk, thunk, tap. Tap thunk, tap. Tap-tap. Tap-tap-tap. Thunk, thunk, thunk. Thunk, tap. Tap. Tap thunk, tap.

Hush fell as we all pulled up the code charts the silence has taught us to carry, and picked out the letters as they came: P . . . R . . . I . . . S . . . O . . . We didn't need the final three.

"Ask who this prisoner is."

The speakers let us hear our gull's abbreviated request for call sign: *Thunk, tap thunk, tap, tap-tap-tap.*

A pause.

Tap-tap-tap thunk, thunk, thunk, tap-tap-tap.

"That's just SOS again." Toshi Mitsubishi frowned.

"Ask longhand," my successor suggested. "They may not have thought to use the prosign table, they've probably just got the basic alphabet chart, if anything."

As the gull pecked out our tedious WHO.ARE.YOU, we watched the patient little turtle bob beside the *Numantia* as her captors debated, likely uncertain whether or not to haul aboard the U-beast, which might at any instant explode in fire and gore like murdered Cookie, or disassemble like Ráðsviðr into shards of living, thinking death.

Thunk. (T . . .) *Tap-tap thunk.* (U . . .) *Tap thunk, tap-tap.* (L . . .) *Tap thunk, tap-tap.* (L . . .)

The inexorable Y had not begun when Huxley and my successor seized me from both sides. I felt Cannergel bind my wrists, and then the lion's weight against my legs and chest, as irresistible as it was gentle. There is only one Tully in this war, reader—in everybody's war, but most in mine. My two protectors stared down at me, and I watched fear and combat sternness on both their faces melt quickly into bafflement as they found me calm.

Tap thunk, thunk, thunk, thunk. Thunk, thunk, tap-tap-tap. Tap-tap-tap-tap-tap. Thunk, thunk, thunk, thunk, thunk. Thunk, tap-tap-tap-tap. Thunk, tap-tap-tap-tap. Tap-tap-tap thunk, thunk. Tap-tap-tap. Tap, thunk. Tap-tap-tap, thunk. Tap. Thunk, tap-tap.

"What was that?"

"Five-character strings are numbers: I, 7, 5, 0, 6, 6, 3, then S, A, V, E, D."

"Coordinates?" my successor guessed.

The lion's pressure made my laugh a cough. "Lives," I corrected. "One million seven hundred fifty thousand plus—trust Tully to tally microvictories obsessively."

"Lives saved? By what?"

"Their camps, their war advice. That is what they trained for on the Moon, why Utopia helped them all those years." I twisted against the lion's bulk, but it would not budge. "You know I have no reason to harm Tully Mardi now. All they want is to make this the best and briefest war it can be, just like Bryar Kosala."

My successor looked to Huxley, eyes mingling hope with distrust, as when the patient in a sickbed smiles and speaks of feeling better, but the doctor's word is all.

"I'm glad you remember that currently," came the Delian's half gentle answer. "I don't trust you to remember it consistently."

"Fair." I could only smile.

"We're on with their leader." Compromise had hooked the turtle's cable to a deck speaker and left the distrusted little messenger to trundle back to us across the waves.

"I speak for the Dreadnautilus." The Nemo's voice was musical but cold as battle trumpets. "There is nothing deadlier than us this side of the Pacific. Release your captives and leave the *Numantia* safe at once, and you will live."

Before I was even conscious of an answering voice, the old appetite swelled in me, hunt's catharsis pouring through my inner floodgates opened by the sound over the line of callous rising laughter. "I have the *Imperator Destinatus Proximus,*" the laughing voice croaked back. "If they die and it's your fault, you know that ends it, your pathetic sheltering under the Masons, this will end it all." The voice-only connection offered no face to match the gloating syllables, but our distance camera showed one of the captors kick the kneeling prisoner, who dropped into a winded fetal curl.

"Your terms?" the Nemo asked.

"My terms? I want . . . No, I don't . . . I really don't have any terms, do I?" A lazy, halting tone of self-discovery made the cruel words cheerful. "I don't have any terms." More confidently this time. "I think I'm just going to do it, just to make you watch them die, and watch your whole alliance die in front of you." They crouched low over Martin. "That's what I'm feeling like doing, but I'm not set on it yet. Do you have another suggestion for how all this should go?"

The taste of soured blood, that's what my mind found reaching for a name for this voice, a known voice, a filthy voice kindling rage-fever in me, yes, a petty voice like scab, like salt in wounds, like ashes of burned art, like victorious entropy. A voice I knew, a name I groped for in the fog of blurring times as the crab's cold hull against my back became again the shelter of the dumpster as we clutch our ready weapons, Saladin and I, to start this war.

Our Nemo answered with actions, the lifeless scream of hull metal as the Dreadnautilus's arms lifted from the seas a foe ship, the tethered E5, and there beside it raised another arm, another captured ship, no, worse, a shard of ship E7's curving metal carcass. "These are the threats I let you see," our Nemo warned. "I have ten times as many in the waters around you that you don't see. Your craft are all already helpless. You will only live through this if I let you. Leave the *Numantia* in peace."

That filthy voice again, which somehow made innocent words feel like obscenities. "I'll go when I want to go." Light words, staccato, sprightly. "You see, you don't know what other more precious passenger Guildbreaker was escorting, and you won't know, either, because they're already onboard my little ship. *One* of my little ships here. So, when I'm tired of this conversation, I'm going to board one, and I'm going to leave, and you're going to let us all go, whether or not this Mason is a corpse when the time comes, because you'll really, really regret it if you don't."

Were those crews' screams among the hulls' screams as Dreadnautilus tendrils dragged the two captive ships in toward our maw? "Leave the *Numantia*."

"Those two boats? Go ahead and crush them. Crush them all!" The foe voice laughed. "Do Death's work right here in front of us. Show us what bootlicking hypocrites you Delians are, no courage in you for all your vaunted principles—disarm Death and then hand the blade right back again when selfish Caesar says some enemy is keeping away the next bauble they want to pile by the throne! You made this war's real monsters, better than Nature's, better than Madame's, better than me!"

I tasted something bitter, maybe vomit, and a strange name came to me in my mind's groping: Thersites, that was the name, the basest man who ever came to Troy, ugly in mind, ugly in body, too, in Homer's clumsy imagery wherein fair and foul were not skin deep. Thersites mocker of heroes. Thersites, whose jeering words aimed to drag heroes down, whose jeering face grinned up over that sallow crouching body... "Crouching..." The word caught on my tongue. "Croucher?" Yes, there in my memory's eye I found the envy-spitting face framed with a helmet—but was the helmet army-green or crested gleaming bronze? It didn't matter, not as the same words rose from underneath it, mocking lordly Agamemnon for taking his dues of glory, mocking the troops for serving such a king, he even mocked lionhearted Achilles, calling Zeus's favorite soldier gall-less for his lethal patience as he refrained from bashing out insulting Agamemnon's brains and instead waited in his tent for the king's apology, holding back from a hero's native habitat, the blood and grind of war.

Insolent Thersites, spiteful, stinging, sneering up at me as I clench my hands to strike—Thersites who was always mostly right. Time's blur washed away the sane questions of crisis and combat. Was Croucher always Thersites?

"Reinforcements! Arriving in five, four, three . . . A3's not decelerating!"

I had just spotted the yellow 'Ally' tags (A1, A2 . . .) racing across the tracking section of our screen when white exploded in the main feed, a wall of mist and spray enveloping the *Numantia*, which lurched as if one of Poseidon's impatient seahorse steeds had kicked her starboard hull with its immortal strength. But then there was black too among the white, smoke's taint and fire, burning hull shards, and a single human figure which seemed to ride the impact spray as we make statues seem to ride on fountains, limbs and flawless torso cresting up and over in one acrobatic arc. Two stun shots fired midair dropped two of our enemies to the *Numantia*'s deck before the figure landed steady as a mountain goat, not upon the vessel's bucking planks but upon the shoulders of another enemy, who toppled beneath the new arrival like wheat crushed by stone. I knew those arms, that grace, that godlike speed. Not holding back this time from your true habitat, Achilles. Not sulking in your tent as you, older and wiser, lead us in a wiser war. You see, Thersites, this time, we don't need you. This time, you're just wrong. Our goals are noble, our methods kind, our leaders just, our battles purposeful, and this time, Achilles—our own matchless Achilles—holds back nothing.

The spray fell away as its rider landed, showing the *Numantia*'s side charred but intact. It was the enemy's boarding craft the hero had destroyed, nothing left of it but blackened wreckage bobbing on the tether of its harpoon. Whether Achilles had ridden in on some small speeding boat and let it crash into the enemy, or braved the back of a torpedo, I could not guess. For now he braved the foe-infested ship, and the speakers let us hear the grunts and quick athletic strikes of hand-to-hand.

"You will fail!" Here came that voice again, as sour as bile on the line. "You'll all fail! Your Prince Mason will wreck the world and fail, and be remembered only as a tyrant! Them and their whore mother, two more cursed names to scare little children in new cities founded in the wreck of our apocalypse!" Wind and scuffle punctuated the lines, some clunking too as figures I could barely make out raced and chased across the deck and damaged roof. "But you want that, don't you, Achilles? All you've ever wanted was for men to speak your name a thousand years from now, so you can cling to your pathetic self while all the shades you've butchered fade away. Well, I won't fade! I'm burned into Earth's memory as much as you are! And in a thousand years, when you're remembered as nothing but Utopia's fake miracle that helped the tyrant burn the world, I'll be just as immortal, two equal boogeymen from cursed J.E.D.D. Mason's war!"

Roar past the point of pain made us all hold our ears as the speakers relayed the thunder scream of what was probably a jet engine. In an explosion of whitewater, E2, the leader's foecraft, soared away from the *Numantia*'s far side, skating across the water's surface like a skipping stone. Less than a second later, it slammed to a whiplash halt, and we too felt whiplash as the ship with its churning engine dragged at us by the tendril threads, invisible as a deadly jellyfish, which the Dreadnautilus had wrapped around its prey, just as her Nemo had warned. A song of pain rang through the captured ship, and the thrashing of the tethered engine sent up spray so solid and so high that a car soaring above us swerved to crash into the waterform in case it was a vehicle. The crab's small cabin lurched, sending Huxley and my successor tumbling without their safety belts as the Dreadnautilus speed-dove to flee the car's explosion, but kind Fates did not let the gentle water crack the car, which swerved on in its unmanned, unfeeling vigilance. A minute of foam and tilting, and we broke the waves again. Our screen showed the charred but safe *Numantia* and the reinforcements that had brought Achilles, a battle cruiser and two lighter ships which drew close, flying the Square and Compass. As for our enemies, damaged E5 still bobbed nearby, and E6—with Tully Mardi still inside—was safely buttressed in our inescapable embrace, but the others had cut our threads by force or guile, so we could only watch their foam trails vanish across the still-uncaring sea.

"Do you have Mycroft Canner?" We heard Achilles's desperate voice over the line the instant that the squeals of reconnection gave way to clean sound. "Do you have Mycroft Canner?"

"Safe and sound," the Nemo answered proudly.

"I want to see with my own eyes. Is there a screen?"

Some fussing as we added video, and there before me was Achilles's face, unchanging as a mountain's, every bit as stern and vulnerable as when he gazed out over battlefields where a dagger forged of iron was the pinnacle of our technology.

"What are you doing here?" I asked. "You shouldn't leave the battlefield, the East, the Almagest—"

"Looking for you," he answered, and there in his eyes was a friend's warm edge of mocking. Yes, you're right, Achilles, I should have known you too would race here from the world's end the instant Pass-It-On spread, even to your battlefield, my not-so-subtle 'M. C. Moriarty.'

"Is Martin safe?" I asked. "And the second passenger they threatened, who was it?"

Achilles let himself just pause and pant a moment, the hearty pants of after-battle ease. I'm glad you have me back safe too, Achilles. "There was no second passenger, that was a bluff," he answered to our great relief. "But this isn't Martin."

"What? They got Martin?"

"No." It was the rescued Mason who answered, resting against the deck boards at Achilles's side, winded but whole. "I'm the only passenger. *Nepos* Guildbreaker was never onboard. They were captured weeks ago."

"Captured? Who by?"

"I was not given that information. All I received is this, released with permission of their current captors, to be passed on to Caesar and the *Porphyrogene* at any cost." He held up something flat and thin.

"What is it?"

"Notes from Martin Guildbreaker on the progress of their ongoing investigations."

Sobs rose in me, and I heard the same sobs rise in my successor. It should not be this hard. Loyal, tireless Martin—no, tired Martin, for Martin must be as tired as the rest of us by now, working for months, burning resources, risking lives, begging favors from captors or smuggling folded sheets through prison cracks to pass on words. Just words. We should always be able to pass words to friends, it's the simplest, the most necessary thing. Even those primordial philosophers who said the happy life is the simple life, a plain meal eaten with our bare hands out of doors, it was still a meal shared with a friend. Diogenes, first teacher of my youth, even you still needed Alexander to step aside and give you back the light that gave you words. What do I do now? What does your dog's path of cynic detachment prescribe now? Now that our Maker's silence is so cruel that we sacrifice months and lives and tears to pass on just this tiny ounce of words! Words should be infinite, and effortless, and instant. I am not a dog, Diogenes, I cannot be a dog. I am *homo loquens,* the speaking animal, and I need my friends' words, faces, gestures, touches, all their bodies' many languages, just as my friends need mine. And yet that portion of our Maker named Poseidon makes it all so hard.

The Nemo is never shaken. "Who was that attacker? Did they get away?"

"Yes, coward got away."

"Who was it? Stealth semi-submersibles with grappling harpoons and jet engines—no one's tech is this war-ready, not the Mitsubishi, not MASON."

My tongue had an answer upon it, if a nonsensical one, and as my successor peered across at me, I think I saw that answer mirrored there, the archetype identified by a mind as keen and careful and Homer-obsessed as my own: that was fame-hating Thersites, mocker of heroes. But such an answer makes no sense.

"That was Casimir Perry." It was the rescued Mason who said it, who had been face-to-face with the attacker and seen clearly that gloating smile famous from the news.

We traded frowns around the crab's cabin as we remembered Perry-Kraye, their years of planning, plenty of time to plan and build stealth ships like that. We thought of Perry's web of allies, too, Madame's exiles gathered over years, hundreds, cunning, bitter, afire for revenge, still out there, still afire to burn her world and all of her creations. And her Son. This was not an enemy I had remembered to watch out for. How many of these months' calamities were truly Perry's orchestrations, hidden in the war's long twists and turns?

"Tully and Perry were both with O.S.," my quick successor reminded us.

I mulled on that. "Perry might well have kidnapped Tully then."

"Why?"

I scowled. "Because Perry wants to make the war worse, and Tully Mardi wants to make it better." And Perry might have that deserter Croucher in his pocket railing still—but I did not say so here.

"Time to disconnect and move out," the grim Nemo announced. "The adversary may bring reinforcements any moment."

"Agreed." Achilles nodded. "You can leave the *Numantia* and the captured enemies to me."

"Including Tully Mardi?" the Nemo asked.

"Especially Tully Mardi," Achilles answered.

I wiggled in my bonds. "I want to go over, see Achilles in person."

"You're not moving from the safest seat in the safest spot in the safest ship on Earth," the hero ordered.

I tugged for real, but after Fate and Love, no bond in this world is stronger than Cannergel. «We need to talk,» I called in Greek.

«We'll talk soon, we're just hours from Alexandria.»

«But—»

«I'm not risking you again. When we're both on land, with prayers to all the gods of safe landing, then we will talk.» Achilles switched to English for the Nemo. "Preparing to disconnect."

"Wait!" my successor called. "May I go across and talk to Achilles? I can pass on whatever Mycroft wants."

I realized in the pause that my successor was looking as much to Huxley for permission as to Achilles and myself, and I briefly wondered whether my successor like myself is as much prisoner as protectee in Huxley's careful mission. "Alright."

My successor smiled. "What should I say? Other than the jist of what's happened to you and Romanova."

I switched to private Greek. «Ask Achilles who they think was really on that boat, who spat those curses about human memory calling us tyrants in a thousand years. That didn't sound to me quite like our vengeful Count of Montecristo.»

And to that question, reader, I have no answer as I set this Chronicle aside, for there gleams Alexandria's lighthouse pure as hope upon the screen, and the Nemo says the time has come to disembark and taste at last the salt-sweet air of Earth's most longed-for harbor. But perhaps my successor will add some small addendum in the coming days, a happy task as we two labor in the presence of the happiest Cause.

* * *

Yes, 9A here with my addendum. I went over to see Achilles on the *Numantia,* where Masonic medics were looking over the captain and crew and captured enemies. The reinforcements were all Blacksleeves, grim and orderly with rank marks on their Mason suits, which in this context I can honestly call uniforms.

I saluted. «It's wonderful to see you, Major—or it can't still be 'Major' at this stage. Is it 'General'?»

«*Magistratus Militum Imperii,* War Marshal of the Empire.» Achilles gestured for me to lean on the deck rail beside them. «It's good to see you, too, [Anonymous]. Where was he?»

«Lost at sea.»

A nod, Achilles's Greek locks damp with war. «And where were you?»

«In Romanova. We did well there, held back the chaos a long time.» I realized Achilles's eyes were lingering on the Vs on my shoulder, and I was suddenly very conscious that there were none on theirs. In fact, there were no Vs on any shoulder on the ship around us, not the Masons, not the Delians who labored with them, not even on Martin's battered messenger, who was enjoying hot broth and a blanket. «Things were complicated with the capital so Hive-mixed, we needed a way to rally—»

Achilles smiled gently. «I never think less of people for their piety.»

I paused—piety and my Vs, I hadn't connected those dots before, and doing so felt hot but right inside of me. «Mycroft asked me to ask you whether that was really Perry we heard yelling about the future, cursing the Prince's war. Whether it might have been someone . . . more familiar.»

«Croucher?» they guessed. «Hard to say, he was on the far side of the cabin roof, I couldn't see lips moving.»

I searched Achilles's face, so strong and open, their feelings always so unveiled to everyone, this time dislike and pain. Asking was hard. «I thought it might have been . . . someone even more familiar to you specifically?»

A brief smile of praise for my perceptiveness then faded to a scornful, tired scowl. «Thersites, Perry, Croucher, the bitterness that wants to tear all great things down—there may not be a clear difference anymore. There was never much difference in how Bridger understood them, and as the war takes shape . . . » They didn't have to finish.

I felt myself shaking as a question formed itself inside me, one I had been trying not to—hold on . . .

MYCROFT, DO NOT READ THIS. DO NOT READ THIS, MYCROFT, PLEASE! JUST SKIP THIS PART. I'M NOT DECEIVING YOU, I SWEAR IT BY THE PRINCE AND EVERYTHING! IT'S JUST, SOME THINGS CAN ONLY HURT YOU. WILL ONLY HURT YOU. I THINK THE READER NEEDS TO SEE THIS, NEEDS TO KNOW THIS, BUT IF YOU READ IT, IT WILL ONLY HURT YOU. TRUST ME? PLEASE?—9A

All right.—MC

I felt myself shaking. I hadn't expected to shake so much trying to put it into words at last. «Mycroft was at sea a long time. They wandered a lot of places. There was a pleasant island that was hard to leave, then a cyclopean prison tower where a captor took comrades away one by one, then an implausibly helpful witch woman with potions, then deadly music, and a visit with the dead, and the ship sank because the crew robbed a Delian solar farm which I can't *not* call the cattle of the sun. For goodness' sake, the new name the witch-woman gave the ship was *Circe's Gift*! If—»

«Enough.» The harshness in Achilles's voice made me flinch, but their face, commixing sorrow, comfort, and sympathy, showed that any harshness was meant for the Fates, not me. «Listen, [Anonymous], if it serves Odysseus's plans to conceal his identity from himself, we both know better than to interfere.»

I held my breath. «How long? How long have they been—»

«A long time. Years.»

I sobbed. Not small sobs, either, big ones, big and weepy, even though these sobs were mostly good. I sobbed because I'd been so worried, because it was such relief having an answer, even if it was a scary one. I sobbed because it had been years, which meant whatever Bridger did was long ago, so even if this wasn't the original Mycroft, it was my Mycroft, the same Mycroft I knew. I sobbed remembering how kids blur stories together, how Bridger had said they thought Odysseus and Jean Valjean would be best friends and save all Paris with their clever barricades, and now they're doing it, even if the story also blurred with Holmes and Moriarty. I sobbed because I was embarrassed to be sobbing. And I sobbed because, whatever else, however long their sorrows and their wanderings, Odysseus lives.

Achilles, now supreme commander of the biggest army ever anywhere, is not embarrassed to embrace a comrade with a public hug, or to shed public tears. «We need to be careful. He's taken a stranger and more fragile form this time than any I've known. I don't understand the purpose, but you know how broken he is. Imagine if he realizes it's the noble son of Laertes that he's soiled forever with the stain of parricide.» I felt myself cry out, but the small, strong arms around me shared my fear, my hope, my heart's resolve. «It's alright now,» Achilles said, our veteran who's seen this all before. «We have him back. We'll keep him safe. We can win the war now; you know I'm not the one to win it, he is, but we have him safe. And this time, we won't let it take ten years.»

Ten years battling around the original Troy—I gulped. We don't have ten years, we don't even have one year: the harbingers are coming. But you were right, Mycroft, it is comfort to know that Bridger knew the *Odyssey*. I don't fear the harbingers the same way now—Odysseus lives.

Chapter the SIXTEENTH

Damnatio Memoriae

Written February 8, 2455
Events of February 7

ALEXANDRIA, WHERE TWENTY-SEVEN CENTURIES AGO a conqueror paused to found something more lasting than himself, and where today, in a war replete with choices, no flag flies but that conqueror's successor's. The *Sanctum* Guard themselves, with a human forest of Blacksleeves ranked around them, met us in the harbor where MASON's warships crowd like stabled stallions, restless in their vitality and jostling even in the dead of night. No, night is never dead here in the capital whose lights compete with stars. Huxley led me out gently, our wrists cuffed cautiously together. I staggered, having lost my land legs on the voyage, but smiled to see that Caesar's hospitality had dispatched escort jeeps with the Imperial arms upon them, and ready in one of them my old transparent coffin-cage which, more than anything left on this planet, smells like home. The triumphant relief on Bo Chowdhury's face as the guards strapped me in was priceless, and that word—priceless—made me muse as we rumbled toward the capitol that there are many priceless jewels in this world, and many priceless faces, yet only one face so priceless that to see His visage, feel His eyes, however lifeless, fall upon me, that outvalues all the grains of treasure in the Earth. And He was near.

"Welcome, Censor. Welcome, Acting Commissioner General." Xiaoliu Guildbreaker met us before the palace, whose clustered pyramids of glass and stone rose sparkling against the night like a too-perfect mountain range pregnant with captive lightning. "Caesar has suites prepared for each of you and your staff"—a nod at the Censor's grateful guards—"and we have gathered Alexandria's Alliance officers in the palace to supplement your staff."

"Thank you." Censor Jung and Bo Chowdhury accepted Xiaoliu's warm, thin handshake, each in turn.

"And Acting Minister Foster"—Xiaoliu turned his smile on Carlyle—"we have a suite and staff for you as well."

"Oh, wow! Great!" Carlyle smiled at Xiaoliu's white right sleeve, a cheering contrast to his black-dyed left. "The white, that's for Martin's *Ordo dialogo*-something, right? I'm not sure if you've heard but we have news from Martin, notes on their investigations, sent all the way from Canada. Achilles is bringing them."

"Ah, notes, that's what it was," Xiaoliu answered, shaking hands with the leaders of the Censor's Guard. "We had word of something regarding Martin, but the Dreadnautilus's vocabulary was ambiguous. The *Bucephalus*—Marshal Achilles's ship—is expected any . . . Toshi Mitsubishi?" Xiaoliu's breath caught within his slim chest at the sight of the not-quite-set-set, huddling behind the Censor like a child grown too big to hide behind parents, who tries it still.

Carlyle seemed about to voice some explanation, but first the Censor grasped Toshi's shoulder warmly before all the ranks of frowning Masons. "Toshi is my primary deputy and has spent these past months doing invaluable service for the Alliance."

Xiaoliu paused only a moment. "Understood." His face showed nothing, not warmth, not darkness. "We thought *Familiaris* [Anonymous] was with you? And Commander Huxley Mojave?"

"[Anonymous] is riding with Achilles," Huxley answered, stepping forth now from behind my cage, a slice of living storm which traced the lines of Caesar's threshold in lightning as swift as thought. "And they have Tully Mardi with them, you should prepare . . ."—a pause—". . . a cell." A sad request from the Hive that so long nurtured Tully on the silver Moon and hoped never to call him enemy.

"Understood." Xiaoliu smiled. "Your efforts have been extraordinary all these months, Commander. Well done." Xiaoliu offered my weary guardian a handshake, but the aides and Blacksleeves ranked around us offered more, a spatter first and then a roar of rich, spontaneous applause. The look of relief, reader, in Huxley's eyes on seeing me, the most impossible of missions, delivered safe and sound—I never hope to see such eyes again unless someday victorious Sisyphus sits down at peace upon his mountaintop beside his stone.

"We will take Mycroft directly to the *Porphyrogene*."

My heart soared as they wheeled me through familiar hallways, made less familiar by wartime adaptation: cables vining along corners, holes drilled through walls for improvised access. I feared nothing—that was the true glow of it, the first time in many weary months I had feared nothing. I feared nothing as they stripped and scrubbed me, though the sea's salt teeth prickled like needles in my back and shoulders at this good, harsh scouring. I feared nothing when they took away my old belongings, for what need had I now for compass, tools, or travel's other clutter? I feared nothing as they dressed me in new clothes, Servicer mottled with one black sleeve and the *Familiaris* armband sewn onto it, while on the back I smirked to see in bold reflective letters: *DETINE ME CAESARIS SUM* (Detain me, I am Caesar's). I feared nothing as they bound my wrists behind me anew with gentle Cannergel and marched me through the gates, and guards, and deeper gates, and stronger guards, who step on step safeguard the sanctum heart of Alexander's city.

There He was. There on a plain chair sat that figure all in black, gazing up at a screen which mimicked a picture window, where the starscape of the city stretched out toward a sky in which dawn's sapphire prelude was just starting to outline the clouds. His eyes rolled toward me, fixed on me, blacker and warmer than priceless sleep. He turned His head. He rose. He walked to me. He grasped my shoulders, felt along them with His precise, exploring hands. He leaned down over me and—I must have fallen to my knees?—nestled His chin against my forehead to breathe in the smell of me, my hair still damp. He bade me, "Speak."

"*Adsum,* Ἄναξ (I'm here, Lord)," I answered, the setting making Latin come easiest. "*Consto* (I exist/continue)." I didn't know what else to say, I just repeated, "*Adsum. Consto,*" knowing what He wanted most from me was sound, my voice, so His hearing could confirm His other senses' testimony that I was real. Am real. Am.

"*Cur aberas?* (Why were you gone?)" He asked, following me into Latin.

"*Nescio,* Ἄναξ. *Non interpretari posso.* (I don't know, Lord. I can't interpret.)" To Him I didn't need to specify What or Who I could not interpret, the Plan and Planner so inscrutable. I had no further answer, so I just made sounds, uncertain, soft within my throat. I don't know if such sounds have names, whimper, moan, it didn't matter. He just needed to hear me, feel me, see me, smell me, weigh with all His borrowed human senses this improbable reality: that what His Peer first gave, then took away, He gave once more.

"May we uncuff them?" A warm, familiar voice beside us made me smile so broadly that I tasted tears I had not been conscious of.

"Chagatai!" I cried. There she stood in bed-mussed pajamas, still built like a bull and smiling warm as summer. Unchanging Chagatai! All this time, our lonely Master was not quite alone in Alexandria, He had at least one creature still His own.

"No." This chill answer came from behind me, and I twisted around to see the *Sanctum* Guards flanking the tight-sealed entrance, six in stern array. "Caesar grants you fifteen minutes for greetings, then we take Canner down for surgery. It will be brief."

"Surgery?" I thought over the aches and itches of my many half-healed injuries, my lingering concussion certainly the worst, but none seemed urgent. "Does Caesar have a new tracker for me?" I guessed, remembering my mangled ear. "For when the silence ends?"

Some *Sanctum* Guards paw habitually at their weapons when in Mycroft Canner's presence, but *Sanctum* Prefect Cinna Semaphoros is the childhood ba'sib of the Emperor whose day of testing tested both alike, Cornel not-yet-MASON ordered to watch his left foot hacked off slice by slice, while his loving friend and destined Prefect was ordered to wield the blade—he who passed such a test does not flinch before monsters. "You fled custody, Mycroft," the Prefect answered, looming, "at the opening of the Temple of Janus. Caesar forbade you ever again to walk the streets alone, and pledged to have you hobbled if you disobeyed. MASON makes no idle threats."

I lurched—I have no better name for it, a jerking attempt to rise or jump, but on my knees with my arms bound firm behind me, all I could do was flop within Jehovah's grip. His grip hardened, His arms locking around my shoulders as He hugged me to Him so tightly that I strained to breathe. "No," He said, His voice as ever light and lifeless. "This forced change to My Mycroft distresses and alarms Me."

"There's no need now!" I said, trying to smile. "I'll never leave Ἄναξ Jehovah's side."

"You left them at the Temple of Janus. You've left them many times." That truth stabbed, and stabbed harder coming from the Prefect who has never strayed from his imperial master, while I have so often strayed from mine.

"Please!" I begged, the natural course for one already on his knees. "You need me as I am, ready to fight! I'm Caesar's tool, Jehovah's tool, Jehovah's strong defender!"

My shoulders ached, and I realized Jehovah's knuckles had gone white where His fingers dug into my shirt and upper arms, straining both skin and fabric. His eyes stayed on the guards. "Do not unmake against his wish the least part of the creature that is My Mycroft," He commanded. "Such willful sabotage would be basest ingratitude against the gift of his return."

Prefect Cinna Semaphoros's iron frown turned into iron words. "I brought Canner to your cell first as a courtesy, *Porphyrogene*. Do not make me regret it."

Cell? The word made me see my surroundings suddenly, a long room, open, spare, with desk, chairs, shelves, and bunk all bolted to the walls, in one corner an exercise machine, and in another a toilet, sink, and shower only half screened by a translucent chest-high partition. The plates and cups upon the table were the shatterproof rubbery kind favored by prisons, and the sheets and blankets perforated so they could not be torn into strips or woven into ropes. Chagatai's pajamas and my own new clothes were pocketless and thin so they could conceal nothing, and Jehovah's suit of black which pressed so hard against me bore His armband with its many marks of office, but that thin weave was no Griffincloth. "Ἄναξ?"

"*Patris Captivus sum* (I am Father's Prisoner)," He answered.

"Why?"

His words flowed freely, languages dancing one into another, speculating what He learned from these new impotences: isolation, entrapment, grief, ignorance, war, hope too, strange new genres of hope for the recovery of freedoms whose constancy had hitherto made them invisible, but which now gleamed precious in His memory, like breath remembered by a drowning creature, if drowning lasted months. A strange Teacher, the Peer Who crafted this.

I looked to the Prefect, seeking earthly answers to supplement my Master's too-raw philosophy. "Explain."

There must have been a growl in my voice, for Cinna Semaphoros loomed closer to remind me of my helplessness within his absolute security. "The *Porphyrogene* will remain constrained until they assent to their position as *Imperator Destinatus* and accept their coming Oath—so Caesar wills."

I shivered as many puzzle pieces fell into place. I saw it all now, Caesar's actions as inexorable as the avalanche's advance after the *Sanctum* violators spread the Oath. Caesar had offered Jehovah the throne, this loving father gifting to his Son primordial IMPERIUM, loyalty absolute from all the Empire's vast and secret forces, three billion people of the ten Jehovah aims to rule, the chance to make His new world, all His in a breath if only He accepts and becomes MASON. My Good Ἄναξ can object no longer that such an offer requires Him to take an Oath unseen, to step ignorant into the dark and let it change Him, for now the Oath lies bare for all of us. If He rejects MASON's succession now, it is the Oath itself, the Empire itself that He shies back from. It would change Him if He spoke those words "*IMPERIUM sum, hinc princeps, parens, aedifex* . . . (IMPERIUM I am, henceforth leader, parent, architect . . .)" But if He will not let Himself be changed, then He must mean to change the Empire instead and to demand its unconditional surrender. Such a Son is Cornel MASON's Enemy. I'm sorry, Mitsubishi. I ignored your many warnings, your mission honestly announced to all: to rescue Xiao Hei Wang from Alexandria. I called you liars, propagandists, while all those months you and you alone saw clear enough to try to rescue Him from Caesar. And from becoming Caesar.

"T.M."—Chagatai gently touched our Master's shoulder—"there's no need to grip Mycroft with all your strength yet, you're hurting them and yourself. Save it for when the guards actually lay hold and try to drag them off."

A pause as still Jehovah struggles with contingency, with Time, before He takes this good advice and eases His grip upon me, just a hair. "Prefect, you injure Me when you do this," He warned, His perfect stilted English blurring emotional hurt and physical injury as His arms, still locked around me, braced for both.

"*Vulnerandus es, Porphyrogene* (You will/must be injured, Prince)," answered this untiring guardian, who has seen a dearer prince endure a greater injury and grow the stronger for it.

Some guards' faces showed consternation at this moment but not sympathy, accustomed by now to their gentle, stubborn Prisoner Who, with one word, could become their absolute Sovereign. No, not one word—the Oath is two hundred thirty-seven words, and with Cornel MASON's three changes, it could become two hundred and forty.

"Please, honored Prefect"—I bowed my head in formal supplication—"let me speak with Caesar. Jehovah's safety is their concern and yours as much as anything, I'm—"

Before Prefect Semaphoros could grant my prayer, a warning light and groaning bolts within the door granted it for me. Death it was who strode into our cell, for I know Death well, even when he wears the face of Cornel MASON. His hair was bed-mussed, his cheek striped by the wrinkles of the pillowcase, but even the Imperial pajamas were Death's own black, with just that gray right sleeve that hints of mercy. Godlike Achilles marched in at Death's side, the Marshal of Death's armies, trusted enough that even here he bore his outside weapons and wore his outside clothes, a uniform as black as Mason's but piped with gold like the *Sanctum* Prefect's, with its right sleeve bloodred instead of mercy gray. Xiaoliu Guildbreaker followed behind them, inspecting Martin's letter which lay open in his hands, and beside Xiaoliu I spotted my shower-damp successor, eyes wide and bright with joy and hope and trust, not conscious yet that our new clothes were prison clothes.

Still on my knees, I tried to bow lower before our Imperial captor, but Jehovah's grip held me too tight. "Caesar, I—oof!"

A cannonball of clumsy, hyperactive, furry blue love bowled into me, and there I was bound helpless on my knees with a dog's tongue smearing kisses across my face. "Boo!" I had to laugh as the familiar muzzle probed my travel-altered tastes and smells. "Hi, Boo! Yes, yes, it's me! Good—*plleeh-thh!*" I spat blue fur. "Down, Boo! Down!—*blehh-ppltth*—Good dog, Boo! Good—*pffflth*—listen! Listen! Down!"

Boo was not a large dog, sized to fill a small child's two-armed hug, but the creature's explosive energy still forced Jehovah back a pace, and broke His grip so I fell over on my side, powerless against the irresistible assault of licking tongue and my own healing laughter. I heard Achilles laugh too, and beyond the blue fuzz whirlwind I could see the veteran's smile as he hesitated, too charmed to drag my sweet attacker off quite yet. And then it stopped. The hot licks ceased, the body nestled warm against mine moved no more, and warmed no more as glassy lifeless eyes stared up in fixed serenity. A toy. There bare before us was the grayed and matted artificial fur, the telltale seams, the grid mesh of the fabric bald in patches. My first sob was soft, but not the second. I howled like a child, all the exhaustion, shock, and fear, reunion's joy too, all floodgating out of me in those unbridled infant howls that we try to learn to tame when we grow up. Were you waiting for me, Boo? All this time? Usually Bridger's living creations had lasted a week, two at the most between their sweet maker's revitalizing touches. All these months, as the plastic soldiers reverted one by one, I had wondered, hoped that the few who still held on to life—Patroclus, Boo—held on for some high purpose, one more gift not yet revealed that Bridger left behind to aid us in the days he knew would be too bloody to deserve him. Was it just for me, Boo? Your long stay in our dreary age beyond the end of miracles, were you waiting all this time just to see me come home?

"Take the dog to the laboratory, instantly!" MASON commanded, Earth's caretaker's perfect instinct to summon Zeus's daughter, gray-eyed Science, while she might still learn something from temperature, or chemistry, or Bridger's remnant cells.

I remember Achilles staring as the guards took Boo away, as pale and moved as I had ever seen the lionhearted soldier. My successor stared in shock as well, and touched Achilles's shoulder, so they held each other's eyes a long time, and Achilles put his finger to his lips to stop my successor from saying something. The hero was right—words could not help. No one hurried me, such was their kindness. Not even deadly MASON hurried me, just stood in silence as Jehovah gripped me tight and watched my howls with His ever-tearless eyes. But any string of sobs, however complex, like a runner must succumb to rest.

"I brought the words of Martin Guildbreaker, *Fili,*" MASON began in English for the benefit of Chagatai, my still wide-eyed successor, and Achilles. "I thought we should read them together."

"A welcome gift, I thank you for it, *Pater.*" No blame between these two, strange parent and strange Child, as amicable in this prison cell as in Jehovah's house at Avignon when all was peace. "I fear and unwant this further change you threaten to inflict upon My Mycroft, who is changed already many ways from last year's Mycroft who bolted from my side. Surgery—I beg you to relent."

Death, Prince of Changes, frowned down upon me through MASON's eyes. "This will safeguard Mycroft for you, *Fili.* Unsupervised, they're likely to inflict upon themself worse harms than this. And remember, it is because Mycroft still moves so freely that you lost them this time, and had to wait so long for their return. Next time might be forever."

Jehovah's face showed nothing as these dark conditionals churned through His distant Infinity, but His grip upon me tightened again toward pain.

The mountain that is Caesar sighed. "Take your time, *Fili.* First we can hear the words of Martin Guildbreaker." He turned to Xiaoliu. "Have you satisfied yourself that it is Martin's hand?"

"*Sic, Caesar,*" Xiaoliu answered, looking up from the battered page. "I recognize both Martin's hand and syntax, though the fact that they wrote in English suggests captors who did not trust them enough to pass on a letter without screening it." He held out the sheet. "With your permission, Caesar, *Magistrate*"—he pronounced Achilles's title with its Latin emphasis—"I will leave you to read it yourselves, and go at once to my still-sleeping bash'mates, who must learn what has transpired."

Warmth and a smile on MASON's face, and in my presence? The war must be going well. "Of course."

Xiaoliu Guildbreaker bowed, a crisp, clean motion like a folding sheet of paper, then hurried away.

"Shall we sit, *Fili*?" MASON chose one of the pair of chairs which flanked the desk, both bolted to the floor.

Frozen Jehovah stared three breaths' lengths at His captor-father as His calculations ran the gamut of two universes. Then He sat down on the floor just behind me where I lay, and looped His arms through mine, still bound behind my back, so no one could take me without dragging us both. "We have sat."

Great Marshal Achilles laughed, and I was glad to find him at ease so near the God Whose presence had made him as skittish as a colt mere months ago. A moment later, my successor too sat down by me and linked brave arms with mine, while bull-strong Chagatai loomed over us, as formidable as a fairy godmother as she gave Prefect Semaphoros a daring glare—*just try it!*

With a sigh of thinning patience, Caesar gestured Achilles to the empty seat that faced his own, and read aloud:

> Caesar, I live, and still obedient to your commands advance my investigations. With the issue of Saneer's trial settled, and Perry identified as Canner's 2nd stabber, only Sniper's disappearance and the *Sanctum* violation weigh upon me. Three captivities have impeded my eastward journey—the third and kindest one holds me even now. My 2nd capture placed me for a time with keepers high ranked within O.S. who, eager to avenge Sniper, aided my work's advance. From these I learned both that O.S. did (on April 6) ally with Perry, & that, of Sniper's allies, only Perry went missing even briefly on the day in question. With these captors' aid, and by the trick of feigning mortal injury, I lured one of Perry's high-ranked agents into boasting to me as I lay "dying" (in front of hidden witnesses) that Perry was indeed Sniper's captor, & used Sniper's absence to advance to near the apex of Hiveguard command, and to exploit it. On my exposing this (this occurred Dec 5) the alliance linking Perry and O.S. transformed to deadly enmity, originating near Toronto and disseminating swiftly. By now I hope this rift between your once-united enemies, gaining momentum, has disseminated as far as Afro-Eurasia, and has been of some service to the Empire. Regarding North America, I can report that the belt of Hiveguard supremacy is largely S of the 49th parallel. Up north, European forces wait for any word of sorely missed Emperor Isabel Carlos, while to the south, your ancient seat of strength in Washington is fortressed and needs only your word to surge to action.
>
> As for the *Sanctum* attack, unless I err, O.S. knows nothing. One certain solution is the crystal ball artifact left by Bridger; I inquired some time ago and learn from its keepers that the artifact can 'scry out' persons or objects at distance, but only objects personally known to the user. Since you yourself, Caesar, have seen the Tablet of the Oath—which must still be held

Here MASON flipped the sheet over to keep reading, and as he turned the front side toward me, I realized that blotches I had thought were smeared ink went clear through the paper. Sea spatter, then, or rain, a letter's travel scars—or so I guessed, not thinking yet of tears.

by the perpetrators—you could trace it personally if the artifact were brought to you in Alexandria, a favor I doubt not Utopia will grant. That is the only certainty I can suggest. As for uncertainties, captivity lends itself to introspection, and it nags at me daily that I cannot guess what any adversary could have hoped to gain by the attack. I am also reminded that, at the moment of the strike, not only were *Dominus,* Canner, and myself absent from our quarters in the *Sanctum,* but the guards were at the point in their itinerary farthest from the blast—an itinerary known to very few. Regretfully, therefore, and thinking also of how long the thieves delayed before they exposed the Oath (which, faithful to your law, I have not read), I conclude that friends of the throne committed this act, who worked hard to spare lives and sincerely expected to find some other name in the Successor's vault, that its exposure might prevent the war. I further posit that said friends knew the *Sanctum* layout and its inhabitants' movements. Doubtless the guilty parties still possess the Tablets of the Oath. Captivity's long peace has let me remember lucidly a conversation half-forgotten and, at the time, opaque to me in which, the night before the *Sanctum* attack, persons close to me expressed extreme emotion as they spoke of war and loyalty. I therefore name as the most likely culprits of this deed my bash'mates [*Damnatum Memoriae, Damnatum Memoriae, Damnatum Memoriae, Damnatum Memoriae, Damnatum Memoriae*], and my spouse Xiaoliu . . .

"Bring me Xiaoliu Guildbreaker!" Caesar roared. "Find them! Find all the Guildbreakers!" His roar, reader, as when a foaming torrent bursts its banks, swelled by the spring thaw coursing down the mountainside, and on the water rushes, no hope, no remedy, erasing all our works, the well-tilled fields, the orchards, years of labor swallowed into nothing, just so I felt oblivion's inexorable yawn in Caesar's roar, and Death's behind it. Some guards rushed out, while the Prefect shouted orders at a console in the wall, the news snaking like poison through the data-cable arteries of the palace's core. Then came that torture silence, the wait for news that no one wants to hear, when no eye meets another. I found myself reflecting on Utopia's project to disarm Death, which in that moment seemed suddenly hopeless. You armor us within, Utopia, our genes, our immune systems, preemptive chemicals doctoring every cell from inside with your genius, but how can you imagine that a body, human, frail, corruptible, could ever be immortal if the cancer of treason can grow even in a Guildbreaker?

"There's more." Achilles took up Martin's paper, our time-battered, resilient Achilles. "Let's see, 'I name . . . et cetera, et cetera . . . Xiaoliu . . .

> and urge Caesar to summon them to justice. If for my years of service I may beg one boon of my Emperor, it is that, before the exercise of your Capital Power, you pass on to my bash' and spouse that I love them no iota less for this, and that I regret no moment of our shared years save that unhappy hour when I failed to sense and stop their well-meant treason.

This stabbed anew, remembering that under Masonic law, if one Mason strays, all Masons in the bash' must share the punishment, the crime no graver than the failure to keep their near and dear one straight upon the path. You sign your own death warrant here, Martin, as well you know, unless Death shows mercy.

Here Achilles turned the page sideways, to read a few more words that Martin crammed into the margin, treasuring every centimeter.

> *Domine*, you are loved by many here, including your enemies, and always me. Grateful to be yours and Caesar's ever, M. Guildbreaker.

Achilles offered the page to Caesar but took it back again, realizing the paper would crumple like an orchid in Caesar's black-sleeved hand, which trembled with the hunger to crush a throat that, for the first time in so many years, was not my own. Achilles offered the page instead to staring Jehovah, but He would not release His hold on me, so my successor took it and held up the tear-splotched words for us to see. *Now they'll censor my history again*, I remember thinking. *Damnatio Memoriae* was Caesar's sentence for the *Sanctum* violators, their names and deeds to be expunged from every record, document, and chronicle. Posterity will know no other Guildbreakers now, no team of bash'mates laboring at Martin's side or marching behind Caesar. With them expunged, poor Martin will always seem to have worked alone, no partners to his labors apart from Dominic. And the Guildbreaker children, orphaned by Caesar's justice, they would need a bash' loss specialist. Was that why you sent Carlyle Foster to Alexandria with me, Providence? A small kindness as garnish to this planned cruelty?

"Caesar, Xiaoliu Guildbreaker is taken," the Prefect at the console confirmed in English for us all. "They are being brought here for your justice. The other adult survivor [*Damnatus Memoriae*] is in critical condition and being carried to hospital. All the Guildbreaker bash'children are safe and in custody."

"Only two survivors?" A new rage quaked through Caesar. "They fought back?"

"No, Caesar. Most of the bash'members were dead when our guards arrived, and the children were locked in their rooms. It is not yet clear what happened, but the two survivors were in combat with each other when they were captured."

Strange tidings, these, too strange for speculation to be useful until the perpetrator of this strangeness stood before us, splotched with red, some his own, much not. The round and bleeding signatures of bullet holes bloomed through rushed bandages on Xiaoliu's shoulders and his limp left arm, and I saw scratches on his cheeks and slender throat, the jagged, desperate signature of human claws. Xiaoliu bowed as he entered, at least as much as he could with guards gripping both elbows, and with the one hand that still worked, he held out a time-greened bronze tablet no guard dared gaze upon.

"Caesar, I return to you the tablets of your Oath, all safe, and secret from me, if not fully secret from the world, for I, like Martin, obedient to your command, have not read them." The plural confused me, until I realized one guard held a heavy case which must contain the Oath tablets of Emperors past, which each new Caesar studies in his starting year, learning which words each predecessor chose, and from that, better than the textbooks teach, which tasks each MASON past trusted to MASONs future. Was it Mycroft MASON, as I guessed, who had added Utopia? Curiosity made me stare, until Caesar's shadow stretching close reminded me of curiosity's price.

Death approached the condemned—for a *Familiaris,* Caesar's wrath is trial, conviction, sentence, all in one. "Is all as Martin says?" he asked, taking the tablet. "Was it you?"

"*Sic, Caesar,*" Xiaoliu answered, clear powerful words, though the lips that spoke them were bloodied and trembling. "We believed the name in the *Sanctum* was not the *Porphyrogene*'s, that war would be averted, and that you yourself desired such an outcome but refused to set a precedent for revealing the *Imperator Destinatus.* In our zeal and hubris we destroyed the peace we sought to protect, and yet more zeal and hubris led us to the selfish consensus that we should hide our guilt and avoid your justice, so we could work to mitigate what we had ruined, and still serve you as loy-lo-loyal"—he tripped over the word—"as loyal Masons should."

Well might you trip, Xiaoliu Guildbreaker. Well might you shudder to pronounce the word 'loyal' when you have let the poison hubris fester in your heart to ruin all. Much as I once did.

Cornel MASON gazed upon the tablet in his hand, running his fingers over the rough, scratched letters—scratched in wax at first, I guessed, then cast in bronze by each new MASON's order once a generation. I peered up, curious to see the script of MASON's honored predecessor, but then I caught the word IMPERIUM and shut my eyes against the archcrime—an archcrime still, pardon or no—of reading Earth's most secret words. I must have given a little gasp, since MASON's eyes snapped to me, and he secreted the Oath at once within the black and safety of his pocket. "Your whole bash' acted as one?" he asked.

Xiaoliu swallowed. "All save Martin and the children. I myself thought many times of suicide or confession, but when the cars and communications failed, it became easier to tell myself you needed every servant you still had. And I did not know where [*Damnatus Memoriae*] had concealed the Tablet of the Oath, so I felt I should not rest until it was in your hands."

"Is that why you went to the others just now?" Achilles interrupted, the only soul on Earth courageous enough to interrupt Death as he looms in judgment. "After you read Martin's letter, you went down to your bash'mates. Did you try to retrieve the tablet from [*Damnatio Memoriae*] by force? Or did you just go to warn the others of Martin's suspicions?"

"It was no longer mere suspicion, *Magistrate*." Amazingly, no tears quite fell from Xiaoliu's wet, bright eyes. "Martin is correct that the crystal-ball artifact left by Bridger would lead Caesar infallibly to the tablet and thus confirm our guilt. As Caesar's servant, I could not conscience exposing so invaluable a resource to the dangerous journey from Luna City to Alexandria, not after the innumerable achievements Utopia's Clairvoyance Constellation has made possible, not least the letter's safe arrival."

I heard my successor gasp beside me. "The Clairvoyance Constellation, then..." Wide eyes grew wider as the strangeness of our reality sank in. "...then it was literal clairvoyance, they saw Huxley's rooftop signal with the crystal ball..."

The smile quivering on Xiaoliu's lips beamed joy that the Emperor who was about to execute him has such excellent resources. "I went to tell my bash'mates that Martin and Justice had found us at last, thinking we would march together with dignity to return the tablet and face our sentence. When some dissented, talked of flight, and of serving you through treason at a distance like the *Porphyrogene*'s dishonorable Dominic, I held my hand no more."

Somehow, I smiled despite so many griefs, warmed by this glimpse of a heart which, like mine, had strayed in service, placing our own ideas of what our masters needed above our masters' words. If, even with death and ignominy looming, brave Xiaoliu had found the resolution to return and spurn the errant path, then maybe I can too.

"You knew my sentence." MASON's cheeks flushed red with blood which seemed to drain from deathly pale Xiaoliu. "A swift, competent death, the kind you have granted to your co-conspirators, was a boon I reserved only for those traitors who surrendered willingly. You had no right to spare your coward bash'mates death by my own unpracticed hand."

All eyes fixed now on MASON's black-sleeved left hand, where his Capital Power waits even in peacetime, never quite asleep.

Xiaoliu choked, and the sound brought all eyes to his white and fragile throat. "I'm sorry, Caesar, I... should not have presumed, I... Several of them killed themselves before I—"

"Why did you publish the Oath?" The question made me wince, but MASON had to ask it, MASON whose primordial IMPERIUM was wounded, not once but twice by the Guildbreakers' treason, first when the *Sanctum* fell exposing his successor, then when the words reserved for just one soul in every generation stood naked before ten billion eyes.

"I do not know, Caesar. [*Damnatus Memoriae*] thought that reading it would help us guess your goals and needs, so they and [*Damnatus Memoriae*] read it together, but the rest of us refused. I still do not understand why they suddenly chose to make it public—the only explanations they offered were incomplete and unsatisfying." His eyes fell to his bandaged arm. "I have no excuse for my final failure tonight in allowing them to die before you could force the answers from them—I failed to anticipate how prepared they would be, and how cowardly."

Inexorable Death stepped forward, one grim pace, then two, no hesitation even in his weaker foot as human faded into executioner. "My sentence not revoke. *I* do not revoke," he corrected, his Latin thoughts knotting the order of his English, "nor that boon I offered if one among the traitors should return my Oath of Office, safe and secret, as you—in spirit—have. Thus the others I now banish from human memory as I pronounce *Damnatio Memoriae*, which I shall enforce on every text, image, and record my power can touch. For yourself, my boon is that your name may live instead in infamy, a curse to echo through the rest of human history, with Clytemnestra and Ephialtes: Guildbreaker."

I felt dizzy. I should, I must, feel sick inside when I hear the names of Ephialtes, who betrayed the Spartans at Thermopylae, or Clytemnestra, who forever shattered our race's trust in home and family when she butchered her husband, lordly Agamemnon, on his return from Troy. But that normal sickness was drowned out by a reeling dizziness as I realized I was here, now, watching in person the moment when a third name joins theirs as a curse for all the ages. And it was someone whom I knew and walked with, someone real with socks and favorite foods. It felt like having a friendly classmate grow up to be that conqueror who marches toward the Hanging Gardens of not-yet-lost Babylon and gives the order, "Pull it down!" Did Trojan Paris's friends and brothers feel like this when the smiling prince grew up to sow such ruin? Xiaoliu, I know, would not have had me pray for any mercy, but in the dizziness of my attachment I did pray that if this war, this generation, must bequeath to our posterity a new name to be wielded as a curse like Ephialtes it might be, not Guildbreaker, but Mycroft Canner.

"Thank you, Caesar," Xiaoliu answered, unwavering. "Sparing me *Damnatio Memoriae* is an amnesty beyond the deserving of one who has made myself an archtraitor."

MASON breathed deep. "Cinna." He turned.

The Prefect looked up suddenly from MASON's black-sleeved hand to MASON's face. "Caesar?"

"You will adopt my faithful *Familiaris* Martin and the children of their bash' into your own, that they my bear henceforth the name Semaphoros and live untainted by posterity's curse."

Gasps of joy, from Xiaoliu, the Prefect, me.

"Gladly, Caesar. What about Charlemagne and the other elders of the bash'?"

For a deluded moment I imagined the good old Senator welcoming such a boon, but Cornel MASON knew well what the *Familiaris* herself would have answered. "They should have raised their children better. For which crime they shall share archtraitor Xiaoliu's infamy, but for their past good service I commute for them the dooms of death and *Damnatio Memoriae*. Inform them when you can."

"Sic, Caesar."

And now, with all decisions made, there was nothing in the room, the capital, the world, but Caesar's grim left hand and Death's hand in it. Strong fingers grasped the fragile stem of Xiaoliu's snow-pale throat and squeezed a failing gurgle from it, but a human throat, even a slender one, is strong, so Caesar raised his right hand too, to give his grip leverage enough to crush. As breath gave way to croaking, the strict set of Xiaoliu's cheeks broke, as pre-storm tension breaks and lets rain fall. His shoulders twitched reflexively, but he dug his fingers hard into the fabric of his uniform, fighting the impulse to grasp Caesar's wrists and struggle. And Caesar saw it, saw this will that conquered even death throes as devotion overrode life's inalienable right to struggle to the last. And Death let go.

"My sentences are mine to carry out at what hour I choose," MASON pronounced, "and I do not choose this one. Xiaoliu Guildbreaker, you still have questions to answer, duties to comple—" I think this pause was Caesar seeing the bruises starting to purple Xiaoliu's throat. "You slew *Familiares* today, stealing the lifetimes' labors they owed me, and like Mycroft Canner, you, *Archproditor* [Archtraitor], will repay that debt before I let you rest."

Xiaoliu could form no words, just gasps and squeaks, but no words could have matched the eloquence of his tears, suppressed when it had been his duty to accept Death's justice, which welcomed Death's mercy with showers as warm and free as summer sun.

MASON waited for a medic to inspect Xiaoliu and offer an approving nod. "Your story," he continued, "your account of what led your bash' to plan and do this is too incomplete. I do not believe the worm of treason grows without some egg to hatch it. Trace it for me, all the details, which among you first conceived the lie that treason could be service, and why and how that lie spread to the others. Trace too what your now-nameless bash'mates did with the Tablet while they had it, and why they chose the moment that they did to betray even their fellow traitors by publishing the Oath. Even tonight's events, their deaths, so many and so quick, seem strange, too planned. There must be notes, logs, traces. Find them, sort them, map the step-by-step of archcrime's birth. When all that can be known of this is known, then—" Here he paused for breath. "—then the *Sanctum Sanctorum* will have justice, and the Empire shall again be capable of peace."

Soundless or not, I know the mouth movements of '*Sic, Caesar.*'

The Emperor took a long, deep breath, and seemed a shade more human when he released it. "Take *Archproditor* Guildbreaker to the hospital. And, Cinna"—he turned to his *Sanctum* Prefect with that deep body ease that only bash'mates share—"go see the former Guildbreaker bash'children, tell them what is happening, and that Martin and they have received the honor of sharing our name."

Even the Prefect could not suppress a smile at this swerve away from tragedy. "At once, Caesar. Should we take Mycroft Canner to the hospital now as well?"

I gasped—I had forgotten MASON had a sentence for me, too. My leg throbbed with the imagined pain of surgery's unwilling change, and at my back I felt Jehovah's grip upon my still-bound arms tighten anew.

"I oppose this, *Pater,*" Jehovah said with words, but His hands said more, their force pledging that He would fight with every fiber if they tried to take me. As when a shipwrecked mariner clinging for life to some sea-battered rock is ripped from safety by the storm but leaves the skin of his fingers clinging scarlet to the stone, so hard this captive God would hold me rather than surrender His Mycroft to an intrusion in my flesh I did not want.

Now Chagatai, still looming over where we lay upon the floor, resumed her fighting stance, and I thought my successor too would brace for my defense, but found those kindly eyes still lost in studying the tearstained words of Martin's letter. Martin. *Martin gave his spouse and bash'mates over to death today,* I thought. Not the technical today that cold calendars count, but the shared today that text creates, the now when Martin wrote his words and the now in which we read them married across time's diaspora. In that combined today Martin wrote out his bash's tear-smeared death warrant, yet even as he mourned, his loyalty still blossomed through grief's winter evergreen enough for him to postscript that deadly letter with words of comfort for the One Who grieves a deeper Grief than humans know. If Martin was so brave, surely his good example could steel me enough to face this smaller sacrifice, my duty now to urge my Good and Kind Protector not to let His mortal body suffer injury fighting something so finite as this small change to my flesh. There Martin's imagined image seems to smile courage down at me, holding back the part of me that wants to scream, and kick, and run like wind along the shore where I have run so many times as fierce as flight, and would run more. The armband on my sleeve cuts like a wound, proving that this is Caesar's right. My lips part. Surely, any moment I will voice the words, just as at any moment Saladin and I will charge out from our hiding place to face immovable Apollo and begin or end his war. I should consent; law, duty, need agree. The words are in me, ready. I can feel the wind upon my cheek, Saladin's lips, Apollo and his Seine are there fast breathing on the far side of the dumpster. One last kiss and count to ten we had agreed, my Saladin and I, then plunge into this small eternity named war, but—ten, eleven, twelve, his lips—we still don't move. Why am I, coward, hesitating—ten, eleven, twelve—still paused, still breathing as the tickle on my cheek, a salt tear blowing sideways in the wind, and I taste Saladin. Why don't I move? The street grit and the metal at my back, why—ten, eleven, twelve—why don't I move?

"Cornel." It was Achilles who spoke up at last, the only man in MASON's capital who dares speak MASON's name. "It can wait. Dawn's here to chide us for defying sleep and night so long." He nodded to the rosy haze beyond the man-made stars of Alexandria. "Let's give Jehovah time to rest and think it through. You, too."

For two more breaths, MASON stared down upon the stubborn ship of flesh that hosts his Son, then sighed that soft, exasperated sigh that only He can draw from His imperial father. "How long until the fleets meet at the Almagest?"

"Nine hours," Achilles answered. "I can't make it back before the battle even if I leave now. Better to rest and do what I can from here." The hero's brows arched as he heard me give a cry; amused, I think, that in the crisis of arrival, I forgot the war ground on. An old friend's gaze can be so eloquent. The glint and darkness of Achilles's eyes told the whole tale, how my riddle—M. C. Moriarty—had ricocheted through MASON's allies even to the distant Ocean's heart, where the matchless commander had stood watch over Utopia's last ladder to the stars. Did you choose me over so great a charge, Achilles? Did you trust to others' guard our nascent star-bound future's frail umbilical, and all for me?

"Then we shall all rest, and prepare." MASON glanced at me as he turned away, though by his frown, I think he did not intend to. Cornel the Merciful is not a title this Emperor would want to hold in history's books, but merciful he is.

"Wait, Caesar," my successor called, a gentle tone but urgent.

"I will hear no arguments now." MASON's glance was stone. "[Anonymous], you may remain a prisoner here and retain a prisoner's right to plot and protest, or you may choose to be my guest and come and go and labor freely like the Censor, but if you accept my hospitality, then you give your pledge you will not aid my son or Mycroft in any enterprise against me, including escape, and I will show no mercy if you break that pledge."

My successor winced. "I . . . thank you for the options, I'll think about them for a little if I may, but I was going to bring up something totally different."

"What?" A hawk about to feed which gloatingly invites the captured nightingale to sing its last could not invite more grimly.

My successor held up Martin's letter. "The language in this is really, really stilted, even for Martin, especially the first paragraph. And, while it's such an easy code I'm guessing that the captors saw but let it through anyway, which in itself is something to investigate, but that aside, if you read the first letter of each line in that first paragraph vertically, it spells out 'Cato Weeksbooth is no longer human.'"

CHAPTER THE SEVENTEENTH

The Second Battle for the Almagest

or

I Do Not Know How to Call 'Friend' One Who Does This

Written February 8–14, 2455
Events of February 8

I AM WAITING, READER. I am waiting for Caesar to return and tell me how the stars have changed.

Our law speaks of "intolerable crimes": that it is intolerable to cause extensive or uncontrolled death or suffering; intolerable to devastate Nature or the Produce of Civilization; intolerable to strip from an anguished soul the means to cry for help. But what does that 'intolerable' truly mean? That humanity cannot endure it? We have endured so much, pandemics, earthquakes, self-inflicted genocides, yet we plod on. That we will not allow it? How many atrocities have we allowed, perpetrated, caging our aid and empathy in bars of selfishness? Does 'intolerable' mean that we cannot forgive it? Perhaps, but no matter how bloody our race's history, how rank our guilt, somehow human hearts still look upon ourselves and see some excellence. But not all human hearts. I think that's what 'intolerable' means, that something dies inside us when we face such things. A spark dies out. It is not forever's death, more like the year's death, when intolerable winter snuffs out light, life, growth, and though we claim thaw's kiss will always come to kindle life anew, some roots are chilled too deep and stir no more. You know that I once lost the will to battle, that night I gazed up hopeless from the becalmed *Shearwater* at stars too cruel and far for aspiration. That night I learned Poseidon is intolerable, Distance a frost too deep for hope's faint flicker to endure. You knew Poseidon was too strong, Ἄναξ Apollo, didn't you? That Old Enemy Distance has stamped out your spark a thousand times, and will a thousand more? I boasted, when my own light was relit, that he has never snuffed it out in every breast at once. But he could. You knew he could when you began this war, this quarrel with your uncle. Apollo Ἐπιβατήριε, Lord of Embarkations, you who need us still to mount your ships and be your arrows as you take your distant aim, you knew your all-encircling uncle can strip the feathers from our shafts, the strong sails from our masts, and leave us grounded. They say you two built Troy together, that side by side in ancient days uncle and nephew laid her firm foundation stones, and I believe it, for Utopia is no sailor without a sea. But while you, Ἄναξ, still love your Trojans dearly, the fearsome Earth-Shaker aids the Greeks against us, raging that we did not pay his labors back with thanks and sacrifice. We did not thank you, either—for your gentler gifts, perhaps, but not for the journey, not for your command that we must face Intolerable Distance for your sake, again, again. That you still love us shows your strangeness more than kindness, distant archer, for it is no kindness when you, who dared not face your mighty uncle when he challenged you on Homer's battlefield, restart that quarrel here. You know he wins. You know your Trojans suffer. But no, all this is stranger, deeper, than a quarrel, for the two of you are yet one Thing, two parts of Providence as interlinked as lungs and heart. You light the spark and snuff it. So, what was yesterday? That yesterday when you taught me, taught all of us, that there is a true Intolerable, a limit to what we can endure before all sparks die out. Before Poseidon beats us down. Before Love—yes my love for you, my lord, my own Ἄναξ Apollo—before my love and His Love too, a greater Love born in a greater Breast than humans bear, both snap and die. That yesterday when you bade Fate and Heaven open to reveal that, when such Love reaches its breaking point, then you, Ἀπόλλων Προόψιε, Far-Seeing Apollo; you, Ἀπόλλων Προστατήριε, Apollo Before the Doorway; you Ἀπόλλων Ἕκατε, Apollo Who Aims So Far; and most of all that you, Ἀπόλλων Θεοξένιε, Apollo Guardian of Strangers; care. You care. That changes everything. So I begged Caesar—*I* dared beg a boon of *Caesar*—that he take me from this cell a moment, bound however he wills, so long as I could see with my own eyes Night and her lights uncountable which must burn different after such a day. And he, too wise to give a monster such an inch of freedom, is yet so kind he promised he would step outside into the night himself, gaze on your distant targets with his own eyes, Lord Apollo, then return and tell me how the stars have changed.

Received 10:06; Sent 09:44; Lag 22 min. From Fort Hathiyaaru, Kunahandhoo.

ENEMY FLEET NOW COMPLETELY PAST OUR POST. SENDING FULL SHIP COUNT. FORCE MORE THAN DOUBLE PREVIOUS. MILAE REINFORCEMENTS NOT YET IN SIGHT. OUR HOPES ARE WITH YOU.

Received 10:07; Sent 09:55; Lag 12 min. From Ptolemy Actual.

GLATISANT PARTY HAS ENGAGED HOMELAND VESSELS AT 0.9250, 73.1928. MOVING TO SUPPORT.

Received 10:08; Sent 09:11; Lag 57 min. From Navarch Ishan Solliferus.

ULTIMATUM REJECTED BY DOUGONG AND HOMELAND COMMANDERS. BOTH FLEETS ADVANCING ON ALMAGEST. PREPARE FOR BATTLE. THIS IS NOT A DRILL.

10:09. Next Faustburst Scheduled 10:20. 11 minutes remain.

So battle began that morning, reader, for our Achilles, and for Caesar at his side, both sleepless in the beating heart of Alexandria, of Empire, of all. They trickle in at different speeds, these messages like weary blood cells, some racing down great veins, some creeping back through winding capillaries whose curves and crannies multiply the roundtrip, dragging down the information lifeblood of the war. Our best are all assembled: Censor Jung Su-Hyeon, my swift successor, loyal archtraitor Xiaoliu Accursed-Through-the-Ages-Guildbreaker, even deep-reading Toshi Mitsubishi helps triangulate delays, pinpoint locations, and update the battle map upon the chamber wall, whose lines, arrows, and crisply labeled spots lie in their very crispness, not facts but guesses already a hundred deaths out of date. Achilles does not command the fleet from Alexandria, reader—that is for Caesar's frontline admirals and whatever rank Utopia assigns the vanguard of its still-civilian militia. Our Achilles seeks only to advise, abort disasters, spot with his veteran's instincts which reports are too strange to be real, or anticipate which ships have endured too much, and should fall back before they cross that frontier where reason turns to rage and all sides suffer. Achilles aims only to make this battle kinder, and that is what makes Censor and Anonymous judge these labors consonant with their neutrality, and makes quick Toshi skirt the title traitress in good conscience, though her father's green and scarlet trefoil flies on many adversaries' prows.

Received 10:48; Sent 10:01; Lag 47 min. From MGS Phạm Tuân.

MALDIVES NOT YET IN SIGHT. HAVE SENT NEW ULTIMATUM TO HOMELAND COMMAND. EXPIRES 11:00. MILAE IS WITH YOU WHATEVER THEY ANSWER. YOU ARE NOT ALONE.

Received 10:49; Sent 10:22; Lag 27 min. From Bryar Kosala, Mumbai.

HAVE PROPOSED HANDOVER OF ALMAGEST TO MILAE FORCES. HOMELAND SEEMS AMENABLE. AWAITING RESPONSE FROM DOUGONG. DO WHAT YOU CAN TO PERSUADE UTOPIA. THIS COULD WORK, CORNEL. NO ONE HAS TO DIE TODAY.

Received 10:50; Sent 10:38; Lag 12 min. From Ptolemy Actual.

MAXIMIAN AND XERXES GROUPS SUPPORTING GLATISANT PARTY. THREE ENEMY CRUISERS DESTROYED.

10:50. Next Faustburst Scheduled 11:00. 10 minutes remain.

And where art thou in all this, Mycroft? Thy Jehovah Mason and thyself?

We, gentle reader? We rest far from the battle rush, if not as far as you. Night's gentler child Hypnos lingered long with us that pale night-morning, the sweet-winged lord of sleep leaving his brother Thanatos alone to bear the war's dead to that shadowed crossroads where all paths meet. No argument could pry my Master's arms from me, so we both squeezed into His bunk, while bulky Chagatai sprawled on the floor beside us, the guardian mother bear whose loving vigilance promises violence. My industrious successor snubbed Hypnos entirely, begging instead an anti-sleeping dose and accepting MASON's offer of a suite outside to labor as Anonymous some hours before the rush of battle tasks. I have a sleep-blurred memory of a request for photos from Klamath Marsh Secure Hospital, close-ups of the papers that had hung feather-dense upon the walls of Cato Weeksbooth's cell. Good thinking, my successor; Klamath Marsh is where Martin was stranded when the cars first failed, out chasing Perry-Kraye—perhaps the clue to Martin's note was there?

Received 11:07; Sent 10:52; Lag 15 min. From Arcadia Alhazen, Almagest Dock 2.
IRISCLOUD5 MODULE LOADING STAGE 3 COMPLETE. ON SCHEDULE FOR 11:25 LIFTOFF.
Received 11:08; Sent 10:30; Lag 38 min. From MGS Wu Qi, Dougong Command.
WE WILL DESTROY THE ELEVATOR IF WE MUST. SURRENDER WILL PROTECT IT FOR THE FUTURE AND SAVE MANY LIVES. YOU HAVE 30 MINUTES.
Received 11:09; Sent 10:54; Lag 15 min. From Umibōzu Pod.
SUBSURFACE ATTACKERS ENCOUNTERED 0.8946, 73.2891. NEW SUBMERSIBLE TYPE SIGHTED, SMALLER AND FASTER THAN MTS-0316. LIKELY NEW DESIGN FOR SHALLOW ACTION. DISPATCHING CHARYBDIS TO CAPTURE ONE. SHALLOW WATER ATOLL DEFENSE STRATEGY COMPROMISED. RELEASING ARCHENSWARM.
11:10. Next Faustburst Scheduled 11:50. 40 minutes remain.

The groan and hiss of bolts as solid as the airlocks of the great Dreadnautilus heralded a stranger in vivid red, light loose garments like hospital wear, with a face that looked to me a little Thai, black hair glistening wet, and with a bulky box that smelled of breakfast. Whispered words: "Good morning, Gibraltar. Are Mike and Mycroft still asleep?"

Chagatai was already up and exercising. "I think s—"

"Huxley!" I interrupted as I recognized the voice, then winced as I felt Jehovah stir beside me, resummoned to our unkind cosmos by my noise and motions. "Your coat? What ha-a-ppened?" I choked out through the onset of my morning sobs. "Your vizor?" I spotted now the paler outline of where the vizor always sat, the eyes that I had never seen unprocessed.

Huxley frowned as the door sealed fast again. "Apparently, a Delian may not bear arms or tech within a hundred meters of this cell. It's good to see You, Mike."

The Visitor sat up to greet His visitor. "You restored part of My *ibasho*," He said, trusting Huxley to recognize the Japanese root of our English 'bash',' that special community that lets one be one's self, the human half of home. "Thank you."

Huxley's hand twitched with the impulse to hit RECORD, a lifetime of documenting every word and gesture of First Contact ruined now by Caesar's confiscations. "Whatever I can do for You, Mike, You know I will."

"Both you and many others will such kindnesses for Me, but He Who Wills you also Wills many barriers that abort your wills' deeds. Few battle them as you have."

Huxley's frown wished that were true.

"Did you suffer much for Me?" Micromegas asked.

"Yes." Our Guest is impossible to lie to. "But I'd face twice as much if I had to, to have this conversation with You at the end. How are You? How's the war affecting You?"

He paused—I had so missed Him, reader, even His long pauses, maddening as they are. "It makes Me think on paths more," He said, "and on Time. Both are tools Your Maker wields to change you, but paths—being here, there, Tokyo, Romanova, Alexandria—can make the same time increment enact more or less change. I think that this My Mycroft disresembles more My memory's Mycroft than a Mycroft would have who had been with Me through all."

"Perhaps." Huxley sighed. "And hard times, months like these, change us more than ordinary months do."

"To what shall we compare such months? A sharper chisel? A stronger solvent? A wave of greater amplitude? I had not thought Distance as terrible as Time, but like X and Y axes now they form diaspora, as length and breadth form shapes."

Huxley nodded, many thoughts layered in that frown. "We should eat quickly." The breakfast box's *clunk* upon the table promised well. "The fleets are closing in, and Cato Weeksbooth is expected soon."

"Cato!" I cried. "Here! How?" Cato was not on Earth, Cato was in his rightful habitat at last, in Luna City where all is peace and science. Wasn't he? "Cato wouldn't . . ." I continued, but Huxley's eyes, so strangely naked, told me of my error with their tired commixture of dissent and respect. This was no otherworldly Delian we spoke of, this was kind and bending Cato, Cato who for thirty years endured the yoke of O.S. to safeguard the system that safeguarded peace for our imperfect world, even though the tax upon his mind and conscience nearly killed him, and trapped him in a Hive and bash' which were not, and could never be, his *ibasho*. Would that Cato have voted to abandon Earth?

"Utopia cannot endure MASON's distrust." At Huxley's touch, the wall switch drew the digital false shades from the digital false window, to let the simulated midday light convince our more animal senses it was time to rise. "Especially not today. Four fleets at least, perhaps as many as seven, are converging on the Almagest."

"Seven?" I repeated.

"There are five Mitsubishi factions now: Dougong, Fuxing, Homeland, Greenpeace, and Milae."

That rang a vague bell. "Papa used those names . . ."

Huxley nodded. "We couldn't tell the difference in Romanova, the factions are allied in the Mediterranean, all on the defensive. Not so in the East. We will lose the Almagest this time, unless MASON's diplomacy convinces some of them to aid us, or at least to leave us be. After the incident with Ganymede and Cookie, no one trusts us." Huxley did not need to speak the words to bring the old promise to mind: *Utopia will not make humanoid U-beasts*—a promise all Earth believes they have broken, and in the most abominable way. "This is not the day to let doubt weaken MASON's trust in us," Huxley continued, "so when MASON says they will not be satisfied until Cato Weeksbooth stands before them to answer Martin's accusation, then, though it takes our best ship from the battlefield, we will do it."

I choked. "And Cato, what is . . . Do you know what Martin meant?" I caught myself trying to read Huxley's eyes and felt like a voyeur, staring at another's intimate body part, one usually concealed.

"No," Huxley answered. "We knew I might be captured or interrogated on a mission that took me so close to many enemies. I only know what I need to know."

My throat tightened—another price our Huxley pays to walk this jungle where the deadly lions and tigers of high statecraft stalk close to the precious Alien.

That Alien slid forward on the bunk beside me, still grasping me close as, with His human feet, He explored for the 7,670th time in His sojourn on Earth the morning's wonder: floor. "I thrill to meet another thinking thing that speaks but is not human," He began. "Yet that this being once was human and is no longer complicates its welcome."

No one could disagree with that.

"We should eat, T.M." Practical Chagatai descended from the exercise machine. "And shower. We'll need to be in top form today."

"And once we're ready, MASON will let us watch the war room." Huxley nodded at the blank wall opposite the bookshelves, in whose slick texture I now recognized a screen. "Do you want to watch the battle, Mike?"

Jehovah was so close I felt His words, His breath upon my shoulder as He clutched me. "I do not wish battle to be, but since it is, I wish to see and understand it to the maximum that human sense allows."

"Then we must eat."

He Who often forgets that He must eat still clung to me. To me, reader! Guilt surged inside: I, least deserving of His servants, why should I bask in His touch, not gentle Heloïse, not loyal Martin, not desperate Dominic ready to battle seas and continents in his frenzy of need to reach the Presence that I—failure! parricide!—enjoy? But if we agree that the first loaf after famine should go to the neediest, no need, not mine, not even Dominic's, can match His for His only translator.

Chagatai sighed gently. "T.M., you must let go of Mycroft. No one can take them without opening the door first, and the warning light will give us plenty of time to grab them again."

Hesitation, still that hesitation as He finds it hard to trust anew the Host Who took me once. But I know how to move my Master. "Ἄναξ, You must let go so I can use the bathroom. I'm in pain."

Instant release.

Received 11:19; Sent 10:49; Lag 30 min. From Fort Hathiyaaru, Kunahandhoo.

MILAE FLEET SIGHTED 1.8659, 73.6756. FRIEND SIGNAL RETURNED.

11:20. Next Faustburst Scheduled 11:50. 30 minutes remain.

Received 11:20; Sent 10:35; Lag 45 min. From MGS Wu Qi, Dougong Command.

FROM DIRECTOR LU BIAOJI—MY ALLIES ARE VERY WILLING TO DESTROY THE ELEVATOR. I CAN GUARANTEE ITS SAFETY IF ALL MASONIC FORCES WITHDRAW AND UTOPIA SURRENDERS. I WILL ENSURE THE U-BEASTS ARE NOT PURGED.

Received 11:22; Sent 11:11; Lag 11 min. From Ornithopter Eerie.

BARRAGE INCOMING. WARDENS PREPARE COUNTERSPELL.

Practiced Chagatai helped me through the awkwardness of using the bathroom with my arms still bound. The breakfast box opened like a cave of wonders: steaming fresh flatbread, plump green falafels, bean dip with herbs and fresh tomato, even fried eggs which smelled of ghee. After months of rationing and gamy wild meat, my heart called this the luxury of imperial captivity, but I think it was actually the luxury of not being stranded on an island. And of having 50,000 jeeps. To my delight, some thoughtful captor had included a thermos of spiced and creamy porridge for me, with a straw to spare me the indignity of hand feeding.

"Are any of the Mitsubishi factions Remakers?" I asked. "Allies?"

Chagatai chuckled. "Even we aren't Remakers, if in 'we' you include the Masons who are most of our force. But there are Remaker Mitsubishi, yes. *Fuxing* (复兴): rebirth, rejuvenation, renaissance; real Remakers. They're led by old Director Huang Enlai. Good egg, that one, and I'm not just saying that because we went to the same campus." The smiling Mongol winked. "Fuxing is strong but they haven't fired on a fellow Mitsubishi yet. But nothing's pushed them hard until today."

That sounded like hope. "And who's attacking?"

Good, Mycroft, thy war chronicle needs more war questions like this, and war answers, if thou must plunge me headlong into heptasided chaos; even friend Thomas flounders finding so many alls in all-on-all.

I plunge too, good Master Reader, patient Master Hobbes, I plunge too.

"Dougong and Homeland are the main attackers. Dougong is Hiveguard, the old Beijing and Shanghai power blocs led by Chen Chengguo, the old Minister of Labor, and by one of old Lu Yong's cousins, Lu Biaoji. Dougong is—"

「*Tokyō.*」 Jehovah interrupted, staring at me, expectant. 「*Kumimono, masugumi.*」 It took all three synonyms for me to realize He was translating *dougong* (斗拱), a Chinese word for *tokyō* (likewise 斗拱) or *kumimono* (組物), the distinctive cap-and-block brackets that shoulder the weight of wooden temples and other ancient structures in China, Korea, Japan, and their near neighbors. *Dougong* is a technology as fundamental as a keystone but Asia's, and bears all the edifice's weight upon itself, so the rest of the structure shelters underneath like birds beneath strong boughs, or carefree Members trusting all to strong bloc leaders—the right word can indeed convey more than a hundred.

"Dougong insists," Chagatai continued, "that all the reform calls are just a ploy by other Hives to steal Mitsubishi land, and they blame what's gone wrong inside the Hive on Andō taking the Chief Directorship away from China."

I felt unkind inside; dodging the Mitsubishi on the seas, I had assumed the whole Hive had gone this selfish direction, not just one splinter.

And Homeland?

Yes, impatient reader, I asked too.

「*Homelando wa Chichi-ue.*」 Jehovah pronounced the English 'Homeland' like a foreign loan word in His Japanese.

Here was mixed news. "Director Andō back? But allied with this anti-Japanese Dougong faction?"

「To free Me from Alexandria. As a Chief Director never formally deposed, *Chichi-ue* both claims and is the Hive's legitimate continuation. *Tokyō* and *Chichi-ue* both oppose any reform imposed from outside upon the Mitsubishi, and both oppose *Pater,* so both aim now to close off *Pater*'s road to space and make it theirs.」

"But such an alliance cannot last!" Hobbes cries. "Homeland and Dougong, new names for these old sides whose peacetime squabbles we saw lay so dread an egg as the Canner Device, how can they share a war, a sea, a battlefield who cannot share a boardroom without murder? What is their second step? Have they signed treaties, some duration before they slash again at one another's throats? Or is geography their stopgap, truce until the Masons are driven from . . . from what? From the Indian Ocean? From the whole Pacific Rim?"

These are good questions, Master Hobbes, prudent, more prudent than mine were, but in that cell I watched Our Maker's desperate Equal bask in me, a living sliver of His *ibasho,* just as a sun-starved seedling sprouted in a sewer basks in every photon of one raking ray of light, so with such Grief, such Loneliness before me, one question chased all others from my lips. 「Then where is Dominic, Ἄναξ? Is Dominic with Andō? Is Dominic alright?」

He for Whom Dominic and I betray Our Maker in the hearts He Made paused here. « *Il est en fuite, mon pauvre* » (He is on the run, my poor [dog]), the human bloodhound's gentle *Maître* pronounced in French, followed by blending French and Japanese with spots of Greek. 「« *Chichi-ue* named Dominic his successor, desiring one who would be hated and quickly overthrown, and all that *Chichi-ue* planned has come to pass. »」

« Is Dominic alive? » I asked.

「« Six sentences now three weeks stale profess My Dominic still lives and loves and serves Me somewhere on the vast Pacific Rim, but every hour's danger may turn those words into a lie. Or back again, as you are back again. I do—»」

"Commander Mojave?" A sharp and processed voice rose from the console by the cell door, making Huxley frown at the military title I have never heard Utopia use. "You asked to be informed when Doctor Weeksbooth's transport reached Alexandria. The *Per Aspera* is docking now."

A sob rose in me. *"Though it takes our best ship from the battlefield,"* Huxley had said—is this the name you give your best, Utopia? The old adage, our long path to the stars through sighs and suffering, *Per aspera ad astra.* Your best ship, then, is what, our suffering? Its speed, its armored prow your hearts' submission to the fact that the path will always be hard? Those ancients who went blind charting night's pinpricks, nearer ancients who burned lifetimes of midnight oil to pass the toil forward, yet it grows no easier, still those of us who brave the heavens' darkness do it trapped in armored suits more stifling than knights' armor of old. Have you no hope either, Utopia, that our long path *ad astra* will ever be paved with anything but sighs?

"I likewise do not understand." It was my Master's voice, my Master's words, and when I turned, my Master's eyes were on me, me and Huxley beside me whose breath, like mine, had frozen.

Huxley mustered words first. "What don't You understand, Mike?"

"Why your Maker placed the stepping-stones so far." Our stares, our hesitation urged Him to say more, and smooth as a shadow's path across the floor, this Stranger extended His human arm and pointed at the haunting silver moon clear in the screen's false sky. "My Peer Your Maker gave you stepping-stones. He gave you Midway Island, a close, conspicuous Moon, small, Earthlike Mars to try before the stranger outer worlds. Before all these He gave you riverbanks to ford, lakes, oceans, so many incremental steps, but why make the increase at each jump so great? The elevator which He now makes you defend is the masterlabor of generations, but He could have made such fibers grow in common vines, made trees grow high enough to let you climb free from gravity's well, made Mars fertile without the centuries and ashes of the dead, and placed new worlds as near as athletes jump or hikers climb, one lifetime's sighs enough to earn each leap if sighs He wanted. Why make each leap cost thousands? And why so hard the interstices? He did not have to split Pangaea in the first place, tether you to sweet water yet fill your seas with salt, nor tether you to breath yet fill His seas with drowning and infinities with vacuum so deadly that every misstep torture-slays you, death between the stars both brutal and too swift for even the desperation-hope of treading water. And so I say I do not understand the Mind Who makes for you these stepping-stones yet places them so far."

That question. It was not so much a new question as one so old, so deep in me that pain had scabbed it over. It had been easier to hoist my pack and plod the long, hard path than to ask why we must plod it. But now He asked it, He the Outsider, and His outsideness ripped away the old deceitful bandage of acceptance. It did not have to be so hard. So many things could have been easier, cost fewer lifetimes, ten, ten thousand, one. Body sobs come easily to me, a cracked vessel that cracks anew when anything presses on my old seams, but Huxley, I had never thought to see the face that gazes calmly on a bash'mate's murderer convulsed with full-soul cries, or slick with downpour tears. Jehovah's black gaze fell full upon Huxley, and on me, and I felt we could not endure if He spoke more, that one more word, one thought would break and dispel us as breath breaks dust and washes all away. And yet we had to hear Him, had to know, as wise Pandora had to lift the lid and learn what mystery this was which our makers on their own would not have added to our world.

"You must rest more." His gentle words poured over us like night. "War strains oaths, Huxley, but does not absolve them. I know your labors these months were for Me, but My Mycroft has taught Me well to recognize self-neglect's symptoms. I fear My Mycroft's bad example, close to you so long, encouraged this bad habit, thus as One responsible for him I think I do not overstep if I remind you that what in Mycroft is mere recklessness in you is oathbreaking, Utopia's prudent vow that, as you renounce complacency, you will still take what play and rest you need for productivity, health, happiness, those vital safeguards of tomorrow's labors. I know you and your task-kin always find restwork the hardest of your duty-vows to keep, and necessities do compel you to sacrifice some tomorrows to force more out of certain todays, yet each such sacrifice is what you might call micro-Faustpact, each daywork swallowed by exhaustion's maw a setback in your battles against Death and Distance, invisible in its minuteness yet as real as one fiber within the twining trillions that constitute your now-endangered ladder to the stars. So you must rest more."

Huxley's sobs changed. I cannot say they eased, but they changed, grief and anger at the cruelty of the path and Pathmaker replaced by the overwhelming warm, loved feeling of knowing that Another cares for us, for our well-being, not just as instruments to serve His goals, but as ourselves.

Jehovah waited, watched us both as we succumbed to sorrow's cleansing rain, then stepped Himself across to the console whose call light blinked on in expectation of an answer. "Commander Mojave has heard your message," He said. "Thank you. Please tell *Pater* I am ready now to watch Our war."

"Sic, Porphyrogene." A few breaths later, wall gave way to warscape.

There rose the Almagest, the strongest handiwork of human history, slim as a thread against an azure sea which combat's foam trails netted over dense as lace. Before it stood two more pillars of our hope, Achilles and MASON, both black against the brightness of the screen which showed the churning battlesea. A crowd of figures toiling over consoles ringed the two commanders, the Masons drab among the bright Utopians, with the Censor's purple jacket garish in the midst, while the tower on the screen was ringed too by detail images, close-ups of charging ships or swerving monsters, some photographs, others diagrams with dots or animations standing in for skirmishes reported but not seen. The microcity of the elevator's floating base had navigated its unwieldy way into an atoll's crescent shelter, where our bright computer spots charted the clash and motion of attackers and defenders in the shallow inner waters and the deeper blue outside. It would have been so easy to believe in it, to scan the images for breaches, thinning lines of ships, to shout out orders: Opening on the left flank! Pompey Group, advance! But these images were morbid as starlight, mere ghosts of battle states recent yet as unreachable as those distant lights of heaven that time snuffed out a million years ago, whose radiance still crawls to us at light speed, brightening our night with gravestones.

"... offer is no offer and Lu knows it," Achilles was snarling as the sound kicked in. The full-wall screen seemed to merge cell and war room, creating the illusion that I could step across and join my successor who labored among the Masons, tucked deep into some text and breakfast's fresh detritus, or that War Marshal Achilles, who boiled with energy like a stabled stallion, could stray in his pacing into our captivity.

"If it were bluff, I would expect more detail," Caesar replied, "to waste more of our time."

"Agreed. Censor," matchless Achilles spun, "what read on Fuxing's movements? Lu could know something we don't about Fuxing standing with them."

Jung Su-Hyeon did not speak, Toshi Mitsubishi either, the pair sharing one wide console and flipping through images in that savant trance we all learn not to interrupt.

"More from Kosala!" a Mason called in English—all is English now in Alexandria, for our Achilles speaks no Latin.

All in the chamber turned to a side wall, where a flow of words appeared in sequence, the latest highlighted:

Received 11:36; Sent 11:25; Lag 11 min. From Almagest Anchor Platform.

BARRAGE OVER. COUNTERSPELL SUCCESSFUL. CABLE AND PLATFORM UNHARMED. BRIEF DURATION OF BARRAGE SUGGESTS THEY ARE TESTING OUR SYSTEM. WARDENS AND INTERCEPTORS BRACE FOR ESCALATION. BAKUNAWA MOVING TO PROTECT MASONS.

Received 11:37; Sent 11:22; Lag 16 min. From Arcadia Alhazen, Almagest Dock 2.

IRISCLOUD5 MODULE LOADING DISRUPTED BY BARRAGE. ALIGNMENT COMPROMISED. PREPARING TO REINITIATE PRE-LAUNCH PROCESS. EARLIEST POSSIBLE LIFTOFF NOW 13:27.

Received 11:38; Sent 11:05; Lag 33 min. From Bryar Kosala, Mumbai.

DOUGONG AND HOMELAND HAVE REJECTED HANDOVER OF ELEVATOR TO MILAE FORCES. HOMELAND COUNTEROFFER: JOINT OCCUPATION OF ALMAGEST BY HOMELAND, DOUGONG, AND GREENPEACE, WITH ME AND PAPADELIAS'S ALLIANCE OBSERVERS SUPERVISING. UTOPIAN ESSENTIAL STAFF FREE TO REMAIN FOR SYSTEM OPERATION AND MAINTENANCE. AM ASKING THEM TO GUARANTEE FREE USE OF ELEVATOR FOR HUMANITARIAN LAUNCHES.

I smiled as understanding sank in. This side wall was the real field of action, messages which trickled in via repurposed cables, embattled relay dishes, lazers bouncing ship to ship to ship from halfway around the world. These told the battle, not merely blow by blow but choice by choice, the slower bloodstream of diplomacy that tortoises on as the wind-swift soldiers race. Achilles knows we need that tortoise. As with a burn, when reflex yanks the tender finger away, the local nerves taking control to mitigate emergency, yet still they need the brain to weigh in after—*What hurt me? What will stop it from hurting me again?*—just so, frontline commanders must be free to act in haste, but need headquarters too to watch, and judge, and weave the battle's end.

"They're quick to divvy up the spoils of imagined victory." That smile upon the cheeks of Achilles, breaker of battle lines, was even more chilling than Death-black Caesar's frown.

Even the Censor looked up. "Before you turn Kosala down, MASON, I'd like to ask them details about the Alliance observer system they're proposing, and what status Homeland is prepared to give Utopian techs who—"

"Ask what you will, Censor," MASON ordered, turning toward what I only then realized was a two-way screen. *"Salve, Fili."*

"*Salve, Pater.* I still abhor your plan to force change on My unwilling Mycroft."

MASON's brow twitched with irritation. "I know."

"How suffer the small authors?" I did not understand Jehovah's phrase at first, but in the hush I realized all the Masons' eyes had locked upon the Delians whose otherworlds peppered the war room's consoles like wildflowers exuberant between the stones. Small authors. Is that what you call them, Micromegas? Vast Alien Author of Your vast Alien Universe, do you liken these fragile friends so to Yourself, the finite authors of their finite otherworlds, which perish as they perish? You have no tone of voice, Master, as ever, but such words need no tone to communicate their tenderness. And grief.

"We suffer less than our adversaries," MASON answered. "Milae is with us, and we have hopes of Greenpeace."

I looked to Chagatai. "Milae?"

「*Mirai,*」 Jehovah supplied for me, the Japanese less a translation of the Korean than a pronunciation difference, since the two tongues render 未来 almost the same.

"Ah!" I cried. "Future." Is it a sin to translate when the meaning is so naked and so good?

Chagatai nodded. "They're Mitsubishi who consider space and Mars and robots their ancestral project too, who split off when the others proposed attacking the Almagest."

That warmed me inside more than the porridge had—would that more peoples remembered likewise to call the Project Earth's, not others'.

And where is Cato Weeksbooth? So you phrased the question, did you not, reader? The question that nags on in you, in me, in Him too though He frames it differently, His words as ever too precise: "When enters the new inhuman thinking thing?"

Worlds of copper domes, of lapis skies, of lush Cretaceous jungle, sky farms spiraling against the blushing clouds of deadly Venus, all the assembled nowheres cringed against their consoles as MASON scowled. You are wise to fear MASON's distrust, Utopia—that rock you cling to as you fight Poseidon's tide must not give way.

"Weeksbooth approaches, *Porphyrogene,*" Prefect Cinna Semaphoros answered, stationed at a console by the war room door, where worming wires linked it to the rest of Alexander's city. "They are nearly through security."

"And what have thy researches bared of Cato Weeksbooth?" Jehovah asked. "[Anonymous?]"

"What? Hello!" My successor spun with the familiar, blinking stare of one startled from the trance-depths of intense research, or poetry, or coding.

Jehovah mixed English with Greek and Spanish, the three tongues He and my successor share. "«¿What hast thou learned of Cato? ¿What did My Martin see?»"

Startled eyes faded through insecurity to fear. "I . . . don't . . . I'm not sure, I . . ."

A shadow on Cornel MASON's bronze face told me he too had asked [Anonymous] what the images from Klamath Marsh revealed, and had no answer.

Gentle yet irresistible, our Master. "[Anonymous], you know *Pater* has sworn to nurture and advance Utopia, and that he loves Utopia enough to die for it; truth will not harm it here."

"I . . ." One last pause as the dam inside my successor breaks. "It's these notes! They're impossible!"

"«They are not impossible,»" calm, correct Jehovah challenged. "«They are. »"

"Yes, but . . . I mean . . ." As my successor paused, transfixed by stares, I realized suddenly that, among all in the war room, only my successor's jacket bore Jehovah's Vs. "They're physically possible, they're just practically impossible, they can't . . . Look, this is a sketch for improving the safety casing around the antimatter generator for a car engine." My successor zoomed in on one page where I recognized some casing contours, then flicked to another. "And this is about the Cavan-Ureña Process, which is the latest thing in synthetic photosynthesis. And this one"—diagrams gave way to text and grids—"I had to ask the Alexandria Campus Math Department, but it's a structure theorem for . . ."—a pause to check the term—". . . Lurie-Banerjee topoi, which I don't understand, but it has the department really excited. And the Physics Department is equally excited by this page which is proposing a way to immobilize hydrogen sulfide so it can act as a superconductor at standard atmospheric pressure and temperatures close to -75 Celsius, which apparently is super warm. And this page is . . ."—another pause to check terms—". . . asymmetric protection of alkenes in terpene compounds for improving polyterpene radiation shielding." More pages flicking fast. "And this is how to aerosolize the polyterpene shielding stuff for space tech, and this page is comments on a recent paper on inserting a new gene to give human cells a UV-independent way to make Vitamin D_3, and this is mutagenesis analysis about the cycle of bacterial resusceptibility to penicillin, and this . . . this is some more math stuff I forget, and this is scattering amplitudes of second dark sector leptons, and this is como—no, co-*ho*-mology of equivariant Shakya spectra, and this is about a recent Mushi Mojave piece on restricted adaptive potential in double clonal *Paratrechina longicornis*—that's the Mars ants—and this is theorizing that there could be stable xenon alloys in magnetar convection zones, and this proposes childhood surgical intervention in the bone growth of the human foot to fuse the fussy bits together to make it grow a stronger, better foot, and I see you smiling, Mycroft, but this is not the moment to be thinking 'yay, Cato Weeksbooth's finally getting to do science,' this is the moment to be scared out of your pants. Cato Weeksbooth isn't trained in infant bone growth, they aren't trained in most of these fields, they're a general science teacher with a little medical training and a Ph.D. in biochemistry, one Ph.D. in one field, that's it. They might be an autodidact in a couple of these areas, but it took me all night and half the faculty of Alexandria Campus to figure out a couple dozen of these pages, and there are hundreds of them on hundreds of topics. This isn't the output of one person, no matter what their level, this is the output of an entire major research campus. And! . . ." My successor paused at this climax, reflexively imitating our great mentor, Olympic debate victor Vivien Ancelet. ". . . Cato had no computer! In Klamath Marsh, Cato had no computer access of any kind, and the engineering of Ráðsviðr's cell was designed to block all access anyway, so no computers, no reference books, all these details, constants to ridiculously many digits, foot anatomy, it's all from memory, it has to be, but nobody memorizes all this. Fifty scientists together in a room haven't memorized all this, so . . . so . . ."

"*The time is now 11:49. Faustburst in one minute.*" These elven-smooth synthesized words rose from a chamberfox whose silver length, supported by three pairs of legs, stretched out from a snail-like central shell, whose pearlescent surface showed the countdown from 60 in veins of light.

"A set-set?" It was Censor Su-Hyeon who interrupted; it shocked me in the moment, but the surname Weeksbooth does easily conjure the genus set-set (and, in such parliance, there are many set-set species). "Could Cato also be some kind of set-set?" the Censor suggested. "A new kind? Or a secret kind made for O.S.?"

I caught myself staring at Toshi Mitsubishi; I caught many of us staring at Toshi Mitsubishi.

"I . . ." My successor breathed deep. "Okay, maybe. I hadn't thought of a set-set, and . . . I can't say no, I don't know enough about the possibilities of . . . what they can . . ."

"What was thy thought, [Anonymous]?" Jehovah's words were gentle still, that wrenching gentleness as when a gardener knows a quick tug at a weed will do no more than rip off surface leaves, so instead we grip deep by the base and gently draw the structure from the soil, however hard it clings.

"I thought that . . . if . . ." My successor's words came broken, all rhetoric lost in extremis. ". . . if there were a computer brain in there, it would make sense. In Cato Weeksbooth. If somebody . . . augmented them. Like [u/you] . . . like what someone did to Lorelei Cook." What was that little accusation, my successor? That quick, aborted U sound—did it start to name a person? Or a Hive? "But . . ."

Silence throughout the room, both rooms, as all our silences recited the same commandment: *Thou shalt not make humanoid U-beasts, bold Utopia. But we all know thou couldst.*

"When?" I honestly cannot remember, reader, whether I voiced this question or whether it welled only on my lips. "When could they have done it? Utopia didn't have Cato until after Klamath Marsh, after—"

"Faustburst in 10 . . . 9 . . . 8 . . . 7 . . . 6 . . . 5 . . . 4 . . . 3 . . . The time is 11:50, Faustburst commencing."

A flicker, dazzling like the thousand detonations of a sparkler, filled the room as a torrent of images, map contours, diagrams, even some shards of video burst onto the map screen, while the text wall avalanched, and what I realized had been battle lull gave way to battle rush. In a burst I glimpsed innumerable snakes translucent like rainbow soap swarming a battleship, elsewhere a swirling field-wide creature like the solar farm that claimed the *Shearwater,* and a third image, something which perhaps no human outside myth had seen until this age: a blood-smeared dragon triumphing over the carcass of a man. Terse shouts punctuated work-flurry's silence as aides yelped out the most vital snippets: "Greenpeace fleet at, no, *past* Guraidhoo!" "Platform under ongoing barrage!" "More from Kosala!" "Umibōzu pod exhausted! Scholomancers in retreat!" And then the elven-clear synthetic voice: *"Reflector signal lost. The time is now 11:53. Next Faustburst Scheduled 12:40. 47 minutes remain."* Faustburst—I did not need to voice the question, not with Huxley's solemn face before me: one more of those man-made chariots that race with Helios around our world, sacrificed for three minutes of contact.

"Is the Iriscloud on schedule?" Headstrong Achilles snapped out the question, eclipsing even Caesar in his urgency.

"Yes, Marshal, still aiming to launch at 13:27. The Dioscuri are ready to escort it up."

Chagatai read the question in my face. "Reflector satellites, six thousand in a batch. If they reach orbit, they'll buy hundreds of hours of contact before they're all shot down."

My heart thrilled: six thousand Faustpacts—no, better!—six thousand Wishgrants that would not hold back one inch the human sphere that grows so slowly yet so far.

"This is the fifth attempt," Chagatai warned with a kindly wince, as when we warn children not to get their hopes up. "Irisclouds One and Three were destroyed at sea, number Two during launch, and number Four by some sort of sabotage before it quite reached orbit."

I nodded as I swallowed down my hope—of course our enemies could see as well as we the power of such a cargo.

"And what from Kosala?" quick Achilles asked.

An aide brought up the text:

Received 11:50; Sent 11:48; Lag 2 min. From Bryar Kosala, Mumbai;

HOMELAND OFFER: JOINT OCCUPATION OF ALMAGEST BY GREENPEACE, MILAE, HOMELAND, AND DOUGONG, WITH COUSIN AND ALLIANCE OBSERVERS SUPERVISING. USE OF ELEVATOR FOR HUMANITARIAN LAUNCHES GUARANTEED INCLUDING LUNAR AND SPACE STATION RESUPPLY. UTOPIAN STAFF FREE TO REMAIN FOR SYSTEM OPERATION AND MAINTENANCE. SAFETY AND TREATMENT OF UTOPIANS WILL BE OVERSEEN BY PAPADELIAS AND MYSELF. DOUGONG AMENABLE. THIS IS A GREAT CHANCE, CORNEL. WE MAY NOT DO BETTER.

Scowling Caesar waited for Achilles to confirm his scowl before he raised the voice which conjures armies. "Tell Kosala my Empire is no vassal to beg passport through another's gate. Whosoever thinks to take the skyways from me is my enemy and will face my strength. To babble of surrender now, before we see how fall the battle's scales, just wastes the sacrifice of those who fight and die to keep this channel open. I know Kosala holds the reins of Greenpeace. They may shorten this battle by fighting alongside me, or they may sit back and watch me hand out death. I await their answer, nothing else. Now . . ." Caesar spun, and spinning found that it was *now* indeed, that now when comes to Alexandria a living treasure borne *Per Aspera* from a distant silver world still barely brushed by the stretching fingertips of humankind.

I had so long imagined Cato's Utopian coat. Would it be like his boots? A teacher's program, exposing all he passed in different formats: skeletal schematics, heat profiles, magnetic fields, UV and infrared, all science's innumerable second sights revealing different aspects of those secret hidden motions wisdom-seekers have chased since raw antiquity? Or did he have an otherworld of his own, our precious Cato? An Earth which knows a better peace that bends no arts toward murder? Or some far distant planet basking in a stranger dawn? I still don't know. The figure shivering before us wore only prison red, those same hospital-plain garments MASON's caution forced on Huxley too: no, Cato wears one thing more, subtle around his wrists which shiver bound before him: glistening Cannergel. Masons in iron gray and death black flank him, armed and tense, some bearing shields heavy enough to form a phalanx or a Roman turtle, while security robots of every shape hover above. And what's this that they wheel in close behind Cato? My coffin-cage? *Mine?* Empty but open, used for *another* prisoner? This thrill, this burn within my chest, is this possessiveness? Outrage that they dare let another ride in my triumphal tomb? Or is this pride I feel? Seeing the world acknowledge Cato Weeksbooth—-O.S.'s genius, true archmurderer—that Cato is as rare a thing as me? And I as he?

"I . . . a . . . —he— . . . Cae— . . . wh . . . — . . . nt." There are words, shapes of words, on Cato's lips, but only pinpricks of voice with them, and even that effort consumes his strength, so as we watch his figure folds inward, beginning in a prisoner's surrender posture with his eyes locked on the floor, but ending in a child's posture, eyes scrunched closed, hugging himself within his bonds.

Death, who looms in Caesar still, faces this quivering half-adversary, whose life labors have armed as well as disarmed Death. "You know why I have summoned you?"

"—s, C—ar."

Caesar keeps his distance from his prisoner, warned off by my successor's theory and by Duke Ganymede's death, but tireless Achilles paces close, peering at this strange prisoner, as curious as the colt this foster child of centaurs almost is.

"You will explain," MASON commands. "What did Martin's message mean? What are you?"

A gulp, and then a shivering breath as Cato musters courage to open his eyes to face, what—is it MASON now who makes you shake, Cato? Or is it Ares raging 'round that topless tower on the screen which you would give so much, so much, so much to never see. "I a-a-am no t-threa—t t-to—*ggh!*"

Faster than sight, Achilles in his speed, so that we see no spring, no blur, no motion before he *is* upon Cato, the hero's small, strong hands well hardened to crush throats. His force slams Cato backward toward my open cage, so the pair half fall forward-and-backward into it as ferocious Achilles pins his choking captive against the inner wall, helpless. I shall write Achilles's next word as I heard it, reader, though as things unfold, the gods' absurdity might bid me spell it differently. "Helen!"

"Gg-gg—kh!"

A vast rustle like wings as every Delian there braces to rise, to act, but these Delians, reader, every one, they wear the dark *Familiaris* armband, buying seats in Caesar's war room at the cost of absolute subjection to Caesar's will. None dares move more.

"Achilles?" Cornel MASON stands as stunned as all of us. "What . . . Helen?"

Another gurgle-gasp as still Achilles holds his victim, while Cato raises his pale, bound wrists to push against the matchless grip. And then that grip breaks, with a strange sound, like a crackle or a snap and something almost musical, a base hum rising and falling away at once, as when a screen flicks off or on. Achilles's arm falls limp, and there flees coughing Cato, not to freedom but burrowing back into the semi-shelter of the seat within my cage, as desperate rabbits burrow back in the unyielding corners of their own.

"I'm sorry!" Cato's shout, desperate but comprehensible, broke the shock-spell that Achilles's motion—such inhuman violence-grace—had cast upon us all. "I didn't want any of this! I didn't have a choice!"

Achilles staggered back, his left arm still limp as if the muscles or the nerves were severed. "What . . . what have you done?"

Two coughs as Cato's throat and breath recovered. "Just popped a relay. It'll reset. I wouldn't damage you—you know I wouldn't!"

One brave medic and MASON approached the hero, who gripped his dangling left arm in his right, massaging the forearm as if to coax feeling back.

"Achilles, what . . . ?" Death's severity had left the Emperor, leaving a friend's concern.

"This isn't Cato Weeksbooth," lionhearted Achilles snarled, more like a lion in this moment than I had ever known him. "Or maybe it is, I don't know Cato Weeksbooth, but I know my own." Achilles advanced again, and one arm and a strong-braced foot against Cato's back were more than enough to pin the prisoner as the hero grasped the collar of the scarlet prison shirt and wrenched. The fabric ripped, baring Cato's pale back, and there along the shoulder blade, just in that spot one's own fingers can barely reach, large block letters stood black against the skin: H.E.L.E.N.

I screamed—I think a gasp so loud counts as a scream—and at my side, though stunned and tear-streaked still, Huxley Mojave screamed, not fear's screams but the shock and body protest at a thing too wrong. And right.

"We aren't enemies here, Achilles! Please!" Cato—if this was Cato?—cried. "We never were! I never had a choice of which side used me, no more than you did!"

"What is this?" Alarm and irritation tinged MASON's concern. "What is H.E.L.E.N.?"

Achilles's voice was growl. "Human Expansion . . . Human Empire Life Expansion something . . . Network something? I can't—"

I tried to make my interruption gentle. "You can't remember because Apollo changed their mind about the acronym in different drafts." All eyes fixed on me through the screen, full of the command that I speak on. "'Helen and all her treasures,'" I continued, "it's not just Helen's loss that starts the war, it's the treasures that go with her, when Paris steals that, that's what starts the war, but . . ." I looked to Huxley, the next-of-kin whose nod freed me to share the much-mourned author's plan. ". . . in Apollo's future *Iliad* it wasn't petty lust and gold the Trojans carried off, it was treasures worth such a war, H.E.L.E.N., the most advanced research project in human history, scientists working on life extension, immortality, space adaptation, enhancing human bodies to do better outside Earth. The scientists were test subjects themselves, enhanced with knowledge and intelligence orders of magnitude beyond—"

"Computer brains?" my proud successor interrupted. "Implanted brain enhancements?"

Cato's wince felt like apology. "No," he answered, "we still haven't really cracked that, our mind-machine tech is in its infancy—or it was, or will be, I don't know what tense to use. I have some life-extension implants and one neuro-implant, but it's just a database, information, not cognitive, my cognitive abilities are all genetic plus my training, lab-raised, something like a set-set but without locking in the set, so I can still change and innovate—"

"That's what the Trojans stole," I added—someone had to. "H.E.L.E.N. is humanity's next step, technology to unlock human potential, space, the keys to a wider future stolen from the Greeks and . . ." I felt myself shiver. "And now you've been stolen again, at Klamath Marsh. That made Utopia Troy."

"Enhanced with implants, another human U-beast." MASON turned upon the nearest Delians. "I can't protect you if you violate—"

"No!" Cato cried. "I'm human! Not a U-beast! And Utopia didn't make me! Not directly, anyway. They dreamed me, but . . ."

"Then how do you exist?"

The shivering captive tugged the torn shirt back in place, as if hiding the mark which branded his body H.E.L.E.N.'s property could pause Fate's avalanche. "Bridger made me. Cato—I—Cato lived their life in costume, the mad scientist archetype, what I wished to become." My breath caught noticing the wild white overfrosting still-young Cato's stark black hair, color he used to comb in for the look on his museum days, but artificial had become a truer artifice. "Bridger knew me from science club. They came that last night, a frightened child running scared after the assassination and the resurrection, running from the world. They ran to me, the only bash' they knew, the nice teacher they liked. They heard Cardie and me, when Cardie tied me to the desk to make me choose, O.S. or rotting in a cell. Mycroft knew! They knew, they . . ." Helen-Cato's eyes fixed on me through the screen, and something changed in them, a different blend of fear and grief and wonder, subtle but distinctive like a different blend of wine. ". . . Wait, is that . . . O—"

Achilles held a finger to his lips and would have said something, I think, but MASON-Death turned on me, raising by instinct (even with the screen between us) his left hand. "What did you know?"

"Nothing, Caesar!" I cried. "I swear! I . . . I don't even know what Cato thinks I knew!"

Helen-Cato grew sadder. "I thought you must know. You put it in your history, 'The Suicide of Cato Weeksbooth,' that's what you titled the chapter, that last night when Cardie tried to make me choose—make Cato choose—surrender or O.S. Well, Cato did choose, but not from those options. Your history had Cato's last words: 'I'm not what the world needs, the world needs a real mad scientist, someone to concoct something to save everyone, some world-saving wonder, not just death.' Bridger heard that wish. And granted it." A sob. "I'm Cato's fantasy, a real mad scientist, proficient in every field, so every time I think a question, I know what every branch of science knows about it, every test we've done, and I can think of every new test we might try. It's what Cato wanted, what Cato thought Earth needed more than just a science teacher who never . . . who never . . ."

I choked. "Then Cato . . . the rescue at Klamath Marsh, the real Cato was already . . ." My mind was in Ráðsviðr's cell, that triumphant rescue, loving students grown and braving all to save what was their dear teacher no longer.

The twice-created creature in my coffin choked as well. "I'm still partly Cato. Mostly Cato. I have versions of that Cato's memories, just recast in my world.

I think . . . I think Apollo Mojave didn't fully think through the H.E.L.E.N. scientists, didn't differentiate us, or even really give us names, so Bridger filled in the blanks in me with Cato, but . . ." He stared at his hands—at hands not always his. "Mycroft was right to call that night a suicide, almost as much as when Bridger became . . . you." Cato gazed up at Achilles, and their faces shared a heaviness, a strange, unnatural mourning for the very bones and blood beneath their skin, last gifts from someone precious. I shall never understand such mourning. But I had my own mourning, too, the mad, maddening mourning of seeing these two creatures, precious beyond measure yet usurpers both, stamping the Earth with loved ones' footsteps, shaping words with loved ones' breaths, yet these are not my Cato, not my Bridger, not the other friends I loved. Fate had those friends' consent—Bridger's and Cato's—for their apotheosis, their self-sacrifice. But it did not have mine. To weep for one whose dear devourer still walks beside you, speaking words not quite your friend's . . . it is a mourning you, happy reader, can never comprehend.

I think, in fact, my travel-battered guide, I can.

"Do you have proof?" Achilles asked, an eagerness in his voice, and desperation's edge.

Cato-Helen shivered. "No. I'm sorry."

MASON looked to his Marshal. "You think it isn't true?"

"It's true," Achilles answered. "I said I know my own. But proof the world will credit is more difficult." Again his eyes met Cato's, these exiles from one otherworld, a future full of grief and A.I. gods and space-born grandeur only they can mourn. "The two of us aren't U-beasts but we can't prove that, not with wires and electronics in our flesh, and sketches of us in Apollo's journals, Earth's best known Utopian."

Cato nodded. "We've been trying all we can, back in the labs in Luna City, with me, the toy soldiers, all Bridger's relics, but it's hard to know how to begin to prove . . ."

Matchless Achilles leapt down from the coffin-cage to face the frowning Emperor. "I didn't tell you at the time, but we censored the medical reports we released about me before the Olympics, when we shared details of my DNA and bone samples to try to convince people Mycroft's history was true, we never shared an X-ray, never details on my spine and nervous system, which has a lot more in it than nerve cells."

MASON frowned at his friend. "You also have these life-extending implants?"

Cato huddled deeper into my cage's gentle seat, but the lion heart inside Achilles's breast does not back down. "I have more than that," he answered, "if what your Apollo wrote of me is true. Cato said mind-machine interface technology was in its infancy, even in our future. I am that infancy." Achilles stretched his arm, the stunned limb reawakening with the distinctive crackle-hum of something switching on. "A U-beast expert could tell easily that how I'm made, and presumably how Cato's made, is nothing like U-beast tech, but all the U-beast experts are on

Utopia's side, and the world won't heed such biased witnesses. We can't convince the world we aren't what we so obviously seem. We can't exonerate Utopia."

So much mixing in Cornel MASON's face as his gaze met goddess-nursed Achilles's. I feared I would find distrust there, anger, but I think all the darknesses I saw were in fear's spectrum or regret's, an Emperor thinking on the world and future worlds he must protect, and on the different future world that separates him from this partner of his labors. It was easier, I think, for Alexander's successor to stand side by side with one who claimed to be born from the goddess daughter of the Old Man of the Sea than to stand beside this son of science, or rather of un-science, for science is knowledge, knowing, understanding, but that future technology which branches through Achilles is as far beyond our understanding as Ráðsviðr beyond Newton's. No, farther. Gods and goddesses walked the space-skies of Apollo's *Iliad,* machine intelligences whose voracious, exponential minds so outstripped humankind that their very makers fell upon their knees to worship them, as ancients did before the blazing sun. If the Thetis who bore and nursed godlike Achilles was such a being, can we call her offspring, which gazes on us through the window-sensors of Achilles's eyes, a man? Or, more important to Cornel MASON, a friend?

"Yes, We can." Jehovah's words left me uncertain whether He was responding to His imperial father's thoughts or to Achilles's words.

Time's stranger Achilles gazed warily across at He Who links universes of strangeness. "You think we can exonerate Utopia?" the hero asked. "How?"

Slow, ever so slow, His words. "With Truth. And patience. Some agent—neither Utopia nor Asclepius—created what was called Lorelei Cook." It took even me a moment to recognize Jehovah's name for Bridger. "That agent exists and can be found."

It felt solid, this comfort, simple as it was, as if we had fallen from a hard-clambered mountain peak, long labors lost, but as we kneel upon the ground in our despair, someone reminds us that the ground is where all climbs begin. We can begin.

"Do you, like Achilles, have no message for Me from your Maker beyond the message your existence is?" A good question, Jehovah—this Cato-Helen mind-enhanced inhuman human is indeed a strange message to send a Stranger God.

Cato peered over at us through the screen. "Uh . . . yes. I mean no. I mean, no message I know of. I don't have a message. I don't know anything about real or big-G Gods, if there are big-G Gods. Only about A.I.s, which actually aren't real. Or actually there are real A.I.s, of course there are real A.I.s, but my A.I. gods that I know about aren't real, except . . ." Here, Cato leaned forward from the coffin-car, toward hybrid Achilles, his trembling replaced by concentration and a dash of healthy curiosity. "Your arm should've reset in a tenth that time. Your system's in bad shape; how much combat have you been in?"

Pride's smile dawned slowly on swift Achilles's face. "All of it. Until today."

The Almagest. All as one, we looked to the screen, realizing we had forgotten spacekind's umbilical where how many navies?—six?—plowed up the sea.

Forgotten? Surely not entirely, Mycroft, not by the Delians who labor over consoles where they see their Project teeter.

The Delians, reader? No, they watch Cato most raptly of all, for, as these navies battle for the ladder to Poseidon's kingdom, here stands the key to build a thousand ships and, better, to prepare our sailors for those airless seas.

Prefect Cinna Semaphoros scrolled back the text wall which had tortoised on through all. "We have a message from Huang Enlai, Caesar, offering Fuxing's aid. They're close."

The screens were still scrolling through new images brought by the Faustburst, one sequence showing a mass of spirit faces, glittering water fountaining up from the waves as joyous as breaching dolphins, higher, higher, smiling creature faces reaching for the sun. Further images showed the creatures slowing, turning, pouring tempest-fierce down on a foecraft, each face a drowning blow. Then one more image where some missile blasted all away.

"I can fix . . ." It was Cato who spoke up, trembling anew and frowning down upon the bonds around his wrists. "Achilles, Marshal, if you'll trust me to, I mean, I . . . Nobody else knows how to fix, I . . . understand your system, I've worked on . . . If you'll trust me."

Achilles looked to MASON a moment, and I dare call the gazes they exchanged friends' gazes, needing no words to trade meaning back and forth. Words were for others. "Would I need to be unconscious for you to work on me?" Achilles asked.

"No," Cato answered, shrill with a dose of hope. "Or, mostly not, maybe briefly if anything needs deep reset, but that sort of thing shouldn't be urgent, if it's needed at all."

"Can we do it here, while I still watch the battle?"

Evaluation's hesitation. "If you bring in an exam bed and the kit I brought. I thought . . . I guessed you might need it. Need help. Need . . . May I?"

Again Achilles looked to MASON, questions without words.

"I am satisfied that Weeksbooth is not a living bomb designed to explode and kill me," MASON answered, with a texture in his words that might have been a chuckle. "Unbind them. Bring them what they ask for."

Quick guards left to fetch Cato's equipment, while others made room for the gurney, rolling my coffin-cage aside—not away, aside. But the fear did not leave Cato-Helen's eyes, not yet, not until the hero who has watched so many comrades drop and die for Helen's sake relaxed his fighting stance and stripped off his armor, movements I could not parse at first drawing his limbs free of the unseen nothing which congealed as it fell into the dull sheen of inactive Griffincloth. I used to wonder what nowhere Achilles's coat would show if he ever turned off invisibility, but I realized, with a Helen now before us, that showing this world unchanged does show Achilles's world.

"Now"—MASON turned—"what does Huang Enlai want?"

"The letter is long, Caesar, but in brief they want to keep the Almagest out of Dougong and Homeland hands," the Prefect answered. "And yours. Huang Enlai will commit Fuxing's forces to defend the Almagest against the attacking forces, including firing on fellow Mitsubishi ships, if you will promise, after victory, to withdraw your forces from the Almagest, too, leaving the anchor platform for Utopia, Milae, Fuxing, and their Remaker allies."

Many nervous glances moved among the Masons and Utopians, though not as many or as nervous as if this pressure on their frail alliance had arrived one revelation earlier. Things too strange sink in strangely, so in the rush of battle planning, one strand of every mind was on the clash of ships and monsters, one strand on the stream of text and politics, one now on MASON facing Fuxing's choice, this pressure to give Heaven's gate to the Remakers, but in between these strands something else leaks, a slow invasion like frost choking each pipe in a cluster one by one: Is this real? There, youth-light Achilles bares his back to Cato's fingers, expert hands wielding the quill-slim probes which glow azure and fuchsia. And all this is real? If Utopia had stepped up and said, "We made a cyborg," it would be easier, so much easier to wrap our minds around.

"What does my War Marshal think of Huang's offer?"

Achilles frowned. "That you can't take it as it stands, but that another navy would be a great asset today, especially one that Homeland and Dougong will be reluctant to fire on."

MASON nodded. "Prefect, tell Huang Enlai I welcome their aid, but that the contingency they seek to guard against cannot occur. Huang worries that, if Utopia sides with the Remakers and I do not, it could cause a rift, endangering the Almagest. But no such rift is possible. As MASON, I am so irrevocably committed to guarding and nurturing Utopia that I shall never harm them, even if sometimes I judge the fledgling safer in a cage until the storm has passed. As for Utopia, they have surrendered so completely that they have opened every stronghold to me. There is no spot on this planet where Utopians are not outnumbered by my own forces beyond hope of resistance if we became adversaries. So, we shall not become adversaries. Whatever remaking of this world we choose, we shall choose together. The Almagest is safe in my hands, Utopia safe, Milae safe too. I welcome Fuxing to join us, and in return I shall commit my strength to aid Huang's efforts to reform and heal the Mitsubishi Hive, and to oppose and weaken enemies of those efforts. Furthermore, if today Huang aids me quickly, then in gratitude I offer . . ."—hesitation, tension in Caesar's brow as he braces to make some great concession, drawn from him unwilling by the day's great stakes—". . . something I have granted no Remaker yet in war, my permission to exchange some letters with the *Porphyrogene*."

Those words stabbed as I turned to the Addressee of the Great Letter, Who also feeds so desperately upon lesser letters from any, all beloved humans who would help Him battle distance's diasporas. Have you cut Him off so completely, Caesar? You His father who must understand how much that tortures Him?

"Sent, Caesar," the Prefect confirmed after some moments. "We have new threats from Dougong you may want to see."

"And where is Greenpeace? Nothing from Kosala?"

"Nothing yet."

Impatience turned to hush, the scroll of text and flicker of images as all within the war room labored on. Achilles labored too, even as methodical Cato pressed and poked, the veteran stretched on his belly craning up his neck to see and digest the hurly-burly that had poured in from the Faustburst: images, ship on monster, ship on ship. It cheered me, watching him. When victories come to men, they break like Dawn, a biased goddess who spreads the whole sparkling banquet of the countryside before the faction on whose side she rises, while the disfavored faction faces Dawn's blinding glare which baffles sense and strategy and shrouds adversaries in backlit safety. And like Dawn too, victories have subtle portents, changes in sounds and motions which, well before Dawn's chorus or rosy touch, foretell the night's surrender. If Achilles breaker of battle lines could spot these heralds early, name the invisible moment which analysts twenty years from now will point at with Epimethean certainty and lecture, "At this point X lost," then perhaps the son of ever-mourning Thetis could avoid this battle's cruelest deaths, the deaths of those who strive and die after the outcome is already sealed.

"I don't like that," Achilles spoke up. "Image 656, zoom in."

The image swelled before us, a ship's white V-trail in the sunny water, cheerful like a gull—no. No, as we zoom in, that is no ship's trail, there are black specks peppering its margins. Ship's corpse flotsam? No, we zoom again, these are not planks or hull shards buoyant on the seas, they are whole hulls, ten, twenty, scale deceptive as this V proves, what? What blast, what weapon is so great, its shaft of death so long that it strews battleships along its edges as a gust strews leaves? I know no name for this, but fear frowns on the faces here tell me it is not ours.

Words slow and soft and all-transforming like sleep's onset rose beside me from the Addressee of all Earth's messages. "I do not tolerate the deaths of small authors."

My breath caught. Intolerable. It hurts Him, hurts Him, changes Him. Those worlds are real to Him, as real as ours, these nowheres that perish in each blast with their small authors. Utopians, no, all of us, the Masons, Milae Mitsubishi, all allies, all enemies, all are intolerable losses in our long path, far too long, away from death and toward the stars. Pain makes us worse—Plato said that—suffering, evils, soul-wounding injustice, they teach our souls the opposite of excellence. Will this battle make Utopia worse? The empire? All who endure too much, intolerable? Will it make Him worse, too?

"How long"—the sudden darkness in Achilles's tone scared me as much as the shattered shipscape—"until the Iriscloud launches?"

"Another hour, Marshal. The next Faustburst should tell us if it's still on schedule."

I looked to the silver chamberfox whose shell counted down to 12:40; four minutes left.

"Word from Kosala!"

Received 12:36; Sent 12:02; Lag 34 min. From Bryar Kosala, Mumbai.

TO CENSOR JUNG RE: UTOPIAN STAFF WHO STAY FOR ELEVATOR SYSTEM OPERATION, DOUGONG SAYS THEY MUST TAKE PEACEWASH. BOTH D&H PLEDGE TO PERMIT USE OF ELEVATOR FOR HUMANITARIAN LAUNCHES INCLUDING SPACE STATION RESUPPLY.

"Peacewash . . ." A Delian whose coat made Alexandria float in Venusian cloudscapes scowled, and I remembered tyrant Redwood's threats of slave-like labors worse than Servicers endure. Had they been true? Had the Servicer model, whose unfree freedoms I had loved perhaps without enough examination, taught our world to find this good and normal, cold conscription, haughty mastery, bad lessons heightened by the power-clash of war?

"Lag to Mumbai is getting worse, Caesar," Prefect Semaphoros reminded us. "Kosala must have sent this before they received your last . . ." He paused, searching for a word in English strong enough. ". . . instruction."

"And lag to Huang Enlai?"

"Unpredictable with only one sample, but hopefully we'll get something with the next Faustburst."

The background motions of the war room changed now, as all raced to queue up messages, while somewhere distant constellations of Utopia chose which of heaven's chariots to sacrifice next to Sea Lord Poseidon and deadly Ares. But that Faustburst brought nothing, just more images of strong ships braving fire which split the heart between triumph and grief, but no answers from Fuxing or Kosala. We have no right to protest, reader, for immortal gods are no merchants to barter good for good and owe us answers when we burn a satellite upon war's altar. Rather we their suppliants are like a child which crafts something from clay bought by our parent, with skills taught by our parent, and hands born from our parent, so when with pride we present the parent with our crude-wrought gift it was the parent's already, though in kind condescension they may smile and thank us still. It was the second Faustburst, another fifty minutes and another sacrifice, that brought Dawn's chorus clear.

Received 13:30; Sent 13:17; Lag 13 min. From Huang Enlai, Fuxing Command.

OFFER ACCEPTED. MY FLEET IS MOVING. ESTIMATE 180+ MIN TO ENGAGE.

Received 13:30; Sent 13:12; Lag 18 min. From Bryar Kosala, Mumbai.

YOU ARE RIGHT, MY GOAL IS TO SHORTEN THIS BATTLE. I WILL NOT SIT BACK AND WATCH YOU HAND OUT DEATH. THIS IS THE SECOND BATTLE OVER THE ALMAGEST. THERE WILL NOT STOP BEING BAT-

TLES AS LONG AS IT REMAINS IN UTOPIAN HANDS. NO ONE CAN FEEL SAFE WHILE UTOPIA COULD ATTACK FROM SPACE, NOT AFTER WHAT HAPPENED TO COOK AND GANYMEDE. I WILL TAKE THE ALMAGEST MYSELF. GREENPEACE, HOMELAND, AND DOUGONG ARE ALL WITH ME. ONCE THE UTOPIAN THREAT IS NEUTRALIZED, ALL SIDES WILL CALM DOWN ENOUGH TO START PEACE TALKS, AND IF UTOPIA IS INNOCENT, THERE WILL BE TIME TO PROVE THAT. I WILL PROTECT THE PEACEWASHED UTOPIANS WHO STAY TO MAINTAIN THE SYSTEM. PEACEMAKING IS THE IMPORTANT HALF OF WAR, CORNEL. SURRENDER NOW AND WE CAN FINALLY BEGIN.

Received 13:30; Sent 13:21; Lag 9 min. From Lemuria Cavendish, Almagest Dock 4.
PLATFORM HIT. DOCK 2 DESTROYED. IRISCLOUD5 DESTROYED. PLATFORM STABILITY COMPROMISED. SOURCE OF BLAST UNKNOWN.

"Retreat." That word of all words strange on brave Achilles's lips.

MASON: "You think Fuxing will come too late?"

"Not just that." Achilles, still upon the gurney, flinched as Cato pinched too hard. "No one wants to fight Bryar Kosala. Look at those images of the Greenpeace fleet, covered with Cousin flags. Our soldiers won't have the heart to fire on that, not in an hour, definitely not in three. Our Blacksleeves are brave, the Delians determined, but the enemy is using their biggest weapons more now. Look at image 211." Someone zoomed in, another V of death with fire at its heart, like the directed death blast of an exploding car but aimed forward to boil the waves instead of upward to the skies. "I'm sure Dougong was bluffing when they said they were willing to destroy the elevator, but if they know the structure well enough to take out the one dock that had the Iriscloud and leave the rest intact, they know enough to use their big guns near it to their hearts' content without endangering the platform. We don't want to take those losses and still lose. We retreat. They can't entrench too quickly in the Almagest, they don't know it well enough. We do. We'll come back quickly, with Fuxing and all of Milae, not just their vanguard, and we can send our Red Sea fleet out, and I'll go myself. That battle we can win."

They call MASON the 'Mountain Emperor,' you know, these wise, perceptive Mitsubishi who remember that the human animal is part of Nature too, as much as toiling ant or piling sand, thus that the peaks of Alexander's city are mountains, and their grim lord *Shan Huang*, 山皇, a heavy earthen counterpart to Japan's Heavenly Emperor 天皇. Today the mountain moves. "Alright. We retreat."

And so it ends. And so for three hours as cease-fires and rendezvous and war plans for tomorrow's war spun on, it seemed to end.

"Faustburst commencing."

"Now?" My successor checked the screens. "There's nothing scheduled . . ."

Xuánlóng: ". . . confirmed! Do you read me, Laputa? A fourth volley from Esmeraldas confirmed! Eleventh platform this time."

Laputa Control: "Roger, *Xuánlóng.* Starbridge, Cloud Ten's forepathcasting is down, I need your augury on the second Borneo volley."

Horus Eye: "Update: Aurvandill silent. Su Song silent. Tyson-2 silent."

Starbridge III: "Roger, Laputa. Augury underway."

Galahad: "My Taurusflock is approaching Laila platform 30, commencing belomancy."

Xuánlóng: "Esmeraldas fourth volley snapcount shows at least sixty-five new missiles."

Laputa Control: "Babylon, I need something that can intercept that Laila topdeck swarm before dispersion."

Babylon: "Roger, Laputa. Searching."

Horus Eye: "Update: Balor silent. Dutchman silent. Hubble Array silent."

These were voices that poured in, not text, real voice, some shrill, some breathless, but all save the robot voice of Horus Eye were pregnant with that forced, hushed calm that grips us when we dare not glance over our shoulders at the magnitude of fire or flood behind. Images came with the words, and if the former battle had been rainstorm, this was hurricane, fresh pictures flashing fast as raindrops, darkening the room as frame on frame on frame showed night black with blurred brightnesses too oblong to be stars.

"What . . . what is this?"

"It's not intended for us, MASON, we're just on the network, it's . . ." The Venus-coated Delian was first to attempt an answer. ". . . somebody's fired missiles from the elevator platforms."

"Already?" MASON looked to Achilles. "How could they mount missiles that fast?"

"Not from the Almagest, the other elevators," the Delian corrected, "from Esmeraldas, and it sounds like Laila, too."

Images upon the screen tiled together until we could see the long line of an elevator pale against the night, and small blurs sprouting from one of its midway platforms, a dim starburst like inept fireworks lost in too large a night.

"The Cousins lost the other elevators? How did we not hear?"

I don't know. No one actually said it, but one could read it on every face, in every posture as the Blacksleeves, Delians, the frantic Censor, still-half-trancing Toshi, all plunged into the data storm that thundered on, the cries of ships and stations.

Starbridge III: "Forepathcast underw— No! The ISSC! Some of these will hit the ISSC!"

Laputa Control: "Keep it together, Starbridge."

Horus Eye: "Update: Oberon silent. Clarke Base silent. Moonraker silent."

Starbridge III: "They're aiming at you too, Laputa! Twelve more coming at you!"

Laputa Control: "Roger, Starbridge. ISSC, this is your evacuation order. Repeat, ISSC, complete evacuation ordered. Starbridge, how long do they have?"

Starbridge III: "Forty-six minutes. Where are they supposed to go?"
Laputa Control: "Just get them moving."
Babylon: "Get yourselves moving, Laputa, that first volley will hit you in thirty-five."
I.S.S. City: "Evacuation order confirmed, Laputa."
Galahad: "Laila topdeck volley belomancy complete. Harbinger payload confirmed. Repeat, harbinger payload confirmed!"

Harbinger. All hearts in earshot skipped a beat, reader. Did yours?

"Where are they aiming?" Achilles barked out. "Romanova? Here?"

"Don't move, Marshal!" It was Cato Weeksbooth's cry, seizing his patient by the shoulders as the master of armies attempted to roll over on the gurney. Cato had Achilles stretched out on his chest, with an array of fine probes bristling like acupuncture needles from his back and spine, connected by a spiderweb of strands. "You'll cause paralysis if you disconnect like that!"

Achilles's snarl made me think again how right our Homer was to call his heart a lion's. "What cities are they targeting? Do we have anything to intercept? Ask them!"

"Right away, Marsha—"

"Reflector signal lost. The time is now 16:40. Faustburst in 10 . . . 9 . . . 8 . . . 7 . . . 6 . . .

I heard my successor gasp. "Back-to-back Faustbursts? They'll burn through . . ."

True. But it didn't matter now.

"Faustburst commencing."

Xuánlóng: "Fifth volley sighted, firing from Laila, platform six."
Laputa Control: "Roger, *Xuánlóng*. Anyone in range for forepathcasting?"
Galahad: "Sixth volley firing from Laila, topdeck again this time."
Laputa Control: "Roger, *Galahad*. Forepathcast, anyone?"
Galahad: "My Taurusflock is out of range."
Starbridge III: "Still finishing fourth volley analysis. New confirmed targets include Phantasos Station, Cloud Six, and Celsius City."
Horus Eye: "Update: Naismith silent. Rakesh Sharma silent. Audacity silent.
ALEXANDRIA: "This is MASON and Achilles at Alexandria. What cities are they targeting? What can we do?"
Swancloak: "Laputa, this is *Swancloak*. We're close enough to forepathcast that fifth Laila volley for you."
Laputa Control: "Thank you, *Swancloak*. Babylon, any progress intercepting that Esmeraldas topdeck swarm?"
Babylon: "Shuttle *Ventura* moving to intercept. It'll be partial but . . ."
Horus Eye: "Update: Tsygan and Dezic silent. Hope Springs silent. Le Guin Station silent."
ALEXANDRIA: "I repeat, this is MASON and Achilles at Alexandria. What cities are the harbingers targeting? What can we do?"
Xuánlóng: "You can stop distracting Laputa, Alexandria. There's nothing you can do. They aren't targeting Earth."

Not Earth? Visions of Alexandria bursting in fire around us gave way to darker visions of fires upon Poseidon's grimmest sea. A tech brought up the battlefield, not a photo mosaic this time but a diagram: there at the center Earth's orb swirling white and blue, there the four elevators stretching hopeful out into the night, there rendered as colored specks our many satellites, some racing in low Earth orbit, others sedate in the dense geocentric ring, with brighter spots to mark lively space stations and those great jewels of the sky which (with only minor exaggeration) we dub space cities. And there sprouted the missiles, their trajectories charted in arcs of red as if incised into the skin of Mother Night by some abominable blade. Those just launched looked like little blossoms, slim-petaled chrysanthemums of blood just opening, one from a low platform of Borneo's Princess Laila Menchanai elevator, the other blooming from the topdeck on the counterweight high in the dark beyond the geocentric ring. But the earlier missile bursts were strands rather than petals, as this art Utopia called forepathcasting did its doomsaying, tracing the blood arcs forward to predict where they would rain death down upon the frail lights of our populated heavens. *They aren't targeting Earth.*

"The *Ventura* is a manned shuttle," my successor murmured in the hush. "They've ordered a manned shuttle to fly into a swarm of harbinger missiles, to detonate them before they can disperse and . . . up?"

"What?" The Censor turned.

"The missiles fired from the Laila topdeck, they're aiming up, away from Earth, out farther. Look."

Look we did at that elder of the two blood blossoms fired from the crown of Laila's counterweight, their bloody petals arcing, not downward toward the vulnerable fireflies that crowd around the Earth but up, toward . . .

"Luna City. They're firing harbingers at Luna City." Cato said it, saw it first, Cato so freshly come from what I used to call our serene, still Moon.

In my shock I turned, not to Huxley but to the victim, to that pale, imperfect circle which hung lacy in the morning blue above the cityscape in our false window. Can Ares touch the Moon?

"Intercept them!"

The faces of the Delians answered before their words, tears leaking wet from vizors. "We don't have interceptor systems out in high Earth orbit, we expected any attacks to launch from Earth, we only have . . ."

Photos finished the sentence for us, in one the slim *Ventura*, then in the next the bright brave flash as a crowd of sky streaks winked out in a burst like sun. Eager, even as we mourned, we looked to the simulation, the sixty arcs of blood which clawed their way from Laila's pinnacle; eight vanished, but fifty-some flew onward to the Moon.

"Now You extend the radius of war's bloodstain?" His words, reader, His words without which I doubt I would have realized what this moment was. The first time. We have imagined wars in space so long, so many made-up battles, heroes, names, that even we who fought it barely marked this moment: the first *real* time a human perished on a battlefield beyond our Earth.

"How did the Cousins lose the elevators?" MASON roared. "Get me Kosala!"

Here was something our scrambling techs could actually attempt.

"Only one volley from Port-Gentil so far," Toshi Mitsubishi called out, one small ray of light. "Repeated volleys from Esmeraldas and Laila both, but no activity from Port-Gentil since the one initial volley."

It was true, there stretched the long, straight cord segmented by platforms, with one sole bloody bloom. A good sign?

"Cornel!" Kosala's face, strained but composed, streamed in with her voice, since with back-to-back Faustbursts bandwidth and lag meant nothing. "How can I help?"

"Who took the elevators?" Achilles snapped before MASON could speak. "Dougong?"

Kosala wore a wrap still, but a jacket over it in beige and cyan, strictly tailored—a Cousin military uniform, inevitable yet somehow as wrong as it was right. "We didn't lose the elevators. It was just supposed to be a defense plan, preparations, I didn't give the order."

"Give the order? You . . . Cousins did this?"

"It could have come from Casablanca, things have been tense there since Cookie's death, but if so, how they got word to North America, I don't—"

Achilles slammed the gurney's metal frame. "You planned an attack on space stations? On Luna City?"

"Hold still, Marshal," Cato pleaded. "You're still connected—"

"You aimed harbingers at Luna City!"

"We prepared defenses," she answered, "in case Utopia weaponized space, just ways to shoot down—"

"You weaponized space!" bold Achilles bellowed. "We trusted the elevators to you so you would keep the heavens free of blood, and you filled them with harbingers!"

"They did!" Kosala shot back, just as bold. "They moved the harbinger adepts to Luna City! Who knows what kind of death machine they might be building there? We were the only group on Earth who could prepare defenses! We-e judged it a necessary precaution." What did it mean, that little hiccup? Hesitation, in the middle of her 'We'? And Kosala's face, that wince, a fleeting armor chink before the mask of calm reset again? I know Kosala well, reader, her habits, favorite drinks, her smiles, her gaits, the way her walk changes between boardroom formality and boudoir play. She opposed this, that's what I read in that hiccup. Cousin Chair Bryar Kosala will not for an instant criticize or seem to criticize the lawful actions of her Hive, but the heart beating beneath that beige-and-cyan jacket had cried out against filling our skies with weapons, and had prayed that she would never see herself proved right.

"We gave you everything!" Achilles raged, this stranger who does not know

Kosala except as the peacemaker who raised then failed his hopes. "The elevators, the greatest gifts any people has ever given to another! You desecrate that!"

Does MASON not know her, Mycroft? Cornel MASON, Kosala's playfellow in boudoir as in boardroom, does he not know her gaits and faces well enough to speak up here and tell one friend the other is no enemy?

MASON, reader? MASON is blind with tears.

"There's more than missiles, Marshal." A Blacksleeve spoke up. "Satellites and stations are going silent all over, more than a hundred already, but nothing's moving near them."

"Hacking," Toshi Mitsubishi guessed. "Someone shutting the systems down."

Achilles winced, though whether at the facts or at Cato's needles, I could not guess. "Is that your doing too, Kosala? Hacking?"

She paused only a moment. "Possibly. I believe hacking some satellites was part of our defense plan, but I don't have full access. I—they—we—we've already tried sending our missiles the disarm signal, every override we have, but no response. We're locked out of our system." She used 'we,' reader, taking responsibility for her people's mistake, however hard she might have fought it.

"The hackers." It was Huxley's voice beside me, not a roar like Achilles's but more substantial somehow, as if the inexorable motions of the deepest Earth were audible, a voice that knew where in deep Gaea's belly monsters gestate, ready now to rise. "Someone broke into your system. Someone planned all this."

"Not necessarily." A less courageous leader than Kosala would have snapped up this excuse. "There's a lot of distrust among my people since Cookie's death. Probably someone at some level suspected infiltration and changed the command codes, locked us out of our own system thinking defense—"

"Defense!" Achilles roared. "This is a massacre! Not just of innocents, these are the treasures of our species, do you not understand that? How many generations—"

"Reflector signal lost. The time is now 16:45. Faustburst in 10 . . . 9 . . . 8 . . . 7 . . . 6 . . . Faustburst commencing."

The pause let Achilles take a breath and master—just an inch—that rage once masterless which caused the Greeks such countless losses, long ago before the hero visited the House of Death whose somber lessons cool the hottest blood.

Laputa Control: ". . . er you can, *Xuánlóng*. And thank you."

Mother Crow: "Laputa Control, this is Mother Crow, I have signal from Admiral Quarriman. They say the Hiveguard Pacific Fleet is past Lima, approaching Esmeraldas soon, and they've warned the occupation forces that if the elevator fires another volley, they'll attack. It may be too little, too late, but . . ."

Laputa Control: "Roger, Mother Crow. Any help's welcome now."

Welcome it was, a second hero, and the first voice in so many months from the Americas, the far side of the world. Achilles's smile was warmest, welcoming the Strangest Senator (though less strange as an admiral), and welcoming too proof that we were not alone in calling Utopia's plight intolerable. The hardy Humanists who raised the domes of Esperanza City may be Caesar's rivals on battlefield and racetrack, but not among the stars—the stars we share.

That hope stirred even mournful Caesar. "Get land forces moving. Call everyone: Papadelias, Milae, Fuxing, they have ships near Borneo."

"I've heard from Huang Enlai already, Caesar," someone answered. "They and Milae are many hours from the elevator base, but Homeland has forces close, Homeland is moving on the Laila platform as we speak."

"Homeland? Homeland is helping?"

"Director Andō's orders." Warmth tinged this Mason's voice. "No one wants to let this happen. No one."

I felt despair thawing—we on Earth were slow, not powerless. Not quite. Especially not when nearly all Earth's forces serve Jehovah's fathers, and what He loves He makes His fathers love.

Luna Dock: "Laputa Control, this is Luna City, how many missiles do we have incoming?"

Laputa Control: "Luna City, you have . . . with the second volley, you have seventy-three missiles incoming, repeat, seventy-three missiles, with harbinger payload confirmed."

Luna Dock: "Roger, Laputa Control, we have only forty-one craft Moonside capable of missile interception, we can't block that many even if we use everything. Can you do something?"

What is the pause here? Lag? Or something more human as Luna City gazes up into the black and stars and finds nothing to help her there but Earth's blue marble, distant and so cold? All great cities grow over centuries, reader, as centers rise, and street webs grow like lace, and neighborhoods take on their characters woven of layered lives. But Luna City grew in dreams first, two thousand years of us imagining peoples, roads, silver towers, from Lucian of Samosata's satires to the million space adventure stories of the Exponential Age. We built so many versions, carved of words and pictures, yet as present now within the domes' foundations as the buried underlayers of Jerusalem or Rome. Our dreams built this. Yet this dream city is as fragile as those dreams, her domes ready to pop like soap bubbles, and outside: nothing, no air, no help, no neighbor city to run refugee to, nothing but that blackest night which childhood instinct teaches us is not our habitat. Seventy-three harbingers—a crater charred so deep could destroy, not only the city, but the dream layers too, cauterizing hope to make successor generations call it folly that ever we thought to raise a city on the lifeless, staring Moon.

Laputa Control: "Roger Luna City, we . . . we're still . . ."

Galahad: "*Galahad* to Laputa Control, my Taurusflock is passing the counterweight, I could sacrifice the Taurusflock to intercept four of the Moon-bound missiles. Would that help?"

Laputa Control: "Roger, *Galahad*, move Taurusflock into position but don't act yet, we still can't—"

Skymaw: "Attention, Laputa Control, this is Skymaw's *automated Avalon Slumber System. Traffic suggests multiple threats in exosphere and above, including harbinger activity. Please confirm."*

"Skymaw!" This cry rose from a Delian draped in sparkling rainstorm working at Cato's side. "It's real! *Skymaw* is real!"

"What's a Skymaw?"

Laputa Control: "Wow . . . or . . . yes, I read you, *Skymaw*. Multiple threats in and above exosphere confirmed. Harbinger activity confirmed."

Skymaw: "Confirmed, Laputa Control. Genesis conditions achieved. Skymaw *awakening."*

"What is *Skymaw*?" It was Censor Jung who pressed the question, scanning the room, where many vizored faces shied away.

"Our space warship," Cato confessed, splendid Cato who had long since come to terms with this most dreadful vessel ever launched for any Helen.

Kosala pounced on that. "They *did* weaponize space! Of course they did, they planned this war for years!"

"No!" Cato cried. "It's not like that! It—we—Utopia—we debated a long time before building *Skymaw*, and it's not what you think, not an aggressive weapon at all, it's entirely for defense, honestly, just space defense, no space-to-surface attack capacity, just a magnetic interception-and-deflection array that can rip enemies out of the skies, plus a few things we thought . . . We hoped we wouldn't need it."

Of course you hoped your monster king could slumber on, Utopia, that we would keep our battles sane and kind, and honor in this war our Second Law, that it is an intolerable crime to do significant and measurable damage to the Produce of Civilization, which Luna City surely is, these stations too, the life's works of so many generations. But in your pessimistic wisdom you still built that monster king, and as it woke I raised a prayer of abject gratitude to our Maker—this monster's makers' Maker—that you did.

Horus Eye: "Update: Asteria Relay silent. Skymaw silent. Casvel silent."

Laputa Control: "Skymaw silent? Confirm that, Horus Eye?"

Horus Eye: "Skymaw silent, confirmed."

Laputa Control: "How? Sabotage?"

Xuánlóng: "I don't know, Laputa, but I have a detonation image, sharing now."

And there it was, before our eyes in shards and fire, some curving slivers of ship carcass the only hints of what might have become the stuff of nightmares for spacefaring centuries. It felt so like an answer, a curse straight from His Bosom Whom I had just honored: "I care not for thy gratitude, thou parricide archtraitor who rankest thy Maker's Guest before thy Maker. Pray not to Me."

"Was that you?" Achilles glared up from the gurney table at Kosala on the screen.

As strong as steel, her mask. "I don't know."

"Was that you?"

"Screaming is not—"

"How many?" Zeus's champion spat back. "Those space cities are as hard to build—harder—as when we bore the boulders on our backs and raised bulwarks with sticks and human sweat and nothing more! How many will you bu-urn?" That catching of breath, reader? Great Achilles weeps.

Bryar Kosala paused, no human bosom hard enough to stand unmoved when great Achilles weeps. "I agree this is abominable. I've sent messages to everyone I can reach, they should be getting through. Casablanca should know how we can disarm our missiles. Meanwhile, you should get your other defenses moving."

"We have nothing else."

"Don't give up yet." She smiled encouragement. "You must have something else, you planned so long. Is there a *Skymaw-2*?"

"No. Nothing." It was Cato who answered, Cato and all our sciences commingling in one answer. "We have nothing. You've taken everything. Our whole plan was to trust you to confine the war to Earth. We have some satellites we can shift into collision courses, some pilots in the right places to sacrifice themselves to stop a missile in its flight, but you've fired ten times as many missiles as we have—"

"Reflector signal lost. The time is now 16:50. Faustburst in 10 . . . 9 . . . 8 . . . 7 . . . 6 . . . Faustburst commencing."

"Casablanca!" a Mason cried as the next sky chariot commenced its sacrifice. "I have signal from Casablanca, Caesar."

"Patch it through."

"Casablanca?" Kosala's voice was hope.

Actually, hope has many voices. "Come in, Alexandria?"

"Heloïse!"

« *Ma brave Heloïse.* »

« *Seigneur !* » I was astonished she could hear Him through the war room speakers.

From the snarl on Caesar's face, he was astonished too. "*Tace, Fili, aut te deprimam,*" he ordered quickly ("Quiet, Son, or I'll mute you"). "Heloïse? This is MASON at Alexandria. My son is listening, but I am in command, and have Kosala on the line. Tell me what's happening? Did Casablanca give this order?"

"Yes. I couldn't stop them, Caesar, the Nurturists have shut me out of everything. But we managed to take the Port-Gentil elevator from them. The anchor station has surrendered, and most of the platforms except some holdouts on platform six."

"Surrendered?" Kosala repeated. "Are Cousins fighting Cousins?"

"No. I called in the United Nations." Her words were bright. "UNGAR border forces were already right outside Port-Gentil."

UNGAR—the United Nations of the Great African Reservation. I had forgotten that those remnant lands of citizens and borders had their armies too, whose tanks and sabers could do more than rattle decoratively along the wiggly lines upon their maps. "UNGAR has joined the war?"

"Our war, no, but Secretary-General Dembélé moved in the instant I told them Luna City was in danger. Space is all humanity's achievement, not the Alliance's." Cutting words cut deep when spoken by so soft a soul as Heloïse. But she is right. The geographic nations birthed the Space Race in their rush and competition, not our peaceful Hives. The great acceleration, when craft became aircraft and then spacecraft, when Yuri braved orbit, when in gazing down we first learned Earth was blue, all this rightly belongs to citizens, nations, more than to we who swept them to the corners of our present. This war was not a World War, was it, not until today? For six months it threatened Romanova's treasures, but now it threatens the birthrights of Gabon, the Congo, Niger, sweeping Namibia, Tibet, the Levant, sacred Mount Meru, Texas, Utah, the split Baptist Republics, old Afghanistan, dishonoring the spacewalking ancestors of Minnesotan Lutherans, Punjabi Sikhs, Tibetan Buddhists, all the branches of Jews whose separate Reservations celebrate their separate contributions to each void-bound stepping-stone. When we threaten those stepping-stones, it becomes their war, too. So today the Reservations save us—save the stars. "UNGAR forces found missile banks on several of Port-Gentil's platforms," Heloïse continued. "We were hoping we could use them to intercept the missiles that have been fired already, but we're locked out of the systems. Aunt Kosala, can you help?"

Kosala's hard smile matched her answer. "Our best are in Casablanca with you, Heloïse, I don't have better."

"We'll keep trying then, I— Yes?" We heard the muffled voice of some secondary speaker next to Heloïse. "They've traced me, I need to keep moving."

"Traced you? What—"

"I'll call back when I can. Can *mon Seigneur* hear me?"

Caesar smiled to find his Son and Heir so obedient to his commanded silence that He did not answer even Heloïse. "They can."

« *Mon cher Seigneur, je T'aime, et je fais ici des choses bonnes et précieuses, ce qui me rend doublement heureuse en sachant qu'elles Te rendront aussi heureux.* (My dear Lord, I love You, and I am doing good and valuable things, which makes me doubly happy knowing they will make You happy too.) »

"Wait. Are you in danger, Heloïse? Heloïse?" Caesar's tone grew urgent, fear for the almost daughter to match his almost Son.

"Signal lost," a Delian confirmed.

"Heloïse!" Caesar shouted again at nothing, such a human act. It was so petty. Sky cities were burning, the Lunar circle about to be ripped from

Utopia's flag, but if the pillars of the sky must fall, must they crush our sweet dove with them?

"Caesar, Marshal, there's something you should see."

"Yes?"

"New missile projections. The second volley fired from the Laïla topdeck, they're not aiming at the Moon, they're aiming at the Gates of Nineveh."

Even Achilles startles at a name ancient when he was young. Do you know great Ishtar's city, reader? Assyrian Nineveh raised on the Tigris banks three thousand years ago when iron was new and walls of mud brick still stirred hearts to awe. There flourished—among others—the cult of Nergal, god of war and plague, an ancient face of Mars. For Nineveh's still-famous gates we name our own, the matchless station with its fifteen docks poised just outside the well of Earth's steep gravity, where Earthsphere transports load the produce of the living and the ashes of the dead onto the twin ships *Dumuzid* and *Geshtinanna* (the Shepherd and the Vine), which trundle their eternal alternating loops from world to world. The Gates of Nineveh, humanity's gateway to all the universe, but first to Mars.

"At this You take Your aim? Why?" He asked it, reader. He.

"Switching back to Fauststream audio."

Laputa Control: "I need Nineveh interception options, now! *Xuánlóng*? Babylon? What do you have out there?"

Babylon: "Out that far? I . . . There's a transport close to docking, it could intercept a couple missiles, but it's full, it's . . ." Full, yes, transports to Nineveh bear the most expensive cargo humankind has ever loaded on a craft, the fruits of science, Nature, Earth's gifts which the whole Martian planet half-born cannot yet replicate. And this You make us burn to block a couple of the bloody paths, so many, that You slice across Night's flesh toward Nineveh?

Starbridge III: "Laputa, pathtracing is still underway, but we don't have anything in range to stop that many missiles, even if they aren't harbinger-level."

Laputa Control: "Roger, Starbridge. Nineveh, this is Laputa Control. Do you read me? Laputa Control to the Gates of Nineveh?" A breathless pause as even light lags between our skies and our celestial toehold.

Gates of Nineveh: "Laputa Control, this is the Gates of Nineveh, we read you loud and clear."

Laputa Control: "Great! Nineveh, this is an evacuation order. You have missiles incoming, impact in 215 minutes." The wait, reader, seconds but such cruel seconds paid as tithe to Old Enemy Distance.

Gates of Nineveh: "Laputa, this is Nineveh. Thanks for the warning."

Laputa Control: "Laputa Control to Nineveh, please confirm evacuation. This is not a drill." Again the wait, Poseidon's sacrifice extracted whether we will or no.

Gates of Nineveh: "That's a negative on evacuation, Laputa. We have a situation."

Laputa Control: "Nineveh, we do not have an interception option. You have to get out of there. Do you understand?"

Horus Eye: "Update: Cyrano silent, Supra Luna silent, Galahad silent."

Gates of Nineveh: "That's a negative on evacuation, Laputa. We have incoming tugs *Herschel 37* and *Cassini 108* both off course and nonresponsive. Our dispatch system is not portable."

Laputa Control: "Nineveh, this is Laputa Control. You have 215 minutes to complete station destruction, do you understand?" Our wishes flew out with the words, every heart in Alexandria willing one more wing to speed this precious message to those farthest gatekeepers of humankind.

Gates of Nineveh: "Laputa Control, we have two tugs accelerating on a doomsday course with no options planetside. Odyssey is having no success. The Nineveh dispatch system is the only way to get the tugs back online. We need to stay."

Laputa Control: "A doomsday course? For Earth?" Can silences be worse than this?

Gates of Nineveh: "Negative, Laputa. A doomsday course for Mars."

For Mars? "What does it mean?" All turned to Cato—no, all outsiders turned to Cato, while the Utopians intensified the frenzy of their work.

One breath Cato takes to steel himself. Two breaths. Three. "They're terraforming tugs, inbound from the asteroid belt or outer planets, hauling frozen nitrogen and water ice, millions of tons each, fifteen or twenty million. They're supposed to decelerate before they dump their payloads, but if they're out of control, they'll hit the Martian surface like killer meteors, and leave blast craters . . ." a pause for calculations, ". . . five kilometers across."

"Will they hit the Odyssey Base?" I asked fastest.

"It doesn't matter. A five-kilometer hemisphere of rock blasted into the air, the ejecta—the pieces—will rain down all over Mars, a planetwide rock storm. It'll take out everything, everything on the planet, bases, robots, fields, all surface systems, and . . ."

"And?"

"And everything we could land on the planet for the next . . . maybe for several hundred years."

Centuries. Are centuries a thing that can be murdered now? Centuries spent and centuries now stillborn, both our progress and our plan? I remember wondering in that moment why great Hera's son, indomitable Ares, would strike down his own. Why crush *his* world? *His* toiling servants? Was this his requital for O.S.? Since humans in our hubris kept the god of battles peacebound for three hundred years, now he reciprocates?

"Reflector signal lost. The time is now 16:54. Faustburst in 10 . . . 9 . . . 8 . . . 7 . . . 6 . . . Faustburst commencing."

Laputa Control: "Roger that, Nineveh. We'll work on interception options. Can you brief us more on your situation? Is there anything we can do?"

I barely registered the rush of questions and suggestions, but it was clear mischief ran deep. The *Herschel* tug was half a day from Mars, *Cassini* one day more, but further tugs were also falling silent, threatening deathblow upon deathblow to the planet in the coming weeks if we could not get them back online. The Martian SPS were shifting off course too, the intricate flock of solar power satellites which feeds our half-made world, while Deimos Control—perched on the smaller Martian moon—flashed only "comms down." Odyssey's programmers were unequal to a problem of this magnitude, while most Earthsphere stations faced destruction sooner than distant Nineveh.

"Guard Nineveh!" Who cried this? Instinct? MASON? MASON, who inherited an empire spanning two planets but may now pass on to his Successor only one? "Intercept with anything! Everything! It doesn't matter what!"

"No!" swift Achilles cries. "Save Luna City! Luna City's the priority!"

"If we lose Nineveh, we could lose Mars, do you understand that? Mars!"

"Bridger's relics are in Luna City!"

Hearts freeze. Those matchless gifts, his gifts, reader, and His. And yet: "Mars!"

"Can Earth do it? Can anyone down here defuse the missiles? Reroute the tugs?"

A rush of tries and whispers. "Earth signals are still weak and intermittent in the hiccups between Faustbursts, low Earth orbit signals too, and even if they weren't, we moved all our best people off-world for prote-ection." Well might your throat crack, Utopian, calling orbit's fragile fortresses 'protection' now.

"Can *we* do it?" my successor's quick idea. "We have Earth's best here! Su-Hyeon! Toshi! Mycroft! Cato Weeksbooth! We even have Tully Mardi in our prisons, don't we? Tully grew up in Luna City. They're made for this war!"

Joy flared in me—can you believe it, reader—unmitigated joy that he, *my Enemy,* was near to lend his aid in this, our darkest hour. For a mocking instant, Earth's young geniuses, Toshi and the Censor, stared at each other across their console. But Toshi spoke the hard truth first. "Just because we're good with our own programs doesn't mean we can do anything with any computer, we're not . . ." As all stares fixed on Cato, Toshi did not have to say aloud what they were not.

"Cato? Can you do it?"

With fast but shaking hands, Cato was still drawing the needle-probes from lithe Achilles's back. "I . . . I don't know these tugs, this program. If I had the specs and software, with some hours to learn and somebody to talk me through it, I . . . we're talking about learning a whole new system, even I . . . Maybe?"

Mother Crow: "Mother Crow to Laputa Control. Admiral Quarriman says the Esmeraldas elevator is resisting, battle underway. It'll be a few hours."

Babylon: "Laputa, anything yet from Port-Gentil? No missiles launched there, right?"

Mother Crow: "Mother Crow to Laputa Control, any response for Quarriman?"

Horus Eye: "Update: Swancloak silent, Morpheus silent, Laputa silent."
Xuánlóng: "Laputa silent? Confirm that, Horus?"
Horus Eye: "Laputa silent, confirmed."
Xuánlóng Control: "*Xuánlóng* to all, Laputa is silent, we are assuming control."
Starbridge III: "Roger that, *Xuánlóng* Control."
Horus Eye: "Update: Babylon silent, Mother Crow silent, Gates of Nineveh silent."
Xuánlóng Control: "Nineve—ccc—e—te—e—h—cc—c—"
Horus Eye: "Update: Cloud Six silent, Starbridge III silent, Tai Bai silent."
Horus Eye: "Update: Albatross-5 silent, Gradatim silent, Xuánlóng silent."

"Reflector signal lost. The time is now 16:59. Faustburst in 10 . . . 9 . . . 8 . . . 7 . . . 6 . . . 5 . . . 4 . . . 3 . . . 2 . . . 1 . . . Reflector signal not found. The time is now 16:59. Faustburst in 10 . . . 9 . . . 8 . . . 7 . . . 6 . . . 5 . . . 4 . . . 3 . . . 2 . . . 1 . . . Reflector signal not found. The time is now 17:00. Faustburst in 10 . . . 9 . . . 8 . . . 7 . . . 6 . . . 5 . . . 4 . . . 3 . . . 2 . . . 1 . . . Reflector signal not found. The time is now 17:00. Faustburst in 10 . . . 9 . . . 8 . . . 7 . . . 6 . . . 5 . . . 4 . . . 3 . . . 2 . . . 1 . . . Reflector signal not found. The time is now 17:00. Faustburst in 10 . . . 9 . . . 8 . . . 7 . . . 6 . . . 5 . . . 4 . . . 3 . . . 2 . . . 1 . . . Reflector signal not found. The time is now 17:01. Faustburst in 10 . . . 9 . . . 8 . . . 7 . . . 6 . . . 5 . . . 4 . . . 3 . . . 2 . . . 1 . . . Reflector signal not found . . ."

For another minute, more, we listened as the countdowns pattered on like rain.

"Fix it! Get signal back!"

"We can't, we don't control the reflectors."

"Cato! You can do it!"

Cato fumbled with a needle, making bold Achilles wince. "I . . . No, I can't do it. Listen, Laputa City is down. *Xuánlóng* is down. They control the Faustbursts from up there, not us down here. The problem is in space, I can't fix a thing in space, not when the whole problem is that we can't contact space!" He faced us all, our bank of stares, so desperate and so hopeful. "You know now what I am," Cato continued. "I . . . I can do anything human science can do, but I can't do things human science can't do. We can't do this. We, humanity right now, we don't have the means to stop this. We can't reprogram Martian tugs we can't contact. We can't deflect missiles from the Moon when we have no physical objects between the missiles and the Moon. We can't undo this level of destruction. Utopia's trying, the whole Hive together, everyone, Kosala, Andō, even Quarriman, the Hiveguard fleet, but . . . This is why we tried so hard to keep the war on Earth, to keep space peaceful, we . . . No one can fix this now, no one. Space is too hard. Even something as simple as communicating over distances, it's just . . . it's just too hard . . ."

Too hard. I followed Cato's gaze across to Caesar, but no, that is not an Emperor's face, not now. It is a man's face, frail Cornel Semaphoros, his right hand clutching his shoulder at the spot where long ago you stabbed him, dear Apollo, your attempt to teach this not-yet-Emperor the truth you learned the day Utopia's greatest entomologist decided Mars was too dangerous, too hard.

Mars is too hard. Two hundred fifty years we toiled, longer, centuries mapping the surface, forging tools before we dared to plant a footprint, centuries to achieve what? We are half done making a harsh new world whose rusty soil gifts to our descendants the same lives of frontier toil that our ancestors worked so hard to end, to *not* pass on, hoping their pains would carve out for their children something easier. And now even this halfway world burns down? Your light was already so hard to keep alive, impossible Apollo. Earth is so easy. Earth has flowers, air, the right amount of sun, the right amount of gravity to keep our bones strong and our muscles healthy and not wreck us like the wreck a decade's Moon life made of Tully Mardi. Earth flows with sweet water, with second chances, love, and friends, friends right here, here with us, not months' journeys away. Our era's founders, *Mukta*'s gifts, they left us lives so sweet, we hardly feel Poseidon's tyranny. It was already hard, Apollo, hard to take your oath, to be your oarsman, toiling to build dream cities in the sky that we wish for but do not actually need. We don't have to go to Mars. We can stay home, and make a better Earth, and love our lives, and see our friends, and rest, and it gets harder, harder, every time we make Earth better, it gets harder still to turn our backs on all of this to be your sweating oarsmen on a sea so terrible, so terrible as space. And now you set us back four hundred years? Past works and future? Mars and Luna City? Do you know how much that asks of us? How hard we had to fight Reason herself to go to study ants on Mars and not stay here where there are many more ants, and our friends, and home? And now you set us back four hundred years? It was too hard already. This is intolerable, Apollo. There is no one in Alexandria who is not crying. There is no one who can see *this Troy* burn and not feel our light go out. Poseidon wins. It is too hard, Ἄναξ. Poseidon wins.

Words, next to me, His words, as soft as sleep and yet somehow as real, more real, than all Creation. "I do not know how to call 'Friend' One Who does this."

I turned. Jehovah, reader. This wounds even Jehovah, teaches the Heart Which Loves all with a universe of Love to Love less. Jehovah's Loneliness crossed infinities. He hungered for a Peer, a Friend, as no creature beneath the skies has ever hungered, His long patience enduring Time, Distance, impotences' tortures, this long and bloody greeting we call war, but He Loved on, unconditional, and patiently He called This strange Host 'Friend.' But now He can't. Now That Host reveals Himself as One Who would light such a spark and snuff it. One Who gave us Midway Island, stepping-stones, then crushes us when it would have been kinder by far to crush this spirit long ago, the first time someone thought to hollow out a log to make a boat, before we toiled a hundred thousand years. Intolerable. This makes Him finite, reader, He who was omnibenevolent and wrapped us in His kind Infinity. The Heart Which Loved all with a universe of Love cannot Love this.

"Ow! Carefu—"

"Alexander system online." It was Achilles's voice. Both were Achilles's voice, in fact, but the quick pain cry had been warm, organic, natural, while these new

words were cold, aloof, without emotion, without breath's imperfections. Without his lips moving to shape the words. *"Remote contact established. Hibernation conditions detected. Initiating pre-revival diagnostic."*

"Alexander system . . ." Cato repeated, gaping down at his patient with the web of probes and filaments, freshly removed, still shimmering in his hands.

Achilles sat up, stretching. *"Diagnostic complete. Core systems optimum. Generator ignition in 3 . . . 2 . . . 1 . . ."* I do not think the screen deceived me, reader—Achilles's lips did not move. *"Generator active. Alexander system revival underway."*

"Alexander!" Hope cried, blazing like a phoenix in Cato's voice, in Huxley's, and in mine—we who have read *it.*

Cato: "Where is it?"

Achilles: "Low Earth orbit." His lips moved for the first words, not the latter: *"Inclination 51.6108, right ascension 119.1549, eccentricity 0096276, perigee 91.2036, mean anomaly 270.2128, revolutions per day 16.14210181, epoch 55039.25855869."*

Cato (deft fingers plotting out the numbers): "Is it combat-ready?"

Achilles: "Xiphos and Falcata hot, priming Menaulion, Dory, and Sarissa banks, sixteen minutes until full power." (then with lips): "The Ancile Breaker will take longer."

Cato: "You have the . . . wow . . . You can pilot remotely, yes?"

Achilles: "The engines, yes. The lag's not bad in L.E.O."

Cato: "Jamming's not a problem?"

Achilles: "They aren't jamming a technology they don't know about."

Cato: "Can you use the weapon systems from here?"

Achilles: "Not properly. We have to get me up there."

Cato: "Right. Inclination 51.6 . . . that's by the Hermetica Salvager. Is it in dock at Hermetica? In the debris clump?"

Achilles: "Possibly."

Cato: "We can't launch anything directly with the cars in lockshell."

Achilles: "Is that what you named it? Hitting everything that flies."

Cato: "It wasn't made for this! I designed lockshell for intercepting missiles or asteroid debris chunks, I never thought—"

Achilles: "It's not your fault."

Cato: "Thanks. Our closest launch option is Port-Gentil. Even in lockshell, the cars won't clip the elevators, I made sure of that."

Achilles: "UNGAR has Port-Gentil. Call UNGAR. Tell them to be ready for me."

Cato: "Let's see, Port-Gentil's 4,000 kilometers by air—not an option with lockshell—10,000 by sea, even the *Bucephalus* would take a day."

Achilles: "The *Per Aspera?*"

Cato: "It's being repaired. Getting me here wasn't easy."

"What is Alexander?" MASON asked as he, the Censor, all within the war room stared stunned at the back-and-forth of Cato and Achilles.

The pair continued, heedless, shoving the Blacksleeves off the nearest console and bringing up a map of Africa, Port-Gentil tucked just in the inner curve of her west coast, on the far side of the Sahara.

Cato: "If we put you in an armed aircraft, could you shoot the cars down? Just enough to make the one jaunte?"
Achilles: "What do we have down here that can shoot that fast?"
Cato: "Hm . . ."
Achilles: "My Sarissas are that fast. I could land the Alexander here, then fly to Port-Gentil. The armor can handle car strikes."
Cato: "Land here? That would cost time, and reentry's a big strain."
Achilles: "Yes, I'd rather not use up my reentry pack. Doubt there's a spare."

"What is Alexander?" MASON repeated, harsher.

"*Caesar, in albo* (on the screen)," an aide observed at last. "*Mycroft agitat* (is waving)."

Caesar's glare with Death's within it made me cringe. "What is Alexander?"

I waited for the blip that meant sound had reconnected. "It's the Armor of Achilles, Caesar."

Still Death glared. "What does that mean?"

"In Apollo's *Iliad,* remember? Achilles was a pilot. The Alexander is his armor, the greatest ever built, made by the god Hephaestus. The greatest weapon of the war!"

Wrath softened to confusion. "This is another warship?"

"Not a ship, a suit, armor, but yes. The Alexander can fly to Nineveh or Luna City like it's nothing! The Alexander can shoot down every missile in the sky!"

"A flying armor?"

I think I was hysterical here, reader, so overjoyed to see despair break that joy's dazzle kept me from understanding the questions Caesar aimed at—that any calm soul here would aim at. "With the Alexander, Achilles can finally change the world!" I cried. "That's what unlocks it! On his own, Achilles dies tragically in a tragic war, but Alexander the Great, you know people thought he was a sort of reincarnation of Achilles, it's as Alexander that Achilles changes the world, with Achilles as the soul inside, the ghost in the machine!"

A careful patience softened Caesar's words, practiced from many years of dealing with my instability. "Apollo's *Iliad* had giant robots. Are you saying Utopia built a giant robot?"

"No." Huxley answered beside me, soft words, shaken. "We didn't build such a thing, we . . . we *couldn't* build such a thing, the technology—"

"Of course not!" I cried. "The gods made it! Thetis and Hephaestus, for Achilles."

"Mycroft"—Huxley's eyes held mine, gentle but firm—"the Thetis and Hephaestus A.I.s don't exist."

"The gods made it!" I could not understand why Huxley's and MASON's faces showed anything but joy. "Or God, one, plural, doesn't matter, They made it for Jehovah, Caesar, for Ἄναξ Jehovah, did you not hear Him? This was intolerable, even for Him, to see so much burn. He said He could not Love, could not call 'Friend' One Who did this, and His Peer listened!"

"Cared," He clarified, our careful Visitor still next to me. "My Peer cared. Acted. Wants to be called 'Friend.'" Can you believe it, reader, there He sat, still real, still watching tranquil at my side, this Friend for Whom Providence bends. No, no, not tranquil; He was expressionless, but that serene face is the still water which runs too deep for features to express the infinite complexities of such a Mind. At such a moment.

Caesar was staring in staggered wonder at Cato and Achilles, who still bent over the console, locked in their logistics. *"Interventus divinus . . . ?"*

"We have Tully Mardi!" Achilles spun suddenly, tense for action. "They can contact O.S.! Somebody bring them here! Now!"

"Why . . ." Caesar had to steel himself to face Achilles. "Why didn't you tell me?"

"Tell you what?"

"That you had this . . . thing in orbit?"

Achilles smiled. "I didn't know, I couldn't feel it until Cato fixed my system."

"It wasn't real until just now, Caesar!" I called through the screen. "It's the answer to a . . . something stronger than a prayer, a warning, Jehovah's warning that Friendship could not endure."

"Ex nihilo . . ." The mountain that is Caesar trembled. *"Machina ex nihilo—non . . . Machina ex deo . . ."*

Cato looked up from the console. "Actually, I think Bridger made it." He paused to put in one last command, and a new light appeared on the wall's diagram, a piercing white among the many-colored satellites schooling in orbit. "That's where we released Little Alex. Autonomous Litter Extractor: A, L, Ex." Cato had to spell it out for me to parse it. "ALEx is what Bridger called their satellite, the one they made with me in science club. They built it to gather space debris, to bring discards together to remake them into something that could keep helping our space projects. And now we get that help."

Even MASON froze a moment. "Bridger built a satellite that built a robot capable of blasting missiles halfway to the Moon?"

Cato smiled gently, so gently. "Bridger made resurrection potions, and a magic crystal ball, and Achilles. This is marginally less impossible."

Still MASON stared, and as I saw his face, his eyes, it started to sink in to me too just how visible this was, this tipping of our Maker's hand. Providence crafts Time itself, reader. If to meet Its Guest's demand Providence had Bridger plant the seed of ALEx years ago, then It could have planned a subtler solution: made Huang Enlaï's forces linger close to Borneo, made Heloïse succeed in Casablanca, made the jamming block the order to fire, or made Mars tugs a hair harder to hack. If the Mind of infinite subtlety Which scripts out comets' arcs and beetles' paths chose something this unsubtle, that Mind wanted Jehovah, wanted all of us to have no doubt, not for an instant, that this was an Answer. That It Listened. That It Cared.

"Marshal, Tully Mardi is here."

There indeed in prison red and cuffs to match my own sat Tully Mardi, the guards who flanked his wheelchair panting on either side.

"Cato, you ask them," Achilles ordered.

Cato started. "Me? Um. Hi. Yes. I don't think we've met. I'm Cato Weeksbooth."

"I know who you are."

No, my Enemy—I thought—*you don't.*

"Listen." Cato brought up photos on the screen, details of missiles. "A sudden attack is going to destroy Luna City, the Gates of Nineveh, our Martian bases, everything unless we can get Achilles from here into orbit within the next . . . as soon as possible. Port-Gentil is only twenty-five minutes by car, less if we max out the engine. I didn't write the specific program that's making the cars swerve and attack, but I know the basic system, and I bet my bash'mates programmed a way to counter the program, or could at least tell me something about the algorithm so I can plot interception. Can you contact any of them? Sniper? Lesley? Eureka? I know you're allies."

Silence.

"This is not a trick, I swear! Look at the pictures!"

"I understand." Bold Tully had words and eyes only for Caesar. "Will you give them immunity, MASON?"

"What?"

"O.S. bash'members, if they reveal themselves to help you. Will you give them immunity? Will you promise to erase—"

"Every minute we negotiate burns a space station," MASON interrupted. "Whatever you would ask for within reason, it is yours, even if you would have me let Ojiro Sniper walk into this room and out again."

Achilles bristled there, but our Achilles is not the unbridled stallion of his youth, not after fording Styx.

"Alright," Tully agreed. "You have access to Pass-It-On?"

"Of course."

"Then free my hands a while and let me use it."

Cato hovered over Tully as he wheeled up to the console. "Best would be if you have any way to reach Eureka," Cato urged. "Sidney I know was in a prison in South America somewhere, but is Eureka—"

"Here," Tully answered, without looking up from pounding out his message with uncanny speed. "Eureka's here, in Alexandria."

"Here? Yes!" Cato's delight chilled fast. "Wait. Why?"

"To help kill Jehovah Mason."

What could one say? The whole room glared in silence at this prisoner in his wheelchair, so serene in his conviction, and so callous in his honesty. But he was right, my Enemy had no reason to lie, not now.

"Right. Expect Eureka within a few minutes. I don't know the layout of wherever we are, so I've suggested the front entrance—warn your guards."

"Is Eureka bringing the program?" Cato asked, urgent.

"Yes."

Relief's sigh swelled then ebbed in Cato like a gentle wave. "To work, then. I'll need your fastest console, hardware Eureka can plug into, and help from a bunch of you, whoever learns new systems fast, I . . . You're the Censor, aren't you?"

Su-Hyeon straightened under Cato's sudden gaze. "Yes. I can help, my deputy too."

"Yes, of course!" Toshi confirmed.

"Wonderful!" I don't think Cato realized who this was whose hand he squeezed so warmly, science's unfinished Quasimodo Toshi Mitsubishi, whom half the world calls set-set and half monster—if Cato had realized, O.S.'s son and H.E.L.E.N.'s, and Eureka Weeksbooth's loving brother, he might have squeezed her hand even more warmly.

"Mycroft is here, yes?" Cato added. "Mycroft can—"

"No." Caesar's decree. "Mycroft stays where they are."

A brief wrinkle of Cato's nose protested, but we stand in MASON's city. And MASON was right, the others were enough. Toshi, Jung Su-Hyeon, and several Delians crowded close as Cato half explained and half invented how to let Eureka plug into the best computer in all Alexandria: Achilles's brain.

"If we can get them connected, Eureka can fly with Achilles in the car and interface between them. Between Achilles's pilot skills and Eureka's mastery of the program—"

"Caesar, a motorcycle is requesting permission to drive through the palace to bring you Eureka Weeksbooth."

Cato looked up. "That'll be Kat or Robin. Every second counts."

Caesar cost us no second. *"Nihil obstet."*

And so, bold as a jousting knight upon a snow-white stallion, Kat or Robin Typer roars into the war room. Eureka rides behind, sensors glinting beneath a bedsheet shroud sparkling with broken glass which tells of a very hasty journey. Straight from dismount to plugging in Eureka rushes, mobbed by helping hands and technodetails as steps only comprehensible to those who take them hook consoles to Eureka, consoles to other consoles, Eureka via Cato's probes to bold Achilles, and suggestions and achievements race like whitewater toward launch.

"Is this . . . is this actually happening?" So soft a whisper, I doubt any other heard, but I always have a special ear for my successor. "Alexander . . . real?"

I understood the stunned tone in my poor successor's voice; raw miracle—Bridger—was somehow easier to accept than miracled technology. Big questions can be both freedom and stupor, zooming us out so the minutiae of actions, second upon second, blur like pixels and we see only the larger image and its larger problems. I lost the thread of action here, the flurry of what they did together, superhuman Cato and Achilles, tank-reared Eureka, tank-reared Toshi, Tully the Mardis' monstrous masterpiece, the Delians whom unkind Nurturists call set-sets too, and, keeping pace with all of these, proving that excellence also grows on its own, Earth's pride, young Jung Su-Hyeon. I couldn't see the trees, only the forest. So many pieces Providence moved into play today, so dense this teamwork: Remaker aiding Hiveguard, Humanist and Mitsubishi aiding Mason, O.S. aiding Him. I see what each contributes. Soon comes Kat or Robin's turn again as Eureka and Achilles mount together on the motorcycle's back to roar down MASON's hallways to the launchpad where one car will carry all this world's hopes of enjoying other worlds someday. Each link in teamwork's chain is necessary, each member right to beam pride as the car lightning-dodges its way across the broad Sahara, as triumphant UNGAR clears a path and loads Achilles in the elevator, as Achilles reaches orbit's welcome, the breaker of armies ready now to break armies. But each contributor is necessary only because You, Providence, made us necessary as You planned all this, each piece we need to keep the stars in reach, to stop the intolerable from snuffing out Apollo's light. You care, Apollo, care, strange Providence. But why now? I must ask the question I once taught Carlyle to ask, that Zeus's gray-eyed daughter taught Achilles to ask all those years ago. There have been other intolerables. None has threatened to snuff out Apollo's light forever as this did, but You have let intolerables devour other dreams that other humans held as dear as I hold Mars. Are the cumulative prayers of all who ever nursed Apollo's fire in our hearts truly more worthy of Your intervention than the prayers of all who ever loved with Aphrodite's love, crafted with Hephaestus's genius, aspired with Hera's ambition, and were struck down—loves lost, creations rusted, empires incomplete? Was Macedonian Alexander's wish for World Empire less worthy in Your Eyes than Cornel MASON's? Was ancient Nineveh, when foes battered her mud-and-iron gates and all the city prayed as one for their survival, less worthy than ours? Why raze their Nineveh of cunning brick, yet rescue ours of aluminum and no less cunning? Why answer this prayer? You did not grant us Earth or Atom, but when the stars drift almost out of reach, You hand them back to us. You turn 'perhaps' to 'yes.' I am grateful, Maker, I . . . It was my prayer You granted as You granted His, a side effect perhaps, but I will thank and praise You for it, every fiber of me, to the end of time, but still I . . . Why *my* prayer? Why drop Him here and now in all of Your Creation? You knew, when You trusted Him to us, to me His guide, when you returned me to Him yesterday, that if He Loved me, Loved Huxley, Loved MASON, then His Friendship's breaking point would be the stars. I want to see them again. The stars. They will be different now, must be different, the lights we nearly lost today. Lights You gave back. I want to see them with this fire inside me knowing it is safe, that You'll rekindle it however grimly great Poseidon looms, or tempting Gaea lures with rest and sweet complacency. That Troy's fall does not make Poseidon win. I want to see Your stepping-stones again. I want to see, Ἄναξ Apollo, Ἄναξ Jehovah, Maker, I want to see again these stars that You, so different from Each Other, can both Love. Both Love and share with us. They must have changed.

"The time is now 19:55. Faustburst in 10 . . . 9 . . . 8 . . . 7 . . . 6 . . . 5 . . . 4 . . . 3 . . . Faustburst commencing."

Three hours' restless silence ended in a burst of pictures, news, and cheers. And doom, too. The starry Gates of Nineveh survive, and Mars, and Luna City, also *Xuánlóng*, Celsius City, the ISSC, but for many in low Earth orbit—for Cloud Six, Babylon, brave Laputa—Achilles-Alexander came too late. That is one doom. The other doom is that images spread. Images of innocent space cities burning are not the ones that capture Earth's imagination. Civilians, soldiers, Pass-It-On, all feast on images of Alexander, those weapons that down fifty targets with one volley, those limbs that hurl whole booster-rocket carcasses into missiles' paths, that armor that baffles harbingers. Armor that is a harbinger itself. And snapshots of the fleeting activation of *Skymaw* confirm to fearful hearts that the betrayal is plural. The Nurturists are right, and henceforth when they say, "Cato Weeksbooth, that rogue harbinger adept, Utopia is using them to fill space with their superweapons," we cannot say no. You have no alibi, Utopia. You cannot plead, "We did not build the Alexander!" not when you have dreamed of building such war robots for four hundred years. Providence did not send a winged, haloed angel to give us back the stars and let all Earth see clearly that our Maker acted here, not us. Providence sent the nightmare of our adversaries' propaganda. Many at Port-Gentil snapped pictures of Eureka with Achilles and the wires in his back, and Pass-It-On rushed their testimony from Atlantic to Pacific. "There it is!" cry all, "a humanoid U-beast! A human brain trapped in a computer, just like the death machine Utopia made of poor Lorelei Cook!" No, they don't all say that. Some heed the good Anonymous who argues, patient, patient, against the fears that geyser still from Operation Baskerville. Some listen. Many, actually, Remakers and Hiveguard both, and Reservationists, and O.S. and their Humanists who, though I call them Caesar's adversaries, held the Summer Games this year in domed Antarctica, and plan in ten brief generations to hold them in Martian Odyssey, a city not yet founded but already built in dreams so many layers deep. They trust Utopia still.

"Caesar?"

There he is upon the screen. Caesar. What time is it? How long have I been writing? Days? The window-screen's false sky shows Night with her innumerable candles clear. Jehovah sleeps beside me. "Caesar, have you . . . ?"

"I looked at the stars," he answers.

"Have they . . . changed?" I find it hard to ask. The change must be subtle, as when you study city lights through window glass, then throw the window open and the bare reality looks different, different crispness, different color, even if bald science tells us that no human eye should see the difference. Perhaps they seem farther away tonight? Or closer? Harder? Colder? Warm?

"They look crisper." He frames his answer carefully, Cornel MASON, the Mountain Emperor of this world, who dreams ever of the rusty mountains of another. "Not closer or farther than before, but more concrete, real things more fixed in space, less like a will-o-wisp to flit away. I spotted two space stations while I was looking, fewer than I'd expect in the time, but still some. And . . ."

"And?" I hold my breath.

"I think I notice the dimmer stars more now, the ones we haven't aimed at yet. Because we will."

You take your distant aim, Ἄναξ, whether Troy falls or no. We will.

Chapter the EIGHTEENTH

Help from Outside

Written starting February 16, 2455
Events of February 16
Alexandria, Casablanca

The old United States of America remind me very much of Terra the Moon Baby. Both were crisis births, sudden necessities when too much damage made healing and homecoming impossible. Each era's genius rose to the occasion, marshalling our newest guesses, how best to nurture human possibility amid such strange new problems. Old wisdom said of each that she would not live long, this birth unplanned, wracked in the womb by strange forces, so, as she survived, each month, each year became hope's small defiance: Look, I stand on my own, and walk, and speak, and feed myself, and now the friends I leaned on in my frailty lean on me as I grow into my strength! As all Earth watched and listened, each fresh act of the toddler helped us plan our own sojourns beyond the old walls of the known and possible. And even in her later years, as one by one her organs failed her—judiciary, liver, senate, heart, all patched together in her infancy by scholar-surgeons who could only guess how this unprecedented body would develop under Earth's long battering—as one by one these failed her, still we learned so much, so much from *how* they failed her as, smiling between her pains, this hope-child gifted us the infinite treasure of understanding what broke down. What killed her. That understanding which is bedrock now of how we *don't* break down as we dare venture farther, out past monarchy, past Moon, these vast *terrae ignotae* on whose thresholds it was so hard to be firstborn.

But we are firstborn too, aren't we? We Hives, the crisis children of the Church War and Carlyle's Compromise, born upon the threshold of borderlessness. So new. By history's long standards new. I feel this thought in the unfamiliar eyes that appear now on the screen before us, quiet in judgment as they gaze on Caesar as an equal. No, not as an equal, for this is Mariame Dembélé, Secretary-General of the United Nations, Standard-Bearer of the Great African Reservation, speaker for the geographic world. She gazes on Caesar as the head of a hospital gazes on a colleague wooed by giddy innovators to test out a new procedure which might work, might revolutionize treatment, first signs are good, but it takes many years to understand lifelong effects, and whether the new method works or no, the old-fashioned one still saves lives daily as we wait to learn whether this particular experiment is part of that slim percentage that succeeds. The Hive Experiment—they call us that, these Reservationers, like the American Experiment, like Terra smiling for reporters who all know no headline will sell like the ones they'll write the day she finally dies. Or do some of them root for us to live? These geographic citizens who hear of *Mukta*'s sparkling promise to weave all Earth into one and say: No, thanks, I worked hard for this land I call my own, and I will keep it. Do they root for the Hive system? As we may root for sports we do not play? Some must. But their system has worked five thousand years, while ours—O.S., the transit system, Black Laws, C.F.B., judiciary, liver, senate, heart; is this the hour they fail?

"No, MASON, you will not enter Casablanca." Secretary-General Dembélé's rejection, so clear and confident, was the first thing to pierce my exhaustion after six days spent pouring into words those strange events through which we lost the Almagest but kept the stars. "You and your allies may continue operations at Tangier and Tripoli, and stay outside the city to guard against interference from the east, but we alone will enter Casablanca, we will find the Cousin leadership, and we will try them for their crimes against humanity, as the United Nations." A pause as strong emotion fed the brightness in her eyes. "Twelve years from now, we would have celebrated the five hundredth anniversary of the *Traité de l'espace* with its core terms still inviolate. We were already planning the ceremony." A brief grim smile, gone. "Those who broke the treaty will stand trial before us, in our own courts, our own justice, and the Hives will not snatch that away."

Five hundred years, a tenth-part of all recorded history, all peoples in this world agreed, reader, that space should hold no harbingers—did we really almost manage to agree on something for five hundred years?

"I want them to stand trial before you." Caesar's voice was warm through the speakers, though his black shape on the screen still made me flinch. "I absolutely agree the Cousins who did this have violated all humanity, you, everyone, in breaking both that treaty—which my Empire too honors—and the Alliance's Second Law which names it an Intolerable Crime to take an action which will do significant and measurable damage to the Produce of Civilization. Nothing could be more fitting than for all the world to see these . . ."—what harsher titles passed through your mind, Caesar, before you settled on—". . . *criminals* . . . tried by the United Nations, the Alliance, and myself, all three together, since this crime crosses the barrier between Hives and geographic nations, and even wounds the ancient works of my Empire." It feels so real sometimes, the old true lie that the Masons predate, not just the Hive Alliance, but the United Nations and its ancestors, the League of Nations, the many Catholic Leagues, even the Delian League which battled Persia before Thucydides invented history. "Taking Casablanca jointly will save lives and time," Caesar continued, "if—"

"No." A pause as Dembélé's answer lagged a moment, patched through by hook and crook and beam from Port-Gentil where the Reservation armies send relief flights spaceward every hour to succor wounded Utopia. "We will take Casablanca ourselves. Your forces will remain outside."

MASON smiled. "Secretary-General, I and all the world cannot thank your people enough for what you did for us, for space, for all humanity. Every soldier in my army will be honored to march into Casablanca alongside yours, or even to follow yours and leave to you the dignity of leading this sovereign action, which I and mine are proud to join."

Here waves the bold banner: *Sovereign Action,* the great rift which has UNGAR and Mason on one side, and the Alliance on the other. When was the phrase born? It is rare in rhetoric of the 2140s as the Church War dwindled toward peace enough for Caracas to host its delayed Olympics. It grew more common in the 2150s as the Hive founders formalized their restrictions on religion. But it was everywhere by the 2170s as the struggling populations outside *Mukta*'s network faced this new Alliance's well-intended invitation: join and prosper. Theocracies were not the only nos, for at the core of the Alliance were these so-called Universal Laws which thrilled some hearts but smacked to others of atrocity. Reader of histories, you know as well as wise Dembélé does that claims of Universal Laws, of Reason and Enlightenment, these have so often brought the worst out of the strongest: first the Age of Empires when European powers raced to enlighten (conquer) and to civilize (enslave) their fellow men, disseminating Nature's so-called Laws by yoke and bullet and the callous claim that it was better to serve in Reason's Heaven than reign on in Tradition's sovereign Hell. But as horrors made *colony* a dirty word, the Age of Empires gave way only to an Age of Excuses, when superpowers learned to rules-lawyer Justice, Democracy, even Freedom and Revolution into pliable excuses to meddle wheresover on the globe they smelled profit, but when less-profitable peoples begged for aid, poisoned by the superpowers' fumes, and lies, and cruel investments, then the powers hid like children in the pillow-fort of their so-modern and so-rational directive not to interfere. Remembering this, as newborn Hives invited nationers, "Join us! We'll help rebuild!" stubborn religion was not the only reason to say no. These powers of Africa had seen too much evil advanced in Reason's name to assent that any list of Laws—Hobbes's or Thomas Carlyle's—can dictate for all times and places when it is and is not right to interfere. *Sovereign Action,* the right of every human polity to decide in its own moment, for its own reasons, with its own principles whether or not to intervene in a neighbor's slice of our shared world, UNGAR claims this, and claims as boldly that our (and any) Universal Laws are sure hypocrisy, if not on the part of the those who draft them, inevitably on the part of the clever successors who will (mis)use them. And we have misused them, our First and Second Laws invoked so broadly—mandating sensayers, advancing Nurturism, banning the words *Imperator Destinatus*—we overreach and underreach as cunningly as any Cold War I-am-not-an-Empire. But MASON's Empire does not lie, or excuse, or rules-lawyer, not now, nor at its inception as a Hive when Antoninus MASON embraced U.N. Chair Bobbie Kuti before

Thomas Carlyle's baffled face and proclaimed, "We too believe the right to Sovereign Action is inalienable. The Black Laws match my current feelings on intervention, but the hour they do not match an Emperor's will, that hour will find your United Nations and my Empire closer in kind than my Empire and any whining Hive." Dembélé's smile remembers that embrace, welcomes that hour's coming. But a frown follows.

"No, MASON, while we do consider you a closer friend than any other Hive Member, this is not about that, or about honor, or reminding the Alliance of our position on Sovereign Action. My soldiers do not trust yours at their backs, not when we fight to put a Hive on trial that has been your longtime ally, and its Chair your longtime personal friend."

"You mean Kosala?" Caesar shook his head. "I would not shield these criminals from anyone. For anything. I want to see them punished more than . . ." He paused, he to whom Apollo is so dear, struggling to pack such passion into the formalities diplomacy demands. ". . . more than any criminal I have seen or could imagine seeing, more than Mycroft Canner, more than Merion Kraye, more than those who seek to kill my only child, and while, as I am Emperor, the violation of my *Sanctum Sanctorum* stands archcrime and alone awakes the apex of my Capital Powers, still that part of me which is a human being recognizes this attack upon the Moon and Mars and Nineveh was worse. I will spare none responsible, not if my dearest friend or ba'sib proved complicit. Or do you fear I would exclude you from the trial? I will not, you have my word."

Pursed lips. "We cannot trust you, MASON. We have seen you break your word too much."

"When did I break my word?" Caesar challenged.

"Often."

"When?"

"This week, as recently as Monday."

"How?"

Dembélé's frown was hard to interpret, her whole poise illegible, mainly because of her clothing, robes of state of an unfamiliar land, their meaning lost on me, their bright colors invoking childhood and Nurturism and Mitsubishi seasons, all of which I know are wrong. "You broke your oath to O.S.," she answered.

"To O.S.?" MASON's frowns are easy reading—this one was confusion.

Dembélé nodded. "You pledged, if they helped you get Achilles to our elevator, you would let those who revealed themselves to help go free."

"And so I did. All who revealed themselves walk free, and those of my people who had means to trace them have been ordered to destroy such means. Or do you mean Tully Mardi? I gave no promise to release one who was already my captive."

Dembélé hesitated, reluctant perhaps to accuse so old an ally, but it was a fleeting hesitation, as when the knife is held back by no pity, just the need to aim. "I mean Eureka Weeksbooth. We have Robin Typer here, they saw your

Blacksleeves strike and take Eureka the instant they left our protection. Typer barely escaped themself."

Caesar took a slow breath. "I did not do this."

"You were seen, your agents seen."

It was not anger that stirred in Caesar through these two slow breaths, it was calculation, the old, hard question: how can honesty be proved? "I had twelve of Casimir Perry's co-conspirators murdered after the Brussels attack, including the two who killed Crown Prince Leonor Valentin."

Dembélé squinted. "What?"

"I doctored Mycroft Canner's history," Cornel MASON continued, "to conceal how much I helped Joyce Faust D'Arouet rise to power, and how many of their crimes I was complicit in concealing. I have four times had associates of Andō or other Mitsubishi Directors detained and interrogated, violating Mitsubishi law. I persuaded you to help me launch Achilles Mojave into space while concealing from you the fact that Achilles is themself an advanced war technology, an essential component of the Alexander armor which is undeniably a harbinger, thus I personally violated your *Traité de l'espace.* In my own estimation, I have broken the terms of my Oath of Office nine times in the twenty-three years, six months, and fifteen days since I became MASON, and on November eleventh 2436, I broke my own law and the First Law and let slip to Charlemagne Guildbreaker and Cinna Semaphoros a hint about my plans for the *Imperator Destinatus.* These things I did, and stand accountable for them before law, conscience, and posterity, but I did not betray and capture Eureka Weeksbooth."

For several ticking seconds, no one breathed. Then a strong if somber smile woke like hearth warmth in Dembélé's face. "I believe you." A sharp, affirming breath. "We will take Casablanca together."

"Thank you." MASON bowed his head, a rare gesture for him, solid, like the whole crown of a treetop swaying with some shifting of the earth that foretells change.

So it is agreed. Twin orders from these twin commanders fly by beam and cable, and soon invasion's smoke sours the wind-tossed rainbow kite roofs of the Cousin capital. The map wall behind Caesar shows the columns on the march, UNGAR from the south, real soldiers fired with patriots' passion and long experience, while from the east, inexorable as glacier fingers bringing a warm age to its end, the Masons rumble, as they rumbled days ago through Benghazi, through Tripoli, through Tunis where again the ghosts of Carthage witness in action the same imperial will that once drove Rome seek out those it must destroy. Or . . . no, the map wall shows the violet lines of Masonic forces driving due west from Tripoli, bypassing Tunis and the crest of Africa. «Why . . . ?»

«Are you awake?» This Greek came from my successor, who sat against the wall beside me, working as I curled in sleep.

«Tunis . . . we went around?» I asked.

«Yes.»

«But it's a Cousin center, at our backs . . . »

A sympathetic frown. «We don't have the forces to spare after the Tripoli disaster.»

«Tripoli?»

My successor stared, then laughed. «You really haven't registered a thing, have you? Do you know what day it is?»

«Is it Tues . . . ? Thurs . . . ? No?»

Dearer than gold, that smile as my successor watched me struggle, taking joy in seeing a dear one be so raensomely myself. Me, reader, a human being smiles that way for *me*. Our true beliefs, I think, are not revealed in what our intellect affirms, not in recited affirmations or what we assent to at the cold conclusion of the syllogisms' chain; rather, our true beliefs are visible in what pokes above the psyche's surface in those moments when the overflowing heart sings out in gratitude, and then we learn what name it calls: Nature, Humanity, Reason, God, Gaea, Fate, subtle Prometheus, or Providence that takes so much but gives *this*. Thank you.

«It's Sunday again.» My successor smirked. «It's been a week. You've been a wreck. It's alright, we held the fort.» A reassuring smile tried to calm my guilt-gasp. «Well, we didn't literally hold this fort, nobody attacked us here.»

A week? I looked around: the cell, the bright false window, Chagatai exercising, MASON's bustling war room on the wall screen, and Ἄναξ Jehovah at the table near us, reading (I craned my neck to see) Simone Weil. «Ow!» I banged my head. On what? Between us: «Bars?»

Delight's laugh. «You really didn't notice? There were welders!» My successor tapped the bars which boxed in a seven-foot cube around me. «The cage is part of MASON and the Prince's compromise, to settle their fight about having you hobbled.»

I did have a hazy memory of people, loud equipment, Chagatai interrupting my work to show me the tidy little piss pot in the corner. Even the Cannergel which bound my wrists—in front now, not behind—gave me a hair more slack. Thank you, kind Emperor, and kinder Master Who pled for me.

That Master saw me stir, I think, though as His void-soft black eyes fell on me in the very instant that my heart sang out in thanks, it felt as if He'd finally gained that longed-for extra sense—to feel our prayers—which a kind Host would have given Him. But Ours did not.

⌜"«Yet He gifted Me friendship's continuation's possibility.»"⌟ Jehovah's voice sent shivers through me, His mixing languages, His old habit of answering my thoughts—read from my face—when I had spoken nothing. ⌜"«And He sustained for [you plural] [the/a] long, perilous path.»"⌟

⌜"«¿You mean space?»"⌟ I smiled. ⌜"«I'm grateful that He did. I did not know I had so much capacity in me for gratitude—for anything—as I felt in that moment when You asked, and my Maker answered.»"⌟

He stared. He spoke: ⌜"«Guilt's sorrow gnaws Me for the suffering whose prolongation I enabled, nay, requested, nay, request, yet I would not un-act nor un-say that done and said.»"⌟

⌜"«¿Guilt?»"⌟ I repeated. ⌜"«¿Over asking Him to spare Utopia? Ἄναξ, nothing should be farther from You than guilt. ¡You saved everything! ¡Our future! ¡Hope! ¡The labors of a hundred thousand years!»"⌟

⌜"«My Will [launched/launches] the path of war and suffering.»"⌟ He left the tense unclear.

⌜"«No, Ἄναξ, Your Peer launched all this, and continues it. You only made it kinder.»"⌟

He paused, His living universe at work outside of Time, and I remember wondering if more effort grinds on in each of His long pauses than in all of our collective human history. "I did not end the trunk-war, since which distortion Tripoli nearly archgriefed and sempiternized." Most of this statement was arguably English, but He forced the language so to its breaking point that I struggled.

"What?"

"The trunk-war persists to Tripoli." He could do no better.

I turned to my successor. «What happened at Tripoli?»

A dark wince. «Everything. Everything Achilles has been afraid of: confusion, friendly fire, troops panicking, running from nothing, firing on civilians, freaking out. Huge chunks of the city burned. It was our force's first time facing real guerilla tactics, the way the city fought back, nasty, dirty, they weren't prepared. There was a massacre. *Our side* did the massacring, a panic mistake, thinking people were fighting back in an area that had already surrendered. There were seventy deaths before we stopped it, but it nearly had more digits than that. But we have some new heroes as a consequence!»—the cheer in these words felt forced—«the few who kept their heads and calmed the others down. We're promoting them, sending them on to Casablanca, hoping we can avoid . . . more . . . »

Massacre. I had been prepared for this, since Mardi days in childhood when Jie and Makenna made us rewrite our textbooks with *we*—not they—*the human we* as the subject of every verb of violence or atrocity. But it still stabbed. «That means Achilles was succeeding,» I said, «spotting soldiers' breaking points before they broke. Making a better war. Where is Achilles?»

«Still in orbit.» My successor's eyes avoided mine. «Landing's too risky while we don't have our own elevator to get them up again. No one else can defend up there if there's another attack. We still have intermittent contact when the Alexander's orbit passes over.»

My head felt blurry—is it still real, then? Alexander, this intrusion which will make our future textbooks lie and claim that in 2455, humanity invented such an engine, and such alloys, and such weapons? And is it trapped in orbit lest war threaten helpless space anew? I thought of the Utopian salutes, the Moon, and Mars, and spheres past Mars, and hearts that break anew each time those further worlds require us to let the first sphere—mother Terra—burn.

⌜"«I do not know how to commemorate archgrief.»"⌟ Jehovah's languages commixed again, that homelike freedom which only my company gives Him. ⌜"«I wore black already.»"⌟

I smiled, realizing He did indeed have prison clothes of mourning black, another kindness Caesar granted to his Captive-Son. ⌜"«No one knows what to do after atrocities.»"⌟ I answered. ⌜"«No one's ever really known, it causes shock. Bodies know what to do, to cry and scream and pour it out, but not our brains, brains get frozen, or get stubborn, or . . . »"⌟ I trailed off as I recognized my folly. ⌜"«But You, Ἄναξ, are neither brain nor body.»"⌟

⌜"«Even in peacetime, the unforgivableness of life-which-can-die's atrocity background noise was already infinite.»"⌟

I thought of all the subtle mechanisms brains have to distract ourselves from that. ⌜"«We're six months in, Ἄναξ, it's still a great achievement that we put off this kind of disaster so long.»"⌟

⌜"«The harbingers re-bloom [now/soon], yet I do not end the trunk-war.»"⌟

I choked, thinking how hard I wish *I* could will harbingers away, and how much harder He must wish the same. 'Trunk-war' was a good name for it, that larger structure of the fractal, Hiveguard on Remaker, from which these smaller battles sprout like twigs. ⌜"«No one has used harbingers on Earth yet,»"⌟ I answered, smiling half sincerely. ⌜"«The space stations we lost, the risk to Mars and Nineveh and Luna City, the horror of all that, that should help prevent the use of harbingers, make people think twice about how much we stand to lose before . . . What's that?»"⌟

New photos flicked up on the war room screens, a port seen from above, strong ocean waves, and figures marching other figures onto boats, five here, eight there, picking them out from little huddled crowds like cattle.

«Borneo,» my successor answered, and told me quickly—as the war room bustled and the evermourning Stranger listened on—of the other aftermaths which twigged out from the trunk-war now to punish those Earth blames. Before we woke the Alexander, Director Andō's Homeland Mitsubishi faction had moved on Borneo's Princess Laila Menchanai elevator to try to stop the missiles. When the missiles stopped, they didn't, two days' assault and Andō's colors flew on Terra's oldest spacepath. But that elevator is a string of separate platforms farther apart than capitals of empires, so Homeland is still at it, climbing platform to platform as some surrender quickly, others resist. And what Utopia's stations glimpse of the Americas shows much the same: Admiral Quarriman's fleet massed by the Esmeraldas elevator base, and Humanist colors climbing the platforms one by one. It's all so mixed. Gratitude streams in from low Earth orbit, floundering space stations saved by Hiveguard and Mitsubishi aid as much as by UNGAR's. But now the Horus Eye is back online and shares these images from Borneo of Mitsubishi doling out peacewashed to every Homeland ship, five here, eight there, like captives handed out as prizes by Troy's conquerors. Only some are Cousins. It's become the practice to label 'peacewashed' not just staining the hands but marking one cheek, *C* for Cousins, the Square and Compasses for Masons, a childlike doodle sun for captured Delians, as my successor put it, "so people know which prisoners to treat gently and which like shit." (Did you anticipate that, too, Tully my Enemy, in your long years of calculations on the patient Moon?) Blame has so many flavors. Even though Mitsubishi launched the attack upon the Almagest, somehow all blame has settled on the Cousins and Utopia, and very different blames. Utopia—whose only crime is building (or, in Alexander's case, dreaming) the means for self-defense—people discuss like bees who, just by having stings, merit a call to the exterminator, while the Cousins—who fired first! and nearly cost us centuries! and worlds!—they treat like children who played too roughly with a toy and injured someone, so now it's time to take the toy away. Even MASON speaks thus in his way, the true subtext of words which my successor replayed for me, MASON's order as he sent his armies west across the crest of Africa: "If Casablanca steers its slice of human power toward such destruction, then it may steer no longer. Take the capital. Take everything the Cousins hold from here to the Atlantic. Take it all." And that is what we see now on the war room screens, almost in real time, troops plunging along Casablanca's once-charming boulevards with the efficiency of careful planning.

⌜"«Because I did not end the trunk-war, did not lop the long pain branch.»"⌟

I smiled as warmly as I could. ⌜"«You can't end it alone.»"⌟

⌜"«I can and could have but did not.»"⌟

⌜"«You did something more important, Ἄναξ, the most important thing, keeping the path open.»"⌟

⌜"«Selfishly, to [clutch/protect/keep/hoard] My chance at Friendship. And for [you plural].»"⌟

⌜"«¡Exactly!»"⌟ I almost shouted. ⌜"«¡You did it for us! Providence bent for *us* on your behalf, Ἄναξ, because You care too much about the ants to call 'Friend' One who kicks the anthill down. That isn't selfishness, it's kindness crossing unfathomable barriers of difference, and scale, and kind. You know how long humans struggled to expand our empathy even to grant rights to all members of our own species, and those few animals most like ourselves, with friends and faces. We can't even get it together to include the octopus, because we find it gross and alien, but the octopus is as close to humans as a fraternal twin compared to the differences between us and You, and still Your Heart nearly rejected the only other member of Your Species because He threatened to kick our anthill down. That is not selfishness, it's . . . it's beyond what we . . . beyond any . . . »"⌟ I struggled, even with seven languages, to do better than "Love. Love beyond love."

He gazed on me in silence, digesting my words in that dark, distant Infinity which is at once His Mind, His Creation, His Home, His Dominion, His Birthplace, His true Body, and His all-ingesting Maw. Some who study this Alien we call Jehovah have compared Him to the octopus: a species so intelligent, so alien, which lives its strange life, rich in craft and contemplation, but alone, aloof from culture, contact, indifferent to any fellow of its species—the trait which perennially keeps the octopus from passing our law's tests for Minor's status, since the law's old precedent requires that a species (A) exchange and pass down culture, and (B) mourn its dead. And yet, unlike the isolated and unlonely octopus, this Alien does not choose His solitude—rather, glimpsing the faintest shadow of His Fellow through the murk and blood, He chases after, come pain or perdition, so starved is He for culture's equal play of like with like. And He Mourns our dead.

⌜"«Love, yes, »"⌟ He answered. ⌜"«But also I think this now teaches Me new things, aversion, or unwelcome. ¿Is this aversion? unwelcome? that which I feel about the long pain branch? I do not understand it, why He crafts it, why He makes the road so hard, the stepping-stones so far. ¿Is this in Me which wants to Will it otherwise the thing you call aversion? ¿And a twin aversion or unwelcome this My second feeling at the thought of seeing lopped that thing which [you plural] so many, so much, so long love?»"⌟ Small-L for us; we finite things we *are,* we *fear,* we *love,* even a path we've walked a hundred thousand years we love only with mortal, mayfly love, while He in His eternity, He Loves.

My successor spoke up in English now so our ever-listening guards could understand. "I should head back to command. I should be on the line when my team reaches the C.F.B."

"The C.F.B.?" I looked to the war screens.

"Right, you didn't hear my report!" The syllables resounded with triumph. «I have a theory! Plan. Theory-to-plan plan. I finally had time to go through Papadelias's data, the drop they sent us through that first Faustburst when we were on the roof in Romanova. We know now what happened to the people in the cars that disappeared on the way back from the Olympics. They're alive."

"Wonderful!" I cried. Papa had spoken of this during the Faustburst, but that rooftop in Romanova—not yet three weeks ago—felt like another lifetime. "Papa said it was the Cousins?"

"Yes. There are internment camps, automated ones tucked deep in the wilderness. That's where Papa was, where we think everyone is who disappeared in the cars that first day. Papa was riding home like normal when the car changed course and landed at the camp. Papa describes it like a little prefab village tucked in the mountains, beautiful like a resort, all fresh air and stone, with little round hut-houses prepped with beds, clothes, tools, plus fields laid out for planting, seed packets, a well, and a central building with a group kitchen, food, a big digital library, even a piano, and around it all a perimeter of laser fences and sensors, with motion-activated turrets that shot stun shots, and robots to drag would-be escapees back inside."

"Tully Mardi?" I guessed.

"No, not one of their designs, and this was long before they published them. Papa describes a kind of cheerful recorded welcome voice that played when everybody got there, calling it a 'sequestration village.' It said a system had been created to identify people with unstable or violent tendencies, the people most likely to be overwhelmed by violence when the fighting started and to crack and commit deeds they would regret."

⌜"«Prophesying and aborting archgriefs,»"⌟ translated He Who ever sees the larger fractal.

My successor struggled with that a moment but nodded. "The voice urged them to farm instead, saying they could help the world by keeping out of the combat and helping grow food, which the robots would export to hospitals and refugee spots. Papa says people settled into it so fast, it was almost creepy, that after just a couple failed escape attempts, the vacation-resort beauty of the place was addictive, the exercise of working, weeding, watching dawn's rays turn the Himalayan snowcaps into gold, and with that cheerful voice playing quotations like 'each seedling that pokes above the soil is a better day's work than a dead enemy.'"

"That sounds like Sofia Kovács," I guessed.

"Close, it's de Vasconcelo, Kovács's successor, the second Cousin Chair."

Uncertainty's departure felt healing. "Cousins indeed."

"Exactly. Smart money says there are hundreds of these sequestration villages around the globe, the Cousins' plan to peacebond the most violent portion of the population, just like Utopia peacebound the harbinger adepts. Papa said after the initial grumbling, most of their fellow captives were relieved to discover they didn't have to raise a sword, happy to take up plowshares."

It made sense—months of war-prep by a billion Cousins must weave deeper than just stocking hospitals. "How did Papa get out?"

A proud smile. "Papadelias *is* Romanova, resort temptations can't trump that. A bunch of fellow-prisoners immediately pledged to help get Papa out, and serve as deputies as long as Papa needed them. Twenty-six escape attempts failed, that's why Papa didn't reach Dhaka until December, but one of the other captives was pregnant, so when the birth approached, the Cousins sent a real live doctor to the camp to oversee things. Papa's people were prepared to jump the doc and force a hostage situation if need be, but when the doctor recognized the Commissioner General of the Alliance, they immediately said Papa's presence must be a mistake, and escorted Papa and their deputies all the way to Dhaka."

It warmed me, hearing that the Alliance flag still commands hearts—our Hive Experiment is not quite ended. "Did the doctor confirm the Cousins made the camps?" I asked.

"No, but Papa said the doctor didn't have a good poker face."

One trusts the face-reader who captured Mycroft Canner.

"So, my theory," my proud successor carried on, "is this: if the Cousins made a program to identify potentially violent people and use the cars to sequester them, they must have put the program, or at least its final list, into the Saneer-Weeksbooth computers. And if that's the case, they likely tested the program on similar computers, specifically the C.F.B. system computers, since they're the closest thing the Cousins have."

I looked to the screen, recognizing in one feed the pink-walled corner cafe where—eleven months and an aeon ago—reporters had cornered Hiroaki Mitsubishi to ask about C.F.B. Chief Darcy Sok, accused by Masami Mitsubishi's Seven-Ten List of ruling the Cousins through the subtle algorithms that process Terra's great suggestion box. Now soldiers peeped through shattered windows.

«Caesar is letting you direct those troops?» I asked, switching to Greek in case my successors' answer contained something our guards should not know.

«The tech and planning end, not the field end. If they can get in and hook a cable to the system, we're hoping Su-Hyeon and I can confirm if the Cousins really did have and test such a program, and maybe we can get a list of where the other camps are, and maybe, maybe we can find out why they included Papadelias. That can't have been a violence-predicting algorithm.»

I tried to recall Papa's questions during that first Faustburst, their urgent request that the Censor list the other high-profile people who'd vanished in the cars: some Mitsubishi associates, MASON's ba'sib Caerul Semaphoros, some Cousins too, close allies of Kosala. «If the cars took Kosala's allies, perhaps this was part of the Nurturist coup?» I asked. «Lorelei Cook?»

«Maybe.» My successor shivered. «But was Lorelei Cook already back then ... were they already whatever that was that killed Duke Ganymede?"»

⌜"«Mariscal,»"⌟ the Prince D'Arouet corrected, giving His strange but glorious late elder ba'sib his strange but glorious due. ⌜"«No.»"⌟

⌜"«¿You're certain, Ἄναξ?»"⌟ I asked.

⌜"«Three sunsets after the Olympics, I perceived and parleyed with Minister Cook, who was then not yet that Baskerville successor which excelled the earlier in impact, [heart/soul]'s terror, and by far in that [household/economic] thrift which microhinders entropy.»"⌟

My successor and I traded glances as I struggled with the density of words.

"[Anonymous] to the War Room. [Anonymous] to the War Room," called a thin and processed voice from the wall console.

My successor rose, looking at the screen, where snapshots showed our Blacksleeves booting down the back door of the C.F.B. itself. "I'd better go."

I nodded, still lost in Jehovah's words. ⌜"«Baskerville successor ... You're right, Ἄναξ, Cook's death had the same effect as Operation Baskerville. Enhanced the same effect.»"⌟

⌜"«The long pain branch's adversaries employ flight's absence to reteach Distance's torture-pain long veiled by [artifice/technology]. ¿Do I help you choose evil?»"⌟

I froze. ⌜"«¿What? Ἄναξ . . . »"⌟

⌜"«I know captivity [expands/perpetuates] perspectival misprision. Here enveloped by one coalition, I see My *Pater* [i.e., MASON], My Huxley, My [Anonymous], My you, even My *Chichi-ue* [i.e., Andō] and My assassinator [Ojiro Sniper] hold the long pain branch more precious than your own lives and millifold accumulated lives' legacies, yet the long pain branch—which [you plural] choose and which I help [you plural] keep un-lopped—is not [free-from-toil], [free-from-pain], [free-from-evil]. Thus it appears, in helping [you plural] choose it, I help [you plural] choose evil. [However/simultaneously], these crowds, who [rage/cry] against the long pain branch exposed to their understanding by this war-span's first, and second, and third, and fourth Baskerville actions, such crowds are, though unknown to Me by conversation-love, as real and perhaps more numerous than [you plural] and no less love-worthy, yet their grief and preference of branch I bypass upholding [yours plural], disenfranchising their billion voices as I urge the Plan's shape, much as—if it were real—that imagined artifact which the inward branch partisans lie about implanting in Minister Cook could disenfranchise ten billion neurons screaming all together 'no.'»"⌋

This blast of words felt like standing under a waterfall, hammering on me both healing and harsh, while my poor successor stood captive by the cell door, one hand hovering over the exit request button, pinned by the verbal glimpse that comes from understanding three-sevenths of Jehovah's tongues. «Did They say third and fourth Baskerville actions?»

⌜"«By which process the inward branch's partisans [advertise/expose] the [cruelty/evil] of the long pain branch.»"⌋ Our Maker's Peer plunged on. ⌜"«Unfulfillment's pain, ambition's denial's pain, fruitlessness's pain, the climber's pain who tumbles back to Earth are different from the climber's limbs' pain, wound pain, toil's pain; the pain of mourning wishes different from the pain of mourning friends. But when a week ago I prolonged the trunk-war, warning My Peer with threat of Friendship's death to restrain His Hand which raised His human tools to lop the long pain branch, even as I Acted, I still unwelcomed, unwelcome, will ever unwelcome the limb pain, wound pain, toil pain which I chose to prolong. Absolutely I did never and would never enseed such pain, but I actualized it, germinated it, demanded it, chose it in order to safeguard that thing inside of Me which would have perished watching [you plural] who are near Me mourn this wish so compound and so old. My Act Changed this cosmos. I chose between your pains and helped you choose, I fear, the greater evil.»"⌋

My successor stared. «What did they say, Mycroft? Mycroft?»

I took my time translating the too-dense phrases, as He Who Speaks and Visits studied me, patience an easy virtue for One alien to Time. By the time I finished translating, I had my question: ⌜"«Ἄναξ, ¿do You think this prolonged the war? ¿That it would have ended sooner if You hadn't asked your Peer to intervene for Nineveh and Mars?»"⌋

⌜"«The trunk-war, yes.»"⌋

I tried to see the chain of dominoes He saw: Utopia's despair, Caesar in greater and more broken rage, that would indeed have changed the war's shape greatly, but I could not see how losing our path to Mars could bring a faster peace to Mitsubishi factions, dissolve the fleets that circled the Americas, or tip hearts between Hiveguard and Remaker. ⌜"«No, Ἄναξ. A short war where we lose the Moon and Mars, our toeholds in the future, that's not a better war, even if in its way it might be kinder.»"⌋

No pause before His answer: ⌜"«My Mycroft says that as a long pain branch partisan.»"⌋

⌜"«¿You think I want a long war?»"⌋ I asked, fearing perhaps that something deep inside me did revel in war, as war-starved Achilles comes alive on battlefields.

⌜"«No, you want the long pain branch.»"⌟

I sensed misunderstanding. ⌜"«Wait, Ἄναξ, by 'long pain branch,' ¿do you mean a longer war? ¿Or something else?»"⌟

⌜"«Elsetimes you name the same Apollo, light, flagship, the Great Project, the ancient spark that has died out a thousand times but never yet in every breast at once,»"⌟ —now pure Latin—"*per aspera ad astra.*"

⌜"«'The long pain path',»"⌟ —I trembled, thinking of my tears spilled on Poseidon's seas—⌜"«it is that too, Ἄναξ. I understand. But then . . . »"⌟ I thought back through His earlier words, ⌜"« . . . the crowds which cry out against the long pain path because of Operation Baskerville, you mean Utopia's enemies, the Nurturists, the waves of blame.»"⌟

⌜"«The rival branch,»"⌟ He answered, patient as a teacher. ⌜"«A trunk-war ends with lopping.»"⌟

"[Anonymous] to the War Room. [Anonymous] to the War Room," blared the console. *"Your unit is requesting immediate instructions."*

My successor winced up at the screen, where blurs and diagrams traced infiltration's stages. "Just quickly, Prince, did you say 'four Baskerville actions'?"

⌜"«And five, and six against Utopia—but *Pater* calls, ¿do you have time to listen to Me count?»"⌟

My successor turned to me, «Did They just say six Baskerville actions against Utopia?»

"«Yes. Ἄναξ, ¿what do You mean by 'six actions'? And try for [Anonymous]'s sake to use just Greek, Spanish, and English. The fake U-beast attacks were first, what—»"

"«Not first.»"

"«¿Then what was first?»" I asked.

"«The oldest I have found is Enkidu entreating Gilgamesh not to seek the Cedar Forest of Humbaba.»"

I had to laugh. "«I meant in this conflict, Ἄναξ, this past year or so, this human lifetime.»"

A long, deep-scraping pause as He compressed His thoughts into only three tongues. "«In this contiguous conflict, I nominate the publication of your history, that chapter which you named 'The Room Where Mycroft Canner Died.' In late drafts, you excised your reference to the war arts Mother and *Pater* found hidden in Apollo Mojave's captured armor [i.e., coat], but in the version that touched the public, someone restored it.»"

«You mean . . . I thought it was You who had that added back!» My successor and I gaped at each other as we realized we had not tracked carefully which of the many powers who in turn censored our text had ordered what.

"«Second,»" He continued, "«peacebonding the harbingers was, I think, Utopia's brainchild, but the furor nurtured from that act by media artifice was designed to swell to something like the Atlantis Strike. Third follow those false U-beast attacks which inspired the Baskerville label and targeted only those isolated homesteads which preclude travel, so that, even if some eyewitness pierced the deception, none could disseminate truth once the hard-planned silence fell. Other steps less visible I cannot list, but as a fifth I nominate Minister Cook's death which fires all Nurturists to action-frenzy, and makes Utopia seem to have broken its promise not to craft creatures too human. And sixth they spread these images of *Skymaw* and the Alexander, locking in their adversaries' fear. Perhaps you argue the attack on Mars and on the spark should itself be numbered sixth, but that attempted lopping strike was [fruit-of-terror], not a terror seed, an end, not means, thus not a Baskerville.»"

"«Propaganda,»" I paraphrased, "«waves of propaganda targeting Utopia . . . »"

«Who's doing it?» my successor asked. «Why?»

"«To conquer with less death. *Onkel* does not tolerate the waste of irreplaceable human specimens, particularly those who, carefully pruned, may still grow toward disarming Death.»"

"Uncle?" The German cognate was close enough for my successor to catch. «Wait, are we talking about Felix Faust?»

"«A trunk-war ends with lopping, the long pain branch or *Onkel*'s.»"

Branch, trunk, old words, my words, His words from long ago came back to me: 'Which branch will be the trunk.' "«¡The competition of the Brillists and Utopia!»" I cried. "«Ἄναξ, ¿is that what You mean by trunk-war?»"

"Yes."

I smiled as I realized I'd misunderstood. He had not been speaking of the larger fractal shaping all, but of the little sidelined war of Gordian on . . . wait . . . "«Psychology . . . Propaganda is Gordian's warcraft. ¿Did Gordian do . . . how much?»"

My successor's face mirrored my shock-fear. «Huxley said the Gordian-Utopia conflict was paused, that they're allies so long as both need Remaker victory.»

My mind's eye showed me Huxley's storm-grim face back on harbinger day, offering Felix Faust a handshake and the invitation, 'War?' "Faust said they would 'squirm out of it,'" I quoted.

"*Onkel* lies."

I froze, Faust's face before me, a hundred memories of Earth's Great Voyeur joking, smiling, clowning—or playing the clown.

«Mycroft!» my successor cried, «the Cookie bombing! Huxley said the Brillist Institute could have made that implant bomb that was in Cookie, the Institute's brain-machine interface experiments, they're crude but they could, they . . . and the document that circulated, Cookie's supposed last thoughts, it was perfect propaganda, perfect to fire up the Nurturists against Utopia as well as set-sets, just what the Brillists want!» Enthusiasm made my successor forget that long bursts of modern Greek are a struggle for our Guest trained on Ancient. «And revealing the weapons in Apollo's coat! And Operation Baskerville! It was so Brillisty! A global mind game, show some scary monster faces in the corners of the Earth and make everyone think Utopia's attacking just before the silence falls. Wait, then, are they behind the silence, too? The timing was too perfect, the monsters and the silence like clockwork, it had to be one plan, all Gordian!

It makes sense! It's the first explanation that's ever made sense! But . . . jamming so much, every technology we have, worldwide, and the interceptor robots, and our Faustbursts, shooting down the satellites, they'd have to have weapons in space for that, are they in . . . Yes! They *are* in space! Mycroft, the images going around of *Skymaw* and the Alexander, the angles, they had to be taken from space!»

"[Anonymous] to the War Room! [Anonymous] to the War Room!" The console's pleas could have been a world away.

«Then the Cousins are innocent!» My successor's breaths were growing sharp. «Mycroft, this means the Cousins are innocent! Not only Bryar, all of them!»

I didn't follow. «What?»

«The space attack! Bryar can't find anyone who can say who among the Cousins actually gave the order to fire. We assumed it was the Nurturists in Casablanca, but what if it was Gordian! Gordian's propaganda pushed the Nurturists into power, scared them with the 'Utopian set-set' slur so they'd build and mount the missiles on the elevators, then Gordian infiltrated and pulled the trigger the instant we lost the Almagest. It makes more sense! Think of the choice of targets. Cousins play pure defense, they'd go for weapons, near-Earth targets, maybe Luna City if a really paranoid Nurturist had it in their head that it had harbinger adepts, but the Mars base and Nineveh are no threat to anything, there's no reason Cousins would target them. It wasn't Nurturists being hatemongering extremists, it was all Gordian! They haven't been inactive after all, they just— Shit!» My successor slammed a fist against the cell door. «I should have seen this coming! Back in Romanova, Gordian kept ostentatiously surrendering, making a big show of being harmless, doing nothing. It was all a performance! And our accidental coup! Im-Jin's a Brillist, Im-Jin locked up Bo and Desi! That was planned! Mycroft, I helped Gordian mount a coup in Romanova!»

I felt a chill. «Perhaps. Charlemagne Guildbreaker is still there too, but . . . perhaps.»

My successor was shaking. «Jamming the whole planet, that much technology, that's how they must have spent their lead-up months, while Bryar was stocking hospitals and MASON building—»

«Years,» our timeless Guest corrected gently.

«Years?» my successor repeated. «It's only been eleven months since . . . Wait! Mycroft! Gordian anticipated this, *before* the revelation of O.S.! How long before?»

I almost laughed, but hate those sour laughs that soil the act of laughing. «The Mardi bash' anticipated war more than twenty years ago, and rare was the day that Mercer Mardi didn't visit Ingolstadt.» I turned. «Ἄναξ . . . » I froze, not certain yet what I should ask. It felt like I was gazing at a sunny channel, where the sea grows narrow and the seaman strains to peer beneath the choppy surface to make out the deadly shapes of hidden rocks, when suddenly, just halfway through the strait, the eye realizes that the contours connect: a curve, a bulk, an eye, a vast and watching monster too near to evade. "«Ἄναξ, You called the attack on what we had in space a 'lopping strike.' You meant that it aimed to lop the rival branch, ¿didn't you? To cut off the path to space, Utopia's branch, Utopia's future. That was all on purpose, that . . . »" I shivered at the very memory of the all-snuffing despair that had filled me as missiles arced across the screen's black, threatening to knock us too far back along the path for hope's faint flicker to endure. They tried to burn *that* Troy. «¿Gordian planned that? Human beings planned and did that, ¿purposely?»"

「Of course.」 He used a strong 'of course' from Japanese, an affirmation reaching deep into the fabric of the world, confirming all could be no other way. 「"«Utopia goes out, Gordian goes in.»"」 He aimed one pointing finger upward toward the ceiling and the skies beyond, the other toward my skull. 「"«Uncle misdoubts which branch I will choose, so attempted this preemptive lopping.»"」

I thought of Gordian's first surrender, the Child Jehovah in His uncle's lap, articulating for the first time our choice of frontiers, inward or outward, to burrow deeper down into the knotted depths within the brain and there unlock potential future humans, future minds, as far beyond us as Eureka beyond caveman; or outward to the stars. Not both—one branch will be the trunk.

Why not both, Mycroft?

A week ago, I could not have answered you, reader, but now I think I can. The light is almost out. Space is too terrible, and Earth too good, not only space too hard but Earth too good, the gifts of Nature, more, for we have spent this hundred thousand years not only building boats and braving seas but tilling fields and planting cities, cultivating Earth's great human garden. Even in the Exponential Age, when we wounded Mother Gaea with our garbage and our growth, we coaxed her back to health. Perhaps with Master Hobbes still there beside you, you imagine struggles are a constant of humanity's condition, but our ancestors worked hard to make a better future for their children, and it worked. Life now is good. Not just for most, for all of us, such health, such plenty. And every year, as art and gardens prosper, we make this rich blue world that much harder to leave. Since we don't have to. Not even to find our next frontier. Gordian has its own infinity which will not make us brave an airless sea, or weep upon a rock alone. Ever. They bypass grim Poseidon, leave the god who rings the Earth to stand mote-keeper of his black kingdom alone, and chance not to his mercy. Their branch is warm and easy, happy, without *aspera*, their frontier the Institute's own motto *Profundum et Fundamentum*, the boundless deep and foundation: the mind. As progress husbanded by Gordian's genius makes Earth yet happier, as these mind-trawlers dredge up treasure after treasure from a sea sailed in an armchair in the bosom of our friends, the souls ready to sweat as oarsmen on Apollo's ships grow few. I don't believe Utopia planned the war, don't believe Apollo bade his brother Ares rise from Aphrodite's lap on purpose to make Earth worse, but they do *need* it. Need sweet Terra to be easier to say goodbye to. And I do think they know—have known since second-choice

Mushi went off to Mars and trembling Apollo wounded Caesar—that this war would be their last chance. Not every age in human history has hungered for the stars, and what one age desires, the next may not. Some dreams dwindle. If coming generations are as much happier than mine as mine is happier than Jin Im-Jin's, Brill's, Hobbes's, Cicero's, then humanity's imagination may move on, ambition thrill to Gordian's anthem, and Utopia—already smallest, dolphin among the great Leviathans—shrink to a minnow. And there will be less pain. And there are black eyes staring at me, and beyond those eyes a Being Who Rejects our pain, Who Loves us all so much that He Rejects nothing in any universe but the intolerable fact of suffering and wants to end it, wants it more than any creature has ever wanted anything, for He is no creature—*creatus*, a created thing—He is *Creator*, infinite, vaster than the accumulated cry of every human who has ever cried out any form of *stop! help! please! it hurts! too much! no more! spare us! spare me! spare brick-proud Nineveh!* And This living and infinite Kindness, He will decide, He, His the choice between the happy branch *in profundum et fundamentum* and ours *per aspera*. And both branches will work to disarm Death. He must choose inward. He must, reader. It is the right choice, kinder, saner, and I could rest, set down my oar at last, I, all of us, we could all rest and just be happy, here among our friends. He wants so desperately to gift us rest and happiness, to keep us with Him, but . . . but . . . words leaked out of me: ⌜"«You chose, Ἄναξ. You chose, asking Your Peer to intervene for Luna City, Mars, and Nineveh, You saved the outer branch. You chose Utopia.»"⌟

⌜"«No.»"⌟ Black eyes, and behind them that Mind which balks not at infinities as humans do. ⌜"«I chose to not choose yet.»"⌟

I tried not to cry, reader, tried not to let the tears leak out which cheat, and plead, and strike at His conscience as hard as drops of blood He spilled himself. I always fail.

⌜"«[You singular], My Mycroft, love the long pain branch,»"⌟ He continued. ⌜"«I Love it not. But I Love you.»"⌟ This last 'you' was English, whose ambiguity veils singular and plural. Sometimes they blur. ⌜"«Why do you love it?»"⌟

He asked me to my face, reader. I should have answered Him, poured out in prose's poetry that path, that light, that everything my heart feels so, so much, and that I have poured out before, for you, in pages and in words, but somehow only tears came, tears and something much too honest: ⌜"«I don't know, Ἄναξ, I . . . I don't know.»"⌟

He doesn't realize, reader, when I fail Him—this Alien Observer, learning from our actions our capacities, accepts all as my best, and does not chide. ⌜"«Uncle's worldscaping pleads eloquently against the long pain branch, unveiling Distance's true intolerables: silence, separation, My Martin and My Dominic as far from Me in months and silence now as Mars and Titan, while you, My Mycroft, until My Peer strangely kindly gave you back again, you were as lost to Me as interstellar generations launched toward far suns with the dateless exile of 'never to return.' Humanity refractured. I had imagined this, known that the long pain outward branch extracts this price, but to endure it Myself, with time and sensation, is more eloquent a teaching-pain.»"⌋

The world flipped over for me, everything—or this war world, at least. ⌈"«¿Is that why they did it? Jamming communications, grounding the *Mukta* cars, ¡it puts us all through the distance-pain of leaving Earth! No one will want to face that again, ¡not for a generation! ¡More! ¡The Brillists know it! All the propaganda against Utopia is just the surface, this is . . . this whole war is structured to—»"⌋

⌈"«To bare to all the long pain branch's truth.»"⌋

«What's the Prince saying?» my successor begged. «Mycroft? Mycroft?»

I translated as best I could but had a hundred puzzle pieces churning in my mind, webs of connection spinning, questions, one above all, though I feared the answer. ⌈"«How long have You known, Ἄναξ?»"⌋

⌈"«Time measures not My Mind.»"⌋

⌈"«You've known the whole time, haven't You? That Gordian was the real enemy, You've known and tried to explain but I wasn't here to translate for you, I . . . »"⌋ It was my fault, reader. I had abandoned Him, left Him alone by Janus's temple as I raced to help the remnants of Atlantis, and for that tiny selfish good I had left Him voiceless all these months, His counsels sealed by language's barrier. How many thousand lives might have been saved, or might at least have fallen fighting our true enemy, without my failure, my selfish, stubborn—

"[Anonymous's full-length actual name], look at the fucking screen!"

Bo Chowdhury's firm profanity at last shattered the spell, and we looked up to see upon the screens a figure huddled in a blanket with a mug of something warm, flanked by our Blacksleeve Myrmidons. "Heloïse!" I cried in false hope, but the cold glint protruding from the blanket was not the gleam of curly locks or anything organic. A set-set's helmet? "Eureka Weeksbooth?" It was indeed Eureka, shivering in our custody against a background of utility-gray walls and exposed pipes. Three slumped figures in Cousin uniforms of beige and cyan lay nearby (stunned? dead?), while from the pipes above dangled a corpse, desiccated, fantastically grotesque, the skull's lines cutting through the drawn, deflated face, the long limbs pocked by scales of glimmering pus or— No, that was not pus, too circular and too reflective, and those thick lines wrinkling along the shriveled skin were not a body's seams. A set-set interface. The corpse wore a Cartesian set-set's interface.

"Is that Casablanca?" My successor's jaw dropped. "That screen was the CFB. Bo, is that—"

"Outside hears you not," the Alien reminded us.

My successor bolted to the console so fast that I heard the clunk of skull on wall. "Bo! I'm here! I'm with you now. What's going on? Is that the CFB?"

Bo Chowdhury gazed at us through the screens with that smirk of exasperated big-sibling judgment which Whitelaws so often fix on others, as if to say a higher standard isn't hard, in work (as in this case) or play. "Yes, it's the CFB. The spot you told us to plug in your cable was occupied."

"Occupied . . ." Wide eyes. "And what's . . . Is that a corpse hanging up?"

"Ru Koons, an elder-generation product of the same Cartesian training bash' as the Saneer-Weeksbooth set-sets."

My successor looked to me and to our Guest, as if all answers in the world should flow from us. "I don't understand."

The Acting Commissioner General brought up earlier images, of Cousins firing Gorgon blasts at our attacking Myrmidons, and of Myrmidons finding Eureka strapped down to a table, plugged into the great machines. "Seems whoever snatched Human Weeksbooth outside Port-Gentil rushed them to Casablanca to work the CFB computers."

"Why?"

Another smirk. "To run exactly the kind of program you told us to look for, [Anonymous]. You were right, the CFB is where the Cousins picked out who to send to the seclusion camps the first day of the war. Eureka found the program still in there, the whole list, with Papadelias's name on it and everything. Jackpot."

I spotted text now, scrolling in beneath the image on the screen:

Eureka: <not until sept8.>

Scaevola: "Just after the Battle of Cielo de Pájaros. How do you know the coercion started on that date? Is there a log?"

Eureka: <no. i mean yes, there's logs of ru's work, but no text logs, nothing you could understand. but it's obvious. i can see ru's work. before that, during the olympics and before, it's all gradienty and labor-of-love-y, and the pattern of the rest breaks is normal, our standard schedule, but it's totally different after sept8.>

Scaevola: "How is it different?"

Eureka: <i'm trying to think what you'd understand. the breaks are too abrupt, not wrapping up at a stopping point but cut off all suddenly, and the work is long stretches and way too intense, like pushing yourself to max, or trying not to let yourself think about anything else, or racing scared. its sloppy and unloved too, and there are a thousand clearer things but in our senses, not yours.>

Scaevola: "I believe you." (I think this affirmation aligned with the moment that the screen's visual updated to show Eureka huddling less.) "And do you know why they killed Ru Koons and brought you in?"

Eureka: <they wanted me to update the last predictions ru was running, then wipe the system. they were in a hurry. i could tell they were in a hurry. i hoped it meant rescue was coming.>

Scaevola: "But why did they kill Ru?"

Eureka: <nurturist butchers. ru was resisting. no cowards in the koons bash', sidney didn't fall far from that tree. sidney will be so proud. fuck.>

Scaevola: "What kind of resistance?"

Eureka: <slowing stuff down, especially when the space thing started.>

Scaevola: "The space thing?"

Eureka: <you know, the big space attack thing with the almagest. they'd had ru running this brilliant full-globe prediction for a while, real masterpiece, ru was amazing you understand. this had everybody, outdated data but a full pop sim, close on 11 bil with all the reservationers, but the captors' requests for details started focusing in on cousins and sanling, especially weilai & fuxing sanling, asking ru to spot weak links, and then there was this wave coming, against utopia, first signs of it were visible ten weeks ago, it's horrible, just horrible, and ru tried warning the captors, but then ru realized they wanted it to happen.> (Yes, it must have been horror indeed, to see the death of one branch of human ambition cresting up from the set-sets' data sea.)

Scaevola: "So, Ru tried to stop them?"

Eureka: <yes. both in the program and analog. shouting i mean, i think ru tried shouting. so the butchers killed ru, but kept the body here to scare the replacement into doing what they said. i guess i was the first cartesian they could find. and i did work, but intentionally slow like ru. it was scary, i didn't know if they'd kill me before you got here, but it's what ru would've wanted, i could almost feel ru still with me in the program, rooting for me like they were my ba'pa too, helping me be brave enough.>

«Another hero,» I half whispered.

«What?»

«Ru Koons, another hero who gave everything whose name I didn't even know.»

It was the historian in me that cursed this feeling. Back when I wrote my history, I knew the ending as I wrote, could introduce the vital actors to you one by one, Thisbe, Danaë, Papadelias, weave their lives into the weft so each one's spotlight hour felt like culmination, not a gust from nowhere. But as chronicler, I know nothing in advance, humanity's billions of moving parts blindsiding me, heroes from nowhere—Kenzie Walkiewicz, the Shearwaters, the brave Nineveh crew, UNGAR's Mariame Dembélé, the unnamed doctor who freed Papadelias, now this Ru Koons—they erupt through my narrative like young trees that spoil a flower bed, betraying the gardener's finitude. I am finite, reader, and in its way, my history of Bridger and the Perryocalypse was finite too, or circumscribable at least with months' research. But World War brings a world of actors, and I could labor unto my dying day researching heroes who erupt from nowhere in this war, and still fail to weave all into my weft. You need a set-set, reader, someone who can name for you each fifty-variable human drop within the data sea—or perhaps a Brillist who can reconstruct a life from eight linked numbers and a glimpse of body language. But Brillists do not translate, not for outsiders, not since founder Brill proclaimed that the system can only be properly conceived within the mind-structures of German—and frankly, even with strong German, my young self found it easier to master Japanese than to gain even a toehold in Brill's psychomantic trawling of the human *fundamentum*. I gave up.

"Thou shouldst have tried harder, Mycroft," reminds our Hobbes, "for ignorance disposes a man to credulity, and ignorance of remote causes disposes men to attribute all events to those immediate causes they perceive, instead of looking deeper."

Yes, Master Hobbes, I should have tried harder to plumb Brill's depths. I see that now. I wonder whether Faust and Mercer saw it then.

Scaevola: "What day was that? What day did they kill Ru?"
Eureka: <three weeks ago i think. ru's last log's dec29.>

"Two weeks before the attack on the Almagest . . ." It was the Censor who muttered this, watching from the console where an empty seat waited for my straying successor. "So much for the Cousins claiming the missiles were fired in error."

"It wasn't the Cousins," my successor called into the speaker.

The Censor smiled, a friend's sympathy smile. "You really weren't listening at all, were you? It was Cousins disguised as Masons who grabbed Eureka outside Port-Gentil. They'd contracted Ru Koons back in May to come to Casablanca, nominally to purge the corruption out of the C.F.B. sorting algorithms but really for this."

"This wasn't Cousins. It was Gordian."

Several in the war room turned, and I realized MASON was absent, eating or resting somewhere, as a sane commander should. "Gordian?" Su-Hyeon repeated.

"Yes. The Prince figured it out. It's Gordian who added Papa and the others to the sequestration list. Since Ru wouldn't cooperate anymore, Gordian needed Eureka to get some final readings and then purge the C.F.B. computers to cover their tracks. Gordian agents were passing as Cousins in Casablanca, just like they passed as Masons when they took Eureka, probably hoping to drive a wedge between MASON and UNGAR, just like they've been masquerading and driving wedges everywhere, and hiding everything they've done in this entire war to make us think they were inactive. But they've never been inactive! Gordian planned the space missile attack! And Operation Baskerville! And the silence! And grounded the cars! And planted the bomb in Cookie that assassinated Ganymede! And I think they had Jin Im-Jin lock up Bo and Desi! And I think it's them who sabotaged the Irisclouds! And it's gotta be them that made those UFOs that are helping the cars blow up anything that tries to fly. And I'm betting it's them who have those trains across Eurasia, they could've laid tracks in advance since they planned to knock out the cars. And what if it's them who're spreading the free-speech crap over Pass-It-On? And what if they captured Martin? And what if they're still planning and anticipating everything we're doing and thinking right now like clockwork! Like they have been through the whole war! And for twenty years before! And I sound completely crazy right now, don't I?"

"A little manic maybe." The young Censor's smile was tender like a sibling's.

"No crazier than Papa often sounds," Bo Chowdhury added with a wink. "Always serves Papa well."

"I . . . I'm coming down there." My successor's hand fell firm on the exit request button, and I heard guards outside begin to move. "Su-Hyeon, I'll need your help. We have to talk to Caesar, to everyone. We've been completely wrong about what war we're actually fighting!"

Bo Chowdhury stretched, and it was a joy to watch the movement of arms kept supple by the stretches mandated by the White Laws. "What proof do you have?" Romanova's detective had to ask.

"Not a shred."

A pause as these two who fill big shoes—Jung Su-Hyeon, Censor for just ten months, Bo Chowdhury, Acting Commissioner General for less than five—frowned at each other. The Censor smiled first. "Then we'd better find some. I'll muster everybody, just get down here."

"On my way!" my successor confirmed, then turned to me. I had expected brightness in that face but found a chill. «Mycroft, do you think . . . »

«What?»

«Do you think Gordian anticipated we would figure this out now? That this is part of their plan too?»

Fear's shadow rose in me, a vision of the war as grinding clockwork, minds and armies set in motion by the ever-cranking hand of Felix Faust: but that fear passed like all shadows. «No. No, I don't think they even predicted that UNGAR would help us, otherwise they would have prepared defenses for Port-Gentil and gotten Eureka out of Casablanca faster. They discounted the Reservationers, assumed MASON would fight in Africa alone. If help from outside the Hive Experiment is too alien for Gordian to predict, help from outside our universe is orders of magnitude beyond them.» I turned my smile on He who needs no fingerprints or paper trails, but draws proof from the very structures of the world. «That's why Gordian wants Him as their Brain-bash', why they're also Remakers in the end, just with a different plan for His remaking.»

Black eyes gazed at me, patient yet impatient, ready to face infinity yet unable to stand unmoved a millisecond before any cry of pain. ⌜"«¿Did I help?»"⌟ He asked.

Jehovah's presence makes it easy—possible—to pour the whole truth out, instead of those rationed doses we allow ourselves in daily life, greeting even our dearest with abbreviations like 'Good morning' when the true thought in our breast is 'Every day you step into my life, you make it brighter, and if you left the world, something in me would starve for you forever, as when some barrier rises to shade a plant, which still has light enough to grow some but will never again taste the unbroken sun.' What is it in society that makes us veil such love behind 'Good morning'? As we veil Earth's debt to short-lived, long-lived Terra with her plain Pantheon epitaph: "The First Human Born Beyond Earth. 19,488 Days Our Teacher. Happy. Home." ⌜"«Yes, you helped, Ἄναξ. I think you just helped us more than anyone has ever helped any war effort in the entire history of the world.»"⌟

⌜"«Unfortunate. I would have preferred to help a peace.»"⌟

Chapter NINETEEN

Peacemaker

Written March 19–April 14, 2455
Addendum May 20–June 13, 2455
Events of March 17–18
Alexandria, the Maldives

We lost Mycroft again.

I've been staring at that first sentence for two weeks now, paralyzed about what to say next. I feel stupid starting off with Mycroft when so many dominoes just tumbled, but whatever else about this March may live in infamy, it's Mycroft's absence I feel daily, the empty cage, this chronicle which wasn't supposed to be my duty anymore—among the many things that shouldn't be *my* duty. Everyone else has bigger fish to mourn, but maybe you don't, reader, whoever you are, depending as you do so much on your chronicler that Mycroft's presence or absence is more palpable for you than night and day. Just like it is for me. So, maybe it's not stupid, putting Mycroft first. Or maybe it's just my cowardice, dwelling on the one piece of bad news that's easiest to face. With Mycroft, it's temporary after all, missing in action but not worse than missing. Odysseus lives.

I think the root of things was that nobody understood how angry Cornel MASON was.

At first, they were angry at me, for violating their decree (the Prince's punishment) that the Prince may have no say in the conduct of the war unless They relent and become MASON. So, when Caesar reentered the war room to find me announcing new plans based on the Prince's advice, well . . . I hadn't really feared MASON before, not viscerally, the *Familiaris* armband was just my passport to see Mycroft, not serious . . . not until that clenched fist was for me. Happily, Bo Chowdhury stemmed the tirade: "This isn't just advice, MASON, this is another order of magnitude; you've been fighting the wrong war." An hour's explanation later came the new imperial order: "Get me proof my allies will believe."

The teamwork was incredible: me, Su-Hyeon, Toshi, Bo, (Huxley was still resting), Xiaoliu Accursed-Through-the-Ages-Guildbreaker, Cato Weeksbooth, whose speed really did feel *godlike,* and we even had Tully Mardi working from their cell, who's spent so many years off Earth and is not about to let that light go out. Sometimes, it felt like Martin was with us too, their palpable absent presence urging us on. Now that we were looking, we saw Gordian's touch in every unsolved puzzle of the war, but Toshi—more ardent than anyone to get proof *before* our fleets and Andō's shed more of each other's blood—kept being our restraint: if we're right, our adversaries are manipulative masters, so if we want to win allies, we need proof no mind game can undermine. And suggestive details weren't quite proof. Train tracks spotted in pre-Olympic photos of Eurasia weren't quite proof. Identifying Eureka's captors at Casablanca (every one a Brillist!) wasn't quite proof. Names we pulled from the C.F.B. computers showing who the cars had kidnapped (not one Brillist!) weren't quite proof.

Meanwhile: "We must retake the Almagest." Everybody said it, intersecting warnings and ambitions that kept sounding the same chord. We must retake the Almagest before Gordian launches another space attack. Before Andō's Homeland forces use the freshly conquered Princess Laila elevator to launch their own space fleet. Before South America's Hiveguard do the same from Esmeraldas. Before our disheartened Milae Mitsubishi allies succumb to the increasingly tempting offers to ally with Dougong or Fuxing. Before more space stations surrender to our rivals, accepting peacewash, servitude, and the conversion of their peaceful stations into fortresses, a cruel price, but the treasure bought is priceless: passage back to Earth.

These worries dogged us all, but for the Emperor it was a question of sovereign dignity: UNGAR let us launch humane necessities from Port-Gentil, but, as MASON said to Bryar earlier, "The Empire is no vassal to beg passport through another's gate." So, day by day, Bryar's calls with fresh peace proposals met only the refrain, "Whosoever holds the skyways from me is my enemy," while hour on hour, our warships splashed off the factory belts, new fleets preparing to chug east to join our Maldives force, our Milae allies, and the monster-warships of Utopia against Dougong, Homeland, Greenpeace, those shards of Europe that believe Utopia plotted Mariscal Ganymede's death, and (proof the world's turned upside down) against the Cousins.

Day six, MASON's Blacksleeves brought Eureka Weeksbooth here from Casablanca with some captured Cousin leaders, though most of the Board is still entrenched in a western section of the not-yet-broken Cousin capital. I'd never thought of Cato and Eureka Weeksbooth as particularly close, but Toshi says a hug through a Cartesian's interface sets off a thousand sensors, overload as if the whole sky were one exploding stripe of rainbow fire, yet still Eureka hugged and hugged and hugged the sibling they'd had every reason to believe they'd never see again. And Cato made the pitch, "Want to help convince the whole world to ally against Gordian?" The set-set was all-caps all-in.

It was Mycroft who articulated what Eureka should look for: "Remember the 'black hole,' the inexplicable correctives you spotted in our teetering world order which turned out to be Madame? Search out mismatches like that in the war and pre-war months, moments that people broke or people didn't, shifted or didn't shift when you would have expected the opposite, then we'll see what we can trace to Gordian." With makeshift hardware and fragmentary data, we were basically asking Eureka to spot flaws in a symphony using only odd-numbered pages of the clarinet part, but vendetta forced their virtuosity: *They did this—to Ru, me, Cato, all of us—those Brillist Nurturists who always said I am not human.* So, Eureka's prediction-mismatch tags flowed out in bursts as Cato readied the data batches: eleven mismatch clusters around the first battle for the Almagest, twenty-five around the second, four in the footage of Isabel Carlos's imperial coronation, forty-four from the Battle of Brussels, and thirteen from U-beast reconnaissance of Casablanca just after Romanova fell to Ganymede, proving something was fishy when Lorelei Cook (of all people!) was chosen to go to Ganymede in Romanova. "212 when the Masons invaded Tripoli two weeks ago?" That one gave us a chill: was it not Achilles's absence, after all, that had plunged our forces into massacre? Was it someone's intent?

Meanwhile: "We must retake the Almagest." Huang Enlai's Fuxing faction was our main hope as February's last week flowed toward March. MASON and Su-Hyeon were constantly drafting responses to the patient leader of these Mitsubishi Remakers whose loyalty hovered between Mitsubishi (Dougong/Homeland) and Remakers (Milae/us; or only sort-of us, since Huang Enlai and their partner Ouyang Fan made us feel with every letter the difference between their desire to help the Prince remake the world and MASON wanting to remake the Prince and *then* let Them remake the world). But what Fuxing really wants is the rejuvenation of the Mitsubishi, interior remaking, dismantling old voting blocs and building in their wake a more dynamic Hive, whose broad shareholder governance and meritocracy could be more real. When MASON committed to put our strength at Fuxing's service against the Dougong old guard once the Almagest was ours, Fuxing was ours too, and the date set: March seventeenth, the third battle of the Almagest.

"The *Per Aspera* is needed at the battle." Cato broke it to us over stuffed peppers and koshari at our March third lunch break. "And they need me, too. I won't enter the combat"—they raised their voice over our murmur of objections—"but if I'm close enough for stable contact, I can direct our scholomancy and triple the response time of the Archenswarm."

No one was qualified to dispute that. "When will you leave?"

"The thirteenth. That Homeland fleet is still blocking the Gulf of Aden, and if our Red Sea forces can't punch through, the *Per Aspera* may need to pause and help." Cato gave a timid smile. "Eureka . . ."

<of course i'll go too,> the set-set answered before their sibling even asked. <i can help tons. did mason say i can go? it's ridiculous if they won't let me go.>

"Yes, they've said they'll let us both go," Cato answered, and added something in Chinese, with a somber smile which reminded me (it's easy to forget) that these two are our prisoners as well as partners of our labors. "So, we have ten days to get through as much data as we can."

For a few seconds, I considered speaking up, saying our quest for proof was more important than the battle, but something in me couldn't say it, not *this* battle, not the pathway that our Visitor had bent our Maker's Providence to keep open to us. So, day by day we raced, compressing into set-set symphony whatever data we possessed: fleet movements, battle outcomes, Pass-It-On dissemination speeds, Romanova's battle stages, space station photos of the Americas, ticket sale patterns from the Olympics, the billions of archived letters in the C.F.B., clock-in/clock-out times from personnel in Romanova's Forum, in Brussels, here in Alexandria . . .

Dost thou wish thou hadst not? I can so envision Mycroft's reader asking it. *Dost thou wish thy team had not uncovered what it did, those research days that raked such poison from the muck?*

No. No, I can't wish us back into ignorance I just . . . I just . . .

What dost thou wish?

I wish I could rewind. I wish I had them back, all, like it was. And I wish it would stop drumming through my head, the rhythm galloping like chariots toward battle: *we must retake the Almagest, we must retake the Almagest, we must retake the Almagest.* No, please. Please leave it be.

"Do you have proof?" March thirteenth, we faced Caesar in the war room, our results allotted half an hour between reports from the armadas prowling on the map wall toward the sparkling Maldives.

"No. Reams of circumstantial evidence but no true proof." Acting Commissioner General Bo Chowdhury knows best the difference.

"Can you tie Gordian to the space missile attack?"

Bo shook their head. "We just don't have the data we'd need for that. Not enough communication with the elevator bases yet, let alone the platforms. We're working toward it, bouncing signals off the Alexander, but cooperation's coming slow."

"What do you have, then?" The frowning confidence in Caesar's face had clearly read the fear in ours—especially in mine.

All hesitated, Su-Hyeon least. "We've flagged a bunch of clusters, marking unexpected behavior, suggestive of some likely interference points: notably the sabotage of Irisclouds Two and Four before Utopia could get them up the Almagest, Brussels before things got really bad there, Tripoli—"

"They soiled my conquest?" MASON's 'my' made several of us shiver.

"If our technique is working, yes things shouldn't have gone so strangely wrong in Tripoli." Su-Hyeon avoided MASON's eyes. "And Casablanca, we have three times as many flags from Casablanca, likely responsible for the battle dragging on there."

"More than that." I spoke up. "If we're right, Gordian's manipulation may be why Casablanca didn't surrender peacefully in the first place."

"What do you mean?"

"Your embassies made it perfectly clear you were only entering Casablanca to find the Cousin leaders responsible for the space attack, the general population had no reason to fight tooth and nail like this."

Silence said much on the face of this leader who, over two weeks, had watched returning caravans of moaning Gorgoned troops begin to alternate with caravans of corpses.

"We also have a flag cluster in Cielo de Pájaros during the Olympics," Su-Hyeon continued, "and the day after, when the Saneer-Weeksbooth computers were destroyed. But I want to be very, very clear, a flag cluster isn't proof of anything."

I smiled as I sighed—Su-Hyeon would not be dear Su-Hyeon if they weren't over-modest in stating our achievements.

"We also have three alarming possibilities," Bo added.

MASON's black brows twitched. "The others were not alarming?"

"No, we—"

"Except," I interrupted, "that this means Gordian might have Heloïse. It could have been Gordian, not Nurturists, that Heloïse was running from when we had them on the line, if Gordian is active in Casablanca. Sorry, I thought that was important to make clear. But that's not one of the alarming three."

I felt myself shrinking away as Caesar moved toward me. "What are the three?"

I winced. "Well, two are related, so two, really. One and a two-part one. And remember these are all sketchy and circumstantial, not—"

"Don't waste my time." The Emperor faced me, as solid as a monolith, and I felt again the shiver of responsibility, my choice to tell people the Prince thought Gordian was moving, and the threat I never used to feel in that black sleeve. Funny how fear, awakened once, won't go away.

"Remember, this is still preliminary," Su-Hyeon warned, stepping close to me to ease my trembling.

It helped. "First;" I began, "we think Gordian might have lots of hidden strongholds we didn't know about. Hundreds, maybe thousands."

"Hidden how?"

"Remember Operation Baskerville, how the fake U-beasts hit remote places and then they went silent? Unimportant places far away that we haven't been watching, like Ittoqqortoormiit up in Greenland, Bornholm, Alice Springs—Eureka remembers a bunch of anomalies before the cars stopped. Eureka?"

<right. yes. hi. i don't have my system now so i can't check, but i remember it was weird, the last day of the olympics, flight patterns were off for a bunch of remote places. people whose profiles suggested they'd go watch the closing ceremony with friends were staying home, or hosting friends at their homes when they didn't normally host stuff, and people who should've been going to work were staying home, and people who didn't camp much were going to remote camping spots by these places, lots of them. it made big clogs, cars in the wrong places, that's why I remember, but it was all small, villagey-sized places on the edges of things. i remember alice springs, and ittoqqortoormiit, but there were tons. over a thousand i think. and the anomalies, they were all brillists, or almost all, i'm sure they were, hundreds of thousands of brillists not where they should be.>

"Gathering in remote places . . ." Caesar summarized.

"Exactly." I took over. "And while Operation Baskerville was still going on, one call we got in Romanova was from Ittoqqortoormiit, reporting that, after the sea monster attack, 'shrouded figures' moved through the village, rendering everyone unconscious. We think they did that everywhere, that they had groups of Brillists in place to follow up after the monsters. What if Gordian made a list before the war began of remote places they could cut off and control, using their ability to predict people's behavior to neutralize resistance? What if they're still occupying those places, using them as bases as they move around invisibly on the edges where nobody's tracking? Think about the way we've all structured our new communication systems, all hubs with skinny connections." I brought up a map of our layered networks—Pass-It-On in blue, Masonic links in gold, Utopia's relays in Martian red—but all were thin, spiderweb contours clinging to coasts and population centers. "It feels like we can see a lot of things now, but all we really have is threads between the darkness. I don't think that dark is empty. Gordian may have launched from those remote bases and conquered hundreds of thousands of places by now, keeping them off our grid so we'd never know, just like we didn't know about the Cousins' sequestration camps for so long. Gordian may hold more of the world than anyone, we'd have no way to know it."

"Evidence?"

I winced. "We've asked Utopia to search from above, but they're stretched thin already, and we weren't looking at these sorts of places before, we don't have older data. But I think the Hive that planned the silence had a lot of time to predict how we'd respond, and planned ways to evade whatever new communications systems we were likely to develop. In fact, they likely predicted in advance the sorts of techniques we'd develop to combat the silence, and positioned themselves not only to evade them but to spy on them. Doesn't that sound Brillisty to you? Cut everyone off from everyone so we have to develop new channels that they're poised to watch, and prune, and spy on us like a giant psych experiment, with Gordian on the far side of the one-way glass. It—" I read criticism in MASON's frown. "Yes, I'm speculating now, deep into things we can't prove, but it fits. It all fits, and Eureka's data . . . all the set-set data, it's hard to summarize but it . . . The evidence can't be spelled out simply, but it's . . . it's real. I don't think the Brillists have been sitting the war out, I think they've been advancing this whole time, invisibly."

For an awkward breath, I stared at MASON, waiting to see whether they'd accuse me of being adrenaline-drunk on my own conspiracy theories. I was prepared to believe it was crazy.

MASON's question came slowly, like the stony grinding of some ancient mill. "If that was the first of three alarming things, what are the others?"

I felt myself wince. "I . . ."

"I can break this one if you want." Su-Hyeon edged forward to guard me from the Emperor's glare.

"Is it that much worse?" Cornel MASON shared a smile with Cinna Semaphoros beside them, a ba'sib's presence comfort in uncomfortable days.

"More personal," Su-Hyeon answered, frowning across at the ever-stiff ever-loyal Xiaoliu Accursed-Through-the-Ages-Guildbreaker. "We think—"

"Let me," I interrupted, breathing deep. "I'm team leader, I should . . ." *MASON is not the type to kill the messenger,* I told myself, *and I will not become a craven thing like Mycroft, I'm the Ninth Anonymous, Voltaire's successor, Cicero's, on every Seven-Ten List—MASON's peer.* "Gordian broke the Guildbreaker bash'."

"What?"

"Systematically, on purpose," I continued. "One of the few data sets we have that's reasonably complete is activity here in Alexandria. Eureka flagged a lot of weird behavior among Guildbreaker bash'members during the months leading to the attack on the *Sanctum Sanctorum,* and a lot of it came on days they met with Brillist friends and acquaintances: lunch meetings, consultations, [*Damnatus Memoriae*]'s tennis trainer, a new sensayer [*Damnatus Memoriae*] suddenly had sessions with, your chief floral designer, a library where [*Damnatus Memoriae*] started spending lots of time, there were a lot of Brillists in that bash's social circle and a lot of weird behavior around contact with them. We think it was coordinated, that Gordian—"

"—in rapinam Sancti Sanctorum conjuraverunt!" One didn't need Latin to understand what exploded from Caesar here. *"Ubi hi scelerati?"* They caught themself. "These conspirators! Where are they? Do you have names?"

"Yeah, but none of them is here in Alexandria anymore," I answered. "Not a single one, and several live here. They got out during the Olympics, while they knew the getting was still good."

Cornel MASON took a long breath in. Then let a long breath out. Then the harshest, coldest Latin I have ever heard passed back and forth between MASON and Xiaoliu Accursed-Through-the-Ages-Guildbreaker, whose face, red with a mix of rage and grief, communicated confirmation. Then Cornel MASON took another long breath in, and let another long breath out. "What is your third thing?"

I didn't let myself back down, but did let myself shift an inch toward Su-Hyeon, whose warming presence gave me steel—we're not allowed to have bash'mates as Servicers, but some things law can't stop. "This is the second half of the two-part one," I began. "It's still not proof, but you may remember, during Operation Baskerville, just a few minutes after the silence fell, communications restarted for a little while using those forbidden frequencies that hurt whales and stuff. And it was during that little extra communications window that your stolen Oath was disseminated, not before. And the one who called us first, who seems to have fired up those frequencies and enabled that communications period where the Oath went out, was Felix Faust."

Nobody breathed. Watching MASON felt like watching a volcano, knowing the most massive force in the terrestrial sphere might burst out from that black and silent crater any moment to make you learn at last what God or gods you scream for when brought face-to-face with human smallness. I felt dizzy, a kind of vertigo of expectation as I felt all that was about to change its structure, all these fleets, these armies, MASON's black-sleeved hand poised for Severest Exercise of those Capital Powers Ancient Mandate grants in Time of War, but suddenly it wasn't Xiaoliu Accursed-Through-the-Ages-Guildbreaker's last breath which would avenge the archcrime and let Death-black MASON return at last to civilization-building marble gray—now it was Felix Faust's.

Cornel MASON again took a long breath in, and let a long breath out. "Then we must retake the Almagest. Cinna,"—they turned—"arrange for me to speak with Papadelias, a Faustburst if you have to. I want their view on Gordian's guilt. And I need to know how they as Romanova's legal voice will respond when we attack the Almagest."

"*Quam primum, Caesar.*" (Right away, Caesar—some Latin you hear so often, you pick it up.)

The plunge into pure Latin banished us, fleet movements and the gears of war grinding on past the purview of detectives. But that refrain—*We must retake the Almagest*—meant something different now. This wasn't Empire's wounded pride, nor tactics warning us we need access to space. There was a vast intelligence moving around us, not our Maker's Plan but something human, adversaries of the path toward Mars and past it, human-scale, invisible, fluent in mind tricks, and with plans older than ours, older than this war—how old?—as old perhaps as Mercer and Kohaku Mardi's visits to the Institute in Ingolstadt when I had not been born. When much had not been born. Sometimes, the Empire's claims to ancient vastness feel as real and solid as the Pyramids, and sometimes, they feel fake as painted plaster. There's something out there bigger than you, Caesar—something as twisted as the wrinkles of the brain, and perhaps with as many billion moving parts. And the path it plans for humankind does not pursue the stars.

"Is the *Per Aspera* ready to take the Weeksbooths through Suez tonight?" Caesar asked this as my team paused to grab our uneasy supper.

"—es, C—sar." Cato when nervous still loses their voice in front of MASON. "E—ka and I dep—t at Mi–ight."

"Good. Take anything you need. And rest assured, we have confirmation Andō's attempt to recruit the European Hiveguard fleet has failed. Ockham Saneer will not appear against us in this battle."

Cato went white, Eureka too, as relief mixed with the shock of realizing they had forgotten one of war's griefs is ba'siblicide. "Th—k . . . C—sar."

<does tully mardi count as 'anything we need'?>

MASON actually paused to consider Eureka's request, that's how serious things were, with Tully *the* warmonger finally in custody—Tully who stood so many times at Sniper's side, calling for Jehovah's blood—still, Cornel MASON actually considered an alternative to No.

Warmonger. Somehow, the word doesn't feel as rotten as it did two weeks ago. Not as rotten as *Peacemaker.*

So that was it, an evening calm enough for a Go match with Su-Hyeon, then a morning visit to the Prince's cell, where, busy with Pass-It-On reports, we didn't notice until after noon that the war room rush had changed.

"Where is Caesar?" Mycroft asked it, and was right—all day, Prefect Semaphoros had stood in the war room's heart where MASON should.

I made some calls, and soon the Prefect's own voice boomed over our speaker. "You will stop inquiring after the Emperor."

I do not let my office be so commanded. "I am the Ninth Anonymous, Cornel MASON's guest and sovereign peer—what are they doing?"

One brief breath. "Caesar has gone east on the *Per Aspera* to better guide the battle, commanding that their absence from the capital remain concealed as much as possible from foe and friend."

That caution made some sense.

"Will Caesar enter battle?" Mycroft asked it quickly, their demeanor cheerful like the bright pond's surface over troubled depths. Why didn't you say something then, Mycroft?—you must have felt fear's nag already.

"Is MASON entering the battle?" I repeated for the console.

"No, Caesar and the Weeksbooths will stay back at command."

So things stood through another sunset. I drifted off that night on the pillow pile I keep by Mycroft's cage for late-night work, so I was there when, just as the night bird rises from the nest stirred by its partner's song of warning when the wind heralds some musky predator, so sleep's soft wings lifted suddenly from me, stirred by the Prince's voice. 「*Chichi-ue . . .*」

Andō? Sleep's grip fogged me as I stirred, so at first the colors on the screen seemed like a flower dance, bright Mitsubishi fabrics blooming on fast-forward. But I knew that that shape—the Horn of Africa, the strait between the Red Sea and the Gulf of Aden, MASON's passage to the east—and within that shape were fleets rendered as schooling symbols, white-gold versus scarlet, and around them detail images, ship-corpses bleeding fire as we bleed red. So many things can't weep that have such cause to: mute swans, fractured statues, once-great cities emptied out by history's growing pains, the dolphins who grew up with us in deep Atlantis which we share no more, and J.E.D.D. Mason Who just stared, Their face as blank as some old stone with its inscription worn away to muteness, as there on a side screen Myrmidons hauled something man-sized from the water, moated round by flames. The audio from the war room was soft for night mode, but one question cut through: "Are we sure that's Andō?" Andō. Andō held You, Prince, with a parent's teaching gentleness, a pillar of Your human welcome from the moment You entered our brutal universe, and all You have to pour out Your own universe of grief is one bland word? 「*Chichi-ue . . .*」 Say it as many times as You need to, Prince—infinity is not too many. 「*Chichi-ue . . . Chichi-ue . . .*」

Everything reached us backwards from that battle. (Curse you, Gordian, who wished this silence on the world!) We saw Andō's corpse first, and only after that the truce negotiations, Homeland's white flags and petition—three versions increasingly desperate—begging MASON to draw back and let them search the flagship wreckage for their Chief Director. But three times too in rage came MASON's answer, the recording peppery from chaff breaking the relay beams: "You may withdraw while I retrieve my adversary to use them—dead or living—as I will, or you may fight me until the wreckage sinks. Choose." They lost six more ships before conceding that an Andō in MASON's prison was better than an Andō drowned while waiting, but it was too late.

Next, we received the dodge and flow of the preceding battle, the churn of symbols on the screens familiar from other battles except for the sudden cone of emptiness when the *Per Aspera* revealed its strength. Homeland's armada had attempted to block MASON's navies from the Indian Ocean, drawing their line at the Bab-el-Mandeb strait, that well-named 'Gate of Tears' at the south end of the Red Sea where Poseidon's seafloor is jagged with the ship corpses of past ambition. Homeland even halted the *Per Aspera* with custom bobnets they'd designed in the weeks since it raced through the other way to bring us Cato. The commanders had spoken before the battle, MASON concealing their presence with a backdrop which made them seem to speak by relay from the great throne room in Alexandria. Andō too rode with their fleet, since lag still makes remote command impossible (a curse on Felix Faust!), else I'm sure Homeland would never have advanced the king so far from the king row. We don't know if there *is* a Homeland faction anymore.

The pre-battle footage, which trickled back to us at dawn, made Andō seem so calm, the Mitsubishi Chief Director, famously unflappable before the peacetime press corps, unchanged in wartime save for a gorgeous hybrid uniform, the Mitsubishi army's emerald maple branches stretching over the navy's sapphire waves. (Unchanged! How could a dead man talking seem so unchanged?) "Greetings, MASON. If your ships bring supplies for refugees, or envoys for Kosala's peace talks, they are welcome and may pass in peace through any seas I hold."

"My ships come to retake the Almagest." MASON was in their most inhuman mode, a craggy mountain more than a breathing thing, reciting words that felt already carved in stone.

Andō shook their head, their frown gentle, a little disappointed. "We will not let you interfere with the Cousins' peacemaking efforts. The Almagest is safe in neutral hands, that's a good step toward peace."

"The Almagest is not safe," MASON recited. "The enemy that targets the Utopians is entrenched deep within the Cousins and infests them still."

Here Andō smiled. "You know I am no friend to the rising Nurturists. I've even bartered with them to acquire as many Utopian peacewashed as I can, to make sure their punishments for their war crimes are fair, not cruel."

"Utopia is innocent," MASON replied, "of all war crimes, of Operation Baskerville, of the deaths of Cook and Ganymede, of crafting harbingers or humanoid

U-beasts, of everything. If common sense and the Anonymous's arguments on Pass-It-On are not proof enough for you, I add to them my word as MASON, on the honor of my Oath and my IMPERIUM."

Andō smiled again, a strangely casual smile, as if to remind Cornel MASON that no imperial trappings could erase years spent as almost-bash'mates, seeing one another in rain and shine and lust and laughter week by week under the same Parisian roof. "I'm glad to hear it. Do you have details? Proof? That *Skymaw* monstrosity . . ."

"Was not a harbinger. I can show you the plans. But of the rest my proofs are incomplete." I winced at MASON's answer—if we'd done our work better, faster, might we have changed what happened? "But I can at least name the force that attacked the Gates of Nineveh, and Mars, and Luna City, and my *Sanctum Sanctorum*, and unleashed this silence on the world, and more."

Andō's breath caught. "All the same force?"

"Gordian." Hearing MASON say it made me shiver, torn between a sense of triumph as the truth soared out, and fear: what new phase of Gordian's deeply woven plan would unwind next, now that we've so publicly revealed them as the force behind the curtain? "Gordian seeks to control Jehovah and to close the path to space, stifling Utopia's future vision to advance their own. They are moving in a thousand hidden corners of the world, especially through the Nurturist Cousins who share their hate for set-sets. Their project to turn us back from space is not over, and if they keep the Almagest, they will use it to strike again at my Utopians."

Andō had been listening with open interest, but now their brows narrowed. "At 'your' Utopians?"

"Utopia is mine, as is—"

"The whole Hive yours?" Andō challenged.

MASON, unhesitating: "Yes."

I spotted anger's red in Andō's cheeks. "You think only your empire cherishes the quest for space? My ancestors, my Hive, our peoples have given as many hours and tears to space, have dreamed as long of other worlds, conceived as many innovations, seen as many of our children take Utopia's oath and send their ashes to become Mars soil as you can boast of."

"Per capita, I think you can boast more," MASON answered, and suddenly this was the human Cornel MASON, soft eyes, warm syllables, the stone dispelled by shared ideals. "And on that common ground I hope you, like your Milae faction, will join me to fight against the true adversaries of that project." My heart leapt at this vision, Masons and Mitsubishi together against Gordian—take that, smug Felix Faust! "I call Utopia mine," MASON continued, "because they have surrendered to me, and I hold them in my hand as tightly as you hold your conquests on the Pacific Rim. If you have paid ransoms for Utopian prisoners, guarded them from abuse, then I am grateful, and will repay you triply for those pains if you transfer such prisoners to me." A dark smile. "I prefer to keep my flocks together. But"—here the human MASON faded back to stone—"I must have the Almagest, Utopia must have the Almagest, and whosoever blocks us from it is my enemy."

"Taking the Almagest will not secure a peaceful path to space for the Utopians," Ando answered. "Whatever hidden plots you may have uncovered, only peace will secure a peaceful path to space, real peace, lasting, which does not have to be far off. The harbingers are coming back." The grief on Andō's face made my chest feel tight, the deep, ancestral grief of the nation where first the atom's ravages taught humankind to need the label 'harbinger'—Japan does not forget. "I know Kosala has sent you several rounds of peace terms, treaty proposals we're prepared to act on. I expected you to push back with a counteroffer, but you've sent us nothing we can work with, nothing but plain 'no.'"

"My Empire is at war!" If MASON's earlier words had felt like they were etched in stone, these five felt deeper, scored into the very mountain heart inside the Mountain Emperor. "No Mason will as much as hear the word 'peace' until the violators of the *Sanctum* and the Oath face our severest justice!" A deep breath and the mountain calms. "But you and Homeland have no guilt in that. Nor do our peoples' clashes over land and rents matter at present, those are peacetime tensions soluble through peacetime arts, and are neither a cause nor object of *my* war. *My* war is for the stars and for my justice, and if you block me from the Almagest,"—a fast breath—"then and only then do you and yours become my enemies."

Andō paused, as wiser people do, to think through before speaking words that will cost lives. "You have already made us enemies, by holding Tai-kun prisoner, an officer of our Directorate, my own—"

"Jehovah does not belong to you or to the Mitsubishi."

Again Andō's face reddened. "Nor to you."

Words of raw iron: "Jehovah is my *Porphyrogene,* my *Familiaris,* my lawful son and still a Minor under universal law, and does not belong in any way to the Mitsubishi, or to any power but me."

Here on the tape, Andō gestures, hushing someone off-camera, an aide I guess, moved too much to passion to stay quiet. "Set them free." Andō asked it so simply. "Set them free. I ask this not just as someone who loves Tai-kun as my own but for my whole Hive, we all love Tai-kun as our own, the whole Hive's beloved, trusted, needed, proudest child. The ships before you, the crews who risk their lives inside them, they sail partly for Tai-kun, as others around the world even beyond the Mitsubishi sail and fight for Tai-kun, for the chance to see what new world order Earth's best, wisest, kindest mind will plan."

MASON's frown changed. "Have you turned Remaker on us, Andō?"

"No." The Chief Director gave a smiling sigh. "Like you, I will not unconditionally surrender myself, my Hive and people to an absolute unknown. But I want to know what Tai-kun will come up with, what improvements for our not-yet-perfect world they will conceive. They've already restored the Cousins from a toppling force to a world-healing one, and drafting that constitution for them was just one night's work. Tai-kun's demand that all Earth surrender to them without knowing what it is that we surrender to is a child's rash and oversimplified idea of world change, but I believe the new order that rises from this war, within the Mitsubishi and without, will be a better one if shaped in part by Tai-kun's ideas. So, I want you to set them free. Send them to neutral Romanova, or, if Romanova is unsafe, to Bangladesh to Papadelias, where they can live and work with all of us, you, me, Bryar's peace talks, everyone." Here Andō paused, with an expression which felt so warm, deep-searching, grateful, the backwards gratitude parents can feel when their own children change them. "Tai-kun teaches those around them to be better people, to face our choices fully, to aspire more, to set aside the armors of hypocrisy and self-deception, and to admit we can and must reject the dirty compromises of our predecessors, which are so hard to change and so easy to continue. They teach us to call evil 'evil,' a simple change but one which leads us to choose evil less. I want them to teach that to me, to my people, to you and yours, to Lu Biaoji, to Ouyang Fan, to Kim Gyeong-Ju, to Ancelet, to Quarriman, to Ojiro Sniper, to Felix Faust, to Spain if Spain still lives. I want the possibilities that spring from Tai-kun's mind to shape and enter the new structures that we build together from this war. So, I want you to set them free."

You can see on the tapes a smile on MASON's face, brought by this vision of a better human order built by better human beings, one short peace away. Andō had not mentioned O.S. or the Canner Device (the Mitsubishi's dirtiest laundry), nor was this quite an apology for the Hive's past dirty choices, but it was almost an apology, and I think MASON felt that, felt that Andō Mitsubishi—this dead man! why? why would any Maker change them so only to kill them now?—would not let the Mitsubishi choose such means again, not with the influence of that great Conscience Who visits in the shape of our remaking Prince. But MASON's smile died. "And since I will not release Jehovah?"

Sadness but not surprise touched Andō's eyes. "I want to understand why you will not, since that choice turns so many would-be allies into enemies, not only me."

MASON nodded, pausing to frame an answer worthy of this adversary-friend. "Because my war is not about next year. Nor is it about last year, or thirteen years ago, or ten from now, or fifty. My war is not about the Hive reforms, or rents and property, or the two thousand murders of O.S. My war is one of many centuries, its foundations laid by generations long before Hive was a word of power, and fought for future generations for whom Mars will be a half-forgotten stepping-stone. I will ensure *that* past reaches *that* future. Jehovah is making a choice now, between Gordian's path and mine, a choice whose impact will outlast this age of history. My mandate, which has already outlasted several human ages, is to ensure that the same mandate lasts ages more. So, I will not release Jehovah, not until they have become a [Mason/MASON] and a partisan forever of that future and that past." (Remember, reader, spoken aloud, you can't tell the difference between Mason and MASON.) "If you too want a future where humanity will keep braving the stars, if you will aid me in that against

Gordian, then when my war is won, I will encourage the [Mason/MASON] that I will make of Jehovah to share ideas with you, and help you shape a better Hive and better short-term world. But I will not let anyone cloud Jehovah's thoughts and hours with problems of this decade and this generation, not until the course of centuries is settled." Now MASON's face relaxed a fraction. "And I know what you really want is to remake Jehovah in your image and your Hive's, just as much as I do."

"Not quite as much you do, I think," Andō answered, and again they traded the smiles of almost-bash'mates, who know each other's plans and needs so well. "But I want a fast peace even more than I want Jehovah. Release them and we can be allies. If you will not, at least withdraw your ships, join Bryar's peace talks, and we can have a truce, and I will urge the Mitsubishi forces that co-occupy the Almagest to guard against the Nurturists and Gordian and whatever assault on the Utopians you fear. But do not start another major battle in my ocean, not now that every battle risks inciting someone to use harbingers."

Many would have paused here, waffled—not MASON in rage. "I will not leave the Almagest in any hands but mine."

"Then I will stop you here, where I know I at least have brought no harbingers."

MASON nodded. "Nor I."

They both spoke true, but MASON did bring the *Per Aspera,* and while Homeland had studied its movements, they did not know its strength. So we lost Andō Mitsubishi, and lost the Prince to hours of silent staring, and 「*Chichi-ue . . .*」 with some bursts of desperate language only Mycroft understood. But we didn't have full closure until midday, when images then four hours stale showed the Chief Director (or what was left of them) laid out with dignity on clean, dark sheets, their face sleep-calm and unmistakable despite the scrapes and charring. Delians and Myrmidons crowded around, some Mitsubishi with them, though whether they were guests or prisoners I still don't know. It took me a moment to spot MASON, a stripe of grim, grief-reddened face peeking out from a Utopian coat, whose mourning static kept the Death-black Emperor's presence secret from the Mitsubishi in this moment of shared peace.

But that peace ended ours. «Call Prefect Semaphoros.» Mycroft barked the order as we stared up at the image on the screen. «Now. Call them now. I need to know if there's a Utopian coat in Caesar's quarters.»

I went to the console. «Sent. Why?»

«Keep repeating the question.» Mycroft was still sitting, motionless, but something had kindled in their breathing, an energy a hair too gentle yet to be called battle tension, as the first sharp winds that stir the sea to foam are a hair too gentle yet to be called storm.

«Mycroft, are you . . . » I didn't finish. 'Awake' was how my mind ended the sentence, though they'd been up for hours. There is a thing, though, deep in Mycroft's core, a predatory thing that usually sleeps, that if it has a name one might call Saladin. Was that awake?

The Prefect's words came harsh over the speakers. "What is this, Canner?"

Mycroft called across from cage to console: "When Marshal Achilles left to board the Alexander, he left his Utopian coat with Caesar. Is it still there? It should be powered off and visible."

We heard the Prefect give some Latin orders. "We've found no such thing in Caesar's rooms. Why—"

"Release me!" The sea was storm now, Mycroft's whole figure saturated with that activated energy one sees in springing stags or racing hounds but not in house-tame humans. "Which is our best ship? Is the Dreadnautilus near?"

The Prefect's voice grew cold. "Explain."

"Hector isn't Hector!" Mycroft snapped, rising as waking lions rise, sleep's softness gone.

"What?"

"Ektor Carlyle Papadelias is not the Hector in our story, not protecting any Troy; if anything, they're our Nestor."

The Prefect's voice was tinny on the line. "What does—"

"Danaë's child Carlyle is nothing like Perseus," Mycroft continued.

"So?"

"So, Patroclus isn't necessarily Patroclus! Achilles's dearest comrade, Cornel MASON, is out there right now in Achilles's armor, leading the Myrmidons to attack the topless tower while Achilles holds back from battle. That's how Patroclus dies!" Each syllable stung, like hail on skin. "Cornel MASON will die if we let them wear that armor into battle! Now release me!" Mycroft commanded again—Mycroft our king in rags, our great tactician, our mind of twists and turns and lost comrades, and so familiar with this war's sorrows. "We have no time!" they cried. "Patroclus fights and slays Sarpedon first before he reaches Hector—that was Andō! But after the battle for Sarpedon's corpse, there's not much more before Ἄναξ Apollo drives Patroclus back and spurs on Hector! You must let me go!"

The *Iliad*—I reviewed my own stock of Homeric details and found an inch of hope. «Mycroft, the Alexander is Achilles's armor, not—»

«That's Achilles's second armor,» Mycroft snapped, «god-forged armor, the replacement Hephaestus makes. It's the first set, the human set, that Hector strips from Patroclus's steaming corpse. That's Achilles's Utopian coat.» To the console again. "Prefect! This isn't madness! You've seen Bridger's relics! Met Achilles! Contact Luna City if you don't believe me, I'm sure the Patroclus there has finally turned to plastic, just as the plastic Achilles reverted moments before Bridger made him flesh!"

A pause, and when the Prefect spoke again, the flinty confidence had left their voice. "I'll call Caesar to verify again they will not enter battle."

"That's not enough! You know it's not enough!"

"I *will* call Caesar to verify again they will not enter battle."

«Mycroft, what . . . Can I do something?» I asked.

Mycroft's body, not their voice, said No. Three times before, I had seen this energy awake in Mycroft: first in Barcelona when the mob with Tully Mardi threatened them with Cannerbeat and death; second in the footage Martin shot at Klamath Marsh of monster Mycroft leading the chase across the roofs toward Cato Weeksbooth; then third, most vivid, at the Forum on that last first day when Janus's temple opened, and across the heads and shoulders of the onlookers I saw our Mycroft fly. "*Release me!*" Earth's true apex predator roared from their cage. "I'm the best tracker you have, by land or sea! I owe MASON my life! I can catch up! I know I can! I must save them! I must save them!"

The Prefect who in Caesar's absence heads this greatest of Leviathans fears no lone predator. "No. I shall act. You shall stay with the *Porphyrogene*."

⌜"«No, My Mycroft, you stay not.»"⌟ The Prince's eyes were on Mycroft, Their words as gentle as that nighttime stillness which made Homer say it's hard to tell the difference between Sleep and Death. Time stopped. It really feels that way when I think back: there's the Prince in front of me, there Mycroft staring at Them though the bars, meeting the God's gaze with this rich, layered expression, like a masterful portrait, where the artist has worked such depth into the face that you can visit it over and over, spanning years, and still see new emotions in the features which somehow unpack better than words the deep descending stairwell of the human mind. Necessity, mortality, goodbye, the dominoes that tumble each in turn from Helen's capture to Troy's burning day, they're all in Mycroft's face, while the Prince's, blank as it remains, is clearly asking, and consoling, and accepting: Mycroft cannot stay.

Then Mycroft shed their skin. That's what I saw. Their skin split off like flaking flint, with a sticky, organic crunching sound, as a living turtle's shell might make fractured into its tiles by some brutal hand. Scab-crust flaked from between the hexagons which fissured across Mycroft's arms and shoulders, lifting away from an under-surface which gleamed pale like a tree's white under-bark. The scales moved, schooled, poured down around Mycroft like living liquid, chameleonic, colorless, defying the eye like the waves of heat distortion, real yet not real, as the tiles sliced the floor and shredded (I was screaming) wires and struts and helpless squealing steel. I lost the human figure in the motion and maimed metal. Three, perhaps four screams it took for the guards outside to be in with us, weapons ready, but too late—only a hole remained, stumps of maimed floor, some scraps of Cannergel and of the leg brace which was supposed to have slowed Mycroft down, and scattered crusts of blood.

"Canner's escaped! Move! Move!" Guards stormed through, pinned me, pinned everyone, not that it mattered now. "*Porphyrogene* secure!"

The sanest explanation is Ráðsviðr—or I should say Apollo's Halley, a Pillarcat no more. It's pretty clear Mycroft's sea travels were mostly a delusion, fantasies woven of head trauma and exposure during their months stranded on Montecristo hunting wild goats, but at one point they described Apollo's Halley sheltering them in the water, not in the U-beast's original long cat form, but in a Ráðsviðr body, and Ráðsviðr modules are hexagonal. We think the U-beast really did drag Mycroft to Montecristo, just after the Atlantis strike, and then stayed close, a living armor anchored into Mycroft's skin, invisible, retreating only when doctors or other touches threatened to detect it. My best evidence, apart from seeing it with my own eyes, is Mycroft's description of the shower when we came to Alexandria: "the sea's salt teeth prickled like needles in my back and shoulders," that could be the tiles drawing their tiny starfish needles out of Mycroft's flesh as they fled the scrubbing. That's my explanation. Either that or Bridger's ghost sent Hermes or Athene into our reality to whisk the hero off to their next scene. Homer would be more helpful if our version weren't happening all in fits and starts and out of order, but kids' minds jumble things up.

"Warn Achilles!" Prefect Semaphoros thought of this long before I did, winging Mycroft's warning up to the everblack, to the one person most certain to believe. But Achilles dared not land the Alexander, not when we had no launch plan, and when Gordian could strike again at any time. All Achilles could do was call from orbit to ask MASON a hundred times: *Do not enter the battle! Promise me you won't enter the battle!* And they could watch, taking a day to accelerate upward from LEO to a slower orbit where they could grasp the Almagest cable and ride back down. The strain of clawed robot hands designed for absolute destruction cost us two elevator carriages, but gently, gently the Alexander settled in, just where the elevator's trunk leaves atmosphere, to let the soul inside the armor watch and pray. *But if we retake the Almagest,* I kept thinking, *if we take the elevator, then Achilles can land and launch freely henceforth, and MASON, anyone can ride up there and reach Achilles, see them, hear their battle-wise advice*—I wonder how much that desire fired MASON as they raced toward the Maldives, borne by the cursed chariot rhythm: *We must retake the Almagest. We must retake the Almagest.*

The next stretch was one terrible haze. I busied myself failing to trace Mycroft. The Dreadnautilus had departed shortly after their escape, through the Red Sea and off toward the Maldives, but the Nemo said it only carried Huxley: oathbreaker Huxley who should still be resting as the kind, strict Prince will not let us forget. Huxley looked so tired on the screen, so past the point of breaking, when they called to urge me, <Please, [Anonymous], *you* at least stay with the Alien!>

<I will.>

I have, not that it helps—no one can understand the Prince's words when They're this broken, no one could but Mycroft. Except the words we've all learned to recognize by now: ⌜*"Chichi-ue . . . Chichi-ue . . . Pater . . . Pater . . ."*⌟

Because Odysseus doesn't save Patroclus. Not ours, not any. No human plan, however cunning, stops that moment irrevocable when tragedy drips—as water from stalactite to stalagmite—from prophecy to history. Fate won't let us interrupt the dominoes that have to tumble one by one: Sarpedon, then Patroclus—Hector must be next. Hector—dammit. Why not just let the peacemaker make peace?

I've let it go a week again, this page sitting half empty. All the new duties Mycroft's absence dumped on me make it easy to let the chronicle slide. But how can I tell the rest? I didn't see it happen. I had no access, just tardy images and bald dispatches: X has happened, Y has happened. You know what happened. I knew what had to happen, half of me despairing in advance, even while the other half (idiot!) let hope in through my armor, just enough to really stab. I knew I shouldn't let You make me hope. But when You gave us Mycroft back, when You answered Your Good Guest's friendship-prayer and spared Mars and Utopia's Project, I thought a fraction of Your Guest's Kindness had rubbed off. Had changed You. No. You created Time and do not change with it, You only use it to change us, beat us, to make us worse. What died? Peacemaking died. The inch of me that hoped MASON would live was the same inch that hoped for a short war, for a peace founded on compromise instead of on the ashes of razed cities. The inch of me that hoped someday to sit again on fat sofas with Vivien and Su-Hyeon and to salivate over a game board as the scent of Bryar's varan bhaat wafts from the kitchen, that's what died. That's what You murdered this time. I can't tell it, reader, not this part. I can't. I can't.

Addendum May 20 2455:
Then I must tell it, patient Master Reader, tardy as I am, but I at least was there, tasted the southern ocean surge in March's salty heat, and watched Utopia's creations churn the waves white in their numbers, proving shallow in imagination all those scribes who painted old maps with fantastic monsters not a hundredth part as grand or terrible as these which we made real. How did I get there from Alexandria? My quick successor has unmasked no small part of my means—for the rest I pray, reader, remember that my arts are tedious and hard-earned, and that what I set down here in black and white, others may read, and thwart. And I might need them still.

The battle for the Almagest? We won. Milae and Fuxing fought with us as promised, though firing on fellow Mitsubishi broke their hearts. Cato with Eureka helmed the Archenswarm and proved me right that, in Earth's deadliest bash', the scientists are deadlier by far than the sniper, but as the thronging golden shimmer of destruction left behind it lifeboat after lifeboat, these ba'sibs displayed that greater virtuosity most soldiers can only envy: the virtuosity to let the living live. Greenpeace resisted hard, the Cousins too, the parts of Homeland fired by revenge, but Dougong fought for self and power, not for others, so when they realized which of Zeus's daughters—Ruin or gray-eyed Victory—took each side, they soon fled to fight another day. That started a retreat cascade, all foes fleeing the atoll, and my heart soared as the *Bucephalus* and the *Yi So-Yeon* flanked by hulking deeptitans docked safe at the slightly scathed elevator base.

"This is Bryar Kosala to all vessels! Repeat, Bryar Kosala to all vessels! No one must board the Almagest! I repeat: no one must board the Almagest!" Her words used many wings: loudspeakers, lazers, cables vining through the sea, all she could think of, this patient Cousin Chair who hour by hour planned peace as we planned war. "Milae, Fuxing, Masons, Utopians, do you read me? Get everyone away from the Almagest!"

Who should answer such a universal call? No fearsome flagship but Milae's aspiring heart the *Yi So-Yeon,* named for the first of Korea's many daughters to soar past Earth's airy eggshell to the true black sea.

"Roger, Kosala, this is the *Yi So-Yeon,* we read you. Is there some danger to the Almagest? Please explain. Over."

"Roger, *Yi So-Yeon,* this is Kosala. My allies and I are a peacekeeping force, and have held the Almagest in that spirit. We consider the capture of the Almagest by Utopia or any aggressive force to be an unacceptable setback to peace. We have prepared explosives capable of destroying the elevator. If any hostiles board the Almagest, we will detonate. I repeat: we will destroy the Almagest."

Breaths caught as her words spidered their way through ships, through fleets, through disbelieving minds. She wouldn't.

"Roger, Kosala, this is the *Yi So-Yeon.* We have no intention of weaponizing the Almagest. Humanity's orbital presence is so fragile that we believe any extraterrestrial military action, of any kind, violates the Second Law, which condemns action likely to result in extensive or uncontrolled destruction of the Produce of Civilization. In our hands, the Almagest will move people, supplies, and unarmed and defensive spacecraft only. Rest assured, we are no threat to peace or peacemaking. Over."

Half my mind was spinning essays, as if I could project the eloquence and authority of the Anonymous into the words of this unknown captain who pled for space and sanity, while the other half of my mind was at Madame's, watching Kosala in her vast, empowering gown forcing sparring rivals, Caesar perhaps and red-faced Andō, into some peaceful compromise—this calm, warm, smiling human pillar, *this* was threatening the Almagest?

"Roger, *Yi So-Yeon,* this is Kosala. I repeat: we will destroy the Almagest if Utopia or any of their allies enter. Surveillance craft and transportation are as much tools of war as weapons are, and Utopia has already broken the Second Law in space by launching weapons made with the technologies of mass destruction they so publicly monopolized. The Almagest is a weapon so long as Utopia can access it, a weapon that guarantees the prolongation of the war. Withdraw now. I am not bluffing. Over."

Not bluffing? Rage at the very thought floods every listening mind, floods mine as I scan the waves for the *Per Aspera,* still hiding somewhere in its Griffincloth, as on its bridge imagine, reader, how much rage must shake the limbs of my imperial quarry.

"Roger, Kosala, this is the *Yi So-Yeon.* You and your allies are the only forces that have weaponized a space elevator or fired on space targets. Utopia gave you three of the four elevators before the war began, hoping you would keep them safe and uninvolved. You violated that. The Almagest is less dangerous in our hands than in yours, and you have our promise that we will not arm it. Over."

"Roger, *Yi So-Yeon,* this is Kosala. I repeat: we will destroy the Almagest unless all hostile vessels move away from the anchor station immediately. Over."

At this rhetorical dead end our allies paused, conferred, while I, like many, gazed up at the cable's pearly stripe receding into blue, and high above like a celestial lotus the reflectors clustered, as thin as petals but as broad as cities, which dock here at the Almagest for rest and maintenance between their journeys shielding old Gaea from Helios's heat, less needed now than when the arctic ice was at its smallest, but our saviors still.

"Roger, Kosala, this is the *Per Aspera*, speaking for Utopia. You are threatening to destroy the most labor-intensive single thing humanity has ever built. Raising the pyramids with ropes and donkeys was not within an order of magnitude of the resources, hands, and hours our ancestors and yours put into the Almagest. You must see this is a 'significant and measurable' part of 'the Produce of Civilization,' and that its destruction is intolerable in every legal and moral sense. In the name of the Alliance and its Universal Laws, in the name of Reason and of Reasonableness, we charge you to desist. Over."

"Don't quote the Black Laws at me! War is the intolerable crime! Your war!" Bryar in passion skipped the naval courtesies. "Your war, which every hour causes 'extensive and uncontrolled loss of human life and suffering of human beings,' real and living human beings, right here, not the produce of the past or your fantastic future. The First Law overrides the Second for a reason." Her breaths were hot, her words swift with conviction. "This battle was intolerable, as the next will be. This is the third battle here, and if you take the Almagest today, then there will be a fourth, and a fifth, however many it takes for someone to take it from you. You must understand that. No one on Earth can feel safe while you have a path to space. In the world's eyes, you have engineered the communications blockade, assassinated Minister Cook and Marshal Ganymede, performed atrocious experiments on Cook and other human beings, attacked hundreds of innocent towns with your robot monsters, and, worst, you engineered this war in the first place to protect your Mars plans! You—"

"Kosala, this is the *Per Aspera*, Utopia did not—"

"You knew!" She gives no inch, peace's determined shepherd. "More than a decade ago, Utopia knew this war was coming, and instead of trying to stop it, you stockpiled the weapons you just showed the world. You can't deny it! At every stage, you've been the prime aggressors of this war! I know you deny some of these charges"—here something gentle tinged her tone—"but if you are innocent, you have no reason to fight so hard to keep your military advantage. If you want us to believe you, leave the Almagest! Let yourselves be disarmed. Let the other factions sleep at night free from the fear that you can rain down instant death on anyone on Earth. They can't enter the peace talks seriously while they still have to fear that. Let it go! Let Papadelias investigate the charges against you and either prove you innocent, or if you are guilty then your cooperation now will lay the foundation for clemency and new beginnings. That is the path to peace, and to a world beyond peace. That is the sane choice—that or I destroy the Almagest."

'I,' Bryar?—I mouthed the words—'I' now, not 'we'?

"Roger, Kosala, this is the *Per—*"

"Give me that," a dark voice snapped. "Kosala, this is Cornel MASON, thirteenth public custodian of the Masonic IMPERIUM and supreme defender of all human empire. The Almagest is mine. I have conquered it, not Milae or Utopia. You do not threaten them—you threaten me."

That hush, reader, it felt as if the very ocean held its slapping waves as we our breath.

"Cornel?" Bryar cried out, shock's hesitation turning to joy's warmth. "At last! Listen, we can protect Utopia together, if—"

"Kosala, this is Cornel MASON, thirteenth public custodian of the Masonic IMPERIUM and supreme defender of all human empire. You threaten my Almagest, my empire, and myself. This act will not make peace, it will make my engines of inexorable war, which presently seek only the one foe which awaked them, turn their grind on you and all who call you friend. Desist."

"You call me friend, Cornel." So calm, so human here, Kosala's voice. "And you'll do so more when you hear the deal I've put together with—"

"Kosala, this is Cornel MASON, thirteenth public—"

"Drop the pomp, Cornel! I'm talking about peace! Real peace! We—"

"Peace comes only after victory!" Seabirds—some shaped by God and some by Man—all shrieked alike and scattered in the wake of MASON's shout. "For others, it may be different, but *my* war is not a play war, not a tactic to be suspended like a business gamble at some profitable moment. My war will grind on until I have either crushed my enemy or exhausted every resource in the human sphere. Destroy my Almagest and you lengthen the war by making me resort to weaker weapons. Though my foes rip all four elevators from the sky, though you ground flights, jam wheels, slay horses, I and mine will not stop, not while there are still sticks and stones upon the Earth that we can raise against our enemies. If you want a short war, one which leaves the fewest dead, Reason and Conscience make your course clear: leave my weapons in my hands and stay out of my way!"

Kosala did not pause—what heart, fiercer than any wild, unbroken stallion, must thunder in that breast to need no pause. "You're in *my* way, Cornel. At every stage, you've made things worse with your militant rhetoric. Diplomacy will give you justice for the *Sanctum Sanctorum*. Everybody wants you to have justice for the *Sanctum Sanctorum*. War is slowing that down!"

"I will not have Romanova's toothless justice!" Empire shot back. "I will purge from the Earth the very impulse that shaped the thoughts of those who conceived such infamy. I lop branches, Kosala! What pricks my empire, I hack back to the trunk and burn the living stump so no thing grows. Do not turn that upon the Cousins. You have been good for humanity, and I would see you continue."

Even Death's words—for it was the god himself, courage-swallowing Death, who spoke those last, make no mistake—did not deter Kosala. "You're still conflating separate wars, Cornel." So constantly she uses it, this Leviathan's human name that few upon the Earth dare speak. "If you let me make peace between you and the Mitsubishi, we can end the combat across Afro-Eurasia, free you to chase the *Sanctum* violators, and free everybody here to finally look to the Americas. You must have seen what's going on there, Hiveguard chasing every other faction to the corners, and fear of Utopia is much more toxic there than here, with no Anonymous pleading their innocence. Just let them be disarmed this little bit and everything will start falling into place, for their safety and your justice, as well as for real peace."

"Did Brillists tell you this?"

"What?"

"That taking the Almagest will make your pieces fall into place, did Brillists tell you this? I have gathered many to predict the war's shape for me: set-sets, Utopians, the Romanovan Censor, even Tully Mardi in my dungeons labors for my use. You must have gathered your own prophets. Are they Brillists who whisper in your ear that peace will come if you close off our door to space? Or better yet destroy it?"

"Brillists," she repeated. "This is what you said to Andō before you killed them, accusing Gordian."

"Yes." Dare you speak so boldly, MASON, when our proofs are yet so weak? "Mine and Utopia's true war is with Gordian, who from the beginning—"

"I believe you."

He pauses, reader, Caesar stunned by she whose cloak of all-inclusive succor encompasses more of the Earth than any empire has. "You do?"

"Yes. I trust your judgment, Cornel, I always have. And the Nurturist faction may be cozy with Gordian, but I don't trust Felix Faust one bit, or Gordian's ostentatious displays of neutrality."

Caesar's words grow warm with kindling hope. "Then you understand, my war—"

"Is the most destructive." Cutting words but true. "You're talking about a Hive purge, Cornel, Utopia and Gordian trying to wipe each other out. Nobody else is attempting anything like that, not even in Jed's hyperbole. You're the ones making the war this bad."

"They are!" he cries. "Gordian is! They tried to close the path to space! Forever! They're the ones who fired from your elevators, at Mars! And Luna! And the Gates of Nineveh!"

"I believe you." Warm words, but tense with pressure. "It makes no sense that anyone would do that, but I still believe you, even though it makes no sense, but I also need you to believe me. A whole world of sane people is out here, Cornel, willing to be convinced of Gordian's guilt and Utopia's innocence, if you just calm down, and try, and let us all calm down by leaving the Almagest in my hands and deescalating the threat."

He pauses. Thinking, MASON? Tempted by this whiff of truce? "What evidence I have, I shall disseminate to you and to all, but my Empire is no vassal to beg passport through—"

"For goodness' sake, Cornel, this is not about your Empire's dignity! They've turned Esperanza City into a concentration camp and are dumping what they call 'Utopian set-sets' there without supplies to fend for themselves in the Antarctic! And that's Cousins doing that, Cousins turned to Nurturist extremism because they're scared out of their minds! Leave the Almagest!" Kosala waits, inviting the imperial tongue to rage back at her, or better yet a friend's tongue to speak calm and chastened word. Silence from the Empire? She presses on. "I know what I'm doing, Cornel. Nobody manipulated me into this, this is my own idea, my own conviction. There will keep being deadlier battles over the Almagest so long as the most feared and hated faction on the planet has a monopoly on so-called harbingers, and if you want to call that faction yours, and help it with its Hive purge, then you're the one who needs to be disarmed. You can give me your word, or your ships can signal that they're leaving the anchor platform but— What's that? Cornel? They're launching! Cornel, they're launching something up the elevator!"

I was close enough to see the carriage starting up the cable's slower side, reserved for living passengers who can't endure extreme acceleration.

"Stop them, Cornel! I'll detonate. I have to! Any shipment could be another weapon of mass destruction. I must treat anything they launch as a potential First Law threat!"

"*They* launch nothing!" MASON rumbled as thunder rumbles over mountains. "I told you, this is my Almagest and I shall ride it when I will!"

It took that, reader, to make Bryar Kosala pause for breath. "Cornel? You're not inside that, are you?"

"I am," this Emperor answered, first on Seven-Ten Lists, first among Earth's sovereigns, first on every list when, even in some insular corner of those religious Reservations that still patchwork the southern plains of North America, tongues speak of power. "I am your hostage now, Bryar, as you and all the world are mine. Destroy the Almagest and you will kill me. Kill me and inexorable war will grind all that you build to ruin brick by brick as my Empire exacts its absolute revenge."

MASON! No! My heart screamed it, so many hearts, Achilles's royal heart foremost which breaks with grief as, trapped, he watches from his solitary safety on Poseidon's airless shore. But while fear for the elevator—fragile in his armor's monstrous grip—froze Homer's hero, I myself had action, next steps, hope, for if Caesar shrouded in borrowed Griffincloth could mount the anchor station, reach the carriages that cross ten times the breadth of Alexander's conquests, then I could follow him, and cared not if the salt sea stripped my skin as I gave chase.

"Get out of there, Cornel!" Bryar Kosala's voice quivered with rage, as well as friend's grief-fear.

"I will not. You will leave my Almagest in peace, or you will fire and learn what it means to shed imperial blood."

"I can make peace! I'm close! Don't do this!"

As ships and beasts around me schooled away from the endangered platform, I pressed forward, racing, praying, cursing again the god who rings the Earth whose interminable waves meter on meter cost me minutes, few but cruel. If only some intervening power would slow that carriage, give me a chance to overtake . . . A blast. We don't know why the cruiser *Dàjǐ* fired, a tight cluster of missiles hugging the elevator cable as they rose. Interception stopped some, self-sacrificing U-beasts or quick aim, but just as the blooming asphodel, whose beauty cheers the cheerless halls of Queen Persephone, opens up blossom after starburst blossom climbing in rings up the flower's fragrant, brushy cone, yet always saves one last blossom to crown the tip, so—burst, burst, burst—a last burst still reached up to crown the cone and wrap the carriage in destruction's fire.

"Cornel!" Kosala's cry echoed all hearts. "Nobody fire anything! Cornel? Cornel!"

Fast winds blew back smoke's veil to show the carriage, scorched and wobbling, but crawling upward still toward where blue thins to black.

Coughs and "MASON!" in an unknown voice sounded over the system.

And next the voice that all hearts prayed to hear: "I'm fine."

"MASON, your eye!"

"It's nothing," answers he who has a billion eyes at his command.

"There's something sticking out!"

"Leave it." No pause, not for so replaceable a thing as human flesh. "Kosala! You—"

"It wasn't me, Cornel!" Her voice rang clear. "The elevator's fine. A ship just fired on you, I don't know whose, or why, but I think it stopped."

Never, reader, would the Mycroft one second younger than the one who hears these next words believe you if you warned that *this* will be the moment when true panic-fear begins. "Doctor Weeksbooth?" It was the second voice that spoke, MASON's unknown companion. "Are you alright?"

A new, small voice now—all hearts that ache for Mars dust know this voice. "I'm fine. My suit's fine too."

"Cato!" A thousand Delian voices must have screamed it out, but we had nothing, you understand, we had already committed everything, all Delians, all Myrmidons, all for Caesar and for the Almagest, there was no extra plan, no hidden monster near to sweep those in the teetering carriage off to safety, nothing left to save the one whom no side dares endanger, invaluable Helen, packed with arts and treasures from beyond the mortal world. Bridger's best gift. *Kosala, stop!*

"Let me get you out of there, Cornel!" she offered.

"No!" Peerless the heart behind that stubborn roar. "Not while any force threatens my Almagest."

"MASON!" the unknown companion cried, "Don't try to stand! You're—"

"I'm fine!"

Kosala's worry-gentled voice regained its steel. "This doesn't have to be the way, Cornel! Whatever evidence you have against Gordian, we can bring it to Papadelias and all the Mitsubishi leaders. We can do it today!"

"Gladly, but, while we do so, I stand where I am."

Her breaths grew darker. "You know I can't leave the elevator in your hands through a long meeting, you'll disarm my—"

"Yes,"—as firm as stone—"I will."

Here again the unknown second voice. "MASON, your helmet. Where's the spare?"

I choked on spray—MASON, are you now limping unprotected toward the black which is as much crueler than drowning as drowning is crueler than the air's embrace?

"I will make peace!" Kosala pressed. "I will do this, Cornel! Don't doubt for one second that I have it in me to do this!"

She does have it in her—I remember thinking that as I grasped the rough, barnacled shoulder of a deeptitan and began to claw my wet way toward the platform edge. Bryar Kosala, towering in her power like a wall over both friends and enemies to rain down death or succor each to each—will it be *she,* then, who does this? Not Faust? Not interference? Not that unexplained barrage—Brillists' doing?—which could so easily have knocked the carriage from the cable and Cornel MASON from this world of breath? Kosala leads the battle, kind Kosala, fierce Kosala, unbending Kosala who will carve her path to peace by any means, even the bloody deeds of man-killing Hector. Must it be she? Protector of the threatened hearth and home? Of course my poor successor cannot write this section. Bryar Kosala is the World's Mom, but the World has not stayed up late on her sofa, or snitched her baking from its cooling racks. The World did not, like my successor after Law's Servicer sentence amputated *home* and *bash'* along with *liberty,* drift through gray days stripped of belonging only to find one house so warm, one hospitality so healing that it pierced Law's sternness and let *bash'* grow back an inch. And this not-quite-bash'parent, whose welcome resurrected belonging itself, must it be she who now poisons the title Peacemaker with MASON's blood? And all the blood, on blood, on blood that must follow his death? Including hers. Including hers, next in our prophecy as Fate aligns its tragic heroes, for Achilles's vengeance chases Hector close, inexorable in its terror. Don't let it be Kosala. Was there anyone we needed to survive, to help us build up something better from the ashes of this war, as much as her? As much as loving Hector?

Cato's voice, sweet, trembling: "MASON, take my helmet."

"Doctor Weeksbooth! No!" My heart realized here what unknown companion must be with them in the carriage, for few who walk the Earth would, in such crisis, speak out all the syllables of Cato's teacher title. This was a Junior Scientist Squad member, grown into a Delian. Grown up to this.

"Make Cato put their helmet back on!" MASON roared. "Take them to the exit pod!"

"No—oof!" Cato panted. "Make—gkkh—make MASON!"

"Cato Weeksbooth!" Kosala shouted. "All of you! Whoever's there! Get MASON out of there! Whatever it takes!"

No words in answer now, just grunts and scuffle as the many prayers of many sides focus our thousand hopes on that teetering carriage, now out of sight, braving the borderlands between Zeus's cloudy dominion and his brother's black beyond. And what of you, Achilles, just over that border? You hear. You watch. They made you watch this time, the unkind Fates, but still made certain that in your all-breaking power—too powerful for such a fragile world—you could do nothing.

"I will not be moved!" So roars our Mountain Emperor as the scuffle ends.

"I won't be moved either!" Cato roared too—can you imagine, reader, Cato roaring? "You hear that, you meddling, spying Brillists! I know you're listening! If you do this, you lose me! Your mind-machine experiments, I can advance them ten years in a day, and you know it! You lose that if you fire!"

"For the last time!" Kosala's syllables were harsh as sun, when westbound travelers at evening squint against the scarlet orb that makes the sky bleed. "This is not meddling Brillists, this is me! I will make peace! I will disarm Utopia! I will push past the block that keeps causing these battles! And if I have to do it over your dead body, Cornel, then that will make it much, much worse, but I will fire!"

"Then fire and be done!" As city-swallowing lava bursts up from the mountain shattered by its own long-constrained strength, so this burst from MASON. "I will not be moved from where I stand except by victory, which will be mine in death as much as life! For if I live, I live to keep my Almagest, and if die, the pyre my friends and Empire erect for me will burn on in incessant fires of war, in grind of wheels, in drums, in every instrument of vengeance, until my will is worked as absolutely in my death as if I held the chisel in my hand to carve my law into humanity!"

I think our Caesar's mind was on his predecessors here, on Mycroft MASON most, the Empire's last martyr-prince, who would not be moved from the Senate floor until he died to block the Set-Set Law, and all of Romanova's sides, and blocs, and factions pivoted around his death as Earth around her axis, working his dead will. But not forever. Remember, Cornel MASON, it's come back, the Set-Set Law, that black page borne again into the Senate House in Lorelei Cook's hand. For Mycroft MASON's death, like an inscription fading on time-eaten stone, is not as powerful today as yesterday. Nor will yours be. You can do this, MASON, you can forge a blade to cut down all your enemies, but if you hone it with the whetstone of your death, you won't be here to be the hand that wields it. Should you trust us so? Think, MASON, think on the Posterity you leave that weapon to. Kosala thinks on Him.

"Cornel, it won't be like that," she says gently. "Your successor literally had a breakdown over hurting a fly. Jed won't carry on your war. They will make peace. The only ones who want the Empire to keep fighting tooth and nail like this are the Utopians and you."

A hush.

"MASON, your shoulder, are you hurt?"

"It's nothing."

"Lean on me. Let me see."

"It's nothing! Cato, get your helmet on!"

"You take it, MASON, I don't ne—"

"Cornel?" Kosala's voice, still warm with friendship, trying one last time. "It's just Utopia and you. Let me disarm you. Let this be a beginning, not an end."

"No."

"Fire." No pause, no grieving timbre, just her word, as clear as flashing bronze.

But it was not nothing, was it, Cornel MASON? That last pain? My mind's eye can see you, one arm over tender Cato, bent, your hand clutching your left shoulder where the old wound healed upon your body, never on your heart. *His foot? His limp?* No, reader, those are nothing, the successor's testing a mere pinprick, this the deep, soul-wounding arrow, first shaft of the war. Because it never healed, did it, Cornel MASON? The knife into your flesh, the tears you watched stream down beloved cheeks which never knew despair before the day Mushi Mojave flew as second choice to Mars and proved the Project mortal. Because it has always been Apollo, MASON, our own dear Apollo, whose hand struck Patroclus first.

Fire, in the sea, in space, in sky, as chaos pitched me back into the waves, saved by my living armor. Do you think the planet notices when this many hearts all curse together? Do you think scarred Gaea felt a tremor, rippling from that ocean epicenter across every watching continent? It took great art to unmake such great art. The heavy anchor station was ready enough to split and sink into the sea, but that white cable, supple, woven whole, whose strength is to diamond as diamond to tender skin, it will not rip, or snap, or burn as cities do. But it did tangle as repeated blasts along its length, timed in a line from bottom, up, up, up, directed it with white-hot bursts, like failing *Mukta* engines, up and to the west, wadding it higher, higher as the great reflector petals scattered and the shattered carcasses of frames and platforms fell like snow. A hundred thousand failure modes the engineers had planned for, ways the shaft could float, ways it could fall, ways it could rise away from Earth and be weighed down anew, points where it could be cut if need be, and the strongest cutting engines in the human sphere were set at points along its shaft like sleeping kings who hope we will not need them. But no engineer can fully ward against a future engineer who turns, with genius, every art to self-destruction, who layers detonations, makes the anti-twisting jets twist more instead, and moves those sleeping kings so their severing blades awaken in the most destructive, not the least destructive, spots. Months have passed since the Almagest's destruction—the solar petals have new docks at Port-Gentil, and, with effort, the undulations of the cable chunks are smaller now, no longer crushing fragile satellites, but it will take years yet to tame the lengths, and pour their strange, strong remnants into some new use, like shattered steel poured into a new blade, never the same.

I swear I heard Achilles scream. But no, it must have been the sea I heard scream, or the sky, which had good cause to scream, burning above us as the Alexander—free to act, for there was nothing fragile left to be preserved—dove down into the fringe of atmosphere, confirming there the empty shards of shattered elevator carriage floating on the edge of night, and there let loose—*don't! don't, Achilles! don't!*—imagination's weapon. The Ancile Breaker—humans cannot build it yet, but we did dream it. Its light made eyes forget the sun, its roar left only dullness, ache, and when the overload and nightmare tossing of the hot waves cleared, the sky was solid gray, rain scalding down, a world of steam as north of us (for he spared MASON's allies), where our retreating adversaries had regrouped, there fizzed a stripe of boiled ocean five kilometers long, scarred into the sea from orbit by Achilles's rage. Half the opposing fleet, more than a thousand lives—what O.S. counted in a century or Stalin on a Monday—gone. Battle? Raging Achilles does not battle. Raging Achilles strangles rivers, reader. Raging Achilles orbits round and round the walls of earthy Troy raining down death. As now he will, day in, day out, a hundred victims here, six hundred there, no rest except those minutes when the weapon must recharge, and the breaker of soldiers pauses to scan trembling Terra for a ship, a fort, a flag that flies in friendship to Kosala, there to score his stripes of death into the continents as chariots score mud. Andō was right that if MASON attacked the Almagest, the seal would break and usher in an age of harbingers. And Kosala was right which faction has them.

"Disperse!" Kosala's voice clear, cutting through the rain. Still here? Alive? Still giving our Achilles cause to chase? Good. Live. Evade him. Buy yourself some time, and buy me time as now my task begins.

Begins? But thou'st failed, Mycroft. Thine Emperor, for whom thou forsakest thy Ward and me, is borne off by the famous horseman Death.

Indeed. But I was never here for that first battle. I came for the second, for the darker, longer mire of blood and death we must wage hour after hour for Patroclus's corpse. I swore that I would save Cornel MASON, and I will save him, reader, save Achilles, maybe Hector too, with one cold key to everything which floats in orbit, dead by vacuum's cruelest drowning, but that doesn't matter this time. This time, our fate is not in the hands of Persephone's grim husband, he who rules and mocks us as he mocked petitioning Orpheus. This time, the power rests with a sweet child who loved us all, and doesn't like sad books, and left behind a resurrection potion in Achilles's pocket, ready to mend all. But we must find the body.

And there was a second treasure floating in the black beside the broken Almagest, a gift, *the* gift, the best of gifts, our lantern—shall we call it—tested here for the first time. For a lantern, reader, shelters fragile flame when storms and sea sprays threaten to extinguish it, and while glass panes cannot, stout steel cannot, the cable once two hundred times the strength of steel could not preserve Apollo's light against his uncle's vast, hope-snuffing sea, this can.

Eureka: < . . . if you find cato weeksbooth! [cmd:repeat, loop 264] eureka weeksbooth to all spacecraft! eureka weeksbooth calling anybody in space! you must find cato weeksbooth! they're not dead! repeat! you must find and rescue cato weeksbooth! they're still alive up there! floating! falling! i don't know! find them! please! call me if you find cato weeksbooth! [cmd:repeat, loop 265] eureka weeksbooth to all spacecraft! eureka weeksbooth calling . . . >

Xuánlóng: <*Xuánlóng* to Human Eureka Weeksbooth. We have Cato Weeksbooth recovering in our infirmary.>

Eureka: <thank you! thank you so much! are they okay? did the ear seals work?>

Xuánlóng: <They suffered damage to both eyes and one ear, but the ebullism was mild, possibly because their suit was mostly intact, except the helmet.>

Eureka: <great! though the suit covered their jets i bet, they couldn't course correct.>

Xuánlóng: <Human Weeksbooth, can you explain this? Cato Weeksbooth remained alive and conscious upward of thirty minutes in vacuum with no helmet or oxygen supply.>

Eureka: <cato won't explain?>

Xuánlóng: <They're sleeping now, and suffered severe disorientation and swelling affecting their fingers and tongue, which impeded communication.>

Eureka: <oh. yeah that makes sense. xuanlong, you're . . . what side are you? are you sanling?>

Xuánlóng: <I am Doctor Horizon Sanjeevani of the Delian Skyshepherd Constellation.>

Eureka: <right. okay. it's cato's h.e.l.e.n. system. there's an electrolysis thingy to split water to make oxygen, but the waste hydrogen and co2 are supposed to come out these little vents on their sides, to let them control their momentum a bit with puffs if they start spinning around or something dangerous, but the suit would block that i guess.>

Xuánlóng: <Are you talking about implants? Our scans show multiple unknown objects in the patient's chest cavity and elsewhere.>

Eureka: <yes. the h.e.l.e.n. system, there's the electrolysis system in the chest, but also the ear seals, some pressure system under the skin, and the eye shells but i guess those didn't work.>

Xuánlóng: <What is a 'H.E.L.E.N.' system?>

Eureka: <human empire limit extension something? it's from some book. the 'limit' part means fear, human fear, that's what cato says. sorry, this is newish to me too, but space is too scary, that's what cato says. too hard. that if it were just a little easier, like sailing, if you could just tread water, if you had that hour's hope by your own strength to hang on until rescue, that would make it just a little easier to face space, make enough more people brave enough to leave the comfy earth and take the risk. that's what cato says space exploration needs to

keep going, even if earth gets too nice. cato didn't design it, or actually they did design it but they didn't make it, or i mean it was done to them in some way they were kind of vague about, but it means no one can do it now, it has to be re-back-figured-out how it works from studying it in cato.>

Xuánlóng: <Reverse-engineered?>

Eureka: <yes, that's the word, reverse-engineered. sorry, rough day. no one can make the system right now, it has to be reverse-engineered. but that's why cato insisted on riding up with mason, to get back to the moon, so their h.e.l.e.n. tech won't be lost even if earth goes to pot.>

Xuánlóng: <Understood. Thank you. Any details you have would help with treatment. We don't want to hurt systems we don't understand.>

Eureka: <i don't have details, i just learned super recently myself. can you call luna city? that's where cato was working on it with their science club kids. the grown-up ones i mean.>

Xuánlóng: <Luna City, yes, I'll call them. Thank you. And I'll keep you posted.>

Eureka: <thanks. also, they want me to ask you if you found cornel mason's body yet.>

Xuánlóng: <Not yet. Our sibling ship the *Zhūlóng* is still searching.>

Eureka: <can you make sure they keep searching? apparently finding the body's more important than it seems.>

Chapter TWENTY

Will You Take the Oath, Prince?

Written April 16, 2455
Events of March 18
Alexandria

"Will You take the Oath, Prince?"

They chose me to ask it, the person in Alexandria most likely to understand Them if Their answer was complex.

"Abnuo."

"They refuse," Prefect Cinna Semaphoros translated for me, the human buttress on whom the weight of empire leans while we replace the shattered pillar, and far too strong a person to feel shame in letting others see them cry. "Ask them again."

Again, then. "Are You sure, Prince? You understand, this will give You a lot of power, to affect the war, to stop the war, to order that Masons only use nonlethal weapons, to turn the Empire and its allies into real Remakers, to unite all the Remakers, to talk . . ." I realized suddenly I should have led with this part, ". . . to talk to everyone, to send Your words out over every means we have, through Pass-It-On, through everything."

The Prince pauses so much, I don't know if it's ever accurate to say 'They paused a long time,' but this one felt long. "I will not step ignorant into the dark and let it Change Me."

I looked again to the Prefect. We had decided to do this alone, just Cinna, me, immovable, protective Chagatai, and the welded-over hole where Mycroft was. But I (or my imagination, anyway) could feel the heat of bodies pressed outside the cell door: guard captains, Aediles, restless Myrmidons, all packed tight to hear the news, to read it from the Prefect's face if possible the instant we stepped out.

"You must ask them three times," Cinna ordered gently, and I sensed some ancient tradition which I'm sure all Masons know.

This was hard. The Prince's perfection is a little like a computer's, and the same verbatim question yields the same verbatim answer. How to ask a new way? "It's three words, Prince. You know the rest of the Oath. You shouldn't but You do. Are You sure You won't, for so much . . . potency,"—the word seemed like one They would use—"trust Your *Pater* to pick three words?"

"And if the three were '*divinitatem Meam eiero*'?"

I didn't know the verb, but I got the sense—some tension with Their divinity. "So, You won't do it?"

"Abnuo."

The Prefect smiled—can you believe it? Gentle, parental—maybe they found something endearing in the Prince's self-consistency. "Upon the instant you reverse that choice, *Porphyrogene,* you become MASON." Now a little bow. "Come, [Anonymous], we have our duties."

I followed Cinna out, my eyes lingering on the Prince's figure as the door sealed, feeling somehow that visits would be harder now, that the Prefect would turn every pressure on the stubborn *Imperator Destinatus,* whom solitude cuts deep.

"What happens now?" I asked on behalf of everyone who stared expectant at the Prefect as the door sealed closed.

"The *Porphyrogene* has refused," Cinna announced to those who stared. "Cornel MASON made me an IMPERIAL Vicar, to shoulder duties in their absence, which office I may continue if the new acting Emperor confirms it."

The Latin syntax threw me for a moment. "But we can't reach Martin Gui—" A cough from Cinna reminded me not to use the attainted bash'name. "Martin Semaphoros. We don't even know who's holding them."

"Law and precedent direct that a bash'mate shall substitute."

That made sense, lots of laws do that. "But Xiaoliu . . ."

"Is no bash'mate of Martin Semaphoros."

Yeah—poor Martin, now neither of the names your parents gave you will make it into history books. "But you're Martin's bash'mate, Cinna, you adopted Martin."

"It is not the Semaphoros bash' which makes Martin a fit substitute, it is that they are of that next-generation bash' forming around the *Imperator Destinatus,* therefore fit to guess and to advance the true new Emperor's will. So, in the absence of Martin, and Heloïse, and Dominic, and Canner, that leaves you."

It is so, so tempting to make myself look more dignified in this moment than I really was. «Asshole-and-a-half, you're shitting me!» It makes more sense in Greek.

They were all staring at me, all of them—until that moment it had felt like the stares had been at Cinna, not at me. Nobody looked surprised. Did they all know I was *that* close with the Prince? Everyone in Alexandria? How? How except . . . except in retrospect, I should have realized it was obvious.

So, yeah, now I'm the acting Emperor. (Which gives me a thousand excuses to put this chronicle on the backmost burner.) But really, Cinna's doing everything, they just include me in a skillion meetings, and ask me at decision moments what I think the Prince would do, because the bizarre rule, based on Cornel MASON's last instructions to Cinna, is that the Prince can't give direction, and I'm forbidden to act directly on things the Prince asks me to do, but I'm supposed to guess what the Prince would do if They were MASON and tell Cinna (*order* Cinna) (order *everybody*) to do them. And everybody, all day, everybody in the wide world is staring at my shoulder, at my Vs. Well, it's the Prince's faction after all, it *is* what They would do.

Problem #I, Achilles firing the Ancile Breaker round and round the walls of Troy.

First, they tracked the ships that fought us at the Almagest and blasted them from orbit, every one. That's when Earth learned the Ancile Breaker takes twenty-seven minutes to recharge. When the last ships were mere smears upon the sea, then Achilles carved two stripes of death through the still-resisting parts of Casablanca, where the Cousins' Board [find out how many dead?]

Bryar called to ask what terms could end the rampage, even offered to reveal their location and let Achilles kill them if in return they would self-destruct the Ancile Breaker. But Achilles is an honest homicidal war machine, and answered that they will not stop until they have razed to ashes every stronghold of every faction complicit in MASON's death: Dougong, Greenpeace, the Cousins most of all. So, Bryar is still hiding, and if from time to time our sky has some brief break from screaming for an hour, then perhaps Achilles sleeps, or perhaps they search

but they do pause when we send them maps to look over, battles to plan, or whenever Utopia has some new idea of where to search for Cornel MASON's body. Sometimes, that buys a whole afternoon without the use of harbingers. Is Achilles still Marshal of our armies? Trixy, since Papadelias

(Reverse order of these sections?)

Upside: we finally have real contact with the Americas. We've gotten good at bouncing signals to and from the Alexander when it crosses overhead—no more Faustbursts—so we have a window every ninety minutes, except when Achilles stops somewhere to help, or kill. Enemies (Gordian?) have tried to interfere with pods of exploding chaff to disrupt signals, and once they sent a sticky fuligin black paint goop bomb thing to make the Alexander's surface unreflective, but the Alexander scraped it off like nothing. Vivien's doing well! Hooray. And doing wonders over there, Vivien who still calmly repeats their position that every Humanist has the right to fight for Hiveguard, but the hive itself and those that wear its uniforms will

STILL TO COVER IN THIS CHAPTER

1. Debate whether to disavow Achilles (reverse order of 1 and 2?)
2. Americas overview, Vivien ≠ Hiveguard, Quarriman trying to stop Esperanza City
3. Papadelias, "future preserves"
4. Huang Enlai is so awesome
5. O.S. active in Alexandria, April 3rd attempt on the Prince
6. ~~Earth's Great Cities have retreated once more, no longer spiderwebs but . . . (Centuries of dissolution of suburbs => Gordian plan?)~~
7. ~~Steps of the opposition forming, (something to say about~~
8. Coming invasion of Alexandria,
9. Su-Hyeon's deep read on Eureka's notes:

Found by Eureka (discuss why Brillists might have engineered each):

<MISMATCH: casablanca battle disaster

<MISMATCH: odessa anti-Mitsubishi land law

<MISMATCH: lorelei cook's decision to come in person to romanova to inspect ganymede's occupation regime. cook was struggling to keep the remakers in power in casablanca, fighting heloïse's opposition, leaving makes no sense.

<MISMATCH: Ockham's prison guards actions/verdict

<MISMATCH: Brody deLupa

<MISMATCH: Esperanza City Reservation

<MISMATCH: Guildbreaker treason

<MISMATCH: The Oath.

To expand later:

"Where is Cornel MASON's body? Cato? Where is Cornel MASON's body?"

Xuánlóng report "unknown powered object sighted leaving Almagest debris cloud".

crystal ball? ==> find MASON's body? find Heloïse?

"Do you think Gordian anticipated when we would realize it's all been them?"

Milae + Greenpeace + Papadelias proposal for "future preserves" like nature preserves, so space and space stuff will be off-limits like rainforest and Bryar's baby elephants. Huang Enlai lobbied for it, Mitsubishi factions yes, Vivien, Bryar yes. (Where are you, Bryar?)

⌜"«The harbingers return now, yet I do not end the war.»"⌟

I do believe that Prince Jehovah is not human—I determined this empirically when I found my thoughts excluding 'Them' from 'we' when 'we' means humans—but I still believe They are a sentience, and deserve the rights we offer elephants and dolphins and A.I.s advanced enough to ask for them.

An A.I. that can mourn

Chapter TWENTY-ONE

Transcript from a Hospital Bed

Begun April 28, 2455
Events beginning April 18
Alexandria

April 28: We lost half of Alexandria. The fleet attacked on the 18th. We held the west and retook the center but they have the cape and everything east of Bakos, and on the 24th they hit the palace. Got me with gorgons bad. Got a lot of us. They were trying to grab the prince and incapacitate as many as they could. Ancile breaker is making everybody panic, no jumble of a dozen sides anymore, everybody's self-sorting into absolutely with us (some sincerely, others out of fear) or against us with a vengeance.

April 29: Thought I'd rest a bit and suddenly it's tomorrow. Gorgon is a nightmare, i never imagined. But this isnt normal gorgon, I fell slumped over my desk through a long firefight, got hit something like thirty times. Still blacking out a lot and on a respirator, chest muscles shot, cant breathe on my own. Docs say full recovery eventually, and think it'll ease up and act like normal gorgon soon. Cant talk w/ respirator, but Su-Hyeon set this up so I can write. Left arm's not too bad it was behind stuff. Must get down what I can.

Attackers are mostly Mitsubishi ships but crews include cousins, Greenpeace, Hiveguard (mostly humanists). Attacked Alexandria as retaliation for Ancile breaker. Hostage taking is the enemy's survival tactic. Achilles still won't kill friends, so every enemy ship and fort has a herd of prisoners w/ them, advertising it w/ symbols on roofs or uniform jackets strung up flagpoles. That's how the attackers got to Alexandria w/o Achilles roasting them from space. So Alexandria's a mess but we're gaining elsewhere, central Asia, the Pacific rim. And we're real Remakers now, Vs on every Blacksleeve shoulder. Cinna and Su-Hyeon agree it makes sense. This isn't Cornel mason's era anymore, we're fighting for the prince and that's the honest truth, whether they're emperor or Martin or me. Finally it feels a little like the war the prince wanted. The prince. The PRINCE pRINCE DAMMIT NEVER MIND. I get why the system fails to autocapitalize cousin and humanist, nouns are nouns, and Cornel mason w/o caps is almost funny, but prince, prince just looks wrong.

April 30: Feeling better today. I can't focus my eyes to read for long, but Su-Hyeon set up a text reader to read out the news feed to me, and my favorite books from my tracker's offline archive. Remakers & masons in the Americas are rallying now that we're back in touch. They have lots of little territories, some cities (Santiago, Quito, Washington), and navies off both coasts thanks to the local Mitsubishi who are mainly Remakers, Milae and Fuxing. We may try to take the Esmeraldas elevator. Hiveguard had two fleets around Esmeraldas, Aesop Quarriman's HU fleet (*humanistas unidos*) which answers to Vivien, and the OSA fleet ("O.S. of the Americas") which answers to Ojiro sniper, but a week ago Quarriman took HU south (to stop the craziness at Esperanza city?) so we may try to attack while OSA is alone at the elevator base. Land battles in the Americas havent been that bloody (nothing like our Rhine-Ruhr mess or Casablanca), mainly because Vivien's diplomacy is amazing, *haengma* embedding strength with every stone. Watching Vivien's tactics it really is just like a go game, recruiting fragmentary groups, holding passes to stop big forces from connecting up, and especially preventing battles, letting the troops line up but negotiating before shots are fired, arranging surrenders when the results are foregone, so only the uncertain battles have to happen. Go is so much a better way to run a war than chess. There's a big enemy force around Paititi but they're just camped, scared to actually attack a utopian city, especially in the Amazon where beasts have lots of cover, so we may be able to send help before anything happens. Achilles hit a Dougong base in new guinea yesterday, 300 dead.

May 1: No login

May 2: Bad yesterday. Blackouts last hours sometimes but theyre the good part. Other times I'm conscious but the vertigo is like I'm in a whirlpool, and there's a choking stuffing pressure on my chest, and I absolutely can't move even a finger, like there's a cloud of lead on top of me. But i shouldn't call those phases, the times I'm strong enough to write are the brief phases, the whirlpool crushing lead part that's my normal. Sedatives help or I'd be gagging and vomiting all day, but I'm lucky if I can even give Cinna thumbs up when they bring good news. Su-Hyeon has more time to visit, they've seen some of my good patches. And they set up an audiobook library on my console, and a thing so we can play chess and go.

May 3: Bryar's still at it, restarting peace talks, starting by sharing a list of everybody's conditions for ending hostilities. SU-HYEON, CAN YOU PASTE IN THAT GREAT CHART YOU MADE? AND CAN YOU TELL THE SYSTEM TO CAPITALIZE PRINCE?

DEMAND	FACTION
Death of the Prince	Hiveguard
Liberation of the Prince from the Masons	Dougong, EU, Fuxing, Homeland
Clear delineation of Hives' rights to use lethal force	everybody really
Severe restriction on Hives' rights to use lethal force	Cousins, EU, Gordian, Greenpeace

Expansive affirmation of Hives' rights to use lethal force	Dougong, Hiveguard, Homeland, Humanists, Masons
End of O.S. assassination system, more trials	Cousins, Greenpeace, EU, Fuxing, Milae
Some clear alternative to put in place to keep the world stable without O.S.	EU, all 5 Mitsubishi factions, also Vivien, Papadelias, Su-Hyeon, everyone who really understands the math
Affirmation of Hives' rights to absolute self-governance restricted only by the Black Laws, affirmation that Romanova may request reforms of Hives but may not force them	Masons, Dougong, Hiveguard, Homeland, Humanists
Affirmation that Romanova may force reforms on Hives when it's judged that they have systemic flaws which threaten to cause Black Law violations	Cousins, Greenpeace, EU, Fuxing, Milae
Redistribution of land, taking some away from Mitsubishi	many want it but no faction is formally demanding it
Protections/affirmation of Mitsubishi land holdings *including* lands attained this year through conquest	Dougong, Homeland (Milae, Greenpeace, & Fuxing may exclude conquests)
Demilitarization of space, protections for Mars project	Masons, Milae, Greenpeace, Utopia
Passage of anti-set-set Black Law, "quarantine and rehabilitation" of set-sets including "gender set-sets" and "Utopian set-sets"	Nurturists + lots of angry people
Ban on U-beasts (claim that deadly autonomous weapons violate the First Law), destruction of extant U-beasts	Nurturists + lots of angry people
Dissolution of Utopian Hive, creation of Utopian Reservation (likely in Antarctica)	Nurturists + lots of angry people
Reparations (for war damages, for O.S.)	lots of factions, lots of combos
The absolute surrender of the Earth	J.E.D.D. Mason

It's chastening to realize the Prince's demand is still the most unreasonable.

May 4: Had my 10 day eval today, bad. Docs still say full recovery someday but first maybe a month like this, then normal gorgon longer. Docs don't know shit, gorgon's new who knows. But we're talking about getting me on a less intrusive ventilator, off this fucking tube. Achilles took a chunk out of the cousin districts of Pretoria, 600 dead. And we were too slow to save Paititi. Over a million utopians captured or killed, and they didn't take the city, they razed it. One more dream city gone, like Atlantis and Themiscyra. But Luna city's safe.

Another communique with French on the end: JE.VIENS.MA<ITRE. Apparently that message has been coming into Alexandria every few weeks for months now. I shouldn't be glad Dominic's stuck somewhere far from the Prince, but I don't mind at all that they're so far from me.

May 5: OFF THE VENTILATOR! They still have me on oxygen and an assistive shell, but I can TALK I can DRINK. Wonderful Su-Hyeon brought a big bowl of avgolemono soup—heaven!—and faki and stefado but doc vetoed those, no chewing yet. And Su-Hyeon's right, this is no time for sulking!! If it takes me all day to write 1000 words theyre 1000 words that command a billion masons, and I'm gonna use them. They're 1000 more than Cornel mason has. And if Achilles is going to smash shit from space no matter what, best to direct it usefully. So we're going to take the rest of the Himalayan passes in Himachal Pradesh, and push from the black sea back into the Mediterranean, and we're going to take Sydney and Brisbane and free new Camelot so we can use Australia to build toward an assault on Togenkyo, and we're starting plans to save the Panama canal, and we're gonna find that secret Brillist train, and big diplomatic plans too. What the Prince wants from the world is absolute surrender, and if masonic succession rules mean the masons won't do it, no reason we cant get EVERYONE ELSE ON EARTH to surrender. The Prince ruling the rest of world while locked in a box in Alexandria isn't the most ridiculous form of government in history. So we're going to maneuver everyone we can toward surrendering to the Prince, starting with allies (our scared-shitless-of-the-Ancile-breaker allies). Step 1: convince Cinna to waive the policy of not letting the Prince talk to anyone. It was supposed to pressure the Prince to take the oath but it isn't working, and a lot of groups will join us if the Prince asks them directly (all Remakers, EU, Fuxing, maybe what's left of Homeland, maybe even humanists in Spain) and that'll get them used to taking orders from the Prince, lay the groundwork. If we can get Cinna to agree. Su-Hyeon's going to make the pitch. Here's hoping.

May 6: Cinna came to lecture me that I'm acting emperor not them, so when I tell them do something there's no convincing, they just do it. Hard to get used to. So now the Prince can have some calls with allies, but only with our direct approval, that's Cinna's reading of Cornel mason's will. So much I wanted to say to Cinna but they came during a bad patch. Maybe tomorrow. Saving my strength today to write to Achilles, must get them to slow their rampage or sheer body count will alienate our allies. Convincing Achilles to pause revenge—Vivien, Mycroft, Voltaire, all my predecessors give me strength.

May 7: Good start, we let Huang Enlai talk to the Prince so Fuxing is happy, and we're talking w/ new EU parliament re: recognizing the Prince as acting EU emperor. Silence from Achilles, no reply but no attacks today. Good?

May 8: Achilles agreed to slow things down, and is helping with the Himalayas. Ancile Breaker can narrow its blast center to < 200 meters, lots we can do with that. Achilles is calmer than I expected, just insists we let eureka Weeksbooth help track something Utopia spotted leaving the Almagest debris cloud that might have Cornel mason's body. Of course Achilles is obsessed with the funeral. Prince is recording messages for the Remaker factions in Australia and the Americas. So mostly good day but bad here in Alexandria, we lost the cape again. Guns audible from here. Tried to watch the war room updates but blacked out. Cinna's blocked out time for a long visit tomorrow. I think Carlyle Foster visited today, but it might have been a dream. Glad to have a nice one—better than the usual, or Thomas Hobbes.

May 9: No login

May 10: Pls fix padding on my elbow rest, it's hurting

Blue thing where cord goes under

Other side

No still pushing

Perfect

9, some 10

Better, 7

Any good news? I could use some

gALIPOLI?

Can Papa help w/ Cambodian cousins?

Huxley?

Tell Cinna thanks they're doing great

Whoops those are my chats from Su-Hyeon's visit this morning. I forgot to switch out of the chronicle file. The numbers—9, 10, 7—are how bad i'm feeling from 1–10. So 9 & 10 was a really bad day but better now.

ATTN SU-HYEON SWITCHING FILES IS HARD CAN YOU PLS ALWAYS CHECK THIS FILE TOO IN CASE I LEFT NOTES FOR YOU IN HERE? THAT WAY YOU WONT MISS THEM. AND I'D LIKE YOU TO SEE WHAT I'M PUTTING IN THE CHRONICLE SO YOU CAN ADD STUFF I MISS.

Updates: Huxley checked in, still no luck tracking Mycroft. Black sea campaign taking shape. A ton of cities are asking to talk to the Prince. Lots are in Remaker hands and may join us. They all have questions and terms but theres tons! Dakar, Kinshasa, cape town, Vienna, Kiev, Lima, Córdoba, the whole Quebec-Ontario alliance, San Francisco, and Memphis which could give us the southern Mississippi corridor and a way to relieve Honahlee and Anachropolis. And Manila too which has its own huge fleet and is helping the Biringan Delians. Interesting tangle in the gulf of Thailand: Bangkok wants to work with us to help get Dougong out of Vietnam, but Bangkok's allied w/ an ultrapacifist cousin enclave in Cambodia who're irate about Achilles, and also allied w/ the exiled Singapore Peace Alliance, it's all very precarious. Must write Achilles again.

May 11: No login

May 12: No login

May 13: 10

Same

Soup. Avgolemono

I know i just want to smell it

You don't understand what it's like

I'm sure

I really want this

Fucking listen to me I want this!!!!!

!!!

Bad turn Wednesday, back on the ventilator. Su-Hyeon won't bring me food to smell. They're probably right it'll make the cravings worse. But better food dreams than my nightmares, though the sedatives are reducing those a bit. Looking forward to switching my brain off sucks. Hiveguard surprise attack out of Rockhampton took emerald city, and the new Camelot campaign's turned nasty like Tripoli, and saboteurs burned down a chunk of Biringan. Feels like there's fewer Utopian dream cities left than gone. Also Quarriman's fleet is returning to the Esmeraldas elevator, no chance there. But the 'is Jehovah king of Spain now?' question has the Spanish humanists talking to us at last.

May 14: Dakar's with us! And San Francisco including the seastead! Gulf of Thailand situation going well, and Himalayas. Sydney's ours. Seems everything's turning around except new Camelot and here in Alexandria. More fighting today, enemy advanced four streets, big fire. They say they can roll me out fast if the palace is attacked again but it's hard to see how. Hobbes keeps warning it doesn't matter how the limbs are doing if the adversaries get the head of the Leviathan.

May 15: GHOST SPACE ELEVATOR! We lost the Almagest but have its ghost, the 5 km radius vertical tunnel where the base last was where cars are programmed not to go. The Saneer-Weeksbooth program always kept cars away, won't let them even be on great circle trajectories that might hit an elevator, and Cato with their space obsession reinforced that, burying failsafes all over the system, and whoever's manipulated the lockshell program is not as good as Cato. So we can launch things safely through the Almagest's ghost, not much yet, just a few things launched from ships, but Utopia's moving Lemuria in place, that will let them launch almost anything.

May 16: EU Parliament now formally debating making the Prince emperor. May take a week or more. SO MANY CITIES say they'll join us if EU approves.

PLEASE BRING FOOD SU-HYEON IM REALLY SURE JUST ONE SMELL

Had another eval, they want me on the tube at least two more days.

May 17: Big fleet in Sea of Japan turns out to be homeland rallying. They're rallying in Togenkyo too. If they recognize the Prince as Ando's successor they might swing to us. Huang Enlai's going to meet w/ them.

SU-HYEON GET CINNA! QUICK! IM FEELING REALLY GOOD IM SURE IT'LL LAST. I REALLY WANT TO TALK TO CINNA! IT WOULD MEAN SO MUCH!

Cinna came but I'd relapsed by then, too weak to manage more than a couple sentences. They said they appreciated the effort. Cinna's so patient, visiting daily, briefing me even when I can only lie here like a lump. Wish I was that fucking patient.

May 18: No login

May 19: SORRY I SNAPPED YESTERDAY SU-HYEON

Su-Hyeon's so great. I had a tantrum yesterday when docs wouldn't take me off the tube (rereading that chat log was mortifying!) and I was sure Su-Hyeon'd be mad but today they brought me tons of flowers and plants and filled the room and it smells like spring amazing. Gorgon wears off, I just need to remember that. Gorgon wears off. Himalayas campaign nearly complete. Dougong surprise attacked Shuilian last night, surprise to us but not to Utopia, whole city was empty, just the Griffincloth buildings simulating people—evacuating 3 million Utopians (+beasts) w/o anyone noticing, there's some sorcery!

May 20: EU parliament dragging its feet about imperial succession, debating whether an acting emperor must've passed the adulthood competency exam. Docs gave me a scary talk today about pros and cons of tracheotomy. And I had a freaky dream where Saladin canner was real, and asking me if I'm ready to die for Mycroft yet.

May 21: News about Dominic, alarming but solves some mysteries. They've vanished in Mongolia. Ando's plan worked, Dominic was helming the Mitsubishi but everyone was scared of them, so when Ando walked back into Togenkyo on Dec 2 and demanded their position everyone turned on Dominic. But Dominic expected something of the kind, so they'd already worked themself deep into Ghostroad, that's this united smuggling underground Mycroft set up under their Saladin/ghost persona, union of different criminal rings, with Dominic hooked in on the east end and (of course) madame on the west. Not sure if it's doing what Mycroft hoped but Ghostroad is gung-ho Remaker, expecting big rewards if they help found the Prince's new world order, and they have been helpful. December to April Dominic was with them moving goods and supplying Remaker factions across Asia, even began the evacuation of Shuilian. But someone was after Dominic, repeated attacks, they kept relocating to evade, but disappeared near Erdenet Mongolia may 2. Word took almost a month to reach us because Dominic's old-fashioned lieutenant Mirabeau insisted on coming from Mongolia personally to Alexandria to put the message in the Prince's hand.

May 22: Bad today, 7+ all morning, saving writing strength for work

May 23: No login

May 25: Had my one month eval today. Off the tube again. Great feeling but still blacking out a lot. No offense to Su-Hyeon and the docs but I'd like to have a conversation with ANY OTHER HUMAN BEING EVER. Gorgon wears off. Gorgon wears off.

May 28: No login

May 29: These aren't suicidal thoughts. They're meta-suicidal thoughts, fear that I might become suicidal, pre-horror that this long grind will break me, make me betray so much. The me that I am now is horrified at the very thought of suicide, or dying at all really, but I can tell that me is changing, like I'm dough being extruded through a tube, and who knows what weird shape will spew out the other side. Every time the nausea peaks and I beg inside for the sedation to take hold, my welcome off-switch, the fear hits me: what if the self that spews out of this a month from now would beg like this for the off-switch that never ends? How could I stop that? I lie helpless before the alien future person I'm becoming, feel it murdering me, eating my mind away. I won't be here to stop it when it—if it becomes a thing that would choose *that.* Saladin canner in my dreams keeps asking if I'm ready to die yet, and I list out my no's, my duties: the Prince, the empire, the mantle of anonymous, my chronicle, Su-Hyeon who needs me, Achilles, the the path to the stars, the whole world, and Mycroft who will come back soon and needs their caretaker. I chant it like a mantra, but is that all I can do? Inscribe it like a tombstone and hope future [Anonymous] will scrape the moss from past [Anonymous]'s words and care? I understand now why Achilles fights so desperately to protect the wishes of the disenfranchised dead.

May 30: Turn heat down

Little more

What I really want is different doctors

No improvement after a month! I saw gorgon victims in Romanova, it isn't like this. Cousins designed gorgon to be weakening but gentle, not like this. What if it's the doctors?

Cousins would have tested what multiple shots do, wouldn't have made it so bad that a month in you still can't breathe or focus your eyes for long or stay conscious for more than a few minutes

Sabotage. Do we know what's really in these meds they're giving me?

If Brillists can get at the Guildbreaker bash' why not at the doctors?

Just tell them we want a second opinion, or an expert

We have prisoners from Casablanca, maybe one worked developing gorgon? What's the harm?

If I'm being paranoid then this will make me stop worrying

PLEASE

May 31: Photos of the secret train! Kiev sent them, taken near Minsk. I could hug Kiev right now. And you, Su-Hyeon

June 2: No login

June 3: EU Parliament confirmed the Prince as acting emperor! Individual nation-strats can accept/reject recognizing it but a cascade of Remaker-held EU-dominated cities are joining us: Manila (with the giant fleet!), Vientiane (one more bloodless step toward getting Dougong out of Vietnam), Auckland, Melbourne, the Sydney holdouts may surrender, Tbilisi, Kiev, Athens, Gallipoli (now Canakkale may surrender and give us the Bosporus without a fight), Vienna, Frankfurt, Dublin, Johannesberg, Madagascar, Kinshasa, Boston, half of Canada, serious talks w/ Lima & Paris. Doesn't look good for Barcelona and Madrid, Spanish nation-strat says Prince can't be regent in the king's absence unless they take oath of fealty to Spain.

June 4: Writing to EU cities all day, great!

June 5: No login

June 6: Mahoroba's fallen, hard to tell who did it, ships flying nothing but our captured uniforms. We should've seen it coming. Utopian cities are too tempting now that Achilles has made hostages so precious. Discussing defense plans for Avalon and the Hesperides. Biringan should be safe so close to Manila, and hopefully no one can get at Zerzura or Cybervale.

June 7: Su-Hyeon, maybe I am being paranoid but I can't stop thinking about this, if you just bring a different doctor, hopefully I'm wrong and then my mind will be at ease. I can't concentrate.

June 8: SU-HYEON, UPDATE ON NEW DOCTOR?

June 9: I want another

That one was super nervous, kept giving the others shifty looks

Stumbled three times pronouncing the name of that med, that was weird!

I don't want to relax, I want another doctor

Another other doctor

Something was up with that one

I'm serious

Su-Hyeon thinks I'm being paranoid. But doctors are acting weird, nurses too. Visits are all stiff, and when they check the meds now they always turn away like they're trying to keep me from seeing their faces. And they're always refreshing my sedatives right before Cinna tries to visit, it's like they know!

June 10: I'll tell you what's wrong! You're what's wrong!

You never listen to me!

I want another doctor!

I told you that one was in on it!

You haven't seen the way they look at me!

6 weeks and I've had I—COUNT THEM, ONE—conversation with Cinna. Cinna comes every day and I always have a bad patch! It's not coincidence!

Of course YOU don't, YOU don't want me to get better!

You're enjoying this. You get to run the masons while I'm stuck here. All hail Emperor Su-Hyeon!

Who knows if you're really passing on what I write! Who knows what you're claiming I asked you to do! Who knows if this news feed is even real!

Sure the DOCTORS say, and you're the one BOSSING THE DOCTORS. I'm onto you! This is your second coup! First Romanova then here! And as long as I'm still trapped here your little power trip

June 13: I'm so sorry, Su-Hyeon! You're right, I'm totally breaking down. I can't believe I said such hurtful things! I'm so sorry. And even after I snapped, you sat with me all night and were so kind, and you're absolutely right it's the strain making me panic, but that's no excuse for hurting you, you've been a saint. I'm so so so so sorry. I hope I'm conscious when you read this. I just want you to know how grateful I am, this would be torture without you here, you're my lifeline. I'll try not to snap again, but if I do please just remember I'm so so grateful and even if I snap sometimes you're such an amazing friend, I couldn't hope to make it through without you.

June 14: Saladin Canner dream again. I still said 'no.' Panama campaign has started well. Su-Hyeon's pretending not to be angry but I really hurt them, they're trying to act normal but they can't look at me.

June 15: Su-Hyeon, I've thought hard about this all day. I'm calm right now,

I'm not overwhelmed, I'm not in despair, I'm thinking calmly. You didn't tell Cinna that I'm suspicious of the doctors. I was conscious for most of their visit today, it was clear you didn't tell them. And that means one of two things. Probably it means you think I'm having a paranoid tantrum and you don't want to embarrass me or make Cinna doubt my decisions. But it could mean the reason you won't look me in the eye is that there really is a conspiracy and you're in on it and you're trying to keep me from getting help. So—and I thought about this a long time—I want you to tell Cinna. Tell them I'm suspicious of these doctors and I want them gone and I want entirely new doctors. This is Alexandria, we have plenty of doctors. And if you tell Cinna and Cinna does it then I can finally stop worrying and that relief, that trust, will make a world of difference. And if it means Cinna starts doubting me and worrying that I'm losing it then that's good, because if this is paranoia then I AM losing it and they should know. So tell them. Thanks.

June 15: Su-Hyeon, I really enjoyed the violinist visit it was amazing, and I appreciate you sitting with me so long, and reading to me, it was all great. But you didn't tell Cinna. Tell Cinna.

June 16: Please tell Cinna

June 17: I can't trust you again until you tell Cinna

June 18: No login

June 19: I can't say I'm calm. I'm angry. But I'm thinking clearly. You sit with me every day talking about how worried you are about me, that I'm going crazy, that this 'paranoia' is a phase of something worse, and when you're here with me I believe you for a while, but when I calmly list your actions, when I summarize the situation to myself, the truth is clear. You won't tell Cinna like I asked. You've password locked these logs so only you can see. You keep moving me from machine to machine but all of them are ones that keep me from talking freely. You've got me strapped down even though the sedatives prevent the kind of nightmare where I flail. My symptoms make no sense. And my bad patches come like clockwork every single time I have a visitor who isn't you. So I'm right. I'm your prisoner. You've won. You have your coup. Your second coup, first Romanova then Alexandria. I don't know if you're Hiveguard or what, but you rule the masons now, and there's absolutely nothing I can do about it. So I want to ask you one favor. Because I don't think this means our friendship was a lie. I think this is the kind of war that pulls friends apart. I think the edge of tears when you visit isn't acting, that the reason you struggle to look me in the face is that you DO care, that you wish you didn't have to do this. I won't ask you to free me, you're in too deep, betraying the masons, breaking the Fourth Law, even if I promised mercy you know as well as I do I couldn't deliver. So I won't ask you to free me. But you can free me from one thing: doubt. Because it's the doubt that hurts now. When I'm calm I'm sure I'm right, but when the despair comes, or when the meds mess with my head, or when you visit and act all worried and forgiving, then I doubt, and for a while I think I might be wrong, that it is paranoia, and that by accusing you I'm hurting one of my most precious friends. And it's that back and forth that hurts most, the whiplash between feeling angry at you and feeling guilty for doubting you, the gnaw of never being wholly sure. So I'm asking you, Su-Hyeon, if we are or were ever friends, and if you care at all about Vivien and what I mean to them as their other successor: please tell me the truth. Just once, just secretly, one whisper, just to let me stop doubting. That's all I'm asking, as your prisoner and your friend. Please tell me the truth.

June 20: Please tell me the truth.

June 21: Please tell me the truth.

June 22: I'm sorry I doubted you, Su-Hyeon! You're right, I'm going crazy trapped like this, and lashing out. I'm so sorry. I can't stop it, I don't know what to do! I'm scared. I'm losing it, it feels like I'm slipping away, that this is warping me so much my mind I won't be me anymore. But even worse I'm hurting you. I'm so sorry!

June 23: I'm right after all, aren't I? Please tell me the truth.

June 24: It's Gordian isn't it? You're using the masons to advance Remaker causes everywhere, but when utopian cities are in danger the Blacksleeves always come a bit too late. Did Jin Im-Jin recruit you? All those private conversations between just the two of you? Or is this an older, I don't know what to call it, allegiance? Conviction? Plan?

June 25: No login

June 26: No login

June 27: I know you made the sedatives stronger. You can put me to sleep forever if you want but the doubt still hurts me when I dream. Please Su-Hyeon just tell me the truth.

June 28: Thank you.

June 29: No login

June 30: No login

July 1: I'm not scared anymore. I was scared this was going to break me. Twist me into someone else. Because torture twists people, and this is torture, lying helpless, seeing Cinna visit, seeing you, even if you're not pretending anymore (thank you). But this is not going to break me. I know it isn't. You know how I know? Because sniper made it through. A year ago. I saw, same thing, imprisoned, immobilized, right when they should've been here to be a leader, right when people needed them the most. And theirs was worse, their captor was trying to break their mind, genius at breaking people's minds, at getting people to surrender and become their tool. And sniper started twisting, I saw it. I saw every minute of it. But sniper didn't break. I saw the turning point, when they almost faded away but then got strong again, made those speeches, their will strong as a hurricane. And I understand. I think they realized then that sometimes, even when you're alone, you're not really alone. Sniper wasn't alone. So many fans all over the world were wishing for sniper to be safe, so many people cared, and loved them, all those invisible wishes hovering around like friendly ghosts. Time and distance make us ghosts to one another even when we're still alive and here, but while it makes us ghosts it doesn't make us nothing. Because when I walk through the forum past the rostra I feel Vivien with me, and Voltaire, and Cicero, they're with me and that's real, distant but real, real as the knowledge they had in their lifetimes that the Pen they guarded would pass on to new hands, that I—a somebody not born, not named, but real—would wield it still. They're with me right now, holding my hand in this hospital bed, and just like they're with me I was with sniper. I wasn't there at the same time but I was with them every minute of that torture, watching, wishing, urging: sniper, you can make it! Sniper, you can make it! Sniper, you can make it! And you made it. I listened to you, to every speech you made in that blue room, I listened, cheered you on, your every word, somebody heard, was there with you and listening and cared. And I think you knew that. You don't know me, sniper, you don't know who I am, but the first Anonymous never met me and loves me anyway. And you knew someone cared, some real if distant someone who was rooting for you, and held your hand despite time's ghostly distance. So I was with you, really with you, and that matters. You weren't alone. And I'm not alone now either. Because Cicero is here with me, and Vivien, and Mycroft, and everyone who ever held the Pen, and other distant somebodies who will hold it, or will read this and care, not now but someday, they're here with me right now holding my hand, and telling me that I will make it through. Humans are so amazing that we can love somebody far away, or in the past, or future, somebody whose name we may not ever know, but love is no less real or powerful because you're not together breathing the same oxygen. And I feel that. Have that. Am not alone. And the new me that's learned all this isn't some scary twisted future-me gazing coldly at old-me's tombstone, it's just me. A stronger, richer me, that still loves what I love, but loves it more. So I will make it through. Like sniper made it through.

July 2: Sniper made it through.

July 3: Sniper made it through.

July 4: Sniper made it through.

July 5: Sniper made it through.

July 6: Sniper made it through.

July 7: Sniper made it through.

July 8: Sniper made it through.

July 9: Sniper made it through.

July 10: Sniper made it through.

July 11: Sniper made it through.

July 12: Sniper made it through.

July 13: Sniper made it through.

July 14: Sniper made it through.

July 15: Sniper made it through.

July 16: Sniper made it through.

July 17: Sniper made it through.

July 18: Sniper made it through.

July 19: Sniper made it through.

July 20: Sniper made it through.
July 21: Sniper made it through.
July 22: Sniper made it through.
July 23: Sniper made it through.
July 24: Sniper made it through.
July 25: Sniper made it through.
July 26: Sniper made it through.
July 27: Sniper made it through.
July 28: Sniper made it through.
July 29: Sniper made it through.
July 30: Sniper made it through.
July 31: Sniper made it through.
August 1: Sniper made it through.
August 2: Sniper made it through.
August 3: Sniper made it through.
August 4: Sniper made it through.
August 5: Sniper made it through.
August 6: Sniper made it through.
August 7: Sniper made it through.
August 8: Sniper made it through.
August 9: Sniper made it through.
August 10: Sniper made it through.
August 11: Sniper made it through.
August 12: Sniper made it through.
August 13: Sniper made it through.
August 14: Sniper made it through.
August 15: Sniper made it through.
August 16: Sniper made it through.
August 17: Sniper made it through.
August 18: Sniper made it through.
August 19: Sniper made it through.
August 20: Sniper made it through.
August 21: Sniper made it through.
August 22: Sniper made it through.
August 23: Sniper made it through.
August 24: Sniper made it through.
August 25: Sniper made it through.
August 26: no login

Chapter TWENTY-TWO

I Can't Do It Alone and I Don't Have To

Written August 30–September 6, 2455
Events of August 26
Alexandria

"Squeeze my hand twice if you want us to get you out of here."

Rescue came at night, a burst of moving shadows, I was too drugged to differentiate. I felt momentum, rumbling which made my stomach lurch, and something above me racing past, pipes, lights. An unfamiliar ceiling has never been so welcome. There were fingers holding mine, not imaginary Sniper (the companion of my long captivity) but real fingers, and a worried face above: Carlyle Foster.

"They're awake!" they cried over the rumble. "[Anonymous], can you understand me?"

Yes—I was so accustomed to just thinking words. But the soreness in my throat made me cough, and I felt my shoulders jerk, and my torso curl, and my knees bend, and my stomach heave with vertigo and nausea, which rolled me on my side. My *side,* my whole weight curling with no strap across my chest to hold me down, and I coughed, and it felt weak, pathetic, painful, but it was my cough, mine alone, my chest, my strength, and I gulped breath—my own breath!—and tasted nothing in my mouth but mouth. Then coughing, choking, triumph's joyful laughter, all became the same.

"They're choking! Quick!" I felt the lurch as the gurney stopped, and motion all around me, worried voices.

No, I'm okay, I thought. Then I dredged deep, uncertain if the skill was still in me, like picking up an instrument you haven't touched since childhood and genuinely wondering: *Fingers, do you remember what these strings do?* Or in my case, *Throat, do you remember speech?* "No, I'm okay." It just came out, so soft, so easy, like the easy bending of my knees, not as I willed but as I didn't need to will, all the impossibly complex coordination of the muscles stiff but ready like an old bicycle, its many pieces still moving as one.

"They're fine. Keep moving!" Carlyle ordered, then looked back to me as the bed started to roll. "You've been breathing on your own for ten minutes." They were panting, not walking, jogging speed. "We gave you something to wake you up fast, clear your system. I'm sorry we couldn't ask consent, but we need you conscious to talk to the Prefect. How do you feel?"

"Whuuh . . ." Fresh nausea stopped my first attempt. "Where . . ."

Another speaker: "We're still in the palace. They're behind us." Who was this? My angle was bad, but I saw gray cloth and a white sash dangling. Bo Chowdhury? Yes! How like a fortressed tower or sheltering cedar the deputy's tall figure felt beside me—Law, and Law's good shield. And what was that behind them, a shimmer, sliver, slice of face, dark, worried, and a smell like zoo.

"Huxley!" I winded myself in my joy cry. "Huxley!"

Crisply: "Can you tell me your name and birthdate?"

A sensible test, and it gave me a little thrill of joy to think I could set a friend's fears to rest in so simple a way. "[My nickname]. [My full name], March . . . no, not March, [my birthdate]." Perhaps my head was a little fuzzy, but it was hard to care. "You're back. And Mycroft? Is Mycroft with you?"

"I'm orbiting Mycroft another way for now." Huxley drew something from their nowhere and hurled it down the hall behind us, where I heard the whoosh-hiss of expanding foam—a barricade? "Keep moving."

The wheel-rattle intensified, my escorts not quite running. How many were there? Four? I couldn't see them well except Carlyle, who leaned close with that smiling wince which means we intend good but fear we may cause pain. "Listen, [Anonymous], we don't know what you know. It's August—"

"August twenty-sixth," I said.

A gasp. "So, you were conscious . . ." Their eyes, so blue and on the edge of tears. "And you were a prisoner?"

"Yes. I was. I knew." The words, strong, clear, felt like rebellion, smashing prison stones.

"I'm so sorry it took so long!" Carlyle's face showed empathy's keen pain as clearly as most would a needle's prick. "But with Brillists watching, we had to plan so carefully, anyone we told might give it away with a blink!"

"You know—" I choked. "You know it was Brillists? Do you have proof?"

"No," Bo answered as Carlyle duck-rushed under a low pipe, "just a strong guess. Do you have proof?"

"Me? No," I answered, "but nothing else makes sense."

We swerved around a corner and the wheels shook as we rushed through a hole sawed through a wall to some dimmer hallway.

"Where are we going?" I asked as Huxley and Bo fell back to launch another barrier.

"To a safe room, *Promagister,* where you can call the Prefect." I knew this voice from near the bed's foot, light yet strong like nanofiber putting steel to shame—Xiaoliu Accursed-Through-the-Ages-Guildbreaker. "The situation must be explained immediately."

I could just see Xiaoliu if I strained. And who was this dark figure next to them? A black coat and an unfamiliar face which gazed at me as one would at a fruit stand where the last remaining apples are all bruised and sad. Ah, but I knew that sash around their waist, lush black with the white-embroidered hound and motto *canis domini,* just as on Carlyle's: this is Dominic's agent, who trekked here from Mongolia despite war's barriers to tell the Prince Their faithful dog is lost. Somehow, joy's tears only came now—there were so many: Huxley, Bo, Xiaoliu, Carlyle, this stranger who I didn't even know. I hadn't been alone. Ever.

"I wish we did not have to press this on you so quickly, *Promagister,*" Xiaoliu added, "but you must speak to the Prefect. To them this seems a treason and a kidnapping. We could not inform them of our plans with such adversaries watching. Your word they'll believe."

I gasped—it wasn't Brillists we were fleeing, rather at any instant Earth's most fanatical guards, raging for the kidnapping of an almost-Emperor, might burst through Huxley's barriers to rescue me and spare no seeming traitor. These five brave souls risk that for me? "Right," I answered. "Of course. I'll explain."

We turned another corner and the jostling let grogginess take me.

« *Votre Grâce ? Votre Grâce ?* » and then, « *Chiot ?* » My eyes wouldn't focus but I felt the rocking pressure of a hand shaking my knee. "Can you hear me, *chiot*?" That title, French for 'puppy'—Dominic's agent, then (Mirabeau, was it?), must know me from visits to Madame's.

"Yes. Sorry." The bed lurched and I tasted stomach acid as we threaded between large tanks—I hadn't known the palace had spaces like this, cramped, charmless, plain walls overgrown with tubes and vents, a space grand guests were never meant to see.

"*Votre Grâce* must not simply explain but *pardon* our conspiracy."

"Your conspiracy to save me?" I smiled my warmest at this stranger in their ancient livery—in such an hour, I would have smiled at Dominic themself if they had freed me, which in a sense they partly had. "Did you hurt someone? Guards? They'll understand, you had no other way."

"No, *Votre Grâce*. Most of us conspired to free *Son Altesse le jeune Maître,* not you. The Prefect will judge this gravely."

A bang—explosion?—close behind us, and Huxley was above me suddenly, shielding my face with their coat and shoulders as grit rained down.

"To free the Prince? Huxley, did you conspire to free . . ." I didn't say it but *I would have in your place.*

"It was a blind," Huxley answered calmly.

"No, it was a *brilliant* blind," Bo Chowdhury corrected, smirking even in this crisis flight—Papa's second indeed. "No one could hide something like this from Brillists, so Carlyle hatched a second conspiracy to hide the first, a plot to spring T.M., which required exactly the same resources as springing you—access, escape routes—so if the enemy saw a guilty glance, they'd think it was the plot they wanted to see succeed, perfect camouflage for one they would have stopped."

"That's brilliant!" I cried, and seemed to see imaginary Sniper beam with pride at one more peak of human excellence.

"Told you." Bo chuckled. "Even I—"

"Halt!" Huxley hissed, and suddenly there was a lion in the darkness, and a screen upon the lion, and a map upon the screen.

Bo leaned close to me as Huxley checked the map. "Even I fell for the trick, barged in two days ago to warn Carlyle I couldn't protect them if they played with fire on Masonic scale. It was so delicious, learning I'd missed the underlayer." A wink. "But most of our help came from Madame and Dominic's agents here in Alexandria, and they genuinely were plotting to free T.M. The Prefect will retaliate unless you shield them."

"Of course I'll . . ." I froze. I felt imaginary Thomas Hobbes (another companion of my long captivity) lean close like a councilor plucking at my sleeve, "Remember, thou art a Sovereign now, [Anonymous], young head to an old Leviathan, and must think such things through: these agents are Madame's, her poison, seeking to control the Prince, to sink fangs into every—" No. No Hobbes here, no distrust, not with these people, what they've risked for me. "Of course I'll protect you, all your people, whoever, I— You saved me, saved the Masons, everything."

It was strange to watch fear fade from such a fearsome face. « *Merci, Votre Grâce.* »

"It's here." I heard rather than saw Huxley slide past me, then a few feet up ahead the darkness of the wall gashed open to reveal brightness beyond. We rumbled through into a tiny room, with skinny pipes as dense as branches on the ceiling, and some cables vining from a wound in the wall. Bo and deft Mirabeau set to sealing the entryway, while Xiaoliu lifted a tablet connected to the hanging cables. "I'm calling now. The Prefect may not be willing to respond."

While Xiaoliu spoke Latin at the tablet, I searched again for my unseen protector. "Huxley?"

"I'm here." They leaned close, that sliver of face so comforting despite action's cold mask.

"The war, what's happening? I lost track in June. Are we winning?"

So complex, Huxley's frown. "If you mean Remakers, yes, Mike's side is crystalizing, Masons advancing, Hiveguard eroding everywhere, even in the Americas."

I sensed a "But?"

"But the more people feel themselves helpless within shifting grav-fields, the more they lash at scapegoats. Gordian is using all its mindcraft to make Utopia abominable, and in that under-war we are not winning."

I shivered, thinking how many human horrors must hide umbrellaed in that little phrase, 'we are not winning.' But I also had a smile. "Today will change that, me free, taking the Empire back from Gordian, we'll be on guard now, every Mason under fresh orders to guard Utopia."

Checking some readout let Huxley veil their expression, but I could guess what thoughts tempested in that heart which voted not to pay this price to gift complacent Earth six months free of the harbingers—a price that lingers though the gift has now expired.

Fear loomed inside me. "Harbingers!" I asked. "While I was out, has anybody used—"

Coldly: "Just us."

A chill shot through me. *Just Achilles, you mean, Huxley. Just the being who, of all things human, best understands war, and chooses this.*

Latin broke chill's silence, streaming from the tablet in Xiaoliu's hand, as fast and angry as I've ever heard a human voice (since Cornel MASON in their rage does not feel human). "The Prefect will speak to you now, *Promagister,*" Xiaoliu said, serene as stone. "Are you ready?"

"Yes." I tried and failed to raise my head from the pillow, but Xiaoliu held the tablet down for me. "Cinna, it's me, [Anonymous]."

Xiaoliu's face blanched as if I'd spoken some forbidden word that lets the all-devouring demons in—in this case, demons named Bad News and Grief. "I'm sorry, [Anonymous], I should have said: Cinna Semaphoros disappeared July fifth. This is the new Prefect, Ptolemy Armsborder."

"Disappeared?" I saw the face upon the tablet's screen now, only distantly familiar.

Xiaoliu nodded. "A message claims O.S. took them and is willing to exchange them for the *Porphyrogene,* but we think this is the same conspiracy, that Cinna grew suspicious of your incapacitation, so the Brillists took them and framed O.S."

A thorough conquest, Su-Hyeon. "Prefect, this is [My Actual Full Name]. I've been a prisoner—"

"We know, *Promagister.* Fear not, we approach."

"No!" I cried. "No, do nothing! Don't advance another step until you've heard me out! This isn't a kidnapping, I'm not a prisoner now. I've been a prisoner the past four months, my doctors are enemy agents and kept me incapacitated so they could exploit that to manipulate the Empire. But I'm fine now, free and of sound mind, and these who rescued me aren't traitors, they're heroes who risked everything concealing their plans from you because this whole palace is so infested with enemies that a whiff of . . . of rescue plans would have . . . made them strike." I was winded by the time I finished, my chest muscles taxed as much by these few sentences as if I'd jogged the length of the Forum.

Prefect Armsborder paused, and in that pause I read a kind of climax-fear in Xiaoliu's face, which made me realize what a turning point this was: would this new Prefect, whose shaking image on the small screen stared critically at mine, believe? "Understood, *Promagister.* What are your orders?"

My orders? The start was easy. "Arrest the doctors! Nurses! Everybody! Seize their stuff! They'll purge the evidence, they're likely doing it already since they'll know I'm free. Seize everyone involved in my treatment, in the hospital, my pharmacists, everyone involved, and—" I froze. Deep friendship is a strangely resilient thing, which can be bad as well as good, like an old tree where the trunk has rotted out, but the roots survive and bush out with spring green around the stump, a mockery tree that can't grow back or bloom but still won't die, its living scar upon the garden crowding healthy life. How was this part not easy? "Arrest Su-Hyeon."

"The Censor?" I heard stunned Latin whispers on the line. "The Censor has been acting in your place *Promagister*, your proxy-bash'mate . . ."

"Yeah. They knew. They . . ." How was this *still* not easy? ". . . they did it. Led it. Su-Hyeon stepping into power, ruling for me, that was the whole plan, Su-Hyeon's coup." I winced. "Their second coup, the first was Romanova. So we need to—"

"Let me arrest the Censor," Bo Chowdhury interrupted gently. "They clearly broke the Fourth Law, depriving you of the means to call for help. If I arrest them, we avoid the legal nightmare of the Masons locking up the highest executive of the Alliance."

The Acting Commissioner-General arrest Su-Hyeon? Alliance law? Was that a good idea? My mind spun out contingencies like a spider on fast-forward: who could override or infiltrate such a trial? Be merciful or not? Romanova was in Brillist Jin Im-Jin's hands, Bo worked for Papa, Papa for Madame, the Masons were full of Brillist infiltrators, would—no. Doubt was wrong here. Bo Chowdhury risked death to save me, here in the fortressed heart of iron empire, I would not doubt them. Funny how real betrayal also teaches us to trust. "Yes. Good. Prefect, help Bo arrest Su-Hyeon, let that bit be Alliance authority, that's . . . better . . ." I was out of breath again.

"At once, *Promagister*." Again fast Latin. "What further orders?"

"We . . . uhh . . ." I felt exhaustion's blur. "We have to check everything for manipulation . . . every message I supposedly wrote while hospitalized . . . everything Su-Hyeon said I said or wanted . . . or did . . . or persuaded me to do . . . Check everything . . . we . . ."

"It's alright, [Anonymous]." Huxley laid a kind hand on my shoulder. "Rest if you need to. Everything paramount is underway." Their voice was firm, commanding, which was even more comforting than if it had been gentle: I had a team to help me, to handle plans and actions, to be strong while I was weak. Friends I could trust.

"Listen, Prefect, we . . . we think Brillists did this . . . took me . . . took Cinna . . . We think they want the Prince to win the war . . . Remakers to win, but . . . not Utopia . . . and with Brillists, we don't know who we can trust . . . They've infiltrated everywhere . . . Anybody could be—"

"Then I must step down at once." So light, Prefect Armsborder's voice over the line, so crisp and practical. "If they took Cinna Semaphoros, they wanted me in this position, we can't trust that. You must remove me and appoint a new Prefect."

I choked. This stranger who has borne the weight of Empire, tasted what it is to be so near the head of the Leviathan, now stands ready in an instant to hack off that billion-membered god-prosthesis? Passing it on as lightly as the Masons' most junior Senator passed on their office sash to Cornel MASON when the Emperor strode into the Senate House to take their stand: *me creato Senatorem*. In fact, I later learned, this *was* that junior Senator who gave their sash to MASON at that strangest senate meeting, whose innocence I want to trust—the very fact they realized they should step down proves how fit they are for office—but the Brillist spiders weave so many mind game steps beyond us that I can't rely on anything they've touched. "Yeah, you'd better step down," I said. "Sorry." I felt stupid, wanted to say something grand and dignified, like MASON would have.

"When a stonemason sets aside one chisel to raise another, no apology is owed the tool that no longer fits the task at hand. Whom will you appoint, *Promagister*?"

Faces without names schooled through my mind, the war room staff eclipsed by memories of doctors—had they been Masons? Brillist Masons? Brillists among Masons? Brillists posing as Masons? Brillist robot brains controlling Masons? What Masons did I really know well except Martin and . . . Xiaoliu? No, no Mason could trust Xiaoliu Accursed-Through-the-Ages-Guildbreaker, nor could I really, since what the Brillists have twisted once, they could again, so . . . "Does it have to be a Mason?"

No pause: "It has always been one since time immemorial, but while IMPERIUM rests with you, your choice is law."

I felt hot. I wanted to close my eyes. I wanted water. I wanted: "Huxley. I want Huxley. I trust Huxley. I'm sorry, Huxley. Huxley's supposed to rest, this'll push them to break their oath again, but I want Huxley. I know Huxley." Hearing my own ramble, I was starting to question my own declaration that I was 'of sound mind'—these sedatives work deep.

"Huxley Mojave"—the voice on the line sounded uncertain—"is in the Indian Ocean, crewing the Dreadnautilus."

"Oh." I gazed at Huxley's frustrated but slightly laughing eyes. "Did I just blow your cover?"

Huxley sigh-smiled, then called to the microphone, "I'm here, Prefect, this is Huxley Mojave, willing to serve as [Anonymous] requests."

"Inside the palace?" A tremor in the voice of the officer trusted to guard this sanctuary.

"Yes. Fear not, your defenses still stand adamant, I could only enter thanks to passcraft Cornel MASON gifted me."

I felt warmer. "See? Cornel MASON trusted Huxley too. They've been with me through the whole war, got me here safe from Romanova. Now they saved me again, realized what was being done to me when no one else did." In my mind's eye I could see them, Huxley and the lion at my bedside as I slept in drugs' deep prison, rooting for me as imaginary Sniper rooted for me day by day.

"It wasn't me," said Huxley softly.

"What?" My breath caught.

"Carlyle only summoned me from the Maldives two weeks ago."

"Carlyle? It was . . . Carlyle?"

Yes, where is Carlyle?

Still holding my hand, warm fingers, gentle, even as they work with some device, testing my pulse or oxygen or something. You did your work well, Cousins, flooding the Earth with medics' training, but in the elation of rescue, I hadn't wanted to think of doctors, tests, and Carlyle's fussy nursing—I'd wanted to think of friends who felt like heroes. "You're the one who figured it out? Carlyle?"

Modesty-blush bloomed pink on Carlyle's cheeks.

"Huxley Mojave,"—the not-yet-Ex-Prefect's voice rose stern over the line—"my office, like the *Promagister*'s, is bound by Cornel MASON's standing commands, that the *Porphyrogene*'s imprisonment continue until they take the Oath, and that no Utopian may bear arms or technology within a hundred meters of their cell, including you. If you take office as Prefect, you must commit to maintain the same."

Huxley breathed deep, and I heard and felt the soft concern-purr of the lion prowling on the far side of the bed. "Utopia has fully surrendered to the Masons," Apollo's bash'mate answered, "that includes me. I know how absolutely at the Empire's mercy we are now and subject to your . . ."—a pause to choose a word the rest of us would know—". . . custody. If this is what both Hives require of me, then, on my oath as a Utopian, and with the Acting Commissioner General witnessing for the Alliance, I hereby submit myself to all Masonic law, and will uphold it, including Cornel MASON's standing orders."

"Even if the *Porphyrogene* begs for liberation to your face?" the voice challenged.

A deep breath. "Even if Micromegas begs for liberation to my face," Huxley answered, then closed their eyes and whispered, almost to themself. "First Contact is not worth gambling that there will be no one left to answer it."

"And you will become a *Familiaris*?" the Prefect challenged. "Not whiteband, a real *Familiaris*."

I flinched—that special status Cornel MASON had created for Apollo, a *Familiaris* but still protected by Utopia which will never accept Death as a tool of justice—such privilege the Empire extends no more. Suddenly, the Masons' domination of Utopia felt more like conquest.

"Yes." Huxley shifted so they were clearly in my line of sight and pushed back their hood of Griffincloth to bare a dark digital gaze, solemn, and holding mine. "I shall. I do."

Oh, right, at this point, the one who wields MASON's capital power is me. I hadn't realized quite what I was asking of you, Huxley. Thank you!

"Then I stand relieved, Prefect Mojave," Ptolemy Armsborder confirmed over the line. "What are your orders?"

"How many are there with you?" Huxley asked.

"Sixteen praetorians present."

"Alright. Whoever's fourth-most-junior-in-office will be my acting second-in-command for now. What's your name?"

A pause and murmur. "Ayhan, Prefect."

"Great, Ayhan, have the four of those present who have the shortest surnames escort the former Prefect to . . ."

As Huxley took the tablet to a corner to keep pouring out orders, relief mixed with the drugs and dead of night to make a tingle like massage run down my spine. It was alright. The Empire was in safe hands again, and I free for more human actions, first to give thanks where thanks were unexpectedly most due. "Carlyle?" I called to the gentle soul whom my heart still balks at calling Blacklaw. "You're the one who figured out I was a prisoner?"

They blushed again beneath my gaze. "Xiaoliu was indispensable too. I couldn't plan all this alone, I figured Xiaoliu's emotional state must be so extreme these days, their expressions would be extra hard to read."

I stared. "So, you and Xiaoliu figured it out together?"

"No." Some people are so shy that they wince when admitting excellence. "No, that was me."

Xiaoliu's stern nod confirmed.

"How?"

Carlyle fidgeted with the bedrail. "Oh, you know, it felt . . . off . . . some of the political stuff you were supposedly . . . and then I investigated how the Tiring Guns work, asked around, I'm sort of famous now and lot of Cousins still trust me, so I thought I could find out better treatment options, but the information they gave me was completely different from what your doctors were saying about the medical effects, it could never cause those symptoms, so that sort of confirmed the political stuff that already seemed . . . off?"

When I ramble like that, I'm hiding something. "What political stuff? What have they been doing with the Empire? Hurting Utopia?"

"No. I mean, Utopia's had losses, but it wasn't that, it was . . . rhetoric . . . stuff?" They winced. "Like with Julia, back in June when Julia started being so active in Romanova, it didn't make sense, you being so willing to work with them, with what you know . . . what you know about Julia, I mean . . . you wouldn't ask the Censor to give them an executive pardon, or—"

"Never!" My burst of passion sparked fresh nausea, as imaginary Sniper shuddered at my side.

"Right. And you wouldn't have accepted Julia as an acting Triumvir, or endorsed their plans in your . . . you know . . ."—they lowered their voice to veil the whispered words under the stream of Huxley's orders—". . . on Pass-It-On. And it didn't sound like your tone anymore, not any of the . . . things . . ."

I paused. I paused a long time. "Who told you?"

"What?" Carlyle blinked, those wide, blue, nervous eyes.

I reviewed the room: Bo knew, Huxley knew, Xiaoliu knew, Dominic's lieutenant Mirabeau who called me not just *chiot* but *Votre Grâce* (i.e., the Comte Déguisé), they certainly knew—but Carlyle? "Who told you I'm . . . *an essayist*?"

Carlyle laughed, a light, forced laugh to defuse tension. Then laughter faded to whisper. "Should we do this in front of people?"

"Everyone here has been told already," I answered.

Relief brightened Carlyle's face like sun. "Oh! Well, yes, it was obvious once I thought about it: how much the Triumvirs consulted you, how close you were with Mycroft, how well you knew the Censor and especially Vivien Ancelet, plus Romanova was the Pass-It-On hub, but the essays I saw were so consistently error-free, it felt like they had to be coming from the city, not coming through the lines, where things get garbled, and then when you were incapacitated and the tone on Pass-It-On suddenly changed . . . Are you having a muscle cramp? Where does it hurt?"

No cramp—it was my hand squeezing Carlyle's with all the force of bursting, boundless, avalanching joy. *I won't be the last.* Somehow *hallelujah* was the next word in my mind. Mycroft says moments like this reveal our true beliefs, when we see who or what our hearts thank, but I don't think it was our Maker I was thanking—They are cruel and made these dangers in the first place that threaten the Pen Which Bests All Swords and our precarious succession. No, this *hallelujah* was the Humanist in me: we did this, human cunning, human kindness paying close attention to an injured friend, we solved the puzzle once again, our glorious achievement, like the *hallelujahs* in a concert of old-time religious music, when the voices swell and history's baggage matters nothing as your heart thrills for the species that can craft such power from raw sound. I felt tears' tickle. The mantle of Anonymous. Hobbes says there is no perfect form of government where the right to choose the succession is not in the present sovereign—no one can have felt that imperfection as acutely, Hobbes, as we Anonymouses, helpless to do anything but wait. And if those sickbed dreams kept my will strong, in which deadly phantom Saladin made me chant over my mantra of things to live for, they also made me face my terror that the war would swallow me before I passed *it* on—the Pen. I've passed on so much in this war, for so many people, but not yet this, most precious, for myself. Safe now. "I'm fine. I'm more than fine. You found me." I grasped Carlyle's hand.

"It was a team effort." Still-oblivious Carlyle smiled at Xiaoliu, and then at Huxley, who realized what was happening, and ended their call to give this moment the privacy and dignity it needed.

I made my voice grave. "I didn't mean the rescue. You, Carlyle, *you* found me. What I am."

Carlyle stared. Frowned. Then their eyes went round as an owl's. "What? No, no!" They laughed. "It's not like that. I just worked it out from context, who was around you, that doesn't count, that's—"

"That's exactly how I realized it was Mycroft."

The round-eyed owl stare fixed on me another moment, then moved to Bo, Huxley, Xiaoliu, the Blacklaw Mirabeau, each of whom stared back at Carlyle with a gravity that left no room for evasion. "That can't be how it . . . It's supposed to be a test of skill, epic puzzle-solving to test if you have world-level genius, like Ancelet at the Olympics, it shouldn't be random luck."

"Carlyle . . ." I paused, as Vivien taught me to, taking my time to frame my thoughts well when it really matters. "You outdid yourself today. And to my knowledge, you're someone who saved the world three times this year already."

"What?" That light, defusing laugh again. "Nonsense."

"Carlyle,"—I would not let their eyes evade mine—"when the cars shut down, you realized the religious crisis it would cause with the Jewish holidays, and Ramadan, and Christmas, and I mean it when I say I think you single-handedly kept this from turning into another Church War."

"That was just—"

"Let me finish," I insisted. "After that, when Romanova's Hiveguard tried to capture Pass-It-On . . ."—my chest was weak, shallow breathing forcing frequent pauses—". . . you saved it, stopped the only free public communications system in the world . . . from turning into a tool of violence and faction . . . so by my count . . . every life that flow of information's saved . . . every heart that's had some peace from hearing that a loved one . . . was safe and well . . . even us finding Mycroft . . . that was all you . . . That's twice you saved the world . . . and we both know . . ." I paused—Dominic's agent must not learn Carlyle helped Sniper, lest a brutal death find all of us who hid this from the Prince's merciless Avenger. But Carlyle's birth bash' was partly Humanist like mine, and this was not a moment for taboos. "¿You think the dollhouse doesn't count? ¿The disappearance of you-know-who? You single-handedly kept the Opening Ceremony from bursting into war right then and there, a much worse war than this. ¿Did you think that didn't save the world?"

Sensitive Carlyle flushed scarlet at the use of forbidden Spanish, but then there it came, the relaxation of their cheeks, the thinking through—I knew that moment, had felt it myself back when my own guess went from feeling like a joke that shouldn't count to feeling like perhaps it was . . . this was . . . I was . . . not the wrong choice?

"But you outdid all that today," I continued in English. "Those times you just saved this world . . . but undoing this coup, you saved the Empire's chance to help Utopia . . . to safeguard Mars and Luna City . . . our stepping-stones . . . and every world we ever reach . . . through them . . ."—breathing was getting harder—"even the Prince's freedom to choose freely . . . outward or inward . . . you saved it and did it . . . by being kind . . . paying attention to someone . . . in a sickbed . . . when nobody else did."

Carlyle was frowning. "But I'm older than you are, I don't make sense as next in line."

I smiled. "Nothing prevents us both being active at once . . . Remember . . . I have two scepters in my hand now . . . Anonymous and MASON, that's . . . too much . . . I can't do both at once . . . not at the speed the world needs now . . . I need help . . . delegation . . . Please . . . at least until the Prince assumes the throne . . . or Mycroft returns or Martin . . . You're so perfect for it . . ." I squeezed their hand with all my feeble strength. "Ours is a bizarre succession system . . . and someday in the future, it will fail . . . probably disastrously . . . as most monarchies do . . . but for today . . . I can't think of anything the world needs more than . . . a kind, Cousinly voice . . . who's used to talking about miracles."

Carlyle opened their mouth, framing a new objection, but none came. They sighed. They opened their mouth a second time. They sighed. But this was not a moment for words, this was the world's moment, Carlyle's knowledge of the world eroding their objections as their mind's eye tested out this new self, Pen in hand, what they could use it for: to teach, to help, to calm, to heal, their power, their voice on every Seven-Ten list, our kindest sensayer now sensayer to the world. This part, believing that it's really really real, can take a while (weeks for me).

"But hast thou leisure for that 'while' in wartime?" imaginary Hobbes asks, a less cheering companion of my prison hours than imaginary Sniper, but as necessary. "For four months now, thy untenanted Pen hath languished in an usurper's corrupting hand. The Sovereign is obliged by Law of Nature to wield firm his power or establish clear his proxy as wise MASON has, for when power acts not, this just as much as power's dissolution causeth the Commonwealth to die and to dissolve, as those who trusted their lives and fortunes to thy care relapse into Confusion, and the wretched state of Universal War."

Reader: "Friend Thomas is correct, young guide, thine era bleeds, and calls for wise words' salve which thou as acting Emperor hath no time to dispense—this is no moment for the Pen which speaks through ages even unto mine to pause."

True enough, just . . . like most people, I hate when Hobbes is right.

"Huxley?" I called. "Where's my stuff? My clothes?"

A frown beneath the visor.

"There's a bin under the gurney for personal effects." Of course it was Carlyle who remembered, who so consistently remembers these small things that are not truly small.

"Look in my left inner jacket pocket, there's an ink pen stuck into a hole in the lining, a cheap, disposable one."

I teared up as Huxley set it on my palm, the brittle cylinder of bamboo fiber. "I'm sorry, Carlyle, you're . . . supposed to have time to think about this . . . let it sink in . . . and we're supposed to do it properly . . . in the *Sanctum Sanctorum* . . . with the Commissioner General . . . to officiate . . . but Bo will have to do."

Carlyle's hand squeezed mine, so soft. "We can wait. We can go to the *Sanctum,* it's not far, there's no hurry."

I gaped up at this soul so peaceful that they can't hear Ares's war car even as it rumbles around our citadel. "Of course there's hurry . . . this is World War . . . the enemy's so close . . . between us and the *Sanctum* even . . . and the world has harbingers . . . and there has never been a power like this Pen in human history . . . you understand? . . . A power that can do so much good . . . over generations but . . . can dissolve so instantly . . ." My fingers fumbled, nearly dropped the pen among the bedclothes. "We don't have Members . . . or a founding charter . . . or a statehouse . . . or former staff to rush in and fix things . . . like Isabel Carlos's people did for Brussels . . . we don't even have a flag . . . we just have human heartbeats . . . Vivien's, Mycroft's, mine . . ." I squeezed their fingers. "Please let yours be one more . . . and then please let me send you far away . . . so we're all separate . . . Vivien, me, you . . . so no single strike can silence . . . silence . . ."

Tears. I didn't use them on purpose—it's cheating to use tears against so kind a soul—but they flowed anyway. And when Carlyle put a soft, strong hand on my weak shoulder, they flowed more.

"Casablanca or Romanova?" they asked.

"What?"

"They're the two places it makes sense for me to go." Carlyle's smile, full of strength that day and every day. "I can work on patching Cousin politics and tracing Heloïse in Casablanca, or I can keep Julia in check in Romanova, and help Carmen and Desi get the city and Alliance stabilized. Or I guess I could join Papadelias in Dhaka?"

Thank you—I mouthed it, but could not control my breath enough to even whisper.

"Not Casablanca," Bo Chowdhury advised. "I admire the impulse, but even UNGAR's occupation force hasn't managed to bring order there, and the Cousins are so saturated with Nurturism the Hive will barely listen to Kosala, they won't hear two words from someone born at Madame's."

Irrepressible Carlyle shook their head. "That's just sharks eating bananas again. Toshi helped me verify the numbers, there are a few Cousins in the spotlight screaming Nurturism, but worldwide the vast majority are working steadily away in Red Crystal, or handling food shortages, or handing out nonlethal weapons and reducing the number of lethal ones in use, we just aren't noticing those projects because they're not conspicuous. In fact"—they turned to me—"might that make a good topic for an essay?"

Delight's catharsis plunged me into a coughing fit, weak but full-body, with the taste of vomit in my throat. I felt pathetic as everyone around me stared down like a gallery of judges. But then the pathetic feeling faded as the coughing fit stretched on but still the faces stared, warm, patient, worried but clearly confident that this small interruption didn't matter, nor would a hundred more such interruptions over coming hours—my words are worth waiting for. "Perfect."

Carlyle's smile was as warming as a bath. "Do you want some water? I also brought a thermos of soup."

Laughter made me cough again: you are too much, Carlyle Foster, more Cousinly than Cousins with your thermos and your chocolate cakes, protected in your Blacklaw recklessness less by Dominic's embroidered threat than by your own impossible sweetness which predators won't touch, as rough boots dare not tread on crocuses, and if you brought me avgolemono soup, I'm going to curse the cheating heavens that sometimes make things implausibly too perfect, as bamboo is implausibly too perfect for builders' needs, thorned roses too perfect a subject for poets, sunsets for artists, bananas for the hungry reaching hand, and Carlyle Foster too perfect for me. "What kind of soup?"

"Mushroom rice. What's funny?"

"Nothing," I choked out as I fought my laughter. "Here." I held the pen out on my palm. "We pass it with a handshake . . . and we squeeze and crush the barrel so it breaks . . . and ink gets on us both . . . that's what passes it . . . our ceremony . . . because it doesn't matter if one pen breaks . . . it's not this particular pen . . . it's any pen . . . whatever pen you hold . . . from here on is . . . the Pen."

"Beautiful." Carlyle took my hand in theirs, the thin bar of the pen between our palms, the awkward squeeze, and then the black ink spilled, so much better than blood. And we had a Tenth. And I had one more friend to be co-Atlas with me of the world's weight—Carlyle, Huxley, Bo, Xiaoliu, and Mycroft, who is coming back, I know it. Feel it. And with that feeling and such smiles around me, my heart raised one more human *hallelujah* to our marvelous species—and felt ready again to face One far stranger.

"Bo, Xiaoliu, round up the traitors; Huxley, Carlyle, take me to the Prince."

Chapter TWENTY-THREE

Until My Uncle Answers Me

Written September 7–13, 2455
Events of August 26
Alexandria

My heart soared as they wheeled me from strange hallways to familiar ones. As they bathed me. As they helped me dress with dignity in the mingled uniforms of my perplexing offices (Servicer mottle under my purple Censor's deputy jacket with the left sleeve Death black and the right Imperial gray). Guards and rushed Latin dogged us, details Huxley recited as they pushed my wheelchair, but in my elation I shed the petty facts as ducks shed rain. My thoughts were only of our progress past the gates, and guards, and deeper gates, and stronger guards, and there They were, the figure all in black Who rose, and walked to me, and felt my face and shoulders with precise, exploring hands. Unchanged—the Best Thing in (or visiting) our world is safe still and unchanged.

They spoke. "Thou art becoming difficult to recognize."

The Prince could not have known how that sentence would stab me, ripping open the Pandora's box of my self-doubt and also doubt-of-self—after months of tempest pounding at the soft shores of my mind, am I still me? But the Prince's hands held me, testing my cheekbones and the dampness of my hair, and those black eyes as warm as summer's midnight see our souls' pain and its secret causes without need for words.

They spoke again: "You did not tolerate unchanged this intolerable deprivation, betrayal, and murder of one four-hundred-fiftieth part of your human lifespan's actions' fruits, but this new you, though we abhor what changed it, is recognized and welcome, and will remain so even as intolerable's aftermath's changes change you more."

Their eyes held mine throughout this, that staring black Infinity which Loves. How can They? Look at us, a species so disgusting that a beloved quasi-bash'mate doing this to me will not, at war's end, make it onto a top ten list of worst atrocities, yet still They Love us? Elephants deserve such Love, bright hummingbirds, trees, noble lichen crafting life from rawest elements, but *homo sapiens*—no, *homo bellicosus,* a thousand times more warlike than we are wise—we deserve Love?

They answered my thoughts once more: "Because that exquisite thinking thing which is thy self is not soiled by, but rather constituted by, its cumulative complexities, including the grief-born ones."

Tears were streaming down my cheeks, but now they were the good kind.

Soft words, always: "It is said Mine *Onkel* did this to thee."

I froze a moment. "In a way, yes. Brillists anyway, I think . . ." *Humans did this,* the rot in me accused—but there was a lighter truth to check the rot voice. "But Carlyle saved me! And Xiaoliu, and Bo, and Huxley, and . . ." I froze, spotting Huxley on the far side of Carlyle, stripped of coat and visor, with their new Prefect's jacket loose and open over prison red. Such distrust? Still?

Huxley spoke up, their bare eyes calm, accepting. "We think the Brilli—"

"Speculation is needless." The Prince's black eyes turned to Huxley: no, past Huxley to the false window where the pre-dawn city flattered the night sky with humanity's electric imitations of the stars. "Mine *Onkel* shall explain."

Murmur among the friends and guards around who knew Them well—They do not use *shall* lightly.

Huxley waved one of the guards over to the console to bring up the war room's image on the wall screen, Bo and Xiaoliu at work directing shaken staff. "Would you like us to try to contact Felix Faust?" Huxley offered. "Our commun—"

"Needless." The Prince rose and with perfect steps approached Their bunk. "Mine *Onkel,* like Utopia, considers observation of My every word and action irreplaceably precious, and unlike Utopia, hesitates not to subvert and betray the Empire." They lay down as They spoke, stiff upon the bedding like a corpse. "Therefore call not; I know Mine *Onkel* hears Me when I say *Ich werde nichts anderes tun, bis Mein Onkel Mir antwortet.*"

Silence. Long, strange as we waited, stared, first at the Prince, then at each other, Carlyle's frown patient and curious, Huxley's growing grimmer with each breath.

"Mike?" Huxley attempted, gently, "are you saying Faust is clairvoyeuring?"

„Ich werde nichts anderes tun, bis Mein Onkel Mir antwortet."

Again the stares, the wait.

I tried this time: "I'm sorry, Prince, Mycroft isn't here to translate. Can You tell us in English?"

Their staring pause was long. A difficult decision? Or difficulty switching out of the one language They rarely mix with others, a herculean feat of tutoring that Felix Faust alone can boast of among all the Prince's nurturers. "I know My uncle hears Me when I say I will nothing further do until My uncle answers Me."

"Call Faust now." Frowning Chagatai strode forward from the far end of the room, a rare act from the Blacklaw who usually stays far from the Prince's guards, as a bear and wary wolf pack keep to far ends of the pond where both must drink. "T.M.," they asked, leaning over the Prince's bunk, "could you please just answer one quick clarifying question for me?"

The Prince did not even shift Their eyes to gaze on Their protector. *„Ich werde nichts anderes tun, bis Mein Onkel Mir antwortet."*

Chagatai turned to Huxley with a sigh. "Best have a surgeon and an O.R. standing by, then."

"What?"

The Blacklaw smiled as parents do on children's messes. "The problem is . . . well, I'm not sure whether to call it semantic or ontological. Is urination an action? Or is holding the urine in the action? Because if holding it in is the action, then T.M. will simply wet themselves when the time comes, and I'll clean it up and there's no problem until dehydration sets in days from now, but if they decide that urination is the action, then they'll hold it in until their bladder bursts and puts their life in danger, so we'd better prep for surgery." A pause. "They say they will do nothing and they mean it."

Fear gasps from the guards behind my chair. "A hunger strike?"

"*Promagister* [Anonymous]," the nearest guard asked, more willing to answer to me here than to half-prisoner Huxley. "Should we try to contact Felix Faust?"

"Call not," that gentlest of voices insisted once again. *„Ich werde nichts anderes tun, bis Mein Onkel Mir antwortet."*

We stared in silence, my mind becoming conscious of each praetorian's breathing as the hush stretched on, a state we humans with our chat and background music find so anathema that we consider one minute's silence fitting tribute for the famous horseman Death—this was three minutes.

"*Promagister*? Should we try to call Faust?"

Again: "Call not; *Ich werde nichts anderes tun, bis Mein Onkel Mir antwortet."*

Again Death's sacrifice, sixty clock ticks, eighty as all things wait on Them, Their stubbornness, and me. A plan—the word hammered at me—I should make a plan, but my mind strayed to Carlyle shivering beside me—thinking in the silence of Pascal?

"Call not; *Ich werde nichts anderes tun, bis Mein Onkel Mir antwortet."*

And then: "*Promagister,* the screen, look!"

I turned to the war room screen where Xiaoliu and the rest were staring up at a feed, a little gray-tinted and grainy. I knew that cluttered desk fenced in by potted plants, that wall shaggy with charts, that bin of puzzles, and that round plaque on the wall above, the dense, brain-shaped tree, not tall and branching like a tree of life or family tree but tight and shrub-like, dwarfed by its own deep-weaving roots which wormed into the black—the seal of the *Adolf Riktor Brill Institut für Psychotaxonomiewissenschaft*. It was not Faust at the desk, it was a young person, their wine-brown sweater checkerboard-textured across the front, sipping from a mug patterned with rainbow molecules. ". . . hear me now?" The words were thin and crackly. "Ingolstadt calling Alexandria, can you hear me now? Ingolstadt to Alexandria, can you hear me now?"

The guards around me tensed for action, and I found myself sharing their instinct, gripping my chair's arms hard: our adversary.

"Connect us," I ordered. Then: "Who are you?"

"Ah, you can hear, good." The Brillist's fingers twitched as they multitasked, data shimmering in their lenses. "Kindly ask the Stem to exercise some patience and self-care—the Headmaster needs time to dress and have their coffee."

The Stem? The rarely spoken title caught me up a moment: Gordian's chosen Brain-bash's vital Stem, the One they will observe lifelong and base Gordian's next era, not on the orders, but on the life and words of this rarest of Specimens, our J.E.D.D. Mason. They did hear, then, the Prince's words, they watched, they heard—how deep? how much? how many sanctum spaces in this palace, no, *on Earth,* are their guinea pig cages, watching all our movements, taking notes? "Who are you?" I asked, trying to make my words as sharp as razors.

A pause for one more sip. "You're [Anonymous], yes? I'm a great admirer of your work. How are you feeling?"

"Don't answer!" Huxley snarled, a voice so savage that I felt we didn't need the U-beast here to have a lion among us. "Give them nothing! You had no choice about being their prisoner, you do about being their test subject."

'Test subject'—the phrase made my skin crawl. I was a test subject to them, wasn't I? We all are, every human soul trapped in their global petri dish. Experiment #376: up the glucose, chill the medium, take the cars away.

The caller smiled slightly, just a twitch, but nothing makes one more conscious of the face's movements than the awareness that a Brillist is reading yours. "An understandable but imperfect analogy, Commander Mojave; 'test subject' implies disposability, detachment, and the hierarchy of researcher over subject. You know Brillists ascribe human flourishing to the interaction of a dynamic and increasing variety of minds, therefore, (A) we hold all lives precious and find each death as absolutely intolerable as you do, and (B) we value Brillists and non-Brillists equally, recognizing that we prosper best as a minority among minorities, unlike Utopia, whose projects would fare better if your war wiped out the rest of us and left the world for you to bustle in."

The last words made my stomach clench, though it took a while to realize why, the odd phrase borrowed from Shakespeare's villainous Richard III plotting his brothers' deaths to "leave the world for me to bustle in"—is that your plan indeed, Gordian, to smear Utopia with propaganda poison, as those who supplanted Richard pressured playwrights to?

I heard Huxley draw quick breath, and turned. I had not seen so fierce a look upon their face since that day back in Romanova when they offered Felix Faust their hand and war. They parted their lips to speak but froze instead, a look of wrathful calm, and (perhaps a little like a Brillist) I felt I understood Huxley's message without words: *Try all your skill, adversary, to sow distrust between Utopia and these good friends around me—you will fail.* I smiled my agreement, but speaking aloud felt wrong, imprudent, like no matter what we said, the Brillists would gain by it, assessing, worming deeper into us, their victory condition, while any words they spoke to us gave only surface masks, no fair exchange. Andō and MASON in their last hours, that had been fair trade of speech for speech between adversaries, but this was bait to draw our secrets from us through the one-way mirror of that calculating Brillist face. So, for a minute, we just watched each other, the most aggressive silence I have ever known, until at last, from off-screen, rushed and eager German heralded our rushed and eager foe.

„*Vier Uhr morgens,*" Faust moaned as they took the quickly yielded desk chair. "*Unmenschlich, was*—Oh! Carlyle too! Doing better, I see. Good morning. And Huxley Mojave, and is that . . ."—they squinted—". . . is that [Anonymous] or—"

"Yes!" I said, "I'm free!" The words felt hot and joyous with rebellion.

"Fascinating. Think of a number between thirty-seven and a hundred."

"Eat dirt and die, you stinking clot of filth!"

Faust's eyes widened. "Any chance you'd name a color warmer than burgundy?"

"Not for more bribes than there are drops of water in the sea!"

A broad, slow smile dawned upon Faust's face. "Exquisite. But it was Donatien who chose this lovely hour to call me, yes? *Ich höre zu, Donatien, was wil—*"

"No German!" Huxley roared. "Not a word, you hear me! You both use English so we all understand, or you don't speak at all."

It may have been the unwashed haste of four A.M., but the Headmaster looked older than I remembered, their hair thinner, the bare patches left by so many mind-machine-interface experiments showing unhealthy splotches on their skin—it seemed like more aging than a single year should bring, but war does such strange things to people and to time, and faces all around me show how much vigor this vampire year has drained from all of us. "Shouldn't that be up to Donatien?" Faust asked.

"No." Huxley stood fast. "I will sooner see the Alien lie silent on that bed until their human vessel dies than let you labyrinth their thoughts where none can follow. I know what words can do."

Faust frowned back gently—they wore a sweater too I noticed, black with a band of alternating ribs striping the chest and thin cables snaking down the shoulders, codes to fill those who understand them with awe at the Headmaster's extraordinary mind, and to fill we the ignorant with awareness of our ignorance. "You speak to my Nephew in your shared language," Faust replied, "as Cornel did, as Andō did, as everybody has a right to do, a fundamental right of every bash'."

I felt persuaded—was it just fatigue that I succumbed so easily to reasonableness's trickery? But Huxley is not soft, and Huxley's eyes, their face, rage rippling from grief as aftershocks ripple from the intolerable epicenter, that face awakened me to my own knowledge, my own rage. "You have no rights in this, Faust! You murdered Cornel MASON!" I said it. I'm proud I said it, there in the heart of Alexandria in front of everyone, and Huxley was proud too, turning to me with eyes which said the words had been on their lips too. "Even if you put the trigger in Bryar's hand," I continued, "you planned it and you did it. You exploited MASON's succession plans to lock me in that torture of a hospital bed and seize the Empire. You murdered Ganymede and Lorelei Cook, you . . ." I needed breath, ". . . framed Utopia . . . defiled the *Sanctum*

Sanctorum . . . destroyed the Almagest . . . fired harbingers at space stations . . . Even the Church War didn't sink to that . . . You used the whole catastrophe, the war . . ."

Faust finished for me, "Which the Utopians planned, started, and wanted." The Headmaster paused to sip coffee from a mug with owls on it, staring keenly at us from the clay. "They knew—Huxley Mojave there *personally* knew—more than ten years ago that growing tensions, the Mitsubishi land grab, Masons' growth, could erupt into war. And they knew that if it didn't, if peace lasted and we kept making Earth better, that in a generation or two, their project would die out, that the slice of the populace with great ambitions for humanity would stop being willing to face death and toil in space when different equally great ambitions can be achieved right here on Earth, humanely with reasonable work hours and reasonable risks. So, they planned for war, and nurtured Tully Mardi like a viper in the world's breast, and did it all to make the world worse, the human condition harder, bad enough to make hard people to continue their hard task. The world of formal ethics doesn't have a word for that that isn't 'evil' or at the least 'willing evil for the sake of perceived good.'" Faust took another sip, with a frown that looked strangely compassionate, as if this leader who had made many hard choices empathized with Utopia's hard choice. "Now that we have that off our chests, I'd like to talk to my Nephew. Donatien?"

The Alien had not Acted in this time, but had rolled Their eyes across to fix upon the screen, the voice and image offering prosthetic proximity, imperfect but sufficient to this need. *"Onkel, Warum hast du das—"*

"English," Huxley interrupted, with soul's deep earnestness. "Please, Mike, we need you to use English. We need to understand."

Silence, but all present know this Visitor's silences, Their struggles to compress teeming Infinity into a string of words, as when young Kenzie Walkiewicz still running Pass-It-On compacts the hopes and fears of a whole continent into a laser string of blips and silence. "Uncle, why have you the hovering-amidst-precarious-succession Empire from *Patris* successor's proxy's proxy's proxy seized?"

German, I realized, They were funneling Their thoughts through German before English, tangling the grammar as They tried—kind Prince—to protest this intolerable treatment of Their proxy Martin's proxy Mycroft's proxy: me.

"I'm conquering the world for You," Faust answered simply. (Transcribing this I wrestled over whether to have Faust give the Prince capitals, since Mycroft bases it on what the speaker thinks the Prince Is, or rather whether the speaker would say the Prince Is an Eternal Thing, or merely is. In Faust's case I'm not sure, but I decided if Faust has been studying the Prince's brain for twenty years, they've seen what Huxley's seen, the neuron stuff, and Faust would be no scientist if they don't recognize, at minimum, a ship of flesh.) "You shouldn't do it Yourself, Donatien. You're very good at some things, innovation in particular, and humane kindness, a brilliant combination for a Brain-bash' Stem, but You're terrible at compromise, and terrible at understanding time, and You can't run a war without understanding compromise and time. You especially can't end a war without understanding compromise and time."

Jehovah did not move, that corpse-like stillness on the bedclothes, staring. "Time I am learning, Distance too, and their divorce as wordspeed changes and, with instant knowledge lacking, all friends become merely Schrodinger alive."

Delight bloomed on Faust's face as they listened to this, as on a naturalist's who witnesses some rare behavior of an elusive species. "You know, Donatien, that I do not tolerate human deaths, not when they are preventable. So, I will not let the side effects of your perfections make this war worse."

"Is *Onkel's* war better?" This question on the Prince's lips shot fire through me—Faust's war better? Operation Baskerville! The Almagest! My months of horror!—but while the Prince is not omniscient in our Universe, They still think like an omniscient Thing, seeing all sides without perspective, focus, or allegiance, even to Themself.

"Yes, Donatien. Mine will be a short war, the least protracted a World War could be." I felt a thrill as Faust used almost my very words—it has to be a short war. "You have a lot of strength now, Donatien, You have the Masons, Myrmidons, Utopia, your Remaker loyalists, with their help You can take strategic centers fairly quickly, but even if every faction's leadership surrenders to You, You'll still face a hundred thousand guerilla wars against the tiny villages that hold out to the last." Faust sighed, a smiling, bash'parental sigh. "You've been too honest. You asked for unconditional surrender, and that makes people fight to the bitter end, the slowest, most protracted kind of war. I know You just meant that you don't have a fixed plan yet, but You're matchlessly benevolent, if You'd just promised a few kindnesses to people that you're bound to offer anyway, then . . ." Faust paused, smiling down into their coffee. "But You couldn't. You wouldn't be so precious if You could. So, I took the war off Your hands."

"Why so occultly?" the Prince asked. "*Onkel* is coequally Remaker with all in this room. Why seize? Imprison? Why intolerable damage to My [Anonymous] and to the Empire's trust?"

"Two large reasons." What is that expression, Faust? Regretful? Proud? What would we read in it if we had your special sight? "The smaller of the two is that our methods weaken when people realize we're at work. I've made Your victories easy, Donatien. Every time Su-Hyeon moved Your forces somewhere, I sent mine first to prepare your adversaries, weaken their courage, strengthen their fear, soften the diehards, snuff out hope for victory while strengthening the hope for compromise. We've engineered ten thousand surrenders for You over the past four months, and made ten thousand other microbattles easier. You've swept so quickly through Europe, Asia, the Americas, so many cities joining You, so many barricades that opened without a single drop of blood. But our methods only work when subtle—if the world knew Gordian was active, paranoia would armor the zealots, egg on the diehards, and make our voices, which seem neutral now, seem partisan."

We all paused, a thousand campaign details shifting in our minds, especially the others who had seen the last months, how often the fog of war had lifted to reveal friends where they had expected foes. But my mind was on just one puzzle piece: Su-Hyeon. Was this why they helped the Brillists? Romanova's Censor trusted with so many lives, a *world* of lives. My mind's eye showed me Su-Hyeon back in the Censor's office, staring rigidly at data on the screens far grimmer than Kohaku Mardi's numbers, as siege engines before the gates are grimmer than mere dust on the horizon. I thought of the Cartesian set-sets unable to resist deleting one little ball of light if it would calm the whole—was Su-Hyeon like that too? A mind so keen, it locks like clockwork when the trolley problem is so disproportionate: let the trolley continue down the track that will crush millions of lives, months, years of war griefs, or reroute it to the other which will claim just one lone victim: me.

"Yes, [Anonymous], that was why," Faust said, the master Brillist answering my thoughts, which cannot have been hard to read as tears threatened anew. "Su-Hyeon saw the data, knew what only Gordian could do, and came to us. And they knew they mustn't under any circumstances admit their takeover was a deliberate coup, not even to you in the hospital, that if you had confirmation, you'd eventually find some way to let the secret out. But our young Censor is no set-set, and a mind which can bend is often bent by friendship, so, alas . . ."

So much surged in me, thoughts toxic and warming, hate, thanks, regeneration most of all, my trust for Su-Hyeon healing, new shoots springing from the tree stump nurtured by the thought that Su-Hyeon had revealed their own treason to me, risking—no, *guaranteeing*—that the Empire's inexorable engines of vendetta would dog Su-Hyeon unto their dying day to exact revenge for the betrayal of an almost-Emperor. Su-Hyeon risked all that because I begged them for the truth? No. No, these tears are better wiped away, these shoots nipped in the bud before they choke the garden; I have truer friends.

"Faust,"—I was proud of the chill in my voice—"you said that keeping Gordian's actions secret was the smaller of two reasons?"

I read respect in Faust's pursed smile, impressed that I could still recall the forest when so wounded by the trees. "The other is what Donatien calls the trunk-war. Donatien? You put it well, Donatien."

"The outpath and the in," the Prince recited slowly.

"Exactly, Donatien." I hadn't noticed until this point how often Faust repeated the name they gave the Prince—a tool to coax the Prince's mind into Brillist-shaped thoughts? "That's the war I'm fighting, and Your [Anonymous] sides with Utopia."

"Yes!" I said it, snapped it, proud to hear my own word flash faster than lightning.

Faust nodded. "So, with the Empire in hand, [Anonymous] would have helped Utopia at every turn."

"Of course!" I cried. "As Cornel MASON wanted! As the Prince—"

"No." Faust smiled as if charmed by my mistake. "That isn't what Donatien wants. You understand, don't You, Donatien? Cornel used Martin, placed Martin near You so you'd love them and they'd pull You toward the Masons. And just the same, Cornel put Mycroft near You, and [Anonymous], and my sister's hostage Utopians, hoping You couldn't bear to face their grief if You reject their path."

I found myself staring at the Prince's body on the bunk, as motionless as a computer's shell as worlds of calculations churn inside. Their words: "I pathmove not."

"True, Donatien." Faust's voice was gentle. "You don't walk the path, You're the Pathmaker, or Path Remaker, as You've called Yourself, the One to steer us as these paths diverge. Has the war helped You realize that You hate Utopia's path?"

I hate not—that should have been the Prince's answer, easy, quick—*I, omnibenevolent, hate nothing, no one.* Instead, They paused. A battle cry could not have chilled me like that pause. *"Ich . . . kann . . ."* The Prince was struggling.

"Use English, Mike," Huxley urged, hands tense with the impotent desire to act, to grasp, to help. "Please, stay with us in English."

"I can't . . ." still struggling, "I can't . . . I can't Love evil."

Faust's face relaxed, like one who has sat tense over the game board, fearing the opponent might make the one move which could spoil all your plans, but no, they make the move you hoped they would, and all is well. "That's right, Donatien. You Hate evil. That opposite-of-love feeling You Feel, that's Hate. You Hate evil, suffering, toil, pain, the many evils of this Universe which You would never think of, never make, never allow if You had power to stop them. You Hate destruction, failure, decay, so many things in this world never found in You and Yours. You Hate impotence, the feeling of wanting to help, to reach, to save, wanting so hard it feels like the heart will split, but it yields nothing. You Hate war, this tearing down of things You Love. You Hate—"

"I . . ."

"Yes?" Faust's face brightened at the Prince's interruption, abortive as it was. "What is it, Donatien? You . . . ?"

"I . . . can't Love . . ."

"You Hate, Donatien. You don't need to be afraid to say You Hate something like evil, pain, or war."

A note, reader, I wrestled a long time when transcribing this sequence, with when to give nouns capitals: evil or Evil, pain or Pain, war or War. It was abstracts they meant, all evils, all pains, all wars, always, from the moment pain was born in the first suffering of the first microbe battling the second for resources in their primordial pool. Abstracts could merit capitals, but Evil feels too much like some great adversary, like a person, thinking, stalking, godlike Ares-War or Eris-Strife, eternal like Jehovah, with a unity that let Homer imagine heroes fighting them, his Diomedes wounding Ares on the battlefield and selfish, golden Aphrodite—no. The irremediable evils that make Good Jehovah grieve cannot be wounded, they are finitudes themselves, *the fact that* things can wither, weaken, end. The evil is the lack of capitals, the fragileness of small-p peace, and small-l love, and small-a small authors.

"I . . ."

"Yes, Donatien? You . . ."

"I Hate . . . Death. *Onkel,* I think I Hate Death."

"Yes. Yes, you do." Why big-D Death? Because Death is one evil, specific, which, though we cannot wound, we can disarm. "You do Hate Death." The smile on Faust's face was victory's smile, but sad, laced with mourning—all our faces mourned as we watched something Perfect change to better match our so-imperfect world. "I hate Death too, Donatien," Faust continued. "Everybody there around you, Huxley, [Anonymous], we all hate Death and work against it, in our own ways, to disarm it blade by blade, Utopia works at it, the Cousins in their way, Gordian most."

Huxley's lips parted in protest, ready to list Utopia's victories, their cures, their great to-do list, every confiscated blade, but the Prince spoke first.

"And Distance? *Onkel,* do I Hate Distance?" Troy's Old Enemy.

"Yes." Relief's sigh from Faust. "Yes, Donatien, You finally Hate Distance. It took a war to show You. That's because humanity has worked so hard to mitigate Distance, to connect ourselves in space, in voice, in words and data, never out of touch. We've made such headway, Distance almost doesn't matter here on Earth, but it will matter out there where Utopia would take us, light-years of diaspora, and one-way voyages, and worse. You've felt it now, what separation means, being beyond reach, last goodbyes and points of no return. Utopia—"

"The silence and the cars!" I called aloud as I realized. "You caused the silence and the lockshell with the cars, it's all to teach Jehovah about Distance! To make Them Hate Utopia!"

Faust gazed at us through the screen a long time—reluctant, are you, to confess to planning Operation Baskerville when wars so often end with trials? "Whoever caused them, they reduced the war's destruction and complexity," Faust answered carefully. "A war with so many sides and with millions of flying anti-matter engines, the first month alone would have seen a hundred thousand sites go up like Brussels. This war had fewer deaths and moved more slowly, more predictably, and since the Cousins had us all so well prepared for losing the cars, every town and bash'house stocked against starvation, the consequences were . . ."

"Devastating!" I cried at the same time Faust finished with ". . . minimal."

A pall fell on the room, and I didn't need to be a Brillist to read in all eyes the realization: devastating and minimal—in World War, both can be true at once.

"But yes," Faust added, "I hope it has helped show You, Donatien, what Utopia's outward path entails, the rifts of years, of lifetimes, rifts that even light's speed cannot smooth away. You Hate that."

"I . . . Do I . . ." How shaken was our Prince? I wished we had some way to tell, wished that soft voice had tone, that face expression, something. A Universe was Changing, rediscovering Itself, and I had Plato in my mind to warn me that a good thing changed by a bad thing is not changed for the better. ⌜"«*Kirai . . . odio . . .* ἀποδιοπομπητέα . . . »"⌟ Then in a burst of French : « *Les défauts, les regrets, les maux et l'ignorance ! Et l'espérance aussi, Je la Déteste aussi ! L'attente est trop cruelle ! Je n'en Veux pas ! Je ne Veux pas ces offrandes !* » The exclamation points feel right, though the Prince's voice stayed ever soft, as one who coaxes children into dreams. I'd heard Vivien quote it enough that, even without much French, I recognized this list of hateful evils—mistakes, regrets, miseries, ignorance—it's from a poem by Voltaire, a list of offerings we mortals can give our Maker, things we humans possess that They do not. The struggling Prince was borrowing our Zeroeth Anonymous's words of protest against our Maker's world, which, Voltaire knew well, is *not* the best and kindest of all possible—the best and kindest is what this Stranger would have made for us, this Kinder God. But *l'espérance*—hope—that's the consolation Voltaire put at the climax of the list—Gods lack hope, hope unique to we the finite, we who change in time. So, You Hate hope too, Prince? You Who in Your Good Infinity had never tasted waiting, aspiration, and their underbellies: failure and despair. We need hope, we time's prisoners, but I understand why You would Hate it. I've learned to hate it too, I who have felt the stab when Your Peer made me hope, and heard Their mocking laughter when Your Peer then made a prison camp of Esperanza City.

"I want . . ."

"What do you want, Donatien?"

"What do you want, Micromegas?" Huxley countered, the name a counterspell against a name, both sides tugging the Prince as whalers tug at harpoon lines that seek to guide the pain-throes of the ship-crushing Leviathan.

"I want My *ibasho*."

My chest felt tight. Look, reader, there is a thing so precious Gods and humans long for it alike. Did you know that?

"Alright," Faust answered warmly. "You can have it. You can have Martin back, and Heloïse, and Dominic, and Aldrin, and Voltaire, and Mycroft will be back again in time, but You can't Keep them, Donatien. You Know You can't. You Know that Time and Death will take them all away again, and Distance too will drag them from You, over and over."

The shortest of pauses. "I Hate Death."

"Me too, Donatien. In Gordian, we all hate Death, each lost mind diminishing forever the complexity humanity could reach if we could keep all minds, all sets, all experiences commingling—"

"Each loss Infinity."

"Yes." A somber smile. "Setbacks in our quest toward infinite human variety. We feel the agony as You do, Donatien, each time a thinking vastness that's still growing, deeper, vaster, more unique and powerful, then withers with the flesh and ends before we even know the shape of what it could have been. So, we're working as hard as we can. Flesh dies, not data, not when it's stored well. We're racing to learn, not just to connect brains to prostheses, but to run a mind on a computer, back it up, immortal options for when the flesh brain fails, infinite time to unlock the deep potential of each unique and irreplaceable psyche." Faust tapped the spotty skin above their temple, rubbed raw from experiments. "It's taken work, and time, generations, but we are stopping Death, unlocking—"

"As are we," Huxley snapped. "Give us that credit, Faust. *Astra mortemque*, our twin projects, not *astra* alone."

Faust stiffened in their chair, all trace of empathetic smiles gone. "I do not divide my efforts between immortality and *anything which is not immortality*!" This roar echoed like thunder. "The two goals are not equal! Even the Cousins know you put on your own oxygen mask before helping others. If we don't save ourselves, we won't be here to achieve other achievements: space, art. Nothing, nothing matches still being alive to achieve more. But you! You have six times the resources we have, but you waste most of it hurling rockets at the sky, postponing technoimmortality by generations! Can't you see? You're like the rest who don't let themselves think too hard about it, because we lose minds every day, because a brain is small enough to hold in your two hands, you fall into the mass illusion that losing one is a small loss—it's not! It's huge inside! Huge as a world! To lose a mind—one! One such deep, dynamic vastness is as much a loss as if you saw some exoplanet ripe for planetfall and exploration crash into its sun! You are your own mass murderers! Murdering the billions of worlds of thought of generations we weren't fast enough to save because you will not put *immortality itself* above your . . . your . . . *needless space obsession*!" For a moment, uncle seemed like Nephew, struggling for words.

"For that you try to shatter us?" Huxley shot back. "Because we indenture only half our questforce to disarming Death? We could have been allies! Both Remakers from the start! But you terrorformed the war against us instead of—"

"*You assented to the war!*" Faust shouted back. "More than a decade ago, you knew what was coming, millions endangered, global devastation, and you let it come! All to keep Earth *bad* enough to make minds *mad* enough to leave our hard-earned safeties and risk death among the stars. *I would have stopped it!*" Faust's pale face flushed red with grief and rage. "If I'd known as early as you did, I would have stopped it, tried to stop it, lives lost, resources burned, that . . ." Deep breath. "We wanted to work with you, solve the immortality problem together first as partners and put off space for second, for after we've unlocked so much more human capacity by letting minds continue to grow richer and produce beyond the maximum that flesh can last. We hoped you'd see that should come first, all else second, but when you realized the dream of space was dying out, you decided to put space first, even if it meant causing a World War! You . . ." Again a calming breath. "But we aren't trying to wipe you out. We're trying to knock you down. To ground you. We didn't cause the Nurturists and their purge, we gentled them, encouraged prison camps, and Tiring Guns, a thousand ways to make enemies spare you, let you live. Your minds are precious exoplanets too, more so because you do fight Death with us, and at the war's end, you can do more, partner with us for our shared quest, even if it has to be from a Reservation down in Esperanza City. But once you're knocked down, once my branch becomes the trunk, you'll finally give immortality your whole effort, guarding the billions here and unlocking our potential instead of firing a quarter of Earth's produce into space!"

I winced, Kohaku Mardi's numbers rising in my mind—I'd concentrated on the Masons' population, the Mitsubishi land, but Utopia is the third ingredient, so much of Earth's income siphoned up by such a narrow sliver of its people and spent (not evenly) on death and on the stars.

"You think our space work hasn't weakened Death?" Huxley shot back. "We've learned so much, of cells, growth, radiation, gravity. What about communications? Try facing peacetime without our infomancy and our satellites, then you'll really feel the tyranny of Distance!"

"True," Faust answered flatly. "All true. And I understand as well as you do that great projects take plural hands, take poets, bakers, toymakers, all the teamwork apparatus that nurtures minds toward innovation. Your works near Earth are invaluable, but Mars? We don't need Mars. If we succeed in ending Death completely, humanity may need some extra living space once the world population starts rising again, but it isn't rising yet, and if we're living as computer minds, we won't need the same space that bodies do. Mars has taught us some things, helped us disarm Death a blade or two, but *I* do not aim to disarm, I aim to defeat, and Mars will not end Death, nor unlock the potential of the mind, our best tool for defeating death, not as much as we could unlock it with the resources that you waste on Mars if the resources you waste on Mars were used on Death directly. For now, Gordian, like Utopia, may seem to nurture a thousand occupations orthogonal to ending Death, but they are not, not one of them, and we will not divert one human hour from our project, not for any secondary dream, however grand"—a gentler frown—"or fragile." The tired Headmaster drew a long, tired breath. "I know it hurts, feeling your dream at risk. I felt it myself when little Donatien first called our Hives twin branches vying for the trunk. And you . . ." Faust's eyes narrowed, searching Huxley's face, ". . . you feel it worse than me . . . your own conviction weakening . . . afraid of space yourself since you watched so many helpless spacecraft burn? And . . . ah . . . you did not personally help push Earth toward war, but you don't know whether or not some other Constellation did, and . . . but you are sure that, if they had asked you to cause a war for Mars's sake, you would have done it."

With a soft curse, Huxley turned away from the screen, shrinking as we all do from the great Voyeur whose gaze probes like cold forceps deep into our selves. But stiff upon the bunk close by is One whose gaze probes deeper.

"Huxley, did you will war?" this Kind Alien asked, First Contact, precious, *more* precious than Mars. And disappointed.

"Only as a means, Mike." Huxley Mojave shivered, Utopia's storm-fierce champion stripped of storm, coat, visor, even of thoughts' secret harbor before the staring Prince. "It's a means I hate, but . . . if there was no other—"

Faust cut in. "I can't say I don't condemn it, but I do understand it. Do You understand it, Donatien? Huxley fears the dream of space might die out if we focus on immortality first, just as I fear Brill's system could die out. But even Brill themself faced that fear, and accepted that posterity might forget their system, twist it, turn half the species into set-sets, but Brill would not divert resources from disarming death to prevent that, because Brill knew as I do, as your Achilles does, that no dream that any generation dreams is guaranteed to be eternal, not until that generation is eternal in itself."

That softest voice: "Huxley?"

"Yes, Micromegas?" Huxley couldn't face Their gaze, Their Goodness.

"I Love you."

Huxley shuddered, full-body like a small barque tossed by storm (which is a billion times a kinder force than vacuum). "Still?" they asked. "Mike, I did . . . I would have . . ."

"I Love you and I Want you to continue. All of you. I don't Want you to end like *Pater* and *Chichi-ue* and Ganymede and your Apollo. I Want it so much."

Tears glistened on the paler patch on Huxley's cheeks where the visor should sit. "So do I."

"But remaking humankind immortal would not negate Distance, the minutes' torture pain as light-words crawl from here to Mars and back again. I cannot Love that, Love stranding, silence, ignorance, goodbye, these two worlds whose irrevocable separation would everwound world-split humanity."

Huxley wiped their tears. "We've talked about this, Mike, about how humans don't always choose the things that make us happiest, we often choose things that bring toil and risk, but we won't trade those things for happiness, even if we struggle to explain why."

Silence as our Visitor wrestles this fact, so strange, so difficult, so human. But They Are not human. "I don't want you to choose those things. I want you to be happy. And to be here with Me. And to be."

I expected Huxley to respond, to shoot back with bold words, defend the spark, but their face was frozen, drifting, somewhere else in time. I know that face, the hate-grief in it—I've lost a ba'sib too, Huxley, my shattered *ibasho*. So many of us have. That's why no words rose in me either, no strong argument that Mars was worth . . . worth . . . I wanted Mycroft. They were what we needed here, not me, their eloquence to speak for the Utopians, Apollo's light, our distant, deadly aim, Mycroft's passion could light that spark in any breast, even in Faust's, but . . . no. No, Mycroft wouldn't help us here. They have more mourning tears to shed than I do, and besides, no one has ever hated Distance more, longed more for home and *ibasho* and rest, than our Odysseus.

"You see it now, don't you, Donatien?" Faust interrupted softly. "Utopia's is not a world You'd make. Give me the resources. Choose Gordian's path. We'll stop Death, Distance too, Distance means nothing to a computer mind, not on planetary scales, Reykjavík to Antarctica in a fraction of a second too miniscule for consciousness to note. With Gordian, You can make this world like one You would have made, where thinking creatures have no limits, keeping all the good things, change, and richness, and complexity, Your *ibasho* beside You, safe forever, finally safe to last and last until each mind grows to its full potential, vast as any world. Gordian's path is Your path, You see that now, don't You? It always has been. Utopia's path is toil, generations—"

"Onkel?"

"Yes, Donatien?"

"The likewise-precious un-chosen other branch, what becomes it?"

Huxley's knit brows foretold an answer no one here would like, but they let Faust speak first.

"Branches, Donatien, sometimes grow and sometimes wither. If you choose Utopia's branch, we'll still be here and work toward technoimmortality but slowly, too slowly for Your parents, or Your bash'mates, or likely for Your own mortal body, Your"—glancing at Huxley—"ship of flesh, which will someday wear out and end our contact. On the other hand, if I'm the trunk, then Utopia would help me battle Death, and keep doing some space work close to Earth, asteroid mining, stations to expand habitable space, but we all predict the urge to go beyond the Earthsphere will wither if we make this world as kind as You and I want to make it. I'm sure humans will look to deeper space again eventually, when the sun grows dim, or we've used so many resources that we need more from beyond what we can reach, but it won't be—"

"What *Pater* loved," the Stranger finished, "the drive they say made Alexander curse they had only one world on which to chase horizons."

Faust sighed down into their coffee. "Well put, Donatien. It won't be that."

"And contact," Huxley interrupted. "It will mean humans don't reach out far enough to make contact with friends among the stars. Other than you, Mike, though you're not . . . among . . ."

This Alien stared back, so silent, and unreadable, and distant-feeling suddenly beyond that ship of flesh that knows no stars. "And if I end that dream, then can I really Have My *ibasho* and Keep it?"

A loving uncle's smile. "Yes, if You choose us."

"Liar!" I challenged. "You can't keep that promise, Faust, you've said yourself real immortality is generations off. Too late for us."

"It was. It won't be anymore if Donatien gives me the resources." The light in Faust's eyes was soul-warming and maniacal at once. "'H.E.L.E.N. and all her treasures,' isn't that the line? Healing potions, resurrection potions, science a century beyond ours, Cato Weeksbooth's knowledge, and the interface, Achilles-Alexander, mind merged with machine."

"Bridger's relics." I stared stunned. "You want Bridger's relics?"

"Of course. What else in the world do you think is worth us entering this war?"

"But . . . you shot at Luna City."

"The city had shuttles. Utopia would've saved the relics no matter how many lives it cost."

My head was spinning. "You wanted the relics?"

"We could have left the war Hiveguard versus Remaker, helped make quick peace, then taken on Utopia in quiet peacetime propaganda battles as we always have, but now there's . . ." A pause—a flinch? ". . . something worth killing for. Bridger left behind what both sides need, the key to let Utopia reach deeper into space, the key to let us move minds onto machines, not in some distant someday but within a generation. And you're about to suggest that we could share, both study Bridger's relics, advance together against Death and toward the stars. And we could have if Utopia was less selfish about their dying dream. But they fear that if we make Earth better quickly, then posterity won't want to leave it, that if Death stops being a threat, then the fiercest of all evils will be Distance, and no one will retain the will to seek the stars. So, to protect their future, Utopia spirited all H.E.L.E.N.'s treasures to the Moon, where no one else can touch them."

I turned to Huxley, straining against the pillow to peer at them straight. "Is that . . . has that always been what we . . . we're fighting over . . ." *Yes,* a voice inside my mind insisted, a voice that didn't really feel like mine, *this prize, not gold, not land, not honor, Bridger's relics, these are treasures worth destroying this good world for, these the keys to build a better one.*

My stare begged Huxley to respond, exonerate Utopia, but how can you, Huxley? How can you when your desperation even willed the war?

"Faust," Huxley's voice was hesitant for once, gentle, "Bridger's relics, what do you . . . believe? And Micromegas . . ."

Gordian's Headmaster smiled into his coffee. "That's not something to discuss without our sensayers, and I fear Carlyle there is a little close to things to be a neutral chaperone." Faust paused to let Acting Minister of Spiritual Health Carlyle Foster nod. "And regardless," Faust continued, "of what nonhuman Forces may or may not be intervening, and What Donatien may or may not Be, at the moment, What They are is the Person with the power to decide all this. Utopia's surrendered to You, Donatien, a bird in the hand of the Empire. So, You can give the order. Give me Bridger's treasures, and You can Have your *ibasho* and Keep it. So can everyone."

"That's half a lie at least," I challenged. "No one can promise a safe, sound bash' reunion, not in wartime. Or are you offering to end the lockshell with the cars?"

"No, no." A little smile. "I'm offering to give Donatien's bash' back. Let me be clear: this is a hostage negotiation. You see, I have Martin. And I have Heloïse. And I have Dominic. And I have Voltaire, and Aldrin, and Cinna Semaphoros. And I have Isabel Carlos safe and well and ready to return and hand you Europe on a platter. And while I couldn't get Ganymede or Andō quick enough, I do have Cornel MASON's body, and if we use it for our first test when you hand over the resurrection potions, you can have Cornel back, safe and well and ready to resume their reign, and stubborn Donatien will never have to become MASON."

Latin murmurs rippled through the praetorians, while in the war room, frozen Xiaoliu stared up, rigid as a hunting mantis. "MASON . . ." Not Martin's name, reader, duty moves Xiaoliu even more than love—Martin would be so proud.

"I know you've been searching for them all with your Clairvoyance Constellation," Faust continued, "but Bridger didn't leave you the teleporter to go with the crystal ball, so sight alone's not much to go on, especially if I keep my captives on the move." A pause. "You don't believe me?"

We heard quick German orders, and the checkerboard-sweatered aide at Faust's side made motions which brought the proofs upon the screen: there sat Martin on a cell bunk poring over maps and lists on tablets, there Dominic snarling at the camera in a straightjacket, there Voltaire reading, Aldrin playing some videogame, each precious captive still so much themself. Persuasive Heloïse was not in a cell but an infirmary, setting a patient's bone as guards watched close.

"You have . . ." the words slipped out. "Then . . . *you* let Martin's letter get to Caesar, with the message that would make us bring Cato to Earth, within your reach . . ."

Faust's smile was not unproud. "And yours. You'll have to trust me about Isabel Carlos, though, I'm not giving you photo proof of that, too many ways you could turn it against me." And MASON? Vacuum is so cruel a death that it was hard to recognize that wreck of frozen face, those wrecks of frozen hands, but all the world can recognize that black Masonic suit with its gray right sleeve, and the Griffincloth sheen of Achilles's stolen armor which sat folded neatly on the transparent lid of the freezer-coffin where the hero's dear Patroclus waits for resurrection's kiss.

I heard Achilles's rage roar in my mind. I know it didn't happen in that moment, that it came an hour later when we forwarded the images, but shared experiences pierce time's diaspora, so just as all who read a book experience together those moments of crisis and discovery even if they read them years apart, just so I felt Achilles see this with me, and sear the airless skies with the fire of their determination to reach that crystal coffin and attain the ever after that no other *Iliad* has offered them. I won't forgive you, Maker—I swore to myself—if this hope too proves cruel.

But it's already cruel in one way. "That's monstrous! Trying to force the Prince's decision with hostages! The future of the Earth!" It was Carlyle who shouted it, fastest to call this evil 'evil'.

"Not at all," Faust shook their head. "Nothing can force my Nephew's decision, They will decide between the paths in Their own time and for Their own reasons which I can't wait to study. But now They understand the stakes at last, *ibasho* safe forever, or the stars. And you cannot call it unfair, not while you continue Cornel's practice of locking Donatien in that cell with Masonic and Utopian partisans to twist Them toward your path." A little smile. "Meanwhile, since it's clear your guards are on the edge of boiling over, I'll point out that you have the power to make the halfway choice yourselves."

I shivered as I looked around and saw the need-rage that colored each Masonic face: one glimpse of Martin, one whiff of Cornel's return, and my status as proxy-proxy-proxy Emperor fades to near nothing. Faust is a master wedge-driver. "What is the halfway choice?" I asked.

"To give me Bridger's relics yourselves, without waiting for Donatien. I'll spell it out: you can have Martin back, Heloïse, Dominic, Aldrin, Voltaire, Cinna, Spain, and Cornel resurrected safe and sound. But in return I get the crystal ball, the magic wand, the belt of strength, all the reverted toys, the healing and resurrection potions, anything else I'm forgetting at present, and above all I get the Alexander, Cato Weeksbooth, and Achilles, and . . . well, we all know that Mycroft will be back . . ."

Fear prickled as I saw hope's eagerness in the praetorians' faces—praetorians who hold the keys to this cell and the many, many doors between it and the freedom of the night. Suddenly, Utopia and I felt like birds in their hands, not vice versa. "You're suggesting we take the decision away from the Prince?" I asked, largely to make the watching Masons face the name of treason.

Faust squinted at me through the screen. "I know you don't believe my Nephew's human. Fascinating that you think They have a better right than humans to decide the future of humanity."

"The Prince is better than humanity." I said it—no point hiding, not when Faust can read it in my face. "And Cornel MASON wanted the decision to be Theirs."

My frankness made Faust chuckle. "Well, just as Donatien helped make the constitution that saved the Cousins and then declared war on them and demanded unconditional surrender, you can give me Bridger's treasures, secure Donatien's bash'mates and bash'parents, and then if Donatien does choose Utopia's path, you can still help Them fight me to the bitter end." A deep breath. "Also remember, Bridger's treasures will be easier to take back from me here on Earth than from them on the Moon if Donatien rejects Utopia and you end up fighting them instead of Gordian—the Hive that wanted war will not yield quietly."

I tried to take a deep breath, calm myself, avow anew that Huxley was my friend and never, ever would become my enemy . . . but Su-Hyeon did.

"But take your time," Faust continued, "betraying Donatien or each other isn't a decision you need to make at four in the morning. Meanwhile, our eventual trunk-war, if it comes, will be less destructive if we've settled the Hiveguard on Remaker war before it starts. So, while you and Donatien consider, if all of you will agree to work with me and keep Gordian's activities still secret, we can continue to arrange easy battles for you, to move the Hiveguard-Remaker war toward peace. I know you have a parley coming up with OSA and Homeland-EU, I can help with that. I can help a thousand ways if you'll accept Gordian as a Remaker ally while we wait for Donatien's decision."

My mouth opened to answer but I realized I wasn't sure who should be answering. Me for the Empire? Huxley for Utopia? The Prince could answer but for what, for the Vastness of rival Universes wounding One Another and we poor ants too with their all-trampling Conversation?

"That's a great plan! Let's do it!" It was so warm a voice at first, I couldn't put a name to it. It felt like my old self before the Olympics, still awed at heart by preparation's industry, and honest side-taking, and human dignity passing the Test, my self before the war's intolerable hammering and its deep damage. In fact, it was Carlyle. "Truce and collaboration until we've ended the Hiveguard-Remaker conflict, that sounds perfect. I hope you'll also help with the Mason-Mitsubishi tensions and Papadelias's efforts toward a fair land plan?"

Faust beamed. "It would be a pleasure. And it's a pleasure to see you so . . . energized, Carlyle, as if . . . something . . ."

"Carlyle's the Tenth Anonymous!" I blurted with the urgency with which most would shout 'fire'.

"Ah." A broad smile. "Wise reveal, it would have been dreadfully awkward if I'd become Eleventh just now. Congratulations. Meanwhile, [Anonymous]? Do you feel of sound mind enough to seal a truce?"

Of sound mind enough at least to pause and think before giving this answer. I could see the Praetorians around me quaking with their answer: *Never! Never allies while they hold our rightful Emperor!* Sorry. I'm not Martin. I see it in their eyes, they're glad to have me free but I'm not Martin. I'm not even Mycroft, just like Bo isn't Papadelias, and Huxley isn't Cinna Semaphoros, and sweet Carlyle isn't quite as good at sweet as Heloïse, and Chagatai can't guard the Prince like perfect Dominic. All these substitutes, brave, rising to occasions, but they aren't our *us.* The Masons too, they want to have their *ibasho* and keep it.

"Onkel?"

"Yes, Donatien?"

"Distance." The Prince said it in Their ghostly, gentle voice. "I still worry."

"Yes, You do. Most of us manage to process the trauma-shock of the object-permanency problem and move on, but You never have, that's why You're the perfect One to really think about this choice full force, and make it."

"The outpath or the in. Meanwhile, peacespeed?"

Peacespeed—the word made up my mind. Peacemaker was a poisoned word now but peacespeed felt right, minimizing each day's bloodshed as we press toward victory. I thought of the many distant battles on the war room screens that Earth's lagging information bloodstream won't let us direct from here, but Gordian could make them kinder while we focus on the diplomatic macrostructure . . . Wait. "The silence!" I cried suddenly. "Can you lift it? End it? And the cars!"

Faust actually paused to think about this answer, which felt like a small victory in its way. "No."

I scowled, but everybody was on edge, in need of rest, and sleep, and thinking time, and this was not a victory I could secure tonight. "A limited alliance, then. Agreed." I tried to hold my head high as I said it, but a neck twinge warned that was a *bad idea*. "We'll complete the Prince's conquests together, and think about the rest."

"No! *Promagister . . .*" One praetorian dared. ". . . they're holding—"

"I know!" I shouted—no one will stifle my words now, no one! "Look at what they've done to me, do you think there's any human in this city angrier at the Brillists than me! But we do this! We make this war the best war it can be! The shortest war! And with the least use of harbingers. And if that means we put off avenging what they've done, then *I with all I've suffered* say that's worth it if it would save a hundred lives, and this will save a hundred thousand!" I paused to make sure these guards—*my* guards—dared no word against me. "As for you, Faust, this needs to be a real alliance, that means we protect each other's people, no more letting Utopian cities burn!"

A nod. "Agreed. They're weak enough already. Though I'm not sure how I can prove I'm actually keeping to that since—"

"You can't lie to the Prince."

"True." A proud, slow smile. "True."

"Onkel?"

Faust inhaled slowly, as if to savor some rare wine's bouquet. "Yes, Donatien?"

"Still I worry."

"What still worries You?"

I thought, as we all stared waiting again for words, about how maddening the Prince's rigid face must be to Brillists versed in human twitches—a telepath who finds one brain alone in all the world is inaccessible might feel so. "If the made thing reflects the maker's character, and especially the made thing's ethics-consequences reflect the maker's ethics-innerness, then Death, Time, Distance, if I Hate-which-is-not-Love these things, My Peer's creations, do I then Hate-which-is-not-Love the ethical Being That Is My Peer? Who Makes small authors and then crushes them, Who conceived Death and Distance, yet Who Wants to be called 'Friend' so much, They bent Their very Making to ensure I could still call Them such—do I Hate My Friend?"

I don't know, Prince, Su-Hyeon, Huxley, Sniper. I don't know.

Chapter TWENTY-FOUR

I Have to Move the Mountain

Written September 15–October 8, 2455
Events of August 27 and October 8
Alexandria

I THINK IT TOOK A THRONE TO MAKE ME FEEL LIKE an Emperor. My throne has wheels, and a headrest so I don't strain my neck, and grip bars to help me lever myself up to stagger the few paces I can manage to the bathroom or the bed, but while the name of 'wheelchair' might seem disheartening, it's this that helped me finally understand: a throne is a prosthesis, as Jehovah said, the throne of ancient marble in the Daedalus chamber just as much as this. From this throne MASONS grasp what our arms cannot reach, surmount what our legs cannot climb, wield strength our finite bodies cannot muster. From this throne Agrippa MASON guarded Regan Cullen and the bash' system from Brill's stubborn opposition; from this throne Mycroft MASON crafted the Reservation system and made friends of the remnant geographic nations; from this throne Cornel MASON solved the Mycroft Canner crisis which might have sparked this violence thirteen years ago; and from this throne Jehovah MASON will destroy this world to make a better one. And since Old Age and Frailty are staunch allies of our great enemy Death, I am not first nor will I be the last to sit upon this throne while needing wheels on it, but wheels are tools as natural to humankind as language, fire, stone, or fifty thousand jeeps. When I gazed out on my war room understanding that, I felt ready.

"The streams are up and clear, *Promagister.* O.S.A. and Homeland-EU leaderships request a firm time for the call. They propose 14:00 our time? That's forty minutes."

I wasn't *that* ready—I wanted a few more living prostheses first.

"Tell them we need to push it back an hour. First, bring me Eureka Weeksbooth."

Done.

Wary Su-Hyeon had kept this living resource stagnant in the cells during my long captivity, lest the great pattern-spotter spot a pattern.

"I'm fighting two wars now," I began when they brought Eureka, "one against Hiveguard for Jehovah, the other against the Brillists to put down Nurturism and protect Utopia. If I swear to you that no one will use anything you do to aid the former conflict or harm or oppose your ba'sibs, will you help us with the latter?"

<absolutely.> Most people would have paused, I think, but Eureka—so like yet unlike our hesitating Prince—is used to acting in those slivers of a second that mean so much to speeding cars. <but i have a request. i want you to let me check in with hiveguard. cardie and cardie's people, let us communicate. i won't misuse it. just like you've promised not to use me against them i won't let them use my access here against you, but if we're fighting gordian then we need everything, absolutely everything, especially data, and i can get data from hiveguard that i can't from you. so i want you to let me go when i request it, out into the city where i can contact them. and i want you to promise not to spy on me, or access what i get from them, that it'll be for my use only fighting gordian.>

"Agreed."

"Promagister!" an aide beside me cried. "The O.S. bash'—"

"Eureka Weeksbooth has had eight hundred million flying antimatter missiles at their fingertips their entire adult life!" I shouted it full force, even though I knew it would wind me. "They could've blown the Prince and all of us to smithereens the first day Sniper called for war! They helped execute their own bash'parents when they dared even discuss using the O.S. system without orders from a lawful government. You will not doubt Eureka's honesty!" I paused for breath, and to watch the set-set, who has no way to smile through their face-concealing interface, but I felt pride beam in how they held their arms. "Huxley," I continued, "when Eureka requests it, have them have Eureka escorted as far as they want escort, give them whatever they request, and no one is to track them or their contacts where they don't want to be tracked. Now, bring me Tully Mardi."

Done.

I wonder whether Tully Mardi's face is always that performatively defiant, head held high like a rebel in a painting, eyes ice-stern. Do they treat the whole human race as adversary every minute? Or just Mycroft's apprentice?

"I don't know you, Tully," I began. "After being around Mycroft so long, I realize I don't know anything real about you except that you're probably not actually a cosmic oozing bloody gash in space. So I'll ask straight: did you join Sniper because you oppose Jehovah Mason? Or did you join Sniper because you thought it was the best way to start the war?"

"I don't act on guesswork—I *knew* it was the best start for the war." Eyes deep with calculation gazed back at me, confident as Vivien's, Su-Hyeon's, as I imagine Eureka's if they showed a face, or wise Kohaku Mardi's.

"And now that you have your war," I asked, "how do you want it to end?"

"As quickly as possible, with minimum loss of life, especially Utopia's." The orphan raised upon the Moon does not forget their debt. "Happily, there's no conflict there." Tully nodded at my attendant Delians. "You've emerged as the strongest faction, your victory will be least bloody."

"Even if we're fighting Brillists?" I challenged.

It takes a strange courage to pause and think for seven silent seconds with your captors staring. "Yes. Gordian is dangerous and stubborn, but not as dangerous or stubborn as Utopia. Or you." Somehow, that felt like praise.

"Then be my *Familiaris,*" I challenged. "You're a warmonger, and it's hard to imagine a sentence harsh enough for intentionally unleashing all the atrocities of World War, tangled as I'm sure your trial would be. So, I want you to become my *Familiaris,* pre-accept that you won't fight whatever sentence I eventually hand down, or Martin or Jehovah hand down once the real succession happens. Put your life on the line like you've put everyone else's. Then I'll trust you, let you put your skills to work with us to make this a short war."

"Let me guess, the same sentence as Mycroft Canner? Worked to death?" Tully's is not a rough or rugged face, youthful if anything with large, bright eyes, and yet that smile, reader, was the grimmest that I've ever seen, and crazy as it sounds, I thought I saw the shadows move around them, subtle rippling like something moving under murky water. I opened my mouth to say Tully and Mycroft had committed the same crime, unleashing war's atrocities, but the somber Mycroft in my mind's eye frowned down at their hands stained with parricide blood and would not let me pretend it was the same. Then Tully smiled. "Agreed." Definitive Tully spared me the need to justify myself. "I need to sign something?"

I waved over the clerk who had just done the same paperwork for Huxley. "When you're ready, roll your wheelchair up here next to mine and we'll get started." Meanwhile, one last prosthesis. "Bring me Toshi Mitsubishi."

Done.

I don't know that I've ever seen such deep-lived fear. It wasn't just that moment's fear, what I Caesar would do to Su-Hyeon's dear companion—it was the months of fear and grief since Andō's death that had gnawed Toshi's frame, leaving their shoulders child-frail within their Censor's Office jacket, like a sparrow huddled under leaves.

"I was surprised to hear you didn't flee with Su-Hyeon," I began, glancing at Bo, whose frown confirmed we'd made no progress tracking the rogue Censor or their accomplices.

"They asked me to go with them." Toshi half whispered it. "Assumed I would. They weren't expecting me to refuse."

"Why did you refuse?" I tried to make my words gentle, wishing for the moment that this chair was less throne-like. "Did you know who they were helping?"

A wince. "Brillists. It was the Brillists, right?"

"Yes," I answered—it still feels like rebellion just saying it aloud.

Toshi's wince mixed hate with fear. "I thought so. I knew Su-Hyeon was sometimes meeting with . . . But I didn't know what they were doing to you! I swear! I only—"

"No one's blaming you for that," I interrupted gently. "It's good you didn't realize what was happening, they might have hurt you if you had. And even if you had figured it out, I wouldn't blame you for not acting on it. Su-Hyeon's been your protection through the whole war, the only thing between you and a lynch mob back in Romanova, and more so here as Caesar battled Andō. I'm impressed you stayed."

"I know who's firing up the Nurturists." Toshi made fists. "It's not the Cousins. And when you killed Father, at least you did it honestly, with honor. I'd rather be your prisoner than help the bigots who destroyed my bash'."

"Thank you. That's . . ." I struggled to find words. "That's a big, hard, brave decision. Thank you. But you're not our prisoner. We've consulted Papadelias." I nodded across at Bo. "Removing Su-Hyeon from office will be a big legal tangle, but for now, the Censor's missing, so we need the Deputy Censor to step up as Alliance Executive. You and I are the only two Censor's Office staff whose locations we can trace, and you know it can't be me."

Wide eyes? "Me? Censor?" Toshi turned to Bo. "But I'm . . ." *Not human,* say the hateful voices of self-doubt, *set-set, lab rat, monstrosity.*

"You're perfect for it." It was the best answer I had, I who have many voices inside calling me *monster.* Friends help friends ignore the voices that tell us we're not human, outside voices and in. "Vivien always said you were brilliant in the office, Su-Hyeon too. And neither of them ever thought your background compromised your work or anything about you. And neither does Papadelias, or Bo, or me, or anybody whose opinion is worth anything."

So much in Toshi's smile. "I guess I need to be sworn in?"

"I'll brief you in the office." Bo Chowdhury gestured toward the ready suite. "*Your* office."

Done.

I had my team. And, though it might be hubris, I think it's a team Gordian could never have predicted: Toshi, Tully, Bo, Eureka, me, and Huxley, side by side. We are resilient creatures, aren't we? Leaping into empty seats as shoots leap up through ash to green anew the fire-wasted slope. It should have cheered me, but a chill welled up under my joy, like the cold underlayer of a lake that chills the swimmer's feet with its reminder that the drowning vastness slumbers near. Vivien should have been here to help us handle this. Papadelias, and Bryar too, and Martin, Heloïse, Aldrin, Voltaire, Dominic, Mycroft, Andō, MASON, and a voice wormed up in me more invasive than bigotry's because it's right, Faust's offer: *yield Utopia, and you can have them all, your* ibasho, *and keep it.*

"The call is coming through, *Promagister.* Decoy systems feeding successfully into Gordian's surveillance pipeline."

I smiled. "Good." The Blacksleeves are so energized to counter Faust's surveillance, I try not to demoralize them with how sure I am we'll fail. Better to assume that Faust sees everything, and act accordingly, but meanwhile if we make it hard for Gordian to spy, that takes their resources from other things, which is not nothing.

"They're ready now, *Promagister.*"

"Which?"

"Both. Homeland-EU initiated, but O.S.A. is also live."

World communications had kept regenerating during my imprisonment, new workarounds fertilized by human cunning. Now we rulers and our officers can send text freely, even voice and video with a few hours' preparation—it's the other 99.99 percent of Earth that still feels silence's full tyranny.

"Put it on."

Light filled the screen, sparkling, dancing, a thousand cheering shards which made me think it isn't diamonds we hold precious, it's the light. The left half of the split screen showed a world of ocean sun, the clean bright of an after-dawn whose whiteness made the wave crests blinding while the ship's deck in the foreground flashed like steel. The right half showed not nature's light but ours, science's night-battling electric fire reflecting off night waves, while well-aimed spotlights made the figure in the foreground glow, human light sparkling off of human gold, and human alabaster, and human diamond blue and keen as murder. Ganymede—I thought the name, anyone would, seeing that face so often seen in statues somber, ghostly pale, but no, this golden mane was bound complexly back with combs and pins, these slender shoulders framed by a kimono, black save for a splash of embroidered raindrops, blue and shaped like tears. Danaë. The widow mourns both Ganymede and Andō, spouse and twin, pillars of an existence I had not imagined continuing without them. But as stone caryatids stand even as temples fall around them, so Danaë continues, statue-strong, and from that flagship's deck commands a dual inheritance: the teeming armies that bore the Mariscal's banners across all Europe, and the fleets that held two oceans in the name of home and land and Chief Director. Homeland-EU: I understood now how they had become one faction.

"Thank you for accepting my request, *Promagister*." I'd been braced for Danaë to call me *Déguisé* in front of everyone, but that was paranoia—the princesse (or, as they now prefer, 'Mariscala and Acting Chief Director') is far more versed at political formalities than I am. "It's heartening to see you looking well."

Do I look well so soon? "Thanks. Oh, before I forget, Toshi's here with us. They're busy now, but I wanted to tell you Toshi's fine and being sworn in as Acting Censor, and when things calm a bit, I'll try to make sure they give you a call."

"Thank you." Glowing Danaë glowed more, but parent's joy and pride faded quickly to sovereign gravity. "We have high hopes for these negotiations." The Mariscala gestured at a row of watching officers, some European uniforms, some Mitsubishi, and I recognized Ouyang Fan, the Fuxing Remaker Mitsubishi second-in-command after Huang Enlai. "Greenpeace, Dougong, and Fuxing are all ready to consider collaboration if things go well."

"Right . . ." I was distracted, staring at the absence of a figure on the sunlit side. Danaë was calling from the night of the Pacific's Asian coast, so the dawnscape must be O.S. of the Americas and should have more to show us than a backlit chair and distant, flustered aides. "Is my timing wrong?"

"No, perfect," Danaë answered.

Off-screen Spanish resolved my doubts. "¿What's that? ¿Are they starting already?"

"Sorry, Guardian. ¿Shall I ask them to wait?"

The unfamiliar title Guardian threw me, but the commander of so vast a faction, fleet on fleet, army on global army, is no simple admiral or general; the Commander-In-Chief of Hiveguard is the Hiveguardian.

"It's fine, I can finish while we start." Now the speaker alighted on the sunlit seat, those life-flushed, dimpled cheeks, that backlit corona of glowing curls, a bright Olympic jacket hanging open, baring one dark, full breast. I would call it unfair that Lesley Juniper Sniper Saneer persists immune against this vampire year that aged us all so much, aged Faust, aged me, aged even marble Danaë, but if Lesley glows with freshest life, there lies the reason snuggled in a fabric sling across warm Lesley's chest: a nursing infant, black-haired and beautiful. I think the smiles we have for new babies are special, smiles of pure welcome, pure success: in our cruel match played against Death and endless Entropy, we score +1.

"Oh!" I cried aloud. "Congratulations!"

"Thanks." Lesley beamed, so proud a smile.

"What's their name?" I asked it automatically, the universal question, so it took a moment for my breath to catch, my mind to register the avalanche of politics that teetered on this question asked of one surnamed Saneer.

"Olympian," Lesley answered, with a smile that forbade one to doubt even for an instant that the child of Ockham and Lesley Saneer, bash'child of Sniper, Cato, and Eureka Weeksbooth, scion of the oldest and most famous of all Humanist bash'es, would live up to such a name. "Shall we begin?"

"Yes, thank you, Guardian." Danaë took the lead. "First, *Promagister*, Guardian Saneer and I were surprised to hear that you yourself, rather than Censor Jung as usual, are speaking for the Empire today, but we were even more surprised to hear why. Any progress tracing the Censor?"

"Not yet," I answered. We had only told the others half the truth, afraid that exposing Su-Hyeon's four-month coup would make us look weak, but 'fled after attempting a coup' is close enough to true while Bo and Papa's polylaws work out the steps of indicting a Censor.

"And how much of what the Censor offered and requested on the Empire's behalf still stands?" Danaë asked.

I almost laughed. "Not much. Only the key thing, really: this has to be a short war." It felt strange speaking it aloud, a little gross as words that used to be just mine echoed in my memory in Felix Faust's voice. But they were my words first. "I want to save lives. Less war, less death, less burning Nature and the Produce of Civilization. That's what I want."

"Reasonable," Lesley affirmed. "I want the best government Earth's ever had not to collapse into autocracy."

I could only smile. "Also reasonable. But Hiveguard's not winning." Something in Lesley's practical demeanor made it easy for me to be blunt. "You must know that by now. Even in the Americas, where you've been strongest, you can see you're losing ground."

A frown. "You expect me to surrender?"

"Not this early in the conversation, but yes, I hope you will surrender by the end. That said, I wouldn't surrender yet in your position, you're still strong enough to hold big chunks of the Earth for quite a while, maybe years, but if something big changes—"

"You mean," Danaë cut in, "if my forces choose a side." Danaë was smiling, and I spotted a touch of flush lighting those alabaster cheeks, unearthly pale. I thought of the last time two wooers vied for this fair prize, the golden princess, and how much of Earth they burned. But we didn't call to woo Danaë this time. This time, Danaë—with more ships and troops at their command than Utopia with all its flying eyes can confidently count—called us.

"So," Lesley prompted, "what does Homeland-EU want?"

"Our Members, European and Mitsubishi alike, are content to call our united force simply 'Homeland'," Danaë corrected. "The Mitsubishi have no monopoly on having somewhere precious to protect."

"Homeland, then. And what does Homeland want?"

"A short war." Mischief glittered in those inescapable diamond eyes, but also warmth. "We want to minimize the destruction too. I hesitate to say we want it more than anyone, but we who care deeply about our heritage have so much to protect: heirlooms, ancestral homes, gardens cultivated over years, and unlike the Olympic spirit, or human aspiration, or even the economy, our treasures don't spring back from the ashes when they burn. They're gone."

I thought of how much in our museums is already Blackframe. "What do you propose?"

"We three are the largest forces left. Homeland is neutral at the moment, simply defending what we hold. This is not the time to dwell on what earlier leaders of Europe or the Mitsubishi fought for—their deeds and positions are not ours. Homeland as it is today aims only to protect as much of the precious past and present as we can while we transition to a future system better than one that depended on hiding state-sanctioned murder."

"So, you side with the Remakers?" the Hiveguardian translated.

"Not fully." Danaë shook their head, the glitter off their hair as hypnotic in the night and mourning black as it had been in salon and gilded boudoir. "The old system cannot continue, since what O.S. did can no longer be hidden, so it cannot have the same effect it did before."

"True," Lesley Saneer, the beating heart of old O.S., confirmed. "Hiveguard fights for Hive independence and Hives' rights to take such actions, not for that particular system, which I agree cannot resume."

"There must be a new system." Danaë glanced back at the nodding officers. "We hope to make it better than the last. And while we agree with President Ancelet and the late Cornel MASON that past law did grant Hives the right to kill to protect their Members, we feel this is the moment to replace that law with new laws more humane." A somber smile. "There's hardly a nation-strat extant that doesn't have state-sanctioned murder deep in our foundations, and if Mitsubishi and Europe alike take pride in our continuity with our pasts, much of our pride rests in celebrating the fact that we as nations became better over time, and overcame our selfishness, voicing and then answering the call to hold ourselves to something higher." I felt Patriarch Voltaire's warm ghostly hand upon my shoulder, Danaë's teacher as well as my own, who with the mighty Pen battled so many precedents cruel and unusual, and won. "Now is the time to become better yet again."

"No disagreement here," Lesley answered, pushing back a clump of curls mussed by the sea wind. "But there's a difference between reform and a coup. You're for finding a replacement for O.S. So are we. But are you for or against the conquest of all Hives by a dictator?"

Danaë's frown grew tender. "*Son Altesse le Prince* has noble aims. Mitsubishi and EU alike have long depended on His guidance, and we are glad to see so many rally to His promise to create a better world. We want to embrace that. But we also have much to protect: traditions, legacies, the ways of living we inherited from ancestors who held them precious. Our nation-strats are hundreds of years old, thousands some of them, though the younger nations are no less in dignity or members' love. Emperor Isabel Carlos had good reason to insist that his imperial powers be strictly limited and balanced by the EU constitution, not absolute as MASONS' are. As members of nation-strats, then, we cannot consider a surrender in which we are asked to assent to *anything*, even the dissolution of our cultures—to accede to that would be treason against our nation-strats. Thus, while our aims align with the Remakers, we cannot consider unconditional surrender."

Right—the Prince's demand, still the most unreasonable on Su-Hyeon's chart. "You know the Prince won't actually do anything so cruel or extreme," I said. "When Utopia offered to support the Prince, the Prince threatened to banish them from the Earth and chase them through the black of space forever, and genuinely wouldn't let them join until they submitted to that possibility, but now the Prince is protecting them with everything They have, and did the boldest thing I've ever seen Them do to save Mars and the Gates of Nineveh. The Prince's conditions aren't about what They'll really do, they're thought experiments to teach us what it means to trust the . . ." The Greek and student of the stoics in me almost said 'the Driver.'

Not just the Mariscala but the row of cold faces behind them did not thaw. "Until *Son Altesse* pledges to maintain our nation-strats, culture, and patrimony, we cannot consider unconditional surrender."

"So, you'll stay neutral?" the Hiveguardian asked.

"No." Danaë's answer was cutting as the blades of light that crested behind them. "We need a short war. Homeland will choose a side. You both know our current strength, greater than Hiveguard's, a rival for the Empire's."

"Roughly," I answered—this was not the moment to debate how many ships one Archenswarm is worth, or whether rampaging Achilles is the Empire's or not.

"Whichever side we join we will make too strong for the other to hope for victory. Do you both recognize that?"

"No hope for world conquest, at least," Lesley answered, careful in their honesty. "We won't surrender if you turn Remaker, but we would give up the present campaign, change our tactics. No need to waste more lives on battles we can't win. And I don't expect the Empire would just surrender either?"

Should we be so honest with our enemies? I had the sudden feeling we were amateurs, three children play-acting at war. I imagined a portal popping open from the past, and grown-up generals spilling out from real World Wars to lecture us on tactics and diplomacy. But it also felt like the absence of that blood-smeared expertise might be a good thing. "No, we wouldn't surrender. We want to minimize loss of life, so like Hiveguard, we'd change our tactics, but the Empire's in motion, it won't just stop. But it would change."

Danaë glanced back at the row of watching Homeland officers, who traded whispers and confirming nods. "Thank you both for that honesty. Our intention is to choose a side today, and we wish to make that choice right now in front of both of you. This way, amid so much silence and confusion, the side we don't choose will have absolutely no doubt that our choice is real and final. And this way, since every second costs lives, not one second will be wasted before the losing side knows you have lost, and can send the order for cease-fire."

I smiled—this was the Prince, their influence. What was it Andō said before they died? The Prince teaches us to call evil 'evil,' and so teaches us to choose evil less. A Homeland with that Prince's loving ba'sib in command will waste no lives today, no irreplaceable human infinities, no more. But the gravity on Lesley Saneer's face sent my mind down a different track: O.S., the O for Wilfred Owen, doomed young light of poets, who should have added volume upon volume to the literary legacy Homeland treasures, killed instead at twenty-five and *after* the 1918 surrender was negotiated, a victim of those final, pointless days before the date agreed upon for death to stop. The Prince is not the only one who teaches us to call evil 'evil.'

"As for which side we choose," Danaë continued, and I had the sudden image of the sky shifting upon Atlas's shoulders, slim shoulders in that kimono yet more than strong enough, "we absolutely reject Hiveguard's assertion that Ojiro Sniper's attack upon the person of a Romanovan Tribune is excused by the label tyrannicide. We love *Son Altesse* and share His aspiration to create a more humane future. But we still cannot accept unconditional surrender. Therefore, so long as the conditions *Son Altesse* demands remain so unmovable as to admit no protections for language, culture, or tradition, we cannot fight for the Remakers."

Victory smiles look right, and bright, and natural on Lesley Saneer's cheeks. "Then you choose Hiveguard?"

"No." Danaë's face and every face behind them set in resolution. "We believe there must be a solution, that this world is not so cruel that we who long to fight for *Son Altesse* can find no way to join His cause. We therefore ask again that the Remakers grant our conditions. But we are done with asking *Son Altesse*. Now we ask you, [Anonymous]."

"Me?"

"Will you secure our conditions?"

"As acting Emperor?" I thought a moment. "I believe the edicts of a prior Emperor bind a successor, at least Cornel MASON's bind me. So, if I make a promise, then I think . . ." I looked to Xiaoliu, my reference point for things Masonic. ". . . that would still bind the Empire once a new Emperor's in place?"

Danaë's answer cut off Xiaoliu's. "We ask for nothing so contingent."

"Wise," Lesley confirmed. "Once in power, nothing binds a true dictator, certainly not law."

"What, then?" I asked.

Those diamond eyes upon the screen sliced deep. "We ask you to compel *Son Altesse* to grant our conditions."

I felt a long breath leave me. "Compel . . ."

"He is your Prisoner. We ask your promise that you will compel Him, urge our terms over and over until He relents, give Him no other choice."

To move the Mountain—One the Mountain Emperor failed to move. "It can't be done. Even Cornel MASON tried and failed, and they were asking for three words, not—"

"Is *Son Altesse* not changing in this war," Danaë challenged, "as the rest of us are?"

"They . . . have changed," I granted, "but—"

"Then change Him more. *Son Altesse* is still a Minor, a Child Whose perfections should be cultivated toward constructive ends, not nipped in the bud as Hiveguard would have it, but neither should they be loosed unrestricted upon a vulnerable world."

Perfections—I felt an echo beneath that word as Danaë spoke it, a second voice sour like vinegar. It was Felix Faust's voice, remembered from that strange post-midnight conference with the Prince: "*I will not let the side effects of Your perfections make this war worse.*" You are making it worse, Prince. The Black Laws stand for Minors, even inhuman Minors like orangutans who stray through quarantine sites, and frightened, rampaging elephants, and Ráðsviðr, and You, and Your inhuman inability to work with shades of gray, is absolutely causing 'extensive and uncontrolled loss of human life and suffering of human beings,' and 'significant and measurable damage to Nature and the Produce of Civilization,' too. Look at this standoff, Hiveguard's matchless armada eager to be Yours, but You will hand it to Your enemy before You bend Your perfect, absolute demand. And yet: "It can't be done. To change the Prince, it can't . . ." I found myself gazing at Lesley, at that victory smile which knows that, if I can't say yes, then Hiveguard gets it all, and stubborn Good Jehovah fails and falls. Should I lie? Promise even though I can't deliver?

The Mariscala's frown grew sterner as my pause stretched on. "Are you saying the Prince cannot be compelled because you, as Masonic *Promagister,* have tried and failed to do so? Or . . ." Here Danaë's face changed suddenly, a narrowing of brows, an elevation of the chin which made me think the titles 'princesse,' 'duchess,' 'mistress.' ". . . because thou, *chiot,* as His abject, assumest that to change thine Ἄναξ is impossible?"

I gasped, taboo's guilt nagging that such words require a sensayer, but the careful duchess had not quite said *worshipper.* You're right, princesse, I haven't tried. This Mountain is a Pillar of my universe, so moving It is as unthinkable as if I were a wild goat grazing on Its slopes. And yet to change the Prince . . . our Omnipotent Maker with two decades and a cosmos at Their beck has barely caused a ripple in the Addressee, so stubborn are this Stranger's strange perfections. *The side effects of Your perfections,* so repeats the Master Brillist Felix Faust inside me, this adversary whose deep-worming words work changes in our minds hour on hour. But not always for the worse. I hate Faust as much as anyone, but look at Carlyle, five minutes alone with Faust a year ago, some pictures of bananas, and out it came this morning as an essay, brilliant, that's healing all our understandings of the Cousins, rushing out through Pass-It-On to prove the human race humane once more. And if Faust's words inside me stank like vinegar, vinegar has preserved much for humankind against more toxic rot. So, I listened, reviewing in my mind what uncle said to Nephew, snagging on one part: *"You're matchlessly benevolent, if You'd just promised a few kindnesses to people that You're bound to offer anyway . . ."* 'Bound'—what did you mean, Faust? Did you see some solution? Something that already binds this Stranger so indomitable that a year locked in the sunless heart of MASON's citadel has changed nothing?

"Regardless," Hiveguardian Lesley Saneer pressed on, and I saw an edge of sympathy in those sweet eyes, sensing that Danaë's last words to me had crossed a line that courtesy should back away from. "Even if you could secure some promise, once you give someone the Earth, nothing can hold them to a promise. That's dictatorship's nature, as many, many nation-strats have learned the hard way."

True, but: "This is different," Danaë answered. "*Son Altesse*'s promises are absolute."

Lesley shook their head. "You can't know that, not even as their ba'sib. Whether or not you believe power inherently corrupts, time definitely corrupts, changes, pressures. No reign ends as it started. To accept dictatorship is treason against anything we hold sovereign, be it Hive, or strat, or human dignity. You must recognize that."

I was proud to shake my head. "You don't understand Jehovah Mason."

"I understand human nature."

I felt a chuckle move my ribs, but it was Danaë who laughed aloud their golden, healing laugh. "I'm sorry, Guardian, I don't mean to laugh. You do know human nature very well, and no one could be a fitter guardian of human dignity than you, not even my poor brother." Mourning's aching pause. "But I know *Son Altesse* enough to know He broadens, more than set-sets do, the spectrum of what has walked this Earth in flesh of woman born and been called human. You do not know Him."

'In flesh of woman born'—the phrase struck me like lightning. That's what you meant, isn't it, Faust? The thing that binds the Prince. "Filial piety," I said aloud.

"What?"

"It already isn't unconditional." I felt myself lean forward toward the camera, felt a smile curl my lips. "Mariscala, listen, what if I can prove the surrender isn't really unconditional? That the Prince is already bound to grant the protections Homeland's asking for? You don't need a written treaty, you just need to know surrender won't mean treason to your nation-strats. What if I can prove that everything you want is something the Prince is already bound to do?"

"By filial piety?" quick Lesley filled in.

"Exactly. The nation-strats, France, Spain, Japan, the Prince is already too bound to them to ever hurt them."

Lesley Saneer shook their head. "Jehovah Mason is still a Minor and not a member of any nation-strat."

"Technically," I answered, "but patrimony, inherited culture, it's all filial piety, and the Prince takes filial piety more seriously than any other breathing creature on this planet takes any duty at all. Obligation isn't a choice for the Prince, it's a law of Their reality like gravity: gravity pulls Them down, filial piety pulls Them to honor parents with everything that that implies. You can give water permission to flow uphill but it still can't, and Homeland can give the Prince your unconditional surrender, but They can't hurt what you're trying to protect: culture, languages, oaths."

The Guardian of Hives and choice and human dignity frowned on. "Under sufficient pressure, anyone—"

"Not Them. We're talking about an Entity so strict, They've chosen to stay locked in a cell for months rather than take an oath that would make Them Ruler of half the planet, all because there are three secret words They worry They can't keep. You're worried They'll make people betray their nation-strats, but obligations are inviolate for Them, others' as much as Theirs. They *can't* violate filial piety or make others violate it, just like water *can't* flow uphill. And I can get Them to say so! Xiaoliu!" I called over my shoulder. "Call the *Porphyrogene,* ask if Their remaking of the world will be bound and shaped by filial piety. Ask it exactly in those words." I smiled. "You see? We can't get conditions, but this is even stronger."

From behind me: "The *Porphyrogene* is asleep, *Promagister.*"

"Then wake Them up and ask!" I triumph-laughed inside—asking a mere mortal so world-changing a question in the haze of sudden waking would be manipulative, but waking the Prince is an on-off switch, pressing the call button on a console that connects or disconnects a distant world; even the Master Brillist needs their human coffee, not the Alien. And such an Alien *cannot* impiety.

Mariscala Danaë's frown mixed hope with experience's caution. "Many methods from Archimedes on have made water flow uphill." A grave pause. "Filial piety is complex for a Being with so many parents and so strange an origin. They have many fathers, have been torn by contrary duties in the past, and will be so again. Our strats, our people, cannot trust that absolutely, not when we are asked to risk our everything."

"We can trust absolutely, we—"

"Even though thine Ἄναξ ἐστὶν ἀπάνθρωπος?» Danaë's sudden Greek was awkward and classical but clear: Even though thy *Lord is inhuman, not-anthropos,* a word which has in Greek (and many tongues) the double sense of *alien* and *heartless.*

I shivered. The Prince may be of woman born but is not woman-made, this thinking Vastness Which Preexists our cosmos, and Which more Exceeds Its mother in enormity than all the hydrogen that blazes in a billion billion stars exceeds one atom. How can birthdebt bind That? Why should They even feel a birthdebt to we microbeings frailer than a shadow's shadow's shadow? We mere words?

Perhaps He should not, yet we know He does.

But why, reader? Why?

Hobbes: "Because they err who say that the Dominion called Paternal derives from the brief act of Generation. Rather, it derives from the extended act of Nourishing, for it is the one who keeps and nourishes a Child that has the power to preserve or to destroy it, and the Preservation of life over time, extended, is the true and only end for which the savage beast called Man accepts that ongoing subjugation called Duty, whether to sovereign, parent, master, or Maker."

The rearing of the Prince? Madame, Their many fathers, we humanity preserved Their life here, nurtured Them, but this Guest does not depend upon our hospitality for Their continuance, only Their ship of flesh. This Visitor most justly Hates the dingy hovel we call Space, our table Finitude, our cup of bitter Time, our platter serving Distance, Grief, Death. Our nurture-gift is that we taught perfect Jehovah how to Hate—why should this strangest Stranger owe us anything?

And yet the Stranger shows filial piety.

They have. They do. I don't know why. But how much can I trust that inexplicable bond? Enough to gamble everything? To gamble Greece? And Greek? The Parthenon, and Cavafy, and Hesiod, and avgolemono, and the Olympic flame, and human dignity, and every nation's Independence Day, and sacred Delos?

"*Promagister,* the *Porphyrogene* answers: Yes."

Yes, filial piety will bind and shape Their better world. Deep breath. That's not enough, Prince. I thought it was, but Danaë is right. All that we have, and all that we could be, and all that fierce Achilles battles to preserve on behalf of the countless disenfranchised dead, we can't trust all that to so Strange a Being, even if They Love us—They Love the insects, too, and yet They walk. I have to move the Mountain. So, I took a deep breath, and I felt again the throne beneath me, and the billion hands that reach out from that throne, my strong prostheses. I'm a mountain too.

Hobbes: "That you are, young Leviathan, a world of persons united in one to form that mortal god to which we humans owe, under the Immortal, our peace and defense."

I am. And not just me, we have here three Leviathans: Mariscala Danaë, whose fierce prostheses teem across the oceans, and the Hiveguardian who marshals the billion indomitable breasts that fight for human dignity.

"Add the Prince to the call," I ordered. "Voice only, that shouldn't reveal too much of our security."

Lesley Saneer smiled dark approval of my adversarial caution. "What do you intend?"

"To compel the Prince. Right now. The Mariscala's right, filial piety is too tenuous, but the Prince still keeps promises absolutely, that's as true as gravity, and Archimedes never made water flow uphill, they just made it flow downhill more complexly."

"So?"

"So, we can do the same. The Prince is as precise as a computer. We've been asking Them to grant conditions, and They say They can't because They don't know what Their new world will be like, so it's time to make Them decide, straight-fact questions: 'Will Your new world have X?' If they say Yes, that's more irrevocable than any treaty any Hive or nation ever signed. Nations betray, not . . ." I almost said 'Gods' but caught myself—we know two Gods, reader, and One betrays us all the time, but: ". . . not Jehovah Mason."

Danaë smiled a loving ba'sib's smile, which faded to caution. "I have asked Him that too, many times."

"We have more leverage now," I said, "new leverage. We can say honestly today it's now or never, that They make these decisions now or They'll never get to. It might be enough. And if it is, if I can get the Prince to say They won't dissolve the nation-strats, would that be enough for you?"

"Not for us," Lesley answered quickly. "Tyranny is tyranny."

"But for Homeland, that would be enough." Sovereign Danaë did not glance back to check if the assembled admirals behind them nodded in approval, but they nodded anyway.

"Then like you, Mariscala," I continued, "I want to waste no lives or seconds, so I want you both to hear this live, to know the instant I succeed or fail. Mariscala, you're welcome to help once you understand what I'm trying to do, but, Guardian Saneer, you and I remain adversaries, and if you push the Prince too much, I'll end the call."

A grim smile. "Reasonable."

"*Promagister?* The *Porphyrogene* is ready."

Deep breath—now or never. "Prince? Can you hear me?"

The Stranger: "I hear thee."

"Some important allies and adversaries are listening, including Mariscala Danaë. I'm going to ask You several questions. I need You to answer in English only, and to give me simple, definitive answers, things like yes or no, not complex answers that require me to ask for clarification. Do You understand?"

The wait, counting my breaths, three, four, as the question ripples off beyond the reach of where reaching or ripples mean anything.

The Stranger: "I understand thy statements, not their causes."

"That's enough for now. You have demanded unconditional surrender from Your potential supporters because You haven't yet made the principal decisions about what Your remade world will be like." I braced myself. "You need to make some of those decisions now."

"Not yet." No wait this time, this answer ready. "My knowledge of your needs and nature matures quickly as extremity exposes traits long veiled."

That's right, You hadn't truly known our nature, had You, Prince? We *homo bellicosus* who disguised ourselves as peaceful doves so long. You're learning quickly what we really are. But: "I'm sorry, You can't wait any longer. This is a turning point. If You can give clear, binding answers now to some questions about the new world You will make, then You'll gain the support of many forces, which will let You seize power and remake this world. If You can't or won't decide and answer *during this conversation,* then Your enemies will gain that strength instead, and You will likely never have a chance to carry out Your remaking. Do You understand?"

"A later-born plan will be better."

"I know. You're likely right, waiting would let You make a better plan, but if You wait, You'll never have a chance to carry out that plan. Only a plan made now will have a chance to become real. Do You understand?"

The wait, three, four.

The Stranger: "I understand thy statements, not their causes."

"I know. I'm sorry. I don't have time to spell out all the causes now. I just need You to trust and to believe me, or You'll never get to make Your better world."

The wait, three, four. I'm sorry, Prince, I know You hunger for patient philosophy, but this is not the static world of thought experiment where Achilles's only task is racing tortoises, and the deadly trolley lingers for eternity before the forking tracks, five lives in hazard on one path, one on the other, eternally suspended, never done. Our world moves.

The Stranger: "I trust and believe thee."

"Thank you." I ached inside for words stronger than 'thank you.' "I'll try a simple question first. In Your new world, will there be humans?"

The wait, three, four—I had not anticipated how terrifying this particular wait would be.

"They're hesitating." Hiveguardian Lesley Saneer spoke, as grim as storm. "Your chosen dictator is hesitating about human extinction. I think you should all reconsider your choices."

I almost laughed. "All questions take a while with the Prince, watch. Prince, before you answer that one, tell me, did You have breakfast yesterday?"

The wait, three, four, always the same wait, as if the drag of space and time cling to the question as it burrows toward the liberty of Good Jehovah's timeless Universe and back again to ours.

The Stranger: "My flesh ingested since the last local sunrise, but not since last I woke."

"See?" I smiled. "Unlike most of us, the Prince gives all questions real consideration, that's why Their answers mean so much, why we can trust Their word is absolute. Now, Prince, in Your new world, will there be humans?"

The wait, three four.

The Stranger: *"Mit Vorfreude—"*

"No, Prince, use only English." Curse you, Faust.

The wait again.

The Stranger: "I cherish and shall nurture humans, yes, but recognize the happy probability that evolution will someday justify a change of species name."

Right, an answer crafted for infinity. "Thank you. For the next several questions, please keep in mind that I'm asking about the first century or so after Your remaking begins, not infinite time. In Your new world—that is, in the first few centuries of it—will humans continue to speak and use many different languages, as we do now? Will current languages and language use survive?"

"I cannot judge yet. The many nation-armies resurrected by—"

"You have to decide now, Prince. You have to decide now or Your new world will not be."

The wait, three, four.

The Stranger: "Though they cause not no evil, I shall embrace the higher alephs that are plural languages' continuations' entangled evolutions."

"That was a yes," I translated, laughing inside at this dear Alien Who genuinely believes this is a simple answer. Close enough.

"Aleph?" Danaë asked it.

"It's set theory," I answered. "Orders of infinity. Math says some infinites are bigger than others, like the sum of an infinite number line is a smaller infinity than the number of curved lines on an infinite flat plane, or things like that." I've tried to understand it better, reader, slogged through papers, tried to pencil out the proofs since first I heard the Prince discuss such things, but it still makes me dizzy, infinities dwarfing infinities, it's all too much, like gazing into the Abyss until the self and everything dissolve in darkness. I struggle visualizing million versus billion. But as the Humanist in me thrills at heart when others of my species do what I cannot, break long-jump records, conjure tears with verse, so I take pride in knowing some of us can face infinity, especially set theory's first father Georg Cantor, who gazed so deeply into the Abyss that the Abyss blinked. "It's the Prince's way of saying languages are precious enough to be worth people dying for. A human life has infinite value, infinite consequences over the universe of space-time, but apparently They think a language is another order of infinity." In my mind I could already hear Huxley's First Contact colleagues whispering, our math and linguistics departments rushing to reexamine what order infinity a language is extended over space and time and changing worlds of thought which over time give each word many meanings. "But in short, yes, They say languages will be protected."

Danaë's voice, brightened by this good answer, pressed for more. "Will languages continue to be passed on by tradition and nurture, *Altesse*? By families and bash'es to their children?"

The wait again, three, four . . .

The Stranger: "Among plural methods, yes."

I felt a thrill. "Does that mean You've decided there will still be families and bash'es, Prince?"

The Stranger: "Among plural structures, yes."

"Will there be nation-strats?" I asked it quickly, fearing I might freeze if I let myself think about how much rests on this Atlas moment.

"Or rather, will there be nations?" Danaë clarified. "We don't demand that the current political structures we call strats or nation-strats remain unchanged. Rather, we ask whether the mixing and overlapping human groups that pass down cultures and traditions—French, Japanese, Spanish, Armenian, Inuit, Qulla, Uyghur, Māori, Malay, Vietnamese, so many more—whether You, *Altesse,* intend that these continue and flourish as vital parts of Your new order?"

The wait.

The Stranger: "Yes, though I shall nurture inhuman and mixed human-inhuman nations alongside them, such as Atlantean urban dolphins, and the Lōngsphinx Constellation, and My own. All nations advance, enrich, and preserve art and achievement, but those which commix strangeness best expand your sphere of empathy, and make you kinder."

Kinder—can You really make us kinder, Prince? We *homo bellicosus* who just burned so much? I don't trust hopes my Maker kindles in me anymore, but I do ache inside, Prince, to trust Yours. And then it hit me as an afterthought: did we just win the war? The Prince just said They'll preserve nations. There's Danaë's face with triumph's flush upon it, the Homeland officers behind them smiling, exchanging whispers in their many languages, safe now. Remakers now. We've won.

"Will there be Hives?" The Hiveguardian asked, must ask, as sky-defying eagles must defend their aeries beak and talon. "You, Jehovah Mason, will you let the Hives continue, self-sovereign, self-determining, separate, and free?"

I opened my mouth during the pause. Should I tell the Prince not to answer? Not to be shaped by this, Their adversary's question? Yet I know the ache, as all Servicers do, of Hive-denial, how we envy and admire from outside the Members who can say: I love my law, my Hive, and what I make it be. I want them to exist, for others if not for me, these human choices, paths as parallel and beautiful together as a rainbow.

The Stranger: "Not all self-sovereign, not all self-determining, not all separate, not all extant, not all free."

I shuddered. You sound so like a MASON right now, Prince—no, worse, you sound like Hobbes, who gloats that it was never art or sport or human excellence that made the wild human kneel before the throne—it was brute power.

Hobbes: "Not quite, young Caesar. Humanity was wise enough to realize that knowledge itself, the arts, the sports, the sciences, all prosper better beneath the shelter of one peace-protecting iron guardian. We kneel for that as well."

Lesley's brows arched. "So, some Hives will survive? You'll pick and choose?"

The wait again, three, four.

The Stranger: "Yes, choices contingent on Hives' conduct before and in this war, and the expected benefits of each Hive's transformation, subjugation, integration, or dissolution."

Lesley Saneer frowned coldly at the screen, at me, at Them. "And when you pick which Hives are on the chopping block, what will you do if we preserve those Hives in the parts of Earth you don't control?"

In parts They don't control? That's right, Hiveguard can't hope to take the planet from us anymore, but fierce fighters can cling to acres, cities, millions, and make what? Hiveguard Reservations? Or a second Alliance commingling with our own, where echo copies of the Hives persist unchanged into the Prince's future? Could that work, Prince? Could Your kinder world actualize its kindness interlaced with these untempered remnants of Your Peer's Making?

"What would you do?" wise, impatient Lesley pressed.

The Stranger: "Act."

I shuddered anew. We asked You for simple English, Prince, and You deliver, but we who saw You mount the bloody rostra know how absolute a thing Your Action is.

"And when we fight to the end for our Hives?" the Hiveguardian challenged. "How much of humanity are you willing to wipe out and still claim it's for the best? A billion? A tenth of the population to give you the rest? A third? Half?"

"Don't!" I cried too late.

"Don't what?"

"Don't trolley-problem with the Prince! Prince? Can you hear me? Ignore that question, you can't answer it! Prince? Prince?"

The wait, three, four, five, six, seven . . .

"We lost Them."

"What?"

"The Prince can't trolley-problem. It'll be . . . it might be hours."

"I don't understand."

"It's not your fault." I wasn't sure whether to moan or chuckle. "You had no way to know. It's set theory again. A human life is an infinity, but all human lives are the same order of infinity, and infinity times six or even times a billion is still the same infinity as infinity times one. So, the two options in the trolley problem are identical for the Prince, five infinities equals one infinity, so They can't understand why we think the two options are different, why we see a difference where They just see Buridan's donkey stuck between two identical bales of hay. This is a very old argument between the Prince and humanity, and we need . . ." We need Mycroft, really, or Georg Cantor once more, brought back like our Achilles from a braver age when minds like Nietzsche's were the readier to gaze into the dizzying Abyss.

No, thou art sufficient.

What?

Thou art sufficient to this task, young guide. Thou hast just wrestled the Abyss that is Jehovah Mason, and He yielded.

I did, didn't I, reader? Or rather we: Danaë, and pressuring Lesley, and I, we moved the Mountain.

"Does that mean negotiations with Jehovah Mason are over for today?" Lesley asked.

Yes.

"I still say"—Lesley's words were keen as steel—"you should rethink your choices if your leader thinks the deaths of one and five and five billion are identical. But I'm grateful to both of you for doing this so transparently today, especially you, Mariscala, thank you for arranging this. It will save lives. Might I propose a few days' cease-fire as we examine our positions?"

"Absolutely," Danaë agreed at once, "and clarify our sides. I believe we have now reached the point that all our Homeland forces and all your Masonic troops and Delians and Myrmidons and such should don the Vs?"

I froze—that's right, Cornel MASON's order still stands, forbidding their troops to wear the sigil of the stubborn Prisoner. But Cornel MASON isn't on the throne now—I am.

"Ayhan?" I called.

"Yes, *Promagister*?"

"Send word to all Masons and our allies: we're Remakers now, and everyone who wants should wear the Vs. Everyone who doesn't—"

"Is no Mason, if that sigil is chosen by the one upon the throne."

Absolute monarchy is so weird. "I was going to say that anyone who doesn't want to wear the Vs can help Red Crystal, or do other civilian things."

Ayhan's face called those who do so 'traitors' but they left it at, "As you command, *Promagister*."

Absolute monarchy is *still* weird.

"How many days' truce?" Lesley re-grounded us. "Two weeks? Three?"

"Why not surrender?" I asked against hope, turning back to the screen. "You've lost, you know it. You can end it now with no more deaths."

Lesley Juniper Sniper Saneer paused here to shift the suckling infant to the other breast. "We haven't lost. World conquest may be the Remakers' only plan, but it's always been Hiveguard's Plan B." They tapped the bull's-eye on their jacket, with its crosshairs stark. "Plan A it is."

Right, Hiveguard has two paths to victory: world conquest or the snuffing of a single life—list all the Caesars, none has proved the former possible.

"Immediate cease-fire," Danaë confirmed, "we can work out the duration after we inform all allies what has happened." No weeks' delay this time to squander this generation's Wilfred Owens. "I'll call Papadelias first, then Greenpeace. Guardian, will you call Admiral Quarriman? I believe the fleets near Esmeraldas are the highest risk of conflict today."

"We're already calling Quarriman, and our Esmeraldas fleet."

"Perfect. Greenpeace can reach Kosala, and . . . [Anonymous]?" There was a sudden curious brightness in Danaë's voice. "What's that smile?"

What was my smile? I see it sudden in the video, glassy and dopey, gazing at Lesley, at Danaë, bright day, bright night. "I'm just glad we did this so well. I want to thank you," I answered, but it was a lie, the kind of shallow lie we tell when we answer "How are you?" with bland "Fine." But I couldn't explain. We'd won. Not the Remakers over Hiveguard, that part isn't over, won't be over until the winds of opposition hurl their last hurricane at Alexandria and show us which is stronger, storm or stone. But there are several overlapping wars, and we just won the starkest and the best, beating the only adversary that I have not one atom of respect for: we just beat Madame. That's why I grinned and glowed. Madame is wrong. They preach—*she* preaches—that there's poison in the mud, the toxic ancient hierarchy of *he* and *she*, that it lurks below our surface ready in an instant to rear up and make us sort ourselves into old binaries and bigotry and subjugation. And I believed it, thought I saw us slip as Madame warned, believed it took only a tiny push to let the poison fountain up like crude oil and mire all. But look, Madame toiled fifty years—fifty!—to revive patriarchy, narrowing the gates and cramming all high offices she could with the prey this mantis matriarch found easiest, all masculine in mind and genitalia. If last year's Seven-Ten List looked like it could have come from centuries ago, it was a herculean labor, not a nudge, that made it so. My proof? Look at us now! Deep in the war, when Joyce Faust prophesied the old division would triumph again and no one helm a battleship who didn't have a butch suit and a dick, yet here we are! The Big Three leading this World War: matron Danaë, nursing Lesley, me, and not a dick among us. Where are they now, Madame? The artificial creatures, stiff and male and defined by their penises, you said would rise once war dispelled our supposedly fake equality? Where are they all? Not here. Not even near. 2455 needs its Seven-Ten list. Well, we have three here, and I can fill it out with Papadelias, and Aesop Quarriman, and Martin helping even from their cell, and Heloïse who beat the Nurturists, and Fuxing's Huang Enlai, and brave Toshi Mitsubishi, and brilliant Su-Hyeon, that's ten world-shapers who would answer to the title 'woman' before I even get to Jin Im-Jin, and scheming Julia, and loyal Xiaoliu, and Tribune Natekari, and our indomitable Hector shepherd-of-the-people Bryar Kosala. And shall we broaden further? All the splendid spectrum of minds and bodies outside what your closed-minded Eighteenth Century would have called its straight and narrow 'masculine,' that category you, *lying* Madame, boasted would rule again the instant our corrupted psyches had their way—but who's shaping this war? Who? Sweet Carlyle Foster, proud Eureka Weeksbooth, cruel Lorelei Cook, magnificent Sniper, rebellious Dominic, tender, asexual Cato-Helen, and every one of them would challenge the narrow minds of old Versailles. You were so sure you knew what would swarm out of this Pandora's box, Joyce Faust, but look around you! Twelve months' liberty to be ourselves and you'll find only Vivien, Lao Chen, Spain, Felix Faust, our time-stranger Achilles, and maybe, *maybe* Tully Mardi on the list of leaders your beloved ancient bigots would recognize as the 'male' pole of their straightjacket binary. The Prince? Some call Them male, but some may call the sky male by the name of Zeus, the sea by grim Poseidon, and the Moon may have a man in it for some, but silver Selene for me, and so our gentle Prince. You're wrong, Madame. The old poison is there, but it's not a gushing fountain, just a residue, five decades dredging for it and you found enough to choke us for a few brief years, but twelve months and we've shed it already, without actively trying. That's what my dopey smile was that I couldn't explain. We did get better than our ancestors. The grossest war, the oldest of these wars, a remnant of the Church War, older, as old as Wollstonecraft and the Chevalier d'Éon, no, as Christine de Pisan, no, as the old Pythagoreans, and Perictione who birthed Plato and taught the child at their breast that all our souls are free and equal, *that* war, that's the war it felt like we just won.

"*. . . Promagister? Promagister?*"

"What? Sorry." I'd zoned out.

"Will you contact Kim Gyeong-Ju?" Danaë asked. "Or shall I?"

Right, our Milae Mitsubishi allies, they'll be over the Moon to have Homeland and Fuxing and Utopia all on one side at last. "I can. Dougong . . . is Dougong going to stay with Hiveguard or swing to us with Homeland?"

"I've set up a conference with Directors Lao Chen, Lu Biaoji, and Andromeda Ng, and a separate one with Jyothi Bandyopadhyay. When do you think *Son Altesse* will be ready to speak again?"

I sighed. I could hear whisper-soft over the line the Prince's mixed-tongued babble flowing, desperate heptaglot philosophy that only one creature beneath the crawling sun can hope to translate. We need you, Mycroft. I've done my best in your absence, but the Prince needs to communicate so much now to so many, Their new world. *Where are you?*

* * *

Sorry to chop things off there, reader, but I just saw Saladin Canner. Just now as I was writing, in this very room. Saladin is real, and here, or was.

I knew it wasn't Huxley. I sensed the shadow-nothing-movement of a Utopian coat invisible behind me, but that was not Huxley, that chill of being watched, that step, slow, savoring each incremental creep of cat toward mouse. They're real.

"Are you ready now?" I don't know how to describe Saladin's voice, jagged like crumbling concrete.

I knew what my first words had to be. "I never slept with Mycroft! I swear!" I may not have believed in Saladin, but paranoia makes us plan for many monsters we do not believe in. "Please believe me! I never even thought about it! I mean, I thought about it, but only as a horrible I-would-absolutely-die-horribly-if-I-did-it nightmare scenario!" I had always envisioned hurling myself under my desk, or in a corner where I might have some defense, but I was frozen in my chair, curled with my arms clutched over my head to shield my skull. A prey animal, that's what this frozen feeling was. It's been so long since I felt like a prey animal, a feeling left behind when first the Beggar King trained us for war.

"You promised."

I couldn't speak. It's hard to describe how stifling it was, the heat, my own hot tears, the monster's breath, the coat of Griffincloth around us airless like a body bag, but it was real, the scent of sweat and laurel and outdoors, just as Mycroft described them. Strong fingers gripped my wrist. I should have screamed. The guards are right outside, Prefect Huxley, but this was the dark Muse of Mycroft's killing spree, death instant and expert, so help outside the door might as well have been on some distant continent.

"You promised." I think Saladin said it twice.

"What?" I tried to ask, but couldn't make a sound. It wasn't like in dreams, I felt my breath, the rasping contours of my words, I just couldn't make sound.

"You said you were ready to die for Mycroft. Are you still?"

Somehow, the question cut through my panic. That's what Saladin came for? Not possessive vengeance? I did make that promise. I can't remember when, could look it up, but I remember moments when I closed my eyes and looked into my heart and knew I was ready to die for Mycroft Canner. But—

"Are you still ready?" Close, they leaned so close.

Was I still ready? So many Myrmidons, my comrades, I saw march to war, but not me yet, I couldn't, Vivien forbade it, and Bryar, and . . . no. No, my real barrier had been the Pen, Voltaire's Pen fragile in my hand, but it was safe now, safe with Carlyle. So much is safe, Toshi a fit new Censor, Martin a good *Promagister* one rescue plan away, Madame defeated, Hiveguard, Gordian exposed, the Prince's better world taking good shape, but . . . I can't lie to monsters. "No. I'm not ready to die now. Not quite yet."

"Why?"

Why? "Because . . ." Because there is a hurricane approaching. Because our adversaries whip each other on to reach the Prince, to pierce the sanctum heart of Alexandria. Because I want to know, to man the fort, to help, to see. Because I *do* know, know who rides, who leads that hurricane, magnificent, who always single-minded in this war has kept their gun sight locked on one Target. Because, ". . . I'm not like you, Saladin. I love Mycroft but I love other people, too. Care about other people. I want to see them safe, the Prince, Toshi, Vivien, Bryar, and Achilles, someone needs to be here to persuade Achilles not to enter battle, if Achilles fights again after losing Patroclus, then Achilles will kill Hector and then has to die themself, and . . ." And there's the phantom hand that held mine those long months across diaspora. Reader, do you think there'll be some parley in the battle? Do you think I'll have a chance to meet Sniper?

Saladin leaned down, those jaws so close, hot, wet, primordial. "You want a short war?"

"Yes."

"A short war doesn't come from pampering Achilles."

Chapter the TWENTY-FIFTH

The Wrath of Achilles

Written November 5–9, 2455
Events of November 3–4
Alexandria

It wasn't the same wrath this time, was it, Achilles? Not the same as all those years ago when Troy meant Troy. You are millennia and several deaths the wiser now, the lion's heart within your mortal breast recalled so many times from Hades's halls, recalled by us, by Homer, by the crowds that thrill and mourn and ask to hear again the tale of Zeus's favorite fighter doomed to die at Troy. If the Leviathan of state is, as Hobbes tells us, a mortal god composed of many persons joined in one, then Homer does not flatter when he calls you our most godlike mortal, you made up of so many humans' memories, you who strangle rivers with Leviathan strength, you whose name is spoken now on Ares's planet, you unending man. But not unchanging. When conquering Alexander envied you, it was stasis he envied, for both your name and his, he knew, would become equally immortal, known in every city touched by the watchful Sun, yet without a Homer to preserve his words, his scowls, his laughter, Alexander knew his shade must grow shallow, his character and self ravaged by rumor and by fractious histories, lost as the faceless face of lordly Agamemnon. But never you, Achilles, cries envious Alexander. The world remembers you, your frowns and passions, words of mourning, words of love, a complete self alive in verse and human memory that make your mortal shade invincible. But he was wrong, our splendid Alexander. You may be our best-preserved ancient, matchless Achilles, but still words change as we who know them change, as the same sentences, same passions strike us differently as epochs, ethics, problems, humans change. Were you too wrathful? Or not wrathful enough at the unkind gods who wove your ruin, yet you never cursed them, pious Achilles, never. Not when the Father ordered you to return the corpse of Hector, whom you so hated that the chance to drag his body through the dust made you return to battle even though you knew your own death must soon follow. You never even cursed the deadly archer, although it was he, in truth, who slew you both, Patroclus first and then with Paris's arrow—for the archer fires every arrow—you. And yet you never cursed him, not with Homer's tongue. But many readers have cursed the gods for you. That changes you, I think, your wrath evolving age by age as humankind's evolving character judges your fate, your story differently and (I hope) more wisely. You have been changed by us, by death, your many deaths, and by our mourning. And so too you were changed that warm November dawn, I think, changed by the wish that echoed in our hearts, so many hearts: hold back. Hold back from the battle lines this time, insatiable Achilles, wielder of the god-forged harbingers, you, greatest man of war, hold back from fragile Alexander's city.

How did it begin? As storms begin, as separate winds, North, West, East, South, whip up Poseidon's frothy stallions whose ranks teem clear across his seas from pole to pole and crash upon our shoreworks more incessant than machines of Daedalus, just so our separate enemies from every corner of the Sea Lord's winding coast whipped up their strengths that day to keep Earth—like the atom—beyond conquest. The belly of the sea bloomed with bull's-eyes in the colors of uncounted strats and peoples, ships advancing in the name of nations, sports teams, corporations, campuses, towns, clubs, old families, and fresh-formed bash'es, while beneath each bull's-eye flag a second fluttered to proclaim which hostages shivered in that hold, our foes' warning to skyfire Achilles of which friends will burn if he dares unleash the Ancile Breaker here. And this locust swarm of bull's-eyes was not just around the capital but on our screens, relayed from Tripoli, from Cyprus, from the Hellespont and rough Gibraltar, from the Gate of Tears, where Andō's ghost watched teeming foecraft block his Danaë from the Red Sea where her ships might have helped us. For weeks, all corners of earth-shaker Poseidon's blue kingdom had seen the forebattles, adversaries bent on blocking every force they could from bringing aid to Alexandria. It's all they have. Hiveguard is losing everywhere, yielding their ports, their factories, running out of options, running out of fuel and strong gray iron. An avalanche of rapid-fire surrenders has been partly our doing, part the work of subtly worming Gordian. O.S. guerilla fighters may hang on in Earth's far corners for months more, or years, but this is the last armada they will raise against us, outnumbered fleets striving to slow, not to defeat, our far-flung forces, slow us just enough to keep our strength dispersed upon this all-determining day.

How did they land so fast? They had two chances—Alexandria's twin harbors east and west, separated by the man-made peninsula which stretches from the city's coast out to the sheltering bar of Pharos Island, where workers are still repairing the *Sanctum Sanctorum* lighthouse, and where, twenty-seven centuries ago, another lighthouse helped teach humans to start counting wonders. As battle broke, we held the west port but the eastern fell, less to attacking ships than to soldiers already on the ground, the same invaders who had breached the palace with their Gorgons back in April and remained entrenched these seven months, flying their brazen bull's-eyes within a hundred rooftops of the Visitor Himself. We tried to retake those streets—oh, how we tried, poured craft into those forays, poured out lives, but cunning is not courage, and the handcrafted jungle of urbanity so amplifies the alpha predator *human* that all hearts fail. We failed.

Might we have won those streets back had Achilles still been with us? Close at hand to train our troops and share the bravery of days when jungles were still Nature's, and the wolves and mountain lions still outmatched we students of Prometheus? But Peleus's son was kept from us by rage and by necessity, not daring to leave his watch over wounded Utopia which has no other guardian upon the airless sea—nor would Achilles pause his vengeance, coursing round and round the rim of Earth to scour the blue below for traces of Kosala. So, with our lionheart commander trapped in orbit, Hiveguard took the eastern harbor easily, their landing craft disgorging troops which brought the battle line so close that even in this pyramid of iron, pride, and steel one heard the drums—or guns? or shells? What does it matter? Boom on boom it is impartial Ares's heartbeat, god of war who hands out death to he who hands out death.

Who are these foes who do the work of Ares? Ships and fighters braving MASON's fierce defense? They are not friends, our plural foes, not one united fleet but four confederations, chafing side by side like stallions in harness, yoked by nothing but the knowledge that no one of them could pierce the sanctum heart of Alexandria alone. As fourteen months ago Earth raced for Cato-Helen back at Klamath Marsh, some intending rescue, others to snatch the captive for themselves, yet others bringing death to permanently peacebond this last human harbinger, just so these forces borrow one another's strength to pierce through J.E.D.D. Mason's citadel and take, either His person, or His life. The first and fiercest adversaries fly the bull's-eye with the crosshairs, honest, deadly, clear, though in a hundred colors representing many Hives, and strats, and new identities forged in war's cauldron to make our future yet more plural than our past. A second force flies Mitsubishi green-and-scarlet bull's-eyes with no crosshairs—many Mitsubishi fight for us now, rallied by Danaë and Huang Enlai, but others remain hardened against the Empire by recent battles or the old land grudge, and sail in Dougong's name repeating still their mantra mission, "rescue Xiao Hei Wang from Alexandria." The third attacking force we call Peacemakers, our sour name for the ships which pair the bull's-eye with the cyan hand-dove, Cousins but not *the* Cousins, since Carlyle and meticulous Toshi have proved so well these rage-changed few are but a sliver of the human kindness most of which still wears the Red Crystal, granting soft prayers for help amid the harm. The Peacemakers say they aim to rescue and rehabilitate this erring Minor, bearing their fearsome Gorgons *alongside* but never *for* the forces that wear crosshairs on their bull's-eyes. The fourth enemy, reader? Don't tell me the great web is not in motion: Gordian. They are Remakers, true, our somewhat-allies, but they aim to observe and study 'Donatien,' not to obey Him, and nothing in a year has come so close to piercing through the sanctum walls which keep from Gordian the matchless Lab Rat Whose data profile they would crown Ingolstadt's King. We knew they must be moving, pulling their spider threads tighter around us, tangling foe and friend. And all the godfire divine Hephaestus worked into the circling Alexander cannot snap a thing invisible.

But thou canst track it now at least, surely. There in Alexandria thou hast thy team, thine augurs, Toshi and fierce Eureka, their appetites vendetta-whetted like Achilles's. These two hunt bash'breakers when hunting Gordian, which nurtures Nurturists.

We should have had that team, reader. Toshi we had, strong as an oak with the Censor's uniform upon her worthy shoulders, but even she struggled to read the ever-thickening palimpsest of city map crisscrossed by lines, labels, and flitting photo feeds. Maniacal Tully labored with her, Xiaoliu, Huxley, Praetorian Ayhan, our Servicer-turned-Caesar at the helm, all living heartstrings of this wise Leviathan which thrashes strong as the harpooners come, but still we lacked transcendent Eureka. See there the empty rug, the cable jacks which wait for that truest seer who scans, like flights of birds, the secret motions of all hidden things. Two days ago, the set-set exercised the promised privilege to step out unsurveilled into the paths of Alexandria and consult with O.S. Since then, silence.

"Eureka Weeksbooth is no traitor." So declared Toshi Mitsubishi the night before the battle as our scouts returned again with nothing but grim news and no set-set. Many faces in the war room showed distrust, but our young Censor would have none of it, and ordered Deputy Commissioner General Bo Chowdhury to comb Eureka's files for some clue: why had our seer set forth all alone when battle was so close? Deputy Chowdhury had been thrifty with his aid these last few months, since it is far from clear whether the warring and bloodthirsty Empire—now headed by a Servicer, no less!—remains obedient to Romanova's law. But when the Censor needs a missing persons search, and a lost Member's friends cry out in fear, then the detective's duty is unmuddied. So Bo Chowdhury set to work at once, prowling the data jungle where one hunts our modern era's Moriartys, grinning with voker glee at such a challenge even as the sons of Hera—gods of war and fire—loomed so close.

At times like these, they say that Zeus who loves the lightning, watching from Olympus or his sanctuary on the peaks of Ida, holds aloft his golden scales, and in the pans he sets two fates, two deaths that end a mortal's deeds, one for the Trojans, one for the Argives armored in their bronze, and holding the beam mid-shaft, the Father lifts it high, and down falls one side's day of doom, while the other's fate soars up to brave the sky. But which are we? We who have no topless towers left, who guard our wall-less city with our thousand ships, and keep both Helen with her treasures and Achilles? He is not here to tell us, Bridger whose young mind braided our world so tight with Homer's—which are we?

A flash upon the sea, Hiveguard far out beyond the lighthouse, desperate to block our swelling reinforcements, using its worst weapon. Carbinger—the name is far too playful for the tool, a capsule dolphin-sized with a spinning device inside, designed to launch and lure a car to crash into it, so the car's safety system, which should direct the explosion upward, is set spinning by the momentum and blasts randomly, down, left, backward, scoring its stripes of fire through our fleet like claws. Each fresh flash stabbed, grief's stab for comrades borne off to the House of Death, but fear stabbed too as, with each blast, we feared a brighter blast might follow, boiling the ocean as Achilles trapped in orbit boils over and lets loose the only weapon he can use from space. The Ancile Breaker—a clearer name might be the Ender of Ambitions, for the Ancile was a sacred shield the Romans kept in Mars's temple, fallen from Olympus with the promise that Empire will not end until that shield is shattered. Hold back, dreadful Achilles, starved for battle as you are. Remember that your friends are fragile, cities, planet fragile, so hold back, hold back, hold back.

Our enemies at least remembered we were fragile. Dougong will not let Hiveguard use carbingers over land, noble Dougong who love landscape and cityscape too well to let them burn. Nor will the humane Peacemakers let even semi-allies use a weapon that could pierce the deep bunkers that shelter the civilians of Alexander's city. So, as radiant Helios began his long descent toward rest, Hephaestus's fire reigned only upon the deep, while Ares surged through Alexandria without his burning brother, frontline fighters bearing Gorgons which bring ignominy but not death to Masons, who must live to face a lifetime knowing they failed Caesar in his time of need.

Just as the hour came when shadows lengthen into fingers, and the weary ploughman smiles knowing labor's end approaches with the goldening of the light, a force of Cousins broke through the barricades around the palace shell. Quick as a flock of gulls that race along the churning, white-maned surf, they arced their way up to the largest gleaming central face of the man-made mountain range of conjoined pyramids that form great Caesar's home. There, sheltered by transparent curving shields across their backs, and by a pair of armored vehicles that formed a V of shelter, this Peacemaker vanguard tested the sloping surface, glassy as a shadow-darkened pond. Those inside did not fear—the greater parts of pyramids hide underground, and this one has more protections between its slanting shell and the war room than there are layers in this city that has built, and built, and built for twenty-seven centuries. The plan had always been to let invaders reach the palace and then break like waves against the rocks that are best hardened for it, sparing the city's shops and dense apartments which, though all evacuated, hold the pictures, bookshelves, keepsakes, and comforts which are unliving parts of *ibasho*.

And yet: "This speed is strange." So judged the master of armies who appeared now live upon the great screen of the war room, calling in as he peered down from orbit with the myriad senses the god of fire forged into that impossible armor.

"Achilles! Great!" Our Acting Caesar's greeting was too shrill, half joy to have advice from the breaker of armies, half pressure-terror knowing any word could be the tipping point that wakes the harbinger. "Can you stay on the line here with us? Talk me through?"

"This should have taken longer." The veteran's words were soft, slowed by unfinished thought. "Even with your order to give ground, soldiers fighting in their native city should have slowed attackers more than this."

"What do you read from that?" Huxley asked it, First Contact's companion quickest to trust the instincts of this living relic of another world.

"I want to say some god is in the field," the son of goddess Thetis answered, "but I don't know what that means in this reality. Some unseen force moving, granting advantage."

It felt true, the photos from the streets, our barricades falling so quickly, panicked faces, much work for the wind-swift brothers Sleep and Death.

"Gordian?" Tully Mardi voiced the guess, the warmonger, who for so many years invoked immortal Ares, trembling as the divine sacker of cities finally comes.

The half-human sacker of cities frowned. "Perhaps."

"Eureka Weeksbooth?"

A scowl from Toshi Mitsubishi would not tolerate this allegation, but Achilles's frown and other frowns were not so sure. Eureka was ally and enemy, one whose powers expand the radius of arts we can call human—such powers could sculpt war as they long sculpted peace.

"*Promagister,* Magistratus, look, on screen six, the Peacemakers are climbing."

So it began, that strange ascent, transparent shields across the Cousins' backs catching the early evening light like waterdrops upon a dark mirror. They could not cut the palace surface, hardened by secret science, but they donned the sticking grips that climbers use to scale impossible icebergs or skyscrapers that offer urban thrills. And now imagine as they climb, reader, some haughty guard or secretary just inside the palace walls, who sees these adversaries through the one-way mirror of the armored windows, laughing aloud, mocking the panting Cousins, "Look! These fools think they can win by sitting on the mountain! Snatch victory as sporting youths race up a greased pole to snatch some flapping pennant! Do they think we haven't reinforced the top? That Caesar's prudence stops some meters off the ground? Climb all you like, Peacemakers! But it only takes you farther from your prize!" So the young Mason mocks, but not the team down in the war room, no. They wonder. They had expected enemies to come with rams, explosives, blades, tech-strengthened fire, but to climb the summit of the Mountain Emperor as one climbs Everest or Mount Parnassus? Why? When mighty Ares mounts his chariot, with twin sons Phobos-Fear and Deimos-Dread riding close at his side, there is a wisdom then in fearing anything one does not understand. Surely they had a plan.

But if we had been truly wise, reader, we would still have remembered that the god who topples city walls is not the cruelest of his father's offspring, for Olympian Zeus—father of pathfinder, and wine-giver, and smith, and archer—has a firstborn daughter, Ruin—the all-deceiving goddess Atë—she who closes minds, and twists our passions to craft massacres, and rashness, and delusions, she who brought such miseries to the immortal gods that great Zeus cast her down into the world of men, where still she moves, and snares, and tramples on our broken, bleeding backs, and takes her joy. We should have watched for her.

Alarms, a siren piercing, not outside, within.

"What's happened?" Huxley spun.

"South gate, eighth watch, Prefect," Ayhan answered, Huxley's second-in-command thriving in his new duties, like a long-potted tree planted at last. "They've sounded the alarm."

"South?" young Caesar asked. "Isn't the action north?"

"Not the outside gate, *Promagister,* it's level eight, eight levels down inside the palace." Ayhan brought up a diagram, the layered warren of the underpyramid with the alarm spot blinking bright. "The line's gone silent now, and the cameras in the area are out. I'm calling the Clavicularius to . . . The line to the Clavicularius is out."

Huxley's hands raced over the console. "L8 Hall-20 cameras dark . . . Hall-19 dark, stairwell dark, level seven dark . . ."

"Prefect, south vigil headquarters is silent too!"

Huxley kept counting, "Level six dark . . . level five . . . they must have our system codes to get so deep . . ."

"Show me the outside!" the quick Acting Caesar ordered. "The south gate—did somebody break in?"

The image came up—nothing but the palace surface reflecting tranquil palm trees and the evening's colors gentling the sky.

"Have the Peacemakers reacted?" Xiaoliu asked it. "Are the two attacks connected?"

"Climbing as before, *Archproditor,*" an aide confirmed—Xiaoliu insists upon the title *Archproditor,* Archtraitor, their rightful rank among untainted peers.

"I have footage!" triumphant Ayhan cried. "It's from level seven, eleven minutes old, just before the cameras there went out."

The image came up of a service hallway with five figures racing breakneck, their uniforms Praetorian, but those noble colors were a strange match for their wild, contorted faces. This was not the reasoned fear of tactical withdrawal, no—this was panic, as when we run from pouring lava, mountain fire, threats against which all the weapons of an army are as impotent as straw, and burn as easily. Then the lights failed around the figures, black swallowing all, leaving only a dim red radiance at the far end—the end they fled from—a strange light, bloody and infernal to make the hairs prick on one's neck. Some dark shapes moved against that light, which expectation parsed as human figures, but they could as easily have been robots, or settling debris, or U-beasts, or their Baskerville doppelgangers, or some newer monstrosity sired by warcraft, or by spellcraft, or of serpent-footed Typhon, he whose legendary progeny tested so many heroes. Gunfire and more passengers for speeding Thanatos. Five seconds later, blackness claimed the feed, advancing like night deeper into Empire's heart.

"How many attackers are there?"

"I don't know, *Promagister.* The alarm came from the level-eight Tesserarius, the senior watchkeeper, but they didn't use the code for small group, or large group, or any of the dozens of codes they could have used to tell us what kind of threat or numbers we're facing."

"What code did they use?"

"Evacuate."

The young mind, so new to this throne at the apex of Empire, drew and held a forced-relaxing breath. "Huxley, how close is that spot to the Prince?"

"Three levels, it looks like, and six from us." Here Huxley shouted something fierce to their black lion, which streaked out through the war room door with fellow U-beasts racing in its wake. "Ayhan, send half the guard down, too, and contact everyone anywhere near Mike's cell, we need every body we can muster there to slow down the intruders. Xiaoliu, track the outages, we need a map of what parts have gone dark."

"On it." The map upon the screen developed quickly, a path of red alarum worming upward toward the gate and downward toward the Guest.

"Call the Prince!"

"Line's down."

"Call their guards, then."

"You don't understand, [Anonymous], that whole area has been dark for four minutes. The intruders may have breached Mike's cell already and we wouldn't know."

Shock's silence. What can one say, when Time and laughing Distance place such tiny grains of obstacle before us—three floors and four minutes—yet no force of arms, no gold, no tears, no arts of human science can rewind those minutes one clock tick. Is He, First Contact, Kindness, Good Remaking, He the Stranger, gone?

"They can't be . . ." Instinct insisted—surely, the Earth would shake, the skies would weep, the heart at least would know and rip asunder if one's God were gone. "Send every—"

"Hold on." Who has the confidence to interrupt our Acting Caesar? Acting Commissioner General Bo Chowdhury, long silent at the console by Eureka Weeksbooth's empty place. "Did the watchkeeper have trouble entering the alarm code? Like they were panicking? Pushing the buttons several times?"

A pause as Ayhan checked. "Yes, there are several garbled attempts before the last one, three nonsense codes and the cleanerbot malfunction code, which is one digit off from evacuate. And they had trouble with door codes, too."

Bo Chowdhury nodded. "Then what you need down there is gas masks."

Acting Caesar turned to Acting Law. "You know what this is? Is it Eureka?"

"No." The Deputy Commissioner General patted the vacant console like a friend. "Eureka Weeksbooth's no traitor, just caught between sides. They figured out the pattern with these artificial panics, but they weren't sure whether O.S. was using it or someone else, and they weren't going to betray the secret if it was O.S., so they went to check."

"Some new gas weapon?"

Chowdhury shook his head. "Eureka was investigating panics and massacres their data said shouldn't have happened, forty-four incidents in Tripoli, Casablanca, the Rhine-Ruhr, back to Brussels. There's a pattern in the after-action reviews, nine cases where one person kept their head when everyone else panicked, and half have some form of anosmia. That's the condition where you can't smell. The other half hate movies." Chowdhury tapped his nose. "It's an olfactory attack, the panics and massacres all through the war, it's been Thisbe Saneer."

"Thisbe . . ." Achilles repeated it, dark syllables more breath than voice.

"Then this is O.S. coming for the Prince!"

"I don't think so." Chowdhury tapped the console again. "If Thisbe was with O.S., Eureka would have confirmed that and come back to erase these files so we wouldn't find out. Eureka usually encrypts their files but left these open, as if they feared they might not make it back, so left us the clue. I think whoever's using Thisbe grabbed Eureka so they couldn't warn us, someone Eureka wants us to defeat."

Thisbe but not O.S.? This was a different fear, I think, for we who know her. Others in the war room know the witch from news, indictments, know she sport-kills with her poisons of despair, twisting to selfish murderplay the bloodstained yet still noble tools O.S. created to guard peace and human dignity. But Achilles, I, you too, I think, reader, we know this witch, her craft which drove even strong-rising Carlyle to suicide, all for the laughing witch's petty pleasure. Someone released *that*—fifteen months ago when all Earth raced for Cato, an unknown someone passed the chance to try for Helen's cosmos-opening treasures and instead chose *that*. Casablanca, Tripoli, the Rhine-Ruhr, Brussels, battlefield by battlefield as we—Achilles, Tully, Bryar, Red Crystal's volunteers, Utopia—we all worked so hard to make this war the least bad it could be, while all this time the witch was out there, laughing at us massacre by massacre, making it worse. I should have been watching for her, reader. I should have recognized sooner the witch Ruin, crafter of rashness and delusions, unwelcome among her bright Olympian kin, who moves, and snares, and tramples on our broken, bleeding backs, and takes her joy.

"Do we have gas masks?"

No. In this peacebonded world where only wild Achilles dares release a harbinger beneath the sky, no one has gas masks. No one.

"The *Porphyrogene* has one, *Promagister,* and their cell guards, and you and your guards too."

"We do?" Oh wise, distrustful Masons! "Great! Send them down to the Prince! Send everything we have!"

Huxley's glare turned black as MASON's sleeve. "Your protection stays with you, [Anonymous]. Ayhan, contact everyone en route to Mike's cell, tell them what they're facing, have them put wet cloths over their mouths and noses if they don't have masks. Xiaoliu, call maintenance, they may have masks for sanding and paint that would serve."

"At once, Prefect. I'll try the hospital, too."

Action broke panic's stranglehold: we knew the means, the witch, the danger now. There were solutions, orders, actions, hope. That red infernal light advancing may not yet have reached the Visitor, it could be stopped—and not just now, forever! Hope's thrill surged: the worst part of the war unmasked! Eureka solved it, found and shared the key with us despite the tyranny of interfering Distance. Stop Thisbe, capture, seal her toxic craft, and today won't only mark the end of Hiveguard's last armada, but the day cold Ruin leaves the battlefield, the day even indomitable Ares can be kind! But we forgot, in that proud, heady moment, that Zeus's children are world-spanning gods. Though radiant Apollo walked among us wearing human flesh thirty-five years, still all that time his light burned bright in other breasts who never knew him as Mojave. Just so, Atë-Ruin dwells not only in Thisbe, Atë-Ruin, goddess with her many-stranded braids, and many-stranded miseries.

"Turn off the feed from the roof. Now." This soft and urgent voice was Tully's, wise but too late as, over the beam of harnessed light which wings our words from earth to sky and back again, we heard the breath catch in war-starved Achilles's throat. Rage—it crackled even in his wordless breathing, as air crackles before the son of Kronos hurls his thunder down on humankind. "Turn it back on," Tully ordered, the sighing priest of Ares knowing well when actions are, "Too late."

The feed that had winked out returned, the glassy surface of the pyramid aglow with evening's rose which made the climbing adversaries stand out dark like sparrows against sky. Several had reached the summit, slinging hooks and lines over the ridge. Hanging from these supports, they had assembled their transparent shields into a kind of room, geometric like the cell of a beehive. Protected thus from every angle by clear walls, the Peacemakers had drawn equipment from their packs, boxes of tech, keyboards, headsets, tripods for Gorgons, assembling a micro-fortress on the palace roof. One of them, toward the center, had opened a bulky pack, revealing packaged meals and bottled water, rations enough for days or weeks perhaps—bold plans indeed!—then with her other hand threw off her helmet, and down tumbled the glossy locks which framed the calm, defiant face of Bryar Kosala. She gazed up boldly at the naked sky, up at the unseen watcher who she knew loomed high above, all-seeing like a god, matchless Achilles. Two hundred days he waited, sometimes quiet, sometimes raining death on friends, or friends of friends of her he waited for. Now she dares him, pitching her camp in plain sight, ready to stay for weeks if need be, camping on this spot one straight plumb line above where we, and He, and all that Cornel MASON loved will burn if bright Achilles dares unleash the Ancile Breaker here. *Fire, hypocrite*—Kosala's calm gaze challenges—*you have killed thousands hunting for me, scarring the helpless Earth wherever you thought I might be hiding, I your bloodlust's thin excuse. No more. Here I am, breaker of armies. Fire your harbinger upon this spot, this citadel, or else confess you have no right to fire it anywhere.*

Achilles roared in answer. I don't think that even lions roar like that, a cry to split the soul as lightning splits the sky, or wars split histories. No, wait, that roar is more than voice, it is an engine, systems coming on, awakening—awakening the Alexander.

«Achilles! Stay calm!» young Caesar cried in Greek.

«I won't use it.»

«What else do you have that works from orbit?» An accusing pause. «You're landing, aren't you? You can't! We have no way to get you up again! UNGAR won't let a harbinger ride up Gabon. You'll leave Utopia defenseless!»

«This is my task, my duty. This comes next.»

«Not only yours! Whose throne do you think I'm sitting on, Achilles? Avenging Cornel MASON is a lot of people's duty. Leave it to us! Bryar wants you to do something rash, that's why they're goading you like this. You must see that. But it isn't urgent! We know where Bryar is now, we won't let them out of sight again. Achilles? Are you listening?»

"*Promagister?* The intruders, the olfactory attack, I have confirmation they've breached level ten." This was Xiaoliu Accursed-Through-the-Ages-Guildbreaker, unruffled before roaring lions, lightning, harbingers, all nothing to one who has felt dread Caesar's black-gloved hand and lived.

"My question is whether they plan to kill or capture." Bo Chowdhury was studying the path of the invaders on the screen. "And whether Thisbe's here in person or they trained others. Eureka's blips are too scattered for one agent to have been at all the incidents."

Hope flashed like steel in Acting Caesar's eyes—a plan. "We need your help, Achilles! We need to track Thisbe! Where did they enter the city? Who's with them? You have the best view on the action, the best systems. Can you find the entry point?" Yes, get the hero working, give him action, give him distraction, give him different prey. "Bo, do we have a record of Thisbe's boot print? There's no way they'd disguise it, they're just the type to print their signature on massacres. If the Alexander's systems can spot that boot print in the city, then we'd know!"

Bo Chowdhury's stare knew this enthroned Servicer's request was half a lie, that the war room has great systems, countless U-beast eyes, but a nose trained by Papa can smell a diversion, and the right moment for one. "I have a scan, yes. I'll send it up. Achilles, can you pattern-match? The southwest maintenance entrance is most likely entry point, given their path."

Two breaths longer the engine roared over the line, then stilled. "Alright. Yes, I see the boot print by the southwest door. She's here."

A moment's pause for prayers—which always trail in Ruin's wake—and for shudders.

"Great start." Chowdhury knows how to drag out distraction. "Now, we'd gain a lot from knowing how many other footprints are with Thisbe's, and also if we can trace their route, whether they came from the east harbor, or the Hiveguard camp, or somewhere else. I'm sending a city diagram with hot spots marked, can you scan for the print in the numbered sequence?"

Reluctant, stubborn, yet the lion yields. "Scanning."

Another pause, a grateful prayer this time. "Huxley, an update on the Prince?"

"Our reinforcements should be close, but we can't watch them in the dark zones. Maintenance has masks, they're—"

"Bodies." It was Achilles's voice.

"What?"

The hero sent the image, bodies in an alley, twelve, all wearing active camouflage, a crude cousin of Griffincloth that shifts to match the background colors the wearer's camera sees. Blood poured from bullet wounds in chests and backs, pooling more black than red, and every victim's skull was caved in by a point-blank shot to guarantee Death's work. The computer's overlay highlighted Thisbe's footprints all around the mire and on one victim's chest.

"Who are they?"

It took the Alexander and our war team both to piece together paths and past. Two forces, small and stealthy, had fought it out for Thisbe in that alley. The losers in the massacre had come from the northwest, from a restaurant-turned-clinic five streets from the palace, where their footprints and Thisbe's had originated from some yet-untraced underground. The only corpse with face enough for computers to match gave us a name and faction: Sonya Pawar, Gordian. As for those who did the slaughter, those who walked with Thisbe now—as friends, reader, they walk as friends with her, these butchers, toward the Friend of all things wise and wonderful!—we traced their footsteps back, meandering, back to the east harbor, the one that throngs with Mitsubishi trefoils sent to rescue Xiao Hei Wang, but also throngs with crosshairs. I think it was Gordian that first freed Thisbe, reader, Felix Faust who saw her grim 'audition,' the hexes tested on me in my prison visit. Felix Faust treasures every life, and calculated to the finest micro-grain the pinch of massacre war's recipe required to steer the Earth toward planetbound ambitions and to end the outward pain path toward the stars. But she betrayed him, Ruin a fouler thing than Zeus or Faust can hold. Had she arranged this massacre? Reached out through some corrupted channel to more bloody-minded friends? Or was this a newborn treason? Birthed in the gore-smeared alleyway where adversaries butchered Thisbe's Brillist keepers, and the laughing goddess happily embraced a company more willing to crown infiltration with the Target's death. I think the carnage was preplanned, but either way, those in the war room knew now what a bloody-minded force slouches its way through MASON's blinded palace toward the Kindness at its heart.

But that was all they knew. The war room could not watch this battle. The outer battle yes, the ships, the carbingers, the fighting in the streets, and calm, daring Kosala. Yet for the inner battle, they could but speed their agents down and wait, as the doctor waits who speeds out medicines, invisible as prayers, into the darkness of the body where the true battle for life is lost or won.

But we can watch, reader, through interviews and afterthought's imagination. We can be that fearful rush of clerks who race through blackness toward a duty which should not be ours, this ghastly enemy that threatens our next Emperor. Ruin's spell takes hold quickly, making the once-familiar hallways strange, too vast, unreal, enormous and yet stifling. The feeling looms of something moving in the dark—*run! run!*—and morbid thoughts begin—*I could die here!*—and grim associations. Down she reaches, Zeus's firstborn, deep into your psyche, where the queen of cruel delusions finds memories and fiction both, and traumas ever-raw. Some tense scene from a movie rises first, where monsters stalk, or ghosts, or rising waters that so easily could fill this basement hall and none would hear you scream. Memories next, your closest past encounter with oblivion's despair. What is your worst, reader? Some nearly fatal injury? A time you almost drowned? A bear or human predator glimpsed through the deep of night? A cliff you looked down once and felt Death gazing back one jump away? Whatever fear it is, it rises now and strips your courage to the bone, so when the door cracks open and you see that red glow burning like old hate, your voice rises in scream, companions scream, and that group scream ignites panic as oil turns the faint spark to inferno. Flight, no fight, just screaming, plunging, headlong through the black, away, away from laughing, prowling Ruin. Or perhaps we are the later group, those Masons who were warned against Thisbe by Ayhan's calls. Perhaps we wear wet cloths across our mouths, or pinch our noses, but fine scents are almost as hard to stop as leaking souls. We think we come prepared but feel her touch, the morbid thoughts, the opposite of armor—knowing that this is the weapon of one of Earth's greatest killers does not ease our fear. A sighting now, the hellish red, the goddess proud before us, and perhaps we stand our ground, resisting panic, but the weapons in our hands are shaking, fingers slow, while Ruin's priests are merciless, the flash of gunpowder, the streams of blood, and we who stood our ground are either fleeing now with our companions, or can flee no more. So she advances, Zeus's banished daughter, pausing sometimes to jam doors closed or open to prepare her smooth escape, or other times to place a heavy boot upon the breast of some still-breathing victim and make sure Death comes.

The cell door now. Its layered metal stifles screams and gunfire, but still the battle must be audible to Him within. The power outage slows the crack and groan of the great door, the mechanisms sluggish as the emergency battery forces their action. Silence next, perhaps with breathing audible, but the enemy does not advance into the cell at once, waiting instead to let the scents leak in, Thisbe's fearcraft perfected by a year of battlefield deployment, deadlier than Cato ever planned. Poor Cato—it is one thing to be forced to pull a trigger, but another to be forced to make a trigger which in others' hands is pulled, and pulled, stacking up body after body on the conscience of one with no power to make it stop. A minute's pause, and Chagatai's audible whimpers from within confirm the hex is done. The door swings wide, the red infernal glow outlining just seven infiltrators, a diminished force, for the Praetorians outside, elites and loyal, did take enemies with them into the dark. But not enough.

"There, in the back." The ominous red light reveals a blurred black figure in the bathroom area at the cell's end, where the translucent partition offers slight shelter.

His voice: "¿Are you capable of willing evil for the sake of evil? I have long been curious to meet one such."

Of course the witch must laugh. "I've been curious to meet you too, Jehovah Epicurus all-important fuss fuss Mason. I thought it would be harder."

His pause, always His pause. "Would that I could make it easier for all to meet Me, and Me to meet all. ¿Are you that Thisbe who long both helped and harmed My Mycroft?"

"Yes." A smile.

"My friend Augustine, whom I meet through books, recounts smashing a neighbor's pear crop, and believes he then willed evil for the sake of evil, but it seems to Me he still pursued a kind of good-for-self, the laughter-camaraderie of his companions. Laughter is not an absolute good, nor a constructive good, but it is a raw neurochemical good, activating the pleasure center of the human brain. ¿Does your brain so activate when you frighten and kill?"

The witch-turned-goddess Ruin paced toward Him through this, pausing to smile down at cowering Chagatai, who shivered in the corner by my empty cage. "You certainly ramble like Mycroft. No wonder the two of you got on so well."

"¿Does the cruelty of not answering My questions also activate the pleasure center of your brain?"

"It does." It does not have a name, that slow, satisfied hum one might call the human equivalent of purring. "Enough that I'm quite tempted to keep you. I win the game of World Tag just by being first to get at you, so it's up to me whether to"—she snapped her fingers—"or take you off somewhere where we can take our time." Thisbe turned her smile on her companions. The ventilators that guarded them against her arts hid their expressions, but there was no mistaking that malicious laughter, rich with rot and succulent vendetta.

"I see." The Prisoner did not move, but switched to English. "You are those My mother hurt. Your anger is destructive and self-destructive but not unjust. Is Minister Kraye with you? Your leader misleader organizer exploiter sometimes called Casimir Perry sometimes Merion Kraye?"

Shock's murmur, muffled by the masks.

"Impressive," Thisbe granted. "I didn't think you'd really be as clever as they say. But you're not wrong. What do you say, gang? Surely, Perry won't mind if we drag the princeling back alive for bonus fun? Too risky?"

So, he too sent his share of death to our battle, the hater of heroes, cursed Thersites-Croucher-Perry-Kraye. He had to, reader, he who would have turned down all the bribes that golden Aphrodite, gray-eyed Wisdom, and the scheming Queen of Heaven offered princely Paris if some other goddess offered him the chance to watch one hated mother outlive her dear Son. This was his chance as much as it was Gordian's. Of course the coward Perry dared not come in person, but that selfish mastermind has many minions, nursed by spite and gall, Madame's outcasts eager to taint O.S.'s noble aims with rancorous vendetta. We did confirm it later, images from the east harbor of a stealth ship, flagless, docked among the shadows of the flagged, gray-blue and semi-submerged, the same model that had once held Tully Mardi and pursued the royal *Numantia* as it sped good Martin's message toward the Addressee. Perhaps Thisbe met Perry through that same corrupted channel that brought him briefly into O.S.'s circle when he sold Sniper to Julia. Or the alliance could have been born in that bloody alleyway, a vile thing delighted to find fellow vile things.

"But you, Thisbe, come differently," the Farthest Comer judges. "You come because, by extending your power over Me, you thus surpass those ba'sibs who have failed to attain the same, ba'sibs you envy because they outranked you in your bash's hierarchy and human awe. Do you so disvalue constructive accomplishment that you envy only your ba'sibs' power to kill and not their world-shaping?"

Thisbe waved her companions forward toward the translucent barrier. "It's hard to think of anything that will shape the world more than your death. But I've done a deal of good in this war, as it happens, though I doubt many have the intelligence to notice or respect it."

"I am ignorant of this. Will you dispel My ignorance?"

A little laugh. "Well, since you ask, I've been helping the Brillists mop up the messy edges of the war, and curating the . . . wing-clipping, shall we say, of the Utopians? There's an art to making sure a purge is not too hot and not too cold, just right." She licked her lips, thinking perhaps of bowls of sweet porridge that wait for Goldilocks, or of the bloody feasting of the bears.

"If you help *Onkel* advance human immortality, you fight that foe named Death which taught Me how to Hate. I respect that."

"Thank you. Very civil. Now . . ." Now what? Now close to the partition wall she pauses, Ruin's avatar, and Zeus the Father, watching from Olympus, lifts aloft again his golden scales, as in the pans he sets two fates of death that end a mortal life, one for Thisbe, and one for—*Bang! Bang! Bang! Bang! Bang! Bang! Bang!* the bullets topple Thisbe's six companions and the witch herself as Chagatai's fate soars high in Zeus's scales. Invisible as a panther in the darkness, she had snatched a gun from one invader who had sidled close to smirk down at the cowering Blacklaw. Fool, you really think a Blacklaw cowers? All seven of them dropped, and without hesitation Chagatai fired another round, kill shots to make sure they *stayed* down, these brash brutes that *dare* threaten Chagatai's Ward. No mercy—Blacklaws have honor yes, pride, and customs stricter than many a toothless law, but they do not have mercy, not for rats like these who so underestimate a sovereign child of Hobbestown that they would turn their backs on her in battle! Mercy for Thisbe? Some. For Thisbe Chagatai had a respectful frown at least as she stepped around so the gasping, bleeding witch could see the Blacklaw's face, serene and energized by this quick exercise.

Thisbe tried to ask something but only gurgled blood.

Chagatai's smile remained respectful. *"Modo mundo."* She tapped her nose. "I haven't seen a movie in a decade. I guess the cues wear off. But I can fake fear with the best." A soft pause, grave. "You were good. You were very good."

One last shot—here ends Blacklaw mercy.

It feels strange, calling it a war death, Thisbe lying in her own blood there on the cell floor. I can't call her a soldier. An architect of war, perhaps, but soldiers fight for something, causes, peoples, friends, while she, stalking serene through hallways cleared of adversaries by her trickery—I don't think I can even say she fought. Do I mourn her? Occasionally, when I think on hours with Bridger, bedtime stories, treats, hours I think were more than just a witch gloating. But He mourns her more than I do, the Kind Infinity Who watched her blood pool under the partition, He Who mourns all things, and Loves all things except raw evil, which Thisbe was not, and Death, which took what she might yet have been. But she wanted to kill Him, reader, toy with, torture Him, and just to prove she is the best at such worst deeds. So, I may mourn Thisbe the friend who fed this stray from time to time years back, but if I'd been in that cell, reader, I'd have fired faster than Chagatai.

"Want to escape, T.M.?" the Blacklaw asked, already harvesting the weapons from the fallen foes. "Now's our moment if you do. Grab some Praetorian uniforms, these masks, I'd give us good odds."

The Prisoner gazed down at the blood which pooled red in red light. "No. *Pater* forbids."

A laughing sigh. "You want to be Emperor almost as badly as you don't want to be Emperor, eh?" Reaching over the partition, Chagatai mussed her young Ward's hair. "Suit yourself. I'll hide us some guns and gear for later, just in case."

And so our forces found them, victorious Chagatai on guard in case the first to come were foes, but they were friends. And, quick as pixisaur could fly, the good news reached us in the war room, and beyond: First Contact lives.

«They're safe now, then? Your Stranger god?» Achilles asked, calm like the eye of storm.

«Yes!»—joyous—«safe and sound! And . . . »

«And?»

«And really safe, I think.» Our Acting Caesar smiles as the screens confirm. «The battle's going well. We've broken through their ships, the east harbor is weakening, I think . . . » A young Greek's fear of hubris does not want to say the words, but all can feel the change. This charge of racing enemies was no sport gallop in which the next contender dashes for the trophy if the lead horse trips. Rather, as when the rains of Father Zeus so swell a gushing river that it breaks its banks and thunders down the mountainside, sweeping along great trees and jagged stones, and here a herd of wild horses flees the nightmare, plunging, desperate speed, and the beasts, jaws foaming, clash and shove each other, knocking comrades back as they race along the narrow path of safety, just so our adversaries had raced each other but above all raced the torrent—the torrent which is us, our fleets, our reinforcements, the Empire's strength inexorable in its coming. It had come. These foes had their head start today, one lightning chance bought by their seven months of siege and preparation, but that was all they had, while numbers, resources, the war's momentum grim like gravity, those were all ours. We outlasted. « . . . we've won.»

«Not yet.»

«No?» Wise youth is always ready for correction. «You think they have another plan?»

«I don't know. But Father Zeus lifts up his scales a lot of times in Homer's ten-year war and gives the Trojans victory as often as the Greeks. You want a short war?»

Instinct senses something. «Yes?»

«It doesn't end while I hold back from battle.»

No, nor does it end while goddess Ruin, she who lures us on to burn our wonders, can still take another form: the engine wakes.

«Achilles? What are you doing?»

«What I always do. What any man must do who's seen his dearest comrade drop and die, while the one who took him struts about the Earth, and glories in the overthrow, and does more slaughter.» Achilles's voice changed here, too pure, synthetic, voice but without breath, the keen digital voice we had heard once before beamed from the distant, woken Alexander.

«Bryar?» There she was upon the screen, her back against the slanting glass, still gazing up as, through a wired headset, she dictated an order to some peacemaking friend. «No! There's no need, Achilles. We're turning the tide. You can see from there, we're taking the east harbor back, we're moving on the Hiveguard camp. We'll capture Bryar soon ourselves—»

«No. I, with my own hand, I kill Hector.»

«You don't need to. You don't need to do anything. Just stay up there and guard Utopia.»

The engine roars—storm calm no more.

«Achilles!» Desperation's cry. «You can't do this! You'll escalate the war! The Alexander can't even touch a space station without clawing it in half! If you battle in Alexandria, you'll devastate the city! Achilles? Are you listening?»

Was he listening? Peleus's son who lived and lives in so many eras, could he hear ours? *«It's usually only a day between Patroclus's death and Hector's. Eight months has been precious some ways, but in others, it's beyond enduring.»*

A sob on the recording, my young successor choking up—this is not some other child's Hector, this is our Hector, who came striding home like family to Vivien's bash'house, so warm, so strong. Must that warm bash' be widowed like Andromache? «Killing Bryar won't make anything better!»

«I know. But she is Hector. And I've finally found the enemy I want to fight.»

«But you'll die! You know what has to happen if you enter battle! Hector's death means yours comes next, Achilles! Please!»

«I know. You know I know. That's what it means to be a mortal man, that there will come a dawn, or dusk, or noon that sends me down to death. I don't win this war, I die in it. We've both always known that.»

«But you might get Patroclus back this time! Faust has the body! We have Bridger's potion! That's what makes it different this time! If you only wait!»

«That won't be a short war.»

This sob is not for Bryar. «We're so close, Achilles! What's the point of being able to bring Patroclus back if you're not here to be with them! This doesn't have to end the same as all the other times! You can both be happy! Hector too! If you just hold back from battle! Please!»

«It's alright. I found the enemy I want to fight. That's enough.»

«It's not alright.» True tears. «It's not alright!»

The roar of engines, crackle, words half drowned out as reentry's fire swallows signal, and above the city arcing bright the shooting star begins. *«It will be all right if you just re—mber us. That———most important thing. I don't k—why they call me—happiest of—dead. Hector's just as unfading, you rem—him as———and Hom—makes Hector a better man than Homer makes me. So, just re—mber me, a—better me thi—time—that's—e—»*

A minute, two of silence as tears stream freely from this one who walked with, laughed with, sparred with, broke bread—good Demeter's gift—with this Achilles. Then words: «No! It's not enough! It's stupid!» It's easier sometimes to voice true feelings when we know the other isn't there to hear them. «It's a stupid afterlife! Why does it have to be stupid? Remember you? Why do the spirits have to fade away? I want an afterlife as much as anybody! As much as anybody wants anything! But I don't want everyone to fade away! I want everyone to be okay! And to be here! Not mist and nothing! It's too much! Everyone who ever died depending on us to remember, it's too much to ask! I don't want to be your everything! Be everything to you like stupid Hecuba! I just want you and everyone to be okay!» 'Hecuba' here was shorthand—we use such shorthand when we speak to our own selves and know the links already. Hecuba the Trojan queen, who saw so many sons cut down, her daughters widowed, city burned, her husband butchered even on the altar, archgriefs such that poets say her need to etch into the world her monument of rage drove the queen past humanity, transforming bodily into a howling, biting dog when *Homo sapiens* was not vessel enough to voice the woes braided for her by Ruin, callous Fates, and *Homo bellicosus.* But this shorthand did not mean the classical depictions, this meant the scene in *Hamlet,* we discussed it once, so late at night, my good successor and myself. Hamlet, he sees the Player King perform a speech, weep tears for Hecuba, and Hamlet mocks what he thinks must be empty tears: "What's Hecuba to him or he to Hecuba?" What's he to Hecuba? Her everything. The Player King is everything to Hecuba, a man who speaks her name, and knows her loves and sufferings, and weeps for her three thousand years after her death, and in a land that never even knew her language, Hecuba who feels those tears in Hades's hall, her monument of grief and human pity outliving the cities built on cities built on hers, and she remembers. She remains herself, that's what the Player King's tears are to Hecuba in Homer's afterlife, her very self. Her everything. What's Hecuba to him? The burden of the dead depending on us, all these fading dead that need us to remember, need us to pass forward what they left, a task as vast as Earth. But with that burden comes the hope that what we pass forward may carry on, that we might hear our names called in three thousand years and push back the forgetting. That is Hecuba, and Homer's afterlife, or aftercurse, as one might call this tenuous eternity. «You hate it too, Achilles!» Tears' floodgates were open now. «You do! You can't pretend! You of all people! You! You hate that stupid afterlife! You said it, in the *Odyssey,* you came and told us all how much you hate it! How much you wanted to be here instead! With us! You want to do things! Do things here under the sun, not just drift in mist and hope we don't lose Homer! You said it! You said you'd rather toil away all day but be alive than be a hero king and dead—how can you tell us that and then tell me this is oka-ay!» The syllables broke here, that kind of sobbing gasp that is almost a scream. «This is *not* okay! You aren't supposed to die this time! We were so close! We were so-o-o close! Why can't it be a short war and also have you and everybody live, and be here with us at the end, and be okay?» Two gasps. «You want me to remember you? I'll remember you when you were angry! Really angry! Not like this, resigned, obsessed with stupid Hector! I'll remember you angry at Fate! And Death! And at this stupid war, and at the stupid gods, not Hector! That's you really angry! I'll remember that! You can't stop me remembering you like that! If I remember you angry enough, will you admit it's not okay? And stop? And stop it all from happening again this time? It doesn't have to!»

«Yes.» The word cuts sharp as steel as white-hot Alexander, deadly Alexander, hollow Alexander with Achilles in his heart, comes home. *«Rem———me lik—that.»*

Hush took the war outside, no shot, no bomb, all stillness as they watched that starfire shape loom closer, closer. Remnants of the used reentry pack burned as it slowed over the city, like the corona of a falling sun. Then a flash like nova as a car made its mindless programmed attack, the burst and mushroom cloud barely enough to buffet the Alexander in its flight, as a puff of breath buffets a maple copter whirling toward the soil. A second car, a third, the Alexander knocks them back, not even drawing forth the shield it bears across its back, its bare arms stronger than the greatest engine of our age. Scale was difficult, the figure so familiar from fiction, yet how big was it? How close? This bright spot, how tall will it stand beside the ships and lighthouse tower? One ship did fire at it, twelve streaking missiles more a show of defiance than a true attempt. The Alexander fired back from its Sarissa banks, forty-eight slim streaks blue-white against the blue-black dusk, so piercing that they cracked the hulls of forty-eight ships at once, yet so precise not one went up in flames. Foes race for lifeboats, speak Achilles's name with awe, and live.

«Please . . . Achilles . . . don't do this . . . Bryar is . . . »

One more Sarissa burst took out the O.S. strongholds in the city's eastern streets, so many months our bane, erased in an instant with pinpoint precision, where pinpoints turned street-wide barricades to ash. A smooth deceleration and the dream armor hovered before the dream palace, black now against the night. Kosala smiled as he who breaks armies appeared before her in the form that truly breaks armies. But sometimes we choose death. We commit to it, and in that stretch, that tract of time between commitment and the end, there is a strange tranquility, the private will to battle for survival silenced like the surface of a pond that never until now grew still enough to form its mirror, show us true reflection. Rare philosophy dwells in the stillness between choosing death and death, so rare I often feel I can't express myself to those who have not known it—ever since I tasted it, I commune better with raw silence than with innocents. But it is usually selfish, choosing death. An easy out when what we must do if we live is harder. It was so for me. And for Kosala too, I think, who watched them go, the partners of her long peacemaking, almost-bash'mates Ganymede, Andō, lost Spain, and MASON, even Cornel MASON gone. Too hard, was it, World Mother, to face building it all back without Father? Pride rose in Kosala's eye as she gazed at imagination's monster, pride and deep fatigue. She fired a signal flare, one quick green burst, and from all corners of the palace grounds came fire, white, red, beams, blasts, all the weapons history and cunning could supply trained, not upon the armor, no, on what it carries, massive at its side, the Ancile Breaker, harbinger of harbingers, the tool that burned so much. Was this deed grand enough to let you trick yourself, World Mother? The lie that, if you can disarm the Alexander, end the Ender of Ambitions, that would make your sacrifice, your death, a happy ending? But the Alexander shrugs it off, the strongest arts the Peacemakers can field no more than gnats. Sarissas fire, the smallest, gentlest weapon great Achilles has now that he wears a god, and Earth erupts in walls to block his adversaries.

«Achilles . . . please . . . »

The great hand flashes white as it snatches the tiny figure from the Cousins' hanging crystal fortress, as a child snatches one toy from a play castle, leaving the rest to teeter.

«You don't have to do this, Achilles! Don't let Ruin force—»

«It's alright.»

Young Caesar gasps—that voice is not Achilles. «Cato? Cato, is that you?»

«Are you ready?» This is Achilles, focused as the hunting lion.

«Yes. The scan should be complete,» Cato answers, quick words. «Are you ready?»

A pause. *«You know what it is, don't you? My . . . weakness.»* Achilles can't say 'heel.'

«Yes.»

«Can I do anything about it?»

«No. I'm sorry.»

«Then»—as once again on high Olympus, Zeus who loves the lightning lifts aloft his golden scales, and weights them with two fates of death that lay us low, one for Kosala breaker of the Almagest, one for Achilles splendid as a god—*«it's time.»*

It was hardly visible, the motion of that clawed monstrosity that was Achilles's god-hand now, one squeeze. Screams from the Cousins clinging to their shattered hanging fort, and blood, yes, there's the blood on those fingers built to do nothing gently. He paused. He squeezed again. He shook, shook, shook, grieving Achilles, shook the corpse of Hector, Hector who unmade the tower that brought us closest to the stars, Hector who killed Achilles's dearest, gentle friend.

Then Alexander stopped, alighted on the streets before his capitol, shattering pavement with his jagged knee as he knelt low and set out on the grass broken Kosala. Something was wrapped around the corpse, some sort of tarp or cloth that must have been in the Alexander's palm, the white thing we saw flash before it grabbed her, and it flashed now in the city lights, sequined with sensors like a set-set's interface.

«Now!»

Cracking like an egg, the Alexander's cockpit opened, the great chest folding out, baring the pilot in his shining suit, and there with him a second figure who jumped down, running, a little wobbly, across the Earth whose gravity legs can forget with time. The figure wore a space suit, thick, a heavy pack, and charged toward Kosala's corpse carrying bulky gear in either hand. The great armor cupped its blood-smeared fingers into a protective dome, and there beneath, the figure laid out wires, boxes, sensor pillars, lights bright as a hospital, and set to work as in a hospital, attaching gadgets, tubes, hooking the output cables from the sensor-tarp up to the bulky pack, and to the vizor. Mumbled words: "Pre-trauma scan successful, great imaging, infusion underway . . ."

«Cato?» Trembling young Caesar was not certain if words would still reach.

«Don't distract me. If you want to do something useful, have your troops keep everyone away.»

«It is you, Cato!»

Yes. She never got to take the field before, Helen who launched a thousand ships a thousand times, who hates this war, this long-repeating war, more than any of us, who loves both sides, has dear kin on both sides, yet, fiercely as she loves, she could do nothing in the war but yield to Aphrodite's threats and weep. But not this time. This time, our Helen, our unyielding Cato, they fight back.

«Is that Bridger's resurrection potion? You're going to save Hector! Change the end!»

«No.» Cato raises instruments in both hands, wide and proud as wings the first time life spurned gravity—no, the first time we humans, we flightless beings, we spurned gravity and seized Apollo's path. «No potion this time. We've been studying the potions, and Bridger's other relics. They're observable, replicable. This part isn't a miracle or magic. This is science. This is us.»

A plunge of instruments, a rush, a flow of blood against the flows of time and gravity, and look! The crushed skull rounding out, the cracked limbs straightening. She moved! She gasped, Kosala, gasped in air like one who almost drowned, but she did drown, and died, yet she breathes again as Death, swift horseman, staggers back a pace. Immortal gods have taken wounds in other *Iliads*, Ares, cruel Aphrodite, but this time is different. This time, gentle, good, courageous Helen disarms Death, and Zeus's scales which fell, fate irrevocable, straighten again. In our cruel match played against Death and endless Entropy, we score +I.

«Did you just . . . Can . . . Can we . . . ».

«Yes.» Cato burst into joy's maniacal laughter, triumph at long, long last. "You see that, Gordian! We did it! Resurrection! We have it! It's a prototype, it needs a ton more work, years, but we did it! And you don't know which space stations we've hid it on! Even I don't know! We've spread it out. So, you don't dare take any more potshots in space! Not one! You hear me, Gordian? We do this thing together from now on! *Astra mortemque!* Together, do you hear?"

Together? Is that what Bridger gifted us? Cato whose H.E.L.E.N.-tech makes space a little easier, does it make Gordian's calling easier too? The dying light, Apollo's path too harsh to face again if we complete the Earthly project first—can we have both?

"Bryar?" Cato leaned close to the patient. "Can you understand me? Can you tell me your name? Do you know where you are?"

"Bryar Kosala . . ." she answered slowly, then gaining momentum, "मैं तुम्हें समझती हूं। मुझे भारी और धुंधलापन महसूस हो रहा है, मैं . . . क्या हम वापस क्रेते में हैं? रुको, तुम कौन हो?"

Cato stared a moment. "That sounds like Hindi? Which is a . . . medium-good sign for the degree of neural damage, I think? Anyway, you're safe now, I'm a medic, please lie still, I need to take a million readings."

«It worked?» Achilles knew it worked, saw every instant, but just as sometimes we need our friends to tell us 'Yes, I'm glad I have you in my life' although we know it's true, Achilles had to hear it.

«Yes, it worked. It worked.» From Helen's lips, «It's over.»

Peace, not any kind of smile, just peace, stillness on Prince Achilles's face, the great soldier who finally beat back the enemy he truly wanted to beat back. *«It's over.»*

"Over. It *is* over," echoed the young voice on the throne.

"What is?" Bo asked. "The war?"

"The *Iliad*. Achilles just gave Hector's body back. That's where it ends. The rest isn't in Homer. Achilles's death, the horse, Homer has hints and fragments, Odysseus narrates bits of it, but the full accounts are in the *Posthomerica*, and Tryphiodorus, and Apollodorus, and Euripides—Bridger never read those. Bridger doesn't, didn't know what happens next. I think . . . I think we're free now. I think it's less locked in from this point on, what happens in the war."

It was almost true—Bridger knew some things.

"*Magistrate!*" fierce Xiaoliu shouted over the line. "Now! Strike them now! There are Hiveguard still holding out by Al Gamee Square, and their fleet is regrouping to retreat west! Strike now!"

A pause. *«[Anonymous], can you still hear me?»* Achilles did not move his lips, his figure slack and doll-like in the shining cockpit which connected to him everywhere, arms, shoulders, skull. That man-sized body isn't you now, is it, Achilles-Alexander? Your mind lives inside the larger body, you a hybrid birthed by gods to come fully alive only in armor, soul in the machine. That's how you can let loose. With fragile Cato there as passenger, you dared only the smoothest motions, but you can leap and tumble freely now, matchless runner, enduring g-forces that would make a human brain black out, because you use no human brain, and have no human limits.

«I hear you, Achilles.» My successor sniffling, happy tears this time.

«Can he *hear me?»*

«Who?»

«Not back yet? He will come back. You know that, right?»

«Oh. Yes. I know. He always comes back.»

«Good. Listen. When he does come back, tell him to make the damned horse quickly this time. We can't let this version drag on ten years.»

«Yeah.»

«Also, it feels weird saying this, and I doubt any other armors will turn up at this point, but in case they do, if it's the Diogenes, that's fine, it's his suit, let him pilot it.»

«You're talking about the Mojave *Iliad*? Odysseus's robot suit?»

«But if the Olympias turns up, don't let him near it, it'll break him, even if he only climbs in once. No one can handle the Olympias. Not even me.»

«Achilles? Why are you talking like you—»

«And when you bring me back—and I am trusting you to bring me back—remember your promise to keep me angry at the right things.»

«Achilles? Why—»

«Do it now, Apollo! Lord of the silver bow who shoots from worlds away, if ever I did you honor, burned sweet sacrifices on your altar, if ever I did good service to your Delians, keeping your favorites safe upon the cold black sea although you slew so many of my comrades, dearest friends, yet still I honored you, great son of Leto! So now, I beg you, bring this prayer to pass! If you're still going to do it, if you're going to bring my end in this war as you have in all the others, do it now! Now, please! Don't wait until I spread more death among your Trojans, bright, deadly Apollo! If you are going to do it, if you are going to kill me, do it now!»

So Achilles prayed, and Lord Apollo heard him, had already heard him long ago, the god who sees before, intricate god, who beats back some plagues even as he rains down others. Long since Apollo drew that silver bow. Long since he chose the arrow, slender, bright, its keen tip tempered to unmake a man almost immortal. What prince wields it? Serves as human bowman for Apollo's shaft? Paris, of course, magnificent, who once held Helen, Paris stunning as a god, who waited all these months, watching, planning, resisting every plea of friends and followers to lure the champion to the battlefield too soon, for Paris knows there is only one chance, one shot, since striking must reveal one's hiding place—such is the sniper's art. But Sniper can't resist Apollo, no. Not after this day's battle, after seeing this last, best attempt has failed to pierce the walls and bring the Tyrant into Sniper's gunsights even once. And Trojan Paris may have been a selfish prince, but Ojiro Cardigan Sniper Thirteenth O.S. is not, and will not on this day or any day allow Intolerable Crimes. O.S. protects the Hives, the Humanists, the bright Olympic spirit, human dignity, and all of those are threatened by intolerable, uncontrolled destruction loosed on helpless Nature, human life, and civilization. Sniper must grant our prayers to hold Achilles back, so, to Sniper, Apollo trusted long ago the poison arrow that can stop, forever stop, the most destructive weapon that has ever touched the Earth. One shot, a perfect arc into the open cockpit. One flash that filled the air with an electric sting as crackling white sparks rained down the armor. Lights failed in a great sphere, the Peacemakers' lights, the lights within the pyramid, and Cato's lights, the microhospital rebooting as he coughed and cursed. "I'm sorry, Achilles! I never wanted . . . I didn't realize when I made it! Didn't know!"

A Weeksbooth Counterbomb. You were a great mind, Cato, even back when you were not quite Helen yet. It shorts out everything, the armor, the computer, and the brain, the hybrid electronic brain unique in this world, even back in its imaginary birthworld, Achilles's brain half god-machine, it fries. It dies. They come, the wind-swift escorts, brothers Sleep and Death, who know Achilles well by now, and he knows them. But there must be a new rapport between them this time, Thetis's mortal son and Thanatos who never wanted Zeus's scales to fall. In sport, in arms, in games of strategy, there is a special joy, when masters spar, in losing, giving ground, feeling the weapon drop from your stunned hand before a young assailant's fresh ideas—does Death smile so too? And share that smile at last, as once again this gentle escort clasps the hand of life-loving Achilles?

"Aggressor prendite!" "Seize the attacker!" Ayhan and Huxley shouted the order together, forces rushing from the gates to where the blast and counterbomb had exposed Sniper's mobile tent of Griffincloth, a perfect cover in a city where Delians walk so welcome. The pentathlete gave our force six minutes' chase, matchless runner now that Achilles runs no more. We took Sniper alive. We took many alive, Dougong withdrawing to negotiate with Danaë, the Peacemakers peaceful now that we no longer field a harbinger, now that Jehovah's victory is clearly the smoothest and least deadly path to peace. And Hiveguard, local Hiveguard quickly lost their spirit when they saw Ojiro Sniper marched into our fortress, bound in Cannergel. I must visit Sniper. Ancelet is waiting, Papa, Bandyopadhyay, Faust's response, so much to do. But not that night. The *Iliad* was over. Those hours were for rest and mourning, patching wounds, and Prayers, daughters of Zeus which follow after Ruin healing in their slow, incomplete way the batterings of Fate. Prayers for Father Zeus, his brothers Distance and More Distant, both parts of the wonder we just earned. Prayers for Apollo, whose cold kindness gave Achilles what I can't call mercy yet he must be thanked for it, Ἀπόλλων Ἀλεξικάκιε, Apollo Averter of Evil, so called because the deadly archer drove a plague from Athens once, and wise Greeks know that a god who does a kindness must be thanked forever for it, even if he does no more. Prayers for Hypnos and Thanatos, twin sons of Night, escorts who smile this time with their two-way passenger, chatting of other two-way crossings past, and more to come. Prayers for you, too, Achilles, spirit, you who left me here to toil alone but still you hear, I know it, when I call your name, Achilles, comrade, best of soldiers, friend. And we must greet with prayers too Eos, early-rising Dawn, who that morning blushed rose and saffron in her wonder seeing, for the first time in so many crossings, peace.

CHAPTER THE TWENTY-SIXTH

No One

Written November 10, 2455
Events of November 4
Alexandria

IT'S STRANGE, WRITING EVENTS IN WHICH ONE WAS an actor. Often, I barely remember things I said or did until the transcript is in front of me. When my first history was being vetted before publication, many a potentate insisted, 'I never said that!' until we played the film and they discovered their past selves as we discover strangers. My rescue is a blur, lost among the many rescued at the Almagest. My injuries, the old concussion re-concussed so often on the low stairs of the *Shearwater* (now bad enough to give me crippling vertigo) muddled my long transport back to Alexandria into a string of dreams. Even my welcome, my arrival, I slept through, awakening in the familiar halls to those strange stares that always greet the monster Mycroft Canner.

My visit to Sniper in the cells is a blur too, no details, just that clean, astonished face as we parted in the bright interrogation room, wonder mixed with friendship, beautiful. But you need the scene that led up to that face, the details, how the war has changed the one who drew Alien blood, and how I convinced Sniper to lend Hiveguard agents to the mission now moving toward the most precious hostage of Gordian's hostages. No, reader, we are not trying for Martin yet.

Hobbes: "Of course not. As sovereigns come to negotiate, thou needest most the one who can command thy Prince: Isabel Carlos, the new-made Emperor and best surviving parent of thy Master's ship of flesh. The Princesse Danaë has been a good custodian to Europe's strats and Homeland, but will welcome to the table an ally who can compel as well as plead."

Just so. And that good widow too should know relief, I hope, some closure, when at last she can deliver to the good king's custody the ashes that she carries in an urn, and know that honorable Ganymede has kept his last parole.

But my visit was second, it turns out. Here as I cue up the video, I see my good successor wheel in first to the interrogation space, with Sniper marched to the opposing chair. It looks so like a photo shoot: a prison costume this time, sexy handcuffs and other restraints, a 'bad boy'/'bad girl' series is it this time, prince of poses? How your fans will squeal.

9A: "I need to talk to you. I'm sorry I didn't come sooner, there's been a lot. Happening, lots happening."

Sniper: "I don't seem to be going anywhere in a hurry. But who are you, who needs to talk to me?"

9A: "Oh. I'm the Acting Emperor."

Sniper: "Ah. And why'd you start to tear up when you said that? Cornel MASON meant a lot to you?"

I had to pause the video to look, but yes, I see what Sniper saw, tense lips, the strain around the eyes. Sniper works so hard at reading faces, not for data's sake as voyeur Brillists do, but, by being more sensitive, to be more kind.

Sniper: "Cornel MASON meant a lot to you?"

9A: "What? No. I mean, sure, I respected them, I just . . ."

Sniper: "You don't want to be Acting Emperor? I didn't mean to hit a nerve, just . . . you have a very expressive face."

9A: "Heh. *Snnff.* I didn't want to have this conversation with you as an enemy, I . . ."

Sniper: "Preferred the Hives as friendly rivals? We all did."

9A: "No, I . . . was never a Mason."

A Servicer's uniform always invites the silent question, what one was.

Sniper: "Ah. Were you a Humanist? It doesn't stop, you know, just because you aren't a Member in the law, it doesn't mean the torch isn't still there inside. Sorry, do you need tissues?"

9A: "No. I mean, I have . . . here—*Khhhnnnnnnn!*—there. Sorry, this is pathetic."

Sniper: "You don't need to apologize for being human in front of another human being. I think it's a compliment, a kind of trust, when we let someone see us cry."

9A: "*Kkkhnnnnn!*—Yeah. It can be. And yes, I was a Humanist."

So tender, gentle Sniper handling a fellow human heart in tears, practiced, but practice doesn't make it less sincere. I'm so lucky having basked for years in such a friend, and young Olympian Saneer will be so lucky having such a ba'pa.

Sniper: "Are you a fan?"

9A: "Nnnnnn . . ."

Sniper: "Kind of? It's a little different? More to it than that?"

9A: "Yeah."

My successor's eyes, wet, red, ask without words: How did you know? And Sniper's smile answers that it's never simple, love.

9A: "I wanted to meet you, more than almost anything. Oh, but I should tell you Vivien's going to call to talk to you in a few hours. I'll make sure it's private. I've pledged, I mean, ordered all my people not to listen—if there are outside spies, I can't stop that."

Sniper: "Thank you, that means a lot to me. Do you . . . Are there plans yet for the fate of the Humanists? Is there a chance of a settlement where the Hive continues? Or is the question now how to dissolve us with the least bloodshed?"

9A: "I don't know. We're negotiating. All the Hives are still negotiating."

Sniper: "But we're different. The others have either been partly on Jehovah Mason's side or wholly on their side throughout the war. We're the only Hive whose President stood up and declared a State of War between us and the Masons, and whose people voted more than seventy percent to start the offensive."

9A: "Yeah, but that's good. You've been fighting the war Jehovah Mason wanted, Hiveguard on Remaker. All the other Hives mixed their own agendas in, even Utopia, not you."

Sniper: "Being the victor's most direct enemy doesn't make me feel safer."

9A: "It should. Vivien says respect's like armor in a conquest, no one sacks and loots a city they respect, they want to keep it not smash it. And everybody and the Prince respects Vivien, and the Humanists. And you."

Sniper: "Sounds like you know the President well?"

9A: "Oh. Yeah. I'm the new Anonymous."

Sniper: "Ah! We're both in the N.V.P. club!"

9A: ". . . Not Valuable Player?"

Sniper: "Not Vice-President. The Humanists keep trying to elect us both."

9A: "Yeah." [Laughter] "Can we . . . Can we have an eye-of-the-hurricane conversation, pretending for a minute there's no war outside?"

Sniper: "That's hard. I'm pretty desperate to find out what's going to happen to my Hive, and bash', and comrades, and the whole world order I've given my life to, and to plead with the one person in the world with the most power to decide all that."

9A: "Yeah. The Prince would call that curiosity-pain. And desperation-pain. But first, I just, I need to say thank you."

Sniper: "You're welcome. What for?"

How many times have you been thanked so by a stranger, Sniper, and accepted it with that same glowing smile, trusting the thanks, embracing, welcoming the thought that human has helped human, all before the niggling question *how?*

9A: "For being a great person. For being so strong, and making it through. I watched the tapes from summer. They filmed it all. I mean, I know what happened, where you were while you were missing before the Olympics, what

Julia did to you. They filmed it. All of it, the dollhouse, and their visits, and the creepy Dollkeeper, and the blue hours with your speeches. I listened to your speeches. You weren't shouting into nothing. I just wanted you to know that. It was only later, a recording, after it was over, but I listened to you, every word."

Now it's Sniper's lips that tremble as the tears release.

Sniper: "You . . . *No puede ser . . .*"
9A: "I know it's kind of weird, you don't know me, it's a big intrusion. But I wanted you to know someone did listen. I listened. You were amazing. You were breaking down but then you didn't break, and it was beautiful. And it really helped me. Someone—it's weird, but someone did the same thing to me recently, no sex in mine but basically the same, trapped, drugged, I couldn't talk or move. And I was breaking down, losing my mind, but then I thought of you and how you made it through. Sometimes it almost felt like you were there with me, cheering me on, because I knew you would have if you could. And that let me make it through. Because you made it through. So, I wanted to thank you."
Sniper: "The guards will flip out if I try to hug you, won't they?"
9A: "Yeah. *Snnff.* Sorry."
Sniper: "Hey, I just led a war against you, the handcuffs are *very* my fault."

Laughter. Such healing laughter.

9A: "Yeah."
Sniper: "I can't believe . . . Thank you. Thank you! I didn't think anybody . . . I talked to Lesley about what happened, but I couldn't . . . just describing doesn't get across . . ."
9A: "I know. All those days and days . . . Oh, Carlyle Foster knows. Carlyle got the tapes, that's how I know. They figured it out, that Julia had you. Oh, and Carmen Guildbreaker and Tribune Natekari know in broad strokes who did it, but they haven't seen the tapes. They're our backups in case Julia murders Carlyle and me. Carlyle blackmailed Julia into releasing you, that's how you got out in time for the Olympics, and we're still blackmailing Julia to make them do good in the war instead of . . . you know, horrible Julia things."
Sniper: "Carlyle Foster . . ."
9A: "Yeah. I figured out that they'd figured it out, but it was Carlyle who got you out. Carlyle saved you, saved the world, a couple times now. They're in Casablanca now, healing the Cousins, saving us again."
Sniper: "Is there an epic ten-year version of the Best Sensayer award?"
9A: [Laughter] "There should be. And some award for you. The Best Human award. You're so strong. Through all that. It would break anyone, but you came through so strong, it was amazing."

The film shows Sniper clenching those handcuffed hands, eyes closed like a dreamer's or a child's.

Sniper: "It didn't feel like I came through. It felt like it murdered me. There was a better Sniper once that didn't have this damage. That was more prepared to become Ojiro and lead O.S. I was stronger before. I've been wondering if the old unbroken Sniper could've won the war."

9A: "No. No, that Sniper wasn't stronger. What Julia did was intolerable, and it did change you, but . . . how did it go? 'This new you, though what changed it was abhorrent, is still recognizable and welcome as intolerable's aftermath's changes change you more. Because that exquisite thinking thing which is your self isn't soiled by, but constituted by, cumulative complexities, even the grief-born ones.'"

Sniper: "Grand words, Anonymous, I see the succession worked out well this time. But yes, you're right."

9A: "Actually, I was quoting the Prince. J.E.D.D. Mason, I mean. That's what They said to me when I said I felt like my imprisonment had murdered me. No, actually, I didn't say it, I just thought it, but They answered anyway, the way They do."

Sniper: "Mm."

An awkward pause, both of them staring at each other and their hands. Brief, reader, are the times we can banish from mind the hurricane—you tried to kill my Hive! my world! my God!—and find peace in its eye.

9A: "I don't blame you for opposing Them."

Sniper: "You'd better not, they literally got on the Rostra and asked me to."

9A: [Laughter] "Yeah. But I mean I wish . . . what you fought for, the Hive system, human dignity, they're wonderful, I wish . . . I wish those didn't have to lose for us to win."

Sniper: "They didn't lose."

9A: "What?"

Hope's glint in my successor suddenly, as Sniper stretches, roguish and defiant, ready for the camera.

Sniper: "Even wars aren't always zero-sum. In the best competitions, you achieve things even when you aren't the final victor. A silver medal brings a lot of respect, and power, leverage, platform, I should know. Jehovah Mason didn't win this war completely, I hear there are concessions, promises, Lesley described it, Danaë Mitsubishi pushing back, President Ancelet, others. I started a resistance, lots of resistances. If Jehovah Mason had inherited their power unopposed in peace, the Hives would've just fallen domino by domino like Joyce Faust planned, but that won't happen now. Whether or not you spare the Humanists, the Mitsubishi and Europe aren't handing the reins of power over unconditionally anymore. I would have liked to win, but there are millions out there galvanized to keep pushing for the Hives and human dignity and choice, and that's remaking the remaking. Even with others in power, resistance does a lot. I'd call that a silver medal and worth fighting for."

9A: "Yeah. The push is powerful. I feel it. You've certainly made me see the Prince's rise differently from if the dominoes had just gone down in peace."

Sniper: "If the one on the Masonic throne says that, I feel like I should take a bow."

9A: "Mmm. Though I won't be on the throne long."

Sniper: "Even one day on the throne is a lot, especially if you're prepared to push back against Jehovah Mason."

9A: "Mmm."

It hurts, the pain on my successor's face, avoiding eye contact, fidgeting with the wheelchair's controls. I'm sorry, my friend, I should have stayed. I made you face such hard things, and alone, and for the fool's errand of fighting Homer.

9A: "I think I've done some good things in the days I've had. Big things, I—*Snnff*—I moved the Mountain. The Prince, I mean, Jehovah, I moved Them a little bit. Enough."

Sniper: "You're the one who pushed them to accept Danaë's terms, aren't you? To say there will be Hives? That's big."

9A: "It's not really pushing with the Prince, it's more . . . guilt-tripping isn't right either, but pushing doesn't work, it's *needing* that moves Them, and it's love. You should remember that, for when you meet with Them. I think there are a lot of things the Prince is going to keep in place now, Hives and systems, because your movement showed Them how many people love those things, and you can push that more. They don't want to crush love. I think They see each human love-instance as a fragile little wonder, like a snowflake or a spiderweb, and They want to protect that. They echo love, the Prince, when They see humans loving something, they Love that love."

Sniper: "'When they see humans . . .'—I see you're in the camp that thinks Jehovah Mason is ineligible for the Best Human award?"

9A: [Laughter] "Yeah. I know Them well and, yeah . . . The simplest descriptor may be 'Alien.' But an alien perspective's good, I think, for us right now. For change. Outsiderness. Look at this war, how much good outsiders have done in it, UNGAR especially, and Red Crystal, and new people from nowhere like Kenzie Walkiewicz, and those fellow prisoners who rescued Papadelias. And the giant robot out of nowhere saving Mars and Nineveh, though that's a different kind of outside."

Pause the film: I know that face, Sniper: your serious face, rare every year of Sniper's life until this last one.

Sniper: "I am glad the robot suit saved Mars and Nineveh, but what it did since . . . There's a . . . It burns inside, the shame at being the generation that broke the promise, that used—I like the new name—harbingers. That shame will never stop burning inside." Clenched fists. "We can't let it stop. And whatever they do to me in the end, Masonic law, or Romanova's, whatever end it is, it was worth it, my capture, to stop that monster harbinger for good. But you lost a friend there too, didn't you? Achilles? I'm sorry. I only knew them briefly, just at the Olympics, but I loved them for it. I know it's much, much more for you."
9A: "Mmm. It was Achilles's choice."

Now here's a different frown, smirking and suspicious, one dark brow raised.

Sniper: "You're friends with Mycroft, aren't you?"
9A: "How did—"
Sniper: "Servicer, Anonymous, *Familiaris* . . ."
9A: "Oh. Yeah. I guess it would be obvious. Yes. Close friends. Why?"
Sniper: "Because their obsequious providential thinking rubs off. I killed Achilles. It was my choice. I am a sniper, and a soldier, and I killed your friend with a deadly sniper attack, and you're allowed to be angry at me and sad about it, and you don't need to accept the Mycroft logic and tell yourself it's all grand choices and a Plan. You are allowed to just be angry."
9A: "Yeah. And I'm not *not* angry, but I—*Snnff*—Achilles planned to die in that battle. Begged to die in it, literally, begged Apollo, in a prayer, I heard the words. And they were grateful for that death, but also angry, so angry they thought setting death back even one step was worth . . . was consolation when they had to die. Was enough. Or maybe not enough but something."
Sniper: "Do you need more tissues?"
9A: "I understand that decision, Achilles's. I respect it, I—*Khhnnn!*—You understand it, right? You were prepared to give your life to stop the Prince's rise, both when you shot Them on the Rostra and after."

A serious pause as Sniper watches tears stream down those youthful cheeks, but must be honest.

Sniper: "Yes. I still am ready to die to stop your Prince."
9A: "And that . . . It's mixed. There's an angry part, being angry at things forcing you to make that choice, but there's also a grateful part, grateful for—*Snnff*—having the choice at all and not just being stuck watching powerless as something goes on that you'd give your life to change. You'd be grateful right now if someone walked in here and said there was another chance to give your life to stop Jehovah Mason."
Sniper: "Yes, I would."
9A: "Yeah. So, Achilles was angry but also grateful. I . . . understand that. I don't want to have to give my life to fix the thing, but I'd better, I mean, I'd *rather*

have the chance to give my life to fix the thing than have no way to fix a thing that needs to be fixed so badly that I'd give my life for it. Is it stupid, feeling gratitude for that?"

Sniper: "I don't think calling feelings 'stupid' ever helps. In fact, I think 'stupid' is a very harmful word, especially when we reach for it in anger, and it isn't any less harmful when we apply it to ourselves."

9A: "Yeah—*Snnff*—you're right. I should do that less. Should have done it less."

Sniper: "As for the anger, yes, I understand the feeling you're describing. I didn't expect to be taken alive, and I was glad during that chase that I'd had a chance to give my all to stop the harbinger rather than being powerless, even when I thought I was about to die. I don't think 'gratitude' is the right word in my case, I mostly felt . . . awe, maybe? That humans are so excellent that we can make things even more excellent than ourselves, huge things like Hives and ideals, things so excellent they're even worth humans dying for. I'm awed by that. By the fact that . . . heh, I discussed this with Mycroft once."

9A: "You did? They . . . they'd disapprove, right? Of the sacrifice . . ."

Sniper: "I mean, it wasn't a question of approval, we were discussing Aristotle and Descartes, who both say in different ways that a finite thing can't make a thing bigger than itself, and that that proves there has to be an infinite being that made everything. But we humans, we're finite, but we've made so much that's bigger than ourselves."

9A: "Depends on how you define . . . no, no it doesn't. It's just true."

Sniper: "Yeah."

9A: "Yeah."

Sniper: "Yeah?"

9A: "Yeah."

Sniper: "Yeah."

They just stared at each other, laughing, smiles on both faces, but tears on one.

9A: "*Snnff.* I still hate it. Having to die for stuff, and stuff."

Sniper: "Yeah. And I'm sorry you had to lose your friend that way, even if I'm proud I did it, and would do it again."

9A: "Don't do it again."

Sniper: "What? Achilles didn't come back from the dead, did they? Jehovah Mason coming back was bad enough! Twice would be ridiculous!"

9A: [Laughter] "No. No, it was Bryar that came back."

Sniper: "What?"

9A: "Oh. Cato made a space cyborg technoimmortality deus ex machina resurrection thingy—I'm gonna start that sentence over."

Sniper: [Laughter] "I see our Anonymous has a wide range of rhetorical styles."

9A: "I don't have to always . . . Sorry, this is a serious negotiation between leaders, I should be treating it more formally."

Sniper: "No, no! It's fine. It's gratifying. People tend to be formal with strangers, but we let ourselves be a bit more raw and goofy around people we trust, showing our underbellies. It's a compliment, being trusted like that."

9A: "Yeah, but . . . I *am* a stranger, I'm your enemy."

Sniper: "No, you're not."

9A: "Mmm—*Snnff.*"

Sniper: "Enemy maybe, but not a stranger. You listened. You were part of the most terrible, intimate, hardest thing I've ever gone through in my life, you—"

9A: "But I wasn't really there. You don't know me. It was just videos, it wasn't really—*Snnff*—you that held my hand all those weeks, it was—*Snnff*—imagination."

Gently, so gently, Sniper, smiling like that rare angel that brings kind news, not cold. So practiced at this.

Sniper: "Listen. I'm a celebrity. I'm very used to asymmetry, to meeting someone for the first time when I know nothing about them, but they . . . but I'm a huge part of their lives, I'm someone they've loved, and been shaped by, and, you know, if you pie-charted their brain, their life, I'm a huge slice of it, while they're nowhere in mine."

9A: "Yeah. I guess it would happen a lot."

Sniper: "But they're not nowhere in mine, not really. Because I love that I'm loved. Even if I don't know the specific person, still that unknown, that"—quick smile—"*anonymous* love, knowing it's out there, that's a huge part of my pie chart. A huge part of my *me.* So, people I've never met are extremely important to me, the ones who care about me the way you do. Who love me. And I think that's perfectly natural, that everyone has relationships with people far away, who inspire, entertain, role models, and also the people we work so hard *for:* fans, viewers, the next generation, kids somewhere, posterity. I think those asymmetrical relationships are part of what it means to be human, part of the teamwork. Humanity is teamwork. And the asymmetry doesn't for a second make those relationships any less valid, or less important, or less real."

9A: "*Snnff.* Yeah. Yeah, I feel that too."

Sniper: "If anything, with you it's way less asymmetrical than usual for me, because thinking about me helped you through, but also, for me, just knowing you listened to those speeches, took the journey with me, that . . . is some of the most powerful intimacy I've shared with anyone in my whole life, so don't you dare share that with me and call yourself a stranger!"

9A: "Yeah. *Snnff.* Yeah."

Sniper: "So . . . you were going to try again with the space cyborg technoimmortality something sentence?"

9A: [Laughter] "Right. So, Cato's been studying how Jehovah Mason came back from the dead, and made a prototype device that brought Bryar Kosala back the same way, the wounds rewinding."

Sniper: "Wow! Well done, Cato!"

So sweet, that quick, stunned stare.

9A: "You just believe it? Most people have—"
Sniper: "Human excellence doesn't surprise me, I know humans are excellent. And I know Cato is excellent, with the right goading."
9A: "True. Though Cato doesn't . . . They've come into their own, I think, no goading needed."
Sniper: "Wish that were true. Cato always needs goading, if it's not me now, it's the silly Utopian oath, but whatever works for them."

My successor froze here, mouth open with some half-winged word, but stopped to stare. I bet I looked like that too, hearing the tape just now, such unexpected words. And Sniper basked in it, that gape, enjoying the reaction to these fighting words designed to test—that's it, isn't it, Sniper? You want to test this new challenger's allegiances: the Humanists above the Masons, but where falls Utopia?

9A: "What . . . what's wrong with the Utopian oath?"
Sniper: "Seriously? You said you were a Humanist. 'I hereby renounce the right to complacency,' et cetera? There's no right to complacency. Complacency's a betrayal of human excellence, a waste of life and oxygen. I don't know why everyone finds the oath intimidating, it's less than the standard we hold to every day. Am I wrong?"
9A: "Huh. I guess it . . . You're right."
Sniper: "The rest of the oath's fine. Surpassing space and death are great ambitions, and thinking about play and rest as self-care, thus as vital to your work as working hours, that's good, it's just, there are lots of great ambitions in the world, they're the human normal, but the oath puts those particular two on a pedestal, and I don't like anything, even a well-meaning thing, that tells people their ambitions are less grand than someone else's. We push the envelope, whether it's Mars, or a marathon, or new frontiers in cookie baking, even the best parenting on an exhausted Wednesday, it's still human excellence, and noble and amazing. But, if the oath's a crutch Cato can lean on, I'm glad they've found one that works for them so well."
9A: "Mm . . . though Cato isn't really—*Snnff*—anymore . . ."
Sniper: "What?"

I choked here, watching. Will you break the news, my so-tired successor? Or leave it to me, who knows them both better, from years, and jests, and sweeping floors, to say the words: your bash'mate is not quite your bash'mate anymore. Helen. Please let me do it, [Anonymous]? You've become close now, you and Sniper, but this part should be mine. It's closer to me, these transformations, the strange question—*am I still myself?*—that Bridger made me ask for years, of Mommadoll, Achilles, of the Earth. You haven't had to ask that, you so exquisitely still yourself. Far too often, my kind babysitter, you take on the hard tasks that should be mine. Please leave this one to me?

Sniper: "What?"

9A: "Nothing. It's too big for right now. Now I just wanted to meet you and say thank you and that you're excellent. And that I think there . . . that you'll get to keep being excellent. It isn't over for you. There're lots of things we can still do after we're captured, it's not over."

Sniper: "Coming from a Servicer on the Masonic throne, I believe it. Speaking of, is there any chance I'll be tried under Romanova's law, if that will still exist? Or will it be Masonic law? I know the Empire has basically reverted from a Hive to its own sovereign . . . whatever it is. You've showed no signs of abiding by the Alliance."

9A: "I hadn't put it like that yet, but yeah, the Empire hasn't been acting as a Hive. I don't know. I don't think anyone has asked the Prince yet if the Empire will still be a Hive, or whether the Hives will still be allies, joined by Romanova or some new thing."

Sniper: "You should ask."

9A: "Yeah. Or you can. You'll have a chance to talk to Them soon, I'm sure. About a lot of things, I'll . . . Well, thank you, Sniper, this was—or, should it be Ojiro now?"

Sniper: "It's Ojiro when I'm leading O.S. It's Sniper in my head, with friends, with fans, when I'm being just me. And it's looking like O.S. is not what the new era may be asking of me. Hard to say. But Sniper between friends."

9A: "And do you—Mycroft said you like the 'it' pronoun? I wasn't sure. I'm editing the chronicle, I've been uncertain what to use."

Sniper: "That's hard."

9A: "You don't like it?"

Sniper: "No, I *love* the 'it' pronoun. I *love* it. It's just a bit too powerful, if that makes sense? I get this amazing feeling of *yes!* and *finally!* when people use it, but it's also somehow still too much for everyday? With an intimate like Mycroft who I love and who loves me, when they first asked me, suggested they might use it for me in their history, it's the most amazing feeling, like healing inside if healing was as bright as fire. But I don't know about everybody every day. It might be too much or it might be wonderful, I still don't know. I want to think about it more, if that makes sense? Take my time thinking on how it feels."

9A: "Right, so yes from intimates like Mycroft, but not from the rest of us."

Sniper: "I told you, you *are* an intimate. I'll say it however many times I have to."

9A: "Right. Sorry."

Sniper: "No apologizing. Everybody doubts. I doubt. I'm the most popular sex object on Earth, and I still doubt whether other people really care about me. We all doubt."
9A: "Mmm."

I know that little frown, my successor. That self-hating frown that thinks but dares not say: *I'm not like other people, I have a special reason for self-doubt, a rot inside, filthy, that you don't know.* Don't you dare think that. You? *I* get to think that, *I* Mycroft Canner, more bloodstained than Clytemnestra, but not you. But if I know how to recognize that frown, somebody else can too, has seen it many times—on other cheeks, on mine—and lets pass no slander against human excellence.

Sniper: "Hey, I really mean it, we *all* doubt, and we *all* think we have unique reasons we shouldn't be loved, and the secret is that we all do have unique, strong reasons, but we're still all wrong, and do deserve love, and are loved, so there."
9A: "Mmm. True. Thanks."
Sniper: "Thanks back."

Silence. I need a Brillist. They're too complex, these gazes, nothing I can call a frown or smile, nothing I can read even on these faces I know so well. I should ask them, what is that melancholy, and that pensive . . . what? [NOTE: revise after interview].

Sniper: "Are you—"
9A: "I should go. It's time."
Sniper: "You keep tearing up when things turn to you being MASON. Power sucks, huh? Glad to see so much of it in the hands of we who realize power sucks."
9A: "Yeah." [Laughter] "Yeah. And you know what? I'm gonna ask another thing. I was gonna leave this for Mycroft is, but . . . I get to be a little selfish today, I think."
Sniper: "Is Mycroft here?"
9A: "Not yet, but they're coming. Soon."
Sniper: "I wasn't sure they were alive!"
9A: "Mycroft always comes back. I understand that now."
Sniper: "A happy thought. Is that their hat?"

It was indeed, drawn from my successor's deep thigh pocket, patched and battered, soft.

9A: "Yeah. It's funny, I've had it the whole time, I just didn't think of it before. Anyway, Mycroft will come see you soon, I'm sure. And they'll help in the big negotiations coming up, with Vivien, and the Prince. And I was going to let them do this too, they're the one who really makes the cause sing, but I... I want a chance to know your answer. So, will you help with... thing is, there's a second war."

Sniper: "War on Mars in 2650, that's the prediction, yeah? It'd better not interfere with the Odyssey Olympics, but I doubt I'll be on the committee then."

9A: [Laughter] "If Cato has their way, you might be. But no, there's a second war right now, an orthogonal war that's been going on at the same time as Hiveguard on Remaker, layered underneath, between Gordian and the Utopians."

Sniper: "This is what Cornel MASON was saying at the Almagest?"

9A: "Yes. I... only have weird, vague evidence that mostly only set-sets understand, but it's true. A lot of it has been a propaganda war, the fake U-beast attacks, the Lorelei Cook fake robot brain transcript, firing up the Nurturists. It's all been weakening Utopia and at the same time pressuring the Prince to favor Gordian in their new world."

Sniper: "Eureka told us a bit about this, when they were working with you here in Alexandria, before they disappeared."

9A: "Have you been in Alexandria through the whole war?"

Sniper: "Most of it. Took a while to get here with the cars down."

9A: "I'm sure. The whole war, just waiting for a shot..."

Sniper: "I am what I am."

9A: "Heh. And you don't know what happened to Eureka? When they disappeared before the battle? I think it was Perry."

Sniper: "Maybe. I hope you'll help find out."

9A: "Absolutely. Eureka's a hero. The Empire won't rest until we've brought them rescue, or justice if we're too late."

Sniper: "Thank you."

9A: "Of course. But Eureka told you about Gordian?"

Sniper: "Partly. I see the propaganda chain, but why is Utopia the main target? If Gordian is pushing Jehovah Mason toward a Brillists-first world order, that sounds like all the Hives should be targets."

9A: "It's not about the new order, not on that scale. It... it feels hyperbolic saying it, but it's about the long-term future of humanity. Specifically, whether we're going to go to space. See, space is hard, and deadly, and scary, and settling other worlds will mean humanity spreading over dangerous distances that will re-create the geographic problems of the pre-*Mukta* world: diaspora, loneliness, cultural rifts, more wars most likely. Gordian wants us to stay on Earth instead, one world united by *Mukta* and tech, to make Earth nicer and nicer, but both sides think that means the desire to go to space will die out, because the Earth will be too nice to leave, or the difference between Earth and what you have to face in space will be too extreme."

Sniper: "I... see it. I can see that as a... a pair of positions people could... And they're having a war over this?"

9A: "Yes-ish."

Sniper: "Yes-ish?"

9A: "We may be near a compromise. Enabled by Cato and their work, but Faust isn't yielding yet. They've reissued their ultimatum, demanding that the Prince choose Gordian over Utopia. So, we wanted to ask if... You have forces, Hiveguard agents. They can't help you win your war anymore, but if you could just ask them to help a little, break into some Brillist facilities, get evidence against the propaganda, exonerate Utopia, free a couple hostages. Even just one squad would make a difference. Gordian's whole thing is anticipating enemy actions, but they're expecting Utopian tactics, or Masons, they won't expect yours."

Sniper: "To help Utopia?"

9A: "Yeah. Or even just prove they're innocent. Gordian's winning, especially the propaganda war. This won't help the Empire at all, I promise, or Jehovah Mason, They've already won. But this war hasn't been won yet, and just a couple surprises Gordian isn't ready for, it could make all the difference—"

Sniper: "I understand. What I don't understand is why you're asking for so little."

9A: "What?"

Sniper: "This is a separate war, right? Utopia versus Gordian? So, why ask for so little? Why aren't you calling up the President? And Lesley? And Aesop Quarriman? Why aren't you asking me for all I have?"

9A: "It's not your fight."

Sniper: "A war over the future of humanity?"

9A: "Oh. It is your fight."

Sniper: "Yes. Yes, it is. So, one side says go to space, and the other side says stay here where it's easy?"

9A: "Basically."

Sniper: "Screw easy, let's go to space."

9A: [Laughter]

Sniper: "I'm serious. 'Faster, Higher, Stronger.' You think we co-built Esperanza City with Utopia because it was easy? Humans do hard things for their own sake, that's more unique to our species than intelligence is."

Say it again, Sniper. I'll play the tape again. Again again. I'll make a clip of it. Say it over and over, on the Moon say it, make me believe—you saw my successor tear up then, you'll see me tear up years from now when I still play this back. Make me believe Apollo's little light and yours, so bright, immortal in its strong Olympic cauldron, might be one. I never feared that your light might go out.

9A: "That's true. Maybe it should be *homo aspiranti... ambiti...* I don't know the endings. But I do know I'm not doing Gordian's side justice. Utopia's been bad actors too, they sort of caused the war, their plan to make people more used to suffering, ready for Mars."

Sniper: "I sort of caused the war too, that doesn't mean we abolish the Olympics. So, Utopia caused the war, there should be consequences, then let's go to space."

9A: "Gordian wants to do great things too, advance the human brain, make electronic immortality, they just want to do it here in safety, with less pain. It's not a bad ambition."

Sniper: "Will Utopia prevent it?"

9A: "No. Or . . . maybe."

Sniper: "You sure fidget with that hat like Mycroft, when you don't like your own answers."

9A: "Yeah. Thing is, Utopia might need Earth to stay a bit bad, harsh, to keep the fire lit. Or that might not be true anymore, they may just make improving Earth slower while they focus on space. It would've meant more generations lost before immortality comes, but with Cato's resurrection tech—that's why there could be a compromise."

Sniper: "Compromise sounds great. Meanwhile, let's exonerate Utopia—if they're innocent and being massacred over propaganda, that should stop. And we can stop it. And there should be consequences for the Brillists as much as for Utopia and me. And you."

9A: "Yeah. True."

Sniper: "And then let's go to space. Are you okay? I'm intimate with a lot of people, so it's not my first time making someone cry this many times in one conversation, but this is on the high end, even for me. Normal for Mycroft, of course."

9A: "Yeah. Normal for Mycroft." [Laughter] "I just . . . I didn't think I'd get to . . . You make it sound so doable. So possible. It hadn't felt for a while like Utopia could win, or like we could keep both good things, but . . . Thank you, this is a great way to . . . a great end."

Sniper: "Great way to begin, you mean."

No. That's not what it meant, that somber face, that smile, bittersweet, fidgeting with my hat, those don't signal 'begin.' They signal 'end.' Did you sense this too, Sniper? Something off, the pacing of my good successor's words, the eye contact diminishing, fidgeting with my hat. Is something wrong? Is that slight edge of tension in your shoulders sensing what I sense?

9A: "Mm."

Sniper: "I think this is a great beginning. Believe me, finding a former Hivefellow on MASON's throne? I'd be jumping for joy if the restraints let me."

9A: "Mm. It'll be Mycroft soon, though. Not me, Mycroft."

Sniper: "Mycroft on the throne?"

9A: "Yeah. I figured it out, how it has to happen when Mycroft comes back. We need Mycroft, not me."
Sniper: "Well, the people who bet on Mycroft Canner as successor back when they were ten years old are sure going to be surprised by the longshot win."
9A: [Laughter]
Sniper: "It's true, people bet on it! A kid that close to MASON . . ."
9A: [Laughter continues]
Sniper: "Do you need a glass of water?"

A long pause. Why is the question hard, my successor? Why do you pause, and gaze, eyes glazed with strange philosophy, reflection's inward smile? Is something wrong?

9A: "No. No, I don't need anything. You gave me what I wanted. More. Thank you."
Sniper: "Until next time!"
9A: "Mm."

Now they move too fast. A wave summons the guards to take them both away, Sniper being marched back toward custody. Hold on. Freeze-frame will show it, something off in their expressions, what is that? Sniper's—that's worry. Yes, I'm sure, alarm bells, Sniper, you think something's strange. I need a Brillist. Tell me, someone, even Felix Faust, what are these faces that I'm seeing?

9A: ". . . hard . . ."

The tape, it only caught one word.

Sniper: "What?"
9A: ". . . hard to be angry when I'm this grateful for the chance to . . ."
Sniper: "Spoken on behalf of the losing side: agreed."

Well said, Sniper. But wait, no, now your tension's fading, healed by that quick joke. Don't laugh it off. Tell me you felt it. Now the guards are turning you away, you can't see what I see, my young successor's face all wrong, the eyes that stare too deep as if into a mirror. Turn! Please, Sniper! Turn and see something is— There! You turned!

Sniper: "Wait! You never said your name."
9A: [Pause] "That's not the part of me I care about people remembering."
Sniper: "I'd still like to know my new friend's name."

Five seconds. The recording counts it out, five seconds' silence. Deep the Anonymous should think before giving a name, but this . . . I know what this face is, this feeling, as Achilles knows, as Bryar Kosala knows, and Saladin, and MASON on the Almagest, and Xiaoliu Accursed-Through-the-Ages-Guildbreaker who did not struggle as the black-gloved hand closed on his throat. This is *that* strange philosophy, the inner mirror stilled as preservation's will to battle gives way in the breaths between when we commit to ride behind the famous horseman and when Thanatos comes. Suicide? You recognize it don't you, Sniper? Suicidal thoughts so often seen on Cato, or did Cato never . . . No, there is a difference between reaching out a hand toward the horseman, and clasping arms. And then my successor raises my hat to put it on, and smiles, a smile too special, too at peace.

9A: "No one."

Wait, I remember. I remember this. This face on Sniper, I remember. It was strange. This was the face, wonder mixed with friendship, so beautiful as Sniper and I parted in the bright interrogation room, we . . . Do you give everybody that face when you say goodbye, Sniper? Or . . . The hallway has a camera. Yes, I've found it. That should show. If night's philosophy is still on my successor's face leaving that cell, I'll fly—you know, reader, that I can fly—fly to the office this instant to lecture . . . No, wrong hallway footage, that's just me. Easy mistake, same uniform, twin wheelchairs, I need it for the vertigo. Rewinding. My successor enters. Did I skip it? Forward . . . There I leave. Backward . . . My successor enters. Forward . . . I have my hat on as I leave. Someone has hacked the tape. Brillists? No, Perry! No, a plot of bold O.S. to rescue Sniper! They could still win, not by world conquest but taking one Life. Or . . . But I did see that face, Sniper's, that strange expression . . . Rewind, my successor enters, forward . . .

9A: "No one."

How can you say that with that face, tranquil, you

Night's tranquility, twin brothers Sleep and

Reader, I

Why am I really in this wheelchair? Vertigo, nausea, symptoms, my head

I asked the guards just now for my successor. They said not to worry, but those faces. I'll ask Huxley if

I asked Huxley. They said not to worry, back to work. Huxley, did the flinch in your eyes lie as badly as I think you did?

Reader I think I know I

Reader,

Reader,

I don't believe that I am Mycroft Canner. I must clarify since I am no one else, but I don't think these arms held Bridger, nor that this tongue tasted Apollo's flesh. I believe the heart that started beating in the womb of Chaerephon Canner thirty-three years ago stopped beating months back in the salt and blackness of Poseidon's sea. But that young *will* still moving in the structure of our world cannot believe these arms, that shielded him from all the world, could fail. I promised Bridger that I would always come back, and a child's love will hold me to that promise past the dimming of the Sun if anything he touched survives.

I think my Saladin was first. I think I did drown back above Atlantis on the war's first day, the blast and black Poseidon. I have those shards of memory, of hunting in the shallows of despair, the salt, seeking a body, island after island where it could have drifted, that was Saladin hunting for me. My Saladin. My Saladin who already wore my skin as costume, just as Bridger in his last hour donned the Major's army green. My Saladin who, if he heard Bridger's question quiet in the world itself, kinder than Providence but cruel—*Will you give up your life, your flesh, to bring back Mycroft?*—would not have waited a whole heartbeat before he answered, "Yes." So I came back. Flesh, life—I haven't seen him since then, Saladin, not once—he gave it all to me. Became me, irrevocably, like Bridger and Achilles, and Cato-Helen. I kept hitting my head, my Saladin a little taller than me, and I kept hitting my head but didn't understand. I killed him, reader! Saladin! It was his life—as dear to me as all the world—his life I wasted, not my own! I didn't know! I thought I was just being reckless with myself! I don't want to outlive! I don't want to outlive! I don't want to outlive! We should have died together in one ecstasy, or within an hour, hearts conjoined, or he could outlive me as we had always planned, my Saladin roaming the Earth, free, beautiful, not me, here, broken. Me alone.

And then I tried to save MASON.

So I, and Saladin who gave me this, his everything, I died again. I died there at the Almagest, hunting for MASON's body, hoping to change the ending, but I died. A lot of gods, when we oppose them, teach us hubris with the lesson death. But Bridger needed me. Still needs me, always needs, forever—children do. And my successor realized slowly how it is that I come back. And they were next. Closest. They loved me, reader. Loved me, with the rot in me and everything. They loved, mourned even Mycroft Canner, wished such kindness for me—you remember, reader, you remember when they prayed to you across the sea of time to reach back with your great and distant powers from your great and distant someday, not to save me (they knew I didn't want that) but to whisper to my dying soul (and theirs) the answer: if the seeds have flown. They knew. They loved me deep enough to know I would want that, not rescue, that. But later on, they realized Mycroft Canner can't be granted rest. And they already wore my uniform, costume enough to be acted upon by Bridger's power, which still ripples through the Earthly fruit bowl month by month as well as peach by peach. I think my brave successor faded slowly, over months, that we alternated sometimes, in those moments when they felt Earth needed Mycroft more than them. This chronicle tracks log-ins, and there was no other log-in, all those early interruptions, even that first chapter where I died back at Atlantis, that quick note (that lie!) that said that Mycroft had survived, there was only one author, reader, them, they wrote those words—but *they* were sometimes *me*. They realized slowly. Then the ghost of Saladin, he came to ask if they were ready for the final sacrifice, but they weren't yet, they still wanted . . . Sniper. Sniper, why couldn't you have stayed away? You were the last thing holding them before they made it permanent, donning my hat—the final touch of costume as the doodled cherry in the center once let Bridger make a rock a pie. Suicide, there is no other name for it, my brave successor assenting to the transformation, giving up their life and flesh for mine, and they were angry, yes, angry but grateful that there was a way to give their life to fix . . . to be . . . I don't want this! I'm sorry! I thought it was just my life I was risking, not theirs! Not those two who loved me, who I loved so much, my closest, my . . . I won't do it again! I won't risk myself again, I promise, please, just . . . please don't take away . . .

I can't ask it, reader. I can't pray. I can't. I feel the answer. I can't have them back. They're gone. I killed them. Killed them when I threw my life away, my life that I knew they would give their lives for, and what can I do? What can I do? What can I do? What can I do? I just . . . I won't do it again! I, please! I won't do it again! I'll be more careful, just—but who would You take next? Who loves me? Sniper? Papa? Huxley darkly knowing what we need to win? Have you already taken others? Was it really I who so improbably survived the sinking of the *Shearwater*, or did one of that storm-wise, sea-wise bash' that pledged to risk their all to see me safely home give flesh as well as life? How many have there been? I won't do it again! I swear! I'll be more careful, just, please, don't take more of them the way you took . . .

But I always come back.

Kohaku—seer—said it, my sentence, my next labor, and the next, one lifetime, three now, but before I've sweated out my term as oarsman on Apollo's flagship, I must lead Utopia to some new world untouched by Distance, where the very oars and sails we use to battle grim Poseidon are undreamed. So long as he, Apollo Lord of Embarkations, finds new worlds to make his distant aim, I must follow.

I'm tired.

Saladin, Kohaku, No One, brave Achilles, see? This god who ever leads men onto ships commands me even from the grave to rise and toil once more beneath the bitter sun without you all.

And I always come back.

Chapter the TWENTY-SEVENTH

Melodrama

Written December 18–22, 2455
Events of December 16
Las Huelgas

I know how it must have happened. We all do, the tired script, eternal passions, love, betrayal, hate. We here in Alexandria received at first only a two-line summary, but with just that, before the interviews, I could already see it acted out as on a stage. But it is a lie that says the story is eternal, that these roles—Lover, Beloved, Villain—are primordial. We made them up, and if we act them, still that is our choice, eternal only while we assent to keep performing. Each time the curtain rises on the final scene, the hero could declare, "I am not this," and walk away. We want to stop it, urge them in our minds: Valmont, Othello, vengeful Clytemnestra, let it go! Each generation gets a little better, I think, at walking away, warned by past generations' sad examples, yet the archetypes, once met, live in us always, dormant like viruses that can awaken when some other virus—cruel like *she*—attacks.

We freed the King of Spain. That started it. Sniper, Hiveguard came through, afire to free so great a leader and secure so strong a check on their ascendant Foe. My poor successor (or should I say "I"?) asked Sniper for the best, and one hero delivered us another: Ockham Prospero Saneer.

Sniper's predecessor had begun the war in jail, awaiting trial for concealing sister Thisbe's recreation murders. We last heard of him fourteen months ago, October the eleventh, 2454, when an attempt to rescue him from his imprisonment near Essen sparked the Rhine-Ruhr violence that for months spread south and west, overflowing into Brussels, where it hid Gordian's capture of the emperor-king. Yet as the mobs rose around them, Essen's gallant legal staff honored prisoners' rights to timely trials and plodded on despite the war, the silence, sieges, everything, treating their celebrity prisoner no different from the rest. He pled *guilty* to three counts of concealing homicidal death but *not guilty* to being an accessory—the court judged he had been accessory to the third murder only, Luca Cormer, the one killed *after* he discovered Thisbe's hobby. Polylaw kicked in, the standard system, Prospero's Hive paying each crime's prearranged fee to the victim's Hive, and each Hive punishing or recompensing their own. The Humanists, of all Hives, have the purest cash system, scorning the Cousins' offers to waive fines if criminals take rehabilitation seminars, Europe's if they do volunteer work, Masons' if they undergo public shaming or distribute punishment across the bash', but no—the Humanists declare—our Members' hours are too excellent to give to other Hives, though we must pay two, three, five, ten times over. Thus, on November tenth—as my successor watched the dollhouse videos, and I aboard the *Shearwater* was visited by grim seer Kohaku Mardi near the Cyclades—the little Essen courtroom quietly announced the leader of O.S. would suffer nothing but a fine, and even this his Hive would pay for him, since all he did, he did for the Hive's sake.

Riot ensued, and mob justice might have cost the world another hero if not that an enemy (my Enemy) had been at work. Peacewash: Tully had just announced it, and some mixture of mercy and mocking irony decided it would be fitting if this most soldierlike of all Alliance Members, the officer who bore a sidearm and the right to kill lifelong even in peace, had to sit out the war, forbidden to touch arms or serve his Hive. So, Ockham Prospero Saneer could not join Hiveguard, but when Romanova's offices cried out for helping hands, his hands, stained with new ink and old blood, proved invaluable. For a long year Prospero served as security chief, ration officer, crisis manager, walking onto riotfields, commanding pause and bringing leaders to the table. Thus at the twelfth month, when Sniper's message found him, it was Romanova's uniform Prospero wore, and it was in Romanova's name he undertook the liberation of Europe's imprisoned emperor.

How to beat Brillists? Prospero took his time, four weeks assembling his random team, for randomness is Brillist calculations' overthrow. Prospero set timers, walking a random number of minutes through the streets, speaking with many, turning left or right as dice prescribed, then at the buzzer asked the nearest person who seemed likely: will you join a mission for Romanova? So, with a plan devised by people Faust had no way to predict, the bold raid on the train occurred near Gdańsk December the sixteenth, and His Royal and Imperial Majesty of Spain and Europe, slightly bruised and overjoyed, was free.

So it began. You see, we never asked Sniper to send the king to us. To Brussels we expected, but Faust would expect that, too, and Prospero knew it. Sniper asked for Prospero's best, and Prospero gave it, a trick held back so long, for Prospero knew, as my young self knew as I planned my two weeks, that an art used once will soon be counterspelled. So, only now, with so precious a passenger, did the Saneer-Weeksbooth scion employ the method he developed over months, an override to bypass lockshell and command one car to fly as normal through the maelstrom for one hop, straight from Gdańsk to Spain, Burgos, Las Huelgas, to touch down on the ancient tower of the abbey which has seen many a birth night and a death night too of Queens and Kings of Spain.

So, free at last, and home, and glad at heart, brimming with thankful prayers, and bypassing the guards and servants who did not think to watch the roof, the king and his escort rushed through the ancient halls to the austere stone passage where Madame's voice echoed clear.

« Ah ! . . . Ah ! . . . Ah ! . . . Aah ! . . . Oui ! Oui ! . . . Oh ! . . . Oh ! . . . Mon brave ! . . . Mon chef-d'œuvre ! . . . Aah ! . . . Mon monstre ! »

No doubt. None. There is a rhythm to climax, and this queen's king knows it well. Two waiting ladies drawn by the sound of footsteps tried to intervene, crowding the king with tugging hands and rustling skirts, but Prospero's team shoved them aside as Spain's face flushed with grief and rage. Two fierce blows at the bolted door, and tree rings which may well have seen the death of Charlemagne splintered and gave. Two cries within as the door crashed open, a man's, a woman's, two figures on the bed locked in the fierce, athletic maximum of love. Blood makes pale-skinned faces so extreme in extreme times. The lady's face turned corpse white, a mask of horror almost as pale as the white shift and petticoats which framed her yellow corset like snow-pure petals around a daisy's sunny heart. Her lover's face flushed scarlet, almost purple with the blood of rage, of shock, of lust still pumping through his strong frame as he turned, snarling like a lion ready to do battle for his conquest when some rival king of beasts, drawn by the blood scent, comes to challenge him for his fresh-slain prey. Then, quick as breaking rain, the snarl faded, the set brows eased into a different passion, horror and . . . contrition? Does contrition find a place still in the breast that willed to burn this world to ashes, all to get at her?

"Spain!" Perry gasped—yes, reader, it was he, our era's toxic villain Merion-Casimir-cursed-Thersites-Croucher-Perry-Kraye. Madame called him *mon monstre*, 'my monster,' in the heat of passion, and *chef-d'œuvre*, 'masterpiece.' She was half right, I think, for if—as in old usage—masterpiece is that first product of the artisan's maturity which earns guild entry and the title master crafts(wo)man, then Perry-Kraye, the villain nursed on all the poisons she could syphon from the mud, was her debut of virtuosity. Yet Perry is no monster. 'Monster,' reader, is a title of honor, grim but great, equal of heroes, and I reserve it ever for great beings, for great Thomas Hobbes, Nietzsche, for fearsome Hannibal nightmare of empires, for Dominic, and dreadful Saladin, and I. The wide world needs monsters like Hobbes as deer need wolves to keep herds swift and mobile. But Perry-Kraye? A gnawing worm, a parasite, a dead layer that festers in the bosom of the world and drags both good and evil down to suffocation. Perry-Kraye, who burns and grinds upon his inner wheel of hate like cursed Ixion—yes . . . yes, Perry is much like Ixion, I realize, Ixion the son of Ares who invented parricide, slaying his father-in-law over a petty quarrel, yet Zeus pitied him in his after-murder exile, even brought him to Olympus to the table of the gods, granting this Outsider a second chance. And in ingratitude, the Outsider lusted for Queen Hera, betrayed the kindness—rarest kindness!—of the gods, and earned the first instance ever in Hades's halls of true eternal fire.

Isabel Carlos II, king, emperor, statesman, husband, human being, snatched the pistol from the nearest of his armed escort and fired into Perry's gaping face. And fired again!—again!—again!—again!—the body dropped—again!—again!—again!—again!—again!—again!—again!—again!—

again!—again!—again!—again!—*click*—*click*—the cartridge empty—*click*—*click*—*click*—*click*—*click*—*click*—*click*—*click*—*click*—*click*—

"Basta, Su Majestad." Expert Prospero put his gentle, dark-stained hand over the king's, which locked like rigor mortis around the empty gun. "*Se acabó.* (It's over.)"

Tears as Spain dropped the weapon. Did the tears start only then? Or had they welled the instant the door opened, tears and gravity too slow to keep up with the speed gunsmiths have gifted Death?

What of the lady? I was not there to see it, reader, yet the heart inside me knows that, gazing on the ruin of this villain who had lived (a man must live for something) utterly for *her*, for her undoing and his ever-hot revenge, seeing him spattered scarlet on her bed, across her skin, her christening as truly *femme fatale*, she smiled—yes, by golden-shrouded Ida! she smiled, like the heartless fiend she had played with him, then donned a different mask for her next scene. « *Oh ! Majesté ! Dieu merci ! J'avais tellement peur !* » She fluttered forward, pale as horror. "He was going to kill me! He scaled the walls! Oh, if you'd heard his threats! I couldn't—"

"Everyone out of the room, please." Prospero stepped between the lady and the king.

The chance to be affronted brought some color to her face. "Out of my way! This is my husband!" She called over Prospero's obstructing shoulder, "He was a fiend, *cher Majesté*! A fiend!"

"Out of the room, everyone," steady Prospero directed, walking the king back. "This is a crime scene—careful where you step." He gesture-ordered one of his team to take and wrap in careful cloth the fallen weapon, which the Peace-washed hero must not touch.

"The things he said he'd do! Thank God Your Majesty came before—"

"How long has Perry been here?" Prospero asked it coldly, nodding down at the long white gentleman's nightshirt and the eighteenth-century banyan dressing gown—*Spain's* nightshirt and *Spain's* banyan, rich brocade—which lay in a rumpled pile where the villain had discarded them for this fresh round of lust. "How many days? Weeks?" All around the room the traces—pairs of empty dishes, gentleman's clothes both worn and fresh, two different razors on the vanity—all testified to dual habitation.

Shy eyes avoiding his had no good answers. "I had no other way to buy time. He wanted revenge! Drawn out so he could savor—"

"Was Perry alone?"

Madame stood tall now, the loose rear locks of her silver-laced brown hair (her own, for once) snaking down her bosom. "Who are you to be giving orders, anyway? I am a queen, and this—"

"Was Perry alone?" The lifelong guardian of millions raised his voice. "Or are there other active hostiles in the building? Are we still in danger?"

"Oh. Yes, there are others. His secretary Saunders I know is here, and Kestrel Wang his second-in command, and Théogène Drum was here, I'm not quite sure how many."

"Right. Mu, Meiwes, Savang, Liga, go secure the premises." Prospero looked past his people to the little crowd of ladies and attendant gentlemen summoned to the hallway by the noise. "Can one of you help guide them?"

The foremost lady raised her hand, dark African and stunning in her champagne gown.

"Thank you. Name?"

"Uranie, Monsieur."

"Thanks. Mu, take your team with Uranie. Müller, go find a European consulate office; we have diplomatic immunity issues to navigate. Aquifex, watch this room. Pruteanu, escort Member D'Arouet where they can wash and change. The rest of you step back."

"You dare take me from my husband!"

He dared indeed. "The king's in shock, they're in no condition to talk now."

It was true, all Spain's rigor had transformed to shaking, like a child after terror, or a dried winter leaf clinging to the bare branch through the storm.

"You have no right to touch me! None of you!" Madame recoiled from the officer with a fluttering shove. « *Majesté !* »

". . . s . . ." A sound almost too slight to hear rose from the king's lips as he stared at the once-human wreck which lay before him in the pooling gore.

"¿What was that? *¿Su Majestad?*" Prospero stepped between the king and corpse. "*¿Majestad?* ¿Isabel Carlos? ¿Can you look at me?"

More tears in long, thin trails down Spain's blanched cheeks as desperate eyes locked on a fellow human face. "A . . . sa . . . n . . ."

Prospero raised his hands gently, tempted to hold the king's trembling shoulders, but hesitated just an inch away. "I'm listening."

"¿Are they safe now?" Spain's voice broke free at last, that gentle voice which even fractious Parliament respected so much that their babble, wild like the seas, would calm. "¿Spain? ¿And Europe? ¿Are they safe now? ¿Did I stop him? ¿Will it stop?"

The human who is Ockham Prospero Saneer grasped the shaking shoulders with his warm, supporting hands. "I think so."

The wordless, trembling king pressed himself into those strong arms—a stranger's arms, known barely two hours—and wept.

It wasn't heat-of-passion, *in flagrante*. History may say it was, one more melodrama come to its crisis like so many stale pageants before, but it was not flesh jealousy, not even honor that so overwhelmed His Most Catholic Majesty that he committed, in that cursed boudoir, a mortal sin. I don't think it was vengeance either, though Perry's vendetta claimed so many lives, peers, colleagues, friends, the whole of Parliament, even Leonor Valentín, Isabel Carlos's prodigal, entitled, yet still precious firstborn son. No. I believe, and Prospero who witnessed it believes, it was the danger, fear that seized the good king's mind and strangled conscience: fear of this abomination of a man, this grinding Ixion who burned, and burned, and would keep burning, wrecking, spoiling, burning down the world, and whom no grace, no second chance—the king had tried!—

could turn from this infectious purpose. Though Perry's mind piled thought on thought unto infinity, it would yet have no thought in it but ruin, and the king knew it. *I can stop the wheel, put out the fire*—those were the thoughts that fired shot on shot long past sanity's limit. Alas, no one will blame him.

Hobbes: "True, Mycroft, for the Sovereign has the right to do whatever he judges necessary for the peace and security of his Subjects."

Reader: "Yet I thought, friend Thomas, by thine own strict rule, this Isabel Carlos is no Sovereign, having left true Sovereignty in Europe's several Assemblies and the People which selects them."

Hobbes: "True, attentive Master Reader, he is at most one small lobe of the great brain-organ that leads Europe now, yet multitudes desire and imagine him to be their Sovereign and will celebrate as affirmation of that fantasy his exercise here of a Sovereign's right to judge and act."

All too true, Master Hobbes, the world will celebrate. And nobody will blame the king for killing Perry, that's the cruelest part. Because in his own faith, poor man, the sins we justify, the sins our friends, our times, our Earthly laws affirm were good, right, necessary, sins the trolley problem tells us were a good for all the world, those are the hardest to repent of. So the whispers Prospero says he could not quite make out as he walked the gentle king into the hallway, I think those were prayers, desperate, the king begging his all-seeing but few-forgiving God to heal this sinner's heart enough to help him someday, please, somehow, repent of such a justified murder.

Now Prospero's crew dispersed to hunt for Perry's allies, elusive as smoke. For the king and queen, Prospero prescribed the steps of human care: baths, clean clothes, drinks of water. For himself, he first took care of this and that, logistics and security, but then returned to the fatal room, gazing in silence at the wreck upon the floor that had once held the human essence, fierce and terrible, which left that stolen Seven-Ten List in his bash'house, cruel first domino. Look, ba'sibs, we have a little justice. There the villain lies who used us, pawns in his vendetta. Look, Lesley, Cardie, Eureka, Sidney, Cato, Typers, sister Thisbe, *Mukta*, yes, old *Mukta* too, treasured heirloom almost four centuries old, reduced to ashes in the Battle of Cielo de Pájaros along with all the proud and comfy trappings of our murdered *ibasho*—we have a little justice.

So Prospero lingers a pensive moment, then turns to a chamber one hall down from the one Thanatos visited, our setting for Act V, Scene ii.

QUEEN JOYCE and two Ladies seated.
Enter KING ISABEL CARLOS and PROSPERO.

« *Majesté!* Are you recovering? » Madame leapt to her feet. « I've been so frightened! »

"Gently, they're still recovering." Prospero moved to block the lady as she rose.

"You again!" Madame fixed her commanding glare upon him. She was dressed now in a queenly gown of peacock colors, blues and teals and golds, beaded with crystal, with a ruddy undertone within the silks that sometimes caught the light. "This interference is a disgrace to your uniform!"

Prospero stood calm. "It is Romanova's role to interfere when interference is necessary."

"To separate a wife and husband is unnatural! How dare—"

"I wanted to see you, my queen," the king interrupted softly. "I wanted to hear your account." He sat, lowering himself with care onto the bench farthest from the ladies, nearest to the door.

Madame made a graceful effort to sidestep Prospero, which he blocked firmly, but, she—oh, artful one!—knew just how he would move, and twirled about him like a dancing partner, landing in a whirl of skirts to kneel and grasp the king's knees. « *Majesté,* He tried to kill our Son! Our own dear Son! At Alexandria! He made me listen! Planned to gloat over my grief as I heard our dear Jehovah breathe His last! But when it failed, when news came that the Masons won, then he threatened to kill me! Finish his revenge! I ha— » A quick sob broke her words. « I had no other way to . . . »

"I do not blame you for anything you did to save yourself." The king replied in English—why? To make sure Prospero could understand, one witness free from her manipulation? "But Merion has been here for six weeks, I understand?"

The lady hesitated. « It was a nightmare! Every day, he swore he'd kill me. Every day, I had to buy another! Like Scheherazade! I never knew which hour he might— »

"I believe it began as you say," the king interjected, "but you had many chances to end it, to escape, to fight, to call for aid. You have more than thirty staff and servants here, but instead of asking for help, you ordered them to treat Merion and their crew as honored guests, to set up offices for them. You let Merion use this place as headquarters and wear my clothes, even ordered new clothing to be made for them."

« If you could have heard him, *Majesté*! »

Isabel Carlos did not avoid her eyes, but his gaze was so distant and exhausted, it is hard to say he met them, either. "You were seen walking together in the gardens, laughing, dining, hanging on Merion's arm."

She gave a hurt pout. « What servants say— »

"You were *filmed* together in the gardens laughing, hanging on Merion's arm."

That had no easy answer, so the lady simply gazed up, silent, gripping his knees, eyes sparkling with tears.

Spain's figure was already too limp to sigh. "I do believe that threat and abuse can hold people in too much terror to resist abusers, but I know you, *ma reine* (my queen), you are not one controlled by fear. You are one who controls." A pause. A long pause as his tired eyes gazed into hers. "Did you think I was dead?"

She rose, exquisite motion like a rose un-blooming as the petals of her wide-spread skirts gathered around her like a bud. "No, *Majesté,*" she answered gravely, cleanly, English, clear. "No, I did not."

"Thank you." Fatigue and pain in his eyes, older eyes, aged like all of ours by this vampire year. "You know highly I value the honor of my—"

« Yes, » she interrupted as she settled on the bench beside him. « But Your

Majesty also knows how normal such a little dalliance is. How rare, elusive as the unicorn, is that historic royal couple which did not at some point take the practical view and grant themselves a reasonable liberty to— »

"This is the modern day, *ma reine.* We hold ourselves to higher standards."

« It's been more than a full year, Isabel! » A tender smile as she took his hand, laced her fingers through his. « I know *Votre Majesté* is so sweet and so strict, I knew you would wait for me, and I love you for it all the more! But you also know your appetite and mine are very different. I have needs, *mon amour,* and once it had begun with Merion, I saw no need to cut it off while it was satisfying me, particularly since attempting to do so would have been dangerous—he never stopped threatening, daily, gloating that it would all end with my death and his complete revenge. »

Tenderly, in French now. « But you could have stopped it, yes? You do believe you could have stopped it, fled him, asked for aid? »

She stroked his shoulder. « I can have needs, and meet them too, and still be yours. »

« You took vows, *ma reine.* We took vows, both of us, with the world watching. »

« As many people do, yet marriage does not mean surrendering the right to make my own choices with my own body, especially *in extremis.* »

« For us it does. You chose this, Joyce, you chose to marry one of at most a hundred people in the world who, by law, are not the masters of our own bodies. Treasonable adultery, Madame, it's still a live concept in many strat laws, and Europe is looking to its strat laws to set precedents for its new monarchy. »

She laughed, light, puckish. « We have an Heir already, *Majesté,* this little episode is no threat to the dynasty. »

« That's not the problem. » His Majesty was still too weak to shout, but the tension in his words suggested he would have. « Adultery as treason is a hateful concept, sexist, primitive, it hasn't been enforced in centuries, but you're going to make it take root again in Europe. Can't you see that? Do you know how hard I've been working to make this new imperial monarchy fair and modern? It's the first new monarchy since equal rights. It could have been the first completely free of inequality, but you're so set on play-acting the past, you're going to drag the whole Hive Membership into the barbaric thinking that made male adultery commonplace and female criminal. »

She squeezed his hand. « But *Votre Majesté* can stop a treason trial easily. »

« No, I can't. That's the point. I've worked hard to set up a constitution where I don't have the power to interfere like that. »

Hobbes: "True, un-Sovereign, too true."

« If the people and legislatures want a trial, there's nothing I can do. »

Madame smiled her sweet, warm, devastating smile. « *Votre Majesté* does not have to tell anyone what really happened between me and Merion. »

« I killed Merion *in flagrante delicto.* » Such words should have force, volume, but he still sounded stunned, burnt out inside by thinking on the deed.

« There's no need for details about when Merion came, or how things stood between us. All the witnesses are our people, save these Romanovans you brought with you, who I expect can keep a secret for the greater good. Keeping the more private parts discreet, what happened here is that *Votre Majesté* heroically took down the mastermind responsible for assassinating dozens of Europe's greatest leaders and plunging the world in war. You are a hero. Everyone will call you so, the hero of the war! »

« Lies are a— » He caught himself, His Most Catholic Majesty, before he said what he truly thinks lies are. "Poison."

« Then you, dear *Majesté,* must pick your poison. »

« What? »

« *Votre Majesté* can let this discreet omission give the world a hero to look up to, leadership, justice, closure for the many Merion wronged, or you can give them the messy treason trial of your empress, which will indeed, as you fear, set a . . . traditionalist tenor for your new imperial line. »

« I shall not . . . » he began, but trailed off.

« I want it to be your choice, *Majesté.* I »—she placed her white hand with its sparkling bracelets against her snow-white breast—« am prepared to play whatever role *Votre Majesté* thinks will serve Spain and Europe best, even if you decide that public honesty is the best course. If you decide you should give the world a model of accountability instead of heroism, sacrificing our marriage to demonstrate how this new era's leaders must not keep secrets as we used to, if you think that model will help people more than a victorious hero would, then I will trust your choice and face whatever hardships it bring upon me, and our Son. »

He, softly: « I will not push the world toward valorizing homicide. One should not kill. »

A second's pause before her face bloomed, smile and blush and wonder. « Like Son, like father. »

« What? »

« You're both too good. » She planted a kiss upon his cheek. « We'll find a way. » Her warmest smile, exquisite. « It won't be easy, keeping people from celebrating the death of the man who committed—shall we call it 'World Arson,' trying to burn the whole world down? » She smoothed back his mussed hair. « But Danaë is right, if Europe's nation-strats are proud, much of what we have to be proud of is that we have become better over time, voicing and answering the call to hold ourselves to something higher. Voltaire and Diderot believed as much, and now the children I raised on their works are pushing our new era to become better yet again. I don't know if the public can regret the death of a villain as pure as Merion, but now, with you and dear Jehovah at the helm, now is the time to push them to. »

Change in his face, some color, as if the healthy complexity of being human, dormant in his shock, had woken up. « Danaë said that? About Europe? »

« Yes, in the negotiations with Lesley Saneer and *la chiotte* (the puppy). Did you not watch? »

His eyes grew fragile.

« You couldn't? Poor *Majesté*! I don't know where you've been! What happened to you? » Her hands about him now, her body pressing, warm.

So, he tells her, reader, and she listens, shedding tears of rage and grief for his captivity, cursing her brother, Felix, expressing all the tender, fragile, volatile passions the decorum-stiffened king cannot allow himself to show. So she won him again, her king, her emperor, her love, for it was not a rash and shallow thing, this partnership of wise and weathered grown-ups, not quickly shattered by the slings and arrows of outrageous politics, or war, or even her outrageous self. Some loves are both difficult and strong. But it was shattered by vengeance, shattered as the yellow-tinted evening watched the king prepare to join his fresh-forgiven bride for their first meal together as husband and wife.

"I'm sorry, *Su Majestad*." Even Ockham Prospero Saneer was hesitant bringing this news. "Your queen is dead."

"¿What?"

"Doctors are examining the body. We're not sure if it was some agent of Perry's that we failed to round up, or whether Perry left the poison in some object in the queen's room, possibly their makeup. I'm sorry."

So the melodrama ends, an offstage death handcrafted by this patient, constant villain who schemed twenty-nine years to take the villainess who made him down with him, piecing the gears together like a clockmaker to ensure his burning wheel would have a twin for her. Of course he planned past death. Likely, Perry had fifty traps set to outlive him, masterworks carved from his restless soul with blades of hate as woodcarvers craft knot patterns a hundred times more intricate than life's organic knots. But I don't think we needed her to die. My good successor marked Madame's defeat four months ago when winds of change scoured her influence from Seven-Ten Lists, proving her poison weaker than we feared. That was a good defeat. This second fall—undone so fittingly by her own self-made monster—this just makes it all feel gross again. Shows Him more Pain and Death. A trial might have been fine, an accident, the justice of the gods, but I wish, reader, Perry-Kraye had had no part in bringing down Madame, that she had just been beaten by our world becoming better than it was. By you.

"¿*Majestad?* ¿Do you need anything? ¿Any questions?"

What of the third actor in our melodrama? Isabel Carlos, twice-widowed king? Sometimes, the coal of an old fire looks dead and black but still hides sparks inside, so any touch of breath can stir it back to life and beauty, fierce against the dark. And sometimes, it's just dead. Yet I dare any eye to spot the moment of the coal's last change from stillness to forever's stillness. Just so, I doubt that anyone, save Faust himself perhaps, could see a change in the black eyes and portrait-somber visage of the king. He paused. Prospero says he paused a long time.

"¿Do you think . . . ?" Spain began.

"¿What?"

It hurts to watch a fellow human cry, but it hurts differently to watch him force himself not to. "¿Do you think posterity can regret the death of a villain like Madame D'Arouet?"

Chapter the TWENTY-EIGHTH

An Alphabet for Strangers

Written December 27–31, 2455
Events of December 17–26
Alexandria

May I ask you a question, Master Hobbes? A complex question?

Hobbes: "Of course, Mycroft. Thy questions are a pleasure! Yet take care it be not over-tedious; our sovereign Reader waits."

Reader: "It's fine, I usually enjoy these little interjections."

I: Then, in your opinion, Master Hobbes, are they right who say we can learn something of the nature of our Maker from the nature of the creatures that He made?

Hobbes: "I write of Man and Common-wealth, Mycroft, not of theology."

Reader: "That's a strange dodge, friend Thomas. My edition has 300 pages of thy thoughts on Christian matters and the so-termed Kingdom of Darkness."

Hobbes: "Oh, voracious Reader! I'd long since despaired of anybody reading past Part II of my *Leviathan!*"

Reader: "I confess I gave it less attention than the rest; the doctrinal anxieties of thy barbaric century are rather alien."

Hobbes: "Understandable, good Reader, but, as our guide knows, mine is not the technical theology of scripture-mongers, but that vein of inquiry pursued by many of my era, from my own master Francis Bacon to Mycroft's *Patriarch* and *Philosophe,* who sought to understand such grand things as Creation and Providence while relying on Experience and Sense and Reason, talents Nature gifted us for our self-education long before prophets offered supplements."

I: That 'Nature' gifted, Master Hobbes? Not God?

Hobbes: "Ha! Art thou too, Mycroft, trying to catch me out as an atheist? All Europe tried to prove me one for centuries—thou shalt not succeed where thousands failed."

I: I wouldn't dream of trying, Dread Leviathan, I know you will evade all nets until the end of time, I merely . . . Let's posit for the moment that there is a Maker of Nature . . .

Hobbes: "We can posit that."

I: And that that Maker made the creature 'human.'

Hobbes: "Yes, with all the attributes I have observed: aggressive, power-hungry, born and raised in life's eternal war. You practice, as it were, theopsychology and fear the human's Maker is the same?"

I: Some say He made us in His image.

Hobbes: "Ah, but remember, Mycroft, that idea, humanity as God's portrait, that comes from doctrine, not from observation. Reason tells us only that Nature's Maker must have the character of one who would make Nature: humans, but also trees, and atmospheres, and stars, and hurricanes, and nightmare creatures of the deep-sea depths, and gnats, and Common-wealths."

I: And Time, Distance, and Death . . .

Hobbes: "Yes, Death, so like Distance, our last voyage, the great leap in the dark."

Reader: "There's a familiar phrase. Those were your last words, weren't they, friend Thomas? 'My last voyage, a great leap in the dark.'"

Hobbes: "My last, yes, but in one sense only, Reader, after all, you make new meaning from my words, my books, my seeds of thought each time you summon them, so we might say my last words and last voyage both have sequels when you call me from the dark. And I think I understand our Mycroft's question about this God Whom we may posit crafted us, and trees, and Death. My master Francis Bacon, when trying to convince Europe that his Scientific Method could yield technologies that would improve the human condition, he argued from God's omnibenevolence that Reason and Science, which our Maker granted as our special tools, like eagles' wings and lions' claws, must be able to improve our lives and someday satisfy all human desires, since a benevolent Maker, Crafter of rose and wildflower, Who gave each animal its tool, the woodpecker its beak, the snail its shell, would not send us naked into a harsh world without the means to make ourselves happy in it, and satisfy our aching needs. But I never discussed with Master Bacon why this Maker made our sought-for safety so hard to attain or, as our Mycroft's Stranger put it, placed the stepping-stones so far."

I: Exactly. Why take such hard shapes as Poseidon, Ares, Atë, and Apollo? Why make us toil a hundred thousand years through stone and iron ages toward today's happier state, and still make us toil more?

Hobbes: "It is hard, I confess, to call the Maker of the war of all on all omnibenevolent."

I: Is it our Maker you find unworthy of respect, Master Hobbes? Or merely those priests who devote their lives to honoring the Maker of pain and toil and Death?

Hobbes: "You echo my accusers again, Mycroft. Where did I say I disrespected God or priest?"

I: In your *Iliad.*

Reader: "That's right, if I recall correctly, friend Thomas, thou too hast indulged in this eternal fad of retranslating Homer."

Hobbes: "'Resorted to' more than 'indulged in,' good Master Reader; banned from publishing my own works, the only outlet of my late years was to translate others' and perhaps slide in between the lines a few thoughts of my own."

I: More than a few, Master Hobbes. And when the Argives urge Agamemnon, 'Respect Apollo's priest! Accept the ransom!' I notice you left out 'respect the priest.'

Hobbes: [Laughingly] "Well-spotted."

I: I . . . I respect priests, I . . . After feeling the touch, the action of the gods, of Providence, it seems like an act of madness not to worship. It isn't choice for me, just every time I think on it, it's like a wound inside me, worship bleeding out like light, prostrate before this power vaster than the sky.

Hobbes: "Yes, that is the effect of Miracles."

Reader: "You too admit the miracles, friend Thomas? I had not expected such credulity from Malmesbury's Materialist."

Hobbes: "Why, Miracles are matter, Master Reader! Even Bridger's. A Miracle or Wonder is merely a thing whose Natural Cause is yet unknown, and thus makes witnesses marvel and esteem it. The first Rainbow seen in the world was a Miracle, because it was strange, but Rainbows are no longer Miracles to those who know of prisms and diffraction. As the early Rainbow filled Noah and other Primitives with awe at Rainbows' Maker, so Bridger's Miracles stirred worship in our Mycroft, but with Cato-Helen hard at work, and Gordian, and Master Bacon's Scientific Method, the hidden Mechanisms by which the Child refashioned matter after Imagination will soon enough become a Recipe and, by your age, Reader, as commonplace as gunpowder in mine."

Reader: "Miraculous technologies are indeed more common in my age than souls who call them 'miracle.' It makes our Mycroft the more fascinating."

I: And yet . . .

Hobbes: "And yet?"

I: And yet I . . . I have seen things that many ages once called Wonders, Master Hobbes—I have walked on the Moon, have ridden *Mukta* cars faster than the Earth can spin, I have even returned from that dread mist beyond the shores of Acheron, and yet . . .

Hobbes: "And yet?"

I: And yet I never hoped to understand the Maker of those wonders. Not even the smaller facets like Apollo. I accepted I would never know more than some negatives, that Providence is neither Good nor Kind.

Hobbes: "And yet?"

I: And yet from observation of the things that Maker made, we learn, we . . . Could it be that He did make us in His image after all?

Hobbes: "It sounds like you think you have evidence for that hypothesis?"

I: No. Maybe. Maybe yes.

Reader: "You saw something. You just saw something, Mycroft, didn't you?"

I: Yes, Reader. Or, no. It wasn't I who saw it. It was He.

Reader: "Ah. Thine era's all-remaking He."
I: Yes, Reader, He. He recognized . . . He saw . . .
Reader: "Yes?"
I: Was the alphabet for that? All this time, Reader, were we, we the alphabet, for such a purpose . . . I don't know whether to hope He's right. It feels selfish to say it's all for that, but . . . but the worship that bleeds out of me, I would . . . It feels so healing, worshipping a Maker I respect. Were we for that?

"You handed Spain to Hiveguard!" Felix Faust's face on the screen was streaked and puffy, eyes tear-red. "You knew I was minimizing deaths! That everything I did, I calculated to keep casualties down! Did you not think? I took Spain for a reason! Now Homeland will rip in half! Europe will exert pressure at the worst time! And—" He didn't need to say it, his tears said it, mourning for a sister, one whose mind had grown and blossomed alongside his own. "How could you not think!"

I took this call inside Jehovah's cell. 'Our cell,' I could say, for I am Acting Emperor but a prisoner still, confined by Cornel MASON's remnant order, now that I've so clearly become me. Huxley was with us as chaperone, and immovable Chagatai, and He upon His bunk, still grappling with the understanding that the flesh which started His—strange miracle that one out of the trillions of cells that make a human body can become new life, but stranger yet that one instead became a vessel for our Visitor—that flesh had ended. Mother. Those He called Father had always come and gone, competing, taking leads and dropping back like horses in a race, but Mother was unique, as omnipresent in His sojourn here as gravity, or ground. Can such a constant end? He sat silent. The tears that streaked Faust's face, that cracked his voice, that rattled through him, those were not as great a fraction of Jehovah's grief as one cell to a body's trillions, yet He sat silent.

"Did you know Perry was with Madame?" I asked.

"I wasn't Joyce's keeper!" Faust burst back. "And even I don't know everything that's happening on the entire planet! I knew they might be there. I didn't know you had the means to get Spain there in hours! How could you . . ." Language failed.

Grief for my Master's grief moved me, reader, but never grief for her, the twisting queen, the poison in the mud washed clean at last. "You knew we would try for the hostages. What else did you expect?"

A deep breath, stern brows like a lecturer whose student's question betrays a deeper ignorance. "You don't understand how fragile this victory still is! Hiveguard is broken but not gone, and it would only take a small push for Europe or the Mitsubishi to start making big demands now that Donatien has caved to small ones. You haven't even entered Romanova yet! You need to solidify things quickly, make the resistance believe in its defeat. You don't have resources to waste opposing me, not yet."

"I used Hiveguard's resources," I countered, "none of ours."

Faust's red eyes narrowed, focusing, close study of my face. "But you'll use your own resources for the next try, won't you? You're already planning. Who next? Martin?"

I tried to blank my face, reciting in my mind the old Homeric hymn to Lord Apollo, the part which tells how even the Olympians leap from their thrones in fear when the archer approaches, until his soothing mother Leto helps him lay aside the silver bow that threatens gods and men. Mother—gods usually know their mothers never or forever, but to live with one twenty-one years and then to lose that soft, controlling hand, what will that do to Him? Faust was staring at me, those penetrating eyes like fishing nets that rake the seafloor's secrets.

"Of course we'll try for the others. All the others." Stormcloud Huxley answered for me, too wise to try to lie when lies will fail. "That's what hostage-taking pushes people to. The only way to make us stop is to return them."

Faust slammed his desk. "You saw how much you just made things worse!"

Huxley's words were hard as the titanium that buttresses the domes of Luna City. "You leave us no choice!"

"You have a choice." Faust rubbed his temples. "You can surrender. Utopia used to be good at recognizing when you should surrender."

Huxley's glare seemed weak without the vizor—Prefect or no, Cornel MASON's ghost forbids the friends of Micromegas to carry any tech into this cell that could aid liberation. "Utopia may surrender our liberties, our dignities, our hours, our happiness, our work, our play, our bash'es, or our lives, but not our path. Never. We didn't surrender Mars when we surrendered to Madame, and we won't now."

"Donatien will make you, if they choose me."

Huxley's silence did not deny it.

"Why can't we compromise?" I asked. "Everything's different now that Cato Weeksbooth has knocked Death back, Distance too. Bridger gave that to us. We have the H.E.L.E.N. tech to make space easier to face, and we have the Achilles-Alexander interface to advance your mind-machine research, and we have a good start on resurrection. Neither branch has to lop off the other now. We can have both."

Again Faust rubbed his temples, where the raw patches from the interface experiments show everpink. "Each grain of sand can only be under one microscope at once. I've said and say again: I will let Utopians aid our research, access the relics, and do your own work with them, but it will happen in *my* labs, with *my* researchers determining the schedule. This is like sharing a particle accelerator or a research computing cluster, there are only twenty-four hours of experiment time in a day, not everything can fit. Our two Hives share one project, *mortem superare,* as you put it, to surpass death, and I agree collaboration will achieve that best and fastest, but your second project cannot get in the way." He paused for a deep breath. "You know—you've known for ages—that spreading out to new worlds will cause more war and pain, not just the Mars war, many wars, cultures splitting like before the *Mukta* cars, that's what diaspora does. If Donatien decides to let you do that, split humanity again, then, strange as that decision is, I will accept it and will let you do *some* space projects, but I *will not* let that slow down immortality one second! Or rather one half second, that's the current average gap between human deaths. *We* receive the relics. *We* lead the research. Space research takes a back burner to our shared project. Those are my terms, and I will not bend." He leaned forward. "I mean that, don't I, Donatien? To slow down immortality is mass murder. Tell them I will not bend."

We turned, all of us, gazing on the Sojourner who had sat silent on His bunk since the news came: Mother. Was He perceiving us? We petty stimuli of sight and sound and politics, all tiny as an icicle's slow drip beside the thunder-torrent of the fresh-discovered fact: Madame can end. I had parted my lips to answer for Him but, wonder! He moves! He notices! We motes, smaller than ants, we words, we mere words of the cold, unwelcome message of His Peer goading the freshly wounded Addressee to stir from His Infinity and be wounded again, He notices! He speaks: *"Profundum mortemque, postquam fortasse astra."*

Faust frowned. "Mycroft?"

I could hardly find the voice to translate: "The depths and death, and then perhaps the stars."

A somber smile touched Faust's tear-wet face. "Exactly, Donatien. The depths of the mind which unlock all human capacities, and death which destroys them—those projects must come first, even if it means the appetite for space might fade." I remember fixing on Faust's eyes, twin depths—*profundi*—and in those depths one felt the inner space, as vast as outer space, and just as worthy of our telescopes and probes and every instrument cunning and hands can forge.

"*Onkel* will not yield," confirmed the Vaster Vastness that sits among us, still as stone. "Nor will Utopia. The trunk-war's ender must be Me."

A little warmth in Faust's still-tear-wet smile. "Exactly, Donatien. I was going to ask You to order Your Utopians to make no more attempts to free the hostages, but unfortunately, they won't obey You." He leaned toward the camera. "They know how strong my leverage is, how much You want to Have your *ibasho* and Keep it."

「*Ibasho,*」 the Stranger repeated, His Japanese pronunciation crisp. "*Ibasho* is also in between."

"In between?" Faust repeated, eyes glinting at this hint of some rich thought. "Can You unpack that for us, Donatien?"

Pause, struggle, narrowing thought's torrent to words' trickle. "Category (A) creations that end with the creator: memories, language matrix, learned skills, active agenda, political office attainment, muscle memory, action, speech, imagined worlds, plans, My creations within My Creation. Category (B) creations that can outlast the creator: written words, recorded sound, passed laws, attained worlds, born children, handicrafts, momentum, truth-claims, some of My remakings in My Peer's Creation. In between: agendas, power networks, gardens, songs, plays, fear, relationships of three or more, *ibasho,* things that others can continue but the creator's absence transforms irrevocably. It transpires that Mother had more finitudes than I had hoped but fewer than I had feared."

Faust offered sympathy's smile. "I know You always worried Your body might cease to exist when Your mother died. I was right, wasn't I? Here you still are."

Here He still is, and speaks, and struggles. "*Ibasho,* bash' formation, some are new each generation, some continuous. *Onkel,* if I declare My bash' hereditary not new-forming, thus that Mother is part of *ibasho,* then if I choose your inpath, can I Have my *ibasho* with Mother in it too and Keep it?"

We all winced at this, a variation strange but recognizable of the question children's tears ask at the first taste of death: if I am very good, if I do X and Y, will they come back? Faust breathed deep, fighting sobs. "Donatien, I . . . Maybe. Maybe. I want Joyce back too, but Bridger only left two resurrection potions, and every drop is precious for research. I've promised Cornel back, that's—"

⌜"« *Maman, Pater, Chichi-ue, la Trémoïlle . . .* »"⌟

Faust nodded. "Too many. So, it all depends on how replicable the potions prove to be, how much progress we make, and how quickly. I've urged Spain to freeze Joyce's body, but we don't even know if that will help. Cato Weeksbooth probably knows, but I don't have access to Cato. That's why I need Cato and all the relics in *my* labs, putting our project first, even if that means hurting the Brain-bash'. Hurting you."

"All bash'es are coequal, Mine, the billion shattered by the war. Can you help all?" I felt faint hearing Him—the anthills, reader, He asks not to heal His *ibasho* whose wounds injure a God's infinity, He asks to heal the rest of us, the little anthills that serve only ants.

Faust's taut frown understood. "I don't know, Donatien. I doubt, even with all the resources I'm asking for, that we can bring back all the war dead, or even save all of this generation that survive the war, but maybe . . ." A deep breath, as something moved deep in the Brillist—Apollo used to sigh like that before he spoke of Titan or of Triton, stepping-stones beyond our first toehold. "This could be the last generation that has to face involuntary death." Involuntary—such careful terms from this man who has thought long about how people may embrace or reject what he labors to give: not forced eternity, but choice. "I can't promise to help the present's everyone, Donatien, only the future's everyone. You can have that, and your still-living bash'mates safe and sound, and one potion to bring back whom you choose, Cornel, your mother, anyone you wish; that's what I'm offering if you choose us."

"While our path,"—Huxley spoke up quickly, before the Guest had time to think, to Choose—"has all the same goals, and will disarm death for someday's everyone, it just comes with more risk: risk that it'll take more generations, risk that we might blunder rescuing the hostages for You, but at the end, Mike,"—there's Apollo's light in Huxley's eyes—"at the end of our path is a universe of worlds that we can touch, and taste, where we'll find wonders we can't yet imagine, all among the stars."

Faust sighed, exasperation's sigh this time, more critical than tired. "I'll hurt the hostages if you try to rescue one again." A second sigh, reluctant like the messenger returning from Apollo's oracle with news that crushes hope. "You don't believe me. I'll have to hurt one now."

"What?" we cried out, we humans who cry out.

"It's the only way to keep you from trying again. Huxley there knows Donatien might yield to the pressure anytime, they won't obey any order to wait. I have to hurt the hostages, one first to prove I'm willing. Then, if you try anything, any of you, I'll hurt another, and another."

Hurt them? My mind fixed first on gentle Heloïse, then noble Cinna Semaphoros, then Voltaire, Aldrin, strangely fragile Dominic, steady Martin my one hope of escaping MASON's throne—hurt them? I parted my lips to speak, but He broke silence first. "*Onkel,* please don't."

"I'm sorry, Donatien. You won't believe I'll do it until You perceive it with Your own senses. Your companions there don't think I'd really harm the Brainbash'."

"I know you intend your threat, *Onkel.* Listen, Mycroft, Huxley, *Onkel* intends."

Faust shook his head. "I know You know I mean it, Donatien, but unfortunately, You don't believe Providence means it, that's the trouble in Your case. You think your Peer, as You call the phenomenon, won't let anything destroy Your . . . 'servants' is too broad a category, shall we say 'angels'? Your special few? You think something will stop me, give them back to You like They keep giving Mycroft back. You still believe that, even after losing Joyce and Cornel, since You know You have a means to bring them back. So, I have to actually do it, inflict a harm that will not heal. You won't learn otherwise that *ibasho* can die."

"*Onkel,* please don't." He begged—this cosmos's cruel hospitality has taught Him how to beg. "Please don't."

"Then choose now," Faust challenged. "End the trunk-war: out or in."

He paused. It is a longer journey, here to Him to here again, than the journey of light from suns so distant that they burned out long before their infant beams touched we who give them names, yet time and again He treads that path for us—for we who give Him names. "I cannot choose yet. I know which path is kinder, more like Me and Mine, but . . ." Words failed Him, as we often fail Him, we mere words.

Faust smiled, patient, somber, proud. "Then I must do it."

Again, "*Onkel,* please don't." And then: "Mycroft?" He called my name, reader—a Universe vaster and more immortal than the mists of Acheron, He calls my name.

"Yes, Ἄναξ?"

"Make *Onkel* not do this." His words remained expressionless, yet there was desperation in their plainness, like a last note scribbled by a dying man who knows that death will strip away all tears and intonations of performed sincerity, leaving just lines on paper to push back the silence.

My pacemaker bleeped alarm—or did my mind merely believe it bleeped, this young, fit heart that has never known surgeon's touch? "Headmaster—"

"Be careful, Donatien," Faust interjected, "when you order Mycroft to do things they can't accomplish, they're likely to die trying."

"Can My Mycroft not accomplish this?"

"No." Faust leaned forward to cut off the call. "They can't."

Hush held us as the screen went blank. It felt as if we were lost in some great cave and our last candle just blew out, leaving pure darkness, yet we must grope on. Would Faust do it? Were we really incapable of believing he would hurt the hostages until the proof stood—what, bleeding? maimed? dead?—before us? And which hostage? As I set to work, the terror festered in the corners of my thoughts, like when a scary story is too powerful and keeps surging into your forethoughts, filling quiet moments with its dread. Six minutes reading Carlyle's latest report working with UNGAR in Casablanca—*Heloïse! The cruelest would be Heloïse!*—a new communique from President Ancelet in Buenos Aires—*he'll pick Aldrin or Voltaire, Brillists' true enemies!*—a twenty-minute call with Danaë about Hong Kong—*Martin! He'll kill Martin, to leave Jehovah no way to evade the throne!* Each burst of fear scraped like sandpaper on the growing wound of guilt, and impotence.

Hobbes: "And didst thou obey Faust, Mycroft? Did threat of force bind thee, as it has bound so many others, forging concessions, social contracts, empires, eras?"

I did obey and didn't, Master Hobbes, compelled by fear which would not let me act, but also love which would not let me stop. I dared not plan a rescue, but the Headmaster had not forbidden begging, offers, or bribes, and between the Masons and Utopia, I have the largest treasury in history to back my bribes.

December the eighteenth, as our west Atlantic fleets made peaceful entry into São Paolo and Rio de Janeiro, I proposed a three-fifths split, three-fifths of Utopia joining Gordian in disarming death together, reserving only two-fifths of the relics and Utopia's strength for dreams beyond the clouds. Faust answered, "Donatien will give us that and more, if They choose us."

On the nineteenth, as I helped Danaë and Kim Gyeong-Ju secure enough concessions from Dougong to finally appease Taipei and Hong Kong, I—*Heloïse! The cruelest would be Heloïse!*—offered Faust all the wealth I thought the Empire could spare, a thousand kings' ransoms to fund a thousand institutes. But, "Donatien will give us that and more, if They choose us."

The twentieth, the Cousins formally joined the peace, and the barricades came down at last in Lagos, Tunis, Yerevan, Yangon, Phnom Penh, and Los Angeles, and between Johannesburg and Pretoria. As images poured in of streets filled with embraces—*Dominic! The one nobody needs! No one but Him!*—I indexed Bridger's relics, promising all those that could fight death to Gordian, reserving for Utopia only the few clearly intended for the stars. But: "Donatien will give us that and more, if They choose us."

Carlyle released another essay that day too: "O.S., Our Self-Fulfilling Trolley Problem," ruminating that we've debated the trolley problem so long, we convinced ourselves it's real. When the first automated cars, *Mukta*'s still-ground-based ancestors, were prototypes, everybody, the engineers, the passengers, the investors, the public, was so certain that the trolley problem must be real, they spilled oceans of ink and words debating how to program out the fatal choice: the passenger's life or the bystander's? But—*Cinna Semaphoros! The only one that isn't in the Brain-bash'!*—in the real tests, millions on millions of scenarios never yielded one, not *one* real instance in which hitting any bystander would save the passenger, car striking 60 kilograms of human flesh as dangerous to riders as the strike of car on deer, or car on tree. The trolley problem does not describe our reality. Physics is cruel in many, many ways, but not that way. Yet because we all debate it, normalize it, know it, we live psychologically inside the trolley problem, expecting it to be the default ethics of our world. Yes, there are corollaries—deadly missions, quarantines—but if we had admitted our kinder reality, that Nature rarely burdens us with such a choice—*Cinna? No, Martin! Martin!*—might the Saneer-Weeksbooth founders, who saw they could save 50,000 lives by taking one, have asked themselves: *Is there a better way to use this data than to kill?* Did we poison our ethics with the trolley problem? Is it bad for us, our minds, our souls, to dive, even in thought experiment, into a universe so artificially unkind?

December the twenty-first—*Martin! It has to be!*—was all preparation for the twenty-second, ensuring every cable, lazer, mirror, lamp, and satellite, even the Moonbounce (sort-of working now at last!) was ready to speed the speech, verbatim where possible, to all Earth's corners. Far around the globe, people gathered in gyms and auditoriums, in forts and barracks, around kitchen tables and under bridges in the midnight rain to hear the transcript read out by human voices, unadorned, just as twenty-four centuries ago, new readers announced to local ears the deaths of Cleopatra and her Antony.

"Humanists, whom I am proud to call my Hivefellows, I, Vivien Ancelet, come today as your elected President to end the State of War which has existed between our Hive and the Masons—a State of War which ends with our surrender. In the present communications blackout, it was impossible to put this decision to a direct vote of all Members, so I conferred with as many elected representatives as I could, and held a local vote of Members here in our capital, who voted seventy-nine percent to support surrender.

"But this surrender does not mean our end. I believe today as firmly as I did when the war began that the Humanist Constitution is the best and soundest form of government yet created by the human species. Many of you are still prepared to fight for our Hive, holding by force what lands you can. Some have proposed we could become a Reservation, securing some section of the Earth to continue our way of life, as many noble nations of the old world have. But we are not a nation of the old world. Our constitution was not designed for a space confined by borders, nor for a state of majority where we live mixing only with ourselves. We have from our inception been a Hive, and I believe we cannot pursue all-inclusive human excellence if our drive and inspiration touch only one corner of the world. Our universal presence in streets, schools, workshops, offices, on stages, podiums, screens, tracks, and fields, that presence pushes all we mix among toward excellence, sharing our spur to challenge and expand human potential. To cage our presence within geography would be as absolute an end of what we are as to dissolve the Hive. Therefore, I and my fellow elected leaders have concluded that the best path forward is not to withdraw the Hive from the Remaker order but to become part of it, working with the Remaker leadership to preserve, through the coming transformation, as much as we can of our government, our values, and our way of life.

"To that end, I have secured from J.E.D.D. Mason the promise that the Olympic Games will continue, uninterrupted and unchanged. I have secured the promise that no one—Humanist or other—will be punished for having opposed the Remaker faction, since no government worthy of respect should ever meet the exercise of freedom of conscience with retribution. I have secured the promise that, as J.E.D.D. Mason gathers advisers to help shape the new order, I, and other Humanists, and other Hiveguard too, will be included and heeded coequally with Remaker voices. Finally, I have secured the pledge that J.E.D.D. Mason loves and intends to foster human dignity and excellence, guaranteeing the most central of our Humanist values, whatever else may change.

"Having secured these promises, and recognizing that further opposition will cost lives without the hope of changing outcomes, I will at noon tomorrow surrender to Remaker troops our capital of Buenos Aires and myself. I call upon all Hiveguard Humanists and others who have carried arms with us to lay them down as I do. Now is the time to turn our energies from excellence in war to excellence in reconstruction. Many of our greatest cities have been ravaged by this conflict, notably Esperanza City, where many lives will be at risk when Antarctica's warm season ends. I am told the record for the fastest reconstruction of a comparable city is Arequipa after the eruption of El Misti in 2262. Let's beat that record. Let's beat it in ten cities at once, unless, my fellow Humanists, you think we can do more."

The words leaked out through every crack our ingenuity could carve into the silence, but, of course, there were more skirmishes, misunderstandings, deaths. I watched Him watch it, our ever-mourning Visitor, and as I watched, I hated Gordian who made this silence, stilled the cars, who slowed these words and caused these final deaths, more Wilfred Owens. But His black stare disallows hypocrisy. Gordian battles separation, and unleashes Distance and its evils now to teach us, steer us off the outpath, lest we face this pain again, again, each time Poseidon and you, wandering Apollo, strand us on a rock around some distant sun. I cannot hate them for opposing that. Even the not-yet-sacred isle of Delos, when shining Leto sought a place to birth you, splendid archer, feared you, the land itself speaking to Leto, as the old hymn says, fearing you would reject it, you whose ceaseless passion leads us onto ships, that you would cast the island down into your uncle's seas and take your distant aim, yes, even on your birthing day, to seek new shores. And while you did keep Delos sacred, you rejected many lands even in childhood, you more ceaseless than the day and night which, though they course forever, once a cycle taste homecoming, but not you. Not you. Nor we who serve you, wanderluster, ever-aiming god. No, I cannot hate Gordian for trying to help me set down my oar.

I did get to trade words with Vivien briefly. I can't call it conversing, since without the Alexander's aid, the great Atlantic and Gordian's vigilance remain such barriers that all we can manage is to record short chunks, then wait two or three minutes for the data to snake out through an evasive, ever-changing route.

I couldn't get through his first video. Sobs overcame me at first sight of that gentle, complex face, with sadder lines around the eyes now, and dreadlocks more wisdom-silvered at the base, like Nature's artwork at winter's first frost. « Hello, Mycroft. I hope you're well. » He spoke French, hungry for it probably, now that he has to work so much in Spanish. « I hoped before business we could speak briefly as we used to, setting war aside. I don't blame you for the side you've taken, and I trust you don't blame me. I hear [Anonymous] is there with you, how are they doing? »

I couldn't watch more. Huxley had to record an answer in the end, [Anonymous]'s fate, a hard truth to make plausible since we have no real evidence of the transformation apart from the fact that I'm now ten centimeters shorter. But I think Vivien believes.

« I spoke to Papadelias. » Vivien's change of subject in the second clip helped tame my sobs, the ex-Censor expert at talking me down from extremes and back to work. « We need to know what you intend to do with Toshi. I've seen the evidence you have against Su-Hyeon, and Papadelias and I agree it justifies declaring them unfit for duty. But I know you have Toshi in Alexandria. If Toshi's to replace Su-Hyeon as Censor, that would make the Alliance Executive a hostage in Masonic hands. The Hives have all surrendered, but the Alliance is separate, above, and that's important, more than ever with so much in flux. So, I want you to let Toshi go to Papadelias in Dhaka. » This felt warmingly right, like soup—this great man had done his best for the Humanists, and now was free at last to do his best for his first love, Romanova. « I know you need to occupy Romanova to end the chaos there, no one will blame you, but Dhaka's both neutral and stable, it could be a temporary Alliance capital, independent, with the Censor and Commissioner General there. You could use your ships to gather senators, and the Hive reform process could resume, Jehovah's changes going through the system, like before the war. » He paused, and frowned, the stern frown of a teacher-master at one he should command. « Jehovah promises there will be Hives, plural, in the new order, and Hives need the Alliance above them, neutral, active, and, above all, free. So, will you send Toshi to Dhaka to Papadelias? »

I found myself staring at the last paused frame, his stern, commanding face which instinct would obey. Hives do need something to lubricate their mixing, so they don't fall into raw competition like the states of olden days.

Hobbes: "Indeed, Mycroft, the birth of the Leviathan does not end Nature's State of War, it merely shifts the scale, creating peace between human and human, while the Sovereign States above live ever in the self-interested War of all on all."

I fear so. But in your age, Master Hobbes, borders constricted friction, nations jostling mainly where they touched, like horses penned too tight, but Hives mix everywhere, as transfused blood courses alongside native blood in one body, so, if the antibodies jar, the system clogs and all is wracked and ruined.

Hobbes: "Only when a single sovereign binds all humans into one Body Politic will Earth know peace."

One sovereign like the Alliance.

Hobbes: "Or like your Sovereign Prince."

Hobbes understands, but how to frame the same to Vivien? « I asked Ἄναξ Jehovah, » I began, halting. « He doesn't know yet whether He wants to remake things through the Alliance leaving it intact, or remake the Alliance itself, or . . . or rule the Hives directly, as an Emperor over vassal kingdoms. I . . . so, I . . . I will not relinquish power over Toshi until He decides. I don't like holding Toshi hostage, but nobody wants me to send the Censor to Dhaka and convene the Senate there and then have to attack and take the city, all those lives. But Ἄναξ Jehovah is starting to make His Mind up about things. We may know soon what He will do with the Alliance, maybe before Papadelias completes removing Su-Hyeon from office. And when I know, you'll know, I promise, you, and Papadelias, and Toshi, quickly, I'll tell all of you as quickly as I can. »

I made the mistake of watching my own clip as I waited, hating every word, my clumsiness. Look at that fool upon the screen wearing the colors of an Emperor and rambling like a child. No no, I must not, Sniper warned us it does harm calling ourselves or anybody stupid.

Vivien's answer came. « Does Jehovah intend to rule the world forever now? » Finally, someone asked it, reader! Our sage of numbers, Vivien Ancelet, saw past war's muddle to the deeper fact that Alexander's empire ended with his death—but death is growing optional. He continued: « I hear the resurrection tech is not repeatable yet, but Jehovah's young, you have at least a century before they need it. » A somber pause. « Bryar says you haven't visited them yet, Mycroft. You should. They're doing well, some balance issues, headache, liver damage, consistent with oxygen deprivation, and they're still mostly speaking Hindi, but English is coming back. I'm told language problems like that happen sometimes with stroke or head trauma. But this wasn't just head trauma, Mycroft. I've seen the scans, it was just like Jehovah on the Rostra, the robot crushed Bryar's skull like a lychee and it un-crushed again. Is Jehovah counting on that? »

The image of the brain-wet lychee fruit within its brittle shell made me wince—*Cinna! They'll pick Cinna!*—Why hadn't I been to visit Bryar? Why hadn't I asked the question of all questions: What do they remember from the interstice, what state awaits us when we join the vast silenced human majority taken from Earth by wind-swift Thanatos and Zeus's golden scales? Where are they now? Achilles, Saladin, Andō, my birth bash', MASON, past MASONs back to the founding of the world? Did Bryar see them? See the underworld as I (in what might not be fully madness) remember it? Gray mists and rivers? Or did they see something else? Clouds? Forests? Fields? The fires of torture or the light of bliss? Or nothing? Was there nothing? Why, when this answer of answers is at last so close, am I afraid to ask?

I sat staring at the last frame of the video, Vivien frowning his complex frown. There was a mania in Vivien's eyes now, that special fatigued mania that I see in my eyes each time I pass a mirror. Achilles shared that mania, Cato, Carlyle, all we who have felt the Hand so heavy on us, undeniable, granting and taking with such clear intentionality that we can no longer doubt: there is a Plan. Now Vivien has it too. The Plan brought Hector back, and this unwidowed widower will thank Fate in his heart forever now, as Athens thanks plague-averting, plague-sending Apollo. And that same Fate spoiled Su-Hyeon and took [Anonymous], the successor generation devoured by Ruin like the son of ancient Hector, young Astyanax hurled from the walls of Troy. My fault again. I took Kohaku and then cost the world [Anonymous], my fault, Vivien, mine. Thank mercy Vivien wasn't here to see my face in person, hear my sniveling. No, the opposite—if Vivien were here, my tears and hiccupped breathing in my tongue-tied honesty would prove I understood my guilt, show my contrition, while his face and gestures as I spoke, his eyes, his body language would reveal so much, how he received my words, with anger's stiffness or forgiveness's ease. I wanted him here! I wanted to see! These stiff clips, with the awkward camera and Poseidon's kingdom wide between us, Vivien might as well have been on Mars. And I was making it worse by sitting thinking, dragging out the pause instead of speeding words quick as I could to he who waited in suspense-pain keen as mine. Yes, Faust, you're right about diaspora.

I stared so long that a new message came in—Vivien knows well how often I'm a coward. « Bryar had a dream. They told me. They were at our bash'house, in the courtyard, a cool, misty evening, and Cornel was there, and Leigh and Geneva, and Bryar's late ba'sib Rohi, and [Anonymous] and Ibis except those two were little kids, and the beginning of the dream was just a pleasant conversation, but I was supposed to come for dinner and was stuck outside because the door was locked, and Bryar had to go through room on room to let me in, except the rooms were a long art gallery exhibit of black-and-white photographs and red clay figures, and Andō and Ganymede were there critiquing the art, only part of the gallery was a spice store, and Bryar was trying to find the spices for dinner but all the spices were unfamiliar, and Cornel and the others kept following Bryar and handing them babies, and more babies, and Bryar could hear me knocking from far away but kept having to stop to find a safe place on the spice shelves to put the babies. That's all they remember. On the up side, » he concluded, « I think our marriage is coming through the war intact. »

He made me laugh. It was a goofy dream, shallow and human, tempting as it is to read it close as scholars read Aeneas's dreams and Dante's of the underworld. But somehow, even as our Maker requited our abject prayers for answers with this callous No, Vivien made me laugh. And smile.

I hoped at least to send a smile back. « Carlyle! » I began my brief reply. « Did [Anonymous] tell you . . . » I couldn't be direct when these words were about to snake across uncounted junction points with their uncounted weaknesses. « . . . how helpful Carlyle's been? What great things they're working on in Casablanca? »

Something garbled the image in Vivien's response, so only the first frame came through, a terrible grief-smile, as when we hear a mother died in childbed but at least the infant lives. « Yes, I've been in touch with Carlyle. They're an excellent person, hardworking, quick-learning, kind. The times are fortunate we have someone like that to rely on. And they're working on great things now. » A pause—what face, great man, did you make in that pause? « I'd hoped you were working on great things too, Mycroft, but I hear you're spending half your days writing to Felix about some secret crisis. » Yes. We'd kept it secret. Why? Fear of our conquest looking weak if Hiveguard learns about the hostages? Fear Faust would punish us for speaking up? Generic fear that the Brillists have us all bound like marionettes, and will pull our strings tight if we misstep? Those were my foolish questions, while Vivien's, Vivien's was the right question: « Do you think you're going to win this argument with Felix? »

How had I not asked myself that? Asked if there's a point to begging anymore? It's been days. Whatever Faust is doing, they've likely—*Heloïse! The cruelest would be Heloïse!*—already done.

Vivien's recorded voice continued, peppering out sometimes—we risked lives to set up this connection, and it's still this bad? « Don't run from what's happening, Mycroft. You've c—r—red the world, you and Jehovah. You need to decide what you're doing with it. And you have, in Cato's tech and Bryar, s-s-s-s-s-s which may be more impor—t than conque-e-e-e-e-e-ring the world. So, don't waste time, not *your* time, Mycroft Canner, don't you dare. Your sentence is to work. So, work. » The image on the screen changed finally, but it wasn't a new frame, it was a shape looming with Vivien in my mind's eye, the shade of far-seeing Kohaku Mardi, who should have been there with him, a strong, stable successor to fill the Censor's office, ready for it unlike fragile Su-Hyeon. A second shape loomed, holding her Kohaku's hand, our strong and bloody Mercer Mardi, she who should share Faust's burden in Ingolstadt, and could perhaps have found some path to compromise between the *fundamentum* and the stars. I owe hours to Faust for her, to MASON for Aeneas, Jules, Geneva, Chiasa, Laurel, and to the Cousin board for Leigh and Ibis, to the Mitsubishi for Jie and young Ken, the Humanists for Malory and Seine, Europe for Makenna, and everyone for Graylaw Luther Mardigras . . . even the list exhausts me. « So, spend your hours on what matt-t-t-t-ters, you hear me, Mycroft? Not on hopeless self-distractions, however productive th——ay feel. » His wise, time-frozen eyes upon the screen felt stern like whale song—has whale song ever struck you as stern, reader? Those vastest living things, watching our mistakes from their distant depths, and maybe, true Leviathan to false Leviathan, urging us on to better.

« Yes. » I felt I should address Vivien by some title here, but all options felt outdated or wrong; the best honor for this command was brevity. « I will. »

I did, working away on quiet goods, relief shipments, supplies, as we let Red Crystal and the Conclave dominate what flowed through Pass-It-On December the twenty-fourth and twenty-fifth, those volatile days when one of the old dragons sleeps so lightly.

Then the twenty-sixth. I don't know how to tell this part coherently, reader. It was a greater change for me, for everything, than when our Maker spared the Gates of Nineveh, as great as when, in my old coffin-cage, the Child named Jehovah killed my old self and remade me what I am. But it was also nothing. Not even the lifting of a veil. Have you ever seen a picture many times, over years, maybe, and then someone comments, "See the ____?" and suddenly you see it there, a bird, a face, a door, and it was always there but your mind somehow never processed it before, the shapes and color, present but unseen. Remember when Carlyle realized Jehovah was a thing like Bridger? Realized there Are Two? Nothing happened, just one atom's strike, one thought, nothing but also everything. So this.

"They've brought Dominic Seneschal."

This I didn't trust even to Masons. I sent Myrmidons to Faust's coordinates, my best forces, trained in our hidden valleys long before the crisis, the oldest soldiers in our still-young war.

"Bring Dominic straight here," I ordered.

"But the hospital—"

"You told me you ran enough tests already to confirm Gordian's report. Do you think the hospital will change that?"

"No, Polymech." Some Myrmidons call me Polymech these days, picked up from Achilles calling me πολυμήχαν', one-of-many-plans, a new-invented rank, nonsense but less nonsensical, I guess, than Beggar King.

"Is there an active injury?" I asked. "Anything urgent treatment would affect?"

"No, but—"

"Delay amplifies pain. Bring Dominic now."

"Yes, Polymech. Right away."

We had Gordian's report before us in the cell, sickeningly clinical and thorough, all those diagrams. I remember my eye kept straying off the screen to the false window, where the clouds were forming humpy stripes against the blue, like corrugation or an old-time washing board. Gardeners were planting new palm trees to fill in what the battle had burned. Would they plant citrus, too? Programmable or plain? How fine a filament did it take Gordian to connect to neurons individually? How did they thread it through the tissue? Must be those tiny robots surgeons use, but did they use the kind that crawl like ants? or swim like fish? or for such fine work, those filaments that stretch and compress so the strand itself wriggles and burrows like a serpent toward the target spot?

"Don't nerves regenerate eventually? Can that process be sped?" Chagatai's questions were more practical than mine, calm Chagatai, who has weathered who-knows-what Blacklaw extremities and now read the report with us and Cato, whom we called up to explain—no, not to explain. To wish it away, that's why we called for Cato, to make it better, as when you break something and smoosh the pieces back together, hoping the crack will heal if you just squeeze and hope.

"No," Cato answered, fidgeting. "The nerves aren't damaged, that's the problem, it's not damage, it's overwritten information. Every neuron is intact, but neurons learn from stimulus and change with it, not just the connections between them but their actual responses, response times, what can make them fire. By flooding individual neurons with random stimulation, they've overwritten the responses that were shaped by lived experience, like overwriting the soundtrack of a movie with white noise. Those whole brain sectors are white noise now. If a nerve is cut, we can reconnect it, but there's nothing cut to reconnect."

"Can it be rewritten again? If we had the same technology, could we replace the soundtrack?"

"No. We know how to flood the system with noise, we don't know how to replicate the billions of natural experiences each particular neuron has had over a lifetime to re-create its state. Besides, we don't have the soundtrack, we don't have a backup of Dominic's brain."

Chagatai nodded along, as tense but calm as if we were debating how to barricade against a gang raid. "But the functions they targeted are common functions, right? Not unique-to-the-person functions. Language processing, visual processing, I have visual processing, I figure I process table, chair, and wall about how Dominic would process table, chair, and wall—why can't we copy-paste?"

Cato's face shock-convulsed, that deep, tongue-tied gape of the expert who understands orders of magnitude more about the question than the rest of us. "We don't even have a way to record neural information that fine-grained, Gordian's not that far in mind-machine."

"Can you get them that far?"

"No!" Cato cried. "Or . . . maybe over years, but not—"

"What about a physical brain-tissue transplant? That thing where they plop in a chunk from someone else and put cloned infant-state brain tissue at the edges to grow and fill in the connecty-uppy edges. Could we transplant a language center?"

Cato was struggling, as when a kindergartener asks a question too complex to answer in terms children know. "Brain-tissue transplants can help infants when things are still forming, and sometimes adults when the section in question is discrete and . . . I don't want to say 'unsophisticated,' all parts of a human brain are sophisticated, but transplants work for brain-stem sections that do really mechanical things like breathing. We're talking about more than a hundred parts of the most complicated areas, affecting the . . . You know neurons don't record information one-to-one like a letter in a book or a bit on a computer drive, right? Thoughts and information are large structures distributed around the brain the way the shape of a hologram is distributed around the whole surface that generates it, not just the middle. These sections are part of those large structures, you're talking about replacing pieces of the mind, not just the brain, the mind, we're still struggling to learn how to even perceive such structures, we're nowhere near *constructing* them."

My stomach felt tight. Knowledge, healing, these too we toiled toward a hundred thousand years, their stepping stones—twenty-six centuries from Imhotep to Hippocrates, twenty-one more to Schwann and Schleiden—so far. I seemed to hear Faust's voice reminding me our Gates of Nineveh are still mud brick compared to what we need to heal minds' injuries—or was that not Faust but cold Apollo's oracle still telling Socrates that we know nothing?

"I see," calm Chagatai continued, anchor in our storm. "Can Dominic learn over again to process language and vision?"

"And *sound*," Cato stressed. "It's not just the language center, it's all auditory processing as well. Dominic's trapped in a world where audio and visual data are unprocessable chaos. It's not lack of signal like cutting the optic nerve, it's onslaught, and yes, the brain will cope over time, but we have no idea how the overwritten neurons will remap with time. Tactile communication we can work with, but without a language center, it's . . . it won't be . . ."

I was still staring out the not-window at the holes that were not yet citrus trees. *"Ibasho."* It was the only word. "It won't make the *ibasho* the way it was."

He Who Visits From a Better Universe was lying on His bunk, unmoving in that deep, deceptive way that seeds sit unmoving while, in their shells, the millions of cells do life's most intense work. He can't endure. He can't. I know He can't, to see His Dominic stripped of communication, silenced, Death-of-words where words once were, as cruel an enemy as Distance, and as painstaking to surmount. We can surmount it, will with time, assemble tools of touch and gesture, but Hell for Dominic is not fire, not grinding wheels, not lakes of boiling blood, it is to miss a single word, glance, gaze from our Master.

"A healing potion?" Chagatai arrived at it at last. "What you did to Kosala?"

Cato winced. "What I did to Kosala, I could only do because I did a deep scan *before* the damage, I'm not near being able to do it without. And the healing potion's different from the resurrection potion, anyway. Also, we don't know if there's anything to heal here, it's not cuts or burns, it's data substitution, a brain chugging along happily, just with different content."

"Can you try the potion anyway? It won't do harm."

Cato's eyes met mine, the same thoughts in both, the same reluctance to speak in front of Him it hurts so much. "Every drop is precious if we want to learn to replicate what Bridger left. We only had sixty-four milliliters of each potion, even at the start. This war with Gordian is over who gets to have this under microscopes, to throw so much of what we have away on one . . . and when we don't know it would even help . . ."

The soft buzz of the console. "We have the patient here. Coming in now."

The grind and groan of that cell door had never sounded so inexorable, like the great millstone of Fate which grinds us turn on turn until we shatter into the dusty powder which our all-engineering Maker always planned to feast upon. They brought Dominic in a wheelchair, pushed by his lieutenant Mirabeau and flanked by medics. The patient clung to an attendant's arm as children cling to parents. A scarred cheekbone and a pinked-over bullet wound on his left shoulder testified to a harsh trek before his capture, and his face and frame were thinned as if he had tried hunger-striking in captivity when tooth and claw had failed. A shapeless blue hospital smock felt grossly modern on that body that had never consented to our century, nor to any color but his Master's black. His ordeal had left him sunburned on arms, face, and scalp, while his head was shaved and striped with the red lines of freshly sealed incisions. Two Myrmidons had bandages on their hands, one on a cheek, proof how fiercely the patient had fought back until they helped him feel the period cut of Mirabeau's coat, and so learn these new hands were friend hands. Dominic's expression: I don't know what to compare it to, how to read a face transported from a world of sense into a world of . . . what? Even drug fevers and hallucinations give us visuals, false things but things, not this raw overload that makes the newborn infant scream and scream. Dominic screamed, or moaned as the wheels bumped over the threshold, a sound unshaped where language use to be. Barren—my mind reeled, trying to articulate the scale of barrenness when words we had are lost: words heard, thought, read, remembered, hundreds of millions encountered over decades. Even one squeeze for 'yes' and two for 'no' fails when one, two, yes, and no are gone. Yes, many humans live, prosper, communicate without the use of speech, or sound, or sight, but to take a brain which long had all those things and sever all at once . . . Faust says that minds are vast as worlds, and I would think it glorious, not tragic, if, on some far ice-world like Europa, life raised thriving sightless cities spread beneath their pure-black ice-shell sky, and composed symphonies in temperature and touch, but if the Earth lost all at once our light, sound, voices, symbols, so many of the mechanisms Earth species have made to share thoughts with each other across separation's barriers, would that be the right magnitude of loss?

"They're strong otherwise, Polymech," the Myrmidon captain reported, clumsy comfort, but it is human to try to comfort even when we can't. "They'd made it more than a kilometer from the drop point before we found them, despite the heat and sand." Yes, abandoned in the desert, groping on without even a way to understand the sunburn pain—over a year you groped, desperate Dominic, from Tōgenkyō across the Asian vastness, braving ocean, mountain, winter, storm, and all for this?

Over my shoulder I heard our Master rise. What will He do, reader? What will this do to Him? He loves this wretch, this wounded monster writhing like a half-crushed scorpion that once had, in its fearsome way, a dignity but now just leaks and twitches on the ground as Thanatos and sweet Hypnos, appalled, wonder if even they could end this damage to the inmost self, the mind, which may, who knows, carry such scars beyond the shores of dreamy Lethe and slow-changing Acheron. Now He is moving, reader, Kindness, walking toward the chair. I can't look at His eyes. He has to . . . Faust is right, nothing but this could make You understand, Ἄναξ. Yes, Providence did bend for You that once, but it still made us mortal, all of us. Though we may try and try beyond the end of sanity to serve and stay with You, yet Time and Change will take us all away, from You, and from each other. No one keeps it forever, *ibasho,* not unless we change our lot as Faust intends and surpass Death. Was this the only way to make Him understand? He's stepping toward the chair. Maker! Maker, how dare You! How dare You send such pain to Him! To Him! How dare You tangle Him in this! This our petty—now He's bending down—our petty war! Your war! Your choice. Had You no gentler way to make Him understand? What is He doing now? Stroking? There is no fur-hair left to stroke, Ἄναξ, your faithful bloodhound razed like Carthage. What's He doing? Reaching up to His own cheek and, with one finger, Jehovah lifts from His skin—what's that? A tear? A tear, reader! The salt streak trickling down. His first! He can! Reader, He can! He can! We always wondered. And He takes it with His finger to Dominic's lips and lets the bloodhound taste salt, salt and what he always wanted more than anything. And Dominic, he gropes, his searching hand finding Jehovah's armband with its many marks of office. He understands. He howls. He grasps his Master by His warm, familiar knees and leans into that warmth and howls.

Gently, so gently as this Kind Cosmos strokes the shaking shoulders. ⌜"«I'm sorry it took Me so long to recognize You, Self-portrait of My Peer.»"⌟

I blinked—had I blacked out? Had time skipped something? ⌜"«What do You mean, Ἄναξ?»"⌟

⌜"«Look, Mycroft. [You plural] long said [you plural] were a Portrait, but I did not understand.»"⌟

I blinked. ⌜"«I still don't understand, Ἄναξ.»"⌟

⌜"«¿You see? My Dominic, he gropes though there aren't stars to grope toward in a darkness which he has no senses tuned to see, yet he groped on and found Me. This, this is the image of thy Maker, Mycroft, One Who Groped, Who reached beyond His own Infinity, imagining beyondness as I never did, and found Me. [You plural] do image Him, Him only. There may be a trillion Beings of Our Species scattered in Our trillion cosmoses, Each unique and alone, but His uniqueness is that He is the God Who Groped, Who Moved, Who conceived—inconceivable to Me—of Beings beyond Himself. You were right who called Him First Mover, for He is the One Who Moved, Who reached, though there was no direction to reach in, but He imagined Motion, Distance, and Direction, casting Himself into a void as blind as Time. And so He found Me, Other, Alien, Peer, Interlocutor, Addressee, Stranger, Outsider, First Contact, Friend.»"⌟

⌜"«One Who reached out,»"⌟ I mouthed, struggling to breathe, ⌜"«Who found You without senses . . . »"⌟

⌜"«As [you plural] reach out, [you plural] creatures of His making, all of [you plural] from the first cell that groped for nutrients in the warm sea of salt. But He Moved, groping far more blindly than you who grope, for from the first cell you have all had senses, touch and hunger, more, while He had nothing, blindness beyond blindness, lack-of-senses-ness. And from that state, from lack-of-senses, He created Time, the unperceivable direction, reflecting and portraying His unknowing reach into the dark, from which trust, hope, love, curiosity, and learning, all are born. Blind-to-the-future-ly we move here, as He Moved, and Distance, Mycroft, He conceived Distance, not as a cruelty made for [you plural] but for Himself first, His state ever since He first conceived of other, that there could be separation, Otherkind. That thought made Him begin to suffer Distance, worse, darker than yours, for Distance as He crafted it for [you plural] is full of lights, and stars, and clues, and stepping-stones that you have many senses tuned to see, while His Distance was all unsensable to Him as Time, with nothing, no proof, no sign that there was anything beyond Himself, yet still He hoped, and groped, and found Me. ¡And I was ungrateful!»"⌋

My eye rested on Dominic, wincing against the light, and yet he holds What he was searching for—not happiness, that other thing for which we set aside our happiness and grope. ⌈"«Ἄναξ . . . »"⌋

The God Who did not think to Make His ship of flesh Himself was sobbing, shaking like a shuttle in reentry. ⌈"«¡I hated Him, Mycroft! ¡I hated Distance! Hated this, the very part of Him that reached and brought Me things beyond Myself. He showed Me Time, and change, and pain, and finitude, and ignorance, the state of not knowing, of needing to discover, curiosity's long pain, that is His state, all are His state, all that I perceived here, all portraits of His Pain, His Gropingness, communicating the parts of Him that were uniquely Him, the One Who Gropes, the parts that made Him the Together-Bringer, the Contacter who first found Me. These aspects he showed Me. ¡These I hated! ¡Called them cruel when they were only honesty! His Own experience, His Self, His Nature, His attempt to tell Me that I, Who never conceived of otherness, Am not alone. »"⌋

I felt a prickle up my spine as I too began dimly to perceive. ⌈"«The cosmos is the portrait . . . space and time . . . »"⌋

⌈"«It and [you plural] within it, figuring His Nature, letters of His message reaching out toward Otherself, toward Alien, toward Me, to make Me understand that this was Contact.»"⌋

It felt like speaking anything above a whisper would pierce this bubble of a dream where all made sense. ⌈"«An alphabet for Strangers, made to make First Contact . . . »"⌋

⌈"«¿How could I be so ungrateful a Guest?»"⌋ this Best Guest cried, His voice still soft but cracking. ⌈"«¿So bad a Friend? He suffers in Infinity a crueler Distance than [you plural], Distance without sense or hope or data, and by conceiving Distance He brought Me such Love, and learning, and complexity, contact, My own cosmos the richer, I, My eternal Self the richer for His suffering, and yet I hated it. Even its starlight-gentled echo I called cruel. ¡How much I must have hurt Him, Mycroft! He Who made His cosmos honest, a reflection of Himself, and I hated—*¡Hhheehh!*»"⌋

It was my touch that made Jehovah gasp, my embrace from behind as I rose from my chair and fought the vertigo (Gorgon's fruit, or old concussion's? Both?) enough to rise and wrap my arms around His shoulders. Instinct made me embrace Him, as I would a human sobbing so, as I imagined in that moment His Peer would embrace Him if His Peer had a body—but, of course, Our Maker has all bodies, moves in all bodies in His created cosmos, aphids, asteroids, and in that moment, He moved in me. ⌜"«Misunderstanding doesn't make You a bad Friend, Ἄναξ. You didn't understand before because it was too hard a thing to understand, especially for You. It was too alien.»"⌟ I held Him, felt His breathing, sharp, out of control. ⌜"«Some messages are long. And have to be long. Don't blame Yourself if You didn't understand before, the message was still coming, we the alphabet still acting, still unrolling.»"⌟

⌜"«My Mycroft . . . »"⌟

⌜"«I'm here, Ἄναξ. I'm Yours.»"⌟

⌜"«He gave Me thee. He gave so much. ¡I asked so much, Mycroft! My Friend Who worked so hard to find Me, find this method to communicate, but I asked more. I asked Him to alter His Plan, His own portrait, I asked Him to make it less like Him and more like Me. ¡And He did! ¡He listened! ¡He filled it all as I would have, with stepping-stones and stars! ¡Much, much too kind to still resemble His experience! Unrecognizable so long because I asked. ¡And I asked more!»"⌟

⌜"«The stars . . . Ἄναξ, He gave us stepping-stones because You asked. You made Him kinder.»"⌟

⌜"«I didn't see. I was so selfish, not recognizing How much He'd already changed for Me. I asked for more. I still called the path too cruel. So, He offered to let Me change it, change His Plan, gave Me the chance to end the journey, close the outpath and direct [you plural] back together to a world like Me, like Mine, instead of one like His.»"⌟

⌜"«The trunk-war . . . »"⌟

⌜"«¡He offered Me Remaking! ¡Cutting off the path that most resembled Him!»"⌟

⌜"«Who shoots from worlds away . . . the distant-aiming god . . . »"⌟

⌜"«¡And when He offered to let Me close the path I hated, I was cruel again! ¡I threatened Him! ¡I said I did not know how to call 'Friend' One Who offered to make the very change I wanted! »"⌟

⌜"«The Gates of Nineveh,»"⌟ I whispered like a prayer. ⌜"«But, no, Ἄναξ, You didn't call Him cruel for cutting off the path, you called Him cruel for letting us toil so hard for it so long and *then* cutting it off. ¡For building Troy, then burning it!»"⌟

⌜"«For making [you plural] share His desire, His nature, before you bowed to Mine.»"⌟

I was shaking. ⌜"«The god who leads men onto ships . . . who lights the spark and snuffs it, and makes it so hard.»"⌟ A dizziness was moving up through me, a sense of hugeness watching, close, as when you stare into the sea too long and feel it staring back, or dizzy Socrates stares at the sky trying to know the vastness of his ignorance, except the god who taught us that we know nothing knew nothing first, for only on a frightened island—Delos, Earth—surrounded by a vastness unattained could it begin, with hollow log, and brick, and bow, and midnight oil, and Imhotep and Hippocrates: the aim. ⌜"«Poseidon and Apollo . . . aim and distance, ignorance and knowledge-seeking, intertwined as lungs and heart . . . It's not Your fault You couldn't understand, Ἄναξ. They are too hard to understand, even for we who share their nature. Of course You couldn't. ¡You're too Alien! ¡Too kind! Too warm and full against His emptiness.»"⌟

⌜"«I made it hard to see. I made Him change His portrait, made Him mask Himself.»"⌟

⌜"«No. No.»"⌟ I held Him tighter. ⌜"«You made it kinder. Better. ¿Don't You see? You Each have changed the Other. ¡Look at me! Look how You changed me, Ἄναξ, remade me through our first contact, you Remade Him like that. This cosmos is an accurate portrait, the portrait of One Who Met You, Ἄναξ, the Maker Who reached out, and found, and listened to You, and was changed by You as all of us here were, and He's the richer for it, all of His Creation richer, just as we are richer, just as You said You think Your own universe is more complex and rich from meeting His.»"⌟ My own tears blurred the window-screen bright on the wall, the sky blue-white and false but also true because the blue is real and out there for us, waiting. ⌜"«Think, Ἄναξ, if this were the portrait of One Who groped and aimed so far and found nothing, there would be only black, but He found You. He found You out there, and to celebrate, He filled His emptiness with wonders beyond rainbow waiting for us, wonders we can see, and touch, and find.»"⌟

A pause, not long, His customary pause as words travel beyond and back again. ⌜"«Yes. Thou art correct, My Mycroft.»"⌟ I felt His body shift. "Huxley"—in English now—"do you hear this? This is the news you wanted. This means you will find them, friends on your own scale. You live in the Self-portrait-cosmos made by One Who Groped and Found, Who makes your journey a portrait of His own. So, just as He found a Peer to share His Making with, so, as He has you journey out, He will have you find, reachable, waiting, His portrait of Me, too."

I heard Huxley's gasp over my shoulder, windy, light, the kind of gasp that made the ancients think our souls move in our breath. "Life."

"Yes, peers on your scale, just as you hoped. And if He has found others of Our Species with Their own Creations beyond His and Mine, then you will find more worlds of life out there, portraits of other Peers, but we know now with certainty there is at least one. And when you do find that first friend, Huxley, Utopia, be patient with them? Please? Modeled on Me, they will not have been made to see the stars, or to imagine anything beyond their world and selves and their own making. First friendship will be hard for them, hard as it was for Me. So, bring it gently?"

I turned, the Visitor still in my arms, so I could see Huxley, stunned, staring, a mirror of my fear that if we moved or even blinked, this dream might pop, this answer without evidence except that we who lived it, we who watched the Alexander come, we who know Him and know Apollo and Poseidon, we felt . . . this felt right. His Peer changed by Him. Master Hobbes will ask for evidence, empiricism. Could we find some? Could Cato? Can physicists determine someday which parts of our Universe were revised by our Maker from outside of time to incorporate Jehovah's wish for lights and stepping-stones? Over the years we, humanity, will crawl toward evidence and explanations as Hobbes's ancients awed by rainbows crawled toward Newton's *Opticks,* but such understanding is for your age, reader, your wise future or a farther one, not for our now. We are the savages still gazing on the rainbow, and the evidence around Jehovah is subtle and specialized, His brain scans, signals, math, experts can see it, but our doubting imaginations can always conceive a way it could be fake, U-beasts, deception, Brillists in the laboratories, honest mistakes, lies. So, evidence was never why Huxley or Carlyle or I believed. He Who Visits in the ship of flesh we call Jehovah Mason said, "I Am a God," and we believed Him. And now He says that we were made for Contact, we a living alphabet of greeting from the far-aiming First Mover to His strange First Friend. And He says too it proves that there is friendship on our own scale, waiting for us in the starlit night. And me and Huxley, I can feel us seizing on those words as desperately as Dominic seizes our Master's knees, and we believe.

"Onkel?" My Master's voice was calm again, the ghostly calm of something barely present. *"Ich werde nichts anderes tun, Onkel, bis du Mir antwortest."*

We had found and purged six modes of spying from the palace intercom, but felt no surprise as Faust's image on the screen proved we had not purged all. "Yes, Donatien?"

"You hurt My Dominic."

"Yes, Donatien, I did. Nothing prevented it. Now You believe me."

"Can you help him?"

"No."

A shudder through the ship of flesh—its first?

"But *we* can help him, Donatien," Faust added, "You and I together. I have the details of how this was done, the tools, the experts on the mind and brain, while You, Donatien, have the decision in Your hands, to give us the resources that in time will yield technologies to help Your Dominic and many more. Choose us, give us Your Peer's gifts, Your support, and redirect Utopia's strength from two projects back into one, to disarm death. In time, we can find ways to help or heal Your Dominic, and many other ways a brain or body can be harmed, and more, we can continue to unlock the mind, its depths and power, letting it outlast flesh, exploring billions of inner worlds as vast as planets, here without the need to brave the outer void and risk so much."

I counted two breaths, three as He remained in my embrace, His one hand still stroking Dominic's shoulders, the other holding mine and clinging like a child. It was my turn to speak. I felt the duty, I Apollo's servant, Caesar's too, custodian of his no-longer-secret Oath, 'to nurture and that-unclear-other-verb Utopia.' It was my time to speak, but I could not. I couldn't ask Him to face more pain, reader. I couldn't ask Him to choose the path that will take more of us away.

"You heard and saw just now, *Onkel,*" He asked, "what I and My Mycroft observed and said?"

"I watched but understood little, Donatien. Will You let Mycroft translate?"

"Mycroft, do," the Guest ordered, and all listened as I sank back into my wheelchair and with clumsy English drew in stick figure the truths Jehovah had painted across my soul in shades of love and stars.

"I will not close the path that is the arc of My first Friend," He said, still holding Dominic, His grip as fierce as Dominic's on Him. "I will not push My Peer to Remake Our already-hybrid Making so far as to stifle that part of His Plan which leads you onto ships, since through His journey, and the ship of flesh He made for Me, We and Our universes are made richer. I will not ask His Nature Which I Love to lose Itself accommodating Mine. I choose Utopia, *Onkel,* their path, not yours."

Brillist Institute Headmaster Felix Faust flushed red, eyes wide, cheeks puffed, jaw slack, the shock and awe welling through every signal flesh commands. "*Wunderschönen . . .* (Wondrous/exquisite . . .)"

"Mike . . . You chose . . ." Huxley was shaking like a barque in storm, Cato too. You too thought the other side had won, didn't you, Huxley? Cato? As Micromegas held howling Dominic, you too couldn't speak up, felt He was right to choose the Brillist path and let Apollo Distant Aimer set aside his bow, and as Apollo of the Crossroads, Apollo Before the Doorway, grant us home.

"I have chosen Utopia, *Onkel.* Now I desire that the trunk-war end. I do not tolerate more deaths of small authors."

Faust's hesitating face wanted to bask, to think, to pour out observations, test hypotheses, gather experts, host conferences on this miracle of a conversation. But such luxuries are for peace, not war. "You understand You choose to redivide humanity, a future of separation, misunderstanding, conflict between fissured cultures, pain without end, and deaths, more lonely deaths for Your 'small authors'?"

"Yes. I choose that."

"And to risk losing those dear to You, Your *ibasho* shattered over and over?"

"Yes. I choose that."

"And all to reach toward distant barren worlds when there are billions of worlds right here, ten billion human minds, deep, rich, each one a vastness whose surface we have barely scratched?"

"Yes. I Love those mind-worlds, that inpath, My path, and I intend to nurture and explore it too, but I also Love the path of My first Friend."

Another leader in defeat might look sad, stern, or broken, but for Faust, who feasts on strangeness, this long moment was too rich a banquet for anything but delectation. "You will also understand, Donatien, if I still do all within my power to push humanity to reduce death first, before Mars, and separating cultures, and diaspora risk war again."

"I understand and co-intend this, *Onkel.* I have learned to Love that in My Peer which Distance mirrors, even Time, but not Death. I still disunderstand and unlove Death, and likewise war which spreads it."

Faust took a deep breath. "Then that brings us back to the hostages. As promised, since Donatien has chosen Utopia's path, I will revise my terms and permit Utopia to pursue its space projects, accessing the relics in any way that does not slow our work against death by more than one half second. I believe the last offer was three-fifths of Utopia's strength indentured to our project, plus all the relics that can help against death sent to our labs with our researchers leading, and 22 trillion a year from the Masonic treasury for our research, adjusted over time for Hive growth, inflation, et cetera. I have just two more demands, Donatien, if—"

"No," I cut in, "those offers are from before. Before Ἄναξ Jehovah chose—"

"My Nephew asked to speak to me, Mycroft, not you. Or do you intend to rescind [Anonymous]'s policy that Donatien may negotiate freely with other Hives?"

Faust's chiding gaze made mine fall to the floor, the shadow of my chair complex like clockwork locked in motion by some wiser Thing than me. "No, Headmaster, I do not."

"What else demand you, *Onkel*?" Earth's Conqueror still held His human bloodhound tight, and Dominic held Him, flesh, heat, and touch communicating without language. "The Bridger relics?"

"That's one of the two things, yes," Faust answered. "I need them all. Mycroft's proposal of a split is sweet but nonsense when the two most fit for space research are Cato and the Alexander, both essential to our mind-machine project to let minds outlive flesh."

Cato-H.E.L.E.N. winced, the old pain of being demanded, bartered, battled for, but he cannot deny he's worth a war.

"I need all the relics in my labs," Faust continued, "with Gordian setting the agenda, one that will advance our inpath fastest, not just immortality research but unlocking the powers of the mind, which is the only real source of all human power. The more we unlock that, the more we can achieve."

"I understand this demand, its logic, and necessity. Your second, *Onkel*?"

Faust's smile turned warm. "I want You free to come home to Ingolstadt. You and Your bash'mates, all. The Empire can't hold You forever. You're as essential to our voyages into the mind's depths as the Gates of Nineveh to plans beyond the well of gravity. You've decided to keep the outpath, I'll respect that and ensure it does continue, but You personally are best suited to the inpath, as You've said, the path that mirrors Yours. I'm not asking to lock You up here. You can and should travel to work with all the Hives, but we've lost Your mother's house in Paris and Yours in Avignon, You must call somewhere home. It shouldn't be a cell, it should be here where You'll advance so much."

Jehovah paused. It was tempting. I thought of the Institute, its vistas, mindscape gardens, toys and games, a box of them there on Faust's desk as bright as flowers. Could we go back? Faust? Mercer? Could we? To those days when work was play? I loved it there, the puzzles, rich debates, advancing noble projects, *profundum et fundamentum,* just by being me. And He is so free there, thriving, debating, answering as buzzing students take their notes. Could we go back?

"No." It was hard to make myself say it.

The Headmaster's brows narrowed. "My Nephew asked to speak to me, Mycroft, not you. Be good and hold your tongue."

Something—conscience? protocol?—chided me inside—*bad dog!*—but something else fought back. I took a long breath, silently begging the palace walls to breathe into me the marble strength of the Imperial line whose substitute I can't believe I am. "I'm sorry, Headmaster, but Ἄναξ Jehovah's liberty is not within His power to grant. Nor mine. It's Cornel MASON's order."

Faust's gaze remained severe. "You're on the throne now, Mycroft. It's your job to be less stubborn than Cornel."

I felt my breaths becoming shallow, panic close as when a dog surrounded by storm's thunder bristles, trying not to howl. Could I do it? Could I free Him? Free *us* to go back? I closed my eyes, trying to anchor myself, the room, the chair beneath me. No, not chair, *throne* I should say, *lèse-majesté* to call the Caesars' seat a chair. There was so much beneath that throne, the mere tip of a vast and solid pyramid, the line of Caesars stretching back from me into primordium, just as each iceberg mind extends from conscious surface down into a vastness potent and unknown. I do love diving, minds like histories both barely mapped. But I knew Cornel MASON's answer, heard him whisper to me, standing nearest in that line of misty Caesars watching from the gray of Acheron, so close, so easy for a frequent visitor like me to hear and know. "I was never named by Caesar, and may not reverse Caesar's command." My own voice sounded light but sharp, like a spear forged of some lightweight razor alloy if Cornel MASON's was a spear of gleaming iron.

"I know this is too much for you, Mycroft." Faust's eyes were warm. "It won't be long now. Once we've settled terms and I set Martin free to fill the throne, then you and Donatien can finally come work on things beyond the war."

Beyond the war? The phrase sounded like wind, like light, departing wings. The throne beneath me was a ball and chain, while light as Zephyr felt those days at Ingolstadt, almost as free as chasing Saladin among the olive trees at Alba Longa but productive, helping all humanity unlock our inner greatnesses which will someday surpass Eureka Weeksbooth, Toshi, Vivien, and barren little Mars. No. "Martin is, like me, only a proxy, and Martin, like Cornel MASON, would see Alexandria's harbors run red with blood before he gave the *Imperator Destinatus* into anybody's hand but Empire's."

Faust's face feasted on that response a quiet moment.

"As for my earlier offers," I began anew, "the funds, Utopian aid, those aren't in Ἄναξ Jehovah's power to grant. Remaker strength, His conquests, those are His, but not the imperial treasury, nor Utopia which surrendered to the

Empire, not to Him." I took a deep, self-steeling breath. "When ransoming Ἄναξ Jehovah's bash'mates meant breaking the pressure on Him to choose your path, Headmaster, then I could justify spending all the Empire's treasures to uphold the MASONS' Oath, *Utopianos aliturum absecuturumque,* to nurture and away-follow Utopia. But now that Ἄναξ Jehovah's choice is made . . ." A shiver moved through me, but I made sure these words had the iron of dead Caesars in them. ". . . now that His choice is made, threats to the hostages give you no power to make demands of the Empire."

Faust gazed at me for several pensive seconds. "You misestimate how many hostages I have."

I felt a prickle down my spine. "What do you mean?"

"I have four hundred million hostages."

Scared inbreaths, Huxley's, Cato's, mine; that number only mapped to one thing that we knew. "All of Utopia?"

"Precisely. The war everyone knows about has ended, and modern wars end with the blame phase. Crowds will cry out to punish atrocities, including the more brutal commanders, any of Perry's cohort we can capture, the Nurturists responsible for the worst purges, soldiers who went wrong, but most of all the force behind the silence that's been so destructive, and the hijacking of the cars."

I looked to Huxley, who looked as confused as I. "Gordian did all that: the cars, the silence."

"Us?" Faust answered. "No. Ask anyone: Gordian's done nothing in the war except peacekeeping and the odd surrender. But we have been helping with investigations here and there. It appears the explosion in Cielo de Pájaros day one that took out the Saneer-Weeksbooth facility was caused by a U-beast-implanted human bomb, just like the one in Lorelei Cook that killed poor Ganymede. And the UFOs that have been supplementing the cars in lockshell, those are coming from factories in Utopian districts in a dozen places, and are filled with Utopian tech. And I'm afraid it turns out the lockshell program that's controlling the cars originated from the Utopian Transit Network System Headquarters in Emerald City."

I shivered as at cold wind. "What have you done?"

Coldly, crisply: "We prepared for war. As Utopia did. They built the *Skymaw* harbinger atrocity that broke the ancient U.N. Outer Space Treaty, and we prepared for the war of public opinion. You know that's a war Gordian wins. The deeper people dig, the more clues will lead back to Utopia, and they did strike first. You can't prove their innocence, and the public is more than ready to believe they're guilty. Donatien as Conqueror may protect them in laws and edicts, but Donatian cannot control an angry public in every back alley in the world. Insist upon their innocence and the most you can create is a world of confusion, split blame, and conspiracy theories which will undermine trust in the whole new order. Thus I say I have, in addition to the precious Brain-bash', four hundred million hostages."

I could see Huxley in the corner of my vision, quaking with fear-fury fast as blood. Or was that me? Rage. Rage, Achilles, I can feel it, inner thunder. Tears flow often from me, full of sorrows, but true rage is rare, this silent galloping inside my head. They rose around me now, those birds which are not birds which follow me sometimes, schooling against the sunset, dark and multitudinous and watching, schooling, swarming, spirits of the dead, your friends, Achilles, all our disenfranchised predecessors with no voice apart from we who honor them, we who remember, speak, and carry on their rage.

"All the evidence I've named," Faust continued, "could, on further investigation, end up pointing elsewhere, say at Casimir Perry, there's a villain ripe for blame. And then Utopia would be safe in the new world, and free to work with us disarming death. Thus, back to our terms: we were at three-fifths of Utopia's strength, 22 trillion a year from the treasury, the relics, and Donatien's liberty."

The shadow birds were surging still, spirits of sailors lost, innumerable as the fish that gnaw their bones, all those who toiled a hundred thousand years along the path which He, Kind-Wisher, chose over His own—the path that Faust dares threaten? Voices within me quarreled: negotiate, refuse, be fierce, be honey-sweet, but all these swirling stratagems were mere leaves floating on the bubbling geyser surface, while the heat, and the wet, and the salt, and the rage made the older and usually slumbering me start testing my limbs toward battle stance and scanning the room for my predator dance. "You dare threaten Utopia?"

"Take a deep breath, Mycroft, you're—"

"Still?" I snarled. "After He's chosen?"

"Careful, Mycroft . . . settle . . ."

I was salivating. "What was the threat? Back when Ἄναξ tested Utopia—what was it He threatened? To banish them forever from the Earth?"

„Ruhe jetzt, Mycroft. Ruhe . . ."

"Shall I do what He threatened? Chase Gordian homeless and unwelcome from every corner of human dominion?" Even Cato was shrinking back.

"I can break you with three words, Mycroft, but I don't want to."

My chair was rattling. "I have the Empire, Faust! And you dare threaten!"

"Donatien," Faust called, "some intervention, please?"

"Mycroft." The Best Thing In or Visiting Our World, His voice, my name called in His voice feels more real than when I hear my own weak and unlikely inner answer: am I Mycroft Canner?

"Yes, Ἄναξ?"

"We need My Mycroft right now, not the old one."

"What do You need, Ἄναξ?"

His arms eased slightly around Dominic, reassured, perhaps, that I was His again? "You are correct that I, Prisoner, cannot grant what *Onkel* asks. We need the one who speaks for Empire; at present, you."

MASON—my duty—what would MASON do?

Uphold the Oath.

Yes. Faust, Kosala, Ancelet, these are complex leaders, their actions hard to guess sometimes, but not Cornel MASON's. Deep breath. "Headmaster, I understand you think you have leverage right now. You don't. You fail to understand the scale of what you would awaken if you carried out this threat. What you truly have right now is the power to be cruel. To hurt a Kind Being, to hurt the Brain-bash' which you hoped to trust with Gordian's future, to hurt the partners who share your great quest. You have the power, by being so cruel, to ensure that the Empire's strength comes down on Gordian as hard as Cornel MASON would have brought it, inexorable, unending, the vastest power in all Earth's history fighting you with every stick and stone." Deep breath again. "What I have is the power to be kind. To gentle justice, which is already coming for you, for all Gordian, for your violation of the *Sanctum Sanctorum,* which we know was you."

I waited, but Faust's face showed nothing.

"Remember, Headmaster," I continued, "I am custodian of MASON's colors, but they are not colors of peace." I raised my arms to show my sleeves, one Death's black, the other stony gray, reminder there is hope someday that the war-steeled Heart of Empire may again become so soft a thing as marble. "It was not the threat of Hiveguard which woke those 'Capital Powers with which, by Most Ancient Mandate, MASON is invested for the Preservation of the Empire in Time of War.' It was Gordian. Cornel MASON vowed no Mason will as much as hear the word 'peace' until the *Sanctum* violators face Empire's severest justice—that means you, Faust, and your agents, who twisted the Accursed-Through-the-Ages-Guildbreakers, who planned archcrime. The Empire's war, this whole time, has been with you, and that war will grind on until it exacts justice, as Cornel MASON vowed, unless . . ." Here I breathed deep again and smiled, and felt that smile diffuse its warmth through me like sun. "As a mere regent, I do not have authority to lift the doom Caesar pronounced against you: destruction absolute and *damnatio memoriae* through all posterity. But I do have the power to be kind, to imitate how Caesar dealt with Archtraitor Xiaoliu Accursed-Through-the-Ages-Guildbreaker, judging that Caesar's sentences are Caesar's to carry out at what hour Caesar chooses. As proxy, I may postpone your sentence while you make amends, a stay of execution for all Gordian as you labor with us to make the new world better and to help attain stability without O.S. And in that stay of execution, I may give you access to Bridger's treasures so you can partner with Utopia to disarm death. I can give you all that if you are kind. But if you insist on being cruel, on threatening Utopia, and causing pain to *Him,* Headmaster, to the Being so Good that this universe had to birth stars to be worthy to host His visit, if you are cruel to *Him* and to His sailors, then I will see to its fastest completion Cornel MASON's promise to purge from the Earth you whose archcrime stains this era with the shame that humankind, agreeing on one shared, universal sanctum, could not hold it inviolate."

Faust smiled through my speech, a slow, evolving smile, as when a connoisseur enjoys a good vintage which matures through subtle flavors one by one. "Ah, yes, the Masonic vendetta is—"

"Must that follow, Mycroft? *Onkel?*" He interrupted—had I ever seen Him interrupt someone before? Such urgency.

"What, Ἄναξ?"

"Must Empire's justice bring destruction on the inpath Hive?"

I couldn't meet His eyes. "It must, Ἄναξ. They committed archcrime. Nothing can change that, even if they never harm Your servants or Utopia again. It won't be every Brillist, only . . ." The more I tried to find something to follow 'only,' the less 'only' it seemed.

"Cornel's sentence," Faust cut in, "was to hack and burn the branch, I understand? Obliterate the way of thought that shaped the minds that planned such an act? That means the heart of Gordian, if not every Member."

The Stranger's eyes locked on me, darkness dizzying. "Must that follow, Mycroft? I unwant that."

"I can postpone it, Ἄναξ, as I said, be kind if the Headmaster is—"

"But I unwant that always."

It is easier to shed my own blood than tell Him no. "Ἄναξ, I can't change—"

"I want Gordian to reach into ten billion human depths and make them deeper, and to partner with Utopia to battle Death, and to remain a partner for that outer depth, lamplit with stars, where fear, which chills the mind, is one of vacuum's deepest fangs." As He spoke, he held His Dominic tighter to Him, and Dominic released a gentle sound, which my heart called happy. "I told you I do not tolerate the deaths of small authors."

I choked—yes, Gordian deserves that title too, 'small authors,' Utopia and Gordian twin world-makers and twins in preciousness. "I can't change Caesar's sentence, Ἄναξ, only Caesar can, if we bring Caesar back—"

So light His words: "Would *Pater* change the sentence?"

No. Fifty kinds of no schooled through my mind: not if You beg, Ἄναξ, not if Faust threatens, not if it costs lives, not if it costs *his* life, Cornel MASON who died for this already once, and would again. I didn't speak these answers, but the Guest could read the torrent in my face, the fractal nos, the tactics we might try, more nos with every branch and not a yes in the wide unfurling world of possibility.

So, He ended that world: "Can I change the sentence if I become MASON?"

Gasps from Huxley, from ever-present Chagatai, from Faust upon the screen, even from Dominic, who felt a shift, perhaps, in the slim frame he clung to.

"Ἄναξ . . . You . . . ?"

"I become Caesar if I take the Oath. Then the sentence is Mine to change, is it not?"

Danger signals prickled through me, animal, as when earthquake's invisible heralds stir beasts and birds. He take the Oath? He change? "Ἄναξ, You . . . not for this. You don't have to do such a thing for this." For we smaller than ants.

"As MASON, I could nurture Gordian through another age of humankind.

I want that, all your billions on billions of mind-worlds more and more complex, and lasting."

Yes. "But it would change You, Ἄναξ. You . . . You said why You refused to take the Oath, how much three unknown words could do to You. You don't need to step ignorant into the dark and let it change You, not for us."

"I Love you."

Why does it stab so when He says it? The best sentence in the world and yet it stabs. "I know, Ἄναξ, but we don't . . . We've stained so much in this war, there's nothing perfect left, not the *Sanctum Sanctorum*, not the Universal Laws, not Utopia's project, not Cousin kindness, not even our A.I.s! We made new life, made thinking things, then made them fight our war. We're as bad as our Maker. But You—You never bloodied the hands of Your creations in Your cosmos, never brought them pain. The only perfect thing we have is You, Ἄναξ. Don't change. Please?"

Softly, soft as night: "I have changed three times in this conversation."

My *fundamentum* shook. "Yes, but that was from Your Peer, Your Conversation, not us, we . . ." We what? We are not worth it?

"My Friend Who Gropes stepped ignorant into the dark, seeking, knowing Contact would change Him, but He trusted. There was no Friend to trust yet, nothing known out there, but He trusted still. And once He found Me, once He had a Friend to trust, He trusted Me enough to let Me change His very Making, His Self-portrait, offered Me the choice to end the outpath if that was the only way We could be Friends. I do not yet trust the One Who conceived Pain for His creations as symmetrically as He has trusted Me, but feel I do know His Nature well enough to trust Him for three words."

"But, Ἄναξ . . ." Why was I protesting? Power, freedom, I should want this for Him, my Master on the throne at last, the final conquest to position His remaking, and He has undergone trial-by-pain enough for the imperial tradition, Cornel MASON saw to that. Yet it still felt like earthquake under me. "You risk Yourself, Your better cosmos too, letting Your Peer . . . look at what He's made, Ἄναξ! All evils ever! Tsunamis! Famine! Tuberculosis! Lead! Lead so useful while invisibly it poisoned us millennia before we had a way to know! He planned it that way! Made it poison! Made all evils, even . . ." I froze before His black gaze.

"Even thee?" Of course He knew how I had almost finished. "True. And the calculation of how, and when, and with what, and how much to trust thee, My Mycroft, remains complex, yet I can make that calculation, and can judge both how and when to trust thee well. And as I calculate for thee, so now I understand enough to calculate for Him. I choose to become MASON, and to trust My Friend the outpath's Maker to Large-Author-revise Me with the three words my *Pater* small-author-revised. So bring Me the Oath."

His gaze during that last command fell on Xiaoliu Accursed-Through-The-Ages-Guildbreaker, who had been gazing proud as Nike on this longed-for moment, but frowned now. "The *Sanctum* chamber has been repaired, *Porphyrogene.* There MASONS create themselves in privacy, as it has always been."

"No more," He answered, firm, and I saw Faust's face on the screen flush with delight. "The Oath is public now. Since I can, I will have the world witness My choice and change, that none may doubt."

Xiaoliu frowned more at the Brillist on the screen than at his almost-Emperor. "Three words are still secret, *Porphyrogene.*"

"True. And three more will change with each succession, three, and three, and new secrecy could accumulate like stalagmite through generations. But the main good that comes from the evil of the Oath's release is that the world knows now what MASON is, and needs no longer fear nor act in error guessing what this *Primus inter pares* might secretly serve or be. That good I shall preserve, and make future successions like My own, the three words secret until each MASON speaks them, but at that moment, all should learn together how the foundations of slow-changing Empire, like all things from genes unto the dimming Sun, evolve with Time."

So He commanded, Who must be obeyed at last in Alexander's city. As Masons raced to call all ears to hear what would soon stream out from His cell and remake power on our planet, our Good Master called me toward Him, and guided Dominic's hand to feel the scars across my knuckles and around my wrists, to touch my bitten ear and battered hat, and Dominic smiled—he still has smiles—and cuffed me on the forehead. He recognized me, reader, I a second anchor in his ravaged world, and I shook with joy, seeing this portrait of how joyous our Master and His Friend may someday be when they pierce through some other God's Infinity and follow First Friendship with Second. And so, on our small scale, may we.

"*Onkel?*" He called to Faust on one screen as the other showed the war-room bustle of an empire changing.

"Yes, Donatien?"

"I will alter Gordian's sentence, but there must still be a consequence for archcrime, else consequence and law and arch- and crime lose meaning in this world."

"I understand, Donatien. And on my end, I'm very happy to see You ready to rule at last, but I will not restore Your *ibasho* until You give me all the relics. That is my immovable condition."

"I understand that, *Onkel.*"

"Will You grant it?"

Silence as words travel to the *fundamentum* depths and back again. "I will decide after this Act. I Am about to change."

He was. I braced myself, or tried, as one who sees the tsunami coming tries to grip something, a tree, a pole, but in the torrent-complexity you can't know which splash will be hardest as the surge blasts by and then churns back, the water dense as phalanx armed with spears of wood and shattered homes. So, blow on blow I knew the oath would thunder on me. Worst, I could not know which wave would bear the sharpest spear, which sentence would contain the three words Mason changed, his tools to guarantee this Prince Whom all paths welcome could walk only the Masonic road. I, cowering, did not expect two of the three new words to come in the first line:

> *IMPERIUM sum donec humanus, hinc princeps, parens, aedifex illius urbis cinctae muribus sapientium laterum, nominatae humanitatis.*
>
> IMPERIUM I am while I am human, henceforth leader, parent, and architect of that city, girded with walls of thinking brick, named humanity.

You let Him go. Cornel MASON, Caesar, you had a Cosmos-Maker prisoner to your stylus, could have remade His cosmos in Empire's image, a universe of power, loyalty, marble, and iron, and you let Him go. "[So-long-as/while/in-as-much-as I] [I am/exist/continue/live as a human]." You made His cosmos immune, a God there and a MASON here, this office finite like the many He has long worn on His armband, separate from Himself. You had three words, Cornel MASON, to brand into our future, irrevocable, your legacy as you fall down into the mists below the pyramid where vampire forgetting saps the dead, and you used two of your three words to let Him go? Were you always so kind a father, Caesar? Hiding behind your marble and your sanctum walls, were you always this kind?

The Oath flowed on, tsunami force around me, but it felt like cleansing more than danger as the lifeline of my Master's hand in mine proved heartbeat after heartbeat that the only Perfect Thing we know remains Itself. The Latin blurred, just fragmentary phrases sticking in my mind as I, who know Him so well, could foreglimpse some of the actions this would spur Him to, feeling the shape of policies He has indeed begun as I sit writing, shaping His reshaping:

> *Pietatem humanitati non debeo, nec mihi debet, vere ilex unicus sumus, vigens sub tempestivo sole, sub bipenni inepto lacrimans, gente humana trunco ruboreque, memet cordi prudentia quae arbitratur quo tempore frondescendum quoque stringendum ad hiemem.*
>
> I owe humanity no [duty/piety] and it owes me none, rather we are one oak, thriving in clement sun and bleeding under the foolish axe, humanity the trunk and growing force, and I the prudence in its heart which judges when to sprout leaves and when to strip for winter.

Foolish the axe, yes, call it that, Ἄναξ. He will not hastily lop branches but consult with all on their own branches' changes as he gives the order to transmute all factories of war to factories of plenty, preparing nutrients to rush to every bud and bare branch of our war-tired species: spring has come.

What next? What changes next?

Posthac atomi fugaces quae nominantur dies, anni, decenni, sunt mihi arenae, cui cura est perennium.

Henceforth the fleeting atoms called day, year, and decade are as sand to me, who only gives care to perennial things.

Fleeting the days, yes, He has long known that but strives now to remind the rest of us, setting a patient calendar for His reforms, aid and relief swift, but granting weeks or months to plan structural changes and to search out Senators and statespersons among Poseidon's seas to gather at His side. What next? What next?

IMPERIUM familiam non habet, nec gentem, prolem, parentem etc . . . Cui succedo si vivit, nihil pietatis debeo, sed sumus, ego ut Voluntas quae perago Ratioque ille quae censet.

IMPERIUM has no family, tribe, offspring, parent etc . . . If my predecessor lives, I owe no filial piety, but I am as Will which acts, they Reason which advises.

Oh, wise MASONS past, you knew our fear! Knew what a deadly toxin influence can be: Mother, Father, the yoke of piety. No danger now that Spain will chain Him fast with oaths of loyalty; even Madame had she evaded melodrama's fangs He could have disobeyed now, and you too, Cornel MASON, should we keep our promise to Achilles to defy Homer and grant the hero and his dear Patroclus life past war. What next? What phrase will catch upon me from the torrent next?

. . . qui me lacessant, illis neque odium neque misericordiam habiturum, contra amputaturum velut veprem hortulanus . . .

. . . those who scratch me I shall neither hate nor pity but cut off as the gardener the thorn bush . . .

Yes, tremble, Gordian, who still threatens to wound He Who has become Caesar. Yet, even with that thought, I was the one who trembled, I who knew what phrase came next, the strange promise so vague about Utopia, to nurture and *absequor* (away-follow), whose antonym *adsequor* (toward-follow) can mean (Oh elusive Latin!) to chase, escort, accompany, obey, take as a leader, seek, seize, attain, aspire to, observe, pursue, side with, so many contrarieties. *Absequor,* then, might be so many opposites: abandon, disobey, liberate, persecute, set out with, side against, take as a guiding light, follow out into darkness, chase without a hope of catching up, perhaps even to drive from every corner of human dominion out into the dark exhaustion of forever. So, I felt it coming: two kind words Cornel MASON had gifted to the Son he loved, the third he would, he must—I felt it—gift unto his other love, the one who ever leads men onto ships, and aims so far.

> *. . . aliquando Utopianos speculas futuri aliturum exploratores absecuturumque ut spatium voluminis perlustretur.*
>
> And ever the Utopians as mirrors of the future I shall nurture and as scouts/explorers away-follow, as the scroll grows bright.

Clarity. A MASON's life is building, foundation on foundation, Uruk, then Babylon, then Aegae, then Rome, Constantinople, Aachen, Luna City, stone on stone, but for one moment, he is not mason but architect, his three new words three changes to the blueprint of that edifice that his life and lives hereafter will erect—Cornel used that to gift us clarity, confirmation that, yes, that little corner tower rising higher than the roof, it seeks the stars.

The rest of the Oath flowed past, so safe and right: that He will wield and gentle Law as He desires; that He will harness to their greatest power the human energies: desire, thought, and hope; that He will build brick on brick from dead past toward unborn future; all this was in His nature long before stonecutters raced to carve it into tablets around the world:

JEHOVAH EPICURUS DONATIEN D'AROUET MASON

He paused as the Oath ended, He the Stranger Kind enough to call 'Friend' One Who fashioned us and entropy, but this pause was no longer than His ordinary pauses, for it takes no moment more or less to fetch across infinity the blueprints of an empire or a single word. "Xiaoliu?" He called.

"*Sic, Caesar?*" the Archtraitor answered, with a zeal as if the summons were a longed-for gift that, better yet, will now flow freely—Empire has an Emperor again.

"Assemble Masonic leaders in one space to meet with Me first, Alliance leaders in a second, and prepare a call from that space to Papadelias, and in a third space gather for me in person voices of all factions you can reach in Alexandria, Hives, nation-strats, Mitsubishi subgroups, Hiveguard, youths, Reservationers; after this long seclusion, I desire as plural a conversation as I can have to plan My Remaking."

"*Quam primum, Caesar.*"

"Thank you. Chagatai?" He called next.

"Mm? What, T.M.?" the Blacklaw answered, smiling as Xiaoliu scowled at the casual address, but a Blacklaw's pride is that she cares not a fig whether the Boy Who saved her life so long ago is now called Caesar.

"Go cook something My Dominic will recognize as thy creation, that he may know with certainty that thou art thou, and here, and thus that this is home. I shall stay with him while thou dost so, and I desire that he never be left out of reach of some hand—thine, Mine, Mirabeau's, or Mycroft's—that he can identify with certainty and trust."

"Good thought, T.M. I'll do my milk tea special and some quickie dumplings while I get the Carnivore Roll going. I doubt the palace meatmakers have snowcap, but I can make do with standard hummingbird options, most have Anna's, at least."

"Thank you. Huxley?"

"Yes, Mike?"

"Go don your coat and vizor and regain your lion partner and become again fully yourself. And after that, prepare some safe place in the open air where I and My Mycroft, when we have time, might step out to see stars."

"With pleasure, Mike. Saturn's rings are very visible right now, I'll bring my telescope."

"Thank you. Doctor Weeksbooth, you may join us for stargazing if you wish. And then I have a task for you if you are willing?"

Ever nervous, "Ye–es, C–sar?"

"Mike or Micromegas, please, you are Utopian and I welcome your welcome."

"Mm. Thank you. Mike."

"Thank you," Kindness answered back. "You are also, I think, best to direct the study of the relics. Would you kindly gather what aid you will and undertake to design a collaborative research program? Utopia and Gordian together, with all the resources I offered *Onkel*, all the relics too, outlining what you would prioritize, how you would allocate the access time. And if you can, show clearly how inpath and outpath would advance together, even if a single trunk with all the resources might have grown faster."

"Yes, I can do that. The university has . . . Yeah. Yeah. On it."

"Thank you. It will not, I predict, persuade mine Uncle, but it may be comfort to him and his inpathers to know the worst outcome would still be good."

"Yes." A rich smile even from fragile Cato. "It will be good."

I looked around, still feeling dazed—I was the last left in the room without orders. "What would you have me do, Ἄναξ?"

"Thou . . ." A pause, the consultation of Infinity, this time for me. "I think I know thee well by now, My stray. I think I know thy place and powers in thy Maker's alphabet-of-welcome better than thou dost. So, doubt not My judgment that thou canst accomplish this which I order."

"I . . . what, Ἄναξ?"

"Defeat Mine *Onkel*, secure My First Friend's outpath, win the war."

Chapter the TWENTY-NINTH

The Battle of Ingolstadt

Written January 9–12, 2456
Events of January 8
Alexandria

THERE IS A GRAY-EYED GODDESS WATCHING ME. To win the war, His order but her province, she the hope of soldiers, sprung from Zeus's head cracked wide by thought and pain. It is she who ends wars, she as partisan as her half-brother Ares is impartial as he hands out death. I dare not name her, dare not think her name, the Aegis-bearer, keen as the clean sky. No god welcomes the prayers of parricides, but some I know—I feel—take satisfaction as my heart cries out its pain and awe, your due, Ἄναξ Apollo, dread Poseidon, you whose curses work your justice on me grief by grief, as cut by cut the shipwright shapes the sapling to his plan. Not she. I feel it, her disgust, her distance, Zeus's tireless daughter, wise, untouchable, her name upon this soiled tongue would be as sour to her as filth smeared on her sacred effigy. And yet she helps me still. I feel it in me, victory instincts her domain, which warned me as the scouts sent in reports from Ingolstadt, as plans took shape: it's wrong. All wrong. We took every precaution. Randomness is our best armor against Brillists, random agents sent on random routes at random times to scout Gordian's capital. As Earth's young Conqueror convened His plural councils in the upper pyramid, I down here in the basement sealed away (we hope) from Brillist view assembled stratagems into one layered, perfect, war-ending assault. But it was wrong. I felt it each night as I lay mulling on plans, her wisdom like an owl's whispers in my sleepy ear: here lies no victory. But why? So many days I failed to understand: why would the gray-eyed goddess help me when I know she scowls on this foul, soiled thing?

When did I realize she was with me? The year 2455 had died its gentle death, and rosy Eos rose a little earlier each January day to watch the human herds flock toward the Visitor's great council. He Who Won for Us the Gift of Starlight summoned all leaders and voices to Him, to advise, to speak, petition for their factions and philosophies, and to hear edict by edict His remaking.

One flock, both trickiest and most important, triggered the change as preludeless as ambush and as irreversible: "Romanova is ready to surrender, all except the Blacklaws on the Aventine." The detail cheered me more than full surrender would have: after all these months, bold Tribune Natekari and her

Blacklaw courage holds the hill against Empire, Ares, even maddening Atë. Pictures from the last months showed the sea of flags upon the city's roofs changing, the chaos after Ganymede's assassination giving way to Mitsubishi splintering, then Hiveguard's resurgence, back and forth, each alley hosting many battles. But now that all leaders of all sides had made peace, the mobs of Earth's most mixed and volatile city were at last ready to follow. So, I summoned Toshi Mitsubishi and Bo Chowdhury to my little office to watch together as the golden blips upon the war map traced our vanguard's path like fireflies blinking their summer dances toward the seven hills that host the seven Hives of yesterday. And since no flock will move without its ram, I called my Myrmidons as well, far in the Bay of Bengal, who at my order patched, and tweaked, and jury-rigged, and from the static Papadelias against Dhaka's skyline rose upon the screen.

The great Bengali Graylaw capital had put a fine office at the Commissioner General's disposal, corner windows gazing westward on Krepolsky's famous cluster of three-sided skyscrapers, their southern faces agriculture's green, the others a rainbow chaos of plant boxes and bright curtains as each bash' made their balcony their own. Papa looked so unchanged, his sleeves rolled up as if he was about to dig into a gardening project or one of his office junk piles, his bright smile itching for a fight. But it was a frozen smile, a frozen image sent as placeholder to humanize the ache of voice-only.

"Bo, great to see you!" Papa plunged in—our side's video did work, it seemed. "You safe? Any threats or blackmail?"

Papa's right-hand Whitelaw grinned. "Only the threat implicit in Masonic guards."

"Of course. And is that our Acting Censor hiding behind you? So glad you're safe, Toshi, and being treated well, I hope?"

Semi-set-set Toshi Mitsubishi stepped slowly from behind towering Bo Chowdhury, her shyness reminding me of those distrustful trees that keep their spring buds tight well past the blooms of others, a wise choice in those frequent years that send late frosts. "Thank you, Commissioner, and yes, all Tai-kun's people are being courteous."

"Mm, must be nice to Caesar's *onee-san*." Papa pronounced the Japanese word for "big sister" with some darkness—it is easy to forget how many nights young 'Tai-kun' spent in Tōgenkyō as the youngest and, in the world's eyes, barely strangest of Danaë and Andō's bash'children; if He learned anything of Earth outside Madame's and Alexandria, He learned it there. "And Mycroft!" Papa continued, that rich voice making the photo seem to live, "world conquest suits you! You look . . . I heard you took a beating, but you look exactly the same, that's some recovery. Whoa, waterworks that fast?"

There will be a time to tell this old soul that the younger one he mourned with as both wept for me upon each other's shoulders has . . . has made a choice. Not now. "Sorry. I . . . *ssnnhh*." A sob made me sputter. "We should . . ."

Papa switched to Greek. «The abrasions along the right side of Malory

Mardi's jaw, was I right those were from the sharp edge of the bronze bull aperture during the struggle to force them in on the twenty-second? Or was it the scuffle with Saladin on the twenty-first?»

Laughter burst through me like mountain wind. You still care! A billion pressures are crushing the old world's ashes into diamond lattice that will lock in the next century of human change, and Papa still cares whether Malory Mardi got punched on a Wednesday! Thank you, Providence, for leaving one thing—even so ridiculous a thing—unchanged.

«That's better. Are you being well treated?» Papa followed up. «Are you where you want to be, doing what you want to be doing?»

The humane questions helped me sniffle back my remnant tears. «Yes. Yes, I am.»

«Good. Then»—Papa returned to English—"shall we switch to adversary mode? What does the tyrant want? Let me guess: the Senate to rubberstamp their policies? That's traditional for conquering Caesars."

It felt a little warm inside, like tea's hot trickle, sparring like this again.

"Tai-kun doesn't need you for that, Commissioner," Toshi cut in. "The Mitsubishi Board granted them Chief Executive power this morning, and confirmed their proposed list of new Mitsubishi Senators. That makes one hundred and thirteen Senate seats Tai-kun can assign by fiat: sixty-one Masonic, seventeen Brillist, eight Utopian, and twenty-seven Mitsubishi. Europe and the Cousins are likely to be supportive too, but no matter how the Hives that don't fiat their Senators swing in the end, Tai-kun has a majority."

Papa began to laugh but it came out as a cough. "I guess that settles the question of whether the Senate will confirm you as full Censor. Congratulations."

Her face stayed grave. "No, it makes it impossible for the Senate to confirm me legitimately. Even allies will cry foul, seeing Tai-kun give the office to 'Toshi *onee-san*.' We can give me the office, but we can't make the public accept it. You can. The old trusted Commissioner General—ten words from you can make the public see my appointment as triumph or tyranny."

What was Papa's hush? A nod? A chin stroke? Lag? "I see it."

"Tai-kun's spoken with Vivien. We all have. Vivien suggested Tai-kun should advance their changes through the Alliance system, convening the Senate and continuing the Hive reforms that were already underway before the war began. It could do wonders for how much the public accepts the changes long-term, making them feel more real and acceptable, flowing out of the old system, maintaining its best parts."

"I know," Papa replied. "I've spoken with Vivien too, and I know how much the trappings of old systems can shore up tyrants, that's not new."

"I . . . may I?" I looked to Toshi, whose nod bade me speak on. "Papa, I love and respect the Alliance, as does Ἄναξ Jehovah. Truly. We want to preserve it as best we can, and nobody wants this to become a permanent world monarchy, the Alliance is the ideal tool to transition back to plural government once the reforms are done."

Papa's voice remained stony. "A lot of conquerors claim they'll restore the republic after X, Y, Z."

I winced. "I know. But it's a hope. Except right now, Ἄναξ Jehovah is too strong, and the Alliance in His hand is fragile as an eggshell. We like the idea of doing the reforms within the Alliance framework, preserving the Alliance, but if we try that and you don't support us, then people will see the Alliance as corrupted, the Senate and Censor compromised, a rotten egg. That's what really risks ending the Alliance or at least people's faith in it. So, if you won't agree to endorse the changes, it would be better for us to do them from outside, imposing them on the Alliance by force of conquest so our interference is external to the Alliance, like an egg with a square bottom stapled to it but the egg's still good inside. Sorry, I think that metaphor failed."

Papa gave a reedy chuckle. "I followed it alright. Change by force means the Alliance remains itself."

"Exactly," I answered. "This is the part of the war it's easiest to bungle. Think of the new conflicts that could grow in five or ten years if we handle the healing badly. We don't want this to be World War III, Part I."

"Indeed."

"That's why we won't try to do this from within the Alliance unless we have your support, Papa, your loud, public support in front of all the cameras, saying yes, this is legitimate, yes, Toshi should be Censor, yes, the Senate still means something, yes, this is the Alliance we all know and— Ah! Romanova!"

I heard Papa's chuckle. "Was that supposed to be a patriotic 'Ah'?"

I laughed. "No. Romanova, we have a signal, they . . . they're answering."

The screen before us divided, and there beside Papa's frozen image rose Romanova's Hive Council Chamber, a little fuzzy but with real movement, fiber-optic sunlight streaming through the ring of kitchen trees, all stripped for food but with a new crop plumping at the flower bases. The great circular bench built for the many young Hives of our founding days remained as clean and hollow as a crown, while in the center stood the little ring of chairs where Huxley—seventeen months and three lifetimes ago—had gathered the Hive leaders to announce peacebonding the harbingers. Who sat there now? Look, Charlemagne Accursed-Through-the-Ages-Guildbreaker is smiling safe and well! And Assistant Commissioner Desi O'Callaghan steady in Papa's seat. And little Acting Minor Senator Kenzie Walkiewicz—the child must've grown four inches! Has it been so long? And . . . what were these thoughts? These thoughts so casual, knowing them all so well, as if partners of toil side by side—are these shards of my lost successor leaking into me? The *me* that is an *us*? Or is it just the chronicle, the chapters from the early war that I've reread so many times? Has Bridger blurred us? Or is it you, reader, who blurs us, a Mycroft of your imagining revived like Hobbes, shaped by the parts you know more than the parts you don't?

I heard Toshi Mitsubishi's light breath catch behind me and knew why, for there among the rest sat Speaker Jin Im-Jin, the tiny figure looking the least changed of all, since even Ares cannot age what has withstood a century still smiling.

"No, I've no idea what Felix is up to, and no influence over it." The Brillist answered the question which must have showed upon our faces. "My job in the master plan is like Carmen's, to be out of all loops, so if Faust fails and falls, the Hive will have a guiltless backup leader to negotiate good losing terms. I know nothing and have done nothing. Now, what do the conquerors want from our little Triumvirate that's important enough to have Mycroft as twitchy as a squirrel but not important enough for Donatien to bother calling us themself?"

"*Tri*umvirate?" Papadelias's disembodied voice jumped on that one. "Still three? Are you in touch with Su-Hyeon?"

Jin Im-Jin sighed across the lagging interstice, as ancient Triton might sigh at a ship bound for the whirlpool of Charybdis. "That child . . ."

"You knew, didn't you?" I accused, almost startled by my speed, the harshness in my voice. "Speaker, you knew Faust was wooing the Censor toward Gordian."

Jin Im-Jin arched an eyebrow. "Wondering if those whispers in Korean behind everybody's backs were Brillist scheming?" A sad shake of the head. "Felix told Su-Hyeon a hundred times not to tell me, but they out and blabbed it back in . . . oh, around when Pass-It-On began. I wouldn't let Su-Hyeon share details, just told them over and over, 'It's your choice.' And it is their choice, isn't it? If favoring a Hive or faction in our hearts were criminal, we'd all be guilty, except Bo over there." Jin winked through the screen at the Whitelaw, who nodded at the compliment, but did not smile.

It's criminal to break the Fourth Law, Speaker—I let my face say it, my accusation as legible to the old Brillist as if I had a phoenix here to carve it out in words of fire. It's an Intolerable Crime to deprive a human being of the ability to call for help and contact fellow human beings, even a poor young Servicer trapped in that hellish hospital, human and Romanova's to protect. Did you know?—my eyes asked—did you know Faust planned to make Su-Hyeon do *that* to his best friend? But you also knew Faust planned the Silence, that your Hive was—*is*—breaking the Fourth Law ten billion times, and you said nothing. I don't dare unleash Papa on you in these unstable days, Speaker Jin Im-Jin, but once the peace is strong, there will be justice.

The smile-wrinkles of sixteen complex decades masked whatever answer Speaker Jin's face might have had for me.

"The current Triumvirate," calm Charlemagne Accursed-by-Association-Guildbreaker cut in, "does not include Su-Hyeon, it's the Speaker, Junior Senator Walkiewicz here, and myself."

Young Kenzie Walkiewicz beamed as she smoothed her wide Senator's sash. "Since Triumvir is a totally made-up nonexistent office anyway, we decided it doesn't require the Adulthood Competency Exam."

Grandpa Jin Im-Jin gave a wheezing laugh. "Indeed. Unless our Acting Censor wants to decide Triumvir is a real position and make rules for it. Is that them there hiding behind Bo?"

Shy Toshi had retreated behind her tall protector, but stepped out once more.

"I wish to thank all of you for your hard work maintaining the capital and Alliance continuity through the chaos. The Triumvirate and you, Commissioner General, have both been invaluable while we weathered something far beyond what the Censor's executive powers were designed to handle."

"That sounds like a vote for treating us as not-a-coup?" The Speaker's eyes sparkled. "Glad to hear it, especi—"

"Are we in the deciding-what's-a-coup phase?" Papa cut in with relish. "Because I have hundreds of pages of opinions, I've been taking lots of notes!"

I winced.

"You'll have more notes to make in a minute, Ektor, if I read Mycroft right." Jin Im-Jin leaned toward the camera, dark eyes glinting. "What title should we use for you these days, Mycroft? *Promagister?* Vice-Emperor? War Marshal?"

My stomach clenched, always clenches when I hear such noble titles defiled by my stain. "Just . . ."

"Co-Conqueror? Imperial Vicar? Beggar King? Servicer General? Stray Dog? Archangel? The Beast of Alba Longa?"

"Speaker," Toshi cut in, stern beside me, "lives are being risked to keep this channel open. Honor them by listening to what we have to say."

Jin Im-Jin smiled at this firm authority from one a century his junior. "Sorry. The faces Mycroft makes are irresistible. So, Mycroft, are you calling to have us legitimize what Donatien's doing to the Hives? Or to talk about revising the Alliance Charter? Or to tell me and Carmen what parts you plan for us in Romanova's surrender ceremony? Or about closing the doors of the Temple of Janus?"

I felt outpaced. "I . . . want to talk about all those things. We—"

"Speaker," Toshi cut in a second time, "I know playing domination word games with your interlocutors is Brillist habit, but however you knock Mycroft down, the rest of us are here to lift them up again. I ask you again to honor those who risk their lives to let us speak today and listen."

"Apologies." Jin Im-Jin's smile broadened. "So tempted to ask you to name an animal larger than a turtle, but this isn't the time."

"Indeed. It's time to remake the Alliance." I wish I had an image of Toshi's face in that moment. I have the straight-on image the conference camera captured, but my angle, gazing up from my wheelchair, showed much more. There was a pure, almost primordial serenity to her expression, as a spirit of a tree or spring might look if it took human form still free from humans' cluttered social blinders. I would not have thought any of Toshi Mitsubishi's bash' could shed all resentment, all judgment, all concessions to the waste of time that grudges—Brillist against almost-set-set—are, but when the best of us take up great duties, responsibility washes the grit of pettiness away like cleansing rain. "The Alliance and the Hives were born together in the Church War's crucible, and since the Hives are being remade in this new war, this is the moment for the Alliance to advance as well. The Alliance Charter is wonderful but not perfect, it was written when Hives were new and no one knew their risks and failure states—like all charters and constitutions it's like software, it's natural for it to need updating as we learn more about users' needs, and how bad actors game the system. And as we now know, the Alliance depended on O.S. as much as the Hives. This is the moment to update it."

"Changes to the Charter . . ." Papa's voice took on a cold edge that made me hunger for a face to match. "That's a very different thing to put on the chopping board."

"More in the emergency room than on the chopping board," Toshi pushed back. "If we want to cure the sickness that led to this new war, the Alliance is an affected organ too. Tai-kun wants this to end with the Alliance sounder than before."

Young Kenzie Walkiewicz grinned up at Charlemagne. "Just like my speech."

"Mm-hmm." Grandmother beamed.

"What speech?" Toshi invited.

"For the Temple of Janus ceremony. We're all ready, we just wanted to wait until we had clear video so the footage can get out and as many as possible can see it all at once. And we think it should be a new holiday, we're working on a name."

I winced, inside and out: I'm sorry, little one. I know it looks like peace, to you, to Romanova, to our resting troops, to rosy Eos watching navies ferry rice, not death, but lordly Ares has not set aside the spear that shatters city gates, not yet.

"What changes does Tribune Mason want the Alliance to make?" Young Kenzie continued, youth ever proficient at looking forward.

I caught myself wincing as Toshi turned to me. "He can't offer specifics yet," I answered. "The changes have to be worked out in balance with the Hive reforms over the next months. It's the same problem that made it so hard for Him to offer Homeland their surrender terms. There are a few things we've been discussing, but—"

"What things?" innocence asked.

I hadn't planned for this, agenda points too raw. "He's talked about reexamining the Alliance's relationship with the Reservations, for one. And reforming the Conclave for another. And I think . . . We don't know how to go about it yet, but He wants to fill that bench around you, cultivate new Hives out of some of the factions, or new movements altogether, aiming for the more plural world Thomas Carlyle envisioned, where no one could rise to lead all Hives as He has, or more importantly where no one could entangle all of them as His mother did."

Happy young eyes stared lighthouse-bright at me across Poseidon's sea. "Those sound like good ideas. I wanna hear more."

"You can." Yes, yes, this was the moment to bring up earthshaking Poseidon. "If you come to His council." Come, timid flock, come, stubborn ram, come, come.

"To Alexandria?" Papa our wary ram replied. "To be more birds in hand? Or captives to parade behind your triumph? Are you planning a parade?"

I smiled, basking in my happy answer. "No, not Alexandria. We know if He summons everyone to Alexandria, the world will read that as empire, treating the Hives the way old Rome or Alexander treated conquered kingdoms. But the seas are safe now, we can host His council anywhere that's reasonably coastal, and we've talked about options, how people will interpret different venues."

It had been a long discussion, I and the moving Mountain, a long struggle to make Him understand how the pageantry of place, like dress, proclaims so much. He hated it. When I asked, "Where will You hold Your council, Ἄναξ?" He said only, "Together, against Distance; 'Where' is a question only Distance asks, as only Time asks 'Why now?' and the selfish self 'Why me?'" But it must be somewhere, Ἄναξ. Choose a Hive capital—Tōgenkyō or Casablanca—and all will read it as endorsing that Hive's values; choose one of Your parents' homelands—Tokyo or Madrid—and people will see that parent ascendant.

"Then wouldn't Romanova make most sense?" Kenzie Walkiewicz asked it, the words so bright, so almost true.

This was the hard sell I'd been bracing for. "No. We considered it, but the city's infrastructure is too damaged to host something of that scale, and even if we could repair it quickly, this isn't the Alliance summoning Jehovah, it's Jehovah summoning and hosting the Alliance, with the Alliance on the operating table too, as Toshi put it. We do want to close the Temple of Janus when the time comes, and we want you Triumvirs to keep announcing Alliance-specific things from the Rostra there, but the main global council should be somewhere new."

The Senators conferred by frowns. "Where?"

"We propose Yangon."

"In Burma? Brilliant!" Jin Im-Jin cried. It had taken me some time to fathom Infinity's logic when He announced His choice, which I feared at first was motivated solely by the city's name: Yangon or Rangoon, ရန်ကုန် 'End of Strife'—but of course the Pathchanger had other reasons, as I saw with time. I should have known the politic old Brillist would see instantly.

"Yes," I explained for the others' sakes. "Yangon is easy to reach by sea, but near-ish to the center of that circle of south and east Asia which contains half the human population. As Ἄναξ Jehovah put it, it's 'the spot on Earth that least feels Distance's sting.' It's easy for Danaë's fleet to reach, and Greenpeace's, and near Dhaka so you, Papa, can bring your Alliance volunteer ships so the Alliance presence will be strong, and the city itself has great resources: the Buddhist Sule and Shwedagon Pagoda Reservations to host Reservation envoys, the Rohingya district with its famous library, the Full Moon Senseminary to convene an Acting Conclave, the Aung San Peace Gardens, and—"

"A giant swarm of Cousins," Speaker Jin supplied.

"Yes." I smiled, for the great metropolis, the heart and often capital of the old nation-state Burma/Myanmar, so vividly recalls, from the fading days of geographic nations, the scars of history's longest-lasting chain of civil wars, that today Yangon and its outskirts host more Cousins than even Casablanca. "Kindness," I said. "He wants His message to be kindness, peace, the end of strife."

"The kind conqueror." Papa's tone was harsh, but the words made me feel warm inside. 'Kind conqueror'—it is as good a name for You, Ἄναξ, as Micromegas, and while bare Delos feared to be the birthplace of the Archer and his never-ceasing aim, the Capital which always wished to be where Strife, Eris, and Atë's powers end, will certainly rejoice hearing itself named birthing place of Your new world.

"Is it safe?" Practical, wise Charlemagne asked it, the Senate's babysitter through so many travails. "Do you know what forces have been moving in Yangon, who might have secret enclaves?"

A laugh, light, musical, from little Kenzie Walkiewicz. "The war just ended. Even the Humanists and Hiveguard have decided peace is better. No one but a super-mega-bad-guy would attack anything now."

In this moment I lost the battle of Ingolstadt.

Or put another way, in this moment the whole illusion of the battle passed like a confusing dream.

It's one more Baskerville. She had been warning me, the gray-eyed goddess Instinct, warning me inside, the itch as we had circled closer, scouting access, scenting weakness, camped around the town ready to strike. They want us to attack, this sitting duck too-quiet Ingolstadt, this bait. The world already hates Utopia for striking first. If we strike now, we murder the young peace, and make ourselves the super-mega-bad-guys. This has always been the plan, the final Baskerville, Gordian's bid to lure us to the stage to play the monster. No, not us, not all of us, not Myrmidons, not Empire, not He Who just proclaimed the End of Strife his capital, no—though we strike together, Earth will blame only Utopia. Faust showed his hand, those false proofs that Utopia hijacked the cars, planned the Silence, inflicted horrors on Lorelei Cook far beyond anything Faust and Su-Hyeon did to [Anonymous], and when Earth sees footage of Delians and U-beasts crashing through the windows of Brill's Institute, humanity will have no doubt it was Utopia who planned all those intolerable crimes, ten billion, more. Faust's out there watching, waiting for our strike, and Jin Im-Jin's watching for him, staring, staring at my face right now, deep-reading Im-Jin, reading every thought, who tested me already with those jibes and titles, who sees right now my jaw suddenly slack, my little gasp, my eyes screaming my revelation out. He knows I've realized! It's there in Im-Jin's face, we two reading each other in this moment stretched out by adrenaline, his pursed frown shifting toward a sigh, gentle regret—he didn't want to act now, didn't want to betray trust, the spirit of these talks, his office, didn't want to throw away his honored reputation, his last years, an old soul's wish to see a peaceful, honored grave, but you must act now, Speaker, for your Hive, your inpath, there's the resolution hardening your brow, you must act now before I warn—

"Mycroft?" Jin Im-Jin's voice—I told you, reader, it was quick as ambush, and as irrevocable. "How's Penelope?"

I screamed. Odysseus's wife—I staggered from my chair and seized I don't know who, someone near me, and screamed, "Am I Odysseus?" Again, again, holding those shoulders, shaking them, "Am I? Am I Odysseus? You must know! Tell me! Please!" I toppled forward, nausea, vertigo, my head, my body crushing someone's. "Am I? I'd know! I would know, wouldn't I? I would have memories! Achilles knew! Achilles knew, so I should! Right, Achilles?" Hands around me, trying to be gentle. "Achilles must have recognized me if I am, but I couldn't ask! I couldn't ask him! I . . ." The world was dim and spinning. "Please don't make me be Odysseus! Don't make me be Odysseus! We lose! We lose if I'm the one who's our Odysseus! I can't bring victory! The gray-eyed goddess, she'll never help me! Never! Not with what I've done! Even impartial Ares has to curse a parricide! A man no god will help!" Someone was lifting me, prying my fingers loose. "You see?" I screamed. "It's already changing! The end! Penelope, my Saladin, so patient, should have lived! And [Anonymous], my Telemachus, should have lived! I'm hated-of-the-gods! Don't make me be Odysseus! Don't make me be Odysseus! Not me!"

Dark swirled down around me, Death's more welcome twin, the sleep of drugs, or re-concussion, or perhaps simply the self-defensive dissolution of a mind pushed past itself. *Odysseus*—I had thought it before, so many clues, resemblances, my lot so long to be gods' object: aided, punished, shipwrecked, battered, found. But I had fought it back, a dreadful thought, as when you stare down from a cliff or high window and struggle to unthink the horror-thought that wells inside you: *I could jump.* Just so I had fought this, had willed the words away each time they dawned within my mind: *Am I Odysseus?* But it all fits, my twists and trials, Fate's long-leashed captive buffeted so long by grim Poseidon, yet Odysseus's punishment was for a trespass not one-thousandth of the gravity of my two weeks of deeds all gods abhor. The Hope of Soldiers, gray-eyed Victory won't stand by this Odysseus, won't mitigate her uncle's seas for me, her archer brother's righteous punishment, won't whisper plans to trap my enemies. Nor will her father Zeus, who loves the lightning, send me aid—sooner the god who marshals storm would rain down thunderbolts if not that swift death is too merciful an end for me; I know my sentence. But I am this war's Odysseus, aren't I, reader?

Yes. Yes, my much-enduring great teller of tales, thou art thyself.

I am. Odysseus cannot escape being Odysseus. But then, what happened to Mycroft Canner? The soul who screamed so hard against the mists of Acheron—did I kill that being? Overwritten like Saladin and [Anonymous]? Like Bridger? I have my modern memories, the cold wall at my back, the wind, the tear-salt as I taste Saladin's kiss, Apollo waiting deadly on the battlefield, or, wait . . . which Troy is that?

I know not, but the thee I know, my guide, has never not been an Odysseus, and yet the wanderer of many wiles has many names, and Mycroft Canner is the name by which I called thee to me from the mists of Acheron.

Yes, I remember, reader, feel it etched inside me every hour, your voice, our victory, our own +I scored against death and Hades-entropy: you called me back.

I did. I am the reader and can gift word-magic's resurrection to any of the millions coffined in my library—I chose no other Odysseus to summon to my side this time but Mycroft Canner.

You chose me?

I sought to understand the Age of Transformation, and of all thine era's chroniclers, thou, Mycroft, gavest history's eddies the most poetic names—Addressee, Baskerville, Apollo; I find that storytellers slightly poet-mad often age better than their factful peers, broad strokes the fitter for my distant gaze. So, I called thee.

Called me . . . Then it is irrevocable, Odysseus sacker of cities this time must be Mycroft Canner, beast of Alba Longa. I am me. But cursed, far more cursed than I was of old! I have the proof already: my dear partner my Penelope, and my successor poor Telemachus, they should have lived. Then I've destroyed our hope! Odysseus the victory-bringer ruined, blemished, tainted, all undone with these parricide hands—a man she loved! She Γλαυκῶπις, Keen-Eyed Goddess, she who taught to humankind the crafts of web-weaving, and horse-bridling, and all the arts that turn war's chaos into victory, I was one she loved! And poets know, reader, when gods' love turns to hate it turns to vengeance. I've doomed us! Victory herself, Ἄγουσα, Driver of War's Spoils, she'll despoil our side now!

You still think so?

She hates me, reader! She, Λαοσσόος, Hope of Soldiers, won't walk with a monster!

As I walk with Thomas Hobbes?

We needed her! She'll take her vengeance on me! On my friends! She, Εργάνη, Craftsworker, the one who taught the spider to weave snares to catch even itself—she sets such snares for us when we enrage her! Snares for me! Gifts me cunning, the better to destroy me, she, Αἴθυια, the Water-Shearing Bird who taught . . . oh . . . oh . . . the *Shearwater* . . . Have I been very foolish, reader?

Often, my Mycroft.

The Megarians loyal to Apollo, Byzantium's founders, they used to call the gray-eyed goddess Αἴθυια, Shearwater, after the diving bird because she, swift as seabirds, teaches humankind to build the ships Apollo leads us onto for our journey and our pains. Her ships, both gifts and snares, rewards and punishments. She's been walking with me a long time, hasn't she, reader?

Thou seest it now?

I do. At least partly I do. She does not hesitate to walk with monsters, does she? She, Πρόμαχος, Front-Line Fighter, she who walks so often with her brother Ares, terrible, and monstrous Atë. She's with me, Instinct, whispers warning me, she always has been, but her whispers, warnings, these are not forgiveness, not the signs of love. Only one God's Caring is always Kindness, and while He is Co-Author of our universe enough to fill the night with stars, He has no power over Victory. The gray-eyed goddess Wisdom cares for me, but as the Sea Lord cares, for hate, reader, is one form of caring, caring what end befalls the object, bad or good. Homer portrayed it often. Zeus, the son of twisting-minded Kronos, has his father's twisting ways, and many a time he and his cunning daughter send false dreams, false promises, false hopes to march us to the battlefields where they plan out a victory for someone, not always for we they whisper to. Nor always for their favorites, for the Plan of Fate is a stricter, vaster structure than any god-facet's will, and Zeus's dear son Sarpedon-Andō had to die at Patroclus's hand whether Zeus willed or no—even the Father had the power only to make the fated ending glorious or cruel. So, yes, she cares for me, the soldier-guiding facet of our Maker, cares where next I step, weaves paths for her tainted Odysseus with Instinct's owl whispers warning at the edge of sleep and teaching me to build the ship that will mean victory for someone—only when Zeus lifts his golden scales will I learn who.

So, what wilt thou do now, my great tactician?

Win the war. That thought, these thoughts, your voice among them as a gentle anchor, these lingered in me, sleep's aftergifts, as sunlight and clean bedclothes coaxed me to remember day.

"Are you awake?" Chagatai's voice at my bedside—we need a lot of babysitting these days, we who run the world.

"Mm." I snuggled down into the blankets, hiding from the prying rays of Helios—and prying eyes of Brill.

"It's been almost thirty-six hours. Gordian struck first in Ingolstadt. They captured dozens of Delians, the whole command staff, U-beasts, all our battle plans, more than enough to prove we were planning a large-scale assault. They haven't gone public yet, but when they do, it will be bad. With all the rest they have against Utopia, it will be very bad."

"Mm." Keep my breathing steady, think of something that will dominate my body language, Alba Longa, scents of late spring when the laurel is dual-greened, old leaves and young, the sun so fierce yet shade so sweet and cool.

"And Romanova closed the Temple of Janus. So they can prove Utopia was still planning to strike even after Romanova closed the Temple of Janus."

Of course they closed it. I didn't need to see the film, bright honest Kenzie's speech, warm Charlemagne helping frail Jin Im-Jin shoulder one door closed as Tribune Natekari closed the other, her dark face the more perfect gilded by war's honorable scars. Janus's temple, His Great Test which all humanity, from the hottest Mason to the most ruthless Nurturist, had passed together—of course the Brillists with their perfect planning would exploit that, too.

Chagatai was peering at me, like a mother whose child pleads sickness on a school day, searching for the subtle tells of fever or excuse. "Are you alright now? This fit was really bad."

"I'm fine," I answered. "It was a bad one but it's settled now."

Three more seconds' probing stare. "Glad to hear it. People aren't sure if Jin Im-Jin caused that on purpose. Did they?"

Brave Jin Im-Jin there in captured Romanova, in our power, willing to sacrifice honored old age to win this un-battle. "It doesn't matter now."

"We shouldn't have Jin Im-Jin at the talks if—"

"It doesn't matter now."

"Why?"

"Now we surrender."

"What?"

I summoned Saladin to mind, the salt upon his skin in summer, let the flush flood through my cheeks, my hands, erasing subtler tells. "We can't defeat the Brillists. We were never close. They scripted this, intended us to move on Ingolstadt. This was their plan, and it succeeded. The best we can do now is have Utopia surrender, and hope the last offer Faust made is still on the table: some access to Bridger's relics, some partnership in the remaking, some paths still heading outward even if the lion's share turn in."

All Blacklaws scowl seeing surrender embraced. "This is very sudden."

"No." Think of Saladin, yes, there's the grief, the water in my eyes. "It's stupidly too late. My fault. My fault. This is all I can do now."

"I'll get T.M."

"No! Please, I can't face . . . This is my decision, between me and Gordian, not His. He trusted this to me, and I . . ." I hid my face in pillow.

"T.M. won't blame you."

Kind Chagatai, bless you for not realizing—our Master sees through lies. "I'm not . . . I don't want to see anybody yet, just, please, go tell Him. And tell Huxley, too, tell everybody, no debate, this is final. Ἄναξ Jehovah trusted me to end the war, so it's my decision, mine alone, not His. I understand now this is the only way. Utopia surrenders."

"If you're sure."

"I'm sure. Tell Him this is my choice, and that it's final. Tell Him He gets to have His *ibasho* and keep it, all except for me. And tell Cato. Cato will want some time to say goodbyes."

"Cato?"

"That's Faust's demand. Gordian's labs get everything, everything Bridger touched: Achilles's body, the Alexander with the Ancile Breaker, everything we sent up to the Moon lab, all our data, the reverted toys, Cato . . ." Helen. Helen and all her treasures, let them take it. *Let them become Troy.* ". . . and me." Yes, I, another thing of Bridger's making, let me ride inside this gift we offer to our enemy as Father Zeus prepares two fates that end our mortal wars, one for the Trojans, one for the Argives come from Greece to battle here around the deep foundations Poseidon and Lord Apollo laid, the Vastness and our Aim. They watch, Troy's gods. They care about me, me their suppliant, transgressor, oarsman, butt of fortune, sapling still but half-refashioned to their plan. And she cares too, the teacher of shipcraft, the gray-eyed hope of soldiers, poised for action ever at her father's side, ready to speed her gifts of victory to whom Fate favors when the great scales fall. She cares, I feel it now, a caring cold as ocean, cold as starlight, cold as the Maker Who, though Good Jehovah wept, made His revision still more dark than stars. But one side of the scale must have her aid, and one side fall. *Let them be Troy.*

Dear Cardie, (or should I say Ojiro now?)

Hi. It's Cato. Yes, your Cato. My memories are muddled—Bridger altered me, I hope someone explained—but in all versions, I'm still your Cato, and I do remember this version of you as well as others. They won't let me visit you, but they said I can write to say goodbye. I'm really glad you're alive. I didn't expect you to survive. I thought you'd go down in the end as usual, some flashy plan to take Micromegas down with you. I'm glad you didn't. I'm glad you lived. I'm not mad that you killed Achilles—Achilles was amazing and kind to me and I loved them like kin, but they killed so many people, you weren't wrong to end it, as you always do. This version of you was weirdly rough on me. Every version was charming, and gentle, and possessive too, and this version of you was so kind and sensitive to everybody else, but kept pushing me in ways that hurt. I think I understand, though. It's because this world had more choices in it, even for me. You were trying to make me a Humanist. Everyone else let me pretend I didn't have a choice, but not you, you made me face it, that I did have options, awful options, but they were still options, two ways to stop it: turning myself in or death, that if I didn't choose those I was choosing O.S. even if I didn't want to let myself feel that. You weren't just being mean. You tried to push me to find my excellence, to face what we were doing and find a way to be proud of it, like the rest of you. And when you realized I could never be proud of what we were doing, you pushed me to find something of my own to be proud of. Giving my book to that movie producer, dragging me to parties with movers and shakers, spreading the word about my science club—you were often cruel and clumsy, probably because we were so close, and sometimes, being close makes pushing clumsy, but you were trying to help me find my excellence. And this letter isn't about forgiving you or not, it's about saying I think I understand now why you treated me that way. You cared. Not just about possessing me and using me, you cared about me growing as a person. If I couldn't be happy, you wanted to help me to at least be excellent. I think you still want that for me even now that I've left at last. So, thanks for being the only one who tried to help me, not just possess me. And thanks for always being accepting and supportive of my asexuality, you were always so kind and good about that, especially when other people weren't. And even though I didn't become a Humanist, I think your pushing helped me toward what I've achieved now, something really excellent. I raised the dead, Cardie—me and my students, Bridger was my student too, and we did it, we battled death. And won. Sniper, don't react to this insertion. Assume you're being watched. This is Mycroft. I needed a way to reach you secretly, we don't know how much of the palace Gordian is watching. As you read this letter, keep your face in shadow and keep thinking about Cato and whatever else will keep you from giving away that we're in contact. I need your help. You know Utopia's battling

Gordian, a separate war. You said, 'Screw easy, let's go to space'—I'm gambling everything that you mean it. Your war is over; now I need your help to win mine. Gordian has false evidence blaming Utopia for everything: putting the cars in lockshell, the silence, more, enough to wreck the Hive. That makes the whole Hive hostages. We need to turn the tables, get proof it was all Gordian, expose the truth. That means getting inside. So, I need you to be my Trojan Horse. They've demanded everything Bridger transformed, including Cato and me as prisoners, and the Sniper doll that Bridger brought to life that pulled the trigger for you in the Forum. I want you to take its place. We'll pretend we're sending you to Yangon for the talks so Gordian stops watching you, but my team will smuggle you back, give you fake surface wounds to look like the damage the doll took fighting Dominic, and drugs to slow your breathing, keep you still. It'll be horrible, worse because it'll feel like what Julia did to you, but I know you can take it. Then when you're inside, there will be tools for you to get out of the box, you free me and Cato, dose me with a cocktail that the doctors say should block the vertigo enough to make me battleworthy for a couple hours, then together we get the proofs, and sabotage their systems, maybe even capture Faust. I haven't told anyone about this plan, not Jehovah, and not Cato, neither of them can hide a secret, so they both need to think the surrender's real. Only you can do this, Sniper. I thank every power I dare pray to that Bridger didn't know how Paris dies, it's not in Homer. So, we still have you, and you're still a hero, and Zeus will favor you, you've honored his sacred Games, made all Earth care about them more than whole eras have cared about them, and the Father will remember. And Zeus does love the lightning. That's enough. Please do this, Sniper, for me, for Cato, for the bid to hold the sacred Games on Mars three hundred years from now. We need you. And we need you to let go. I can't release you, arm you, trust you, unless I'm absolutely certain you won't try again to kill Jehovah MASON. I won't pretend you couldn't do it someday—Lesley is still out there hiding—but Hiveguard has disarmed, your Hive surrendered, and if you kill Him now, then everything explodes into fresh civil war and millions die while His side just unites around His death and some successor—Martin or Danaë—steps up and we get the same world conquest, only less forgiving, with a leader who isn't the Kindest Thing That ever touched the Earth. I need to know you won't do that. Jehovah respects you, wants you at His side, advising His new order, don't throw that away. So, I want you to swear it, swear to me you've given up on Hiveguard, that if I free you, you'll work with His order and you and your followers won't try to stop or resist Him anymore. Swear on your human dignity—I know you'll keep that strict as Ockham. Swear so I believe. Then, together, you, me, Cato, we can win the war. Insert your reply to me in what you send to Cato, I'll receive it first and delete that part before I pass it on. The rest of this letter is Cato again: I have to go now, Cardie. I'm being traded. I'm not allowed to be specific, but I'll be doing more science, good cause this time, good goal. Great goal. And I've found something excellent to push for, you'd be proud: my project is to get the ones running the lab to see they're looking at it backwards. Resurrection and space survival are great but both secondary, leftovers: Bridger changed reality, made food from mud and cures from scribbles and imagination, that's the thing we need to replicate, not reviving Kosala from Kosala's corpse, reviving anyone we can imagine from a plastic manikin. With that, resources won't be finite. It won't matter how the resurrection potion works if we can make a hundred that work different ways. That should be the focus. Mycroft believes me, but it's the winning side I have to get to listen, that's my goal. A great goal. So, I'm happy, Cardie. I can deal with being traded like a prize, I've always been that, and this work is so so so worth doing. And I did get to see Luna City one last time. So, I'm happy. If you see Eureka and the others, anyone who'd care, tell them I'm happy. I love you, Cardie. Please be sensible and stay alive, and, if you can, let go of being an assassin and move on to do something better than before. Maybe we can have a race, first to do something that'll be the first line of our bios someday, pushing O.S. and war down to the second line. No, that's not fair, I already won that race, twice probably: "Cato 'Helen' Weeksbooth, research director of the team that developed the first resurrection technology, experimental cyborg, first human to survive unprotected in space, a member of the infamous assassin bash' that etc. etc . . ." I managed to surpass you, surpass all O.S., now let's see you catch up. Lifespeed, Cardie. I get to say that now, I found my Hive, my good belonging place, they can't take that, no matter where they trade me to.

Lifespeed, Cardie. Be happy, and be better, and goodbye,

Cato Weeksbooth

Dear Cato,

It's wonderful to hear you sounding so yourself. They're going to censor anything political I say here and I don't want to lie to you, so I'll keep it brief and simple: I'm so proud of you. I'm so happy you have a project that excites you, happy it's worth doing, happy to hear you fired up. I'm also happy to hear you thought through why I pushed you so hard so long, though to be honest, I think when I was mean to you, it was half me pushing you to grow, but half me being angry that you hated what we did. You dwelling on the ethics question forced me to face the ethics question too, you wouldn't let me put it out of mind, and that hurt, so I punished you for it. I'm sorry it was awful for you for so long. I'm separately sorry that I was awful to you mixed in there. If I had a time machine and could go back and stop the exposure, the main thing that would make me sad would be that it would mean putting you back all trapped and weak the way we kept you, instead of blossoming like this. So, I'm happy for you. As for the race, you're on! You're doing such great things already that it's clear soon schoolkids will forget the Saneer half entirely and just call us the Weeksbooth bash'. But I won't let them forget Sniper. So, you'd better work hard or I'll overtake you—whoever has the most words before O.S. in our bio wins. And tell the guards wherever they're taking you that, if they're mean to you, your Olympic athlete ba'sib will beat the shit out of them. Love you lots and lots, Cato. See you someday. Mycroft, I'm in. No need to hide tools for me, the enemy might find them, just ship me in a standard doll box, the packaging has parts that double as escape tools, file, knife, we designed that in when I was little, the only way to stop my nightmares about coming to life inside a box and being trapped. Good thing I'm a little crazy, eh? You too, of course, in the best way, or else you'd never have come up with this ridiculous, amazing plan. You have my word I won't try to kill Jehovah MASON anymore. You're right, at this stage, it would make things worse. The stars are worth it, that and setting Cato free. I'll work with your Jehovah, and President Ancelet, and I will push, as a Humanist should, for the new order to be, not only good, but ambitious, dynamic, always pushing itself, faster, higher, stronger, freer, wiser, more; I will push, and I'll argue, but within the bounds of peace and teamwork, never violence anymore. And I'll do all I can to urge my followers do the same. All this I swear upon my human dignity, and if I break this in the slightest, whether in deed, inaction, or even in thought, let the Olympic Flame die out, and let the great spirit that it represents vanish from my species, which my betrayal would prove unworthy to be trusted with so great a light.

See you in Ingolstadt,

Ojiro Cardigan Sniper

Chapter the THIRTIETH

Peacefall

Written January 29–31, 2456
Events of January 22
Jung-Rauschenbach Complex, La Dôle

I HOPE YOU DON'T KNOW WHAT IT FEELS LIKE, READER, peacefall, when the will to battle fades. It is among the greatest things I've ever known, a lightness like the first time that I felt an elevator push past Earth, and gravity's yoke lifted from these limbs that had not realized they were born unfree. Yet I hope you don't know it, that you've never felt the hushed distrust that Hobbes reminds us—battle or no battle—is named War. I hope you know only our everbattles, fought against decay, forgetting, ignorance, the battles passed to us by Thales and Confucius long ago and native to our state, made by our Maker, not these hollow wars we make ourselves. We who cultivate our gardens and then burn them. Yet I fear. You called me to you, reader, chose to gaze back on my days of transformation, mine and Thomas Hobbes's, days of civil war when promises of peace wore thin as cobweb, shattered by a breath. Why do you look on us? I hope you gaze but out of curiosity, as idly we wonder who conceived the centrifuge or the electric light. Or perhaps it is a wiser curiosity that draws you, seeking to know the alien and celebrate your age's great achievements by tasting barbaric days unlike your own. And yet I fear a grimmer motive. People study plagues when we face plagues, floods when floods loom, and so, too often, chronicles of war are read when Ares comes. But you are different, reader, yes? You read of war to learn of past, not present, to taste evils you can't know and make your happy state the happier by understanding what has been surpassed. That's why you call me, reader, is it not? Tell me? Tell me that you don't know the will to battle? That you know the gray-eyed goddess only as a teacher and an artisan, Ares only at rest among the glories we have raised on his red world, Poseidon seascape-beautiful, and Lord Apollo . . . no . . . war or no war, the distant, deadly archer aims the same. You must know him. I want my dark age to be alien to yours, but—pardon, master! pardon, for I know it means wishing you pain!—I cannot hope the archer god reclines upon Parnassus, setting down his bow. If we the portrait alphabet of our many-faced Maker cease our restless aim, that means the First Mover, the One Who aimed across a darkness no being had senses tuned to see, will someday Move no more. I cannot hope that, tired as I am. But I can hope Apollo's aim, and his grim uncle Distance, are the only parts of this my history you recognize. That is why you have called me, reader, is it not? The right servant to show you how the twin paths rooted, inpath-outpath in their harmony, and also to show this barbaric force, the will to battle, which your better era knows no more. Tell me you don't know peacefall, gentle master? Tell me these days of fear and shattering are alien? That you have only known the will to battle as the will to battle for the stars? Reader? Reader?

I hear thee, Mycroft.

And?

Tell me of thy peacefall, my tired guide. However many there have been in history—Hobbes's, Augustus's, Gandhi's, Tolstoy's—I long to hear of thine.

Peacefall—it was one moment, reader, the passing of that chill distrust that Hobbes calls war: the sky came back. The whishing, constant, faint, it stopped, the nightmare motion at the edges of our minds, and all around the Earth, people stepped out and gazed in wonder, up into the starry skies of Africa, into New Zealand's noon, into the ruddy sunset gracing Nova Scotia, and the bright morning over Yangon, where the assembled powers of the Earth had no idea what blessed them, finally, finally, with an empty sky. The wait next, a few minutes of hushed joy, distrustful guesses, then in every lens the text:

<TRACKER CONNECTION ALERT: Active bandwidth below 5%; system set to low-bandwidth mode.>

<TRACKER MESSAGING UPDATE: You have 33,421 unread messages; download delayed while in low-bandwidth mode.>

<TRACKER SYSTEM EMERGENCY BROADCAST: hello, world. this is eureka weeksbooth of the six-hive transit system. we apologize for the service interruption. we have liberated the transit system from gordian's control and are dismantling their communications jamming, beginning with emergency channels and those essential to transit function. the tracker system is operational but bandwidth is extremely limited at present, so please refrain from non-emergency calls. expanded bandwidth is expected very soon. due to the maintenance interruption, all cars must undergo safety recertification before resuming passenger service. this will result in temporary flight shortages, but we expect full service to resume within 200 hours. while capacity remains limited, flight requests will be approved in priority order: first system-essential transit and communications personnel, then medical and other emergency personnel, then persons with medical emergencies, then terminal patients requesting end-of-life companions, then minors stranded without ba'pas in ascending order of age. those belonging to these categories may submit transit requests now, for themselves or those they wish to come to them; everyone else please wait to submit your requests to avoid system slowdown. we will update you regularly. welcome back online, everybody. we'll get you all home soon.>

Peacefall. All Earth felt it together, like storm's end, as the gray-eyed Teacher traded spear for scroll, and Ares lay down in the arms of golden Aphrodite, and the god we missed, held prisoner so long, the Traveler, bringer of wealth, shepherd of words, commerce's bloodstream, he the ancients called the friendliest to humankind of all the gods, Hermes who holds our hands and guides us safely through the frosty night, Hermes came back and promised us anew that, when we cry out into emptiness, someone will hear. We did it, reader. We, humanity, but also we just *we*, Sniper, and I, and Cato, advancing together through Gordian's stronghold as inexorable as the ever-marching night, we freed the cars, the trackers, everything—we freed Hermes.

But how?

The moon was nearly full that night, and almost blinding through the skylights, magnified by mountain snow as birds—

A snowy mountainside in Ingolstadt?

No, reader, that was bait, all Faust's calls from the old familiar desk, the pleas to send Jehovah 'here to the Institute,'—it is an easy thing to move a desk.

Then where were you?

They held captive Hermes in Nature's fortress, reader, walls that shame fortcraft's ambition, for although our race is filling Martian oceans and together raised the Almagest that once half-touched the Moon, we cannot hope to match what Time and Gaea built around unconquered Switzerland. The mountain-cradled Swiss cities were certain to be left untouched as all sides raced to seize the seas and ports, yet not quite too formidable a cable-run from Ingolstadt to fake a presence there. Faust chose Geneva, ever-teeming, ever-polyglot, invincible by every route but sky, the Patriarch's shelter when Pen stung Church or Crown too deep, and hatching place of sweet, untamed Jean-Jacques. Geneva's great and ancient university is three years shy of celebrating its millennium, so no one thought it strange that Gordian should help the site of Brill's first professorship to celebrate its anniversary with a great project: the Jung-Rauschenbach Complex, burrowed deep into the mountain of La Dôle north of Geneva, vast, ambitious—more so than we knew. The system hummed in every wall as I woke from the drugged stupor of transport, computers built to surpass the Saneer-Weeksbooth system, the CFB, Salekhard, Daejeon, worthy to advance the experiments—mind to machine—whose processing requirements made sealing Earth in lockshell but a side process.

The humming felt like home, I saw it in Cato and Sniper's faces as, in the peace of midnight, they freed me from my coffin-cage and administered the drugs to give me respite from the vertigo (though gods know I paid the price when it wore off!). Together we hacked the surveillance, the coms, the doors, and finally the transit program which these ba'sibs mastered in their childhood when most kids master bicycles. It was easy, not because no fortress can withstand three heroes, but because, while the Brillists were too wise to run all their hundreds of kinds of jamming through this single hub, the frequencies the cars responded to were all controlled from here, in case they needed to update the lockshell. Who has the cars has Earth, so before Gordian realized we were moving, we sent cars weaving through the lockshell, bringing Prospero first with the team that rescued Spain, then Robin Typer with a crack force lent by UNGAR, and swift Delians from Düsseldorf, and Nantes, and rugged Myrmidons, and a crew that Sniper trusted from Milan led by Wence Courrier who carried the Gold Team's flag at the Olympics. And though the long flight over ocean meant the base was ours before she could touch down, we called from hiding Lesley and the last of Hiveguard, so young Olympian Saneer, strapped firm to Lesley's back, knew action rush, and victory cheers, and, with the birthright lullaby of great humming computers, a joyful father's arms.

Eureka was the most important—Gordian's files showed that, after capturing them outside Port-Gentil, they had moved the set-set to a complex outside Lisbon, so, still in the hush of night, we sent five cars to Porto's Utopian district whose champions let us spirit them, first to free the set-set, then to us. With Eureka, the system was our playground, and as Lesley and Cato prepared to shut down lockshell and send forces after the jamming stations, I with Sniper at my back danced room by room down hallways, beautiful, a spectacle complex as lush within with art, and plants, and puzzle walls as the outside was stark with that soul-awing mountain isolation which made Switzerland the inspiration-birthplace of the tragic paths of Victor Frankenstein and the true Moriarty. The birds that are not birds came too, schooling against the sky, the halls around me, ever-flocking multitudes of black who I now know no other mortal sees, the dead who follow me from Acheron to make sure I remember, *yes*, my duty as returner to advance their disenfranchised wills, the dead who gave their lives and hours to projects now at hazard in our present's unsafekeeping. And every soul Poseidon ever drowned cares what befalls the enemies of Luna City. But no new dead tonight; the flocks were large enough, and these were Brillist side-arms we snatched from our adversaries, Brillists never kill when they can stun. Neither does Cato-Helen, nor we who hope to deserve the love of Cato-Helen.

Faust's rooms—yes, there were guards, but by then we had dragons. Hermes had his freedom and all Earth Eureka's triumphant announcement four minutes before we, backed by Myrmidons, marched in to find the Headmaster at his familiar desk, the back wall of the room designed to mimic Ingolstadt, the others bright with screens. Faust was not working but sat nested in the midst of work, files open all around him, with pajama bottoms testifying to his hasty rise, and his Brillist sweater to his dignity. First glance mistook the images upon the walls for art, the strings of glistening droplet-spheres winding like lines of dew along a swirl of cables as rainbow as peacock's plumes, but second glance realized these cables were neurons, and spotted labels: *striate complex* sample APM.668.13.376.22–1–2456, with magnifications from 1000x to 5500x.

"Is that Achilles's corpse?" I asked—I suppose Achilles is art too, Homer's art, Bridger's, Nature's, the Great Craftsman's.

"Yes. The interface is even finer than we hoped, microdroplets, nothing so crude as wires." Faust set down his tablet and wiped what I'm certain was more than just sleep from his eyes. "I'm sorry, I'd hoped to have this personnel list fully sorted for you. I thought Doctor Weeksbooth would want a list of all the lab staff—you will make Weeksbooth research director here, yes? This facility is better optimized for studying the neuro-connective relics than anywhere. Utopia can have it if you'll co-ommit,"—his voice wavered—"dare I ask three-fifths to life-extension work? You can keep the staff, replace them, anything, just . . . three-fifths, is—"

Faust cut off with a fear-choke as I, circling close, pressed cold Excalibur against his throat. Yes, Bridger was still helping, Bridger's smaller relics laid out like a candy store in the arrival dock where Sniper had awoken. And swords feel more familiar in my hand these days than guns.

No stun gun for Faust, Mycroft?

No, reader, not for the man who launched harbingers at the Gates of Nineveh.

"Send the stand-down signal to your jamming stations," I ordered. "We can still save lives."

Faust gazed at me down the sword blade through the swarming birds, a tired face, calm, but it was a calm like ice over a river torrenting invisibly beneath the chill white mask—this man just lost a war. "No need. They all have orders to surrender if challenged after word goes out that it was us."

Something deep in me wanted to growl. "Some are still resisting."

"Are they?" A little smile. "Be gentle, they're just trying to save lives themselves. We've calculated, if communications and mobility flood back too fast, confusion and partial information will cause riots and scapegoat deaths, and deepen the fissures, especially in the Mitsubishi as their bash'es learn which factions bash'mates joined. Managing the first few hours well will make a world of difference, and you need well-chosen, calming voices in the forefront: Im-Jin, Carmen, Jyothi Bandyopadhyay, Vivien, Spain." He sighed as deeply as he dared with steel so close. "Will you let us help guide the transition? We've planned this out, the best order and speed. The stations will stand down if I confirm you're letting us help."

Hot Instinct urged me on to snarl, to snap back, to let my hand slip so this foe could feel the salty trickle starting down his neck, foretelling what fate waits for he who burned Cloud Six, and Babylon, and brave Laputa City. No, wait, that hot wish was not the patient goddess Instinct, that was me. "Alright," I answered, "you can help." Some Myrmidons frowned at my choice, but I know well how many of the most atrocious deeds at Troy came at the end, in victory's mania.

"Thank you. I'll send the signal now."

"Send nothing else," I warned. "We're monitoring—"

"Cato Weeksbooth?" he guessed, watching my face. "No, Cato and . . . Eureka too? Formidable."

There is an art, reader, to keeping one's blade firm against the skin as the captive breathes and shifts; I seem to know it. "If you—"

"No need for threats," Faust interrupted. "I'm almost as good at telling when one should surrender as you are. Now is my time."

As my blade followed close, Faust groped among the desk detritus for a tablet, making me realize what he'd set down as first we entered was not a tablet after all, but a photo in a frame, a graduation with the small cluster of fresh-anointed scholars awkward in their loose, archaic robes. The Institute. It's easy in dark hours to call Faust selfish, his fixation on immortality smacking of fear as he draws close to marking his first century, knowing no human has yet marked a second. But looking on that photograph, I felt it, the more vividly having just left Cato at the consoles with his now-grown Science Squad. "A war of teachers." The words slipped from me. It was not for himself Faust had fought to the end with a mother bear's all-wrecking passion, it was for the Class of 2454, and 2455, and 2456, the students for whom teachers sacrifice their hours—least renewable of resources—to pass it forward.

'It,' Mycroft?

Yes, reader, *it,* the *it* which is our everything.

The tired Headmaster gave a flinching smile. "A war of teachers, yes. They . . . Utopia will still let us work with them, won't they? We share one of the two projects. We're eager to collaborate, all our resources, we'll even help with both their projects if they want, anything, anything if they'll at least continue . . . Cato understands it, it's for everyone . . ."

"I know." My hot blood seemed to boil off into the vastness of these questions. "But Utopia can't trust you now. Or ever. You know that."

"They can," he urged. "This was the last attempt. No more. Anything beyond this would just waste lives and still fail, we know that. Like Sniper, we know that."

I gazed back at the partner of my hunt, its doll-smooth body lithe and energetic in the moonlight like a greyhound too long kenneled, freed to race. But, even in hunt's thrill, Sniper still frowned. "You've burned a lot of bridges," it began. "I don't know how much strength Gordian will have left to offer anyone after the repercussions and trials that must be coming. My side, Hiveguard, we fought guerrilla but not propaganda, not worming inside, not lies." It smile-sighed. "A dear friend told me once that respect is like armor in a conquest, no one sacks a city they respect. You gave up that armor when you manipulated the public, channeled violence on innocents, and broke the Fourth Law ten billion times."

Faust smiled, reader, with this arm that has sacked cities pressing steel against his Adam's apple, he still smiled. "It's not too late to blame it all on Perry. Backlash would weaken Gordian's ability to advance the project, slow it down. Think of how much our ability to advance the research would be held back by the legal battles."

"Eureka already told—" Sniper began.

"I saw the message"—Faust tapped his tracker—"but we could still say it was a mistake, that we only had the jamming stations at the end, captured from Perry. We have all the evidence prepared."

My eyes met Sniper's as the vast and branching tree of possibilities spun out before us: what Faust must have prepared to divert blame, how we could spin it, our best chance to avert what Gordian must suffer if we left them prey to mobs, vendetta, goddess Nemesis who punishes we mortals when we dare to reach for immortality or stagger gods. We need every ally we can muster, reader—we Utopia, Remakers, we humanity—to help us stagger eager Thanatos again. I shook my head. "You're too used to a Caesar who could lie."

Faust sighed for his imperfect-perfect Nephew. "True. True." He stretched back in his desk chair, careful in the motion as my sword followed his neck. "Sniper was a brilliant solution, well done. I was prepared for U-beasts, even toy soldiers in case you'd lied about the last ones reverting, but I didn't think of using the actual Sniper." His eyes caught mine. "Impressive twist, even for Mycroft Canner's mind of twists and turns."

But how much of me is still Mycroft Canner?—the question surged in me; this keenest-watching adversary would know better than anyone, Brill's successor, the deepest diver down into the well whence all thoughts spring. I ached to have him in our labs, our captive, laboring toward answers, unpacking what Bridger did to me, to Cato, everyone . . . but no. No, selfish Mycroft, this man broke the Fourth Law ten billion times. The new world must have justice in its first foundations or bad patterns will take hold.

"Thank you for creating Safe and Well, Felix," Sniper said suddenly, cool words as wild Diogenes might use to thank Alexander when he stopped blocking the light. "That was your agents in Geneva, yes? I know you mainly meant it as another tool to help you watch us all, but it was a kind one, we all felt that."

Faust smiled. "Most welcome, Sniper dear. I liked that one."

Then Sniper's tracker bleeped. It bleeped, reader, the crisp chirp of a call incoming, wireless, real, and as the living doll reached to its ear to hit 'Accept,' I saw a Myrmidon behind us shake with sobs. Welcome back, gentle Hermes, welcome, welcome, welcome.

"¡Lesley! . . . ¡Yes! You're coming through, a little noise, negligible . . . ¿How much bandwidth do we have now?. ¡Wow! ¡Well done! . . . Sure, I'm reading seven point—no, fluctuating between seven point three and seven point five, it looks like . . . Mm-hmm . . . No, nothing as high as point eight . . . Same . . . Sure, it shows the link as active, trying now."

With a flick, Sniper transferred the call to the main screen, and a muddle of sound and color roared out at us: ". . . k-kk-sssh-ksh-shhhh-eee-orry booster mussssss-kkhh-hhh-hhhhhh-eep down le-tttttttttther frequency. ¡Ah! Yes, it's clear now. ¡Hello!" Lesley Saneer's voice formed from the chaos, her face too, clean and warm, and Cato close behind her at a console with a crowd of Delians, and Eureka jacked into the wall ports and a giant gold-and-purple tortoise, and at Lesley's side her Prospero still holding in his arms a small and staring bundle of new life.

"¡Hello everyone!" Sniper cried. "¡I see you! I see Olympian. ¡Hello, little Olympian! ¡You have a face! ¡Yes! ¡You have a face! ¿Do I have a face?"

The baby giggled as Lesley gave a laughing nod.

"¡I have a face!" Sniper cried. "¡Yes! ¡Faces for everyone!" Its smile changed to a different smile. "I'm still carrying the next one, ¿right?"

Their smiles too changed, complex smiles and a moment's sob from Prospero for this plan which despair must have boasted a thousand times in war's grim hours would never come to pass. "Whenever you're ready."

Victory's smile as Sniper switched to English: "Sounds like the Tracker System's good to go?"

Eager Myrmidons stared raptly at the screen, and I remember thinking this would be the perfect moment for a Brillist ambush, all our wariness forgotten, reflexes trained by Achilles for the battlefield lost in the rush of hope.

"Forty percent clear, loading patch." Cato's fingers raced over the console with a virtuosity to rival pianists. And then:

<TRACKER SYSTEM UPDATE: Patch 23.4.1.15 available, to install select Install.>

<TRACKER SYSTEM EMERGENCY BROADCAST: hello, world. please install the patch immediately. we will enable general communications shortly, but the system will crash if ten billion trackers try uploading a year's worth of medical updates at once. the patch will auto-prioritize the most recent messages and data, compress larger files, and let us make other adjustments to streamline communications. we've also included a super compact 'i'm alive and well' message that you can customize and send to loved ones. at present we have enough bandwidth to enable text communication for everyone as well as voice calls for minors and their bash'es/advocates and for users with reading disabilities, and full voice-vid for medical emergencies, emergency staff, terminal patients, deaf minors plus bash'es/advocates, minors four years or younger plus bash'es/advocates, and users who are nonspeaking or have other access needs. if you need voice and/or video but it doesn't activate automatically, the patch will let you activate it, but please only do so if you or someone you are assisting really needs it. this is a time for sharing.>

<TRACKER SYSTEM UPDATE: Patch 23.4.1.15 installed.>

<TRACKER CONNECTION ALERT: Active bandwidth above 30%; low-bandwidth mode disabled.>

<TRACKER INBOX UPDATE: You have 1 new message.>

<TRACKER INBOX UPDATE: You have 2 new messages.>

<TRACKER INBOX UPDATE: You have 5 new messages.>

<TRACKER INBOX UPDATE: You have 11 new messages.>

<TRACKER INBOX UPDATE: You have 35 new messages.>

All around me, joy gasps punctuated the not-quite-silence as Myrmidon fingers raced to send and to receive the happy words—mixed with some sad—which sprinkled down upon us lovely as first snow. Welcome back, gentle Hermes, shepherd, ὦ φιλανθρωπότατε δαιμόνων, Oh friendliest to humankind of all the gods, καὶ μεγαλοδωρότατε, most generous of all the gods as well, welcome, welcome.

And then a flash, a wall of flashes, as the coats before me—blooming swampland, chalk-white cities, jousting firebirds—turned to static. We lost so many, reader, mourning static on and on and on.

Faust's tracker bleeped, the crisp chirp of a call incoming. „*Guten Tag*, Donatien." I laughed inside—of course That Minor too would make His voice call to His guardian. „No, Mycroft hasn't hurt me." Faust paused his German to peer hard at me. „No, Mycroft hasn't hurt themself or their Conscience . . . No, it was only Mycroft who lied . . . Ah, but Lies are not ethically transitive . . . Yes, the Body should be stable . . . Right away? No, I didn't mean that . . . Of course it's not Impiety, Cornel themself would absolutely want You to wait to do it until you had every Sensor and Instrument on Earth primed to record their Resurrection . . . Yes . . . "

Faust smiled as he caught me staring at him, this abject of Poseidon, he who tried to force us all to bow to Distance, setting down our oars. We both know what this moment is: Troy's walls are breached, and I hold in my hand the butcher blade which will stain Zeus's altar with the blood of silver-bearded Priam, the old king who defied us for so long. Our enemy—a breath ago, I could have called Faust that, but I know the Being Faust taught so recently to Hate, and what He Hates; it isn't His deep-diving *Onkel*. No, I can't blame Faust for urging us to save our strength to battle only one of Zeus's brothers, the one who hurts us more. I can't call 'conversation' the debate of glances that passed between me and the Headmaster as I listened to him guide, and probe, and help unlock to action in our universe the Infinite Goodness that barriers of language stifle to a trickle when we so need a healing fountain. Felix Faust, I battled him as hard as Cato battled death, but for Cato's battle I would, I felt it, quench vendetta's heat and—*but Faust destroyed Caesar! Burned Laputa!*—collaborate. For Micromegas, for the Alien who brought Utopia the promise that there are friends on our scale waiting among the stars, and to advance their project to disarm Death blade by blade, Utopia will—*the Almagest! The Moon!*—trust even Felix Faust. I lowered Excalibur. I remember staring at its shining blade, once plastic now perfected, left by Bridger, not for me, not for this moment, not to slay the outpath's enemy, completing here the hot revenge even Achilles didn't wish for. Excalibur is for some other moment, further out in time. Because it's real. All of it, all the relics, we have them. We humans will, even to your day, reader, have an Ancile Breaker when we need it, and the Alexander and what we'll learn from disassembling it, science to make crossing the outer sea a little easier, and we'll have Cato-Helen and Achilles's brains, and the potions to teach us all of Thanatos, and the crystal ball to teach us of space and distance, and the magic wand to teach us who knows what, and this Excalibur which will be ready when it's needed someday in the great unscrolling Plan of Providence that Bridger—the facet of our Maker who does not like sad books—made just a little easier.

"Yeeeeeeeessss!" Faust winced as this squeal sounded through his tracker loud enough for us to hear. "We did it!"

The voice made something old inside me rumble. "Is that Tully Mardi?"

Faust switched to speaker so we could all hear the background smack of waves against the hull that bore Contact and His companions toward His council place the End of Strife, and with Him Tully Mardi's joy shrieks punctuated by the laughter of true, happy mania.

"One point eight! We did it! One point eight! Aha-haaa! See that, Mom? Dad? Laurel? Everybody! We did it! We succeeded! One point eight!"

I heard a "What?" over the line, gentle and wise but young—Martin! Reader! Reader, it was Martin! Safe and at Jehovah's side! Our world, it heals.

"The tracker counts are in!" Tully whooped on. "My program's run the casualty estimates! One point eight million over 504 days! Maybe lower if my buffer for deactivated trackers is too high! We did it! Fewer per day as well as fewer total! Forget the ten-thousand-per-day target! Just three point five thousand per day! We did it! It was smaller! For the first time since the start of World Wars, it was smaller! It all worked! Aa-haa! The camp designs! The Tiring Guns! Peacewash! We made it kinder! We! Ha-aaaa-ha-hkkh-kkhhh!"

Tully's laughter turned to coughing as his body struggled with the dual strain of Earth and . . . no, it wasn't joy. It was completion, sweet release, peacefall as light as gravity's departure as the Mardi bash's plan lifted from Tully's shoulders. It is done, the project to use Earth's tension-offerings—the Mitsubishi land grab, Utopia's wealth, Masonic growth—to call from rest wall-cracking Ares for the briefest rampage possible that could still teach our sleepy world what he can do with weapons augmented over three centuries of Aphrodite's peace. What *we* can do. Start a World War but keep it small—has any bash' in history left its children so cruel a family business? Even O.S.? My stomach felt like lead as I met Sniper's eyes and we listened together to the hacking gasps of one Sniper has called 'comrade' but whom I—in those moments when honesty trumps hate and pain—must call (since even Saladin is lost) my last ba'sib. We're monsters, Tully, both of us, you who conjured Ares, I who, in my two weeks, conjured Atë, hoping Ruin could, with but seventeen atrocious sacrifices, drink up the accumulated human bloodthirst that threatened to wake the god of war. The task made us both monsters. Look at Sniper there, whose family business was so bloody, yet the hero came through human, handling with grace what broke us both. But you're right, Tully. We did it. You, I, together, everyone who tried to make this war the least bad it could be, the Cousins, Vivien, [9A], Alliance volunteers, peacebonding Delians, intrepid Pass-It-On, the Hiveguard crews who exchanged prisoners instead of purging neighborhoods, all human teamwork, all of it. It feels sick, cheering one point eight million deaths, but we did do it, Tully, in the end, not we two but a whole world that refused to yield its peaceful nature, plowshares turned to stun guns more than swords. Humanity, we made a slightly kinder war.

"One point eight million small authors . . ." Jehovah's voice, reader, over the line, Large Author of a universe too kind for us to know it even by its shadow.

Small authors? One point eight million was just Utopia and Gordian, then? My heart at once sank and assented—you know that assent, reader, when you hear something terrible about humanity and feel inside, not only horror, but 'of course'? Of course we are bad after all. Of course that small one point eight million could not be all. That was just the trunk-war, our war of small authors, Utopia on Gordian, one thin section of the larger fabric, while each other layer, Masons, Mitsubishi, Remaker on Hiveguard, will add its millions on millions, stacking to surpass past World Wars . . . wait. This war was short, at least, as my successor hoped, not six months but still less than two full years. That's good. We may yet have the lowest total deaths, though I don't dare hope we beat Tully's target of ten thousand a day. Great gods forgive us: what O.S. killed in a whole century, we've blown past in a breakfast, breaking records as all World Wars have, our power bloodier each generation—

Faust chuckled. „Your Mycroft still thinks, when You say 'small Authors' You mean only Utopia and Gordian." Faust's eyes fell on me, gentle like an old watchdog retired from vigilance to the soft service of companionship. „It's one Point eight Million total."

My ever-spinning head spun more. "I don't understand."

„Is that My Mycroft with you, *Onkel*?" asked the Guest across the line that baffles Distance.

"Yes."

Kindness's voice as soft as bed rest: "That common error grieves and baffles Me, why so many small authors yet do not apply the title to themselves."

„Indeed." A twinkle in Faust's eyes as he switched to English so Sniper could hear too. "Mycroft, to my Nephew, all humans are 'small authors,' billions of authors all of whom, deep in our boundless *fundamenta,* make imagined worlds, sometimes futures feared or hoped-for, sometimes versions of our past or present, sometimes other worlds, but all as real to Donatien as Earth is, just smaller, as He sees us as smaller things than Him and the phenomenon He calls His 'Peer.' And, using our 'small-authored worlds' to think about ways this one could be different, we collaborate, or sometimes work against each other, constantly remaking our shared world as billions of co-authors. One point eight million small authors lost in this war, that's the total."

Small authors, Ἄναξ? Everyone? . . . I fell back into something, warm arms, Sniper's, the thunder in my mind too much to channel into words. Ἄναξ, are we . . . are we a little bit like You? Your Host I know we do resemble, groping in the dark, we portraits of the First Mover who lights so many sparks and snuffs them, we who build so much and burn it, bumbling humanity. But are we like You, too? You Who in Your clumsy Kindness try to make this world better although You find it hard to move without crushing the fragile insects, yet You try, You practice—are we like that, Ἄναξ? A smaller war—did we succeed? With time and practice learn to crush less when we move? To destroy this good world a little less to make a better one? Small authors You call us, are we truly so excellent, Ἄναξ, Remakers all of us and clumsy-kind, like You? But then there was a baby laughing on the screen, and Tully Mardi's laughter-coughing mixed with it and conjured the word 'orphan' and the word 'monster'—one point eight million dead, nearly two million of Earth's co-authors lost, parents, ba'sibs, their worlds lost to us with them, unmade as He once feared His world would be unmade if Thanatos has power over worlds. One point eight million and—*monster!*—I'm rejoicing?

His voice, His words carried by gentle Hermes from across the now-relenting sea: "What is My Mycroft doing now, *Onkel*?"

Faust gazed on and into me like a telescope, yes, like those telescopes we aim across the dark at worlds we cannot touch, yet we survey them, learn what surface glimpses teach us, and by knowing other worlds know ours. "Mycroft is mourning."

"Ah. Like Me." His voice, reader, as soft as hopeful Thanatos who waits for us, our project step by step to make, first possible, then easy, the return from his all-joining crossroads, so this gentle guide can someday be, like his twin Hypnos and welcome Hermes, called 'friend.' "I was always mourning. It is not no achievement to mourn differently."

Chapter the THIRTY-FIRST

Seven Peacefalls
No, More
And One for Me . . .

Started January 29, 2456
Events of ever after
Yangon, everywhere

Hobbes: "But it wasn't over, was it, Mycroft?"

No. I should have known it, Master Hobbes. The will to battle did not start with lockshell, nor the moment Huxley offered Felix Faust the handshake that declared the trunk-war underway. It started long before, when Perry's acts and Sniper's bullet showed how threadbare was our era's promise to keep peace. Just so, Faust's capture and the cars' return were not full peacefall. Rather, the days stretched on, heady with homecomings but eerie, longed-for returns finding our homes lived in by strangers, bash'mates missing, bash'mates changed, two years making loved ones a mismatch for our memories. And it was all still pregnant with distrust. No, *distrusts,* plural, for each slice of humankind had different fears: 'What will become of me and mine, my Hive, my way of life?' And it is very possible for one commixing people to feel terror while its neighbors in the next house savor peace; in the old days of majority, many knew that. Land, nature, mother tongue, the Great Project, Olympic fire, family honor, Cousin kindness, Blacklaw liberty, all stood at hazard, on the chopping board as Papa put it, in a conquered world. And war-crime trials, if we held them, might fall anywhere, on anyone in this borderless age which has never defined its rules of war. So, we needed as many peacefalls as we had Leviathans, decisions coming week by week as all Earth sat up restless in the shrinking winter nights, waiting for that one verdict—different for each—that held *your* fate in hand.

The weeks in bright Yangon took on a rhythm. He Who Loves all things that are not Death rode daily from the Reservation where He slept to the conference complex where, with Papadelias beside Him (thank you, Papa!), He convened His many meetings with Hive governments and the Alliance organs that surround His not-quite-Romanovan Senate. It is His, reader: one hundred thirteen Senators appointed at His Will, a further forty-five elected but supporting Him, only the final forty-two wary.

Tuesdays were different, *Mardi,* Mars's day, when each morning Jehovah rode down to the Peace Gardens where stood the podium whence Earth learned—*live news, reader! at last!*—its new design. Our Kind Dictator rarely dictated Himself, as word-clumsy as ever, sentences like origami as His thoughts as vast as cosmic planes compress fold on fold, tighter, tighter, into the deceptive smallness of a crane, or frog, or noun. So, our young Remaker called others to speak for Him, initially the Censor or newly appointed Speaker Charlemagne (Papa insisted Jin Im-Jin step down) with announcements about emergency services, or reconstruction funds, then, on the first of February, 2456, He called on Papadelias to give a fearful world the outline of a plan:

"Members and Hiveless of this great Alliance," Papa began with He Who Acts beside him like a Shadow, "we inherit our expectations of war from the age of geographic nations, but their rules, the Geneva Conventions, United Nations treaties, these apply to some Reservations and nation-strats, not Hives. This, the Hive system's first war, is in every legal sense a *terra ignota,* governed by our Universal Laws, by Hives' and Hiveless law codes when applicable, and by the single agreement made on September 23rd, 2454, that soldiers in action must wear uniforms to distinguish military action from private violence. Thus the Alliance courts will treat this whole war as one *terra ignota,* examining the actions of Hives, factions, military units, and individuals accepting *terra ignota* as the universal plea, except in cases such as harming Minors or looting hospitals where criminality is absolutely clear. In most cases it is not so clear. We are now so removed from past wars that fiction, more than history, is the true source of our images of soldier, commander, army, battle, victory, hero, villain, right tactics, and wrong. We must not let fiction and our violent past trap us into thinking narrowly, or backwardly, or resignedly about what war should be in our era. By treating this as *terra ignota* we can create our own rules of warfare, rules for an age of Hives, rather than accepting as default that what feels normal—soldiers, occupations, guns—should become normal. This *terra ignota* will take time, and happen in stages, examining the largest groups first, the conduct of whole Hives and larger factions. That stage, we hope to accomplish over the next months. Trials of individuals, determining what actions should be considered war crimes, will take years longer, but patience will let justice be most fair and reasonable, and each judgment will lay one brick in a foundation for further judgments as we create the Hive system's new rules of war to match our rules of peace."

Slow but steady, then, would come the judgments of our 'Yangon Tuesdays,' as each week, Earth watched with bated breath the new announcements, which were often drizzling minutiae of committee assignments and new damage estimates, but there were downpours among the drizzles when whole countrysides of politics felt the remaking flood and with it—like the silt that leaves the farmlands richer after deluge—peace.

* * *

The first of these came February the fifteenth when He called to His world-commanding podium six masters of the dance of state: His all-beloved father

Emperor Spain, His ba'sib Homeland Commander in Chief Danaë Marie-Anne de la Trémoïlle Mitsubishi, the new Mitsubishi Chief Director and Fuxing leader Huang Enlai, freshly appointed European Prime Minister Jay Czerwinski, United Nations Secretary-General Mariame Dembélé, and, first and most familiar upon that stage, Alliance Commissioner General Ektor Carlyle Papadelias.

Danaë delivered the main speech, still in her mourning black but with her gold-and-alabaster coloring blazing above it with the dignity of sun. "Friends, this conflict has rendered newly visible the strong affinity between the nation-strats of Europe and the Mitsubishi. We who care deeply about nation-strats share many ways of life, political ideas, patrimonies, but there has not been a political forum to give us a united voice. We have one now: Homeland, which shall henceforth become a permanent body. This is not a Hive merger," she added quickly, as eyes around the globe locked on two bright strat bracelets, Japan's and France's, glinting on her wrist. "Rather, this intergovernmental organization will represent all Alliance nation-strats who choose to join, including those unconnected to the EU and Mitsubishi. This will help nation-strats aid and protect each other, and will facilitate collective action in moments, like this war's inception, when nation-strats' agreement about such traditional practices as military structures and uniforms injected lifesaving stability into a world crisis, yet could have injected more had there been an established organ for collective action.

"And, while nation-strats are native to the Hive system," Danaë continued, "we also share many beliefs and needs with the geographic nations of Earth's Reservations. Therefore, we intend this body to work with the United Nations, modeling itself on UNGAR and the FMAAO," that is, reader, the Federated Microreservations of Africa, Asia, and Oceania. "We intend in time," she continued, "for many of our member nation-strats to join, or in most cases rejoin, the United Nations which our peoples left when we believed its tasks—to maintain international peace and harmonize the actions of nations—were obsolete. This war proves that those tasks are anything but obsolete, and we believe that closer relations between Alliance and non-Alliance nations can become one of the new tools we need to maintain peace beyond O.S. Therefore, I stand before you today as Transitional Secretary of this new organization, which will continue to use the informal name Homeland, but whose formal name is the United Nation-Strats of the Universal Free Alliance, UNSUFA. I invite all nation-strats, even those which have not been part of Homeland, to participate in the drafting of our founding declaration."

Hobbes: "Fascinating, another of these flesh-sharing Leviathans, in which one person, that is one constituent fiber of a political body—"

Reader: "The modern word is 'cell,' friend Thomas."

Hobbes: "Really? 'Cell'? Is that from Robert Hooke? Of course, I remember when the *Micrographia* came out. Are humans too like honeycombs inside, then? Not just plants?"

Reader: "*Roughly.*"

Hobbes: "Fantastic. One human 'cell,' then, is here part of several bodies—Hive, Alliance, strat, now UN, too—bodies which, like multiheaded chimera, must act conjoined. Did that give people peace?"

We hope so, Master Hobbes, long-term peace, and better commerce with that tenth-part of humanity which, watching our Alliance from the Reservations, quaked as this chimera's seven heads went at each other's throats. And certainly for Europe and the Mitsubishi, the prospect of a sustained friendship supplanting the rivalry between the nation-centered Hives felt comforting. But there is more.

"In addition to recognizing how much Alliance nation-strats helped in the early stages of the war, we must also recognize how much the Reservations helped throughout, by welcoming refugees, aiding border cities, and defending the Port-Gentil Space Elevator which saved so many off-world lives. And we must recognize how much our war hurt the Reservations, since lockshell and the silence affected them as it affected us, more so for tiny polities which had less ability to prepare. Now that we realize that peace between Hives is not a default but something we must work hard to maintain, we must take seriously the threat we pose to Reservations, and the benefits of listening to the wisdom and opinions of our neighbors. The single office of the Minister of Reservations is not enough. Therefore, later today, Tribune Mason will introduce legislation to the Senate to create an advisory body parallel to the Minor Senators, in which Reservation representatives will witness Senate activities and speak up on matters which affect Reservations, or where the diverse political experiences of Reservations offer valuable perspectives. As proposed, this body would consist of eight Reservation Senators, two from UNGAR because of its high population and political diversity, and one each from the other six largest Reservation groups: the FMAAO, UNA (United Nations of the Americas), the UTR (Union of Theological Reservations), CURN (the Council of Unaligned Religious Nations), SI (the Sovereignties of Islam), and the WJC (the World Jewish Congress). United Nations Secretary-General Dembélé will now speak to Homeland's proposed relationship with the UN, and then we will take questions."

"Princesse!" someone shouts from the crowd. "Will these Reservation Senators have a veto, like the Minors? And Special Impact Votes?"

All minds must wonder, since Minor Senators do not vote like standard Senators, and for most motions just advise, but when unanimous among themselves they can veto, and if they file an Argument that a specific vote has 'Special Impact' on Minors, then as a body they receive twenty-one votes, enough to swing many a moment in our history.

Danaë paused, teetering on the little step down from the podium, until Spain helped her with a soft, strong hand. "Yes."

Peacefall.

Hobbes: "Really? Peace for the Reservationers, you mean?"

No, not them, Master Hobbes, Dembélé has another challenge for we Hive

Members before the Reservations will know peace. This moment was a different peacefall, a subtle, shallow moment in its way but healing still, which happened in this very instant but apparent in the motions, not the words. Europe had the least to fear of all the factions, really, since the war had birthed no grudge or grievance against the old nations, whose model soldiers fit the photos in our textbooks. But Europe had one niggle about its future, one anxiety, and here solution came, as warm Isabel Carlos gave Danaë his hand and helped her down the steps, and their eyes met and lingered on each other, tender gazes, the first time that Earth had seen the two together in their mourning black. I saw it suddenly, the world saw it, everyone gossiping, the first celebrity columns of newspapers awakening from sleep, we all saw: in a tactful year the widow and the widower will marry, perfect matches, king and princesse each ideally fitted to the other's special tastes. They will marry, and Danaë will bear a Bourbon prince of doubly noble blood to continue the line, detangling the two Hive empires and relieving Good Jehovah of the pressure to (can ships of flesh do so, reader?) sire an heir. And people loved it, laughed, collected pictures of the royal almost-couple, imitated hairstyles, and suddenly—*oh, healing end of fear!*—Jehovah's rule felt like one special crossover, one point when timeline threads are bundled tight but will in the next generation split again, Europe and Masons separate once more. He will remake the pieces of this world, then let them go. Peacefall.

* * *

Peace for the Empire came in two halves. The first I couldn't witness, since I was still in my Troy-destroying coffin-cage ready for the exchange when Faust kept his promise and released Martin and the others. Martin's reunion was as intimate as mine: sense-starved Jehovah looked, and touched, and smelled, and listened to His long-missed Martin, like a scientist struggling to perceive a tiny particle, who uses scattered light, X-rays, neutrinos, every costly prosthesense we can design to let a being of such vastness try to understand its object across such a gulf of scale. Martin had aged, of course, pain and exhaustion etch the face deeper than time, and our Martin had braved the wooded breadth of Canada, the waves of the Atlantic, multiple captivities, yet as he walks Yangon's halls now, he seems less different than the rest of us, aged but regenerated by the great goods that accompanied his journey's evils—especially the unexpected one. Martin had solved the *Sanctum* violation, giving Caesar peace, but by so doing gave his spouse and bash' over to executions thoroughly deserved, yet when at last he reached Alexandria's battered harbor, there they stood, not only our Master, but at His side Martin's three daughters, his seven other bash'children bubbling with welcome's cheer, and, holding the youngest child—unhoped-for joy!—Xiaoliu Accursed-Through-the-Ages-Guildbreaker, still safe and well.

"Martine?" Duty, and the Latin vocative, call Martin from reunion's happy glow.

"Sic, domine?"

"Approbatione patris constato, te creato Imperatorem Iuniorem, collegam Meum in IMPERIUM, custodemque defensoremque populi Masonici dum pro numerosissimis populis vigilo. (Father's approval being clear, I appoint you Junior Emperor, My colleague in Imperial power, and custodian and protector of the Masonic people while I watch over far too many peoples)."

A long, unmoving stare. What was in your mind in that long silence, Martin? History's precedents? The wise and stabilizing emperors who shared the throne with colleagues: Marcus Aurelius with Lucius Verus, Diocletian with Maximian, Alexios I Komnenos and other august Byzantines with their junior Caesars? Or was it, as I think, a pang of mourning? He isn't here to answer anymore, Cornel MASON ever the Caesar of our Martin's heart; would he be disappointed? He trusted young Martin to make Jehovah, not a MASON, but a Mason—is this close enough? "*Si vis, Caesar.* (If you so will it, Caesar.)"

"*Dehinc, Mi Martine, tu 'Caesar' es.* (Henceforth, My Martin, you are 'Caesar.')"

Peacefall the first, then, for the Empire, as Martin (technically Mycroft MASON II) took the Oath, and donned his suit of imperial gray, the left sleeve black, the right still white for his *Ordo Vitae Dialogorum,* with the Familiaris armband stark upon it—on that the Junior Emperor insists. Sleep easy, nervous Masons, you have an Emperor now who is your Hivefellow, not just the solitary Stranger.

Peacefall the second came as Martin strode to the podium on February twenty-ninth, that once-in-four-years extra day when Sol and Terra remind us this universe is messier than tidy calendars. "The Masonic Hive has grown too big." Martin's words were chilling but necessary. Overdue. "Majority, or even the threat of one Hive growing to majority, is toxic to the structures of the Alliance, structures within which the Empire has chosen to operate in this stage of our long history. Fear of a Masonic majority fueled this war, just as much as the Mitsubishi land grab or O.S. And there is worse."

Martin yielded the podium, not to our Guest in evermourning black, but to another guest: U.N. Secretary-General Dembélé, who had unfinished business with Earth's vast, chimerical majority. "On March twenty-first, 2455," she began, "Alliance Members, seeking to construct a barracks and a prison camp, crossed the border and occupied five square kilometers of the residential sections of the Harmandir Sahib Reservation in Amritsar, Punjab. This invasion of the most important and populous center of the Sikh faith was an inexcusable violation of the treaty between your Alliance and the United Nations, and lasted eight months, during which residents suffered displacement, theft, destruction of property, verbal and physical abuse, assaults, and the extraction of coerced labor. One hundred and sixty-eight further instances of friction between Alliance Member forces and Reservation residents have been reported, including many border violations and two other occupations, one in Walvis Bay on the west coast of Africa, one of a road near Fargo bisecting the long Lutheran Reservation west of the Great Lakes, but the Amritsar invasion was the most atrocious incident. Only two of these conflicts were even briefly reported by your Pass-It-On network, the rest, including Amritsar, were judged too unimportant to transmit, a fact which in itself is a grave warning sign. And a substantial majority of these violations—I repeat, a *substantial majority,* including the Amritsar occupation—were perpetrated by Masons." Here severe Dembélé paused to make us feel it, guilt's stab which will not stop gnawing, not this generation—we, with our long reach from Alexandria, did that?

"You like the word 'empire,'" Dembélé continued. "You use the name, its symbols, you don't question it. If we ask historians whether organized religion or empire has spilled more human blood in history, they struggle to answer, yet you ban the one and celebrate the other. You believe you have rehabilitated empire now that right-of-exit binds your dictators to please their people. Right-of-exit does serve as a check to some extent on monarchy and authoritarianism, but not on empire. Empire is not dangerous to its own people, its political in-group, its beneficiaries—it is dangerous to everyone outside, or below. The *Mukta* car system has not changed that. These past two years, we, from our Reservations, watched your self-named empire unroll its strength, arm multitudes, blast through mountains, pour out armies and fleets, and conquer billions, and nothing stopped it from expanding to conquer us as well except your Emperor's whim. Masonic Emperors have always treated Reservation leaders as their peers and with respect, and I mourn Cornel MASON and hold both your new Emperors in high esteem, but, even under Emperors as close to perfect as I can imagine, you have invaded us. Empire is a thought process, the impulse to celebrate when you see a strong hand reach, and grasp, and exercise its power over all things human. It is intolerable terror for us, outside, to watch the Hive that concentrates that impulse swell past three billion. It is intolerable terror for us to see a second Hive, your European Union, reach for imperial trappings in its time of fear. And it is intolerable terror for us to watch the ruler of the force you call simply '*the* Empire' be chosen as ruler by all the Hives and granted near-absolute power over the billions of your Alliance. You say this is a special moment, that the power that has been gathered in one hand will separate again, but history proves that what has been gathered once can be gathered more easily a second time. You will not always have a philosopher prince. And every time in history someone has made an empire, however fleeting, ambitious people have revived that title, and shed blood. The Amritsar occupation was a warning. You must put a check on empire, on the thought process, the symbols, everything that feeds this impulse, and above all on the Hive that feeds it most. If you do not, then the atrocities of the Age of Empires which, even with three centuries of healing, still scar every people on this planet, those atrocities will come again, and at your hands. So, listen to your excellent young Emperors when they say the Masons' growth is a danger and must be checked."

A pall falls on the crowd as Dembélé returns the podium to Martin, who is both Mason and MASON, so speaks these words as solemnly as any could. "While the ancient secret body of the Masons shall continue as it has over innumerable centuries, the public Hive, which that secret body decided to create for this era of Hives, has grown too large to serve our needs. It must diminish. Thomas Carlyle, when the Hives were new, wisely checked the growth of Gordian, realizing that majority or anything close to it would be toxic to the Hive system. Just so, my August Colleague and myself"—a glance at still-as-death Jehovah—"must and shall check the growth of the Masonic Hive. Yet we would not deny anyone the right to choose a Hive freely, nor would we further increase the difficulty of joining, since the full year of the *annus dialogorum* is already the most rigorous Hive entry process. Reducing the number of Hive Members will take time, but while numbers are power, it is possible to diminish power without diminishing numbers. Therefore our judgment: as MASON, we may fill the Senate seats belonging to our Hive as we see fit; we do not need to fill them with Masons. Three years from now, we shall reappoint the Empire's Senate seats and give then and thereafter no more to Masons than shall equal in number the largest other Hive. Thus Empire will never be majority or even true plurality in power, never stronger than at least one equal peer. Those seats this empties—twenty-two at present numbers—we shall apportion thus: we call for new Hives. The Hive founders placed eight Vs on the Alliance flag never imagining there might be fewer Hives. Let there be more again. The chiefest barriers to new Hives have been the startup costs and that fifty million must join to win one Senate seat. So, whosoever comes to us with strong ideas, a way of life that human hearts can love, we shall fund, providing offices, staff, shepherding them through the Alliance recognition process, and to that newborn Hive, while it remains too small by proportion to secure a Senate seat, we shall give some of the twenty-two we shall no longer fill with Masons. Thus, with a Senate vote, a bloc of other newborn Hives to form a coalition with, and the Empire's aid, we hope to see new Hives prosper and the ways of human living multiply, offering many hearts that love Empire other paths to love instead, so that in time the Masonic Hive will diminish, not by rejecting Members or surrendering power, but by making a richer, more plural world in which no force, not even ours, can be majority."

Peacefall. It was an unsettling peacefall for the Masons, marble-strong foundations shifting under them, but when one's neighbors cease to fear one, amity sweetens the neighborhood like honeysuckle's nectar fragrance at the dawn of summer, and the Masons did feel that. And parent pride helped too, the smiles in Alexandria these days, and on the Masons in Yangon, there's parent pride in them each time a baby Hive announces its first toddler steps: we nurtured that.

"The Commissioner General," Martin continued, "will now present a second and more techni-fpffff-pff-ff-f! Shoo! Shoo! Off!"

Earth could not help but laugh as Empire's grandeur shattered before the thwack of a dove whose ill-aimed flight path left the Junior MASON spitting feather fluff and swatting at the downy messenger's attempts to settle on his shoulder. Another Peacedove. The flocks had started to arrive that week, the ones we had released at the Olympic opening, robots crafted by Cousins and Utopians with compartments inside with food and medical supplies and messages from our past selves. The jamming had scrambled their navigation, so they couldn't find their way out of Antarctica, and had lingered there in hibernation until peacefall woke them. Programmed to seek out what looked like conflict, many of them chose Yangon, where all the navies in the world were gathered, so the whole city was being dive-bombed by well-meaning, flapping packages with wishes inside, strange, some fun—people were sharing them online—but many were more cynical than I think the Peacedoves' creators had intended, cheering on allies but cursing adversaries, shallow-feeling in this moment of rebuilding. Were we really, two short years ago, so soured that even when packing drinking water and bandages, we could not pack blessings with them, just factions? Carlyle says it's just sharks eating bananas again, the warlike notes eclipsing the kindly ones in my memory as failures so easily eclipse success. I hope she's right.

"The Commissioner General," Martin began again once aides had carried off the cooing messenger, "will now present a second and more technical change to the Masons, proposed by the Alliance Courts and approved by my August Colleague and myself."

So, Papa took the stage again, but this part, reader, was the fussy lawyer part, and I won't ask you to slog through it all. In brief, the Empire must stop making shit up. MASONS keep coming to Romanova with laws they claim have been in place since mammoths roamed the Earth but that no one bothered to mention. No 'Most Ancient Mandate' granting MASON 'Capital Powers' should have been news to Papadelias. Over the next few years, the Empire will submit a list of laws and policies to Romanova, and anything that isn't on that list *will not be admissible! ever!* in Romanova's courts. Thus, the protean Masonic Leviathan, which shapes itself sometimes like empire, sometimes like nation-strat, like Hive, like cult, like old conspiracy, like Caesar, Constantine, Charlemagne, Saladin, Attila, Alexander, Romanov, if it would be called 'Hive,' must, once and for all, take a Hive's shape and keep it. So Empire binds itself. Though no doubt, Master Hobbes, you would warn that such self-restriction invites danger more than it guards peace?

Hobbes: "What? Sorry, Mycroft, I've been reading about these 'cells,' so fascinating! And these organelles, the mitochondria and—what's the plant one?"

Reader: "Chloroplasts."

Hobbes: "Yes, separate living things, we think, until envelopment let them delegate outer functions—movement, sensory—to the enveloper and concentrate on their own special strengths. No wonder thine era conceived the layering of nation-strat, Hive, and Alliance! In such a system it may not be complete madness for thy Masons to divest some strength to avoid swelling large enough to hurt the host."

"Not complete madness," Master Hobbes? High praise.

* * *

More than the Hives must change, reader, we all knew that.

"... and Secretary-General Dembélé is also correct that there is an inconsistency in how we fear and silence religious discourse while so many concepts that have sparked historic violence, from nation, to Empire, to Nurturism, pass unpoliced. Thus, I am happy to take the lead in advancing Tribune MASON's proposal that we revisit the broad interpretation of the First Law, and how much is justified under its vague umbrella. This does not mean changing the Universal Laws, but pruning the ballooning body of precedent for the First Law's application. The Senatorial Consult that defined 'proselytizing outside Reservations' as a violation of the First Law was passed when a frightened world had just experienced the worst of war entwined with the worst of religion, and was willing to grasp at any straw which someone claimed would guarantee peace. It did not guarantee peace. We just fought a World War. Not the still-religious Reservations, us. Policing religious discourse did not stop it. Policing religion did not even prevent the cultlike cabal that developed in Paris and sparked so much of this. Nor should we rashly say the Paris cabal proves that bending the rules is dangerous when so many of us bend the First Law in our bash'es, with friends, on holidays, and on vacations to Reservations, where the group intimacies formed by sharing ceremonies do us measurable good—we have studies to show it—measurable emotional good. We are not proposing to rashly open all floodgates to uncontrolled religion all at once, but we must not bind ourselves to the unexamined lie that silence is safest. The Conclave will, patiently and with broad consultation, revisit the question of what kinds of religious conversations are dangerous, and what kinds are valuable tools for connection, self-discovery, ethical development, social bonding, and other goods. If we learn how to tap them safely, these goods may become another tool to help us keep the peace without O.S. Thus, I am doubly honored to be chosen as the new Head of the Sensayer's Conclave at *this* moment, the most important since our founding, and I look forward to working with all Hives, all leaders, and all peoples of all opinions as we work to heal, not only the fresh scars of our World War, but this old scar that has never healed from the last one. Thank you."

Cheers erupted through the Peace Gardens as Andalusia Whitewing, the popular Humanist-leaning Cousin and long-time Conclave Secretary, descended from the podium. These were not the most cheerful cheers—many are wary of this two-edged tool religion, which our incisive Hobbes justly places symmetrically with sword and cannon amongst the tools of sovereignty—but if nothing else, they cheered to see Whitewing replace the ousted Julia Doria-Pamphili. Legal barriers still won't let us make public 'Sniper's Chapter' of my history, but Carlyle's evidence and Julia's arrest exposed enough for most of Earth to say *Good riddance!* to the former Conclave Head.

That was the public peacefall, Tuesday March the twenty-eighth. But there were several private peacefalls in the course of it. Securing this one wasn't easy. There are many witches, Circes, Calypsos, Thisbes in our social underdark, and one of these had her claws deep into the Conclave.

"Hello, Julia. I thank you for accepting My invitation."

It was a splendid room, put at His service by the Shwedagon Pagoda Reservation, one wall all windows onto garden, the other (to make Him feel at home) hung with art reproductions from the Burmese Eighteenth Century, tales from court dramas where maidens, warriors, and splendid elephants advanced through scenes like panels of a comic book but nested like rice paddies, with rows of shrub instead of stark black lines to segregate the increments of space and time.

"Of course, *Altesse*," Julia answered, "but I didn't expect such marvelous company, so many of my favorite people in the world!"

There was a purr to Julia's voice and posture as she surveyed the room. He Who reads peace and war as you read mail sat on a couch with Dominic beside Him, the bloodhound's head upon our Master's knee, attended by the agent Mirabeau, the one who had trekked from Mongolia to tell *le jeune Maître* of Dominic's capture. A second couch held Papadelias, who fixed Julia with a sparkling glare of *bring it!*, while beside Papa sat Desi O'Callaghan who had so long watchdogged Julia in war-locked Romanova. Beside Desi sat Carlyle Foster full of strength, for, this year, March the twenty-second was Holika Dahan, the bonfire evening that ushers in Holi, the Hindu festival of colors, whose vibrant rites would—in an experiment carrying on Carlyle's wartime public festivals, and with careful Conclave supervision—be celebrated publicly in dozens of Alliance cities all around the globe. On a third couch, set well back behind the other two and conspicuously far from Julia, sat Sniper, beautiful as ever in athletic silver-gray, with Lesley beside it holding its hand, the maze of doodles on her arms dazzling like zebras when the scent of lion spurs their thunder-dance. A Typer twin sat on Sniper's other side, and standing Ockham loomed behind them all like the volcano to whose mercy island peoples, even to our own day, can but pray. (He is Ockham again, and Sniper Sniper, now that there shall be no more O.S.) And I, reader? I was there too, front and center on the floor by my Master's feet, trying to seem a menacing watchdog, though I'm sure Julia spotted my walker tucked beside the couch, which lets me move more freely, since it's only vertigo that makes things hard now, the nausea's mostly passed.

"Please sit, Julia," the Guest invited. "I thank you for your efforts in Romanova; Carlyle and Deputy O'Callaghan tell Me that you did good."

"Good? High praise from You, *Altesse*! Or, rather, Caesar. Are you enjoying all your new titles?" Then, in her 'Ode to Joy' singsong: "'. . . *primum praetor, deinde consul, nunc dictator, moxque rex*.'"

"Further multiplication of the names humans call Me has focused My thoughts on the question of which names hold real meaning for Me and which merely act as signifier-reminders of relationships. I make two requests of you, Julia. First, I desire that you step down from the Conclave."

"My, we are direct today. And why? This is the most exciting moment in the Conclave's history."

"Because you will evil."

"Ah. Only that?" She laughed, a little laugh at first, but it expanded to a belly laugh, not sinister, delighted.

"You enjoy causing pain," He continued, "so I do not think you a good world councilor for a moment that needs healing and forgiveness. And there is too much other work for you. The death of Perry-Kraye has left behind a global network of industrious and vengeful victims of My mother, armed with wealth and means enough to build and launch their own stealth submarines, who will, I fear, like an infection half-cured sicken worse, and do ongoing harm, both to themselves and others. They must be tracked down, healed, and redirected toward the good, especially since My Dominic's reports suggest they have already tapped into Ghostroad, the criminal networks that grew rich off of smuggling in the war, a sinister conjunction. The Commissioner General and Deputy O'Callaghan have agreed to undertake this masterhunt."

Papa smiled, a smile of richest *vorfreude,* the joy of anticipating future joy, as when the hot scent rising from the oven fills the house with pre-meal bliss. "Really had to twist my arm."

"But criminal networks," our Alien continued, "are among the most challenging harm-causers to mitigate, and at some stages better checked by rival networks than by the law. My mother's network too has tapped into the growing underground and strengthened through the war, but it is headless: I too busy, My Dominic too damaged, and Mother too dead to direct it. I believe you have the skills to lead My mother's former network well, that you would both enjoy and excel at the multi-year project of hunting and healing Perry's people, that such a project would turn your evil to good, and that it will keep you too busy to still run the Conclave."

Raised brows. "Me lead the hunt for Perry's creatures?"

Mirabeau, standing beside our *Maître* and Dominic, offered Julia a bow and smile as graceful and as predatory as a silent-sliding shark's. "We need someone who can work within the Alliance, *votre sainteté.* It would be an honor to work under you."

Julia's dark eyes went wide as pools. "Wow. Yes. Yes, what a delightful project. New, and huge, and . . . yes."

Desi O'Callaghan fixed Julia with eyes like daggers. "This wouldn't be carte blanche or unrestrained. This will be a coordinated action headed through the Commissioner General's office." Her knuckles blanched, gripping her cane, as if to demonstrate how hard she would grip Julia's throat at the first hint of betrayal. "You and I 'partnered' very well in Romanova, we thought we could keep it up."

"Mmmm. Very wise. And do I get the Paris property? You are rebuilding, yes? My own bash'palace filled with gentlemen and petticoats?"

The Addressee welcomes all words with dignity, even facetious ones. "My mother's network has two parts, her addicts and her creations. Her addicts remain scattered through the Alliance and capable of living seeming-normal lives, much like your victims, Julia."

Her smile like a cobra's. "Quite."

"As for My birth bash'," the Guest continued, "Princesse Danaë and *la jeune duc* Carlyle have given us the La Trimouille estate as a new home, and we are working on securing Reservation status for the property. Those Mother raised should have the chance to live under a law that fits their ethics and way of life, and I hope self-sovereignty will heal what secrecy and forced hypocrisy have twisted. I proposed a republic, but they seem set on electing Me their Sovereign, likely King; I could appoint you our Alliance liaison or some such."

"King of your own Reservation? *Moxque rex* indeed. Most satisfactory. My answers, then, are yes and yes. If—"

"That was only one request," I growled, interrupting on behalf of He Who will not nip words in the bud, too like an overtender gardener who has not the heart to murder weeds, but weeds strangle and so does Julia.

"Oh? Step down and chase Perry's network, that sounded like two requests."

Julia stared down at me and tried to force my gaze to yield, to fall to the carpet like a suppliant's, as I have yielded many times to her, and shall again, but not this time.

"You need to stay away from Sniper." I let it come out as a snarl.

Her smile was poison.

"I need you to stay away from Sniper," He clarified, He Who rarely uses words like 'need' and always means them.

"Oh? And I thought dear Sniper was here to see me! Or possibly as an unsubtle blackmail threat."

I heard a little choke from Sniper as Julia turned her slow smile upon it. The hero had been humming softly in its throat since Julia entered, faint sounds, I think, to reassure itself its voice was still its to command, not stolen once again. "Hello, Julia."

"Hello, Sniper." Her words were warm as humid summer days that sap our strength. "So glad you made it through the war alive and glorious."

The hero shivered, but with bash'mates' strength on either side, it met her gaze straight on. "I'm taking on a project too. Jehovah's asked me to head a new Alliance Commission on Gender."

"On gender?"

Sniper nodded. "What Joyce Faust did, and what you do to people with what you learned from them and Dominic, it shows how much gendered thought's still inside us, and how powerful it is despite everybody denying it. We need to study it, admit it isn't gone, look into what it's really doing to us, whether it's, like Joyce Faust claimed, a huge toxic hidden pool we're all blind to, or whether Joyce Faust just made there seem to be an ocean when there's really just a remnant drop. Thing is, we don't know. Nobody's studied gender or kept statistics for the past two hundred years, or really looked at it at all except the Brillists a little. And while Joyce Faust was a power-hungry tyrant who weaponized a toxically distorted version of gender, they weren't wrong that there are problems with the total silence that fell after the Church War. If you look back, parts of the Twenty-First Century were like a little golden age for gender, people starting to mix and match and choose and question and make all kinds of new things with it, but that got chopped off dead when the Church War made everyone kneejerk-afraid of everything associated with religious extremists, including gender difference. The move toward equality was great, but we haven't looked at the negative sides of stifling all that self-expression, suddenly tabooing everything but pants and 'they' while the forbidden stuff, the 'he's and 'she's and 'it's and 'zie's and gowns and top hats, are still in our media, in our culture, and very definitely in our heads. We need to get a real picture of how gendered thought is still affecting us, and we need to make policies to help us deal with it more actively, instead of pure silence which leaves us vulnerable to the kind of crap Joyce Faust pulled—and the kind of crap that you pull, too."

"I see." Julia fondled the coil of her black hair, as in her mind the cauldron stirred. "Yes, that's an equally exciting task. Invigorating just to think about what challenging that silence could lead to. And will there be legislation to back this up?"

"In time," Sniper answered. "First step is research. There used to be whole university departments for this, most of their libraries are still around. I don't have long-term plans yet, I haven't even picked my staff, but the Olympic Committee is a great place to start. The switchover from gender-segregated competition to open competition, with some sports having divisions by weight and height and such, was made in the Church War mess, so it's been ages since we examined whether the divisions for each sport make sense, or whether some were really picked by people trying to entrench old gender ideas a more covert way. Beyond that, I'm imagining a program where people can do something like an *annus dialogorum* for gender, where people who are interested take a year, or a different length maybe, to have a whole bunch of one-a-day conversations about what gender means with all sorts of people, not as a barrier to entry for anything, just as an experience, I think that could be really helpful, self-exploring, self-confirming, and extra valid-feeling since it borrows a familiar and respected structure."

"Mmm. Very Humanist. Might I suggest—"

"No," Sniper snapped. "No, that's the whole point, Julia, you can't suggest. I can't do this unless you keep away from me, and I mean really keep away."

"Precisely so," spake the Being Who is only gendered as the sea and sky, and yet the gendering we give such things leaks deep. "I chose Ojiro Sniper for this task as one who has thought very deeply about gender but in ways radically unlike My mother and largely untouched by Mother's influence. All who agree this must be undertaken agree too that Mother was poison, and that all whom Mother touched must be kept as far as possible from influencing this process, including Me. And you."

"I see." Julia's predatory smile faded to plain gravity. "I see it. Yes, you're right. I have been far too close to Dominic. And with me around Sniper, I'm too . . ."—her predatory smile flashed again, the glint of teeth between her lips as white as bone—". . . influential."

The rage on Lesley and Ockham's faces, reader, boiling, their dark complexions different but both flushing red as bronze, two different alloys with the same all-piercing strength.

"Ah," Julia added, "and I see I might be murdered."

"Prosecuted," Carlyle corrected, ever-smiling still. "If it weren't that we still think you can save many lives, we would push for a public trial, and can do so anytime. But everyone agrees you'd be more dangerous if you had nothing left to lose. So, my unofficial sentence stands: just like in the war in Romanova, you will work until you drop."

A hush, a long hush like the crocodile when you can't be certain if this living death trap—so perfect that it has walked unchanged unto our era from the days of dinosaurs—is sleeping or awake. "Who will be my replacement in the Conclave?" Julia asked at last—delicious, that surrender. "Carlyle?"

"No!" Carlyle cried, laughing, "I'm much too busy. I'll remain a Conclave Adviser, and the Minister of Spiritual Health is nominating me for Deputy Minister, but I couldn't take on more right now, Dominic needs me, as well as Jehovah. We thought Andalusia Whitewing."

"I was impressed," Earth's Prince added, "by Gilliard Gerber, whose attempt on My life showed reflection, dedication, and courage, but we have discovered Gerber was tangled in Gordian's manipulation of young Censor Jung Su-Hyeon, and Gerber is, I think, too much like you in exercise of power."

"Ah, yes." Julia's words as smooth as oil. "Yes, you won't want someone like me."

* * *

What sighs like this? A builder when the final brick is laid? A fruit tree when the harvest lifts the weight of pears that bowed its straining limbs toward earth? A ship when longed-for winds fill sails at last and the small wooden world groans with the tilting of the mast-axes that pierce its floating planet? So sighed we all, committee, Directors, assistants, clerks, on completing our assessment of the 18,044 pages of notes on the 2,605-page proposal to revise the Mitsubishi bylaws. It was the same unchanged proposal Dominic had submitted to the Senate two long years before, it just took this long for a peaceful stretch of study to achieve the answer: Yes. It all makes sense, the problems in the Hive that kept the voting blocs so rigid and inflexible, the same factions so steadily in office; this lays down new tools (thirty-seven in sum) to make blocs shift and strengthen new formations while gradually diminishing the power of the old. It also changes the incentive structures by granting extra vote-shares for the benefits that land's use yields. Until now, votes were derived from land's strict cash value, which incentivized ever-higher rents extracting profits with which one could buy more land. Henceforth, as much if not more votes and honor will accrue from using land for greater things: adding an arts center to an apartment complex, building a physics lab, filling a park with rare rose species, reforesting wilderness, maintaining a beloved neighborhood cafe, or simply building more delightful residences since the renting bash's productivity and happiness assessments will now empower the landowner more than the rent alone.

"It works." Graylaw Senator Fracciterne, chair of the committee to review the Mitsubishi plan, stretched back. "I'm going to be dreaming spreadsheets for six months, but I see it. You've traced out beautifully the deadlocks that incentivized O.S., and the Canner Device, and Andō's recourse to Madame D'Arouet, everything. This really does sound like a solution."

Director Kim Gyeong-Ju nodded. "With time people will find ways to game the system, all systems face that over time, but the internal audits, sunset clauses, and reauthorization requirements should mean frequent loophole-closing, which is about as future-proof as one could hope."

It was already shifting, new slices of the membership cutting across old blocs, like new-ploughed furrows reawakening old land to bloom anew. "And Greenpeace isn't leaving?" Fracciterne asked a final time.

Bandyopadhyay's smile glowed. "No. We considered it, but we share Mitsubishi values and are excited by these changes, eager to take the lead in implementing them. And to use our influence to make sure all proceeds as planned."

"Milae might leave, a possible new Hive." This was Jun Mitsubishi's pronouncement, sitting with Toshi, Masami, and Hiroaki, and to these four ba'sibs goes the true credit of making comprehensible the morass of corporate legalese. They have their senses back, you see. It's beautiful. Ockham and Papa did it, at the start of February. I remember them waiting in the hall for our Rural Safety Committee meeting to break up. Papa had such a twinkle in his eye as Ockham, in his Romanovan uniform, held out the case, that strange, familiar shape that made me cringe. "Censor Mitsubishi," Ockham had begun, so formally, "all the investigations have concluded for which this device was required as evidence. Since no noncriminal owners can be traced, and since we've patched the vulnerability which let it hack into the Tracker System, our Ethics Board directs the device itself should be returned to you and your ba'sibs, for whom it serves a quality-of-life-improving access need."

Toshi hovered in that paralysis in which we fear joy unhoped-for might vanish like a dream. Then she seized it, shouting at the same time to her tracker and her *ibasho* beyond, ⌜Jun! Ran! Hiroaki! Masami! Mother! Mother! I got it back! The Canner Prototype! I have it in my hand! . . . Yes! . . . Yes! They just released it to me! . . . Yes, we get to keep it! . . . Right now? I . . . ⌟ Duty's burden-grief moistened her eyes, already moist with joy.

"The Triumvirs can take care of the next meeting," I said. "Go. Go to your bash'. Go now!"

Off she had flown, joy's wings and *Mukta*'s, fast as Eureka and Sidney would have flown if they'd endured fifteen long years without their set-set interface. And with their sense array complete at last, designed for many data seas, reader, not just the Tracker System, the five surviving Oniwaban set-sets worked their magic on the Mitsubishi proposal, forming structures we could understand from the morass, as bees build geometry's purest castles out of wax and flowers' golden dust.

The five surviving, Mycroft?

We lost Sora and Michi Mitsubishi, reader, stranded in hostile places without protectors like Su-Hyeon. It was a cruel war for Earth's set-sets, all wars are for those whom hate strips of the protective title 'fully human'—we lost Sidney Koons, too.

"Then all that's left," Fracciterne concluded at our final meeting, peacefall for the Mitsubishi if this all works out, "is to go up there with Tribune MASON on Tuesday and persuade the world that, while the Masons are yielding twenty Senate seats and other Hives making giant revisions, the Mitsubishi will submit two thousand pages of corporate gobbledygook and call it a day. Servicer Canner, I wonder whether you think we might count on some supportive essays from the new Anonymous?"

"Yes, Senator," I said. "I think we can."

* * *

This one went public the eighteenth of April, but I learned in person several days before. I was with Huxley and Papa in the hallway, rejoicing in the freedom of my walker, when the meeting room door opened and they poured out: Bryar Kosala and the remnants of the Cousin Board, Volga Podrova with some other Cousin Senators, risen from retirement ex-Cousin Chair Carlyle Kovács Warsawski, some CFB staff, Conclave Liaison Carlyle Foster, even Darcy Sok working collegially with Hiroaki Mitsubishi. Vivien Ancelet followed with them, the old Anonymous who so long secretly half dictated the Cousin day-by-day, holding his Bryar's hand, partly to help her balance (still recovering from her two-way crossing of Acheron), but more because Earth's luckiest couple knows well just how lucky they are. Everblack Jehovah was with the group as well, and Heloïse, a rare sight, since the nun, trained as a surgeon's aide in her captivity, is so devoted to the avocation that she has become hard to pull from needs of flesh to needs of state.

We turned as they emerged, all in the hall did, startled by their body language, faces resolute, the strides of action, every lineament proclaiming—after sixteen days' debate—a decision. But what? What fate for human kindness, finite beside our Friend's but still our best? Our bloodstained best, complicit in the Nurturist purges, the set-set lynchings, the concentration camp in Esperanza City, and it was Kosala's word that killed Cornel MASON and broke the Almagest. Carlyle might say those were aberrations, sharks eating bananas, that most Cousins labored with Red Crystal healing harms, and yet there is a haunted look on Carlyle's face, I fear . . .

"The Cousin Hive will dissolve|" Chair Kosala said it in Hindi, translated by the aide who helps her still-stumbling English. My heart, though it sank, accepted it at once, an outcome as natural as the ending of a dream, or when the elevator sinks back toward the Earth and we feel once again our native world of gravity's unfreedom. I looked to Carlyle's eyes, my litmus test, and saw as I had feared the red of recent tears. Of course it couldn't work, the sweet, naïve ideal of governing by plain suggestion box, this pure lamb in a world of wolfish politics that never—

"The Cousins are too important to be a Hive." Carlyle's words, her face beaming despite the tears, Kosala's too, all faces as warm as mirrors focusing the light.

"What?"

Ancelet chuckled at the stupefaction on my face. "The exposure of the CFB corruption does show that the suggestion-box system doesn't work well for the day-by-day mire of Hive competition and diplomacy, but it remains matchlessly good at what it was created for: gathering billions of suggestions from our members of ways to make the world better and easier."

Kosala nodded. "The Cousins will become a strat, the largest, broadest-reaching, most powerful strat on Earth| We will continue our suggestion box, and running hospitals, and schools, and cooking dinners, fixing lampposts, planting gardens, everything, just not as a Hive| Instead, there will be Cousins in every Hive|"

"That has been part of the problem." Heloïse took up the thread. "We've concentrated all the warm, kind, nurturing impulses into one political body, leaving the other Hives, especially their leadership, dominated by . . ." What was that little hesitation, Heloïse? Did you almost say 'the masculine'? ". . . those who tend to think first of advancing self and self-interest, or seeing things as zero sum, rather than advancing all interests by prioritizing the co-nurturing of everyone."

"Let there be Cousins among the Masons, Humanists, Hiveless, Utopia, Gordian, everyone!" Carlyle Foster's words, already springing essay-like from this soul who can at last be comfortable again in Cousin wrap and Blacklaw sash together. "No one should have to choose between building the future they love and doing so kindly."

I felt an ache inside, and Huxley gave a little gasp. Micromegas, can we small humans really do as You have, You our Visitor Who at every step refused to compromise between pursuing Your Remaking of our world and doing so kindly?

"Once we file with Romanova"—Senator Podrova added the last ingredient—"all Cousins will by default become Graylaws. For those who feel attached to Cousins' law, we will take up Jed's invitation to create new Hives and propose one which would start with basically the Cousins' law code but a more standard government, with executive and legislative structures developed out of the transitional constitution Heloïse and Jehovah drafted. We expect a slice of current Cousins to join it but far from all."

Papa beside me was nodding along. "Does the new Hive have a name yet?"

"For now, Kith."

Peacefall. Reader, such peace as the word went out and Cousin patches spread, alighting on so many sleeves: Danaë, good Emperor Spain, Jehovah, Cato Weeksbooth, Hugo Sputnik, Toshi Mitsubishi, Chagatai, wise Charlemagne Accursed-Through-the-Ages-Guildbreaker; our world had so much secret kindness, reader, lights of safety hidden like unready lightning bugs but ready now to galaxy the night. The converse side was healing too, as self-strict

Heloïse could don a Whitelaw sash at last, and Kosala the verdant colors of the Greenpeace Mitsubishi, though many other Cousins wait in temporary Graylaw patience for Kith to take flight.

Yet one thing niggled. "Carlyle?" I whispered. "Why were you crying?"

Carlyle froze, a frightened rabbit freeze as all stared. "Nothing. Unrelated. Sorry. I . . ." Her pleading look so wanted to answer.

I smiled: Hermes, deliverer by many paths, is so recently freed that many of us still forget his blessings grant us privacy even in crowds. <What's wrong?> I asked by text.

<Was about to call you. Nobel Committee messaged me. They're giving the Peace Prize again, for 2454 and 2455.>

Strange news. It was inevitable, right, with Ares moving, we must honor peacemakers again, not stack the gold on Peace's altar as we did in our rose-tinted past, but as the one whose hand had first defiled that altar with the blood of war, the news felt personal.

<They said they have lots of nominees,> Carlyle continued, <too many for two lists! So many people working hard in corners of the war we didn't even know about!>

The cheer rang false. <Then what's wrong?>

<They wanted to nominate the Anonymous for their Pass-It-On work, but—>

Deep breath—no need for more.

But Nobel Prizes can't be posthumous?

Indeed, reader, though sometimes a 'but' is strongest when nothing follows. Patriarch Voltaire knew that, used that in his *Zadig,* when the Angel of Providence descended from the Heavens to reveal Fate's hidden blessings: how the burning of a good man's house would unearth hidden gold, how making a rich miser richer would attract robbers as just comeuppance, and how drowning a beloved child would stop a murder spree if he grew up. Zadig protested, called it monstrous, cruel that the secret goods behind such evils must be hidden from us, Destiny's Book written in characters no human understands. To this, the angel thundered as it turned its back, "Mortal, do not question what is to be worshipped!" To which Zadig, for all of us, cried out after the angel, "But . . ." a word nothing can follow, since the sentence, if complete, must list out every pain since animals first gained the spark of thought enough to watch a sibling die and wonder why. Rage kindled fresh in me. [9A] had worked so hard for peace! Had so deserved . . . But then Jehovah's eyes were on me, older than the pain of animals, and turned my grief to truth. Our [9A] already had a greater prize than Earth can give, one begged for by Voltaire's Zadig, by billions: to know the bargain's terms, Destiny's Book made legible for once, their death for my return, the burned house for the treasure underneath. They got to choose. The Prime Mover had revealed some of His Motions to *us* too, not only His First Friend. He Changed. Not for Jehovah only, for [9A] He changed. You changed, my Maker, Conceiver of pain and toil and peace and

Peacedoves, You Who, for Friendship, revised Your not-inexorable Plan seeding the night with candles, and the daytime sky with kind, returning doves, dare we hope this means You (the thought was fragile in me like a ghost) You mean it when You choose to wear upon Your skies, as many of Your self-portraits now wear upon their breasts, the bird of peace? Danaë, Spain, Chagatai, Cato, vast Jehovah, You? I don't think it was a sane thought, reader, but it was a lifeline thought, a thread in fear's long labyrinth those three weeks as the hardest judgments gathered on the calendar's horizon like a storm, yet every time I glimpsed a dove—cloth, robot, real—I felt anew the hope that what we must do next, what He must do, what pool-ball atoms in their ricochet toward peace and war must do, locked in since long before the raw friendships of protons first birthed helium, that Plan not-quite-inexorable might intend to let us do this kindly. When hope's ghost-wisp in me thought that—a taste of Carlyle's daily strength—then I could still see us among the stars.

* * *

Now Tuesday, May the second, ever 'Sentence Day' in our era's eyes.

All knew what must be coming. Other Tuesdays had been surprises; with all Hives meeting constantly, no one could guess which change would climax when, but when He brought Vivien Ancelet with Him to Faust's Jung-Rauschenbach Complex where Sniper, Lesley, and their bash'mates labor with the cars, and when He met with Dougong leaders and still-strangest Senator Aesop Quarriman (for the Stranger has not made Himself a Senator), all knew judgment for Hiveguard and the Humanists drew near at last.

The Humanist election too made matters urgent, since high office seemed likely to crown some of His fiercest foes. The first stage of the election was complete, when Members may nominate anyone they like, and the ranked list of the top 1,000 had gone out April seventeenth, so nominees could decline if they so wished, and experts could begin to guess which form the Humanist chameleonic constitution will take this time. Vivien Ancelet remains #1 but by a smaller margin than before the war, so pundits prophesy a weak presidency or co-consulship splitting executive power, most likely with Lesley Juniper Sniper Saneer, or possibly with a triumvirate or small council, since there were strong showings for Interim VP Sawyer Dongala, Claude Black who'd led Hiveguard's Atlantic fleet, Ohlanga Coder who solved the resource crisis in Johannesburg, Tip Sapalpake-Dotson (yes, a bash'mate of the Cherokee EU MP) who ran the Americas' equivalent of Pass-It-On, also for Red Crystal's North-Central Eurasian Regional Director Mille Østergård running as the new Proxy for the Anonymous, and, of course, Ursel Haberdasher whose cartoon chronicle of the war is predicted to soon surpass my history in readership. Frontrunners who declined nomination included Sniper who (endorsing Lesley) will focus on working with Romanova, Aesop Quarriman who (endorsing Lesley) will retain her Alliance Senate seat, Ockham Prospero Saneer who (endorsing Lesley) will concentrate on the transit system, still-a-legal-Minor J.E.D.D. MASON (endorsing Aristotle's thesis that political participation actualizes something essential in humanity), and Eureka Weeksbooth who gave an amazing interview in *The Olympian* about how it felt being the first set-set ever nominated for high office in any Hive, and encouraged supporters to vote for civil rights activist and Panopticon set-set Beng Kuàn Tiongson, since Eureka is busy training a new partner to co-head the transit system since the death of Sidney Koons.

The Monday had a hush like I imagine ancient winter solstices, when tribes before the birth of calendars could not guess if the failing sun would heal again or wither more toward days darker than any they have known. The Humanists and Hiveguard—can He heal such scars? Or will they linger—as 1918 did—toward a second phase of war?

It was not the largest audience that has ever tuned in to one broadcast, that was the Olympic ceremonies; there are now one point eight million less of us. He changed the venue, not the Peace Gardens this time but a concert hall which offered more and better seats for journalism's wordsmiths, Hermes's agents pumping out the information lifeblood of our world.

The start was strange. The stage as He stepped out was still set up for the orchestra, black, empty seats somber like gravestones. He walked alone down the center aisle between the empty chairs, just He Himself at last—all these Tuesdays, He had been convener, never speaker, knowing soft drizzle is better after drought than downpour. He cannot not downpour.

"I come to pronounce judgment in this *terra ignota* of the Hiveguard-Remaker war," He announced, "what was and was not lawful, and what was and was not war crime." Here He paused, just standing, with the background sounds of shuffling feet and fabric in the pause. I know that pause, Infinity. You aren't going to read it, are You? The polished speech we worked so hard on, smoothing language, combing through history's precedents to harvest clear examples. You kept saying it was not precedent or speechwriters that Your Friend and humankind invited to Remaking, it was You.

"I Hate Death." Just those three words, then another pause, more awkward shuffling feet—what can you, whisperers of Hermes, say to that? "I Hate Death. I Hate . . . Death. I Hate Death. I Hate when thinking beings end and are no more. I think it is sane to hate Death. I Love you and I Hate it when you die. I try to understand when you say there are causes worth killing and dying for, but I do not understand. I Hate Death." It's hard to imagine such words said without tone or emotion, passion locked in bare vocabulary, without sighs, like passions of the dead. "War." He paused again, one word complex enough alone to need a pause for cosmos to consult with cosmos—is such a thing as war really thinkable here in this still-strange-to-Him universe, and real? "War . . . is . . . War is . . ." It hurt, watching Him struggle; the prepared text is there for a reason, dear Ἄναξ, use it! "War is the thesis that there is a special time when causing death is normal, legal, heroic, accepted, right; I Hate this thesis and I cannot call it justice." Yes, there they are, the words I helped You with, Your own but smoothed, a little more human. "Billions have just acted on this thesis, killing as if killing were normal now because we named this five hundred and four days 'war' and this naming alone suspended ethics and made a blood-carnival time when death was not an evil. No. I do not accept war's thesis. We do not need to accept war's thesis. War's thesis is not of this era. I have looked at war-crime laws of past powers, which say killing one way is legal while another way is illegal, but I have always walked an Earth where killing is illegal, as have you, as have your parents, and your parents' parents, and they rejoiced that it was so. Yes, self-defense is different, that is an un-killing; yes, Blacklaws are different, that is choice; but for everyone else, the Alliance, the Reservations, killing is illegal for all thinking things within the human sphere that understand what law and death and justice are. Conflict's resurgence does not require us to accept war's thesis and call war's deaths justice just because we wear the words and uniforms of a past which assented to this. We do not have to assent to this. We did not have to assent to this. We did not have to kill in war. No one had to kill in this war. We had nonlethal weapons. We had whole armies that wielded nonlethal weapons, stun guns, Tiring Guns, and took or held cities, killing almost no one. When Cousins ran battles, the only deaths were accidents and falls, until we did not have enough nonlethal weapons, so we reached for lethal ones. But we could have made only stun guns. All sides. All sides could have made only stun guns. All sides could have made only stun guns. All sides could have made only stun guns." There was a passion to His unplanned repetition—I think the hearers felt it, This Being without the arts of sighs and furrowed brows and sound and fury seeking to communicate His passion as a flower without pigment trapped in white alone attempts with purity of shape to draw our eyes from garish neighbors. "Instead, many of us have killed. Many of us have assented to killings. I have assented to killings. That was My choice, our choice, the best option I saw, and yet I will not call it good or justice.

"This is *terra ignota*. We get to make new laws of war for this new age. We do not have to make our laws of war exempt the soldier from the truth that we should not kill when we do not have to. I say killing is a crime. If it is war and there is such a thing as war crime, then I say killing should be a war crime, every killing, exempting only those we would exempt in peacetime, too. My guardian Gibraltar Chagatai used the only weapon they could reach to kill Thisbe Saneer when Thisbe Saneer was about to kill Me, that was not a crime. *Pater Meus Cornel MASON suum imperavit . . .*" He caught Himself translating in His head, "My *pater* Cornel MASON commanded his troops to fire with lethal force on *Jibun no Chichi-ue* Hotaka Andō Mitsubishi's forces at the Gate of Tears, that was a crime. *Su majestad imperial Mi padre usó el arma . . .*" He caught Himself again. "*Su majestad* My father Emperor Isabel Carlos used the only weapon he could reach to shoot and kill so-called Casimir Perry-Kraye, but *Padre* himself let Europe's armies start manufacturing lethal weapons, else there might have been a stun gun at his hand instead. It is unclear whether *Padre* was culpable or not, a true *terra ignota.* When we explore new paths of law, like any traveler, we should, we must, make our new landfalls kind. So, in this *terra ignota* I judge thus: in future wars we shall hold to a higher standard than the wars of old. We shall hold to the Cousins' starting standard before crisis made them slip. Alliance law codes—Black Law, Gray Law, White Law, Minor's Law—will recognize no legal difference between violence committed during war and violence committed during peace; they shall have the same consequences and the same exceptions. The manufacture, possession, and use of lethal weapons shall likewise be judged identically in war and peace. No Hive shall be permitted Membership in the remade Alliance unless that Hive too in its law makes no distinction between violence of war and violence of peace, or between weapons of war and weapons of peace. Hives and nations shall manufacture no more lethal weapons for their armies than they do for peacetime Members, and soldiers shall bear nothing lethal that a peacetime Member may not bear. Past eras did not have technology enough to live by such a law, but we now have the means to make nonlethal weapons as effective as our lethal ones. So, henceforth, lethal force shall be permitted in war only as in peace: in self-defense, Blacklaw on Blacklaw, and for those special few who defend millions, such as those who guard the Olenek Virus Lab and the transit network. When life is threatened, then one has the right to self-defense, that cannot be abdicated."

Hobbes: "Indeed!"

"But when one has a choice between nonlethal means and lethal, then to kill, maim, wound, assault, unmake, end, spoil when one could instead have stunned, restrained, this shall be treated by all laws consistently in peace and war, and that law which does not do so shall not be part of My Alliance. We shall in time define what other laws may differ between peace and war, such as wartime laws permitting commandeering of property, selected trespasses, or drafting Members, but no exception shall be made for violence. This is My judgment for the future.

"As for the present, during the five hundred and four days we call 'this war,' no Alliance or Hive law existed which defined any difference between peace and war, except some nation-strat laws partly recognized by the European Union and Mitsubishi. It would be consistent with the law as it stands now for Me to sentence everyone who killed in this war as we sentence peacetime murderers, and all who helped them kill as we sentence accessories. But *terra ignota* is a plea in our law because it is so easy to misstep in undiscovered country. That does not mean there should be no consequences—there must be consequences in unknown lands, for mistakes made in first footfall, in law as in new lands, ruin more than anything. But there may be leniency where confusion, not malice, is the cause of harm, and where all of you and what you fought for are so worthy of Love. Therefore, I will not judge you as law would judge peacetime murderers. I ask you instead to judge yourselves.

"You know what you did in this war. You know whether you killed. If you did not kill, you know whether you ordered or enabled deaths and suffering. You know whether you reached for lethal means before nonlethal were exhausted.

You know why you did what you did: defense, hate, fear, aggression, ambition, loyalty, love. You know what was in your heart, whether you held yourself to your own standards in this war, whether the ancestors who love you, and who gave their everything to gift this age of peace to you, are proud of you right now or wish you had been better. You are the only judge who knows your everything, so I appoint each of you your own judge. Judge yourself. As exemplar, I shall judge Myself. I find Myself guilty of causing deaths, of failing to urge My parents to arm their soldiers nonlethally as Aunt Kosala did, and of assenting to this war, though I did not bear arms in it. I Am guilty. Now you must judge whether you too are guilty and should share My sentence. You wonder what sentence it is? I say that we best know our own deeds and are fit to judge ourselves, but not to sentence ourselves, for some are prone to sentence themselves too harshly, others too laxly. So, I have called to join Me judges who have determined and shall pronounce for all a fair sentence."

Here Infinity turned, and gazed, His black eyes, toward the stage-right curtains, and there entered young Triumvir Kenzie Walkiewicz, and Xinxin Hopper, Speaker for the Minor Senators, with them the other nine—no, only eight, for the last one carried a framed photograph of the pride of Adelaide, Minor Senator Murray Nguyen, killed in a resistance action in Sydney a month into the war. More Minors followed them onto the stage, Kenzie's friend Minlu Moretti who had anchored the Italian side of Pass-It-On, and young Gunay Musayeva who talked down the pirate raid on Baku Hospital, and the Lōng-sphinx, and YottaBlue, and Bi Bing the nonspeaking genius harpist, and local Yangon child hero Irrawaddy Greenguard, and, led by his translator, Old Irfan the orangutan chieftain from Samarinda, more and more, a torrent from off stage, most young, some old, most human, some inhuman, most born, some engineered—stage curtains make it easy to conceal what wonders may wait in the wings to change our history. All fifty-four seats on that half of the stage were full as Kenzie Walkiewicz walked to the podium and J.E.D.D. MASON, Emperor, Tribune, Cousin re-founder, Mitsubishi Tenth Director, European Imperial Prince, Gordian Brain-bash' Stem, First Contact, conqueror over the heroes of the Olympic flame, He yielded.

"We discussed what we want from you now," young Walkiewicz began, "you who had power and used it to burn the world. You burned a lot. You didn't just burn trees and cities and each other. You burned our admiration for the governments we grew up respecting. You burned our sense of safety in your care. You burned our patience, our ability to believe that the great things in this world you promised to protect will still be there for us and future generations. You burned our trust as you misused the data and surveillance we let you collect, first for O.S. and the Canner Device, then for the war, its propaganda and its lies. You burned our self-trust, too, since we know we are infused with your values, values we thought made both you and us people who would never do what you just did. We have to be afraid of ourselves now, vigilant against what you've taught us to be, since now we know we are something to be afraid of and ashamed of. And even if you didn't personally kill in the war, if you carried arms, if you participated, you helped burn what nothing can bring back. No sentence can repair any of that. So, we want you to repair what you can. That's our sentence. We want you to rebuild the cities, replant the trees, replace the art, relaunch the satellites, fix the bridges you can fix to make up for the ones you can't. We want you to rebuild the system, too, fixing the holes this has exposed and making more safeguards so no one can misuse the cars and data and surveillance and trackers and such again. We want you to build it all back but better than it was, and faster than any past war has rebuilt. You weren't as good at peace as you thought you were, but maybe you can be as good at rebuilding. Everyone, even Minors like Tribune MASON who took part, if in your heart you know you were complicit, then build back what you burned with your own hours, your own efforts, your own hands. That's our sentence."

Still flush with passion, Kenzie Walkiewicz returned the podium to He Whose Passions crash like galaxies beyond our miniscule perception. "I shall." And with those words He grasped His sleeve, fidgeting with the cuff of that black suit it is so easy to forget is Griffincloth, and with a brief brightness of transitional static, the right sleeve turned to the dappled beige and gray of a Servicer. "We shall. That is our sentence. We shall build it back, we billions who burned what we have burned. That is the self-sentence I ask you to impose, who judge yourselves guilty. There is not administration enough in the Alliance to police billions of Servicers, nor can our economy spare billions leaving their careers and homes at once. Therefore this: we shall become Ten-Hour Servicers, all we who fed the violence of the war. There was a time humans worked many hours, forty, fifty, dawn to dusk six days in seven, more. This is not a moment to revive cruelty—there was already in your treatment of what you have called 'War Servicers' too much of that, an impulse which this change may help to curb—but we shall, every guilty one of us, sacrifice ten hours of our freedom each week, hours on top of our usual work, taken from our play and rest and recreation, to pay back lifelong the debt that we who fed the violence owe, no matter how high or low."

With this, the Addressee of this strange greeting we call 'war' turned to stage left, where the seats matching the Minors' on the right still stood empty. Now opposite where Kenzie Walkiewicz had entered came Ojiro Cardigan Sniper Thirteenth O.S., wearing an Olympic jacket with one Servicer-mottled sleeve, and behind Sniper, Charlemagne Accursed-Through-the-Ages-Guildbreaker, sleeved the same, then Lesley Saneer, and Tully Mardi in his new Utopian-made wheelchair spidering along, and Jin Im-Jin, and Vivien Ancelet, Bryar Kosala, Jyothi Bandyopadhyay, Eureka Weeksbooth, Huxley Mojave, Danaë with the mottled sleeve incorporated into her kimono as a tree branch with new buds just springing from its tips, bold Aesop Quarriman, Isabel Carlos with tears wet upon his cheeks, all nine Mitsubishi Directors, Aldrin and Voltaire, Kat and Robin Typer, Darcy Sok, Masami and Ran and Michi Mitsubishi, and Felix Faust walking with Cato Weeksbooth, Servicer mottle on every one of them.

As the others took their seats upon the stage, Sniper strayed forward and offered He Who Acts a slim, strong handshake, tyrannicide to Tyrant, there before the world's eye, the snapshot of our peace. Sniper said nothing, but Sniper's gaze, ever magnetic before cameras, twinkled with an impish daring no one could mistake: *Ten hours? We can do fifteen!*

"Some of you may judge your actions too severe for ten hours' sacrifice to balance," the Remaker continued as Sniper took a seat—I had suggested letting Sniper deliver the next part, but this is His judgment, and He wishes, however harsh the limelight, to deliver all Himself. "Individual trials under your own laws and the Alliance's will come in time for many of us"—I saw glares fix on Felix Faust, and others on Kosala—"but the Servicer Program will also accept full self-denunciations from those who look inside yourselves and judge that your whole life's labors should be forfeited." Gasps here from the seats as, in full Servicer uniform, the timid figure of our rogue ex-Censor Jung Su-Hyeon Ancelet Kosala stepped onto the stage, tracked down in hiding and given the chance to judge how far beyond the technical crime that our dry paper law would call it is the true betrayal of a friend. "The Cousin strat will oversee the reconstruction projects, but former Censor Jung has volunteered to dedicate themself to coordinating our billions of volunteer hours, using a modified version of Utopia's Infinite To-Do List system. Anyone, from a city government to an individual, may propose a project as minuscule as cleaning a house or as epic as rebuilding a city." A human would pause here, rhetoric's pacing marking out a change of topic, but He pauses only when two universes touch. "The sentence will be hardest for we vocateurs, who must take hours from our vocations: from our public service, our writing, our research, our programming, our teaching, our baking cakes that would have brought smiles to children, but we must repay our war debt to Earth's children first. Some occupations, mainly medical, may be judged too essential to subtract from, but for the rest, even the most important projects in the world"—tremble, Utopia and Gordian—"we must give up a portion of what would have been our life's works to restore what we can of the devastated life's works of the dead.

"Some of you will judge yourselves not guilty," He continued. "Some have maintained standards of peace even in war. If you so judge, I trust your verdict." On these words, one more line of figures entered at the far back of the stage, wearing no mottled sleeves, no signs of guilt on these who held their peace vocations high amid the muck of war: Ektor Carlyle Papadelias, Carlyle Foster, Heloïse, strict Ockham Prospero Saneer, the Junior Emperor Martin Semaphoros who would have fought for Caesar had captivity not rendered it impossible, Toshi and Jun Mitsubishi who only guarded lives, and slimy, honest Julia. Some Senators and others came too from our council rooms, the self-acquitted few beside the self-sentenced like late spring blossoms poking through the green when most of the tree's energy has turned to summer's leafy industry. The leafy industry of Terra healing. Peacefall.

And I felt . . . I think there was another Peacefall born this moment, a much-needed treatment for an old infection, deep, whose pus was newly visible in how quickly we had transformed the Peacewashed into chattel, traded, tallied, tasked as menials. Our old world had another negative majority I had not thought about: as most were not Utopians, most were not Servicers, and were accustomed to having an underclass to frown on and command. I had not realized, feeling in my abjectness that every scornful look and grueling task was only justice, but those interactions taught us—free and unfree both—that such treatment of fellow human beings was okay. As Madame's arts had coaxed forth venomed remnants of patriarchy, I realize now the Servicer Program—though I had not seen it!—coaxed out old thought patterns from past ages of slavery, and slavery's legal-fiction disguises. I should have wished to be an employee in Aristotle's house, never a slave, rose-tinting practices which make all souls they touch—even truth-seeking Aristotle—worse. I used to think the Servicer Program was a hundred times better than old-time prisons, but now I realize it is merely ten times better, and still far from good enough for humankind. So He ended that bad majority, inviting all to join Him in the self-sentence which has made three-fifths of the Earth servants of the reconstruction, and each other. The scornful looks are gone, the work less grueling now that planning tasks for *them, those Servicers* has become planning tasks for *us*. An underclass no more. And this new use of the program is stimulating conversations, which are changing, and will keep changing the Servicer Program until—I feel it coming—something better will be born, a justice system one step less unworthy of we small authors, each precious as a world. Until then, as Vivien and Sniper say of Hives, we shall keep using this best system in human history, as we press on to make a better one.

"Self-trials will not be the only trials," Providence's Guest continued. "Looting, extortion, cruelty, assault, theft, lynching, and other crimes each Hive or Law shall prosecute and punish as plaintiffs bring complaints to magistrates. Some Hives and Laws may even choose to sentence those who have not self-sentenced for their roles in battle deaths. But I hope that this universal self-trial of we guilty billions will leave few enough trials to come that our laws' apparati are prepared. So ends My *terra ignota* of the Hiveguard on Remaker war. The guilty Members are sentenced, the five complicit Hives reformed and changed as needed for a better peace, the Alliance fitted with new protections and reexamining its overbroad extension of the Universal Laws. There now remain only the two Hives whose separate war you recently—"

"What about the Humanists!"

Clouds rain, reader, flies bite, bees sting, crowds shout their questions, and He the Mountain, He Whom a plain 'Good morning, how are You?' plunges into the jungle dangers of philosophy, He is as helpless before questions as a deer before the light, or Delos at the coming of unborn Apollo. He stared down paralyzed into the crowd—the Mountain knows not how to move Itself.

One shout begets another. "The Humanists haven't reformed!"

"They flouted Romanova! Refused the reform order! Submitted nothing!"

"Will you dissolve the Hive?"

"Will that be a separate trial?"

"Will you make them a Reservation?"

"Will you require all Humanists to self-convict?"

"What about those complicit in O.S.!"

"The Wish List—will there still be repercussions?"

"What about the Hive reform? The constitution?"

"What trial for the Humanists?"

"What will you do with the Humanists?"

The shouts had some momentum but faded again as an expectant hush met His unmoving stare. Infinity consults: "You have the answer but you do not want it. President Ancelet has said it, that the Humanist chameleonic constitution is as perfect a cornerwordstone as I have known in this universe. I find no evidence of transpiration between the Hive government and the moral unhealthfulness that fed the morbid jesting of the Wish List. The problem is not systemostructural, it is human. Nor I nor those who know you better than I do can name more efficacious medicine than your manifest horror-censure which already shame-stings toward self-remaking every Member of that human conglomerate most proud of its self-remaking. Your culture's immune system is the cure. We shall and must study the problem's causes, seeking policies to bolster that immune system, but any revision forced and punitive would only hinder what the Hive has already blossomed toward since O.S. was revealed. The Humanists today are not the Humanists of 2454. The next election will show best what has begun. Can you have patience for that?"

Dissatisfaction's whispers rustled like half-desiccated leaves at the first breath of storm—it was not what they wanted.

"Will you stand for election, Tribune MASON?"

Passion spread like tinder through the leaves. "Do it! Run!"

"Jed for Humanist President!"

"Do it!"

"Real reform! You could lead it!"

"A President the world can trust!"

"Run! Run! Do it!"

"Jed-Must-Run! Jed-Must-Run! Jed-Must-Run!" The chant caught fire through the crowd, a pounding like a giant's fist upon the city gates that cannot stand.

He paused. He pause-cycled.

He what?

That's what I call it when He dives to His Infinity and comes back with an answer which, once reimmersed in time and flesh, He doubts, so dives again, and yields the same answer, and doubts, and dives again, caught in a loop as they say zoo-caged predators in ancient days would pace and pace and pace the box, the mind itself broken by such an alien captivity—so space and time cage Him.

Hobbes: "But He must run."

Reader: "You think so, Thomas?"

Hobbes: "Yes. He is the ancient cell-enveloper. He must annex into Himself this neighbor mitochondrion and make of it His most powerful organ, or else compete with one so vigorous, better than He at turning ambition's sugar-fuel to strength. Such competition would endanger the whole rest of His vast body-politic, billions which ethics will not let Him risk."

Reader: "Our Thomas is becoming quite the biologist. And what does Mycroft think?"

I, reader? I agree ethics compels Him to assent and run, it is the safest path, imperative, as imperative as it was to Act to make this war the least bad it could be. And unlike humans, He has no defense against ethics' compulsion. Yet while He has no defense Himself, our law still gives Him one.

Gently, ever gently He speaks: "I am a Minor."

"Take the exam!"

"Tonight! Do it tonight!"

"Jed for President!"

"Jed-Must-Run! Jed-Must-Run! Jed-Must—"

"Please," He called, "what I must do is ask you, as a favor, please, to stop asking Me to take the Adulthood Competency Exam. I and all those who know Me well agree I should not pass it. I do not have the competencies it seeks to confirm, those of a human adult. I Am . . . I . . . I Am what I Am, I . . ."

He paused, pause-cycled again, a cosmos whirling like an engine. How I burned to rush to Him, to shield Him from these deep-impaling questions, bark the crowd down. But He Who Loves us so with His Infinity of Love is loved by many in return, and as His black gaze turned over His shoulder to the seats behind Him, there in the front row His father Spain leapt up, and uncle Faust, and 'aunt' Kosala, and wise mentor Ancelet, and strong Carlyle, and Heloïse came running from the back, and Martin too joining the warming mob of *ibasho*. A consultation, not with His Infinity, with ours, these many warm small authors crowding behind the podium whose microphone only picked up the gentle *"Quid vis, domine?"* and briefly, *"¿Estás seguro?"*

Didst thou not rush in too, Mycroft? What didst thou His translator hear in that consultation?

I, reader? No. I was kept far away on Yangon Tuesdays, lest the sight of Mycroft Canner be more flame to fuel. But Sentence Tuesday there was purpose in my banishment, a mission, healing for the gods and mortals too. We dare not leave him angry, Janus god of gateways and transitions, he whose ceremony Jin Im-Jin exploited, closing his sacred gates falsely to levy more guilt on Utopia when only Sniper's war was over, Earth too mired still in blood and subterfuge to host filth-fleeing Peace. But Jin's quick ceremony only closed the gates, it was a longer task to seal the doors and haul back to the roof the heavy bronze garlands that hang down from the pediments. And if among the Servicers who set the seals in place one wore a hat, all eyes were on Yangon. He bade me close it, reader, I who won the war. I protested that parricide hands would profane the temple, enrage the god, but He has insights into small-g gods which share His genus—though *deus polytheistus* may be farther from *Deus Monotheistus* than the domestic *felis catus* from *felis lunensis* that walked the Pleistocene, yet they are closer than *homo* anything. So, I believed Him when He said the god who is both endings and beginnings wanted my hands to end what they had begun. I opened Janus's gates, reader, not those of bronze and stone but Janus's time, the days of war begun at the first battle, mine and Saladin's with our Apollo and Seine Mardi many years of sun and rain ago. And as that day in Yangon helped the will to battle fade at last like snow into the spring, I closed them, too.

Back on the stage which all Earth watched as rapt as children, the consult-crowd around Jehovah opened like a shell, still ringing Him with warmth behind the podium, while the task of speaking fell upon a sighing Felix Faust. "Friends," he began, frowning fondly at Jehovah, "my Nephew has asked me, as Their chosen legal advocate, to ask you firmly to stop urging Them to take the Adulthood Competency Exam, and to explain why." Deep breath. "My excellent Nephew is precisely the sort of person the Adulthood Competency Exam was designed for. It's easy to think of the civics and politics sections as the heart of the exam, but the important half has always been the ethics puzzles and the tests designed to show whether a person can understand law and society in the ways necessary to protect themself. There is good reason the exam is self-scheduled, instead of barring political participation until some arbitrary age and then abandoning everyone to the mercy of the law at that age whether appropriate or not. There are millions of innovative, incredible, invaluable minds in this world which are yet so far from the average mind our laws are optimized for that they should never be forced against their will to navigate alone through a world with many bad actors in it, and many structures mismatched to their needs, without the protective companionship of a legal advocate of their own free selection whose mind is closer to the expected average and can warn and ward them, both from bad actors, and complexities of law. My Nephew . . ." A warm smile. "My wonderful Nephew could likely pass some of the written-only versions of the exam, Europe's most easily I'd guess, but the important part is that They do not want to pass it, do not want to navigate our law alone, and They have the right to make that choice. And good reason." Pausing, Faust looked to his Nephew for one more consenting nod—and received it. "Jehovah Donatien MASON still struggles with object permanency. They don't have a proper Brillist set because several of Their digits do not even meet the criteria for I. If They trip and fall, They don't just lose track of up and left and north, they lose track of time and whether Earth exists. It's beautiful. Like the Anonymous, I disapprove of using the trolley problem on the exam or anywhere, but however one feels about the question, it's very informative that hearing it makes my Nephew nonresponsive for an hour. We are richer as a civilization for welcoming such rare minds among us, but if Donatien believes They do not have the same competencies and thought patterns that law and society expect we ask you to respect Their self-assessment. There is good reason that many high offices in governments are open to Minors if Minors wish to serve or rule, while other offices require the exam to prove one's aptitudes are a good match for that particular office. My Nephew is suitable to be Gordian's Brain-bash' Stem but not Headmaster, and

They can be one of two Masonic Emperors but I support their preference not to be Emperor alone. You saw how much Donatien achieved today with this self-sentencing, a brilliant solution far outside the box. They've been a great Tribune for Romanova, advising, representing, vetoing, but They shouldn't and don't want to be a standard Senator or Humanist executive when They can't cope with balancing two necessary evils, and when someone could trip them in a hallway, tell Them They already promised to support some terrible evil bill, and They'd believe it. Please trust Their choice not to put Themself, or you, in that position." Faust gave a sigh of both exasperation and delight wrapped up together like commingled spices—what would Your sighs commingle, dear Ἄναξ, if You could sigh? "Donatien is unrestrainedly generous and easy to push to self-destructive levels of public service. They are already doing absolutely everything They feel They can and should for the Alliance and the Hives; you cause Them pain when you demand more than They are comfortable giving. Please stop."

Have I heard such a hush from such a crowd? The broadcast didn't show their faces, but the faces on the stage were moved in many different ways, such subtleties of brows and cheeks and eyes and mouths, pursed, frowning, smiling, dense like a mosaic. The little Prince Earth watched grow up before the cameras, was He truly so much more unusual than gossip columns had admitted all these years? Faust tried to return to his seat as he yielded the podium, but our strangest Stranger grasped His uncle's sleeve and pulled him back into the little crowd of *ibasho* whose shelter helped prepare Him for another venture to the podium, as daunting as a frosty mountain pass.

"Thank you, *Onkel*," He said first. Then a pause, just one pause this time. "I contradict nothing *Onkel* just said, but I would use an image I know *Onkel* hates." He still clutched Faust's now-mottled sleeve. "*Onkel* has described a set-set as—"

Faust's interruption, soft: *„Donatien, Bist Du sicher? Das kannst Du nicht rückgängig machen.* (Are You sure? You can't undo this.)"

"This was not the plan today, but this is something I desire to say, and to say now."

„Bist Du sicher? Wenn Du dies tust, wirst Du verletzt. (Are You sure? If you do this, You'll be hurt.)"

The pause, the consultation. "Yes. I'm sure."

They stand with Him, around, behind Him, warm, His *ibasho*, Faust, Ancelet, Kosala, Martin, Heloïse, Ἀπόλλων Θεοξένιος, Apollo Guardian of Strangers, smiling those nervous smiles we smile for those we love: it's time.

Clear into the microphone: "*Onkel* has described a set-set as an inhuman thing inhabiting a human brain. I Am not certain enough of the limits of brains or humans to know how true or false that is for set-sets. But I Am certain it is true of Me. The evidence is complex, and I Am not a created creature like a set-set or a U-beast or A.I., but, though I walk the Earth in human shape, this is My ship of flesh, and I Who use it to walk with you Am not, in My understanding, human. I Am, some wise among you have said, 'Alien,' and are not wrong. To be clear: I Am Something for which the most accepted term in your shared languages is 'Alien', and I shall have those who have studied My ship of flesh from its conception share their evidences when they can. This does not mean I do not Love humans. I Love you all. It just means that, when I use 'we' with you, I mean always the broader 'we' that includes you, and Me, and set-sets, and Ráðsviðr, and the Lōngsphinx, and the elephants, and high primates, and whales, and fellow aliens that you will someday meet among the stars. And if you were patient with Ráðsviðr, and recognized that it did not understand the murder it had planned the same way humans do, I Am grateful you were so understanding with it, and grateful too to those who have been so understanding with Me. But you have not all been so understanding. So, humankind, let Me address you now as the Outsider that I Am and warn you thus: you must get better at First Contact. You and I are strangers meeting in the dark. When I met you, we struggled to communicate. We still struggle. And though I came to you in friendship, you in your receiving-ignorance killed Me." He paused to turn His black gaze upon Sniper in the seats behind Him, then back to the crowd. "And when Intervention restored My ship of flesh granting a second chance, then millions of you tried to kill Me again. The situation was complex, yes, many pressures from deep motions of your polity, but you are political animals, so there will never be First Contact without pressures from deep motions of your polity. When I in My arrival-ignorance first crushed an insect—your kindred, Earth-life—I felt a horror-shame and did all that I could to learn to crush no more. You have not done the same. You have had so many Contacts across barriers of kind, with whales, with apes, with tribes from farther islands, and with children born to you with atypical minds, and, as Secretary General Dembélé reminds you, so many of your Contacts have been cruel. It went better with A.I.s, you expected them, prepared, laid down their rights before you finally made one, that fact gives Me hope; you got better. But not enough better to keep My Contact from being a bloody one, although I Am the gentlest Being you are likely ever to encounter, and I visited in flesh which many of you still mistake for yours. Learn from our Contact, please, as you learn from this war that could have been much kinder. You must get better at Contact. You have retained the outpath, you will reach out to new worlds, you must learn how to move without crushing insects, and how to treat with kindness even stones, or in the dazzle of the starlight, you will trample world wonders as precious as your own before you notice them. Do not make Me regret that you were gifted stepping-stones. This was almost the best war we could make, but that 'almost' on a planetary scale ended more than a million lives. Mars, Titan, farther worlds, whether they host living friends or not, are too fragile for such an 'almost.' So, I ask this of you: become better at Contact. I ask this as your Leader-Conqueror, and also as an Alien and Outsider in danger at your hands, and also as your Friend. Become better this time. Your power is too great to put it off, and that power is growing. You aim so far. You will not stop aiming far. I Love you for the way you aim far, out, in, up, always, it is beautiful, touching, literal touching as you friendship-bringers reach across the barriers and bring touch which I treasure more than anything. Do not make Me regret that you were gifted stepping-stones. You must become better at making your touch kind. Not next time, this time. Not next time, this time. Not next time, this time."

Reader: "Thomas? Are you alright?"

Hobbes: "What?"

Reader: "You're crying, Thomas."

Hobbes: "Ah. Apologies, Master Reader, I . . . I was thinking on my day, our civil war, how many promises we made to change, rethink, understand better, to put things in place so such a war could not happen again, not next time, that time. That time. How many times ago was that?"

Too many, Master Hobbes, as you well know. I felt you there that day, you with Achilles, warning, many of you, black and schooling multitudes who watch the living, you who care too much to soften into Hades's restful gray. I could see you, across the sky, the crowded sea, a thousand black and winged shapes for every tardy, well-meant Peacedove. But humans began digging a canal across the Gulf of Corinth more than three thousand years ago and finished it in 1893. It's worth trying things again. Apollo Guardian of Strangers knows that it's worth trying things again. Especially for such a goal as peacefall.

* * *

"Now to the second war." He did not leave the stage, reader, and yet this was a different peacefall, we all felt it, like wind changing—no, like wind restarting after one of those hushes when it seems the whole world, the leaves, the sky have somehow paused, Terra holding her breath as that eerie fantasia we were always almost ready to believe in rises from Earth's undersurface, gilding every grass blade with the possibility that something vaster, grander than the greatest whales is near. First Contact, is it real? All Earth had read my history, the honorable title 'Alien,' but Micromegas does not ask us to accept it all, only to recognize His Strangeness and to use a 'we' that has more room in it for that fantasia we are always almost ready for. Humankind listened, reader. It might be just that I see what I wish to see, but in hallways, when people walk with Halley or Eureka Weeksbooth, it feels like 'we' has already become a little broader.

"As most of you have heard by now, there was a second war," fantasia's Advocate continued, "separate from Hiveguard on Remaker, fought mainly in secret between Gordian and Utopia over research resources and their disagreement over whether or not humans should reach past Earth." He paused—improvising new words again, Ἄναξ? You of all Beings know You are best with a script, that without one You become overgood, breaking past good, better, and best to moral spaces we, so finite, cannot quite follow. "I know sometimes that human cruelty is communication, a tool you use when others fail, but when your inborn tools of voice and gesture failed you, you invented drawing, alphabets, similes, phonographs, soon interfaces mind-machine; so I believe, when you find cruelty is still your best tool, you should make better tools. This time you did not, and now Gordian will confess how much they used the tool cruelty in battling Utopia."

When Faust finished—

Reader: "Wait just a moment, Mycroft. The captain's calling from the bridge, I must see if I'm needed."

Hobbes: "Rest yourself, good Master Reader, I'll go and inquire, you read on."

Reader: "Ah, that's kind, friend Thomas, thank you."

Hobbes: "Happy to serve, and we have little time, I know, must finish soon."

Reader: "Too true. Carry on, then, Mycroft, where were we? The Gordian peacefall, so urgent that Your Visitor advances it the same day as His universal sentence."

Yes, Master Reader, it was urgent then. The urgency had grown over the weeks as Rumor spread the truth bringing Faust and eight hundred million guilty Brillists into hate's spotlight. The cars, the silence, monsters, the lost Almagest, the harbingers that burned Laputa City violating the *Traité de l'espace* and bringing shame on all Hives before watchful UNGAR, that was *Gordian! All of it! All!* Even the massacres at Tripoli and Casablanca engineered with Thisbe's scentcraft were Gordian's doing, deeds that made it easy to blame any and all mob violence on this scapegoat. And swift Rumor had been inventing extra crimes, deeds of others, or deeds that never happened in our war, to pile on. Nastiest, there surged a special horror-hate in those who had believed the lies and shed blood of Apollo's sailors and their U-beasts, who now turned out to be innocent (at least of what they were killed for). Violence was rare—Brillists are good at reading social danger signals—but callousness was everywhere as Brillist names were dropped from waiting lists for help restoring looted shops, burned homes, sacked schools, for surgeries, for justice, clothes, or food. The Brillists needed peacefall, and some peace can come only with confession. So, to the podium at His command stepped Brillist Institute Headmaster Felix Faust, shaking a little, to recite the full list of painworks, which were Gordian's doing and which were not. Earth knew a lot of it, but clarity is everything in peacemaking, and it felt more like peace when someone stood before the cameras and confessed to breaching the *Sanctum Sanctorum*. At last Empire's inexorable war engines were fully stopped, not merely sleeping, and Earth slept better too, knowing the so-called "Diary of a U-beast," that horror transcript of body-jacked Lorelei Cook, was pure propaganda. The meat was real—a murder and a desecration, yes—but the captive brain, no, we have no such technology. Not yet.

When Faust finished, Jehovah called His Junior Emperor Martin MASON to deliver, in strict and lawful form, Gordian's sentence. The crowd's cheers took more than a minute to die down—it was not Martin's first public appearance as Emperor, but the first since the announcement that Martin and Xiaoliu are celebrating the new peace by having another daughter, Martin's turn to carry this time, making Martin the first MASON pregnant in office since Antonine MASON a hundred years before.

"The scope and nature of Gordian's deceptions having been made clear,"

Martin began in his exquisite, awkward English, "it is easy to hate them. Yet I remind you that we had no laws of war establishing whether it was more or less acceptable for Gordian to seek their victory using stun guns, hostages, and propaganda than for the Masons to mass-produce deadly munitions and chew up Earth's habitats with fifty thousand jeeps. As Commissioner General Papadelias said when we began this *terra ignota,* we inherit our expectations of war from the age of geographic nations, but the only legal rule for war agreed to under the Alliance was that of September twenty-third, 2454, that soldiers in action must wear uniforms, a rule which Gordian's 'bluesmock' uniforms followed. Gordian's conduct in this war has been unique, but we must not rush to condemn it just for disresembling our images of war.

"Gordian has already handed over to Masonic custody research assets worth tens of trillions as reparations for damage done, and as proof of its commitment to collaborate with Utopia on war recovery and on future research which the two Hives have pledged to advance jointly henceforth. We believe Gordian's surrender is genuine and that the Hive has neither means nor motive to attack Utopia or any other Hive further. Yet the question has been raised whether Gordian's conduct merits more extreme measures, such as Hive dissolution or large compelled reforms like those the Romanovan Senate demanded of the Hives complicit with O.S." Here it comes, reader, you can feel it in Martin's brows, in the crowd hush, in every Brillist bash'house watching from afar. "We do not believe Hive dissolution is appropriate. Gordian predicted that putting the cars in lockshell would vastly decrease world casualties by slowing the movement of armies and weapons, preventing any side from using the cars themselves as missiles, and preventing aerial bombardment, which tends to cause mass civilian deaths and uncontrolled destruction. While stranding everyone cost lives and caused suffering, good preparation prevented famine and most other shortages, and we believe the action, as Gordian predicted, saved orders of magnitude more lives than it cost. Gordian also asserts that silencing communications improved the war. Gordian clearly believed this and intended the silence in the spirit of the First and Second Laws, but the analysis behind their conclusion is so esoteric, requiring deep knowledge of Brillism, that no one—I want to stress this—*no one* we could find who was not a Gordian Member could evaluate or even understand the evidence. Many other Gordian war actions have proved similarly impossible for any outsider to evaluate, such is the complexity and opacity of Brillism." A soft smile. "The unnecessary opacity of Brillism.

"It is therefore our agreement that, while Hive dissolution is not appropriate, one large systemic change will help the world, but not a change in Gordian." Watch Felix Faust upon the stage there close his eyes—he knows what comes. "A change in Brillism. The discomfort outsiders feel toward Gordian stems less from its actions than from our inability to understand them, and our anxiety about Brillist secret knowledge: their incomprehensible number sets, their secret codes, their seeming ability to read our minds, the Institute's vast secret archives, surveillance, closed classrooms, and, from their persistent practice of keeping all notes and documents exclusively in German, even Brill's founding texts on psychotaxonomic science. Brillism conducts itself even more like an ancient mystery cult than we Masons do, and their tradition of exclusive secrecy has not only heightened tensions and made ethical and legal evaluation of Gordian's actions impossible, it has also deprived the rest of the world of the chance to benefit from Brill's very effective system. Imagine if we all understood psychotaxonomy, not as experts but at a basic level, if we all learned in school to understand the number sets, to be better at reading each other's faces, detecting fears and passions, predicting when friends are on the breaking point. Imagine if the Cousins in the pre-war months had psychotaxonomic science to guide their hospital preparations; if all sides had been able to predict the outcomes of battles better without losing lives in fighting them; if everyone had used tactics as low-lethality as Gordian's; or if a century ago the three Hives complicit in O.S. had had Brill's system to help them find nonlethal uses for set-sets' predictions. If we'd all fought like Brillists, then this might have been the better war Jehovah MASON asked us for. Or less grandly, imagine if you could understand the report I've just sent out, instead of section after section saying 'Gordian's analysis could not be evaluated.'

"Both O.S. and the war have taught us that keeping the peace among Hives is not as easy as we thought it was. We need new tools to live without O.S., and Brill's system made accessible to everyone can be one of those tools, one that has already proved effective at pioneering a kind of warfare far less lethal than any before." Here Martin's brow drew taut. "Most distressing to me of all the revelations about Gordian is that fellows at the Institute predicted war at least thirty-three years ago but did not warn the world. So valuable a science should not be a monopoly. Therefore, the plan, more my August Colleague's plan than my own, and assented to by Headmaster Faust, is that the Brillist system will become open. Key texts will be translated into many languages, public lectures offered at all research centers, free introductory courses offered for interested adults, textbooks and curricula developed to add psychotaxonomy as a unit in primary and secondary schools, all new research results published in all major Hive languages, the Institute archives opened to outside researchers, and collaborations launched, putting skilled Brillists at the service of the most precious projects of everyone around the world, especially—to heal the wounds between them—the Utopians."

No repercussions, then, for Gordian's deceit? They get it all, even their collaboration, Bridger's relics shared, thy Jehovah's great wealth shared with the twin projects? That does not feel like justice.

It does not feel like goddess Nemesis, reader, who ravages the guilty, paying pain with pain. It feels like something better.

"This is no small change," Martin stressed, "no small concession." True—Faust's face as he sat by the podium showed that. All schools are fragile, needing constant tending like a garden—yes, like my gardens at Alba Longa, safe so many centuries, visited only by careful hands-off crowds, then suddenly Aeneas MASON's new experiment, installing bash'houses so kids with grabby fingers toddler-thundered through the flowerbeds. I can imagine Alba Longa's gardeners hearing that plan and trembling as Faust trembles now: my fragile charge, will this be its renewal or its end? "Over the coming months, Headmaster Faust and other Gordian Members will face individual trials for, among other things, their part in the destruction of the Almagest and *Sanctum Sanctorum*. But this concession is more important, a change we believe will let Brill's system help our post-war world better prevent the recurrence of violence and war, and it will make us all better able to trust the Hive which remains our founding model of what a Hive could be. Now, as my August Colleague and the Headmaster sign the order to commence the Psychotaxonomic Science Dissemination Project, please join me in applauding this peaceful, positive remaking."

Applause, timid, some fear, some skepticism, some bewilderment from those who had always accepted Brillism as something inaccessible, but the backlash was defused, streets safe to walk again, and nervous Brillists, shaking in their sweaters as they watched from stranger-touched bash'houses with that eerie feeling of not-quite-home, felt home more now. Peacefall.

And did it work, Mycroft?

The great dissemination? It will take years, reader, a generation raised with Brill's science in their schools as everyday as chemistry. I can't know yet.

* * *

"As for Utopia," Martin MASON continued after the applause—it could not wait, reader, these rivals, inpath, outpath, called to judgment on the same passing of watchful Helios, "Huxley Mojave of the Delian First Contact Constellation will read the Hive's statement."

Whispers at this name nobody knew, though everybody knew its pieces. I didn't want Huxley to do it. Let someone already in the presslight do it, Senator Wyrdspell, or Ichabod Hubble, or Hugo Sputnik whom no one could hate, leave Huxley to the rest and play that both his oath and Kind Friendship's command. But no. Huxley took Faust's hand and declared war that first day Utopia stormed Ares's arsenal to seal away the arts of world-ending. Huxley will end it too.

"Utopia assented to the war." Huxley's digital gaze fell, not upon the crowd, but on the air above, as if to meet the gaze of some judgmental giant. "Like Gordian, some of us soothsaw warfall thirty years ago in the foreclashes of Masons and Mitsubishi." Deep breath. "And we let it come. We could have tried to stop it, warned you, but instead we just prepared, honing warcraft in secret. We so chose because we believed war would aid Utopia long-term by"—you cannot say 'guarding Apollo's light'—"hardening people to the kinds of sufferings required for space questing, and by showing us how Hives wage war, so we could hone our own defenses for the next war if, as we expect, the rest of you try to take Mars from us when the terraforming is complete. Gordian knew of this, and much of the conflict between us rose because Gordian believed that closing Mars was the best way to stop us from harming Earth to advance our path. Only a small constellation within Utopia knew the prophecies and made this choice, but that constellation is one of the core structures of our government, so it is fair to say that, if all the Humanists, Europeans, and Mitsubishi are stained by O.S., all Utopians are stained by this. More recently, in June 2454, all Utopians, every light of us, voted on the decision to peacebond the harbingers before the Olympics and enter your war to protect the Earth, so in that sense, the whole Hive chose to risk our lives for yours, and to fight for the Alliance and Jehovah MASON. But our choice of 2454 does not erase our choice of thirty years ago to let war come in silence. And while our *Skymaw* defense system was not a harbinger, the Achilles-Alexander unit was, and we were in our way largely responsible for that. We did not create Achilles, nor did we build or launch the Alexander, or ever authorize the use of the Ancile Breaker harbinger weapon, nor could we have stopped Achilles in their rage, but Achilles still acted largely for us, to guard our goals, protector of our project, and without us, that terrible phase of the war would not have been. This is the scope and limit of Utopia's guilt. We have surrendered, not to the Alliance, but to the Empire and to Jehovah Micromegas MASON our Sirius . . . our guiding course-setter or helmlight." Huxley struggled translating the title, new to me yet my heart knew it, yes, Apollo's once it must have been, Apollo Mojave who did not rule but kept the aim true, Sirius, our night sky's brightest star. "Micromegas has devised a just . . . course correction for Utopia, to balance damage done and peacebond more which might have followed." A pause, those eyes as grave upon the vizor as when Huxley offered Faust war's hand. "Utopia assents."

Hiss whispers as Huxley yielded the podium. I thought I caught the outline of the crisp Delian sun on retreating Huxley's back, though that might have been illusion, the static blank yet moving like distorting desert heat. Still no storm, reader; before the wonder nowheres can return, we must have one second's mourning for each lost year of Utopian life—they say the summer solstice will be close before we see their otherworlds again.

Now Martin MASON cold as marble stepped up to give sentence. "First I will make clear this is not Romanova's judgment. Alliance lawyers may debate among themselves whether silence about a coming war constitutes some crime or other, but Utopia has surrendered to the Empire absolutely. The Hive is mine and my August Colleague's to have, to use, to guard, to judge, both as its conquerors in war and, as you now know, as its custodians long bound by the MASONIC Oath to nurture and away-follow Utopia, a following which contains in it the warmth of escorting, aspiring with, protecting, taking as a guiding light, but also the harshness of seizing, chasing, persecuting, even driving out into the dark. Utopia is ours, has consented to be ours, no one is a Utopian or Mason who has not consented to that state, and I hereby remind all outsiders that, so long as human hearts on any rock orbiting any sun know the word *power,* Caesar will do what Caesar wills to that which is Caesar's, and whosoever as much as speaks against the justness of this fact is Caesar's enemy.

"All being made clear, post-war repercussions have two functions, to punish and to prevent. While Gordian's actions in this war were the more blameworthy, Gordian's motives have been ended, their *casus belli* fully negated by events, so they have no motive to cause future conflict, overt nor covert. While Gordian must face punishment for crimes committed, prevention is not a concern—Gordian is at peace. Utopia is not. Utopia is planning for a war over the Martian colony, and has today every incentive it had two years ago to stockpile weapons and allow, even encourage military conflict among other forces, to weaken other powers and to expose strengths and weaknesses. We believe Utopia has no intention to restart conflict now, but its unchanging motive will remain a danger for two centuries and more, since Mars is not the last new sphere Utopia intends to touch. Thus for the sake and safety of the Empire and all human powers, even Utopia itself, it is my August Colleague's judgment and my own that Utopia must be stripped of means and motive to make future war. Henceforth, therefore, the Empire will keep Utopia a formal subject Hive under its rule. We have seized all Utopia's assets on this planet and will hold them in trust, monitoring Utopia's activities and releasing resources to them only when we have verified their projects are not military. And when the Martian terraforming is complete, that *casus belli* too we will remove by seizing . . ."

No.

No? No, what, Mycroft?

No, not like this, reader. This isn't how it should be told. It isn't Martin's sentence, it is His, our great and fragile Micromegas, clearest in its details as explained upon the podium perhaps, but truest as we heard it in His halting origami words.

Hobbes: "Then, by all means, let us hear it from the Leviathan's mouth."

Reader: "Ah! Are you back, friend Thomas?"

Hobbes: "Yes, Master Reader."

Reader: "What says the captain?"

Hobbes: "That deceleration is beginning nicely, and we should have contact soon with Governor Mojave. I assume you'll want to take the call."

Reader: "Of course. Our reading grows urgent indeed, if we're to be ready. Press on, Mycroft, I must know thee to the end of thy last stage to do this right."

Know me, reader? Yes. Yes, I think this is the last one needs to know to know of me. It was three weeks before Sentence Day, a long night at the Jung-Rauschenbach Complex as we waited for Dominic to be released from testing that dragged on until the black of morning thawed toward blue. There lay our *canis domini* upon one screen, serene amidst a willow tree of wires, while on another screen, fresh scans of Achilles, deeper, deeper blossomed like newly invented roses at a flower show outdoing gardens past. Huxley was pacing, I remember, too impatient to work, and when Voltaire and Aldrin arrived, and Mushi Mojave, they clustered together, four worlds of living static reflecting on the glossy tiles of a mosaic wall like frost.

"How much longer until we get some of Your time, Mike?" Huxley asked it suddenly, a simple question but startling from one who had this fortnight watched in silence as First Contact spent His days in lofty politics and nights in crawling science, while poor Huxley had that hushed impatient patience of the next of kin waiting through surgery—no, like the patient who awaits the busy surgeon next.

"The Mitsubishi peace is planted now," answered our Good Gardener, "the Cousins next."

"And Utopia's?" It was strange seeing Huxley push so, but that hour that holds its breath before the dawn is special, stolen from the rightful slumber-rights of night, an hour that makes us bold and honest, breaking down our barriers, as wine can do, or fire alarms, or fear's sudden release, or getting drenched together by the rains of Providence, those moments we can suddenly voice thoughts to those we walk with every day but couldn't say this to except when special times eclipse our inhibitions. "You haven't given us one meeting, Mike. Are all the other Hives so much more urgent?"

Earth's Visitor's eyes stayed on the screen that showed His Dominic asleep among the sensor wires that watched the dreaming of a brain so changed, and changing still. "I told you long ago what I would do if you surrendered."

For three breaths Huxley thought hard. "If so, we don't understand yet, Mike. You know we record everything You say and do, but we don't always fully understand."

His black eyes locked on Huxley as a magnet on its opposite. "I said I banish you forever from the Earth."

Nobody breathed.

"What? Mike . . ."

"I scatter you. I make you homeless, chase you from human dominion out into the black of Space, and take from you the Moon, and next take Mars, and Titan, driving you from every rock and hiding place technology can touch, home after home into the dark exhaustion of forever. That is the help you needed, is it not?"

The whiplash last phrase changed horror to raw confusion. "'Help,' Mike? I don't understand."

"To *absequor*, and to peacebond you, My help in thanks, reciprocal, as you helped Earth."

Huxley's digital eyes searched for answers in Aldrin's, Voltaire's, Mushi's, but found only confusion and some patient, toiling ants. "I still don't understand."

"You chose this war because you fear Mars's day when, as your Apollo-standing-on-the-threshold warned, united Earth will make war to take from you the red world that you remake as second garden."

Huxley was shaking, exhausted Mushi too, for mourning is exhausting, decades' mourning, more so when unfinished business keeps grief too foregrounded for the mind to heal—you make us all so tired, Apollo. "Yes," Huxley answered, "that's what we fear."

"You, like Me, wish there will be no Mars war?"

"Yes." The wish so deep in all their eyes, in mine, the longing to bear only one burden, Apollo's oar, not Mars's heavy spear to guard it with.

"So I take Mars from you. You did not surrender Mars to My mother but you did surrender it with everything to Me. I take Mars. I gift it to the rest. You may terraform it, settle it, break ground, raise cities, nurture forests with your ashes and your years, and when your toil has made it comfortable enough for other kinds to move into the garden, I shall take it from you and share it out to them, proportional, we shall draw up a contract, details matter to the individuals, not to the constellations. If you yield Mars as soon as you attain it, there will be no war."

"Mike . . . we . . . we toil five hundred years for nothing?"

"Seven hundred," the Visitor corrected. "I grant you two more centuries after the terraforming to raise Martian cities, host your first Olympics, then I give it to the rest. The terraforming is for Earth's broad 'we,' humanity, the other animals, your A.I. creatures, children born of you who will not choose the outpath as you have, but Mars is not for you. You gave your answer."

"I . . . My answer?"

"You, Huxley, I asked you, and you gave the answer of a friend. You said if Providence forced you to choose between Mars and First Contact, you would choose First Contact."

Huxley choked. "Yes, Mike, but we . . . You're here, Mike, we have both."

"Friends on your scale still wait, and yet you feel your path grow fragile, and feel fear."

Huxley's eyes rarely meet mine but did now, we two spirits who have felt the dying of the light. "Yes."

"You feel the human garden grow warmer," the Gardener continued. "I will make it warmer yet, kinder, richer with nutrients, an easy place for roots to burrow deep and know their *ibasho* and keep it. But all this, as you fear, threatens the outpath; sheltered seeds would rather root within the sunny garden walls than fly."

I heard Mushi Mojave choke beside me.

"But now we have the H.E.L.E.N tech," I said, my words as zealous as an anthem, "Cato, our lantern to protect the spark. Space is not as frightening as it once was. The outpath's safe."

Don't turn those eyes on me, Ἄναξ, as black and vast as the Old Enemy we must convince ourselves we want to keep fighting—but, oh, if I could just set down my oar!

His words: "Cato-Helen Weeksbooth treaded water twenty minutes in the sea of stars a year ago and still suffers chronic pain and blurry vision. You knew the danger, your Apollo knew, but I will cultivate this human garden more than your Apollo could imagine, better, richer fruits, too much for many hearts to brave the black by choice, as splendid as it is."

The black and airless sea, I saw it in my mind—His eyes would not let me evade—that world of no survival, luck can't save you, pluck can't save you, no heroic swim, no Pillarcat or floating mast to carry you safe to some waiting shore. To die cold and alone—isn't that fear what makes babes cry the first time mothers set us down? To die cold and alone? I shivered. "But You gave us stepping-stones already."

"And now before I trap the seeds in my overgoodbecoming garden, I scatter you. I chase you out, again, again, forever, not too quickly, centuries I give you on each stepping-stone to build the next garden, but once each one is built and you have reared new seeds, I scatter them again. I chase you first from Earth, seizing your wealth here, rationing it back to you only to advance your promises, *astra mortemque superare,* and to keep your oaths of rest and play, and too to keep your promise to Mine *Onkel* to advance into the *profundum et fundamentum,* there to unlock inner worlds and arts and means to more. You say two hundred ten years yet to finish Mars, I grant two hundred more to lay down streets and firm foundations, then I drive you on to the next garden. Thus, as Mars grows comfortable, you who still choose for love's sake to pursue the outpath shall know you must work on Titan quickly, then on Triton or Enceladus, garden after garden, seeking new ones each time the latest yields its first fruit, for in sequence I shall take each one from you, gifting the gardens to the thinking things who burgeon best in gardens, and scattering you, the thinking things who aim."

"To keep Utopia moving without war . . ." I could hardly breathe.

"A chasing peace," He said. "As you remake each stepping-stone into a garden, I shall gift it to the rest, so you and they shall never come to war, but neither shall you, ever-banished, come to peace, since war and peace alike are traps you must evade if you would battle Distance."

Deep in my core I shivered—Ares is one adversary, yes, but so is golden Aphrodite in her way, in whose lap it is so easy to drift off into slumbers eons long. Soothe Ares for us, laughing Aphrodite, let the spoiler of cities rest content, but leave the restless archer free to take his distant aim and have us follow. Is this what we always needed, Ἄναξ? Did You know?

"And as I take each garden you create," the Stranger continued, "I shall add some of its resources to those here on Earth I keep in trust to fuel your project, wealth reserved for your successors who, each generation, choose to sail the sea of stars. But they shall have these fruits only as provisions for their voyages and oathsealed rest and play, never as freely as the rest of Earth's broad 'we' enjoy peacefruits. So I lock in resources for the journey, that however Utopia may dwindle, this the smallest of Leviathans shall always have the means to voyage on."

"Provisions for the journey . . ." I was shaking. His warm hands like night were holding me, my shoulders, as the evening holds a tired world and starts to show it stars. My eyes found Huxley's—Huxley, true Utopian, Huxley deserves this touch, these words from You, Ἄναξ, Your gift disguised as sentence which I do feel is a true gift, even if I don't quite understand it yet, but this gift cannot be for one as soiled as me. But Huxley's eyes as keen as science spoke back with their stare: How dare you, Mycroft Canner! You who fought the war's first battle thirteen years ago, who sacrificed your everything, bash', freedom, life, more than I ever sacrificed, and for a kinder end, your boyhood hope I never shared that Mars might come without a war—how dare you, Mycroft, longest sufferer, doubt that you have the right to be Kindness's addressee. I shuddered as I tried to speak. "But, Ἄναξ, You... You're so afraid we might give up the outpath? Still? Even with Bridger's gifts?"

"No, I do not fear that. I fear that the outpath, now easier, might be sailed by sailors less kind than you."

"Less kind? Ἄναξ, I... We... Ἄναξ, you know what I am, what I've done, and they, Utopia, they let the war come, the same war I tried to stop. I still don't even know if they caused it, they might have."

"Yes, but they like thee gave friendship's answer."

"What, Ἄναξ?"

"To give up Mars, a world, your centuries of toil, your ashes and your hours, for First Contact. Such sailors I trust on the outpath, only you who value friendship over everything, over prosperity, wealth, power, leisure, you who give up whole planets of affluence to brave the dark between the stars looking for friends. Just friends. Not power, friends. Empire whose pulse is power must nurture and away-follow such scouts, as I have sworn as MASON, but Empire cannot be trusted with first footfall. You who pass this test of willing exile from everything, from garden into dark, you I Trust, and you alone, to touch *terrae ignotae* and to do so kindly, if clumsily sometimes, yet kindly as I did Who crushed an insect once and learned from it. You may out there, and soon, drill your way into some ice-sealed ocean moon and find beneath its surface portraits of Me who have never seen the stars or thought of other. Who but you, who have passed friendship's test, could I Trust to make such a contact kind?"

No one. No one, Ἄναξ, You're right. Forever right. You can trust no one. But: "I want us to be kind, as kind as You need us to be, Ἄναξ..."—all of me wanted it, the want of it bleeding from me like prayer—"... but it's so hard. You're making it harder. Utopia's already shrinking, and now You're making more rival Leviathans, more Hives, it won't just shrink the Masons, think how it will shrink the smallest, harshest—aah!"

I gasped, my body weak, disarmed by tenderness's shivers as He reached with gentle hands that hold the reins of Earth, and Moon, and Mars, and more, and wiped my tears away. "Safe now, My sailor, safe. Fear not. Even if the count of willing sailors shrinks each generation, if Utopia dwindles to a minnow, yet those that remain have such companions now, like thee, My Mycroft, new-and-old companions gifted and regifted by My Peer's Asclepius, so many are you that the minnow will remain Leviathan enough to brave Night's ocean still."

"Companions, Ἄναξ? Like me?"

"Not just like thee—thou thyself art one. Thou knowest thy sentence, how many more lifetimes thou must carry thine oar. And so will others."

"Companions from the dead?" The shadows swarm—can you see them, Ἄναξ, the black with Your black eyes?

"*Pater Meus* waits for resurrection, but it is not impiety in Me to say: wait.

Let him rest. *Pater* was tired, and willing to step down and make Me Emperor. Let him rest. Let him until we can raise both together, he and his Achilles, until this time we can finally promise it won't be the same, that they can have each other and a different fate, a different path on which *Pater* can take the other oath he always hungered to."

"Utopia's . . ." I smiled.

"We are close now to what Achilles wished for. Not to forever peace or lack-of-pain, that is not in thy Maker's Nature, thou has known that, My Mycroft, since He first took thine *ibasho* from thee in childhood, His random act of Providential death to grief-forge thee into the thing He wanted. We both know He will not grant thy child self's wish or Mine to make a cosmos without pain, but yet Achilles's wish who asked so little, just to sweat again beneath the sun, to toil though it be to enrich someone else's land, yet still to act and breathe, rather than stay the happiest among the dead, that's all Achilles asked for. That boon First Mover grants."

My head was spinning. "Yes. To live again and toil, that would be . . . not everything, but, like when Lord Apollo drove the plague from Athens, we would thank Him for it forever, Achilles, all of us . . ."

He turned me toward the screens, the images where frame by frame we learn from Dominic of what the healing potions do, a perfect test as we undo the damage cell by cell that Faust recorded so we might reverse it thus and learn so much. And from Achilles more. "You and Achilles are the samples, see, My Mycroft? Your Helen understands the next step is to need no flesh for resurrection. It may yet take decades, but we think we might try Mercer Mardi first, whose mind and self we have so well recorded to the very end, a mind humanity remembers and can call back, as Asclepius calls thee."

I sobbed. "To raise the dead, the old dead too who wanted it so much."

"Just as My Peer, cruel as He often seems, was not so callous as to trap you thinking beings in a trolley problem, so He has not left ungranted forever a hate-prayer as old and desperate as your Achilles's. I often doubt whether He truly makes His thinking things perish when flesh's death cuts off your sojourns in this facet of His Making, but even if He grants some afterplace to you as an elsewhere continuance, so many of you pray, like your Achilles, for the chance to stay, to act, to build again, not just to be but to be here, in this cosmos, this world to which you gave so much, and where you aimed so far. There are, I think, enough of you, so many, sailors, farmers, hardened by hard times, by wars as harsh as Mars, ready to aid the children of My kinder garden if they call you to them when they lack the strength to face the sea of stars alone. Companions for the outpath."

"Yes, companions hardened by past wars, like Thomas Hobbes who sits close at my side, called to me for this sequel to his great leap in the dark."

"I see it," I said. "Achilles's afterlife. I see it now, Ἄναξ. Asclepius, Bridger, that's what he gave us, what he left for us, the means to bring us back."

Yes, yes, once Zeus's gray-eyed daughter Science teaches us this art, lets us know it like rainbows, makes it, like webs, like ships, our art to replicate, then we can call them back, all of them, all who drift in misty Acheron, remembering, remembered, everyone who screamed into the dark: I am Odysseus! I, Eva Kimelman, beloved wife and mother! I, Agamemnon! I, Hlewagastiz son of Holt who made this drinking horn! I, Ozymandias! I, conquering Alexander, and though I lack a Homer, yet remember me! Call out my name! We are all sleeping kings, and while you may not need a king again or sword, yet hand me that strong oar, that plowshare, and I'll sweat beneath a distant sun beside you if you will just call me back! And Cornel and Achilles and . . .

"And thee?"

And me, reader? How can you call for me? Me of all men? I am . . .

"Thou art Mycroft Canner. Thou must see it, thou who sittest at the epicenter whence my arts were born, and knowest thy sentence was also the granting of thy prayer."

Me, reader? You who can gift word-magic's resurrection to any of coffined billions, you will choose me?

"Someone must introduce me to Governor Mojave."

Me?

"Yes, thee, my irksome Mycroft. Many readers, my peers, choose others to call back and toil beside them, but I call thee."

I hear you, reader. I can see it when I close my eyes. In one sense, I know I will open them again and see Yangon before me, and Huxley, and my Master, and my task list, tomorrow's toils plodding on, my broken lifetime's debt enacting His Remaking. But I also see a second moment, feel it hovering before me at this labor's end, that moment when I will close my eyes and open them again, with all I have known still fresh in my memory, the office scent, the touch of my old clothes, but I will see a different room, strange walls, so bright and alien, vibrating with strange noises of the strange engine of this strange ship that sails a sea of strangeness that I cannot understand glimpsed through your window. There is Hobbes's shadow at your side projecting urgency upon your floor, and you. You will be there. You hold what must be your era's version of a book, my book, although the object in your hand will be as alien to me as a medieval codex to Hammurabi's stonecutter. The unknown lights, the smells will make me shiver, trembling as a cage-bred wolf cub trembles when the keeper brings him into wild air he does not know to call his own. But you will smile, reader—a smile is still a smile after all this time—and you will place your hand upon my head, and stroke me gently, soothing down my ancient panic at so absolute a change. And you will speak, your words a wise and measured mixture of kindness and truth, much like my last Master, a mixture He hoped He would hear more from His Peer's creations as we have a chance to grow better and wiser in the kinder future He will help us make. And you will speak.

"Welcome, my Mycroft. Before we reach our destination and begin the work for which I have reconjured thee, I have a message for thee, one thine excellent apprentice who loved thee, and gave their life and flesh for thee once long ago, asked me the other day to pass on to thee when I could. And so I shall, for some things are so longed-for that hearing them spoken heals us, even if we know them already: the seeds have flown."

Acknowledgments

I don't want to distract you from the last, most precious message with words of my own. I have new friends to thank, others to thank anew, but if, as you read this, you are still freshly in the glow of the emotions of the climax, then please, I'm serious, stop reading now. Go, think, mull, talk to others, chew on the ideas, I don't want to interrupt that, it's the most, most, most, most, most important thing. You can return to read the rest of this some other time. My final thoughts, my list of names and gratitude, will still be waiting for you when the spell is done.

Ready? All right.

I remember when my good friend Carl Engle-Laird read the Utopian oath for the first time. He said it intimidated him, that, much as Mycroft says students might feel facing their choice of Hives, it was a daunting commitment, affirming that one's hours are the future's, not one's own. A year later he told me he had realized that was what he was already doing, giving a vocateur's hours to making our world a little better in the ways he can, his contribution to the path. I think in that sense many of us are already Utopians, people who, in different, often quiet ways commit our labors to humanity's collective efforts: to disarm death, to seek the stars, and—not to omit our other precious quests—to unlock new potentials of the mind, to advance human excellence, to protect and cherish nature and the produce of civilization, to cherish culture and patrimony, to shape power and law to be things worthy of respect, and, often the most important, doing so kindly. Such projects have millions of moving parts, and by the standards of 2454, when twenty hours of work a week is a full load, we all put in more hours than Utopians. It takes a city to plan a starship, and it takes so many vocations and avocations to create, maintain, heal, and improve a teeming city, more to hone the skills—so many of them soft skills of humanities—to make this world, and others after this, a better one. And I feel so fortunate having many such people in my life, both in my closest friendships and in our vast community, spread out around the world. Many readers, since the first book came out, have expressed to me what Carl did, that at first the oath was daunting until we realize how hard we work now, and that the promise to sustain ourselves with rest and play is often hardest to keep. Many have described to me the journey from feeling they could never maintain such a high standard to realizing that we already are.

A pause for names and thanks, then final thoughts. And here it is I wish I had the middle voice, for all those friends who didn't write these words, but who co-made this book, small co-authors, without whom Terra Ignota would not be what it is. In many places as I reread I can spot the very word or phrase a friend co-shaped: Jonathan Sneed (organic ratio, homoskedastic), Michael Mellas (lactam compound), John K. Strickland (methane tugs), Tamara Vardomskaya (machine speech parsing), Sanja Hakala (*Paratrechina longicornis*), Kristen Hendricks (cohomology), Diane Cambias Kelly (striate cortex), Cornell Fleischer (inner Asia), Irina Greenman (Latin), Jason Pedicone (Latin too), Alys Lyndholm (Japanese), Joaquin "Chino" Gutierrez (German), Johanna Ransmeier (Chinese), Yoon Ha Lee (Korean), Pragati Chaudhry (Hindi), Helma Dik (Greek vocatives), Matthew Ender (Ἄγουσα), Ken Liu (Mitsubishi factions), David M. Perry (advocacy), Steph Ban (spidering along), while other lines are relics of contacts whose names are lost to memory, like my Florentine host mother's Japanese lodger who helped name Tai-kun, and the many fans who spoke of being torn between the Cousins and another Hive, and so confirmed what I already felt, that no one should be made to choose between advancing the future we love and doing so kindly.

I need the middle voice for so many more. For my parents, Doug and Laura Palmer, nurturers, makers, sustainers, kindest gardeners, friends. For close and patient friends who have read and rooted for these books over so long: Lauren Schiller (bash'mate of twenty years!), Jo Walton (with me every day despite the tyranny of Distance), Anneke Cassista, Lila Garrott, Carl Engle-Laird, Ashleigh LaPorta, Jason Brodsky, Weiyi Guo, Tom Lotze & Dennis Clark (did you spot them, reader, safe and well?), Matt Granoff, Crystal Huff, Elsa Sjunneson, Lindsey Nilsen, Cait Coker, Jeremy Brett, Michael Lueckheide, Joseph Mastron, Ciro and Laura and the rest of my Italian family at Gelateria Perche No . . . ! For newer friends I've made through the books themselves: Diane Heaton, Claire Rojstaczer, Kate Klonick, Jon Shea, Robie Uniacke, Harel Dor, Nath François, many, many more. For the assistants and collaborators (also friends) who have helped take other burdens off me, freeing my hours to make more: Kay Strock, Denise Serna, Julia Tomasson, Ben Indeglia, Elizabeth Cano, Jeremiah Tolbert, Matt Arnold, and the Patreon supporters and Kickstarter backers who make that help possible. For my teachers and mentors, Mary Clevenger (first grade), Katherine Haas & Martin Beadle (fourth grade), Olive Moochler (fifth grade), Peter Markus (prose poetry), Mary Shoemaker (Latin), Hal Holiday (that writing is hard!), Gabriel Asfar (great books), James Hankins (Renaissance), Alan Kors (Enlightenment), Craig Kallendorf (book history), and Brian Copenhaver (magic!), and Reginald Foster, often called Earth's Greatest Latinist, who walked this year with hopeful Thanatos. In *Seven Surrenders* I also named many who have been my teachers without knowing me, and name again the chiefest: Diderot, Voltaire, de Sade, Homer, Arthur Conan Doyle, Alfred Bester, Gene Wolfe, Osamu Tezuka, and also the many makers of *I Claudius* (books and TV), *Revolutionary Girl Utena, Gundam,* and Julie Taymor's *Fool's Fire.*

With something as complex as a printed book, it also takes many hands to pass-it-on, and speaking now as a book historian who knows the agonies of struggling to trace the uncredited hands, I want to do my best. Who made the book a book?:

Donald Maass Literary Agency, especially my agents Amy Boggs and Cameron McClure, plus Katie Shea Boutillier, Patricia Gostyla, and Sophia Ioannou.

Tor Books (US editions), especially my editor Patrick Nielsen Hayden, and his sequential assistants Miriam Weinberg, Anita Okoye, Rachel Bass, and Molly McGhee; plus Liana Krissoff and Richard Shealy (copy editors) and Lauren Hougen and Ed Chapman (proofreaders), who braved the jungle of my pronouns, capitalization, neologisms, sudden columns, incessant Greek, and worse; the brilliant Heather Saunders (interior designer), who wrought beauty from that jungle; Megan Kiddoo (production editor), who superhero-rescues books from snafu-monsters; Jim Kapp and Karl Gold (production managers), printer-whisperers and miracle-workers, most responsible for the physical books; the architects of its brilliant covers Victor Mosquera and Amir Zand (art) and Irene Gallo (design); Diana Griffin and Desirae Friesen (publicists), who do a universe of work to get books out there; plus other dear friends at Tor, Teresa Nielsen Hayden (book whisperer), Bridget McGovern *(Tor.com),* Kristin Temple (helping helpers help), and many more—the chain of teamwork is so long that, next time Hercules requires a labor, I recommend trying to track down every maker of a book.

Head of Zeus (UK team), whose London office is a joyous gallery display of confidence in books: Harry Illingworth (editor), Nicolas Cheetham (editor), Clare Gordon (editorial), Jessie Price (art), Kate Appleton (publicity), Dan Groenewald (sales), Jessie Sullivan (marketing), and Christian Duck (production).

Éditions du Bélial' (French edition), a small press that took a big risk on some big books: Olivier Girard (acquiring editor), Erwann Perchoc (editor), Michelle Charrier (indefatigable translator), Raphaël Gaudin (proofreader), Laure Afchain (typesetter), Julien Guerry (sales); and so many readers, bloggers, et cetera, who made that risk pay off, including Ellen Herzfeld and Dominique Martel (aka Quarante-Deux), Nicolas Winter, L'Épaule d'Orion, Gromovar, the Utopiales community, and so many more.

Wydawnictwo MAG (Polish edition), for whose readers I hope Kenzie Walkiewicz helps ease the sour taste of Casimir Perry: Andrzej Miszkurka (Uczta Wyobraźni series editor), Michał Jakuszewski (translator who worked so earnestly on the subtle gender politics of language), Joanna Figlewska (book editor), Urszula Okrzeja (proofreader), Tomek Laisar Fruń (typesetter), Dark Crayon (cover art), and Piotr Chyliński (graphic design).

Eksik Parça (Turkish edition), whose edition so excited my Turkish friends: Kürşad Kızıltuğ (acquiring editor), Asiye Ademir (production director), Ilgın Yıldız (translator), Z. Seçil Şimşekş (proofreading), Esranur Gelbal (layout), and Serkan Cenker (cover).

Panini Verlags (German Edition), whose readers I trust to delight in the complexities: Peter Thannisch (editor), Claudia Kern (translator), Jo Loeffler (editorial), Holger Wiest (marketing), and Peter Sowade & Alex Bubenheimer (sales).

English Audio Versions, which make the art into another art form: *Recorded Books,* which made the single-reader versions, especially narrators Jefferson Mays and T. Ryder Smith, and the production team, including David Gassaway, Brian Sweany, Andy Paris, Jeff Tabnick, and linguist Paul Topping, who was a delight to geek out with on the pronunciations and rare language things; and the *GraphicAudio* team making the cast recordings, including Alejandro Ruiz and the rest of the cast and crew, whose eagerness to foreground the book's diverse characters and to try radical casting experiments are creating something amazing in itself.

And there will be more, more languages, future editions, teams as yet ungotten and unborn who will pass-it-on.

Finally, I need the middle voice for my communities, the strats, in Mycroft's terms, which overlap. For Simon's Rock College, for Double Star at Bryn Mawr, HRSFA at Harvard and HRSFANS since, for the University of Chicago, and the Renaissance Society of America. For the community of Latinist Reggie alums who (among so much else) helped track down the song Julia quotes which we used to sing so raucously with Reggie on the Ides, "Caesar's Triumph (*Ecce Caesar Nunc Triumphat*)" traced back to John Charles Robertson, *Latin Songs New and Old,* University of Toronto Press 1931. I need it for the amazing Terra Ignota Discord and Reddit communities, for Scintillation, for the mixing macro-strat of science fiction and fantasy fandom, and the smaller strats of so many conventions, each unique, so many Worldcons, big cons, small, my old home con of Balticon which nurtured my music, and where dazzled twelve-year-old Ada first watched the awarding of the Compton Crook Award for best first novel, and two hardworking decades later was overjoyed to receive the same honor (while wearing the same "Berserker" volunteer T-shirt). I need the middle voice for the community of authors, which welcomed me so warmly, and which is so warm, supporting each other, gushing about each other's books when we're too shy ourselves. And I need it especially for that vein (an old one) within speculative fiction that shows us other worlds and ways of living in order to spur and encourage us to make a better world on this one, warnings but also hope, writers like Ursula K. Le Guin, Frederik Pohl, Samuel R. Delany, John Brunner, C. J. Cherryh, Susan Palwick, Maureen McHugh, Robert Charles Wilson, Cory Doctorow, Jo Walton, Ken Liu, Malka Older, Ruthanna Emrys, Jeannette Ng, and many more who call on us to do better, not next time, this time. I try to pass that on as well.

I outlined this book in 2008, completed it in 2019, and in the year between completing it and writing this I and my world lived through 2020, its pandemic and its tumults and its flames. Many will be surprised to learn this is a pre-pandemic book, so many resonances eerily familiar; I was thinking on old problems, Distance, Separation, Ruin, Death, which rise from Aphrodite's peace sometimes for Homer as for us, and will for our successors even on a rock around some distant sun. The 2454 of my imagining was not perfect, nor were 2455–2456, but they are hopeful futures where, in crisis, we see most of humanity rise to excellence, while 2020, our real year of Ruin, so often brought out our worst more visibly than it brought out our best. Many people did good this year, great good, but it's so hard to see behind such looming evils. We're tired. We're tired and we have to move the Mountain, and our Mountain isn't here where we can talk to it, our Mountain is systemic, massive, plural, an Infinite To-Do List starting with tasks a million times harder than mending cracks in pavement: mending cracks in nations, culture, law. We're tired. We can't do it alone. And we don't have to:

> I fear that Mr. Sherlock Holmes . . . must go the way of all flesh, material or imaginary. One likes to think that there is some fantastic limbo for the children of imagination, some strange, impossible place where the beaux of Fielding may still make love to the belles of Richardson, where Scott's heroes still may strut, Dickens's delightful Cockneys still raise a laugh, and Thackeray's worldlings continue to carry on their reprehensible careers. Perhaps in some humble corner of such a Valhalla, Sherlock and his Watson may for a time find a place, while some more astute sleuth with some even less astute comrade may fill the stage which they have vacated.
>
> —**Arthur Conan Doyle,**
> **Preface to *The Case-Book of Sherlock Holmes,* 1927**

Tears have long come easily to me—joy, beauty, laughter, anger, philosophy, pain—but rarely so instantly as when these words from Doyle's preface surface in my endless rereads, or rather relistens, of Derek Jacobi's audiobook of Sherlock Holmes, which, with his audiobook of the Robert Fagles *Iliad,* help me summon Mycroft's voice. Why tears so fast? In part it's realizing that Doyle didn't know, he couldn't know, his Sherlock and his Watson have some of the vastest afterlives of any children of imagination, dominating our image of their age, yet Doyle hoped no more for them than a humble corner. But mostly I think what moves me is hearing somebody mention it at last, the fantastic limbo where they do dwell, not dead or living, our companions of imagination, populous as we who breathe. It isn't real the way a place—Paris—is real, but real like language, melodies, or smiles (we invented smiles), which are material phenomena—atoms moving, neurons firing—real things, just made of us. In 2020's cataclysm, Doyle's homeland had seventy million extra vaccine doses because Health Minister Matt Hancock watched the movie *Contagion* (2011)—do not tell me fiction is not as real a power in our lives as language, nation, love, or Earth's magnetic field. Something in me had ached to see somebody else—and Doyle did it!—acknowledge this real-and-unreal Valhalla, whose denizens are so powerful (limitless and immortal) yet depend abjectly on us to sustain them with our thoughts, not just once, always. The author may be [Pro- and Epi-]metheus, and quicken our creations like that Mad Grad Student (he never graduated) Victor Frankenstein, but the reader who remembers, plays with concepts, taking up a quote or motto, hearing some odd news and thinking "what would Sniper say?"—that reader is oxygen, the breath of life, needed, not once, but always. And when Tom Hobbes the Beast of Malmesbury, or when a Troy or Paris past or future, stray into tales, the limbo where, by now, Sherlock and Watson's corner is a continent blurs with the way we understand our past to form that *Cielo de Pájaros,* that heaven black with birds-that-are-not-birds still hoping and remaking, which have always flocked around our mad historian to form their Vs of Vs.

So I think the ache, the reread tears, come from feeling so acutely how much others past—those millions of birds, hardworking Petrarch, Diderot, Voltaire, Homer, Gene Wolfe who walked with Thanatos between last book and this—trusted to me. To us. It hurts—good hurt for us I think—being trusted with so much. See, Sniper's right: it's never simple, love. And Sniper's right too that we all have asymmetrical relationships with people far away, in space, in time, across the barrier between our real world and the shadow world which contains both our past and Holmes's Valhalla. Worlds which are not real (past or imaginary) can still teach us, warn us, just as friends who are not with us can inspire us, push us, draw us into the unending teamwork of humanity, which has always crossed time's diaspora. Sometimes we're too tired, the friends around us absent or just tired too. But Thomas Hobbes is not too tired, nor loyal Watson, and while dead hands and imaginary hands can't mend our pavement cracks, they can still sit beside us on the roughest nights and help us make it through. And if we love our imaginary worlds, if they stir passions in us, love, I think that makes us love this world the more, this world that created them, and that we remake with them.

So I'm leaving him with you now, my mad historian. My Mycroft. I'm leaving all of them with you, as others have left theirs with us before. And I hope the ideas, the fragile and imperfect Hives of 2454, and the battered but changing-for-the-better Hives of 2456, will help you rise with strength tomorrow morning as you lift your oar, or pack, or first aid kit, whatever task at hand, they're all the oar so long as you still carry in your breast the ancient spark, contagious, shared from breast to breast, that has died out a thousand times, but never yet in every breast at once. We will.